The Guilt Of Wanting

Book 1 of The Guilted Trio

By Rainey Pavo

Independently Published by R. P. Books
First Edition

Copyright Notice:

© 2026 Rainey Pavo. All Rights Reserved.

No part of this publication may be reproduced, stored in a retrieval system, or transmitted in any form or by any means (electronic, mechanical, photocopying, recording, or otherwise) without the prior written permission of the publisher, except in the case of brief quotations embodied in critical articles or reviews.

Disclaimers:

This is a work of fiction, born from the shadows between memory and imagination. While the emotions and experiences may echo familiar truths many women carry in silence, the characters, events, and places within these pages are crafted for dramatic narrative. Any resemblance to actual persons, living or dead, or to real events is purely coincidental. Some moments may feel real. That is their purpose, not their origin.

ISBN (paperback): 979-8-9939983-2-9
ISBN (ebook): 979-8-9939983-1-2

Cover design and formatting by Lanie Brown

Editing by Jenn Lockwood

Special thanks to Beta and Developmental Editors: Gaby Cepeda, Insight Pages, Bespoke Reader Rahmon, and Book Surgeon.

Published by R. P. Books

Printed in the United States of America

Total word count: 65964.

Trigger Warnings:

This book contains sensitive content that may not be suitable for all readers. Please read with discretion.

Content includes:
- Graphic sexual content
- Emotional and physical abuse
- Substance abuse
- Sexual trauma and coercion
- Mental health struggles (including depression, anxiety, and body image issues)

Support Resources

This book and playlist contain themes that may be distressing for some suffering with depression, thoughts of self-harm, or suicide. Please know that you are not alone. Help is available.

In the United States, you can call or text 988, the Suicide & Crisis Lifeline, for free at any time.

Please seek your local crisis hotline at findahelpline.com

Dedication

For the brave souls learning to embrace their desires, confront their fears, and uncover their truth.

To the ones who know our greatest battles are fought in the silence between our words, in the courage it takes to reach for what we truly need.

For those who feel unseen in the moments that matter most. You're not alone.

Acknowledgements

To my husband: thank you for loving me through every version of myself, for holding space for my chaos, my ever-changing hobbies, and the countless hours I spent lost in this story. Your steadiness made this possible. I'm endlessly grateful for you.

To the people who have shaped my life through the experiences they've given me: the good, the bad, and everything in between, every interaction, every moment, and every challenge has played a role in who I am today, and for that, I am thankful.

To those who have loved me, supported me, and inspired me to grow: your impact is not forgotten.

To those who have challenged me, tested my limits, or forced me to confront my own darkness: thank you for pushing me toward strength I didn't know I had. I am forever changed.

And finally, to the one for whom I'm just a blip on the radar, unaware of the weight you hold in my life: you saved me. You may never read this, but this is my love letter to you.

Lydia's Collection

Drink List

Every drink tells a story. Not just of flavor, but of feeling.

For Lydia, each glass mirrors a different version of herself: the woman she was, the one she pretended to be, and the one she's still becoming. And as she moves through each season of herself, every sip becomes its own confession, a quiet record of the storms she's survived, and the stillness she's learned to savor.

And maybe that's the most genuine part of it all: every pour, every stir, and every quiet sip is a reminder that even what once was burned can still become something beautiful.

The Blackberry Sage Smash

When the heart can't stay still: a drink that tastes like contradiction, sweet, herbal, and bruised, just like Lydia before she learns the difference between want and need.

Emotion: conflicted, searching, a little messy

Ingredients:

- 2 oz gin
- 4–5 blackberries
- 3 sage leaves (plus one for garnish)
- ½ oz honey syrup
- ½ oz fresh lemon juice
- Splash of soda water

Instructions:

In a shaker, muddle the blackberries and sage gently to release their color and oils. Add gin, honey syrup, and lemon juice. Shake with ice until chilled and strain into a rocks glass over ice. Top with a splash of soda water. Garnish with a fresh sage leaf and one crushed blackberry for color.

Flavor profile: Earthy sage and dark berry sweetness weave together, grounded by honey and brightened with citrus. It's bold and bruised, fragrant but complex. The taste of a woman trying to steady herself through the mess she still secretly misses.

The Lavender 75

A glass of composure: refined, sparkling, and deceptive in its lightness. It's what Lydia orders when she needs to look like she has everything under control.

Emotion: graceful restraint, outward control, inward ache

Ingredients:

- 1 oz Empress Elderflower Rose Gin (or floral gin)
- ½ oz fresh lemon juice
- ½ oz lavender honey syrup
- 3 oz chilled champagne or Prosecco

Instructions:

Shake gin, lemon juice, and lavender honey syrup with ice until just chilled. Strain into a champagne flute or coupe. Top gently with chilled champagne. Garnish with a single lavender sprig or thin lemon twist.

Flavor profile: Soft bubbles rise through floral sweetness and citrus brightness. Underneath the grace and sparkle, there's weight — a calm façade that hides the ache of restraint. Effervescent on the surface, quietly aching underneath.

The Basil Gimlet

Simple. Honest. Clear. It's the kind of drink Lydia makes when she quits pretending and the fire comes out. Fresh, grounded, and unapologetically her own.

Emotion: clarity, directness, quiet strength

Ingredients:

- 2 oz gin
- ¾ oz fresh lime juice
- ½ oz basil-infused simple syrup
- Small basil leaf for garnish

Instructions:

Shake gin, lime juice, and basil syrup with ice until chilled. Strain into a coupe or martini glass. Garnish with a small basil leaf.

Flavor profile: Bright lime and herbal freshness meet in a perfect balance of clean, aromatic, and direct. It's refreshment without disguise, like the first deep breath after years of holding your tongue. Nothing hidden. Nothing left to prove.

The Quiet Storm (Empress 1908 Edition)

A reflection of restraint and intensity: graceful on the surface, but alive with quiet fire underneath. It's the drink Lydia orders when she wants to appear composed, even as the storm inside her starts to hum again.

Emotion: composed yet alive with suppressed intensity

Ingredients:
- 2 oz Empress Elderflower 1908 (Indigo)
- ½ oz lavender syrup
- ¼ oz St-Germain
- 3-4 dashes grapefruit bitters
- Splash of ginger beer

Instructions:

Gently stir gin, lavender syrup, and bitters with ice until just chilled. Strain into a coupe glass. Add a gentle splash of ginger beer. Garnish with a single lavender sprig or float a rose petal.

Flavor profile: Floral and silky up front, with subtle citrus brightness and a lingering botanical finish. The honey softens the edges, but the gin's complexity gives it a quiet depth with a spicy bite of ginger at the end — *a calm exterior with a storm of nuance beneath. (Empress 1908 Rose Gin can also be used for a slightly more floral taste.)*

The Devil's Margarita

There's a moment when Lydia stops pretending she's innocent. When the thrill outweighs the consequence, this is that moment, poured into a glass: smooth, dark, and daring enough to make her forget who's watching.

Emotion: playful, fiery, unapologetically herself

Ingredients:

- 2 oz tequila blanco
- ¾ oz fresh lime juice
- ¾ oz simple syrup
- ½ oz dry red wine

Instructions:

Shake tequila, lime juice, and simple syrup with ice until chilled. Strain into a coupe or small glass. Gently pour red wine over the back of a spoon to create a blood-red float.

Flavor profile: Bright citrus and clean tequila meet the slow bleed of red wine: tart, giving way to dark, dry fruit. It's beauty with bite, elegance with danger, and the taste of doing precisely what you shouldn't.

The Obsidian

Dark, elegant, and controlled like Lydia when she's past pretending, when she leans into the heat rather than running from it.

Emotion: bold, poised, unapologetic sophistication

Ingredients:

- 1.5 oz Solu Gin or Greenhouse Artisan Gin
- 2 oz Grenadine
- ½ oz fresh lime juice
- ¼ oz honey
- ¼ oz simple syrup (black glitter mix)
- Top with a splash of ginger beer

Instructions:

In a shaker, combine gin, pomegranate juice, lime juice, honey, and simple syrup with ice. Shake until chilled and well mixed. Strain into a rocks glass over a large ice cube. Top with a light splash of ginger beer. Garnish with a cherry or lime twist.

Flavor profile: Dark fruit and citrus play against the gin's bright botanicals, creating a layered balance of power and poise. Honey and syrup smooth it into quiet elegance, but the ginger leaves a lingering spark, the taste of confidence earned the hard way.

The Obsidian (Mocktail version)

Ingredients:

- 4 oz Grenadine
- ½ oz fresh lime juice
- ¼ oz honey
- ¼ oz simple syrup (black glitter mix)
- Top off with ginger beer

Instructions:

Shake juice, lime, and syrup with ice until chilled. Strain into a chilled coupe or rocks glass with one large ice cube. Top with ginger beer. Garnish with a single cherry.

Flavor profile: Deep pomegranate richness meets a flash of citrus brightness, softened by honey and simple syrup. The ginger adds quiet warmth, lifting the darkness without taking away its mystery. It's smooth, sophisticated, and steady, like holding your composure when your pulse betrays you.

Lydia's Spotify Playlist

Books aren't meant to just be read but felt. The Guilt of Wanting is no different. This is a soundtrack for those moments, between guilt and self-forgiveness. Tracks that hold a confession, a longing, a desire, a freedom.

Check out the playlist on Spotify.

https://open.spotify.com/embed/playlist/3oe4bsq1LkZse8DeJvdv2Q?utm_source=generator

Wicked Game – Witchz

Middle of the Night – Elley Duhé

I Get Off – Halestorm

Red Room – Bryce Savage

Desire – Meg Myers

Dirty Little Fantasy – Lilyisthatyou

Closer – Nine Inch Nails

Tear You Apart – She Wants Revenge

Eyes Closed – Halsey

Creep – Radiohead

Everything I Wanted – Billie Eilish

Fallingwater – Maggie Rogers

Heavy – Birdtalker

Control – Halsey

bury a friend – Billie Eilish

DYWTYLM – Sleep Token

God Is a Weapon – Falling In Reverse

If You Leave Me Now – Foxes

Breathe Me – Sia

I Feel Like I'm Drowning – Two Feet

Swim – Fickle Friends

Undertow – Warpaint

River – Bishop Briggs

Staying – Lizzy McAlpine

Death of Peace of Mind – Bad Omens

Lose Control – Teddy Swims

Familiar Taste of Poison – Halestorm

Fire Meet Gasoline – Sia

Dancing On My Own – Robyn

Gethsemane – Sleep Token

Boys Will Be Boys – Dua Lipa

Just Pretend – Bad Omens

Back to Black – Amy Winehouse

Say Something – A Great Big World & Christina Aguilera

When the Party's Over – Billie Eilish

Somebody That I Used to Know – Gotye ft. Kimbra

The cost of giving up – Poppy

All I Want – Kodaline

Falling Slow – Mythic Melody

Oblivion – Grimes

Are You Really OK? – Sleep Token

She Used to Be Mine – Sara Bareilles

As I Try Not to Fall Apart – White Lies

Easier – Mansionair

Can't Pretend – Tom Odell

Like a Villain – Bad Omens

Talk Me Down – Troye Sivan

Love Is a Losing Game – Amy Winehouse

Lose You to Find Me – Deadluve

Vanilla – Holly Humberstone

Mad Women – Nora Mae

I Found – Amber Run

Heavenly – Cigarettes After Sex

Chokehold – Sleep Token

Take Me to Church – Hozier

Alkaline – Sleep Token

Villain Era – Bryce Savage

Earned It – The Weeknd

Glory and Gore – Lourde

I am not a woman, I'm a god – Halsey

    Some of the themes explored in this book touch on mental health struggles that may feel close to home. If you are experiencing depression or thoughts of self-harm, please reach out for support.

    In the United States, the Suicide & Crisis Lifeline is available 24/7 by calling or texting **988**.

If you are outside the U.S., you can find international helplines at **findahelpline.com**.

Table of Contents

Copyright Notice:	2
Lydia's Collection	**7**
Drink List	7
The Blackberry Sage Smash	8
The Lavender 75	10
The Basil Gimlet	11
The Quiet Storm (Empress 1908 Edition)	12
The Devil's Margarita	14
The Obsidian	15
The Obsidian (Mocktail version)	17
Lydia's Spotify Playlist	18
Table of Contents	**22**
Chapter 1	**25**
Present Day	25
Chapter 2	**44**
Chapter 3	**48**
12 Years Ago	48
Chapter 4	**57**
Chapter 5	**64**
11 Years Ago	64
Chapter 6	**70**
Chapter 7	**77**
Chapter 8	**84**

10 Years Ago	84
Chapter 9	**92**
Chapter 10	**101**
Chapter 11	**109**
Chapter 12	**122**
9 Years Ago	122
Chapter 13	**130**
Chapter 14	**139**
Chapter 15	**147**
Chapter 16	**162**
Chapter 17	**170**
8 Years Ago	170
Chapter 18	**181**
Chapter 19	**186**
7 Years Ago	186
Chapter 20	**200**
Chapter 21	**207**
Chapter 22	**215**
6 Years Ago	215
Chapter 23	**227**
5 Years Ago	227
Chapter 24	**240**
4 Years Ago	240
Chapter 25	**250**
3 Years Ago	250

Chapter 26	**256**
Chapter 27	**260**
Chapter 28	**263**
2 Years Ago	263
Chapter 29	**272**
1 Year Ago	272
Chapter 30	**279**
Chapter 31	**286**
Chapter 32	**292**
Present Day	292
Chapter 33	**299**
Chapter 34	**307**
Chapter 35	**313**
Chapter 36	**323**
Chapter 37	**326**
Chapter 38	**337**
Chapter 39	**345**
Chapter 40	**353**
6 months later	353
Chapter 41	**363**
Epilogue	**368**
9 months later	368
Thank you!	**370**
COMING SOON	**371**
ABOUT THE AUTHOR	**373**

Chapter 1

Present Day

I'm going to hell.

By stepping foot into this room, I'm *definitely* going to hell. If ambiance is trying to seduce me into sin, she's already succeeded.

One step inside, and I know somebody built this place for sinners. Long red velvet drapes spill over the windows. Gold and crystal chandeliers hang overhead, casting the room in a dim, ethereal glow. Every crimson reflection whispers temptation. It feels dangerous and sensual, where good intentions come to die.

Nothing scandalous is happening in the main bar, but each step deeper into the club brings a new level of seduction. A few couples, intertwined and lip-locked, are on the plush velvet sofas strategically placed around the bar, creating separate seating areas. I try to watch covertly as they stop to switch partners, as if it's the norm.

Maybe it is their norm.

The thought sends an unexpected ping of jealousy running through my already nervous belly. I don't feel like I fit in here.

Yet, I want to.

The aptly named Red Veil values its clients' privacy and requires all guests to check their belongings into a personal locker at the entrance. I feel lost without my phone to fidget with. If I'm being honest with myself, I really just want to obsessively check my phone to see if he agreed to come.

Anxiety has plagued me since I sent him a text with the invitation two months ago, and I stupidly did not ask for any kind of confirmation. I thought the mystery of will-he-won't-he would be a fun little tease. In reality, I've been a tightly wound ball of nerves since making the bold move.

Me: *Ready to play with your prey. Keep what you catch for the night. Saturday, March 4th. Red Veil Club at 8 PM. Happy Hunting ;)*

So, now I have no indication of whether he will show up, no way to ask, and nothing to keep my hands busy. I need a drink to kill my nerves. I'm sure Adam does too.

Was this all a mistake?

With a small gesture toward the bar, my husband guides me through the crowd. My fingers fidget with the velvet fabric of my dress while he orders drinks for us both: a vodka tonic for him and my usual, a Quiet Storm.

As the bartender sets the drinks before us, my glass catches the low light, glowing in a violet haze swirling beneath the fresh rose petal garnish. Adam places his hand on my cheek, guiding my gaze to his as his thumb traces a slow caress along my jawline.

"Breathe, wife, this only happens if you want it to." He gives me one last look before taking his drink to rejoin our group, knowing I need a moment alone to gather my thoughts.

I lift my glass slowly, savoring the scent of gin and lavender mingling with something deeper, something that tugs at the edge of memory. The first sip blooms across my tongue, floral at first with a touch of sweetness, then deepens into something extraordinary and substantial, finishing with a quiet, spicy lift that hums beneath the surface.

It's a drink that looks soft and unassuming, the kind you'd expect to taste light and playful, but beneath its beauty lies a quiet complexity, an intensity begging to be uncovered.

Like me.

Calm on the outside, but not untouched. There are layers beneath, stories that still pulse with old scars, remnants of nights, of choices, of hurts that I've learned to carry quietly. Pieces of a woman shaped by nights I never talk about, by the fire I try to hide, like the hint of spice that lingers after a sip, warming the edges I won't let anyone see.

Before I set my glass down, the bartender slides me a small, folded card. I blink, caught off guard. He only shrugs, the corner of his mouth curling in a practiced, knowing way before he turns to the next guest.

My fingers tremble as I reach for the perfectly folded note, a million thoughts racing through my mind. It's a struggle to remain with any sort of composure as I fumble to open the letter.

My traps are set. Wonder what prey I'll catch tonight. And I do like to TOY with my prey. -J

My thighs instinctively press together as my hand splays across my stomach, trying to settle the rising panic.

Holy. Fucking. Shit.

He's here. This just became real. *What the hell do I do now?* Part of me hoped he would come—the part that has longed for his touch. But the other, the part that knows how wrong that longing is, hoped he wouldn't. I knew panic and anxiety would take over if he did.

Well, he came. And now I'm panicking.

Where is he? He has to be watching my reaction. I keep scanning the crowd, convinced that, at any moment, he will see me, judge me, and walk away because I am not what he imagined, because I am still...too much, too broken, too afraid. My heartbeat races. Thoughts flash, uninvited and rapid: *What if he sees the panic in my face? What if he doesn't want me after all? What if...*

Without thinking, I tilt the glass back and down the contents in one gulp. The burn hits my throat like claws tearing at me from the inside, as if vengeful hands are gripping my throat with the same weight they had all those years ago. My chest tightens, and my stomach knots, a sharp reminder of every moment someone silenced me, every time fear tried to claim me. The warmth spreads down my chest, both comforting and punishing. The bite of spice is an insistent storm that quietly gathers beneath calm skies.

My heartbeat pounds in my ears. Every worry, every flash of self-doubt, every fear I've carried about being unwanted presses forward. I need to see him. I need to know he's here. I need to believe I can face him.

I set the glass down with trembling hands, my knuckles white from tension, and reach for the note again. I need to read it one more time to convince myself this is real. Reaching for my throat, I need to make sure I'm still breathing, still here, still capable of facing him. But the burn lingers, a cruel echo that reminds me I have always been fighting for every inch of myself.

And still, I crave another. Another sip. Another heartbeat that reminds me I'm alive—one chance to face what I want, what I've been holding back.

Slowly looking up from the note, I lock eyes with Stacy, who wears a curious but knowing look on her face. Raising an eyebrow, she signals toward the bathroom. I offer a small, quiet smile in confirmation before donning what I hope is a convincing mask to conceal my nerves and start walking. With a subtle toss of her natural red waves, she makes our ladies' room excuses to our husbands and follows after me, like my protector.

She has been a confidant, a blessing I met through Adam. I've spilled everything to her about Jason. Every conversation, every promise, every thing he says he will do to me, how badly I want him to. She knows I invited him to our little outing, even encouraged me to go for it. I can only guess she has an inkling of what is running through my mind now.

After stepping into the bathroom and confirming the stalls are empty, I hesitantly turn to face her, knowing that once I say this out loud, it will all be real. *Hell, it's already real.*

"Spill it, Lyds," she starts. "What's with the deer-in-the-headlights look?"

"Fitting phrase," I say, forcing out a dry laugh, "seeing as I am someone's prey tonight." I hand her the note and start pacing the small room, but she doesn't open it.

"I know, babe." Her lips curve into a teasing grin. "And he likes to *toy* with his prey."

She said *toy* with an inflection and a chuckle that contained so much innuendo, yet I almost missed how she directly quoted the note without even reading it.

I stop pacing mid-step, my pulse quickening, confused by her phrasing. "What? How did you…" Turning to face her as I question, she holds a small white gift bag out in my direction. *Did she have that when we checked in? When did she get that?*

"What's in the bag?" I question nervously.

Stacy just smirks.

"Stacy. What's in the bag?" I ask again, sharper this time. "And when did you even get that?"

"Not sure," she responds with a curious shrug. "The bartender gave it to me when he was passing over my drink." Her smirk widens, half amused, half warning. "Your secret likes to toy with his prey, as he puts it," she says, finishing with a wink.

Toy. That word keeps echoing tonight. I should be putting the pieces together, but my nerves are short-circuiting all the logical parts of my brain.

Stacy finally breaks the silence as if she can see my mind running out of control. "He sent me a letter too." She hands me the bag and then lifts the note ceremoniously, as if performing a ritual of the hunt. A playful throat-clearing noise punctuates the moment.

"Get Lydia in the bathroom alone and have her put these in. The Hunter wants to TOY with his prey."

I peek into the bag, and my stomach twists. Inside are two sex toys: a wearable vibrator and a small vibrating butt plug. Instinctively, I know both can be controlled remotely.

Stacy winks and shoves me gently into a stall, holding the door closed so I can't leave until she accomplishes her given task. My mind reels. *This can't be real.* Time slows as I mentally prepare for what comes next.

"Look, Lydia, you are in control here," she says softly. "If you don't want to do this, you can say no."

I close my eyes, taking a deep, deliberate breath, then let it out slowly, forcing some calm into my trembling body. And yet, something in me wants this. I wanted this enough to set this all in motion. I chose to play this game, and I intend to see it through.

I switch on the toys, allowing them to connect to their Bluetooth remotes that I assume Jason has. Slowly, my hand drifts down my body. It glides effortlessly across my thigh, over my hip, the slit in my dress leaving nothing to shield. My pulse races, a mix of fear and anticipation that sends a thrill shivering through me.

By the time my hand reaches my slit, I'm already slick with anticipation of what tonight holds. I let my fingers glide over my pulsing clit, working myself further toward bliss. With no available lube, I use the butt plug like a makeshift dildo, lightly thrusting it in and out of my pussy. My arousal is enough of a lube that I'm able to slide the toy into my tight hole. The pressure is foreign, like nothing I've experienced before, but everything I never knew I was missing. I let out a small moan at the enhanced sensation as I slide the vibrator into my needy cunt, and I give my clit a few more slow circles.

Righting my dress, I take a few tentative steps out of the stall. Then I freeze, remembering Stacy has been there the whole time. My cheeks flare, heat crawling up my neck, as the full awareness hits me: she heard everything, every touch, every shiver. But in true friend form, she gives me nothing but a supportive, knowing look.

I give myself a quick once-over in the mirror, trying to regain composure. My reflection gives me pause, unable to recognize the girl staring back at me. Knowing I'm walking around with these toys inside me, amplifying every pulse and vibration, gives me a high, a strange sense of confidence that I can't hide.

"Damn, girl, you look hot. Confident." She holds my attention to let the compliment sink in. "Now, let's go have some fun and get you laid," she adds as her lips curl into a wicked grin.

Arm in arm, we grab new drinks from our sneaky little bartender and return to our husbands. I know he's here, somewhere in the room, watching as we socialize, waiting to turn on the vibrations when I least expect it. The suspense of waiting is torture, which only makes me wetter as I think about how the night could play out.

As the drinks settle in and I begin to relax, a sudden vibration throbs deep in my belly. I jerk in surprise, and Stacy tries, unsuccessfully, to hide a chuckle. The vibrator presses perfectly against my G-spot and clit, sending a delicious tension through me as the vibrations slowly intensify.

Adam gives me a suspicious look as I fight to keep my face from giving anything away. "It seems I'm being hunted, and my hunter likes to toy with his prey," I explain, holding out both notes for him to read.

His blue eyes darken with what I pray is excitement. But the flicker of fear that it might be jealousy twists in my gut. I don't know if I can stop the rollercoaster I've thrown us onto. And I don't know if I want to.

He lets the moment hold us hostage, the silence stretching between us until it feels like I'm suffocating on it.

Adam's face stays stoic beneath his neatly trimmed beard, unmoving and unreadable, until a sly grin slowly creeps across his lips, making my stomach flip. Gripping my ass, he pulls me toward him, his leg slipping between the slit of my dress, so I straddle his thigh. The tight muscles of his quad are adding pressure to the vibrator in just the right spot. If he's not careful, there will be a wet spot on his pants when I step away. He leans in close, brushing my ear as he whispers, "Have fun, wife. But remember, I get to watch."

Oh. Holy. Fuck.

Between the vibrations and Adam's approving gaze, I'm on the edge, flushed and trembling, close to coming right where I stand, until the vibrations suddenly cut off. I let out a groan, a mix of lust and frustration.

Adam chuckles, low and dark, grabbing my wrist and tugging me toward a dim hallway, searching for the slightest hint of privacy. Although, in a place like this, privacy is an illusion.

As he turns to face me, a rigid body presses against my back, aligned with mine in a way that feels like giving in to a sin I've already decided to commit.

"This must be your hunter," Adam says with a smirk, and I'm not quite sure if it's a statement or a question.

"Jason?" The word slips out, breathy, more of a moan than a question. My mind races, imagining what he will do next and what I might do in response, and the thought of losing control sends shivers down my spine.

"Yes, Lydia." His voice drops into something dark and heated when he says my name, the kind of tone that makes my knees weak.

My eyes lock on Adam's, searching for any sign of regret, any reason to stop. But there is nothing, no hesitation, no jealousy, no pause.

"Please?" I beg, leaning further into his chest, needing the contact to know he's really there.

"Please, what? Good girls use their words." Jason's deep voice vibrates at my back, sending shivers down my spine.

"Turn it back on. I was so close. Please, let me come."

"Good girl," Jason purrs.

His hands haven't touched me yet, but heat radiates through my body from his presence. After twelve years of sexual tension, we are finally here. Finally meeting, touching, and doing all the things we have fantasized about, even if only for one night.

I suppress the myriad of worried thoughts threatening to run rampant in my mind, letting myself melt into his chest as he lightly traces his fingers along my thigh. My pulse quickens, every nerve alight with anticipation, as his touch drifts closer to the slit of my dress and brushes against the edge of the snake tattoo peeking out from the high thigh slit. He moves deliberately, as if he has all the time in the world, each motion making my breath catch.

Jason hums softly. A low sound of approval vibrates down my spine when he discovers there is nothing beneath my dress but the vibrator he provided.

The moment his fingers graze my center, all the anxious thoughts, all the fears that had been clawing at my mind, vanish. Every worry about judgment, about control, about being too much, melts away, leaving only the electric awareness of him and the pulse of my own body.

The sudden start of the vibrations, combined with Jason's fingers working my clit sends shivers racing down my spine, tightening my stomach with a heady mix of excitement and tension. I'm lost in the sensations he brings that I don't notice him loosening the tie of my halter. The sudden cold makes my nipples peak.

"Suck," he commands, and suddenly Adam's mouth is on one of my exposed breasts. Adam sucks and nibbles at my nipples as Jason adds two fingers into my already occupied pussy, leaving his thumb to circle my clit. The way these two men move with me, as if they've been in perfect sync for a lifetime, playing my body like an instrument, is almost too much to bear.

Time seems to stretch, each rapid heartbeat echoing in my ears, while heat coils tight in my belly, winding tighter and tighter, until I can no longer resist. It takes only one whisper in my ear to shatter every last bit of control.

"Come for me," Jason purrs, and that is all it takes. I tumble over the edge with a shuddering cry. My muscles tighten around his fingers, as if afraid he might slip away, vanish, and never return.

I've never lost myself so completely or so quickly, yet I savor every pulse, every shiver of ecstasy they've drawn from me. My body hums with the afterglow, muscles still tingling, breath slowly returning to normal, and my mind swirls with a mix of disbelief, pleasure, and an almost dizzying sense of release.

After a few minutes, my breathing returns to normal, and he removes his fingers. Adam turns me around, forcing me to lock eyes with Jason for the first time. His eyes are black with lust, combined with his lush, dark, tousled hair, making him look dangerously undone, like he's been fighting the urge to touch me until *now.*

He brings his fingers coated in my release to his mouth and sucks them clean with a moan. "I've waited twelve years to taste you, and you taste better than I could have imagined." I feel myself blush at his admission as I stare at him, unable to speak.

We let the silence sit between us, heavy and shattering. It feels like something breaking open, as if years of tension is finally imploding, the way a star ends and something new begins.

Lost in our own world, I barely register Adam righting my dress, fixing the tie gently at the nape of my neck. His hands remain on my shoulder, giving me the strength to stand steady.

The sharp echo of heels approaching finally breaks our moment.

"The exhibition is starting soon. Time to find our viewing room," Stacy says, walking up behind Jason.

He hesitates for a moment longer, as if he refuses to let the moment end, before turning to follow her, making polite introductions to her and her husband as if nothing happened. Adam steps around to stand in front of me, creating a barrier between us and the rest of the world.

He leans down and kisses my forehead, his eyes locking with mine in a silent check, making sure I'm okay with what just happened.

"Thank you," I barely manage to whisper, still floating in a post-bliss haze.

Adam exhales in relief and returns a wide grin. "You're a goddess when you let go. Let's go have some more fun." I take his hand and follow the rest of our group toward our private viewing room.

Feeling Adam's eyes on me, seeing the silent reassurance and approval in his gaze, a wave of relief washes over me. The tension I had been holding, the fear of judgment, of crossing a line, melts away. His acceptance lets me surrender fully to the moment of what just happened, and to the excitement of what is still to come. My chest lifts, my pulse quickens, and I can't help the flush of warmth spreading through me that has nothing to do with the heat from earlier.

The viewing room is arranged with four love seats facing a window that overlooks the main stage. The master of ceremonies walks on stage and begins his introductions and instructions as Jason pulls me onto his lap, and Adam occupies the seat next to us. My focus is on the couple on stage where the man wastes no time diving in to feast on his partner like it's his last meal. Fascination and jealousy run through me as I sit fixated on the erotic scene unfolding in front of me.

A deep vibration hums to life in the rear, a sensation I've never experienced before. I lean back against his chest, my head dropping to his shoulder as I surrender to the pull of sensation. With a slow sweep of his hand, he shifts my wavy brown hair aside, claiming the curve of my neck with his mouth. He's slow, deliberate, knowing precisely what he's doing to me.

BEEP...BEEP...BEEP

No. No. No. Nooo.

Chapter 2

I roll over, slam the snooze button, and squeeze my eyes shut tighter as if that will take me back into the epic dream I was having.

Newsflash: it doesn't work.

Now I'm awake and aching.

Adam stirs to my left, and hope flickers. *Maybe this time.* Perhaps he'll pull me close, kiss me the way Jason did, the way they did, in my dream—hungry, desperate, like he can't get enough. I roll toward him, brushing a hand along his thigh, waiting for any sign that he wants this, that he wants me.

Nothing.

Desperate for connection, I rest my leg over his, positioning my hand dangerously close to his manhood. I make lazy circles, grazing over his cock, waiting, hoping for him to take control.

Still. Nothing.

He turns his head toward me, giving me a quick kiss, and slips from the bed to his home office to start working forty-five minutes early. *Of course.*

I can't do anything but stare as he walks from the bedroom, leaving me alone. I'm not angry exactly. Not anymore. It's something duller, heavier. The quiet ache of this reality, the way things always are. I shouldn't be surprised by his rejection. He loves me in other ways, but that love never reaches the part of me that craves to be desired.

That ache isn't just about Adam. It's the echo of years I spent silenced, beaten down, learning to hide the parts of me that screamed for freedom. I've survived, I've overcome, but the scars linger just below the surface. A constant reminder that I need to fight for every inch of myself.

My dream was unrestrained, raw, a place where touch and need collide—his primal need to have me no matter what. But life doesn't happen as they write about in books.

Books are what the author crafts them to be, fantasies to play out where even the curvy girl gets the perfect man. And by curvy, they mean she's gorgeously thin with a generous amount of boobs and ass, maybe a little more in the thighs, and a stomach that's not a perfect six-pack but still looks great naked.

But that's not me.

I am never that wanted, never that seen. Doubt creeps in, the same voice that's haunted me since high school, reminding me that I'm too much, or I ask for too much. Perhaps I'm just invisible.

I can fake a selfie, making the angles work just right, hiding the features of my body that I despise to fool others, but not me. Mirrors remind me that the weight comes and goes, the apron belly, the minor imperfections, they always remind me who I really am—a girl who wonders if she can inspire that kind of desire.

Every imperfection feels louder in my head, a leftover from the years of being told I wasn't enough, that my body wasn't mine to love. I've learned to survive that voice, but it never entirely goes away.

I crave someone to want me so fiercely that they can't control it. But that's not Adam's personality. Maybe that's why I still talk to Jason, still dream about him, even knowing I shouldn't, even though I know it's wrong, even though Adam is here. He does that for me, even if it's just in my head.

I thought marrying Adam would silence that voice. He chose me. He loves me. That should finally make me feel wanted. It does, but it doesn't. Not in the way I crave. Not in the way that makes me feel alive.

I could survive this life as it is. We have a great life, and Adam has taught me so much about myself, helped me heal.

But why survive when we can live?

With a sigh, I reach into my drawer, grab a vibrator, and sink back into the Red Veil fantasy, chasing the attention, the desire, and the need that's been denied to me so many times before. I just pray the dream can fill the emptiness that Adam and my past never have.

Back to Jason.

Maybe one day I'll be brave enough to ask for what I need.

Chapter 3

12 Years Ago

Staring out the window at the neighborhood pond across the street, I try to hold back a groan as Emily tells me more about this new boy she is crushing on and the conversation they are having. I'm happy for her—I am—but if I'm being honest, I'm jealous.

We are wrapping up our sophomore year of college, and I've never had a boyfriend or even a guy remotely interested in me. It's stupid, but every time she talks about him, it just reminds me how easy it seems for everyone else. Like I'm invisible, or worse, forgettable. I tell myself I'm fine being patient, but the truth is, I just want someone to look at me and *see* me.

A girl just wants to feel wanted.

"Girl," I sigh, turning to face her, "am I going to have to listen to you talk about him all week? I haven't seen you in months, and you flew out here to hang with me and keep me company at my sister's long-ass graduation. It's going to be *so* boring tomorrow if I have to sit through this thing while you have your head in your phone." My voice comes out whinier than I intended.

"I know, I know. But I've had a crush on this guy for a while, and he's finally over his ex. We started talking a few days ago, and I don't want to lose the momentum." I fight the urge to roll my eyes at her when she finally looks up from her phone. "You just need a guy to talk to."

Okay, now cue the most dramatic eye roll.

"Easy for you to say. You get dates. You know, for someone who went to a tiny high school, you have had way more boyfriends and dates than I have. And I went to a massive public school. Remember," I say, pointing a finger at my face, "I had one date in high school, and it was a freaking blind date, might I add." I toss my hands in the air in frustration. "Something must be wrong with me. I mean, I know I'm not the prettiest to look at, but I have a good personality. Right? "

Still, good personalities don't make hearts race. They don't make guys stay up at night wondering what it would feel like to touch me. I've never considered myself pretty. I've spent years fluctuating between a size twelve and an eighteen, existing somewhere between "almost confident" and "never enough." I've learned to laugh about it, to shrug off compliments like they're jokes people tell to be polite. But deep down, there's always been a part of me that wonders what it would feel like to be the girl someone can't stop thinking about.

"Quit with the dramatics. Nothing is wrong with you. And not *all* guys like the model-thin twigs." She gestures at herself as if she's a prime example. She's not a twig, but she is the curvy that guys actually want. "Give it time. You're too shy with guys, but that doesn't surprise me with how reserved you've always been."

"It's called introverted…or social anxiety. Or maybe a combination of both. Who knows?" I say, turning back to the window so she can't see the tears forming in my eyes.

"It's most definitely something like that. You're selective about who you give your time to, but once you open up and make friends, you're loyal to a fault." She pauses, and I turn back to her, moving to sit with her on the bed, her assessment of me healing my heart just a little.

"You just need some flirting practice to build your confidence." Her head drops back to her phone as she types away.

"I'm not going to start flirting with myself in the mirror and making out with a teddy bear to practice. That seems a bit pathetic." I flop back across the bed, watching the ceiling fan spin.

"Ha, ha," she laughs dryly with a deadpan as she looks up from her phone. "No, I mean practice with an actual guy. Even if you don't want to date him, a little flirting practice would be good for you."

"To do that, I would actually need to talk to a guy. And how do I even go about finding this practice dummy?"

That's my problem. Guys don't typically talk to me, and the ones that do firmly plant themselves in the friend zone. The ding of my phone snaps me back to reality. It's likely Mona asking when I'll be back in town to go out drinking with her.

Unknown number: *Hey ;)*

Who the hell...

Just two words and a wink, but my heart stumbles. It's ridiculous—I don't even know who it is—but for the first time in, well, ever, someone reached out to *me*.

"Must be a wrong number," I muse out loud to no one in particular.

Me: *Who is this?*

"You're welcome," Emily says in response. I jerk up to face her, spotting the Cheshire Cat-sized grin or possibly even wider.

"Your face is creeping me out. What did you do?" Her face contorts as she tries to suppress her grin and feigns a mask of innocence.

Ding. Ding.

Unknown number: *Jason*

Unknown number: *Let me guess. Emily didn't tell you she gave me your number?*

Me: *No. Excuse me while I find a new best friend...*

Me: *Who are you, and what did she tell you?*

"Emily. Who is this person you gave my number to?" There's a hint of panic in my voice.

"Stop thinking, or you'll hurt yourself. It's just my cousin."

"Which cousin? We have been friends since Pre-K, and yet, I have no idea what cousin you're talking about since they're all younger than us."

"His family lives in another state, and they don't visit much, so you've never met him. He's our age, so we talk now and then, but he can be a big flirt. Perfect practice dummy since you can chat and flirt without the pressure of a romantic relationship."

Ding.

Jason: *She asked me to keep you occupied so she can talk to that guy she's into.*

"For the record, I think this is a bad idea."

"College is for bad ideas. Just have fun with it. It's not like he can get you pregnant through the phone," she chuckles, adding a wink for emphasis.

"Uggghh! Fine. But don't think I'm letting you off the hook for this." And when the line between practice and fantasy becomes a little too blurred for me to see it's different from reality before the inevitable heartbreak ensues, I'm going to blame Emily for starting this mess.

Me: *Ah, so she's pawning me off on you so she doesn't feel bad about coming to visit then ignoring me to text with some guy.*

Jason: *Yep, now you can be texting some guy too.*

Jason: *Plus, I know plenty of ways to keep you entertained ;)*

Me: *Such as?*

Jason: If I were there, we'd be finding an empty room, and I'd be kissing the hell out of you.

Well, shit. He's just jumping right into this. Panic starts to creep in. My chest tightens, and my stomach flips, half from shock and half from thrill. *What should I do? How do I respond?*

The urge to say something snarky is strong, having never done anything like this, and yet, a small part of me can't deny how alive it makes me feel to be noticed for just a moment. Like maybe, for once, I'm not the invisible girl in the corner.

I was raised to believe purity was power, that waiting made me worthy, that desire was something dangerous and shameful. But right now, all I can think about is how powerful it feels to be wanted, even if it's just a game, even if it's fleeting.

I should Google how to respond, right? How to sext or something?

No, that's a terrible idea. Who knows what kind of craziness will pop up!

Working up the nerve, I type out several different messages before chickening out on each one.

Me: *Well, that escalated quickly.*

Good Lord, that's such a lame response.

"Hey, Em. Did you...What exactly did you tell him to do with my number?"

"Just to flirt a little with you and get you out of your shell. It's not like you're committing to anything you say. Go with your gut."

Go with my gut? What if my gut is wrong? How does my gut know better than my brain, when my brain screams, *This is a bad idea!* My gut feels reckless. Hungry. The kind of hunger that comes from being starved of affection for too long.

"Stop overanalyzing this." She knows me so well; I almost questioned whether I'd said all that out loud. "Just say what you feel or the first thing that comes to your mind."

Jason: *Do you want me to?*

Yes. Yes, I really do.

Me: *Yes.*

Jason: *And if I try to do more, are you going to stop me?*

Me: *Like what?*

Jason: *I will try to get my hand under your shirt and play with your nipples while I kiss you.*

Me: No.

Me: I wouldn't stop you.

Me: I might even let you take my shirt off ;)

Jason: Can I take your bra off too?

Oh, jeez. How honestly do I respond to this? Should I be accurate or just tell him what I think he wants to hear? Or what I wish was happening.

I type out a response, staring a bit before changing my mind. With trembling hands, I hope for the best and choose to say what I wish were true.

Me: I'm not wearing one.

Jason: Shit, that's hot, baby.

Well, I guess that's how. I might be better at this than I thought. And just like that, the invisible girl doesn't feel so invisible anymore.

At least, not tonight.

Jason: This is going to be fun.

Chapter 4

Emily wasn't wrong; he is a flirt. He didn't waste time on playful teasing and dove straight into sexting.

At first, I thought he was joking. People didn't just say those things outright, did they? Flirting was supposed to be coy, subtle, drawn out like the slow unraveling of a ribbon. But Jason didn't unravel anything; he ripped it off in one quick tug.

In just a few weeks, I've said things that would have once made me blush—scratch that, most of them still do. I re-read our chats late at night, half in disbelief, half in anticipation, recalling how my skin prickled as I typed out replies I never would have dared to before.

It's thrilling, intoxicating, like I'm getting away with something. The old me would have agonized over every word, second-guessed every response. But with Jason, there's no hesitation. He asks, and I answer. He dares, and I follow. Even in this risky, secretive game, I'm learning to explore my limits, figuring out what I like and don't like.

And if I keep this up, I might need to invest in some adult toys. My fingers could use a break.

Jason: *I wish I could taste how wet you are for me, baby. I bet that sweet pussy is already dripping for me.*

I close my eyes, imagining how he would feel with his head between my legs and the sounds we would make. The power of his wanting me like that is intoxicating, even if I don't deserve it. I feel seen, even if only for a little while. I push the thought away, telling myself to just live in the moment. Sliding my hand down my body, I tease my clit, feeling the heat and power of my own desire before I start to type out a response that I hope will drive him crazy.

My body jolts as my phone rings, snapping me out of his trance. Talk about a mood killer.

"Hey, Em. How's life back home? Get that guy to be your boyfriend yet?"

"Girl, yes, I have so much to catch you up on. So, he picked me up at the airport when I flew back from my visit and took me to dinner," she starts, giving me a play-by-play of the last few weeks.

She's gushing over this guy and the start of her new relationship. My phone vibrates in my ear as more messages come in, and I can only imagine what dirty things he's whispering in my ear.

Jason: *You better not have come without me.*

Shit. It's been like twenty minutes since I last responded. I lost track of time, listening to Emily.

Me: *Sorry, Emily called. She's still giving me updates on her new boyfriend. But I can multitask.*

I put the call on speaker to text while Emily continues her update. A new message comes in. I expect another teasing line, his usual smooth and wicked words designed to make me squirm. But when I tap the screen, my breath catches.

Jason: *<Image>*

My breath catches somewhere between my chest and my throat. Instinct makes me look away, but curiosity drags my gaze right back, hungry for another second. Emily's voice fades into a distant hum.

My fingers brush the picture, as if I can feel his hard, velvety cock through the phone. I should've seen this coming. I mean, I knew what kind of conversation we were having.

But knowing is different than seeing, and now I never want to look away.

Do I respond? Do I ignore it? What's the etiquette here?

I swallow hard, hesitating only a moment before curiosity wins out. My thumbs hover over the keyboard as nervousness twists through me.

Me: *What I wouldn't give to be sitting on your lap right now.*

I type out another message but hesitate before sending. My chest tightens, not just from excitement, but from realizing that for once, someone actually wants me, *just me*. He's bold—that's something I've learned. *But am I?*

I bite my lip, debating. My nerves scream no way, but the way my body hums says why not? I shift in my seat, the heat between my thighs making the choice for me. *I want him to see me.*

Me: *How about I show you how wet you make me.*

Jason: *You're going to send me a dirty picture? And while you're on the phone with my cousin? Damn, baby, you're dirty.*

A dozen thoughts race through my mind. I've never done this before, but I'm realizing I can decide what excites me and how far I want to go. I know it's risky; it's reckless. There's something intoxicating about the idea of him wanting to see me, just me. He makes me feel desired and sexy, even though I'm not.

I glance at the door as if someone might burst in and catch me, although I'm home alone. My heart races as I slide a hand under my shirt, just enough to feel the skin of my stomach. My hands shake. Is that normal? God, I need to relax.

I take a breath. Hold it. Exhale.

Then, before I can overthink it, I snap the picture.

It's nothing crazy, just the tease of bare skin, the suggestion of more. But still, my heart pounds as I hit send.

I know this will never be more than a late-night game, a stolen thrill. But why does my heart race every time he asks for more from me? This is purely about using each other to satisfy a need. A time when I can believe that a guy wants me for me, regardless of what I look like.

I'm starting to believe Emily was right. I need this practice to build my self-confidence.

My hand is still in my panties and I start lightly stroking my fingers against my pussy lips. I shiver at my own touch as I feel the slickness building, needing this conversation with Emily to end.

"So, enough about me. What's up with you? Still talking to Jason, I hear?" Emily's question snaps my attention back to the conversation.

"What! He told you?"

"No, boo. You just did."

Shit, how did I fall for that?

"Hmph. That was mean, but yes, we are. It's going fine. Good practice."

Ding. Ding. Ding.

"Oh my god! Are you talking to him now? Is that why I keep hearing your phone ding? Is that him?"

"Yeah, yeah, it is. Don't make a big deal about it." I sneak a look at the text.

Jason: *Damn, baby.*

Jason: *How about you remove your panties?*

Jason: *And I'll tell you what to do with that hand of yours.*

Suppressing a moan, I quickly mumble into the phone, "You were right. We are just having fun. Don't let it go to your head."

"Ah-ha! I knew it. I love to hear that I'm right."

"Fine, you were right. *For now*. Listen, I love you, and I'm so thrilled things are going so well with your new boyfriend, but your cousin's being needy, so I've got to go."

She gives a genuine laugh that makes me chuckle. "Sounds like him. Have fun. Don't do anything I wouldn't do!" She hangs up in a hurry before I can even ask her what that is.

Following his instructions, I remove my panties and toss them on the floor next to my bed. For fun, I send him a picture of the pile of clothes.

Me: *<image> Tell me what to do.*

And just like that, I realize something: this game isn't just about practicing with him. It's about me. Learning who I am, what I want, and that somebody can want me.

Jason: *Cute. But I want to see those fingers you wish were mine sliding into that hot pussy.*

Holy. Shit.

Chapter 5

11 Years Ago

Everyone talks about how fun college is, but no one warns you about the loneliness that comes when all your friends become boy crazy and suddenly don't have time for you.

For the last year, my weekends have consisted of either studying alone or being the third wheel. Neither option is exactly exciting, unless I throw in a little stimulating conversation with Jason to distract myself.

It's strange how quickly a year can pass when someone keeps finding new ways to make you blush.

Just thirty more minutes of class, and I'm home free for the weekend. I'll have time to head back to my apartment for a nap, make dinner, and get dressed before meeting friends at a nearby bar after their dates end. A nap is the perfect plan, because right now, I'm struggling to keep my eyes open.

I need something to keep me awake, but I refuse to drink the 5-hour Energy in my bag. It's for emergencies. If I drink it now, I'll never get my nap, and by the time I get to the bar, I'll be crashing. Mona would kill me if I bailed early again. She's the kind of person who stays until the very last call.

Me: *I can't stop falling asleep in this class.*

I turn my phone over in my hand as I wait for a reply, more aware of the seconds ticking by than of the professor's voice. At least the anticipation helps to keep me awake.

Jason: *And what do you want me to do about it?*

Me: *Entertain me.*

Jason: *You want my kind of entertainment during class?*

Me: *How would you keep me awake during class?*

Jason: *Oh, this will be fun. But remember, you asked for this.*

Jason: *If we were in the same class, I would make sure to save us seats in the back of the room.*

Jason: *How quiet can you be?*

Me: *You'll just have to touch me and find out.*

Jason: That's my dirty girl.

Me: Just for you.

My heart kicks up a notch. There's no denying what his words do to me.

Jason: What do you have going on after class?

Me: Um. Home for a nap then drinks with some friends.

Jason: Perfect. I'm going to tell you all the things I want to do to you until you're squirming in your seat, dripping with need. Then get your ass home so you can touch that pretty little pussy of yours until you scream my name as you come.

Me: Yes, sir.

Jason: Good girl.

The way he says *good girl*…it hits somewhere deeper than just arousal. The warmth that spreads through me has nothing to do with the room temperature. I shift in my seat, trying to ignore the ache building low in my belly.

Ten more minutes of class.

Jason: I'm not taking it easy on you today, baby. I'll bend you over the couch, that pretty little ass in the air, just waiting for my handprint. And after I make your ass red, I'll kiss it better. Kissing lower until my tongue finds that wet, needy pussy. I'll tease you with every stroke until you're begging. And when you can't take it anymore, I'll slide inside, stretching you, fucking you until you forget your own name.

His words, in fact, cause me to shift uncomfortably in my seat. There's no chance I'll fall asleep in class now. The way he talks to me makes me forget where I am, my body responding before my mind catches up. Heat spreads through me in slow, wicked waves. It's dangerous how easily he can reach into my world and pull me under. His words shouldn't have that kind of power, but they do.

My breathing turns shallow, and I shift in my seat, pressing my legs together for any amount of friction I can find. I can almost feel his breath on my neck, his words lingering like a touch I can't see, but I can feel.

I try to get my breathing under control, to ground myself. I place my phone on my lap and jot down a few notes in an ill-fated attempt to focus. My heart jumps every time the phone vibrates against my leg.

Jason: <image>

I glance around, sure someone can see it on my face, the flush, the guilt, the wanting. My hand shakes as I open the image, but I do it anyway. Curiosity always wins when it comes to him. A bead of wetness at the tip of his cock catches the light. My breath stutters. I shouldn't stare, but I do because I can't get enough of him. My tongue darts out to wet my lips without permission.

Me: *I've got to get out of this room now before I explode in front of the whole class.*

Jason: *Do I turn you on that much, baby?*

Me: *You know you do.*

Jason: *Show me.*

That does it. My pulse pounds in my ears as I shove my notebook into my bag, barely waiting for the professor's "See you next week."

I sling my bag over my shoulder and fire off a rushed text, aching to set my afternoon plans into motion.

Me: *I'll be home in 5*

Jason: *Good girl.*

As I hurry out of the classroom, I realize something that scares me a little. Jason isn't just my distraction. He's become the place I go when the silence gets too loud, when I need to feel seen, wanted, alive. And right now, I'll take that over loneliness any day.

And that's what hooks me. It's not just the sex; it's the validation. It's that he looks straight at the parts of me no one else seems to notice. For the first time in a long time, I don't feel invisible. I feel wanted, even if it's through a screen.

But beneath that rush is the quiet whisper of something else, a reminder that attention isn't the same as affection, and wanting to be seen isn't the same as being known.

Chapter 6

Finally, a break from college life. As I step out of my last class for the week, a smile tugs at my lips, the weight of deadlines and exams lifting from my shoulders.

With the long weekend ahead, I am making the five-hour drive to my parents' house. I had my car packed before class started, so I could get on the road right after and make it home by dinner.

It's only been about an hour on the highway, and I'm already bored. Even belting to the radio with the windows down isn't keeping me entertained anymore. A slow smile spreads across my lips as an idea takes shape. I unlock my phone and fire off a quick text before letting it fall onto my lap.

Me: *Call me.*

A few minutes later, my cell phone rings, but I have no intention of answering. The call stops, and a text comes through. Using my car's Bluetooth feature, I have the message read to me.

Jason: *Why ask me to call you when you're not going to answer the phone?*

Thank goodness for Bluetooth and speech-to-text.

Me: *Oh, I didn't need to talk to you—I just needed you to call.*

Jason: *ok…*

Me: *My phone is in my lap…pressed between my legs.*

Jason:…

Me: *Right against my clit. You just turned my phone into a vibrator ;)*

A few seconds later, my phone buzzes again. The vibration hums through me. "Good boy," I whisper, a wicked curve tugging at my lips as the surge of control pulses through my veins.

Jason: *Fuck. You're such a dirty girl.*

Me: *I'm in the car for another 3 hours. Now I wish I had some actual toys with me.*

Jason: *I'm surprised you don't.*

Me: *Actually, there is a store right off the interstate. Want to come shopping with me?*

Jason: *Absolutely.*

I've passed this place dozens of times on my drive to and from school. Curiosity piques as I wonder what it would be like to go inside and see things meant for pleasure. I used to think that wanting stuff like this made me bad—or at least, the kind of girl who needed forgiveness afterward. But now, it feels less like sin and more like freedom.

Secretly, I've been itching to go inside and make a few purchases, to expand my own little collection. Now seems like the perfect opportunity. Adult toy stores always make me a little nervous. I've been to a store or two before, but the feeling never fades. There's something about walking in and knowing exactly why you're there, knowing that everyone else in the store is here for the same reason. It's thrilling and embarrassing all at once. And yet, here I am, scanning the shelves, already imagining how I'll use what I buy.

Inside, the store is smaller than I expected, almost suffocating. The air hums with the low buzz of the fluorescent lights over the display models. A clerk shifts behind the register, and I'm suddenly aware of every step I take, exposed as if everyone can see the thoughts playing behind my eyes.

Still, I walk the aisles, hands hovering over the possibilities as I fight the urge to run away.

I continue to look, to touch, to choose.

A simple vibrator, nothing fancy, nothing loud. Just something to keep me company. A classic 6-inch slimline multi-speed vibrator with twist control, along with another intriguing-looking clit stimulator, because why not? I add a pack of AA batteries, toy cleaner, and a small hand towel, convincing myself it's all practical. I'm not doing anything *wrong*.

That's what I tell myself, anyway.

Back in the car, I tear open the packaging, slide in the batteries, and snap a picture of the lime-green vibrator.

Jason: *Tell me that thing glows in the dark.*

Me: *Duh. It was either that or pink.*

Jason: *I'd love to see it glowing while buried deep inside you.*

Jason: *What are you wearing?*

Shit. I didn't plan for this, so I'm not exactly dressed for the occasion. A skirt or dress would've made this easy, but of course, I'm wearing shorts. Not ideal.

Me: *Shorts.*

Jason*: That's unfortunate.*

He doesn't need to ask me to take them off. I already know what *I* want. Determined to make this happen, I set the car on cruise control and unbutton my shorts.

The rational voice in my head, the one trained by years of "good girl" rules, starts whispering again: *This is reckless. This is wrong. You should stop.*

But I don't. Over time, Jason has rewired something in my brain. Every time he calls me his *good girl*, the praise reshapes the old rules. *Good girl* no longer feels like someone else's expectation. It isn't about obedience or shame anymore; it's about what it means to me in this moment, about owning it on my terms. A title I get to define.

Lifting my hips just enough, I shimmy my shorts and panties down to my knees, regripping the steering wheel as I kick my shorts to my ankles. The lace of my panties stretches across my lower thighs like a secret I'm tired of keeping—good call on wearing something sexy today.

With the vibrator and steering wheel in one hand, I use the other to snap a picture of the scene, making sure to capture the lace of my panties stretched around my knees.

Me: *I think I can make it work <image>*

Jason: *Damn, I wish I were there to help. Put that toy where it belongs, baby.*

Giving the dial a quick twist, the vibrator jerks to life on a low setting, sending a thrill through me. The hum of the vibrator fills the silence of the car. The sensation shoots through me, pleasure tangled with panic. Anyone could see. I could get caught. But the fear only heightens the thrill.

Spreading my legs as much as I can, I glide the toy over my clit, down to my entrance, gathering the slickness already pooling there before dragging it back up. I knew I was wet, but I love seeing just how wet my toys get before they even take a dip.

I've made him wait long enough. No more teasing, him or me. Pushing down the panic thoughts threatening to rise, I ease the vibrator in just enough to feel the vibrations deep in my core, leaving the end visible as I snap the picture I know he's waiting for.

Jason: *My dick is so jealous of that toy right now.*

Jason: *<Image>*

Jason: Rub your clit while you imagine that vibrator is my dick.

Me: Passing cars are sure going to get a show.

Jason: Then let's show them how sexy you are when you come, my little exhibitionist.

The word hits me harder than I expect. *Exhibitionist.* A part of me recoils, raised to think modesty was holiness, that desire was temptation. But another part of me, the one I've spent the last few years learning exists, sits up straighter. She likes the sound of that. New kink unlocked.

As I move with the rhythm of the road and the steady pulse of the toy, I realize something. It's not just Jason's voice or his words that I crave. It's the permission he gives me to *want*.

Chapter 7

Getting up early for classes is something I often complain about, but thanks to the new semester schedule, having my Friday afternoons free makes it worth it.

Instead of heading straight home, I stop by the store for groceries. If I don't do it now, I'll talk myself into staying in for the rest of the day. For once, I even planned ahead, made a list and everything.

As soon as I settle into my car, the loneliness creeps in. My friends have plans with their boyfriends. Mona, if she even wakes up before dinner, *might* want to hang out later. But right now? It's just me. And there's only one thing guaranteed to distract me from this hollow feeling.

I stare at my phone, thumb hovering above the screen. My stomach twists into knots. That little voice that's been drilled into me since childhood whispers all the familiar warnings: be good, be modest, don't be *that* girl. Guilt prickles up my spine as I press send anyway.

Me: *Hey, what's up?*

What was that? Real smooth, Lyds. Might as well have sent a "u up?" text in the middle of the day. I toss the phone onto the passenger seat, immediately regretting how eager it sounds. My pulse spikes, but I'm not sure if it's from embarrassment or anticipation. By the time I pull into the parking lot, I've already rewritten the text a hundred times in my head, each version worse than the last.

Grabbing a basket with my list in hand, I head into the store, trying to drown out the anxious chatter in my head. I drift through the aisles, pretending to shop, anything to keep busy, to keep from feeling like I'm waiting. My rational mind tells me to end this, to stop reaching out for something that only makes me feel more exposed.

But when my phone vibrates, all that noise disappears.

Jason: *Not much. I'm in class.*

If anyone looked at me right now, they'd see it, the mischievous little spark in my eyes. The tension between guilt and thrill hums through me, and more often I choose the thrill. I'm about to make Jason's life very hard—pun intended. And the idea of him squirming in his seat, struggling to keep his composure in class, is just a *chef's kiss*.

Me: *Perfect. This will be fun.*

I abandon my empty basket near the entrance and make a beeline for the bathroom. If I'm doing this, I need to do it right.

Stepping into the stall, I start snapping a few photos in various states of undress. I start slowly, a hint of cleavage, each photo revealing just a little more—a playful tease. Then, I go bolder, slipping my top lower, letting the camera capture the swell of my breasts. Finally, my fingers graze my skin, teasing my own nipples, imagining his reaction. When I'm done, I fix my clothes, delete the rejects, and keep the best photos to save just for him.

As I leave the bathroom, my phone buzzes again.

Jason: *You are going to make this class very hard, aren't you?*

Me: *No, not the class.*

Me: *Just you.*

Me: *<image>*

The first photo is harmless enough. Still, my heart beats like I've broken every rule I was raised with. A photo from my shoulders down, angled in a way that shows just enough cleavage. Maybe a little more than I would show when out clubbing. The angle intentionally makes it pretty obvious that I'm in a bathroom stall.

Jason: Where are you?

Me: The store.

Jason: You're in a store bathroom taking dirty pictures for me while I'm suffering in class?

Me: Yep.

Jason: Someone's in a giving mood today.

I grab a few more items from my grocery list and drop them into the cart. As I round the corner to the next aisle, I select the next picture to send. The next one's riskier with my shirt off, bra barely in place, my arm angled to cover just enough to fake some sense of modesty.

Me: Just returning the favor. <Image>

Jason: Now you are just being mean, baby.

I grab the last few items on my list and head to the checkout queue. By the time I reach checkout, my hands are trembling with adrenaline. Every photo feels like an act of rebellion. Every message, a quiet declaration: I am not that good girl anymore. But I am *his* good girl.

As I carry my groceries to the car, I send the last one. My shirt and bra are gone, my arm draped across my chest, fingers pinching a nipple. My breath catches as I hit send.

Me: *Oh, I'm just getting started. <Image>*

His reply is almost instant.

Jason: *You just want me hard in class, don't you?*

Me: *Oh, there's no just about it. I want your cock so fucking hard it hurts. I want you struggling to focus, desperate to get through class without running to the nearest empty room to satisfy your desire for me.*

Me: *I want to own your frustration.*

The confidence in my words surprises even me. It's like my fingers type faster than my fear can stop them.

Pulling into my reserved apartment parking spot, I make quick work of unloading and putting away the groceries. It's well past lunch, and I haven't eaten all day, but I have another hunger to feed first. Rushing into my room, I grab my favorite vibrator as my phone vibrates once again.

Jason: *You may be the devil.*

I was planning to send him the final bathroom picture next, the one with my hand dipping below the top of my shorts, but I changed my plans. If he wants me to be the devil, that's what I'll be for him. I strip off my clothes and position myself on the bed. I knew I was wet, but my panties proved just how much. With the vibrations on low, I slide the end of the toy between my pussy lips to gather some wetness. I smirk as the proof of how wet I am drips from the toy, knowing Jason would be drooling to see. So I let him see. A close-up, the toy glistening with proof of what he does to me.

Me: <Image>

Jason: *I hate you so much right now. When I get home, your ass is mine.*

Me: *Promises, promises.*

I slowly slide in the vibrator as I create a mental image of him opening the text. I imagine him slamming the phone down as he tries to subtly shift in his seat to adjust his pants, as I turn up the vibrations.

Jason: *I'll let you touch yourself right now, but you better not come.*

Jason: *That's for me to see later.*

Me: *You're so mean.*

Jason: *Just returning the favor.*

Me: *Touché.*

Jason: *Now, be a good girl and get yourself on the edge, and I promise to make us come later.*

"Fuck you," I whisper in frustration as I pull the vibrator away just before release.

I'll obey for now.

Me: *Yes, sir.*

Jason: *Good girl ;)*

His words settle over me like a spell. For a moment, the guilt fades. In its place is something close to peace. Maybe even power.

Chapter 8

10 Years Ago

"Come on, Lyds. You promised me a night out last weekend, and you bailed on me. Tonight we're going hard!" Mona whines, as if her perky persistence is enough to break me.

"You say that like I'm a shut-in. I had plans last weekend."

"Oh yeah? And what was that? A date with your TV?"

"No!" My response sounds a little too defensive, even to me. Mona raises an eyebrow in a silent challenge to prove her wrong. "A…computer date," I mumble in response as I turn to hide the smile that crosses my face. My cheeks flush as I mentally relive the night. She doesn't need to know it was really a late-night video call with Jason. Not that I would call it a date or even a relationship. And we are not trying to be. It's strictly sexual. Nothing more than mutual masturbation. Interactive porn at best.

Since Jason and I started talking a little over two years ago, our 'playtime' has escalated from just text to phone and video calls. Even after I shut the laptop, I couldn't stop replaying every filthy detail. He may have control of what I do for him, but seeing his reactions to my pleasure might just be the hottest thing.

Plus, I'm not naive enough to think that I'm the only one he does this sort of thing with, even if he is the only one I think about these days. I have been on a few dates in the last year. Nothing serious, but Emily was right about needing practice. Talking with Jason has made me feel things I never knew I needed.

"Girl, Netflix and chill only works if you're not the only one on the couch. Go home, take a nap, then get your ass back here at eight. Rain and Skye are going out. Plus, I have a DD for us tonight, so you don't have to drive us this time. A night out will do you some good."

Sounds like we are getting into trouble tonight. When Mona and I first met, we decided to go by nicknames at the bars. They are full of strangers, and we didn't want to just go around handing out our real names. So, Rain and Skye were born. And of course, they came with a whole backstory. Inseparable cousins and best friends. Their moms are sisters and full-blown hippies who wanted to give them both earthy names. Our names fit our personalities. Rain tends to be more moody, while Skye is the social butterfly and all-sunshine type. The two balance each other out.

"Fine. Rain and Skye are painting the town tonight," I conceded. Mona bounces up and down in excitement. Her blonde hair flows as she retreats to her closet to dig for an outfit.

A few hours later, I'm back knocking on Mona's third-floor apartment door, already ready to get this night over with. She swings the door open, perfectly put together, radiating confidence and those sunny, perky vibes I can never quite keep up with.

"There she is!" Mona grins, shoving a shot glass into my hand. "Cheers bitch!" I chuckle, tap her glass, and down the shot.

"Oh damn." I cough, shuddering. "A little warning before shoving tequila down my throat would have been nice."

"But you took it," she says with a wink. "And that's what's important." She adds a light pat to my cheek. "Let me grab my phone, and we can head to Chad's."

"Wait. I thought he was driving. I walked here! How far am I supposed to drive us to meet him?" I huff as I follow her down the hallway to the elevator.

"Relax, drama queen. He's literally just downstairs. He lives on the second floor."

Mona bounces down the hallway like she owns the place as I trail behind. Her confidence far outshines mine. Sometimes I wonder how we ended up as friends, given how totally opposite we are. But somehow, we work. She drags the fun out of me, and I keep her chaos at a non-dangerous level.

In true Mona fashion, she steps off the elevator and marches straight into a random apartment. "Chad! We're here!" she yells into the apartment as she makes herself comfortable on the couch. I linger by the door, awkward and unsure, while Mona's confidence stains the air.

"Rain, meet Chad. Chad, this is Rain AKA Lydia." Mona gestures casually as he strolls out of what I assume is his bedroom, pausing in the doorway. His look is polished yet straightforward: dark-denim jeans, a plain black tee, and an effortless confidence in the way he moves, like he doesn't have to try to be noticed; he just is. It's magnetic.

I give him an awkward smile and a weak wave, unsure what to make of the total stranger.

"Hey." He grins, brown eyes roaming in a way that feels both curious and assessing, like he's trying to figure me out without giving himself away. His dirty-blond hair falls just right, annoyingly effortless, maintaining his assessing gaze with an intensity that makes my nerves flutter.

He crosses the space in a few long strides toward me, accentuating the height difference between us. He's only a few inches taller than me, but with him this close, his presence feels ten feet tall. I have to tilt my chin up to meet his eyes, catching a glimpse of his thin lips as they curl into a hint of an easy smile.

My palms feel clammy, and my stomach twists in a knot. The way he looks at me, like he has me under a microscope, every breath on display, makes my chest tighten. I shift nervously, unsure whether to meet it or look away.

"Are you ladies ready for a night out?" He says the words without breaking eye contact, gesturing his hands to usher us out the door.

Once we arrive at the club, Mona grabs my wrist and makes a beeline for the bar. With surprising ease, she squeezes her way to the front of the line, ordering a Long Island for herself, Gin and Sprite for me, and a beer that she hands off to Chad. I must have concern written all over my face because he leans in close.

"Just the one tonight, since I'm the designated driver," he says, his voice low but steady. "After that, it's water for me. You two have fun." He gives me a wink before making his way toward an empty table by the dance floor.

I take a few sips of my drink, savoring the warmth of alcohol as it slides down my throat, just as the music shifts. Mona's eyes light up, and she squeals. We love this club for its variety; they play everything from rap and dance mixes to hip-hop and country line dances. Grinning widely, Mona grabs my arm and yanks me toward the dance floor, just in time for a line dance to start. Mona knows the quickest way to get me on the floor. I'm a sucker for a good line dance.

Once the line dances come to an end and a rap song starts to play, I take it as my cue for a break. I head for the bar to grab another drink and some water before making my way back to the table to meet Mona and Chad.

"You really get into it, huh?" Chad leans in, his voice just loud enough over the music. I'm grateful for the dim lights; otherwise, he'd see the blush creeping up my neck at his closeness.

We continue to chat, nervous small talk woven between moments on the dance floor with Mona. Each time I glance at the table, Chad's eyes are on me, yet he never joins us. Still, the room feels a little warmer each time I catch him watching me.

By the time the bar finally closes and it's time to head home, I'm exhausted, yet my body is still humming from the glimpse of his attention.

As soon as we park, Mona practically jumps out of the car and turns toward their apartment. "Chad, next weekend we'll get someone else to drive so you can drink with us."

"Sounds great, M." He grins before turning to me. "Nice meeting you, Lydia." His voice lingers on my name, soft, deliberate. Without hesitation, he leans in, brushing a quick kiss against my cheek. My body stills at the touch. My eyes fall shut at the delicate intimacy, savoring every moment of the lightest touch.

A few long strides backward, he flashes a heat-laced smile before turning toward the apartment doors. But before I can respond, he's already gone.

Chapter 9

After a few nights out with Mona and me, Chad finally asks me on a date.

It's not some elaborate production, just dinner at a local hole-in-the-wall place and a walk through the park after. But he *planned it*. He picks me up, opens doors, asks about my classes, my family, and what I plan to do after graduation. He listens in a way that makes me feel like I matter.

At the end of the night, he walks me to my door and kisses me. It's not rushed, not pushy. Just...sweet. And when he pulls back, he smiles, looking hopeful. "I'd like to do this again."

I rush out a yes before I can overthink it.

A few months have passed, and we've fallen into something that feels like a relationship, even though we haven't officially put a label on it. We text throughout the day: good morning messages, memes that make me laugh, and random check-ins that let me know he's thinking about me. He calls me at night sometimes, just to talk, his voice low and easy as we ramble about nothing and everything.

He meets me after class some days, walking me across campus even when it's out of his way. The first time he did it, I felt self-conscious, like people were staring, wondering what a guy like him was doing with someone like me. But he just slung an arm around my shoulders, easy and confident, like it was the most natural thing in the world.

"You don't have to walk me everywhere," I told him once, half-joking but also genuinely curious why he bothered.

"I know," he said with a grin. "But I want to."

That simple statement made my chest tighten in a way I wasn't prepared for. *He wants to.* Not because I asked. Not because he felt obligated. Just...because.

For the first time in my life, I felt *chosen.*

Jason makes me feel wanted in a specific way, desired, craved, like I'm the center of his fantasy. But

Chad? Chad makes me feel like I exist in the real world. Like I'm not just a body or a voice on the other side of a screen. I'm someone he actually wants to spend time with.

It's intoxicating in a completely different way.

We've been taking things slow—slower than he would probably like—and not for his lack of trying.

We make out, we touch, and we give each other pleasure in ways that don't involve actual sex. And to his credit, he's been patient. Pushy sometimes, yes, but he always stops when I ask him to.

Like last week.

We were on his couch, kissing, his hands sliding under my shirt. My body was responding, heat pooling low in my belly. As his hand moved lower, fingers hooking into the waistband of my jeans, panic flared.

"Wait," I said, pulling back slightly.

He froze, his hand stilling immediately. "You okay?"

I shook my head, my breath still uneven. "Yeah, I just...not that. Not yet."

For a second, I braced myself for frustration, for him to pull away or make me feel guilty, assuming he would leave me for not giving in to what he wants.

But he just kissed my forehead and said, "Okay. No pressure."

And it felt like he meant it. We went back to kissing, to touching in ways I was comfortable with, and he never pushed again that night.

That moment mattered. It made me trust him. It made me think, *Maybe he's different. Maybe he respects me.*

Honestly, ever since Jason and I started talking, I've found myself more open, more willing to push boundaries I once thought were firm. But actual sex? That's still off the table.

Tonight, Mona's dragging me out again. It's Thirsty Thursday, and staying in isn't an option.

Mona: Happy Thirsty Thursday, my dear sweet Rain. We are going out tonight!

Me: Sounds good. Tomorrow's class is canceled, so I don't have to worry about being productive!

Mona: I love it when you're so agreeable. Wanna come over and pregame until then?

Me: Yup. My last class ends at 4. I'll run home and grab clothes, then we can grab some food and go back to your place to get dressed.

Mona: Works for me! See you then.

Mona: Oh, do you think Chad will drive us?

Me: I'll ask! If not, we can just Uber.

I pick Mona up around 4:30, and we head out to find something for dinner. Chad has a late lab and project meeting this evening, so he won't get home until 8ish, leaving Mona and me plenty of girl time.

"So. How's the sex?"

Mona lives by the beat of her own drum. If she wants to know something, she'll just ask with no embarrassment, no filters. But somehow, the way she asks makes you feel comfortable, like there's no judgment, just genuine curiosity.

I envy that about her. I, on the other hand, overthink most, if not all, of my interactions, mentally preparing for every possible outcome then replaying it endlessly for years to come. I worry too much about being judged or mocked, even though I know I shouldn't care. Their perception is their reality, no matter how hard I try to change it.

"So you two haven't fucked yet?" she presses when I don't answer right away. Blunt, but not crude. It's evident that she's genuinely curious, like she really wants to know me.

"Uh, no. I mean, we have fooled around and stuff, but no sex. I'm... I'm not ready for that."

"How does anyone know when they're ready?"

"I don't know. I always thought I'd have this 'ah-ha' moment when I'd just know it was right. For me, though, that'll probably be after I'm married."

She's silent for a minute as she finishes her makeup. "Why until after you are married?"

I can understand why she's asking. Most of our time together is spent at bars, where deep conversations are few and far between. It's unfortunate that we don't get enough opportunities to talk like this.

"I grew up in a pretty religious house," I say, offering the most straightforward answer I can. She stares at me for a beat, waiting for more but not pushing.

I let out a small sigh. "I was taught that sex isn't something you do until after you're married," I add, ending with a shrug.

"But you'll do other stuff?" Mona asks, her curiosity still clear in her voice.

"Yeah, some stuff," I reply, shrugging. "But I'm still figuring out what I want and how far I'm willing to go. My family didn't talk about sex growing up, other than 'don't do it until you're married and ready for kids.'"

There's no judgment on her face, but she looks at me with an expression I can't quite place. Her eyebrows furrow slightly, her head tilting as if she's upset for me. "I get it. I just wish more parents had a sex-positive household instead of scaring their kids into celibacy. But I'm happy you're finally getting to sexplore."

At that, all the tension in me melts away, and I burst into laughter. "Sexplore?"

"Yeah, exploring things of a sexual nature." She wiggles her eyebrows at me, and I laugh even harder.

"Skye, my dear, you are a hoot." Mona throws her head back in laughter at my comment before handing me a shot of vodka.

"Rain, babe, you and I are just getting started. Cheers, bitch." With that, we clink glasses and down our first shot of the night.

Mona and I are already two shots deep and pouring the third when Chad finally makes his way up to Mona's apartment.

"You ladies ready to roll?" he asks, coming up behind me, spinning me around, and planting a kiss on my lips. I stumble just slightly, caught off guard, and have to grab the edge of the counter to steady myself.

"Alright, enough of the make-out session, you two. Let's head out," Mona giggles, pocketing her phone and ID before we down our next shot and head toward the door.

"You look good," Chad whispers in my ear as he places his hand in the small of my back, guiding me toward the door. I give him a shy smile in return, still unsure of how to accept a compliment.

The night passes in a haze. Drinks blur together, laughter comes too easily, and I can't quite remember if I'm on my second or third drink at the bar. My steps are a little uneven, and my head feels pleasantly heavy, light, and dizzy all at once. The music and chatter seem louder, closer, and somehow muffled at the same time.

We arrive back at Chad's apartment building after closing down the bar. Mona shouts her goodbyes and heads upstairs to her place, and I cling to Chad's arm a moment longer than necessary, feeling my balance wobble. At least we had enough sense to eat before we started drinking, or I'd probably be on the bathroom floor by now.

Chad hands me a t-shirt to sleep in. I fumble with it for a second, making myself giggle as I struggle to get the fabric over my head. Once I manage to get myself dressed for bed, I finally make my way to the bathroom. The faucet feels cold on my hands as I splash water on my face, the mirror waving slightly in my hazy vision. I stumble toward the bed, the room tilting a little with every step, relieved to find it already dark.

The faint glow from the bathroom is just enough to guide me as I slip under the covers. My body is warm, heavy, all edges softened by the alcohol. Chad hums a song I can't quite place from the bathroom, and I let the melody lull me deeper into a haze.

My body feels heavy, the alcohol dulling my thoughts and making it easier to ignore the nagging feeling that something is about to change.

I close my eyes. Tomorrow, I'll figure it all out. Tomorrow, I'll make sense of what I feel. But for now, nothing matters but the slow, heavy pull of sleep.

Chapter 10

My mind is sluggish, trying to piece together where I am, what's happening. My head is pounding with the throb from too much alcohol.

I float between the realm of awake and asleep, letting the strange sensation of heat and pressure envelop me. I let out a soft, involuntary moan, and then hear a deep, satisfied hum that doesn't belong to me. My eyes flutter open, confusion giving way to sharp, sudden awareness. Chad's head is between my thighs.

My brain scrambles to catch up, to make sense of the scene unfolding. When did…? How did…? I don't remember agreeing to this or being awake before this moment. Panic flutters at the edge of my thoughts, but it's trapped behind the haze. My body knows something's wrong before my mind can name it.

His tongue moves with purpose, and my body reacts on instinct, shooting my hand to the back of his head, pushing down, trying to push him away. But my arms are weak, heavy, like they're not entirely mine. The alcohol still dulls everything, making my thoughts slow. My movements feel borrowed and clumsy, like I'm watching someone else flail inside me.

"Chad, stop…" I try to say, but my voice comes out small, uncertain. It's like the sound doesn't reach him. Like my voice doesn't exist in this space anymore.

He doesn't stop.

His tongue finds my clit, deliberate and focused, and my body betrays me, hips twitching, breath catching. But my mind is screaming. *This isn't right. I didn't say yes. I was asleep.*

He slides two fingers inside me, and I jolt, a whimper escaping that sounds too much like surrender even though it's not.

"No…wait…" I manage, louder this time, trying to pull back. The word barely lands before his movement swallows them, like the air itself is siding with him. He pulls back just enough to look up at me, his eyes dark, his expression unreadable. Then he moves up my body, capturing my mouth in a kiss before I can say anything else.

My stomach twists in disgust as I taste myself on his lips. I try to turn my head, to say something, but his weight is on me now, pinning me down. His kiss is insistent, demanding, and I feel paralyzed, caught between my body's slack responses and my mind's rising panic.

His hand moves between us, and I feel him, hard and pressing against my entrance.

"No, I can't," I squeak, shaking my head. I try to tell him to stop, but my voice sounds distant, as if it's coming from someone else. The words don't match how my body feels, how it's pulling me forward, betraying what I want.

"Okay," he murmurs, but his lips don't leave my body. He kisses down my jaw, my neck, his hands already pulling at my shirt. I feel him lift me slightly, tugging the fabric over my head before I can protest.

I'm naked. When did he take off my panties? I don't remember. I must have been asleep.

I was asleep.

The thought claws at me. Maybe I shouldn't have fallen asleep. I shouldn't have drunk so much. The guilt slips in before I can even call it what it is.

"Chad, wait…" I try again, but my voice is so quiet, muffled by the fog in my head and a metallic sound I can't place. My limbs feel too heavy to move the way I want them to.

His mouth finds my breast, tongue circling my nipple, and my body responds, back arching slightly, breath hitching, but it's not consent. It's just biology. Nerves firing without permission.

I feel the pressure again. Lower. At my entrance.

"Sto…" I try to say, but the word catches in my throat.

His lips find mine again, swallowing the protest before it fully forms. His kiss is harder now, more urgent, and I feel him push forward.

The sharp stretch makes me gasp into his mouth, my hands flying to his chest, trying to push, trying to create space, but I'm too weak. The alcohol has stolen my strength.

"I just want to feel you," he murmurs against my lips, his voice rough. "Just a little. If you want me to stop, I will."

"St.." I try again, the word barely a whisper, my hands trembling against his chest.

But he doesn't stop. He's already inside me. Moving. Slowly at first, then faster. My body adjusts, the pain blending into numbness as my mind disconnects.

"Do you still want me to stop?" His voice is deep with frustration and desperation. But he doesn't pause. He doesn't wait for an answer. He just keeps moving. My mouth opens to respond, but nothing comes out. The realization hits; it was never really a question at all.

His breathing quickens. His movements become erratic. Then he stills, a low grunt escaping his lips as he finishes. It's over.

He pulls back, plants a quick kiss on my forehead like this was normal, like this was something we both wanted. "That was good," he murmurs, rolling off the bed, walking away from me without another glance.

My body feels heavy. I feel something press into my palm. The cold metal of the purity ring I forgot I was wearing presses an imprint, like a burn, into my clenched fist. The ring digs harder into my palm as a reminder of every promise I made to stay pure, to stay good. I thought it would protect me.

But good girls still get taken.

Now, it feels foreign, heavy, suffocating. The weight of it, this promise I swore to keep, becomes too much to bear. But maybe goodness was never a shield, just another way to be blamed for what someone else took.

With trembling fingers, I slip it off, letting the metal catch the light before I place it on the nightstand. My fingers feel empty now, like I'm letting go of something. I don't know why I do it, why I take it off. It doesn't matter anymore. I can't hold on to it when everything feels so out of my control.

Was the control ever mine to begin with? Was any of this ever my choice?

I should feel something. Anything. Regret, shame, anger. But all I feel is numb, a hollowness that makes everything else feel so distant. It's like I'm floating above myself, watching someone else live out this moment. I want to scream, but I can't find the words. The weight of it all feels so heavy, the numbness pressing on me, yet I feel nothing—just disconnected.

I hear the snap of latex as he removes the condom. At least he had the sense to use one. Within minutes, he's back in bed. His breathing smooths out into that quiet, steady rhythm he falls into so easily. But the second he drifts off, panic floods the gaps his calm leaves behind.

I tell myself it wasn't...That I didn't say no clearly. That he didn't mean to. The lies come easy, like it's a way to survive the night. Each lie feels like another blanket over the truth. If I don't call it what it was, maybe it won't crush me.

I lie there beside him, staring at the ceiling, my body still and numb. I want to cry, but the tears won't come. I want to scream, but my throat feels sealed shut. I just lie there, listening to his soft snoring, feeling the weight of what just happened press down on my chest until I can barely breathe.

I said no. I said no, and he didn't stop.

I close my eyes, trying to steady my world, wishing for sleep to take me, to pull me under so I don't have to feel this anymore.

But sleep doesn't come.

Just the suffocating quiet, the emptiness, the knowledge that something has been taken from me that I can never get back. And in the dark, I realize it isn't just my body that feels empty; it's the part of me that still believed love and safety could ever mean the same thing.

Chapter 11

I wake before any alarms. Not that you can wake up if you never really slept.

The room is too quiet, too still. My body feels...wrong. Heavy. But it's not just the alcohol lingering in my veins. It's something deeper, something I can't quite name. I stare at the ceiling, willing myself to feel normal. To feel something.

Chad shifts beside me, his breathing slow and even, like nothing happened. Sleeping like everything is fine.

I slip out of bed, being careful not to wake him. Something about last night doesn't sit right. My stomach twists as regret settles in. I need to go. I need to get out of here.

I scramble to find my clothes and scurry into the bathroom to dress. Maybe I can sneak out of Chad's apartment before he wakes up for his first class, assuming he's even going to go. How a senior can skip that many classes and still graduate is beyond me.

I can't believe that happened last night. Refusing to look at myself in the mirror, I wash my face and quickly dress. I flip off the light and ease the bathroom door open, hoping not to wake Chad. My eyes have yet to adjust to the darkness when I bump into something solid as I pass through the doorway, and my body jerks.

"Shit!" I say, startled both by the collision and his presence. My heart slams against my ribs, realizing Chad's awake. He's right in front of me, but I can't look him in the eyes.

"Hey, you okay?" He checks me over as he grabs both arms to steady me. I fight the urge to wrench away from his touch.

I force myself to really look at him, searching his eyes for something. Guilt or remorse, maybe? But there's nothing—just a casual morning-after ease.

"Yeah," I manage, my voice tight. "You just scared me. I thought you were still sleeping.

"I have class in thirty," he says like it's any other morning. "But I figured you would still be out after last night." He does nothing to hide the smirk on his face. "I was going to let you sleep in a little. Isn't your class in about two hours? You can stay in my bed for a bit until you have to leave."

"Yeah, it is." The lie slips out a little too easily. I never told him that my class was canceled. "Thanks. That's sweet, but now that I'm up, I want to head back to my place to shower and get clothes that don't smell like a bar."

I observe him carefully, still waiting for some sign of acknowledgement.

"Okay, I'll call you later," he says, planting a quick kiss on my forehead. My body flinches, but he doesn't seem to notice. I freeze. His lips press against my skin, and every muscle in my body screams to pull away. But I don't. I just stand there, rigid, until he pulls back.

Every movement feels rehearsed, like I've done this a thousand times before: get dressed, say the right things. Pretend everything is fine.

He doesn't notice. Or maybe he does and just doesn't care.

"See you later, babe," he says, already turning toward the bathroom, already moving on. The shower starts. Within seconds, I hear him humming.

I grab my bag and slip out the door, moving on autopilot until I'm in my car, hands shaking as I grip the steering wheel.

By the time I get home, the numbness has started to crack. I stumble through my apartment door and head straight for the bathroom, already pulling off my clothes before I even reach the shower.

I need to wash this off. I need to get *him* off.

I twist the water as hot as it will go and step under the spray before it's even warm. The shock of the cold makes me gasp, but I don't move. I just stand there, waiting, as the water heats.

When it finally turns scalding, I don't flinch. I let it burn. I grab the soap and start scrubbing every inch of my body, working the lather into my skin with rough, frantic movements. My hands shake as I scrub harder, trying to erase the feeling of his touch, the weight of his body, the memory of his breath on my neck.

But it won't come off.

I scrub my thighs, the tender skin between my legs, wincing at the soreness that reminds me it wasn't a dream, that it happened. That it was real. I scrub until my skin turns pink, then red, the soap slipping through my trembling fingers.

I look down at my body, but it doesn't feel like mine anymore. Now it feels marked, stained. Like something has been written across my skin in ink I can't see but will never forget. But no matter how hard I scrub, no matter how hot the water gets, the feeling doesn't leave. The guilt clings to me like a bloodstain I can't scrub out, seeping deeper with every pass of my hands.

I sink down to the floor of the tub, pulling my knees to my chest as the water pounds against my back. My skin burns. I just sit there, letting the water run over me, hoping that if I stay here long enough, it will wash away what happened.

But it doesn't.

My chest tightens. My breath comes in short, sharp gasps. My hands feel heavy, despite the missing ring.

I need air. Fresh air. I need to drive with the windows down, radio loud, sun on my face. But the January sky looks moody, cold. If I keep moving, I won't have to think about it. If I drive far enough, I can outrun the feeling that something inside me has been scraped hollow and left to bleed. *Maybe.*

I've lost track of how long I've been driving around town as I head nowhere in particular, trying to keep my mind clear, when a ring interrupts my melancholy music.

"Hey, Emily." I don't particularly feel like talking to anyone, but Emily is my best friend. Talking to her should help.

"Hey, Lyds, I have to tell you about the dream I had last night."

"Okay, shoot."

"It was like a bunch of dreams in one. I can't even remember half of it, but mostly it was so strange." She's rambling so fast I can hardly keep up and miss half of the dream events she describes. "Anyway, none of that is what I wanted to tell you about. You showed up at the end of the dream, and you were pregnant!"

My stomach drops. Please don't let this be an omen.

"I just thought it was funny that it was you since there is no way that's possible."

Awesome. Now I have to tell her. I was already planning to, just not today.

"Shit." I pause for a minute. "I really hope your dream is not a premonition."

"OMG! Spill."

Best get this over with. I need to talk to someone about it.

"Mona, Chad, and I went out last night." I pause, my grip tightening on the steering wheel. "I got a little too drunk. I was already planning to sleep at Chad's, so we got back and…" My throat closes. I swallow hard, forcing the words out.

"We went to bed. And he…he started…" I stop again. *How do I even say this?* "I was asleep, and he started fooling around." The words feel too small for what I'm trying to describe, like language doesn't stretch that far.

"Okay…" Emily's voice is gentle, patient, and waiting.

"But then…" My voice cracks. I clear my throat, trying again. "He started to…I mean, he actually…started having sex."

The words tangle in my mouth. I can't say it. I can't say *he raped me* because that sounds too harsh, too final, too *real*. That's not what happened. It couldn't be. Could it?

"I told him no," I finally squeak out, my voice barely above a whisper. "I said no, and he...he stopped for a second. But then he..."

"He what, Lydia?" Emily asks softly.

"He tried again." The words come out flat, detached, like I'm describing something that happened to someone else. "And I...I tried to tell him to stop again, but I couldn't... The words wouldn't come out right. And he..."

I falter, searching for the right way to say it. The way that doesn't make it sound as bad as it felt.

"He said...he said if I wanted him to stop, he would. But he didn't actually stop. He just..." My voice breaks. "He just kept going."

I wince as I say it, feeling ashamed that I let myself get wrapped up in this situation.

"And did you...want him to stop?" Emily's voice is careful, like she already knows the answer but needs me to say it.

The word hangs there, caught in my throat. Of course I wanted him to stop. I said no. I tried to repeat it. But if I say that out loud, if I admit it, then I have to face what that means.

"I did," I finally whisper, tears burning behind my eyes. "I wanted him to stop. I just...Everything was so foggy, and I...I couldn't make the words work."

I swallow hard, hating how weak I sound. How pathetic.

"I guess...I guess since I couldn't say it clearly enough, he thought...he thought I was okay with it. That it was okay to keep going."

Even as I say it, I know it sounds wrong. I know it doesn't make sense. But it's easier than admitting the alternative.

The silence on the other end stretches long enough that I wonder if the call dropped.

"Emily?"

"I'm here." Her voice is thick, careful. "Oh, Lydia...I'm so sorry."

"It's fine," I say automatically, even though nothing about this feels fine. "I mean, it's not like—"

"Lyds," she cuts me off gently but firmly. "You said no." She pauses for a moment, as if she wants me to respond, to agree with her without having to say more.

"You said no," she repeats, more insistent this time. "And he didn't stop. That's not...that's not okay. You know that, right?"

My throat tightens on a sharp inhale as I grip the steering wheel tighter, knuckles turning white. I absent-mindedly tilt my head in response, forgetting she can't see me. But she doesn't need to. She can feel it in the echoes of my choppy breaths.

"Did he use protection?"

The question jolts me back to practicality, away from the bigger, scarier thoughts. "Yeah. I don't remember when he put it on, but I remember him going to the bathroom after and taking it off."

"Okay. That's...that's good, at least." She pauses. "You two have been dating for a little while now. Do you...Do you love him?"

I stare at the road ahead, the question settling like a stone in my gut.

"I...I don't know."

"You want my opinion?"

"Always."

Emily takes a breath, and I can hear her choosing her words carefully. "You've always said you were going to wait until you were married. And he's your first boyfriend, and I'm not his biggest fan, you know that. But Lyds...the way you talk about sex, you can't even say *penis* or *vagina* out loud sometimes."

I can hear the sad smile in her voice, trying to lighten it just a little, but the weight is still there.

"I don't think you were ready," she says gently. "And from what you just told me...I don't think he gave you a choice."

The words hit like a slap. I want to argue. I want to tell her she's wrong, that it wasn't like that, that I'm overreacting.

But I can't.

Because deep down, I know she's right.

I can hear Emily breathing on the other end, like she's searching for the right thing to say and coming up empty.

"Lyds..." she starts then stops whatever she was going to say. "Do you want me to come see you? Or you can take a few days off and come over here?"

"No." The word comes out too fast, too sharp. I soften my voice. "No, I'm okay. Really. I just...I needed to talk to someone about it."

"So..." she starts, her voice shifting to something lighter, more hesitant, "aside from all that...was it at least...I mean—" She stops, then tries again. "How was it? You know, if we're ignoring all the other stuff?"

The absurdity of the question hits me sideways. After everything I just told her, she's asking if the sex was good? But somehow, it works. The ridiculousness of it cracks something open in my chest, and I let out a sound that's half-laugh, half-sob.

"Fine, I guess," I manage, but my voice is shaky. "It's not like I have anything to compare it to."

Emily laughs softly, nervous, relieved that I'm not falling apart. "Well, that's...something?"

"Yeah," I say, the ghost of a smile pulling at my lips despite everything. "Something."

The moment passes quickly, the heaviness settling back in, but it gave us both a second to breathe.

"Promise me you'll call if you need anything," she presses. "Anytime. I mean it."

"I promise."

"I love you, Lyds."

"I love you too."

The call ends, and suddenly the silence in the car feels suffocating. The radio is still off. The windows are still down. The sun is finally starting to shine.

But none of it reaches me.

I pull into a random parking lot and put the car in park, my hands still gripping the steering wheel like it's the only thing keeping me tethered.

Emily's words echo in my head, louder now that I'm alone with them. I close my eyes, trying to push them away, trying to focus on anything else.

Deep down, deeper than the denial, deeper than the excuses, I know she's right.

The world keeps moving, like nothing's changed. But for me, everything has.

I just don't know what to do with that yet.

Chapter 12

9 Years Ago

Time's a funny thing. It moves relentlessly forward, and you just keep putting one foot in front of the other, pretending like you've got it all figured out. But the truth? We're all just faking it until we make it.

After that night, the night where Chad...I should have left. I know I should have left. But where would I go? Back to being the girl no one wanted? The one who sat on the sidelines while everyone else dated and fell in love? At least Chad chose me. At least someone wanted me enough to stick around.

I tell myself I was overreacting, continuously reminding myself that I'd been too drunk to really know what I wanted, that maybe I'd given mixed signals. Maybe I hadn't been clear enough. Maybe it was my fault for not saying "no" louder, for freezing instead of pushing him away harder.

And besides, he is my first real boyfriend. What do I know about how relationships are supposed to work? Maybe this was just...normal. Maybe I'd built it up in my head to be worse than it was. Other people have real problems, abuse, cheating, things that are actually serious. This was just one awkward, uncomfortable night that I can move past if I try hard enough.

I know I'm holding onto something that hurts me, but I can't let go yet. Maybe I never will. So I bury it. Convince myself it doesn't matter. Because the alternative, admitting that something is wrong with me, that I let this happen, feels too pathetic, too humiliating. If I leave him over that night, what would that say about me? That I can't handle a real relationship? That I am too damaged, too difficult, too much?

Mostly, I stay because I'm terrified of being alone again. As if being alone proves that I really am as unlovable as I've always believed. If I leave him, who else would want me? Better to stay with someone who wants me than risk being wanted by no one at all. The thought makes my chest ache in a way I don't think I can survive.

Chad graduated a few months ago, moved to the city an hour east of the university, and started a job that's supposed to make him "important." Now that my graduation is days away, I plan to move near him in the city and *hopefully* start a new chapter of our lives. But only if I can get a job—big if. The search has been a nightmare: slow, exhausting, and soul-crushing, especially when I realize how few options there are that actually match my degree.

Most of my days are spent in a monotonous loop, bouncing from class to study session to a part-time restaurant gig. It's not fancy, but it pays the rent. Taking advantage of my fairly light load with all afternoon classes, I pick up a lot of evening and weekend shifts. The night-shift pay is better, and drunk math adds up to higher tips. The drunken chaos is a kind of entertainment, though it's a bit of a hollow pleasure. Watching silly, drunk people has become a favorite pastime, but I find myself longing for a time when my life was simpler and unburdened.

Our schedules are so mismatched that we struggle to find time together anymore. I rearrange my life around his schedule, driving the miles just to steal a few minutes with him. It's rushed. Little moments I manage to squeeze in throughout the week. I make the majority of the trips, spending late nights on the road to see him. I arrive before dawn to catch a few hours of sleep next to him.

Then I wake just in time to see him for a few short minutes before his shift starts, before I have to head back to campus. It's draining, both physically and emotionally.

The distance is hard, more complex than I expected. When we finally see each other, it's like we're playing roles, kissing, having sex just to feel close, pretending everything is fine. But in between, there's this quiet space, this growing emptiness that lingers in the moments when we're not touching, not speaking.

A distance that isn't just physical, but emotional too. I remember when we first started seeing each other. There was a spark, something easy, something comfortable. Even the silence back then felt full, like it had meaning, like we didn't need words to feel connected.

I try to hold onto that. I keep telling myself that once we're back in the same city, once things settle into place after graduation, it'll be different. The emptiness will fade. We'll find our rhythm again. But even as I hope for that, a nagging part of me wonders if we've already lost it, and I'm just too scared to recognize it.

"Happy graduation day," Chad lightly cheers when I answer the call.

"Thanks, babe! Are you on your way to the university? What exit are you near?" My excitement for the day causes a rapid-fire barrage of questions. "Exits 104 and 130 have the best bathrooms and gas stations."

"It's weird that you know that."

Not when I'm the one making the effort and driving it multiple times a week. "I make that drive a lot," I say, trying not to let any bitterness seep through.

He hesitates. "Yeah…so…"

"You're not coming." My disappointment stains each word.

"It's Tuesday. I couldn't get out of work."

"It's fine," I say with a huff, even though it isn't. "Did they say why?"

"I don't have enough PTO."

"You've been there a few months now. I would have thought you had some PTO built up by now." Anger bubbles in my stomach that I force down. *Did he even ask for time off?* He's known about this date for weeks—plenty of time to ask off…Or at least let me know his request was denied.

"Don't be mad."

"I'm not mad." *I'm a little mad.*

"You sound mad."

"I'm not mad," I repeat, trying to convince myself as much as him. "I just thought you'd be here. It's kind of a big day for me, you know?"

He sighs, and I can hear him shifting on the other end. "I know, Lydia. I wanted to be there, but they won't let me take off. I don't know what you want from me. I would be there if I could."

I force a smile, knowing he can't see me. "I'm fine. Really. Just...a little disappointed. But I'll get over it."

"I'll see you Saturday to move you into your new place here."

"Yeah, okay," I say as I hear the call end before I get a chance to say goodbye.

Great. This week has been one disappointment after another. Another job rejection—one I really wanted. The latest rejection email came this morning, from another company that couldn't even be bothered with a phone call. And now my boyfriend can't even show up for one of the biggest days of my life. This week just keeps getting better. And it's only Tuesday.

At least I was finally given a job offer. It wasn't my first choice, or even my second. But it's something that will at least cover bills and rent for my own little place, which, to be fair, my mother will be thrilled to know that I'll be living alone and not in Chad's bed before we're married. I tell myself this job will do until I find something else.

I remind myself that we'll be back in the same town soon. Chad and I can finally do all the everyday couple things like actually go on dates rather than just hook up when our schedules align. It will give us a chance to reconnect and rebuild our relationship.

I stare at the ceiling, blinking away the tears that threaten to spill and ruin my fresh makeup. I take a few slow, shaky breaths. Chad isn't coming. Of course he isn't. But I refuse to let him ruin this day.

I push myself toward the closet, forcing myself to move forward. Graduation awaits. Standing tall, I pause, naked in front of my graduation gown, my mind wandering to something—and someone—completely different.

I start to plan the perfect seductive photo. My cap and gown slide over my naked body as I get into position, letting the front drape open to show just the right amount of naughty with one hand wandering south, where I know he likes it. I adjust the angle then snap. No time for a breakdown today. Not when I know exactly what can put a smile on my face today.

Me: <Image>

Jason: *Damn baby, you're killing me. Congratulations on your graduation day. But, honestly, that gown is doing you a disservice. Lose it so we can properly celebrate. You've earned it, and I want to see all of you.*

With Jason, I can take control, choose when and how I feel desired. It's the only place I feel alive.

Chapter 13

It's been a few months since my graduation, a few months of living in the same city again. I'd hoped things would settle, that the proximity would fix what distance has strained. But something about our relationship still feels uneasy.

We spend more time together again, but the shift has become jarring. Chad's energy, his outgoing, extroverted spark, has dimmed, replaced by a distance that his eyes can't hide.

It's not just his mood either. There's the drinking. I didn't notice it as much when we were apart. I wasn't around enough to see a pattern. But now, living in the same city, spending more time at his place? It's harder to ignore. I can't say it's excessive. He's not stumbling around drunk all the time, but it's more than it was in college.

Is this why he always made me drive to see him?

When the workday ends, I'm bolting out the door, already feeling the hunger set in as I head to dinner with Chad. The drive there has become something of a ritual now. Alone in my car, I let the silence of the road swallow me for a bit. My mind calms with each passing mile. The sunset is unusually stunning today, creating a watercolor effect in the most beautiful shades of orange, pink, and purple across the sky. It's magically calming in the solitude of my car, grounding me to the Earth's natural peace.

The day is winding down, and the sky deepens, turning to stormy blues as the sun sinks lower just as I reach Chad's place. The air feels heavier as I walk toward the door; a chill has settled in the atmosphere.

"Hey, babe, did you see the sky as the sun was setting? It was beautiful." I'm still caught up in the peacefulness of my drive over, holding on to the calm that exists outside of this apartment. I toss my keys on the coffee table next to an empty glass and plop down on the couch beside him.

But something's different. The usual warmth, the sense of connection we've been slowly rebuilding, is missing. His posture is off, slumped and closed off, and he avoids my gaze as if the very idea of meeting my eyes feels like too much.

"What? Oh, no, I didn't." His voice is distant and unbothered.

I force a smile, trying to hide the discomfort that's slowly creeping in. *I should have known the calm wouldn't last.* It's easier to pretend everything's fine than to face whatever has shifted between us. I lean back into the couch, though it doesn't feel as comfortable as it once did.

"Bummer. Anyway, how was work?"

"Fine. Are you ready to eat? I'm starving."

"Yeah, sure," I say with some hesitation, a little put off by his curt attitude. "Where did you have in mind?"

"I don't know. Let's just drive around until we see something that sounds good. Can you drive? I'm tired." His words feel rushed and dismissive.

"Yeah, sure." I eye him cautiously as I scoop up my keys and head for the door. "Maybe we can try out a place we haven't been to yet."

The drive has been relatively quiet, except for the few food options we take turns pointing out. "Oh, you know what?" he stutters out, pointing at a cafe across the street. "Let's just stop there, Jamie."

Did I hear that right?

"Jamie? Who the hell is Jamie?" I say, the words slipping out before I can stop them. In that split second, my chest caves in.

"Huh?" He looks up at me, his eyes unfocused.

"What did you just call me?" My voice shakes with disbelief.

"Jamie. I mean Lydia."

"Jamie? We have been dating for over a fucking year, and you call me Jamie? What the hell?" My hands tighten on the steering wheel. Over a year together, and he just erased me. Replacing my name with another as if I never existed. I feel small. Microscopic. My existence has been downgraded to a placeholder in his story.

"I didn't...It's not what you think...I've just been drinking."

I mentally retrace my steps since arriving at his place. The empty glass on the coffee table, the quiet sleepiness, the faint acidic smell growing stronger. Together they tell me more than I want to know. His drinking is getting worse. Not excessive yet, but on its way there.

"I'm sorry," I say in disbelief. "Is that supposed to be a good excuse? Who is she?"

"My ex. Let's just go home. We can talk about it later." He rubs his forehead as if he's frustrated with me.

"I will gladly take you home," I say, throwing the car in drive.

He doesn't argue when I put him in bed, but he tries to convince me to crawl in with him, which I refuse. The audacity to think I would sleep in his bed after the disrespect. He falls asleep quickly, like my presence isn't worth fighting for. How can he look so peaceful when I feel like my life is unraveling? Maybe I was always just a shadow of someone else.

Light catches the bottle on the table as I pass. Picking it up, it's almost empty. Closing my eyes, my chest tightens as I try to recall the memory of being here yesterday.

Wasn't this bottle unopened when I left yesterday morning? I'm sure I saw it sitting there, seal intact, when I left for work.

A beer after work is one thing—hell, I drink a glass of wine myself to unwind a few nights a week—but almost a whole bottle of vodka? That was less than twenty-four hours ago. That's...excessive. The word claws its way into my thoughts.

Yes, excessive is definitely the right word.

Don't most people start growing up after college? Don't they stop drinking and partying so much once they realize that working with a hangover sucks? Maybe that's just me. After working all day at a job that is emotionally draining, the last thing I want to do is fake social energy at work the next day, feeling like my head might explode, trying to make nice with customers while all I can think about is crawling back into bed with a cold compress over my face.

I sigh, staring at the bottle again, wondering if he even knows how much this is starting to affect me—or if he even cares. Either way, the distance between us is growing wider, and I don't know how to bridge it anymore. Maybe I never knew how.

I can't stay here. Not tonight. I grab my keys from the coffee table where I'd tossed them earlier and leave without saying goodbye. He's already passed out anyway.

I pull out my phone, my fingers shaking as I type. Not just from anger, but from the weight of it all. Loneliness, shame, guilt, desperation. I can't stand this anymore. I need to talk to someone. Someone who won't make excuses. Someone who will make me forget. Someone who will see what I need.

Me: Why are guys such assholes?

Jason: We just can't help it. What did he do this time?

Me: Got drunk...and called me by his ex's name.

Jason: Lydia, baby. It's Wednesday.

Me: I'm aware.

Jason: He's that drunk on a Wednesday?

Me: Yep. We were supposed to be going out to dinner. He was already like that when I got to his place.

Jason: Does this happen often?

Me: Do you really want to talk about my boyfriend?

Jason: I'd rather help you forget him.

Me: You're good at that.

Jason: Making you forget him?

Me: Yes

And making me feel like I matter.

Jason's words bring a fleeting sense of relief. He's the distraction I crave, even though it feels wrong, like I'm reaching into a fire I know will burn me. But when I talk to him, even if it's in the most disjointed way, it feels like I'm actually heard. I shouldn't want this. I shouldn't want to talk to him, especially when every part of me knows it's crossing a line. But I do. I need it.

"Stop it! You know this can never be anything more," I whisper to myself as I unlock my apartment door, trying to convince myself the boundaries I've drawn are real. I sound like I'm giving myself therapy, as if speaking the truth could somehow make it easier to accept. Jason is my source of therapy, helping me explore and mend the broken parts of me that I never knew needed to be healed.

My stomach growls, but I feel the hunger for something more urgent than food, something deeper. It's not just the need to be touched, to be wanted. It's a hunger for control. For satisfaction. The kind I can't seem to find with Chad, no matter how much I convince myself that we're fine.

I rush inside, letting my phone buzz with Jason's response, but I barely register it as I strip away the layers between me and what I need.

Jason: Always happy to help you

Me: Actually, I got a new toy with you in mind.

Jason: Oh?

Opening the app on my phone, I send him a link to an app-controlled vibrator designed for long-distance couples. He will now be able to control the vibrations multiple states away.

Me: *Download this app and add me*

Jason: *You are right. I will definitely enjoy controlling your pleasure. Get your computer ready, baby girl. I need to watch you come.*

It's thrilling, the way he says it, the way it makes me feel like I have power again. But underneath the pulse of desire is something darker. I'm not sure if I'm reclaiming myself or losing more of myself with every message I send.

Chapter 14

I return home from work the following evening to find Chad at my door, full of charm and apologies. He's the version of himself I fell for, the one who knew just what to say to make me feel like I mattered. I believe him, praying that it's the truth. For now, I need it to be.

He leans in with that familiar grin, the one that always makes me melt. He grovels, saying he's sorry, that he didn't mean anything by it, showing me his phone, scrolling through the messages to prove that the last time he'd talked to her was over a year ago.

He looks so earnest, like he is genuinely sorry. I watched him, listening to his words. Maybe I overreacted. After all, it's just a name, right? People slip up. It could happen to anyone, right?

But there's a flicker of doubt, deep beneath the surface, that I can't shake. Was it really just a slip-up? Or is there something more? I try to push the thought away, convincing myself it's not worth losing sleep over.

To keep myself distracted, I throw myself into helping Emily with her wedding plans. The whirlwind of finalizing details and organizing the event gives me some much-needed space, both from Chad and from myself. It feels good to be needed by someone who isn't wrapped up in his own mess.

The wedding is days away, and I can finally look forward to something exciting. A weekend of fun, of celebration, of pretending the cracks are not slowly deepening in this relationship, at least for a little while.

I feel a heat rise to my cheeks, and for a split second, I scold myself. I shouldn't be thinking about him now, not while Chad is sitting just a few feet away. But the thought refuses to leave me, curling in my chest like a secret thrill. *It's wrong*, I say to myself, but my fingers hover over my phone anyway, craving the messages that make me feel alive again.

Me: *Are you going to Emily's wedding?*

Jason: *As of now. You?*

Me: *Well, since I'm the maid of honor, yes, yes, I am.*

Jason: *Then I'll need to find us a place to sneak off to at the reception.*

Me: *Indeed, you will.*

Jason: *What are you going to let me do to you? All those people partying around us...anyone could catch us.*

Jason's words spark something inside me. The idea of sneaking away, of letting go, even just for a moment, stirs a part of me that's been dormant for far too long. It's a fantasy I shouldn't indulge, not with Chad right there beside me. It feels like a betrayal waiting to happen. But the sweetest escapes are always laced with a hint of poison, aren't they?

I could fight it. I could remind myself who I'm supposed to be loyal to, what I'm supposed to protect. But is that a fight I want to win?

Me: *Anything.*

The day of the wedding arrives, and everything unfolds just as planned. Nervous energy churns my stomach, not from standing in front of a crowd or giving a speech, but from knowing Jason will see me walk down the aisle before I'll even get a chance to spot him.

I try to ignore that feeling, pushing emotions down like I always do. Today isn't about me. It's about Emily, my best friend, marrying the man she loves. The man who, without knowing it, triggered a strange shift in my life just by pulling her into his orbit.

When the ceremony ends, we exit back up the aisle, and I try to get a glimpse at all those who attended without being obvious. I smile at my friends and Chad, but I don't see him. My mind speeds through possible scenarios as we finish taking wedding party pictures. *Maybe he's sitting on the edge where I couldn't see him, or he's running late. Maybe he's not coming, or he's here and doesn't like what he sees. Why do I care so much?* I resolve to enjoy the reception, eat, drink, and dance with Chad and my friends. If he's here, he will find me. If he's not, I'll give him hell later.

But as the reception goes on, the toasts are made, the first dance is held, the cake is cut, each event deepening the grip of disappointment. The music swirls around me, laughter bouncing off the walls, but it all sounds muffled. I smile, but it's a hollow gesture. Inside, my chest tightens with the absence of someone who should be here.

I keep checking the door, scanning the crowd between dances and photos, but there's no sign of him. My phone stays frustratingly silent. Each time someone new walks in, my heart jumps then sinks when it's not him. I watch couples twirl and clink glasses, and the sparkle in the air only magnifies the dull ache inside me. The room is bright and festive, and yet I feel invisible.

He's not here.

After the reception, a few of us close friends and family head to a nearby bar with Emily and her new husband. We continue partying as Chad sits stoically at the bar. To most, he seems bored, maybe tired. But I know better now. That distant look, the way he appears to be nursing the same drink for the last hour, but I've lost track of his actual number. That gut feeling tells me he's straddling the line between drunk and too drunk. I made sure to stop drinking at the reception so one of us was okay to drive home.

He's not a loud, obnoxious drunk, but he is too intoxicated to pay attention to anything I'm doing as I stare at my phone, still trying to make Jason feel guilty for not showing up. *I really wish he had.*

Emily, however, noticed. "Who has your head in your phone all night? Your boyfriend is sitting at the bar, drinking by himself, so it can't be him."

My fingers freeze, and my eyes dart to her before glancing around the room, confirming Chad is too preoccupied to care what I'm doing.

"Jason," I finally confess, drawing out his name as if I'm unsure I should be saying this out loud.

"Y'all should just fuck already and get it out of your system."

Oh, my dear sweet friend, if you only knew.

"Ha. Yeah, well..." I pause to consider if I really want to admit this.

"Well..." she urges me to continue.

"Remember, you started this," I remind her, pointing a finger in her face. "But I think if he had come to your wedding, I would have."

Emily's eyes widen, and for a moment, she just stares at me. I can see the wheels turning in her head as she processes what I just said. Her expression shifts from surprise to something softer—concern, maybe, mixed with curiosity.

"Wait." She holds up a hand. "Would you have slept with him?"

I respond with a quick smile, although I know the question was rhetorical.

"Wow." She exhales, shaking her head. "A few questions. What about Chad? How do you feel that he didn't show up? Where would you even have...? How would that have even worked?"

My face widens with a smile despite the gravity of what we are discussing. I love my best friend and her support of my brand of crazy. Subconsciously, I think she wants us to happen. Is that why she started this whole charade to begin with?

"Hopefully, I would have had the sense to break it off with Chad before I did something like cheat on him." I pause, letting out a large breath. *Or used cheating as an excuse to leave.* "Where and how, I don't know, but knowing Jason, he would have found a place to make it happen. But he didn't show, and it stopped me from doing something stupid," I quickly respond, hoping she doesn't notice I avoided the major question. The feeling claws its way up my chest, sharp and unrelenting.

Disappointed. I feel disappointed.

I wanted him so badly I was willing to implode my entire life. His absence hits like cold water, a harsh reality check I need that snaps everything into focus. It reminds me exactly what this relationship really is. We use each other, both giving and taking what the other needs.

Whether he knows it or not, he has single-handedly restored my self-confidence—at least some of it. Fueling my fantasies and showing me what I need. While I, in return, provide him free porn both in words and pictures.

"You didn't answer the one question."

I wish I could say I didn't care.

But as I look at Chad sitting alone at the bar, barely aware that I exist, while I text another man, something in me starts to crack under the weight of my ever-present guilt.

I realize I'm caught between what I crave and the life I believe I deserve.

I care so much more than I want to admit. And I don't know how long I can keep pretending I'm okay with it.

Chapter 15

The night winds down. We exchange goodbyes with hugs as Emily promises to send photos soon. We see the happy couple off and head back to Chad's for the night.

As if on autopilot, Chad undresses, quickly showers, and tucks himself into bed. Light snoring fills the room almost immediately.

I take my time in the bathroom, letting the hot water run over me as I replay my conversation with Emily. Her words still echo in my head—*"Y'all should just fuck already."*

I kept checking the door, scanning the crowd, wondering if he'd appear at the last minute. He didn't. But he did text me later. I'd felt my phone buzz against my leg just as we were arriving at the bar. A simple message, nothing over the top, just a 'Sorry I couldn't make it. Thinking about you.'

I'd stared at it for too long in the bathroom, rereading it more times than I care to admit. Two sentences. That was all it took to make my chest tighten, to make me wonder what might have happened if those words had come with him actually showing up.

The room is dark and quiet when I finally step out of the bathroom, wrapped in a towel and with too many tangled thoughts. I assume Chad's still asleep, unaware of the emotional mess I've become. I tread softly toward the dresser, still not sure if I'm glad tonight ended the way it did or if I'm just telling myself I am. My mind is so preoccupied with thoughts of what could have been that I don't hear Chad leave the bed.

One moment, I'm standing alone with my thoughts, reaching for the drawer handle, and the next, there is a pressure I can't comprehend. His hand, warm and heavy, wraps around my throat, the force pushing me back against the wall.

At first, I think it's meant to be intimate, a touch, a kiss on my neck, something tender after the tension of the night. But then his grip shifts, tightens, and I realize this isn't any type of caress.

The pressure builds fast, like a vise closing around my windpipe. I try to speak, to say his name, but no sound comes out. Just a strangled gasp that goes nowhere.

My hand flies up instinctively, grabbing at his wrist, his fingers, anything to relieve the pressure. But his grip is unyielding.

"Chad!" I try again, managing to force air through the narrow passage he's left me, but it comes out as barely a whisper. A plea he doesn't hear.

I blink hard, trying to focus, but the edges of my vision are already going blurry.

This isn't happening. This can't be happening. But it is.

I look up at him, searching for recognition, awareness, anything, but his eyes are vacant. Glassy. Like he's looking through me instead of at me. Like I'm not even here.

He's going to kill me. The thought slices through the panic, sharp and cold. *He's going to kill me, and he doesn't even know it.*

My heart hammers so hard I can feel it in my skull in a frantic rhythm. My hands are still on his wrist, pulling, scratching, but my strength is draining fast. Everything feels heavy.

A burst of adrenaline floods through me, raw and primal. I stop trying to pull his hand away and shove against his chest instead, using every ounce of strength I have left. At the same time, I hook my thumb under his, prying at the weakest point in his grip.

The pressure releases all at once, and I suck in a ragged, desperate breath. It's loud and ugly, more like a sob than a gasp. I crumble against the wall, my legs giving out as I slide down to the floor. My hands fly to my throat, trying to protect myself from a second attack.

Chad doesn't say anything. He doesn't apologize. Doesn't ask if I'm okay. Doesn't even look at me.

He just...turns around and walks back to bed. Like nothing happened. I sit there on the floor, gasping, shaking, staring at his silhouette as he climbs under the covers and settles in bed. My chest heaves with each breath, too fast, too shallow, like my body still doesn't believe it's safe.

What the fuck just happened?

The question echoes in my head, but I don't have an answer. I don't have anything except the hammering of my pulse and the suffocating silence of the room.

I don't know how long I've been sitting here. Minutes? Hours? Time feels broken, stretched thin and warped, but eventually, my legs remember how to move.

I push myself up, wobble, and stumble toward the bathroom, fumbling with the lock. My hands won't stop shaking. I twist the handle once then twice, checking it's really locked, while leaning my whole weight against the door like a barricade.

I flip on the light and immediately wish I hadn't. The mirror shows me everything I didn't want to see. My face is blotchy, eyes wide and red-rimmed. And oh god, my neck.

Dark-red marks are already forming where his fingers pressed in. By morning, I know they will be purple. But even now, I can count them. One. Two. Three. Four. His thumb on one side, fingers wrapped around the other.

I stare at the girl in the mirror. Who is the girl who let this happen? This woman who's standing in a bathroom at 2 AM, too afraid to leave, too ashamed to stay. *When did I become her?* I reach up, fingers trembling, and touch the marks gently. They're tender. Painful. Real.

The evidence is right there, blooming across my skin like some dark flower, irrefutable yet unbelievable. The idea of having to explain this makes my stomach twist, but the fear they won't believe me... That's the part that truly terrifies me.

I turn away from the mirror, unable to look at her anymore, and turn on the shower. The pipes groan and sputter before the water comes, and I step in, letting the scalding spray hit me.

There's something about falling water that's so therapeutic, like rain washing all the bad away, cleansing the soul. I just stand there, eyes closed, trying to wash away what just happened.

The events start piling up in my mind, each one stacking on the other. The drinking. The lying. The nights Chad came home too drunk to stand. The times I had to put him to bed. The mornings he didn't remember The empty promises.

And now this.

Things I know I should leave him for.

The thoughts pour in, each one louder, more insistent than the one before.

But when he's not drunk, Chad's really sweet and funny. And even when he's drunk, he's fun. It's only when he blacks out that things go wrong, and it's not that often. Right?

I press my palms against the tile, head bowed under the spray.

Besides, what do I have to offer that anyone else would want?

The question sits heavy in my chest, familiar and cruel. I've asked it so many times before that it feels like the truth now.

He's the first and only guy who's really shown me this much attention. This is probably as good as I will get. Right? Maybe it's karma for having sex before marriage?

The thought slithers in like poison, and I hate myself for even thinking it. But it's there. The guilt I was raised with, the shame that's been woven into my bones since childhood. I deserve this. Maybe this is what happens when you break the rules.

Or I'm just making excuses again, the same way I made excuses for that first night, the same way I'll probably make excuses tomorrow.

The water starts to run cool, then cold, snapping me out of the spiral. I don't know how long I've been standing here. Long enough that my fingers are pruned. Long enough that the tears have mixed with the water, and I can't tell which is which anymore.

He's snoring when I finally come out of the bathroom, the sound cutting through the silence like a taunt.

I stand there for a moment, staring at the lump of him under the covers, and something hot and sharp twists in my chest.

How dare he sleep.

I tiptoe to the kitchen, bare feet silent on the cold tile, and pour myself a glass of water. My throat is raw, every swallow painful, but the cool liquid soothes it just enough. I lean against the counter, taking slow sips, trying to calm the trembling in my hands.

That's when I see it. The home bar. I stand on the cold tile, my eyes locked on the bottles. Every instinct screams to leave, to run, but my feet stay planted. *How did it come to this?*

He did this because he was drunk. He blacked out. He didn't mean it. The excuses echo in my head, hollow and infuriating. And suddenly, I'm not sad anymore.

I'm furious.

My feet carry me to the bar before I even realize I'm moving. I grab the first bottle, some expensive whiskey he's been saving, and unscrew the cap. The sharp smell of alcohol burns my nose as I take a drag from the bottle before tipping it over the sink, watching the amber liquid swirl down the drain.

One bottle down.

The second bottle follows. Then a third. A fourth. I lose count somewhere around six. I'm hypnotized by the vortex, watching his carefully curated collection swirl down the drain—or at least what he's managed to replace since I was last here. Whiskey. Vodka. Rum. Each one feels like reclaiming something he took from me.

I don't care that it's loud. I let the chaos and noise made by the shattering of each empty bottle fuel my anger.

I want him to wake up. I want him to come out here and see what I'm doing. I want him to try to stop me so I can scream at him, so I can make him see what he's done.

But he doesn't.

It's still early morning, around 2 AM, by the time I'm done, according to the microwave clock. The apartment is dark and silent except for him. I creep back to the bedroom, careful not to wake him, afraid to cause another attack, and start grabbing the few things I have here. A toothbrush. A change of clothes. My phone charger. The book I left on his nightstand.

Another night that I refuse to stay here. I can't stay here. Not with him like this.

As I zip up my bag, I catch sight of his keys on the dresser. My apartment key is still on his keyring, the one I gave him months ago, back when I thought we were building something.

I slip it off. The metal feels cool against my fingers, and I tuck it into my pocket—for good measure, I tell myself. It's mine again. My space. My safety. I won't be able to sleep worrying about when he'll show up. Or if he'll just let himself in and crawl into my bed as if nothing happened.

I sling my bag over my shoulder and walk out, closing the door softly behind me, hoping I'll be able to sleep the nightmare of this day away.

* *

It's almost 11 AM before I finally wake up. My throat is sore, a dull ache that sharpens when I swallow. For a blissful half-second, I can't remember why. Then it all comes rushing back.

Only one text from Chad, about a half hour ago, saying good morning. Does he remember anything about last night? Not ready to fight, I go about my day, ignoring the texts that keep coming from Chad as a flood of questions comes through: What are you doing? Where did you go? When did you leave?

Then a call.

Then another.

Finally, silence.

The sweet silence lasts for a short time before there's a knock at the door. My whole body tenses at the sound. My heart rate spikes as I back against the wall.

"Lyds, open up. It's me. I can't find my key." I wait a little to see if he leaves, but he persists. "Come on, babe. I see your car, so I know you're here."

Stupid assigned parking spots.

After a few more knocks, I give in and open the door, trying to appear as if I was just awoken from a nap.

"There you are. I was getting kinda worried. When did you leave this morning? And why are you not answering your phone?"

"I was sleeping," I force out the lie.

I stare at him for a few long moments, studying his face. Does he really not remember? Or is he just pretending? His face gives nothing away. Or maybe I was never good at reading him to begin with. My fingers drift to my throat, tender to the touch, the skin just starting to darken. It's subtle, barely noticeable unless you know what to look for. But I know. I feel it.

Fighting back tears, I finally muster up the courage to have this conversation. "Do you remember anything from last night?"

"Wedding and the reception, then to an after-party, then home to bed."

"Yeah, that's what I thought," I say with an aggravated huff. I don't know how he's standing right now and not nursing a serious hangover.

"Why?" His brows knit together with confusion.

Furrowing my brow and pinching the bridge of my nose, I spit out, "You got home and blacked out. Or maybe even at the after-party, but that's beside the point. Chad, you tried to strangle me last night."

"No." He says it as more of a question than a statement. I stare at him, tears welling up as the weight of it hits me. He can't even remember it, can't even process what he's done. His voice is calm, almost like he's trying to convince himself more than me. But the look in my eyes, the silent plea for him to take responsibility, slices the air between us, too heavy to ignore. He claims he doesn't remember, but the way he avoids my eyes makes me wonder if that's true or a strategy.

"That explains why all the alcohol bottles were shattered in the trash. Did you pour it all down the sink? You know what, it doesn't matter. I probably need to start drinking less anyway."

He steps forward to hug me, but I instinctively take a step back, not ready for his touch yet. He freezes mid-step, confusion flickering across his face like he didn't expect me to flinch. Slowly, he lifts his hands, palms out in surrender.

"Right. I shouldn't have tried to…I'm so sorry, babe. I never want to hurt you." He hesitates, swallowing hard. "My dad was a drunk, and I don't want to end up like him. I'll work on it. I promise."

The excuse is thin, as if naming his father's demons absolves him of his own. His words land heavily, full of emotion but hollow at the core. An empty promise dressed in remorse. I want to believe him. I need to believe him. Because if I don't, then what does that make me if I stay?

I'll believe it when I see actual change.

"You've said that before," I say. My voice wavers barely above a whisper. "But you keep making the same choices he did."

He flinches at the accusation, and I hope it hits as hard as I intended.

"I know," he says quietly. "I know, but I mean it, Lydia."

I want to scream at him. I want to tell him that promises don't mean anything without action. But I'm so tired. Tired of fighting, tired of being afraid, tired of wondering when the next time will be.

And maybe this was just a terrible accident. A wake-up call. Maybe this is the moment that finally changes things. *It has to be.*

Because the alternative, that this is who he is, that it will happen again, is something I'm not ready to face.

"Okay," I hear myself say, though the word feels like it's coming from someone else.

"Okay." He exhales, relief flooding his face as he steps closer. This time, I let him. His arms wrap around me, and I close my eyes, trying to convince myself that this hug means safety. That his promises mean something.

But deep down, beneath the hope I'm clinging to, a small voice whispers: *You should have left.*

I ignore it for now.

Chad is more attentive over the weekend, sweet and apologetic, promising things will change. I haven't seen him drink once or seen any alcohol in his house. And part of me wants to believe him, wants to believe things can get better. But another part of me wonders how much longer I can let this go on before it's too late.

He's trying. That has to count for something.

But the bruises on my neck are still there. Fading but not gone. And every time I catch my reflection, I see them. A reminder that no matter how hard I try to forget, my body remembers.

And so does a small, persistent voice in the back of my mind that I'm working very hard to ignore.

Chapter 16

The next few weeks go...okay, but I tell myself they go great. Chad stays sober. He's attentive, apologetic, and everything he promised. I almost convince myself that night was a fluke. A terrible, isolated incident we can move past.

Well, except for the job I hate and the nagging feeling that won't go away.

It's a Thursday afternoon in late October when everything shifts again.

"Hey, Lydia, I have something to tell you."

Oh God, the shoe is about to drop. "Yeah, what's that?" I force an attempt at a curious tone, hoping it doesn't come across as suspicious.

"I, uh..." He rubs the back of his neck as if he's trying to soothe his nerves. The self-soothing act causes my nerves to spike. "I kinda lost my job."

Kinda?

Internally, I panic for him. What's he going to do? How is he going to pay bills? "Okay. Like you were let go or...?" Not wanting to ask him outright if he was fired.

"Yeah, fired, I guess."

Then I double down on the internal panic. How does he not know? I can't support both of us on my salary. What will my parents think when they find out he got fired? Why did he get fired? What did he do? How will he get another job after being fired? Is my face showing my panic?

"Did they say why?" I ask, trying to sound casual, though my voice cracks slightly. What if he was let go for reasons I don't want to know about? My chest tightens at the thought.

"Not really, just that it wasn't working out."

What does that mean? There has to be some reason, right?

"But look, I've already started updating my resume. Can you proofread it for me? I'll start looking for a new job. I'm sure I'll get something soon."

"Yeah, of course."

He's right. It doesn't take long for him to get a new job offer. Within two weeks, he accepts a position starting in December. That's only a month away now. The pay is definitely better. One major problem, though, is that it's halfway across the country—the West Coast.

Everything happens fast after that. Too fast, maybe. But I don't let myself think about it too hard.

After accepting the job, Chad asks me to consider moving with him, and now I find myself weighing every option.

Part of me sees this as a perfect out, a clean break, a chance to start over. But then there's the other part, the part that watches him trying, telling me to go with him. He's been putting in effort, cutting back on the drinking, saying all the right things. Ever since that night, he swears he's realized something about himself—that once he starts, he can't stop. And maybe he's right, and he's getting better.

I need to believe he is. Because the alternative—that I'm making this decision out of fear rather than hope—is too painful to admit.

What if I leave him and no one else ever wants me? The thought nags at me more and more lately. I know it sounds irrational, but the fear is real. I've always been afraid of being alone, of not being enough for someone, of being forgotten or replaced. Chad is the first person who's ever really wanted me, the first one to make me feel like I matter. Even if that validation comes tangled in drunken outbursts and emotional distance, it's still something. And sometimes, something feels better than nothing.

On the other hand, I really hate my job. I've been toying with the idea of taking online classes, finding something I want to do with my life. If I move, I can get a part-time job and focus on school. It sounds almost...hopeful. This could be a fresh start. A chance to chase something that feels like mine.

The idea of starting over in a new city, with no expectations, is tempting. I tell myself this is my choice. I'm not just following Chad. I'm stepping into something new for me. It's a nice story. I almost believe it.

But the voice in my head whispers: What if this is a trap disguised as freedom? The idea of being financially dependent on Chad, even for a short time, terrifies me. What if things get worse? What if I'm stuck across the country and can't leave?

Still, the fear of staying stagnant and alone here feels heavier. So I take the leap. I agree to move in with him in January, a few weeks after he settles into his new role.

Breaking the news to my parents is difficult. They aren't thrilled when I tell them. My mother's face tightens in that particular way that means she's biting back everything she wants to say. My father just sighs, long and heavy, like he's already resigned to watching me make a mistake.

"You're moving in with him?" my mother finally asks, her voice tight. "Before you're even engaged?"

"It's across the country, Mom. I can't afford my own place out there right now, not until I find a job. And besides, we've been together for years. It's not like—"

"It's not like what, Lydia?" she cuts me off, her tone sharp. "It's not like y'all haven't had problems before?"

The words hang between us, heavy and uncomfortable. She doesn't know about the choking. She doesn't know about half of what's happened. But she doesn't need to know to be worried. She is a mother, after all.

My father places a hand on her arm, a silent plea for her to ease up. "You know we don't agree with this, but we just want you to think this through," he says quietly. "That's all."

Mom's eyes linger on mine longer than necessary. I can feel her anger and disappointment threading through my chest like tiny needles.

"I know," I say, my voice smaller than I want it to be. "I will be."

They don't push further, but I can feel their disapproval settling over the conversation like a weight I'll carry with me. Still, they don't try to stop me, but I know their guilt trips will continue.

At least the move gives me the perfect excuse to quit my job. I give my two weeks' notice with barely concealed relief, citing the relocation as the reason. My manager doesn't seem surprised. Everyone knew I hated it there.

Chad's moving in November, and I spend the month tying up loose ends, packing up my life into boxes, and saying goodbyes that feel heavier than they should. Every box I tape shut feels like another layer of my old life being left behind, hoping this is for the better.

While helping Chad load his apartment into the moving van before his move, my hand brushes against something small and velvet in his sock drawer. I freeze, knowing immediately what it is before I even pull it out.

An engagement ring. Simple, understated, probably within his budget. It's meant to be a surprise.

I stare at it for a long moment, this tiny circle of metal that suddenly feels impossibly heavy. He's planning to propose. Maybe even soon. The thought should make me happy. Isn't this what I wanted? Someone who wants to keep me?

I slide the ring out of the box and onto my finger before I can stop myself. Lifting my hand into view, I should feel something for this moment as I watch the light catch the diamond and scatter rainbows across the room. Instead, my stomach twists in a way I can't decipher. Why does it feel more like a trap than a promise?

I tuck it back exactly where I found it, careful to leave no trace. I don't plan to tell him I found it. But now I know. And knowing changes everything. Or maybe it changes nothing at all.

By the time January rolls around and I'm loading my car and making the drive to join him, I've convinced myself this is the right choice. A fresh start. A new chapter. A chance to finally be happy.

I just wish I fully believed it.

Chapter 17

8 Years Ago

Sitting at the coffee shop, sipping a cup of coffee in the late-May sun, the new city no longer feels like an adventure.

We've been here four months now. Four months of trying to make this work, of telling myself things are getting better. Four months, and I still don't know anyone here. No friends. No support system. Just Chad, his coworkers I've met twice, and the baristas at the coffee shop who know my order.

I spend my days piecing together part-time retail shifts, tutoring gigs, and whatever else I can find that works around my master's program. The student loans are already piling up, but school gives me something to focus on. Something that feels like mine.

June creeps in quietly, heavy with more than just the summer heat. After another long day of work and classes, Chad finally proposes. It isn't anything grand, just a quiet night in, pizza boxes scattered across the couch, our usual routine.

But when he pulls out the ring, the whole situation feels forced. Not how you expect a proposal to feel. The way he stumbles over his words, barely making eye contact, his fingers twitching nervously as he fumbles with the box. It isn't like him. The man I fell for, that I moved across the country with, was confident and decisive. This version feels like a stranger.

When he finally manages to get the question out, it sounds more like an apology than a proposal. "Will you...I mean, I think we should...Lydia, will you marry me?"

I want to feel something: joy, excitement, even nervousness. Instead, I feel numb. Like I'm watching this happen to someone else.

I probably should say no, but what choice do I have now? I have no one else here, no steady income yet, and now student loans from my online master's program are piling up. I can't go home without looking like a complete failure. Plus, I've never told anyone about the issues in our relationship. How would I explain it suddenly crumbling? The pity looks. The inevitable "Why didn't you talk to me?"

And what would I even tell people? That I moved across the country for a guy who can't remember strangling me, sometimes can't remember my name, and hugs the bottle like it's his one true love? And I choose to call it quits now? That sounds pathetic even in my own head.

My mind cycles through every what-if version of telling my mom that Chad proposed and I said no. They flood through my head, unrelenting. Each one plagued by the initial relief followed instantly by waves of guilt and shame. She means well and wants what's best for me, but the idea of disappointing her... I can't.

So, I keep the mask on.

"Yes," I hear myself say. Because what else can I say? I already started building a life around him. I say yes, not out of love, but because I didn't see a way to say no without losing everything. I say yes out of obligation, to him, to my parents, to my upbringing, to my reputation.

He slips the ring on my finger—the same ring I found weeks ago in his sock drawer—and it feels heavier than it should. Maybe he isn't drunk; maybe it's just his nerves catching up to him, the pressure of our future together crashing down on him. But my mind constantly questions if it's the alcohol doing the talking. He certainly could have had a drink or two while waiting for the pizza. I can't decide, but the ring on my finger feels more like a trap than a promise. The weight of it is suffocating, a constant reminder that I'm stuck, and now, I have even less of a way out.

My mother starts calling the next day, wanting to talk about venues, dates, and guest lists. I tell her I want a long engagement. Time to save money, time to plan appropriately. In reality, I just can't bring myself to pick a date. Every time she brings it up, I change the subject. "We're not in a rush, Mom. We want to do it right."

She's thrilled regardless. At least the wedding planning keeps her happy and stops her guilt trips, since I'm no longer living with a boyfriend, even if every conversation about it makes my chest tighten.

The weeks slide by in a haze of work, classes, and wedding research, looking at venues I can't afford, scrolling through Pinterest boards that all look the same, pretending to care about napkin colors. It's easier to focus on the superficial details than to think about what I'm actually doing. What I'm actually agreeing to.

By the time the heat starts to break and the first back-to-school ads appear, I've traded wedding magazines for hand wraps and a heavy bag. I start working out at a local boxing gym, ostensibly to lose weight for the wedding, but really because hitting something feels good. Feels like control. The gym has become my refuge—the one place I don't have to smile. I usually go early in the afternoon, but today I went later. By the time I get home, Chad is already there, changing from his work clothes into something more casual.

"Hey, Lyds. I've got dinner plans with some work buddies tonight. Then we are going to play pool at the pool hall down the road if you want to join us there after dinner."

"Yeah, sounds good. I was just planning on leftovers anyway. Let me know when y'all head to the pool hall, and I'll come meet you." I pause then add, trying to keep my tone light even though we both know how I really feel, "Don't drink, please," I beg as he makes his way to the door.

He waves a hand dismissively. "Yeah, yeah. See you later." I barely catch a glimpse of his eyes as he leaves, almost missing the subtle eye roll he tries to hide.

The moment the door clicks shut behind him, I feel an unexpected rush of relief. Some time alone. My own space. I immediately pull out the bottle of wine I've been saving, one I'd hidden away so Chad wouldn't drink it before I had the chance. He's done that more times than I care to admit. This bottle isn't cheap, and I've been looking forward to it, savoring the idea of a quiet evening.

The irony isn't lost on me, hiding alcohol from an alcoholic then drinking it myself to cope with life. But I don't let myself think about that too long.

I pour myself a generous glass. It goes down too easily. Too quickly. I tell myself it's just to unwind, just to get through the night without overthinking everything. But deep down, I know it's a distraction, a way to numb the weight of what's been building up inside me—a way to forget for a little while.

I should call Emily. Or Mona. Talk to someone about how I'm feeling. Instead, I reach for my phone and open the one conversation that always makes me feel wanted.

I snap a picture of the mostly empty bottle to send to him, anything to spark a conversation that'll pull me away from my spiraling thoughts. A reminder that I'm not as alone as I feel.

Me: <image>

Jason: Someone must be enjoying herself.

Me: Oh, I'm about to.

Checking the time, I need to start getting ready to meet Chad and head for the shower with my glass of wine in hand.

Jason: I'd love to see that

Curating the perfect shower image, I snap a photo and edit the color. There's something sexy about black and white photos. Then I hit send.

Me: <image>

Jason: What I wouldn't do to you in that shower.

Me: Are you doing anything tonight?

Jason: I'm all yours.

Me: Video call when I get out of the shower?

Jason: Love to.

Still wrapped in a towel, hair dripping droplets down my neck and shoulders, I pour the last of the bottle into my glass and set myself up for a video call. For these few minutes, I can forget about the ring on my finger. Forget about the wedding I'm supposed to be planning.

Forget about Chad and his friends at the bar. Here, with Jason, I'm not trapped. I'm wanted.

Positioning myself on screen from the chest up, I make the call. Jason answers with record speed.

"Hey, sexy. Mmmm." He licks his lips. "What I wouldn't give to lick those drops of water off of you right now," he purrs as his eyes track a drop of water down my neck and into my cleavage.

I take a slow sip of my wine, licking the remnants from my lips as I watch him watching me. With one hand, I unwrap the bath towel that protected my last bit of modesty and lift it between two fingers up the middle of my body before tossing it to the floor. I have my laptop sitting on the dresser that faces the bed, but standing this close, he can still only see me from the top of my cleavage and up.

"Finish that wine, baby girl. Then back that pretty ass up to the bed and show me how wet you are for me."

Taking a sip of wine, I place the glass on the dresser and slowly back up until the backs of my legs hit the bed frame. Settling on the bed, I position both feet on the footboard with my knees up, ready to open wide for him. My hand roams slowly down my chest and stomach, pausing right before I reach the part of me he really wants to see me touch.

With the laptop screen still in perfect view from this position, I watch as he re-adjusts his camera to give me a view of his beautiful cock. He starts to lightly stroke himself as he expertly instructs my movements to coax us each into our separate orgasms together.

He licks his lips, eyes fixed on me as I lick my fingers clean, letting out a small moan at my taste.

"There's something seriously sexy about seeing you come undone like that for me while wearing another man's ring."

"You are supposed to be making me forget my troubles, not reminding me how dangerous this is."

"Fine, let's go again."

Checking my phone, I let out a sigh when I see that Chad sent a message five minutes ago that they were paying the bill and heading to the pool hall. "I would, but I have to get dressed to meet Chad and his friends."

"Ah, I was wondering how you had the alone time to come for me."

"He had dinner with some work guys, but I'm going to meet up with them after. You can watch me get dressed, though."

He hums in appreciation as I turn to the closet to fetch my favorite summer dress, ready to savor its last wear of the season. It's a purple, mid-thigh dress, nothing too short or revealing, but it's designed with a dual zipper in the front that allows for some sexier adjustments, like an added slit or a deeper V-neck showing a little more cleavage.

Bringing the dress back in front of the camera, I slip it on before making a show of zipping it up. I take my time, letting the tension build. I'm still riding the high from the orgasm Jason gave me, the thrill of his words swirling around me like the wine in my glass.

"Nothing underneath?

"Nope," I say with a flirty wink.

"Mmm, I like that dress. It's perfect if I were to stand behind you while you're belly up to the bar. I'd unzip the bottom, giving the dress a nice slit for me to slip my fingers on that perfect clit of yours while you order your drink."

"I wish you could," I say as I take a sip of wine, hoping it hides the blush.

"Text me when that fiancé starts ignoring you. I'll be here to keep you company. I'll get you in the bathroom so you can unzip that dress for me." With a final wink, he ends the call. Every word from him feels like a lifeline I shouldn't need but can't let go.

Twenty minutes later, I'm walking into the pool hall, wet again, just thinking about his words. I scan the room and spot Chad at a corner table, surrounded by his coworkers. He laughs with them, drink in hand, despite my "don't drink" request. He doesn't even notice when I walk in.

Wondering why I even bothered coming out, I pull out my phone and text Jason, knowing Chad's too busy with his friends to notice me.

My phone buzzes almost immediately. Jason is already responding. I smile at the screen, feeling more connected to a man multiple states away than to my fiancé ten feet in front of me.

This is fine, I tell myself. This is normal. Lots of couples have periods like this.

And I almost believe it.

Chapter 18

It's a crisp, cool day in late fall as I jog around the neighborhood. The air bites just enough that I can see my breath, and the trees along the sidewalks are streaked with leaves of gold and rust.

I'm not a runner by any means. I kind of hate it, actually. But when my depression hits, I get the urge to run. And it's been kicking in more and more lately. At least I can run away from my problems, if only for a little while.

In, two, three, four. Out, two, three, four. I focus on my breathing as songs shuffle through the music-streaming app. Letting the app shuffle in its own suggestions helps me find some new music. I slow to a walk as the next song starts. The song is new, but I recognize the voice. Then the lyrics hit me. Hard.

It's about a woman who no longer recognizes herself. Who's broken but won't ask for help. Who's lonely even when she isn't alone. Who gets used by a man who can't love.

I freeze mid-step. My chest tightens. My breathing, which had been steady with the rhythm of my steps, turns shallow and uneven. Each line feels like it was written about me, for me, pulling back layers I've been trying to keep covered.

I don't register the cars passing by as I stand on the side of the road, tears trailing down my cheeks from the overwhelming emotions swirling in my head. When the song ends, I realize I've been standing here for over three minutes, frozen on the sidewalk. I hit repeat. I need to hear it again. I need to understand why it's affecting me like this.

Even on the surface level, this song mirrors my life too well. It used to be mine, but now it's gone. I don't recognize myself anymore. Maybe I never really did. I thought I was lonely before, that I needed a man to love me to be happy. And I was happy, for a while. But now it's all changed. That need sank in and carved me into a shell of myself, leading me to believe this hollow existence is happiness.

Would I give this back for a chance to start over? I know I should. This isn't what I imagined my life would be, but I can't bring myself to do it. It took me long enough to get to this point in life. I'm scared to start over. I'm scared this relationship is as good as it's going to get for me. I'm afraid that if I leave now, I'll be alone forever.

My legs feel heavy. I start walking again, slowly, letting my body move while my mind races.

Another part of me believes that I have to stay because we're already sexually involved. Growing up, all I heard was no sex till marriage, and I'd fully intended to wait. That purity ring I wore felt like a promise to God, to my parents, to myself. Since that first night, the night he didn't stop when I said no, the night I buried, trying not to think about it, when I made myself believe that I had to stay. As if leaving would prove that everyone who warned me was right. That I'd failed. That I was damaged goods. Now we're engaged, planning a wedding I can't bring myself to set a date for.

I'm broken, but I won't ask for help. The lyrics echo in my head, but now it's my own voice singing them.

My fingers dust my neck, remembering the bruises that once stained my neck. The nights I've cleaned up his messes. The bottles I destroyed so he couldn't drink them. The ones I hid so I could drink them myself. The parts of myself I've trimmed away to fit into his life. Each one is a mark he didn't mean to leave—or so he says. Each one is a scar I've learned to rationalize.

How many more scars do I have to justify because I supposedly love the man who is holding the knife? A man who should love me but can't. And it took a stranger's song to make me see it clearly.

Something has to change. I can't keep living like this, engaged to a man who can't love me because he's too busy loving the bottle, too consumed by alcohol. A man who needs me to be smaller, quieter, easier. A man I'm terrified to leave and terrified to marry.

Standing here on this sidewalk, tears drying on my cold face, I don't know what change looks like. I don't know how to start. All I know is that I can't keep running from this. Eventually, I'll have to stop and face what I've been avoiding.

Just not today.

I turn toward home, my footsteps heavy, the song still playing on repeat in my ears. By the time I reach the apartment, I've wiped my face clean and masked it with my practiced smile. Chad's on the couch when I walk in, scrolling through his phone, a beer on the table beside him.

"Hey," he says without looking up. "Good run?"

"Yeah," the words are automatic. "Good run."

The realization sits heavy in my chest, but I tuck it away with all the other things I'm not ready to face. Not yet. Maybe tomorrow. Maybe next week. Maybe never.

For now, I go through the motions, shower, change, start dinner, pretending that nothing has changed, even though everything has.

And I plan.

Chapter 19

7 Years Ago

"Hey, you're home early," I yell from the kitchen as I prepare dinner to go in the oven for later.

"Yeah, not feeling well, so I took the afternoon off," Chad mutters without looking at me.

That's been the same excuse for the last few weeks when he comes home early. I try not to read too much into it. I don't want to be that girl, the one who is always suspicious, always waiting for him to mess up. But I can't help but feel something isn't right.

"Again? That's the third time in the last week. I hope you're not getting sick." I attempt to add a touch of concern, testing the waters.

"I'm fine," he snaps, letting out a small grunt as he passes by. "I'm not sick. I'll be fine after some sleep."

I start down the hall after him, drying my hands on a dish towel.

"It's just…" I hesitate, feeling the weight of the words stuck in my throat, unsure if I should press him further or let it go. I don't want to start a fight, but something in my gut tells me I shouldn't let it slide.

"It's just what, Lydia?" His tone is harsh, almost daring me to say something critical of him so he can react. It's so unlike him that it makes my skin prickle.

I look down at my leggings and t-shirt, buying myself a second to think.

"I was just about to finish getting dressed and head to the gym. Let me grab my clothes out of the room so you can nap in peace." The words come out rushed, deflecting. I'm chickening out, wanting to avoid a confrontation. First, I need to blow off some steam.

I grab my gym bag quickly, shoving in a sports bra, socks, and shoes, my mind already racing. I pause at the bedroom door, looking back at him one more time.

He's out cold. I wish I could fall asleep that fast, but the anxiety and insomnia won't let me.

The whole drive to the gym, my mind races. I pray I'm wrong, that the song I've had on repeat for weeks has me paranoid.

No. I know what I saw in his eyes. The defensiveness. The deflection. I've seen it before.

Within ten minutes, I'm dressed, wrist wrapped, and gloves on, staring at the heavy bag, planning my attack. After a long, frustrated exhale, I slam my fist into the bag, willing the anger out of my system. Each punch is a release, but nothing feels quite enough.

Jab. Cross. Hook. Jab. Cross. Jab. Spinning back fist. Repeat. An hour later, I leave the gym with a clear head, yet still no idea of what to do. He's lying. I can feel it.

After parking my car next to his and moving to grab my gym bag from the back, a glimpse of something out of place catches my eye on the front seat of his car. Something that doesn't belong. I freeze, squinting through the window.

I can't quite make out what it is, but something in my gut tells me I need to investigate. Heading up the stairs to the apartment, I drop my gym bag and keys on the floor by the front door and search for his car keys. He dropped them in the same spot on the end table as he does every day, just next to the key bowl, but not in it—no matter how many times I ask him to. My body sags, annoyed at the thought, as I head back toward the car.

My hands shake as I unlock his car and pull open the door. I rummage through the clutter of grocery bags, half hidden under a jacket, hoping to find forgotten groceries. I should be surprised when it's not.

Mini bottles of wine. Vodka. Whiskey.

My stomach drops.

I rip open another bag that lays hidden on the floor. More bottles. And receipts. Dozens of them. Gas stations. Convenience stores. All from the last few weeks. I check the times tamps. 4:47 PM, 5:43 PM, 2:52 PM. Always late afternoon. Always on workdays. Always right before he'd come home and go straight to bed.

And mints. Little tins of breath mints are scattered everywhere, as if he is trying to cover the smell. *Oh my god.* The pieces fall into place all at once, sharp and sickening.

He's been drinking in the car and in the parking garage before he comes inside. That's why he "takes the afternoon off." That's why he falls asleep so fast. That's why his breath smells like mint instead of alcohol.

He never stopped. He just got better at hiding it.

I flip through the receipts, my eyes scanning dates. Two weeks ago. Three weeks. A month. All of it is evidence. *He's been lying this whole time.*

My legs give out. I sink onto the curb next to his car, bags of evidence scattered around me like crime-scene markers. My hands are shaking so badly that I drop the receipts and have to chase them as the wind carries them across the parking lot.

One lands face up. I bend to grab it, the time and date hitting me like a punch to the gut.

Today—three hours ago.

How many times has he looked me in the eye and lied? How many times have I asked if he's okay, if he's been drinking, and he said no with that earnest, wounded look on his face for doubting him?

I want to scream. I want to throw these bottles at his windshield one by one. I want to...

Even the beauty of the afternoon sun doesn't calm my rapid heartbeat as I pound up the stairs to the apartment. My brain is trying to think rationally, to come up with a plan of approach, but my body clearly has other plans as I slam the door open and head toward the kitchen.

With no regard for the noise, for my sleeping fiancé in the other room, I rip the under-sink cabinet open, pull out a trash bag, and slam the door closed again. I hope he wakes up with the noise, but if my suspicions are correct, he's too passed out to be awoken by a few doors.

Before long, I'm sitting on the couch, staring at a white trash bag full of empty bottles as it sits stoically on the coffee table.

It's mocking me.

I suspected this was what life had in store for me when I agreed to move here with him, when I accepted the proposal, but I hoped I would be wrong. It reminds me of all the things my insecurities force me to keep buried deep down.

It's mocking me. *You deserve better than this.* But will I listen?

I've lost track of how long I've been staring at this bag. My mind races through thoughts, yet I am empty at the same time. The dark of night has long since crept in, chasing away the calming sun. This bag has me in a trance.

"What are you doing?" Chad's question finally breaks the spell. I was so lost in thought that I never heard him walk into the room.

"Regretting," I mumble so inaudibly that I almost miss it myself, but I know Chad did not hear me.

"What's with the bag?" he says as he turns to the kitchen for a bottle of water. I can't even look at him when he returns. My only response is a small gesture toward the betrayal, an invitation for him to see the contents for himself. He caps the bottle as he makes his way to the table. His unsuspecting demeanor shifts, and the room instantly chills as his face drops in disbelief. "Where...where did you get these from?" His nervous gulp tells me he already knows.

"Don't pretend you don't know the answer already." My voice cracks, just a little, but it's enough to let him know I'm no longer in denial.

"It...it's not what it looks like, baby."

"Don't." I jump up and prepare for a fight.

"I didn't want you to worry!"

"Worry?" I let out a bitter laugh. "You think hiding it makes it better?"

"My dad was an alcoholic. I don't want to end up..."

"Stop," I cut him off, my hands curling into fists at my sides. "You keep saying that. You keep saying you don't want to be like him. But what are you actually doing about it, Chad? You hide your drinking. You lie to my face. You sneak around like I'm too stupid to notice. You say you can't control yourself once you start drinking, so what do you do? You drink in secret, with no one around to stop you. You come home and pass out before I can see how drunk you are. And you expect me to believe you're trying?" I'm yelling by this point, arms flailing for emphasis.

He looks down, his shoulders sagging. "I'm sorry. I was going to tell you."

"When? When were you going to tell me? After the wedding? After the next time you strangle me?" The words hang like a guillotine, ready to fall.

He flinches like I've slapped him, stammering, "That's not fair. I'm so sorry about that, baby!"

I pause, pinching the bridge of my nose to steady myself. "You're right. It's not fair to me. You're always sorry." My voice cracks, and I hate that it does.

"But sorry doesn't mean anything if nothing changes."

I make my way to the front door, grabbing my discarded gym bag and keys. With my hand on the knob, I turn to face him. "You say you don't want to become an alcoholic, then man up and do something about it."

I let the silence linger for a moment, waiting for something, anything. For him to yell, to fight, to care. But nothing comes. Silently resigned, I open the door and walk out.

"So, what, you're just going to walk out right now?" I finally hear from behind the door before it closes, and he continues to call after me. "Lydia, where are you going to go? It's 9 PM."

He's right. Where can I go? I don't know anyone here. No friends, no safe places. It feels like I've been running in circles, trying to outrun this feeling, but I can't escape it.

I drive around until I find the only place still open at this time.

How ironic that it's a bar.

The bartender slides a menu in front of me. I don't even look at it.

"Whiskey. Neat. Please."

She gives a quick tilt of her chin before reaching for the whiskey, not asking questions. I like her already.

As I wait for my drink, I pull out my phone. I shouldn't. I know I shouldn't. I know what happens when I reach for him like this. But loneliness is louder than logic tonight, and my thumb finds Jason's name anyway. My heart races a little. What am I even hoping for? A distraction? An excuse to feel wanted, needed? It's crazy. I shouldn't need to.

But I do.

Me: Hey

I stare at the screen, waiting for something to give me an answer. Something, anything, to pull me out of this fog of disappointment and depression. I need a distraction from my downward spiral. Self-doubt is creeping in, a poison slowly seeping into my veins as my life unravels.

I question my life, my purpose...my existence. Thoughts I swore I'd never entertain gather at the edges of my mind, whispering ideas I know better than to follow. *What if I just end it all?* The idea sits on my chest like a stone, heavy and unmoving.

And then my phone buzzes, vibrating twice on the bar top. Each vibration chips away at the stone, breaking the trance, pulling me back from the darkness.

Jason: Hey, what's up

His response is casual—no underlying sexual tension. There's something comforting in the fact that Jason's there, still there for me in some way. Maybe it's all just words, but it's better than silence.

Me: Just thinking.

His response is slow. I assume he was almost asleep due to the time difference.

Jason: About me?

Me: About everything that's happened over the last few years. About Chad. About whatever this is that you and I are doing, about where my life is headed.

I immediately regret hitting send. I've been sexually vulnerable with Jason but never this emotionally open. I've casually mentioned some of the things Chad has done but quickly changed the subject, reaching for a distraction. Is a real conversation something Jason and I are capable of having?

Jason: What happened tonight?

Me: *I just feel stuck. And Chad... He's been getting worse. I don't know what to do.*

I stare at the screen, waiting for his response. Part of me expects him to change the subject, to say something flirty to deflect. That's our pattern. I unload, he distracts me, and we both get what we need without actually feeling anything.

But his response surprises me.

Jason: *Fuck, baby.*

I can almost feel the frustration in his words, the rawness of his reaction to my pain. It's surprising when he seems like he cares about me, not just about the dirty things we do. It hits differently. Like he's been waiting for me to come to this breaking point.

Jason: *You deserve more than this, Lydia.*

The words settle into me, heavy and undeniable.

Me: *I don't know what more looks like.*

Jason: *I don't know what more looks like either, but you do deserve more than what you're settling for.*

He's right. I've been settling for far too long. I let out a breath, feeling the pressure of it all start to loosen just a little. Maybe, for the first time, I'm beginning to hear what I've been afraid to admit, that I can have more, but I have to stop feeling guilty for wanting it first.

Me: *Thank you.*

Me: *Will you be my distraction right now?*

Jason: *For you, always.*

I stayed at the bar until closing, needing the isolation of strangers and the numb comfort of whiskey more than the suffocating silence of that apartment. The click of the bartender's bottle, the hum of muted conversations, and Jason and I falling back into our normal rhythm of conversations…it all felt easier than facing Chad.

By the time I finally pull into the parking lot, it's past 2 AM. I sit in my car for ten minutes, working up the courage to go inside. When I finally do, he's passed out on the couch, an empty water bottle on the coffee table. The trash bag of bottles is exactly where I left it.

I don't wake him. I just walk past, lock myself in the bedroom, and try to figure out what comes next.

If I'm going to survive this, he has to change. If he wants me to stay, he'll have to prove it. AA meetings, counseling, something real. I'm not the type to give ultimatums, but I'm running out of options.

Tomorrow, we'll have that conversation.

Tonight, I let myself fall apart, pretending that falling apart isn't the same as giving up.

Chapter 20

Sleep does not come easily, not that I expected it to. By 6 AM, I give up trying. A few hours of restless half-sleep is all I'm going to get. My stomach growls as I slip out of the bedroom.

Chad stirs on the couch as I pass through the living room to the kitchen for some breakfast.

My back is to him when his bare feet squeak against the tile floor. He enters the kitchen just as I drop a slice of bread into the toaster. I need something to do with my hands. Something normal. Something that isn't screaming or throwing things.

I keep my back to him, pretending to focus on the toast, but my heart is racing. I can feel him hovering behind me, just close enough to make me uneasy but not enough to force a confrontation. I don't turn around, afraid that if I do, I'll explode.

"I have a problem." It's the first time he's said it out loud, admitted it without deflection or excuses.

I drop my head with a slight shake. *No shit, Sherlock.*

Keeping my focus on the toaster, I silently will it to heat faster, to give me something to occupy my hands, as if this inanimate object can help me with this conversation. "Yeah. Yeah, you do."

"What do I do?"

"That depends on what you want." There's no inflection in my voice. No hope. Just exhaustion.

Chad sighs behind me. I imagine he has his head hung in thought while he mentally tries to string the words together. "I don't want to lose you. And I feel like what I'm about to say will be the breaking point."

When I don't respond, he continues, his voice cracking. "I...I got fired." The words land like a punch, and I feel the air in the room shift. My hand freezes on the counter. For a moment, I think I've misheard him. But the silence that follows tells me I didn't.

Deep breaths. Deep breaths. The toast finally pops, and I add the slice to a plate. After a long silence while fidgeting with the jar of peanut butter, I find the courage to ask the questions that I should have asked the first time. "Why?"

"I was absent too much." This does not surprise me. I had some suspicions when he was coming home so early in the last few weeks. Employers don't like workers who aren't there to do their job.

"And by that, I assume you mean all those times you came home early because you were not feeling well?" He hums in agreement. "Why were you not feeling well, Chad?" Somehow, I manage to keep my tone even with the question.

"I was tired...and a bit hungover."

Still facing away from him, I smirk at the validation of my suspicions as the scraping sounds of the knife against toast resonate in the room. Not that I should be smiling about this, but at least I know I wasn't just making things up.

Dropping the peanut butter knife in the sink, I frown at a new thought. Was he drinking at work too? The thought makes my stomach turn. How long has this been going on? How much have I missed?

"All the bottles in your car...When did you drink those, Chad?" I don't know if I'm asking to understand or if I'm just trying to make sense of this wreck of a life.

The question is met with a long silence. Unwilling to let him avoid answering my question, I turn to face him, arms crossed, staring him down until he finally speaks.

"Mostly I would stop at a gas station on the way home from work and drink in the parking garage before I came inside." He rubs the back of his neck to soothe his nerves. "Then I would go to bed before I became obviously drunk."

I stare at him, trying to reconcile this image of my fiancé, sitting alone in a parking garage, downing mini bottles before coming home to lie to my face. How did I not see it?

"So you drank so much in the car after work that you were not hungover enough to get to work in the morning but hungover enough that you had to leave work in the afternoon." My mind races through the timeline. If he was hungover in the afternoon but made it to work in the morning...Either he was still drunk when he got to work, or...

No.

"Were you drinking on your lunch break?"

His head drops with a sigh, and I have to assume that is confirmation. My eyes stay locked on him as my lips purse, and I will myself to keep calm. Rage will do no good in this conversation. "I need you to say it."

"Yes."

"When did they fire you?"

The air in the room is heavy with the crushing weight of silence. Chad stands still, head down, avoiding eye contact.

"When, Chad?" My voice is now heavy with the anger I let slip through.

"Last week. It was last week, and I was ashamed to tell you because I let this happen again."

My hands curl into fists.

Last week. For seven days, he's been lying to me. Seven days of pretending to go to work. Seven days of me asking, 'How was your day?' and him answering like nothing was wrong.

This conversation needs to be done. It's time to man up. For us both to man up. No more excuses. My hands need something to keep occupied, so I pick up my peanut butter toast and take a few strides to close the distance between us.

"You want me to stay? You want to be better? Then prove it, Chad." I take a step closer, toast still clutched in my hand.

"You admitted you have a problem, and that's the first step, but not the hardest. So, here's what happens next: First, find a program. AA, counseling, rehab. I don't give a shit. But get help. Second, find another job—and fast, because I cannot support both of us at my part-time job and grad school. Third, prove to yourself that you are not your father. Show me that you can change, that you're willing to fight for us."

This stupid piece of toast was supposed to help keep me grounded, give my hands something to hold onto, something to keep me from shaking or hitting something. Instead, I've been waving it around like a weapon, jabbing it toward his face with each point I make. It's absurd. We're having the most important conversation of our relationship, and I'm brandishing toast like a sword. Each point I make sharpens the blade.

"If you want me to stay, then prove you deserve to have me stay." I don't stick around for a response. With a final bite of my toast, I walk away, each step feeling heavier than the last. I pack my gym bag, but it's not about the workout. It's about running, about getting away from the suffocating weight of everything that just unfolded. I don't know what's next. But right now, I just need to punch something.

As I reach the door, I hear him behind me. "Lydia?"

"Don't," I say without turning around. "Just...don't. Not right now."

The door closes behind me with a soft click. I don't slam it. Somehow, that feels worse.

Chapter 21

It's been three weeks since I issued my ultimatum. Chad found an outpatient treatment program that started him right away. I assume his treatment is going well. He doesn't tell me much about it. I don't know if that's because he wants privacy or because I stopped asking. Either way, there's a wall between us now that wasn't there before.

He has also been on a few interviews and is currently out for a final interview for a new potential job. Things are starting to look up.

I'm trying to focus on my coursework, but my mind keeps wandering. To the bills piling up, the lease that ends next month. To the ring still sitting on my finger that feels heavier every day.

The phone rings, slicing through the quiet hum of my studies. I glance at the screen, expecting another mundane distraction, but it's Chad. I pick up, bracing myself for whatever news he has this time.

"Guess what?" Chad's voice comes through before I even get to say hello.

"What?"

"I got the job. I will go in for the drug test tomorrow at 8:30 AM!"

"Oh...good. That's good," I say, but my voice doesn't carry the excitement I wish it could. I want to be happy for him. I want to feel relief, but relief is dangerous. What if he ruins this too? What if I let myself hope, and he destroys it like everything else?

"Yeah. The office is a little farther away than I would like for a commute. It took me an hour to get out here this afternoon, but I'll take it. Anyway, I'm about to head back and will go straight to my AA meeting, so I'll be back late."

"OK. Sounds good. My brain is fried from studying all day, so I think I'm just going to eat a quick dinner and go to bed."

"I'll try not to wake you when I come in."

"Thanks."

There's a slightly awkward silence for a few seconds. Neither of us seems to know what to say anymore. When did talking to each other become this hard?

"Okay, well, I'll see you when I get back, then."

"See ya...Oh, and Chad..."

"Yeah?"

"Congratulations," I say before ending the call. I save my work and flip on the TV for some background noise as I make a quick dinner before heading to bed.

When I wake up, Chad is already gone for his pre-employment test. By the time he returns, he should have his start date confirmed.

"Lydia." I'm so lost in my schoolwork that I don't hear him enter the apartment.

"Oh, hey. How did it go?"

"Fine. I should hear something soon. Did you eat lunch? I thought we might have lunch together." His smile is hopeful as he holds up some takeout bags.

"Uh, no, I haven't. I could eat."

Chad puts the takeout on the table and grabs some plates. Just as we are starting to serve ourselves, his phone rings.

"Oh, this is the job," Chad says, his voice laced with hope. He hits speakerphone, and I can't help but feel a pit in my stomach. This should be good news, but somehow, I don't feel like it is.

"Hey, Chad." The man's pause carries a reluctance that makes my stomach drop before he even delivers his news. I push the food around on my plate, pretending not to listen as they discuss our fate in real time. "So listen, we cannot move forward with your job offer. The results came back and…"

Chad interrupts before he gets a chance to finish. "What does that mean? I failed the drug test?"

"Uh, no, you passed the drug test. No issues there. However, they found you had a rather high BAC, blood alcohol concentration, for an 8:30 AM test." My fork freezes mid-air at the admission. Their conversation fades into static as my mind spins as the words register.

He shouldn't have any kind of BAC.

My stomach drops. He went to an 8:30 AM drug test drunk—or still drunk from the night before. Either way, he showed up to secure his future, our future, with alcohol still in his system.

After everything. After the ultimatum. After the promises. After treatment.

"Look, with the kind of work we do…we just can't take any chances with someone coming in with a hangover."

I vaguely hear the end of their conversation as I quickly redo the math in my head. My part-time income. His unemployment is running out. Rent due. Student loans. It doesn't work. None of it works anymore.

It's time. Time to enact the plan I've been holding close to my chest for months.

"Yeah, I get it," Chad mutters, his voice suddenly small. The call ends with a faint click, but it feels like the air in the room has thickened. He curses under his breath. "I'll keep looking," he says, but there's no conviction in his words.

He says it like this is just a minor setback, like he didn't just blow our last chance at staying here, like he doesn't understand that this is it. The final straw.

"No," I say immediately. "I mean, yes, keep looking, but we can't stay here. We can't afford to stay in this state anymore."

"So, what, you want to move back to the university area? We both know there are no jobs there for me."

"No," I say, pausing to take a breath. "I'm going to move back in with my parents for a bit. You should go to your mother's until you find a job somewhere and can get back in control of your life."

"But..." He lets out a sigh and hangs his head in defeat. "Yeah, Okay."

There's a long silence as I just sit, staring at the food on my plate.

"Lydia, what...What about the wedding?" Chad's voice cracks on the last word, like he's trying to hold on to something slipping through his fingers.

I know what I should say—that the wedding is off and I can't keep doing this. I don't know how to marry someone who can't stop destroying everything we try to build. But the words won't come. I don't know how to tell him it's over. All I know is that I can't do this anymore...not like this.

The thought of him drinking himself to death because I leave him paralyzes me. I don't want to be the one to condemn him with my selfishness. But is staying any better? How many more chances do I give? How many more times do I watch him promise to change and then fail? At what point does my compassion become complicity?

"Let's...postpone it. We need time to figure this out, to get our lives together." The weight of my words makes my chest tighten, but it's all I can offer right now. I'm not calling off the wedding. I'm not breaking up with him. I'm just...pausing. Stepping back. Trying to breathe. I tell myself it's temporary, that we'll figure it out once he gets sober, once I can think straight. But deep down, I know that by walking out that door tomorrow, I'm admitting something I'm not ready to say out loud.

I can't look at him anymore. I can't sit in this apartment that was supposed to be our fresh start and has become just another place I'll need to escape from.

I pick up my plate, still full of food, and deposit it by the sink before grabbing my computer. "I'm going to respond to the landlord to let him know we will not be renewing the lease next month. Then I'm going to pack up my things. I'm leaving tomorrow morning."

"What about the rest of the stuff?"

"All my things will fit in my car. The rest..." I pause, staring at the room filled with memories of us. "The rest of the stuff is yours anyway. You will have until the end of the month to get it out." My voice is steady, but inside, I'm crumbling.

I don't wait for his response. I can't. If I stay in this room any longer, I might change my mind.

Tomorrow, I'll go home. Back to my parents' house. Back to square one. The thought should devastate me, but mostly I just feel...empty. Like I've been hollowed out, and there's nothing left to hurt anymore.

Chapter 22

6 Years Ago

"Welcome to your party!" my sister and cousins shout in unison as Emily and I step through the condo door. They arrived a few hours earlier to set up the condo for a weekend of bachelorette fun by the beach.

The trip had already been planned before I decided to postpone the wedding. We discussed it and agreed to go ahead with the trip, though we'd downplay the whole bachelorette theme and keep it low-key.

Emily and I drop our bags in the room we'll share before rejoining the group in the den. "So, fam!" I clap my hands together, walking in with a grin. "What's the plan for the weekend?"

"Well, today will be a chill beach day. I'm going to get the blender going with some margaritas to take down to the beach. Our moms sent us with plenty of food, so we don't have to eat out every meal." One of my cousins starts listing off the plans like an itinerary checklist. "Tomorrow, we didn't plan anything since you booked that scuba trip. Are you still doing that?"

"No, it got canceled. The first tropical storm of the year is stirring up the water at the dive site, so it won't be good diving conditions. But the beach is far enough west that the weather around here will still be fine. A little overcast, if anything."

"Well, that's a bummer. I know you were excited." She pauses, regrouping. "So, then, tomorrow we can do a beach and pool day. Or rent jet skis at the lake behind the condo. We do have a 7 PM dinner reservation. Saturday's your bachelorette night out. We will eat and pregame here then hit the bar strip where the locals hang out. Sunday, we sleep in and hit the road."

Not going on the dive is a little disappointing, but I'm actually glad it was canceled. Chad and I had decided to get our scuba license as something to do on the honeymoon. As exciting as it would be, I know the day would be a reminder of what I was about to walk away from. Drinking on the beach sounds like a better idea.

"Sounds perfect! Let's crank up the blender and get beaching!"

Ten minutes later, everyone is dressed, and the ice chest is packed for the beach.

The condo has a private beach area with umbrellas and chairs already set up. We find two empty spots next to each other and stake our claim. I sink into a chair, stick my feet in the sand, and let out a deep breath. I'm not sure if it's the beach that brings me peace or just the distance from Chad and the wedding.

There's no guilt when I decide the first thing I'll do is compose a slightly suggestive picture to send to Jason. Angling just right to show my long bare legs, the beach, the waves, and a particularly spicy page of my book, I snap a shot and send it off.

Jason: *So, where exactly are we vacationing?*

Feeling bold, I send him a location pin.

Jason: *Oh, really? You know that's like less than two hours from me?*

Me: *Mm-hmm. We are on my "bachelorette trip." Emily is here too.*

Jason: *Need a stripper?*

Me: *Only if it's you ;) And I can do more than look.*

Jason: *I hope you do more than look.*

"Hey, Em, do you know if they got a stripper for this weekend? With this group, I'm assuming that was a hard no."

I'm close with my cousins. We grew up together, same church pews, same whispered warnings about temptation. I can only imagine their reactions if a stripper actually showed up, especially if that stripper were Jason. And especially if he somehow ended up in my bed for the rest of the trip.

"No, you said to keep the bachelorette stuff to a minimum, so we didn't get one. Why?"

"Just wondering if I should prepare for any surprises."

"Hey, so how are you really doing with everything?" Emily's voice softens. "You don't have to talk about it if you don't want to, but...do you think you'll still get married? I'll support you in whatever you decide."

That question has been on my mind for almost a year now. Deep down, I always knew the answer but could never say it out loud. These last four weeks apart have solidified the answer.

"I...No, I'm not getting married."

"Good." Emily doesn't miss a beat. "Because I really don't like him at all. You deserve better. I know this isn't the easiest time, but I really think you should tell him now, not later."

"Yeah, you're right. It's best not to drag this on any longer than necessary. Plus, then we can turn this into a 'Lydia's single' trip!" I stand, brushing sand off my legs. "I'm going to head back to the condo where it's quiet and get this over with before I start drinking too much."

"Do you want me to come for support? I can just sit in the other room while you do it."

"Yeah, that would be nice, actually. But come sit on the balcony with me. I may need someone to keep me from backing out."

"Of course."

We make a bathroom excuse to the rest of the group and head back up to the condo. I take in a few deep breaths before hitting the call button.

"Hey, Lydia!" He sounds excited that I'm calling. We have been mostly silent for the last two weeks, with a few texting moments.

"Hey, Chad." I let my voice feel heavy, hoping he knows before I even say it. "So, listen, I've been thinking about us for a while…I can't do this anymore."

There's a long silence while I let it sink in.

"So that's it? You're just done?"

"There's no *just*, Chad. I've been feeling this way for a while, maybe even before we moved. It's been so long since our relationship was good that I've forgotten what it's supposed to feel like. I can't live my life, a life with you, in constant pain."

"I'm trying to get better, to be better for you."

"I know you are trying, but I can't look past all of this pain, and I can't live my life in fear that we will fall off a cliff at any moment. I've given everything and received nothing in return. I can't hope for you to give me the love I deserve when you can't love yourself first."

"Then why did you move with me?"

"I hoped it would be better. I should have listened when you drunkenly broke up with me a few years ago, but I couldn't see how self-destructive you were then. I think it wasn't until we were living together that I really understood what our life would look like, and that's not what I want for myself."

"Fine. I'll back off for a little while, but I think you'll change your mind once you're alone." I can't tell if that was meant to be a jab, like he's trying to say that, without him, I'd be alone forever, and he's the best I'll get. For a while, I believed that. But whether he had a hidden meaning or not, his comment only solidifies my decision.

"No, Chad. No, I will not change my mind. Goodbye." I don't wait around for a response before hanging up.

I turn to face Emily, who's already waiting with a shot stretched toward me. "Let's drink. Celebratory shots!" *And that's why she's my best friend.* I cheer with a chuckle as we clink glasses.

"Let's bring some back down to tell the others," I say as I fill up an empty water bottle with vodka before we leisurely make our way back, a new lightness in my steps.

"Yeah, I should have known when I would have cheated on Chad at your wedding with Jason that I shouldn't have been with him," I admit to Emily as we make our way back down to the beach. "Well, that and the fact that he had sex with me when I didn't want to, and he tried to choke me."

"Wait. Wait. Wait." Emily halts her walk, eyes wide. "There's so much to unpack in that statement. I don't even know where I want you to start. On second thought, I know you and Jason have a weird, flirty relationship. I want an update on that, but first, start with Chad choking you."

Oops.

"Oh, I'm sure I told you about that," I say, knowing full well that I didn't tell anyone.

"Um, no, you did not. I would not have forgotten something like that. Nor would I have let you stay with him." She playfully slaps me on the arm, chastising me and my life choices. "Why would you not tell anyone? Why would you not leave?"

"That's a loaded question." I take my time, breathing deep as I find the words that would best explain why I felt like I had to stay. Words that took me a long time to say to myself. My feet kick up sand as we walk, the static movement grounding my thoughts. "At first, I stayed out of guilt. Guilt for sleeping with him, like I had to stay."

"Okay, but do I need to remind you that he forced you to have sex with him? I know you didn't really want to admit it then, but you needed time to process and come to that conclusion on your own."

"Yeah, I know, and I see that now. I think part of me wanted to rebel a little and use it as an excuse to keep having sex because, as it turns out, I really like sex. Plus, his mom always made comments about me being a good wife and staying by his side through his addiction. I was also worried about what he would do if I broke it off. I still am, but I can't let that scare me into a life I don't deserve."

I pause, staring out at the waves. "I was so deprived of any romantic connection that I latched onto the first guy to show me an ounce of affection. So deprived that I let myself look past the flaws and soak up every morsel of attention I was tossed. As women, we're conditioned to sacrifice for everyone else. To cater to their needs and happiness at the expense of our own. Or at the expense of our own safety."

"Why didn't you tell anyone? I get that it's a hard thing to admit and talk about, but you have people who love you and would have helped you with anything."

There's safety in the silence, as much as there's safety in noise. It's different but equally as powerful. You can shout it from the rooftops, ask for help, but you risk being labeled as crazy, gaslit into believing it didn't happen, or didn't happen the way you experienced it—until your reality no longer exists. It's broken into fragments and rearranged into something unrecognizable.

Silence lets you live in your truth. Your reality remains intact. It's you and you alone. No one to criticize your beliefs. No one to tell you you're wrong.

Yet, there's no one to hold your hand.

"I think I wanted to believe it wasn't that bad. Some people have it worse than I did, and I hoped it would get better. Now I just hate that I wasted those years of my life on that relationship and have to start over."

"Don't see it as starting over. Use this as a guide for what to do, or not do, in future relationships."

"Yeah, I guess you're right. Anyway, enough of that. Now we enjoy my 'I'm single' party trip and get some sun on the beach." Turning back to the water, I recline in my chair and pull my hat over my eyes, trying to end the conversation.

"Oh, no, girl. We are not done." Emily pulls the hat off my face. "What's happening with you and Jason? I can't believe you two still talk."

I knew I couldn't escape that part. I grab my hat back and sit up with a chuckle. "Yeah. Honestly, I tried to stop, but whenever Chad did something Chad-like, which I'm now realizing was way more often than I thought, we would talk."

"Talk about what? Never mind, don't answer that. Does he know you're only two hours up the road?"

"He does, but he thinks I'm on my bachelorette trip. He offered to come be our stripper."

Emily lets out a full belly laugh. "Is that why you asked about strippers earlier?" She says it a little too loud for my comfort. Looking around, I check to see if any of my cousins heard. "No way in hell is my cousin stripping in front of me. Are you going to tell him you called off the wedding?"

"Yes. Later. When we're getting ready to go out, I can drink and make bad decisions. For now, I want to take a nap on this beach."

But not before sending off one last message.

Me: *So, you're coming to strip for me, then?*

Jason: *Oh, I'm not driving over there just to strip for you.*

Me: *Aww, why not?*

Jason: *If I come, it better be to do more than just strip. I'd be doing you too. And I'll come for you as many times as I can until you pass out.*

Me: *You better drive fast, then.*

We both know he's not coming, but his words serve as a reminder of what it sounds like to be wanted.

The weight of what I just did still feels raw, but a part of me knows it was the right choice. Chad is no longer my concern. For the first time in a long time, it's just me, and I'm okay with that.

Letting the waves and laughter surround me, I realize that this weekend, this trip, isn't just about celebrating my relationship with Chad—or rather, the end of the relationship. It's about reclaiming my life, piece by piece. The beach, the sun, the silence...It all feels like the beginning of something new.

Chapter 23

5 Years Ago

Life has a way of moving forward, even when you're not sure you're ready.

I finished my master's program last spring, walked across that stage with my parents beaming in the audience, and started a new job shortly after. The kind of job that actually uses my degree, pays decently, and doesn't leave me crying in my car during lunch breaks.

I'm still living with my parents, not ideal at twenty-seven, but after everything with Chad, it felt safer to regroup here. My mom hovers, my dad pretends not to notice when I come home late, and I'm slowly rebuilding the person I lost somewhere between college and moving across the country.

Dating has been…an experiment. A few coffee dates that went nowhere. One guy talked about his ex the entire time. Another who seemed great until he asked if I'd considered losing a few pounds.

But I keep trying because staying home every weekend, scrolling through my phone, feels like letting Chad win. Like letting fear win. Even though I still text Jason when the loneliness gets too loud.

Me: *Dating sucks.*

Jason: *I have something that you can suck.*

Me: *Mmm, that sounds way better.*

Jason: *You're so sexy, baby. Any guy would be lucky to have you.*

I wish that were true, that people would see me the way Jason does—or at least the way I pretend he does. His existence is dangerous for me. Something in me can't help blur the line between our reality and the fantasy I've created.

Over and over again. It's just in my mind. If only. I think about him in my sleep. Dreams that I ache to become reality. The false promise he represents, eternal disappointment disguised as carnal bliss.

I've gotten myself far from Chad's chains. Started healing from his mental torment. I could go running to

Jason for comfort. But I don't dare, grounded by the fear of what-ifs.

What if I pursue this indulgence only to find it's all a lie? What if it's perfect and I'd eventually have to walk away? Either way, I've ruined the narrative I've created. I don't think my self-esteem can take that hit.

So I stay in love with the idea that we could be good for each other. I'll take what he's willing to give me from afar.

Me: *Don't say things like that.*

Jason: *Aw, baby. You know it's true. That pussy is perfect.*

Me: *Then come and get it.*

Jason: *If only. But I will tell you what I want to do to you. Make you all hot and bothered for your date tonight.*

Me: *I think you just want me thinking about you while I'm at this party tonight.*

Jason: *Can you blame me?*

My talks with Jason have become almost routine, something to look forward to, but something I try not to build my life around. I don't want to admit it, but part of me is tired of feeling close to someone I've never actually met, even if my body still craves the release he can pull from me.

Reluctantly, I resist the urge to fall into Jason's hold tonight as I let the steam of the shower settle around me. It's rare that I feel like socializing, but the girls at work convinced me to go to the office party with our sister facility across town. It'll be nice to put faces to the names of the people we work with every day.

I'll use Jason as a rescue if I need an escape.

When I left the house, I intended to go to this party. Now that I'm sitting in the parking lot, my social battery is draining. Just thinking of having to come up with small talk has me on edge. The girls have already texted to see when I'll get here. I did promise I'd come tonight, at least for a little while.

I need a drink first. Something to occupy my hands.

Exiting the car, I send them a quick text to let them know I'm here, then I make a beeline for the rented bar and straight to the first empty spot I can find.

After some thought, I settle on a Blackberry Sage Smash as tonight's drink of choice. It's something sweet, savory, and a little bruised all at once. A quiet contradiction that feels familiar, still unfolding, still reaching for the shape of what it longs to become.

    I place my order before taking stock of my surroundings. It's loud, but not in the typical bar way. The music is low enough to talk over. Vaguely familiar faces mingle across the room as servers weave through the crowd with trays of appetizers.

    As the bartender slides my drink over, I spy my friends pushing through the crowd. One grabs my arm, pulling me toward a small circle of people chatting near the center of the room.

    They introduce me to those they've already met, trading small talk about work and mutual acquaintances. The noise swells as more people from both companies filter in, and I feel myself shrinking a little beneath the buzz of conversations.

    I could text Jason right now. No one would notice if I slipped out early. My thumb hovers over his contact before I lock my phone and opt for a refill instead.

    Head down, turning my phone in my hand, I make my way back to the bar. My mind is so preoccupied I don't notice the man I'm about to walk straight into until it's too late.

"My fault," he says quickly, bending down to pick up the phone that fell from my hands. Clearly, I'm the one who should be apologizing.

As he hands it back, something about him catches me off guard. There's an ease about him, something that's self-assured but not arrogant, like he's confident without trying. And then he smiles, dimples appearing on his cheeks, and it hits me harder than it should. My shoulders relax on instinct. "Thanks," I manage in a shaky whisper as I stare longer than I should.

I don't know how long we stand there, his blue eyes locked on mine, before he starts to take a slow step back, almost reluctantly. "Nice bumping into you," he says with a quick wink, turning toward a group of what I presume are his coworkers.

Flustered by the encounter, I linger for a moment, eyes fixed in the direction he went before retreating to the bar. The moment replays in my mind as I wait for a fresh drink. I rest my back against the bar, scanning the room. I tell myself it's to find my way back to my friends. Technically true, but subconsciously, I'm looking for the mystery man again.

After the unsuccessful search, I turn back to the bar with a soft sigh, mindlessly twirling the straw in my now-full glass. My thoughts spiral deeper with each rotation, drifting back to the mystery man, his neatly trimmed beard that lends him an air of maturity, the way his eyes lingered on me, curious...almost intent. I exhale, convincing myself I've probably read too much into it.

"You may want to drink some of that before leaving the bar," a velvety smooth voice says from beside me. "Just in case you want to bump into me again."

My face contorts into a shy smirk as I turn to face him. "Thanks for the advice. I'll try to keep my collisions to a minimum."

He chuckles at the response, playing along with the banter with a small hip bump mimicking a collision. Instantly, the air feels lighter around him.

"I'm Adam," he says, offering an infectious smile.

"Lydia."

"Lydia," he repeats slowly, like he's tasting it on his tongue. "I figured I should know a girl's name if she's going to keep running into me."

"It was one time!" The words come out louder than I intended but still playful.

Our conversation is easy, flowing from the basics of work, and shared frustrations that come with it, to friends and hobbies. He actually listens, like every trivial thing I say somehow matters.

"You look like you'd rather be anywhere but here," he says, his voice low but teasing. It's a strange feeling, the way he makes space for silence without needing to fill it, allowing the conversation to naturally deepen.

I study him for a moment, trying to read the intent behind his words. His eyes hold a steady, grounded energy as he waits for my response.

"Umm, yeah, maybe at first. I'm not big on parties. I promised some of the girls at work I'd come and pretend to network."

He smiles, taking in the weight of my response. The pause stretches between us, giving me a moment to breathe.

"And now?" he asks, genuine curiosity softening his voice as he places a gentle touch on my arm.

"Now…" My lips curve into a smile before I can stop them. "Now I'm glad I came."

"Me too," he whispers just loud enough for me to hear. His eyes linger on my lips as he hesitates before continuing. "As much as I hate to walk away right now, I've got to go."

Disappointment hit me harder than I expected. I came to this party already wanting to leave, but now I don't want it to end. "Oh, right."

"I drove a few coworkers here, and they are...well, let's just say they need to leave before they are forcefully escorted out." He's laughing as he says this, pointing in the direction of a few guys starting to draw a crowd, and I can't help but laugh with him.

"So...I guess I won't get another chance to bump into you tonight, then?"

He grins, leaning slightly closer. "How about we skip the accidental collisions, and I just take you to dinner?" He hands me his phone.

I enter my number, trying to act casual. "Dinner sounds nice." I'm internally smirking, hiding a little thrill.

He smiles, tucks his phone away, and gives me a quick wink before drifting back into the crowd. There's no goodbye, just the unspoken promise that he'll see me again.

I linger a moment, replaying the sound of his laugh, the steadiness in his gaze, and then finally turn to find my friends.

Over the next few weeks, our phones bridge the distance. At first, it's casual. Flirty texts and inside jokes. The kind of banter that makes me smile at my desk.

When I tell him I'm stressed about a work presentation, he doesn't try to fix it or tell me I'm overthinking. He just says, "You've got this. And if you don't, at least you'll have a good story." It's such a small thing, but it catches me off guard. With Chad, every conversation eventually circled back to his problems, his drinking, his needs. With Jason, everything is charged with sexual tension, an escape from reality rather than grounding in it.

But Adam? Adam asks follow-up questions, remembering the name of my difficult coworker, sending me a photo of a terrible coffee shop pun and saying *thought of you*.

Tonight, we are finally going on our first real date, dinner at a quiet Italian place. I'm nervous in a way I haven't been in years. Not the anxious, walking-on-eggshells kind of nervous. The I-actually-want-this-to-go-well kind of nervous.

He orders wine without making a show of it, asks how my presentation went, and when I fumble through the event, blabbering on about work, he listens like I'm the most interesting person in the room. At one point, I catch myself mid-sentence and laugh. "Sorry, I'm rambling."

"Don't apologize," he says, leaning forward slightly. "I like hearing you talk about things you care about. Your enthusiasm is infectious." His smile tells me he means it.

It's such a simple sentence, but something in my chest cracks open.

By the time dessert comes, I realize I haven't checked my phone once, haven't wondered if I should be someone different, smaller, easier. I'm just...here. And he seems genuinely happy that I am.

Within a month, we're inseparable but in a way that feels natural, not desperate. He meets my friends at brunch, and they pull me aside afterward with wide eyes. "Okay, he's actually nice," Emily says. "Like, suspiciously nice. What's wrong with him?"

"Nothing," I say, half-defensive, half-amazed. "I think...I think he's just a good person."

When I meet his friends, they welcome me easily, make space for me in their conversations without making me feel like an outsider. Adam's hand stays on the small of my back the whole time. It's not possessive, just present. Steady.

One night, watching a movie on the couch, after we've been dating for two months, I turn to him in the dark. "Why me?"

He's quiet for a moment, fingers tracing lazy patterns on my shoulder. "What do you mean?"

"I just...I don't know. Sometimes I feel like I'm still figuring out who I am. And you seem so...sure."

He shifts to look at me, his face barely visible in the glow of the TV. "Lydia, I'm not looking for someone who has it all figured out. I'm looking for someone real. And you're the realest person I've met in a long time."

I don't know when we became a couple. There was no grand declaration of intentions, but all of our conversations, life goals, and the big things that matter, aligned. We simply were. I haven't felt this calm, curious, or safe with anyone in a long time. Each date builds on the last: small touches, shared jokes, the kind of quiet moments where words aren't necessary.

I sit back in my bed, phone buzzing lightly with Adam's latest message, and feel something unfamiliar:

hopeful. Not reckless or needy, just...quietly, expectantly hopeful.

Jason is still a shadow in the corner of my mind. I haven't stopped talking to him entirely, a text here and there, never crossing lines, but never quite closing the door either. It's easier to tell myself he's just a friend, a harmless outlet, than to examine why I keep one foot in that fantasy even as I'm building something real.

But with Adam, I'm learning what it feels like to be chosen. And that may be enough to quiet the part of me that still craves the validation Jason offers from states away.

Maybe.

Chapter 24

4 Years Ago

My body moves on instinct through Adam's house, drawn toward the smell of freshly brewed coffee wafting from the kitchen. Adam stands at the fridge, pulling out a fresh pack of bacon as I reach the last step.

"Mmm. Coffee smells great. A girl could get used to waking up to this." I slide in behind him, wrapping my arms around his waist.

"I like you waking up in nothing but my t-shirt, reminding me of what we did together last night." Adam spins in my arms to face me before pulling me into a deep kiss.

I laugh against his mouth. "I'm sure my breath is nasty, and I look like a zombie," I mumble, pressing a hand against his chest.

He grins, unbothered. "Wake up like this all the time," he says easily. "Move in with me."

His words catch me off guard. A jolt of excitement flashes through me before the familiar weight of guilt follows close behind.

"Wh...what?"

Adam moves effortlessly around the kitchen, fixing my coffee just how I like it before handing me the mug. "Move in with me. It's been two years since you moved back in with your parents after escaping that ex. You pretty much stay here every night anyway." He pauses, studying my face. "Unless...that's not what you want?"

"No, I mean, yes. I do want to." I clutch the cup like it's a lifeline. "But you know how much grief I'll get from my parents if we move in together without being married. It's already bad enough with how much I stay here."

"So, you want to move in," he says carefully, "but you're worried about what they'll think."

"It's not just that..." I start, but the words tangle.

Adam takes my coffee cup and sets it down to take both my hands. "Lydia, I'm not trying to pressure you into anything. But I need you to hear something." His voice is low and steady, drawing my focus. "You've spent your whole life trying to make everyone comfortable, even when it meant shrinking yourself. Your parents love you. But love doesn't mean they get to choose how you live your life. You do."

The truth of his words settles heavily on my chest.

"Every time they disapprove, you start questioning everything. Us, yourself, what you want." He squeezes my hands gently. "But this…"—he gestures between us—"this isn't wrong. It's ours. And I want you to want to move in because you believe in it. And I don't want you to choose not to move in just to avoid disappointing your parents."

I want to protest, doubt creeping in from every corner. Every question my mother asks about Adam makes me doubt a part of myself, a part of our relationship. I don't think it's intentional, but it still makes me question what I know.

I dip my head, staring at my coffee, as the cream swirls into a muted beige. "You make it sound so simple."

"It is simple," he says with an air of empathy. "It just isn't easy."

That makes me laugh, a short, shaky sound that catches on the edge of my throat. Adam leans against the counter, arms folded, eyes patient.

Something in my chest pulls tight. He's not telling me what to do. He's not fighting my battles for me. He's just reminding me that they're mine to fight. That I have the right to choose.

I stall, taking another sip of coffee and set the mug down carefully, tracing the rim with my finger.

"I love you, Lydia." He laces his fingers through mine. "I want to wake up with you every morning and go to sleep with you next to me every night. But only if that's what *you* want. If you need more time or need to figure out what you want first, I'll wait. I'm not going anywhere."

He loves me? Of course he does. He's been showing me all along: in the way he listens, the way he makes space for me to be myself, the way he never asks me to be smaller.

And I love him too. He makes me feel safe, grounded, and cared for in ways no one else ever has.

More than that, he makes me feel like I can make my own choices. Like my wants actually matter.

"I love you too." I kiss him hard, pouring everything I can't articulate into it. When we finally pull apart, breathless, I take a steadying breath. "Yes. I want to move in with you. And...I want to tell my parents myself.

No sneaking, no hiding. I'm tired of living like I'm doing something wrong when I'm not."

His smile is soft, proud. "You're not. You never were."

Living with my parents, I don't have much to bring to Adam's. Over the next week, I gradually start moving my clothes and belongings to Adam's—no, our place. Each box I pack feels like reclaiming a piece of myself.

My mom notices, of course. Moms always do. She stands in my bedroom doorway one evening, watching me fold clothes into a duffel bag. "Sleeping at Adam's again?"

"Yeah." I don't elaborate. Don't apologize. Just keep folding.

She lingers for a moment then walks away without another word, judgment hanging thick in the air, even after she has gone.

That night, lying in bed, I fixate on the ceiling, anxiety coiling in my stomach. I could keep doing this. Keep the truth vague, keep avoiding the conversation, let them piece it together slowly until it's too late to object.

But that's not the person I want to be anymore.

Adam's arm is draped across my waist, his breathing slow and even beside me. He's already given me everything I need: the space to choose, the support to stand firm, the reminder that I'm allowed to want things for myself.

Now it's up to me to take the next step. Sunday, at lunch after church. No more putting this off.

Sunday comes too quickly. I sit at my parents' kitchen table, Adam beside me, his hand wrapped around mine in quiet support. My mother sets down plates of food with more force than necessary. My father won't quite meet my eyes.

I take a breath. This is my choice. My life. "So…" I start, proud that my voice doesn't shake. "Adam asked me to move in with him. And I said yes." Silence. Heavy and thick.

My mother's jaw tightens. "I just don't understand the need for this. I wasn't happy about you living with Chad, but at least you two were engaged and halfway across the country. Financially, you didn't have a choice then. But what you have now is a good thing—great, even. Keep things the way they are until you decide to get married—if you two decide to get married. Do things right this time."

Do things right, as if there's only one right way to live.

The silence thickens as I rehearse what to say over and over again. "I know you don't understand," I say carefully. "And I'm not asking you to agree. But this is what I want. Adam and I want to build a life together. We want to know we're compatible, that this is right, before we make a permanent commitment."

My father sighs, leaning back in his chair. "Right? Lydia, you said that before too. Feelings change. Marriage gives you stability. Living together without that..." He shakes his head. "It never ends well."

"What if we get married and find out we're completely incompatible?" The words come out stronger now. "Then what? Are we trapped in a marriage neither of us wants? How is that more stable than being honest about where we are?"

As the words fall from my mouth, I know the argument won't hold much weight with them. It's not what the Bible says, what our religious values say, and that's the only way that counts in their house. But after Chad, there's no other way for me.

My throat tightens as the thought lingers. I glance at Adam, hoping just looking at him will ground my climbing anxiety. He gives my hand a gentle squeeze in support.

"With all due respect," Adam says evenly, "this isn't about doing things the 'right' way or making a statement. It's about building something real. Lydia deserves to make her own choices about her life."

My mom's lips press into a thin line. "She can make choices. But that doesn't mean we have to agree with them."

"No," I say quietly, finding my voice again. "You don't. But I'm not asking for your permission. I'm telling you what I've decided because I love you and I want to be honest with you."

I take a shaky breath. "I know this isn't what you wanted for me. I know you think I'm making a mistake. But it's my mistake to make. And honestly? I don't think it is one. For the first time in my life, I'm choosing something because I want it. Not because I'm afraid, not because I feel trapped, not because I'm trying to please someone else. I'm choosing this. I'm choosing him. And I'm choosing myself."

Silence stretches across the table. My father looks down, jaw tight. My mother's eyes glisten with unshed tears, but her expression doesn't soften.

"I hope you're right," she finally says, voice tight. "I really do."

It's not acceptance, but it's acknowledgment. And right now, that's enough.

I stand, pulling Adam's hand as I do. "We should go."

No one stops us as we walk out the door.

Once the house disappears behind us, I release a long, shaky breath that I'd been holding for a long time. Maybe years.

"You okay?" Adam asks softly, reaching to still my hands. They're trembling with something that feels like release. The first breath of freedom.

"I don't know," I admit. "That was...harder than I thought it would be."

He reaches over, lacing his fingers through mine. "You were amazing back there. You stood up for yourself. For us."

"I kept waiting for you to step in and save me."

"You didn't need saving," he says simply. "You needed to know you could do it yourself. And you did."

Tears prick at my eyes. Not from sadness, but from relief. From the realization that I just chose myself, maybe for the first time ever. From his support.

"Thank you," I whisper. "For letting me fight my own battle."

"Always," he says. "But I'll be right beside you for every single one."

As we drive back to our apartment, I feel something shift inside me. The guilt is still there; years of conditioning don't disappear overnight. But underneath it, there's something new: the quiet, steady knowledge that I made a choice. My choice.

And I don't regret it.

Chapter 25

3 Years Ago

Life with Adam has been a whirlwind of emotions, but he's supported me in every way. He feels steady, calming the chaos that lives in my head.

After a few months of living together, the tension with my parents mostly faded. They've seen how patient he is, how he adds peace rather than creating tension. My mom even admits that this "experiment," as they liked to call it, has been good for us, noting that my smile seems genuine these days. My dad nods a little too firmly when he agrees, like he's trying to prove he never doubted it.

Honestly, things are good. Too good.

And that scares me.

For the first time in my life, I'm not walking on eggshells, bracing for the next explosion. Adam and I share a rhythm built on respect and appreciation. He believes in me. And I believe in us.

So why does part of me feel so restless?

It's a Tuesday night, unremarkable in every way. We're on the couch, his arm draped around me as some crime show plays in the background. I'm not watching. Instead, I'm hyperaware of the warmth of his body next to mine, the familiar scent of his soap, the way his thumb absently traces circles on my shoulder.

I shift closer, pressing a kiss to his jaw. He smiles but doesn't look away from the screen.

I try again, this time letting my hand drift down his chest, fingers playing with the hem of his shirt. "Hey," I murmur, my voice deliberately low.

"Hmm?" He's still watching TV.

My hand slides lower, more intentional now. Finally, he glances down at me, recognition flickering in his eyes. "Oh, sweetheart." He pulls me in for a soft kiss. "I'm exhausted. Work was brutal today." I recoil slightly at the rejection.

"Okay," I say softly, trying not to let the disappointment seep into my voice. "I just...I miss you."

He raises an eyebrow before pressing a kiss to my forehead. "I'm right here."

"I know," I say instead, pulling back and settling against the couch cushions. "Never mind. It's fine."

"You sure?"

"Yeah. I'm tired too."

He turns back to the TV, and I sit there, feeling the distance between us even though we're touching. Three months. It's been three months since we last had sex. And before that? Maybe another month or two.

I keep telling myself it's normal. People go through dry spells. Life gets busy. Stress happens. But this doesn't feel like a dry spell. It feels like...indifference.

It started small, noticing that our kisses didn't linger, even when I tried to pull him back in. Playful touches started becoming less frequent, and sex became even further apart. His love still pours out with the things he does for me, the way he supports me, but the fire iss not there.

And that's what I miss. The feeling of being wanted.

With Chad, sex was like currency. My value was measured in how willing I was, how often I said yes—as if no was really an option.

Jason represented curiosity and fantasy. He showed me what it felt like to be wanted—craved, even. He did that with only words, without ever touching me. Every text was a reminder that someone found me desirable, that my body could inspire hunger.

But with Adam, sex has always been gentle, occasional, as if too much of it might taint what we've built. At first, I thought that was healthy, a sign that our relationship wasn't just about physical need. But now I'm wondering if it's something else, if maybe he just...doesn't want me that way.

Does wanting more make me selfish? Is my past so warped that I can't recognize healthy intimacy when I have it? Or is my guilt so ingrained that it's shaping how I let him love me?

I'm still learning. Learning how to live for me. Learning how to stop living for everyone else's expectations.

But this? This feels like a test I'm failing.

I lie awake, staring at the ceiling, Adam sleeping peacefully beside me. My phone sits on the nightstand, screen dark, but I can feel its pull. The TV's glow stretches shadows across the room. His steady breathing fills the quiet, a rhythm I've come to love. But beneath the comfort, there's a collision of love and confusion.

I love him. I know that. But we are missing something between us.

I shouldn't. I know I shouldn't. But my thumb finds Jason's name anyway, scrolling through old messages I haven't deleted. Words that once made me feel alive, desired, and seen in ways I'm struggling to feel now.

Jason: *I'd worship every inch of you if I had the chance.*

Jason: *You don't even know how much you turn me on, baby.*

Jason: *I want to hear you beg for me.*

I close the messages quickly, guilt twisting in my stomach. I'm not cheating. I haven't talked to him in what feels like forever. But the fact that I'm looking, that I *need* to look, feels like a betrayal.

Adam is perfect in so many ways. He supports me. He gets me. But in bed...I just don't feel the spark I expect. And I keep questioning if that's normal. Am I expecting too much because of my past?

I have to fight against the voice of guilt. *I am not broken for wanting more. But I have to be honest with myself, and with him, about what I need.*

It's time to face what I've been avoiding. Time to figure out whether this relationship, with all its beauty and its limitations, is enough for me. I don't know the answer yet, but one thing is for sure: Adam and I will face this together.

Chapter 26

It's taken me a few weeks to work up the courage to talk with Adam. The idea of disappointing him sits heavily on my chest.

But there's never a right moment to tell someone you love that something feels off between you. The longer I wait, the more frustrated I'll become. And that's not fair to either of us. This needs to happen now.

Adam lies stretched out on the couch, head in my lap, as we watch a show we have seen several times before. It's something we do often, a quiet ritual that usually brings peace to the evening as we wind down before bed. The words feel heavy on my tongue as I try to find the courage to get this out in the open.

"Hey, babe... Can we, uh, talk about something?"

He sits up, instantly attentive. "Of course. What's up?"

I turn on the sofa to face him, twisting my hands in my lap out of nervous habit. "It's not...I just..." He puts a hand on my knee, rubbing soft circles with his thumb, a silent encouragement to push forward. "I'm feeling like we've been off lately. Not emotionally, just...physically."

Adam stills his hand, quietly processing my words as he waits for me to continue.

"I know you love me," I say, pressing on. I have to get this out. "You show me every day, in the little ways you take care of me, the way you see what I really need and support me getting there. I just..." I swallow hard. "For so long, it was ingrained in me that sex before marriage was bad, shameful. Then, when I actually started having sex, it subconsciously became something I needed to feel wanted and useful in a relationship. It's become intertwined with my self-esteem. So when you're not intimate, or when I try to initiate and..." I pause, knowing what I say next will bring him some heartbreak. "And you don't reciprocate, I feel rejected. I miss feeling wanted. Not just loved, but desired."

Adam exhales slowly, standing up from the sofa to pace as he digests what I've said. When he turns back to face me, his eyes convey everything: vulnerability, guilt, and love as he holds back tears.

"Oh, sweetheart, I am so, so sorry that I have made you feel this way." He kneels in front of me, taking my hands as if to ground us to the moment. "It is never my intention to make you feel unwanted and rejected. I want you. Only you." He blows out a shaky breath. "I've never been an overtly sexual person. Sometimes I get so wrapped up with showing how much I love you every day in little ways that I forget the other parts that matter just as much."

His voice is calm, not defensive, just honest. That's one of the things I love most about him.

"I'm not trying to pressure you," I say softly. "I just want us to be close in every way, not just the easy ways. Your love language is acts of service, but I think mine is physical touch. And I don't mean just sex but all the little things: playful slaps, day-long foreplay, sexy texts."

He hums in agreement. "I'll work on it. We'll figure it out. Together."

His words cause me to wince. They're too familiar, too close to the promises Chad made over and over again. But the sincerity in his tone breaks through the wall I refuse to acknowledge I'd built.

Tears sting my eyes as I lean into him, my head on his chest as his arms hold me close. The silence surrounds us, warm and full of promise.

Chapter 27

Over the next few weeks, I see the changes, the way he lingers when he kisses me, the playful smack on the ass when we pass in the kitchen. It's not perfection, but it's effort. It's seeing me. Choosing me.

We both feel the changes his effort has made in our relationship. There's a new lightness between us, an ease that feels earned.

The sun's already gone down by the time we leave, the early darkness of fall wrapping around us as we walk hand in hand toward the restaurant where we had our first date. Neither of us felt like dressing up for a night out, so we decided to pick up our meals to go. Back at home, we work in tandem, dancing around the kitchen as we set the table and plate the food.

"Okay, plates are set. I'm going to the restroom while you finish fixing drinks, and then we can eat," I say as I pass by him, giving him a quick kiss on the way.

When I step back into the kitchen, the whole mood has shifted. The lights are dimmed, wine is poured, two candles flicker in the center of the table, and a soft glow reflects off the wine glasses he's already poured.

I let out a small gasp as I take it all in. "Babe. What's this?"

"Lydia," he starts, voice steady but soft. "I know we've had to learn how to meet each other halfway. But I don't want just halfway with you. I want all of it. The rest of my life."

It takes a moment for the words to register before I see the small velvet box he's pulled from his pocket. My heart stumbles, warmth flooding through me. "Lydia, will you marry me?"

Time stills. I think back on my life, the chaos and pain. How much Adam has helped me to rebuild, how much fuller my life has been with Adam in it.

Those moments deepen my belief in us. Belief in a happy marriage, not free of conflict but working together to make it to the other side.

Adam makes me happy. Maybe that's enough. The rest can fall into place.

"Yes. Of course I'll marry you!"

Neither of us likes being the center of attention, but my parents insisted that a church wedding was the right way to do things. Adam didn't argue. He just smiled that calm, steady smile and said, "Whatever you need, sweetheart."

So we kept it simple. A small ceremony at my family's church with just our parents and a few close friends. No big reception, no wasted money on elaborate decorations. Just vows spoken in a quiet moment one April afternoon, when the air smelled like rain and new beginnings.

When Adam takes my hands and says his vows, there's no need for grand gestures. His voice is even, sincere, radiating the kind of love that feels steady.

I never imagined myself having a grand fairytale wedding. This was my dream. It's honest. It's real.

And it's ours.

Chapter 28

2 Years Ago

It's been a year of marriage. A year of strengthening our life together.

Sometimes it feels no different than the last year of dating, since we'd already figured out how to combine our lives. I guess that's why people say not to live together before marriage, so you can feel the difference. But I'm not mad about that. We still learn new things about each other, working as a team to solve life's problems and celebrate our successes.

But it's also been another year of feeling unsatisfied. Adam put in effort for a while, but eventually fell back into his same routine. I keep reminding myself that his consistency is how he shows his love, but it doesn't touch the part of me that craves something more.

As we lie in bed, I cozy up to Adam's side, my head on his chest, as my hand begins to roam. I trace lazy circles on his skin while he watches the last few minutes of a show. My fingers drift lower, sliding down the inside of his thigh before moving back up toward his center.

The show credits roll, and Adam reaches for the remote. "Good night, wife," he says, pressing a kiss to the top of my head. And just like that, I've been rejected. Again.

That move usually works about once a month. Right now, we're going on two but devastatingly close to closing in on a third.

I roll over to face away from him so he doesn't feel my tears hit his chest. Each breath gets harder, tighter, until I can't hold it in anymore. My eyes find my phone on the nightstand, praying it will vibrate with a message from the one person who always seems to take this feeling away.

Before I do something I'll regret, I slip quietly out of bed and curl up on the couch, leaving my phone far away from my reach. Right now, I need distance from both of them before I do something I'll regret or Adam finds me crying. If he does, I don't know if I'll be able to hold back the anger.

I don't know how long I've been hiding on the couch before I hear Adam's steps coming down the hall.

"There you are, sweetheart. What are you doing out here?"

"Can't sleep," I mumble, hoping he doesn't hear the tears in my voice.

"You don't sit on the couch, staring into the darkness, when you can't sleep. What's wrong?"

"I'm too tired to have this argument right now. Not again."

Adam comes around to the front of the couch, kneeling in front of me. He sighs, rubbing the back of his neck. "Lydia, talk to me. Please." His voice is soft, a hint of worry threading through it.

I lift my head back toward the ceiling, avoiding his eyes. "You really want to talk about this right now?"

"Yes," he says. "Because I think you need to release whatever this frustration is that you have built up."

Something in me snaps. Maybe it's his calmness when I feel like I'm falling apart inside. "Don't tell me you don't know what this is. We've been here before. It's me trying, Adam. It's me trying to feel close to you and getting rejected over and over again."

He opens my mouth to respond, but I don't stop. The anger flows out like a busted dam. "I saw how hard you tried in the beginning. You made an effort. It wasn't perfect, but it made me feel wanted, even just a little bit. But I feel like that's stopped. It's like now we're just roommates who kiss goodnight out of habit."

Adam looks down. "That's not fair."

"No, it's not. But I'm being honest about how I feel." My voice cracks. "I've tried to be understanding. Talking myself through every excuse for you. Stress, exhaustion, maybe it's just a phase. But how long does the phase last? Because the longer this goes on, the more permanent it feels. Every time I ask for sex, it's always 'maybe,' but I've learned your maybe really means no. Every rejection makes me feel smaller, more unwanted. Like sex with me is an obligation."

He winces as he stands. "Lydia, stop. That's not what I want you to feel."

"Well, then, how is it supposed to make me feel?" I demand, hoping his response will clarify everything. "You say you love me, and I know you do, but how do I rationalize this when you can't even touch me? If you really wanted to, you'd figure it out. You'd find a way."

"You think I haven't tried?" Adam's voice is louder than I've ever heard it. "You think I don't lie awake next to you feeling like I'm failing at being a husband? Your husband."

My tears won't stop falling. "Then why? Why does this keep happening? It's like we are always taking one step forward and two steps back with this."

He exhales, long and heavy. "I...I don't know. I wish I did. Lydia, I want you. God, I do. But when the moment's there..." He pauses, rubbing his face in frustration. "It's like my brain shuts down from trying so hard to make my body do what it should for you. I don't understand it. And every time it happens, every time my body doesn't do what it's supposed to, I hate myself a little more for letting you down."

I hate that I make you feel this way too.

Silence stretches between us, thick and suffocating. Finally, Adam steps toward me, placing a hand on my cheek. "I love you, Lydia. I just don't know how to fix this. How do we fix this?"

And for the first time, I don't have the energy to tell him it's okay because it's not.

"I know you're angry right now, and you have every right to be," Adam says, his voice soft, almost timid. "But please, come back to our bed. Let's try to get some sleep, and we can figure this out tomorrow with clear heads."

He holds a hand out to help me off the couch.

"Yeah, okay," I murmur, the fight gone from my voice. I take his hand, not out of resolution but out of exhaustion.

I wake the next morning to an empty bed. When I make my way to the kitchen for some much-needed coffee, I find a fresh pot made but almost empty.

Adam sits at the kitchen table, focused on his computer. The sound of me pouring coffee pulls him from his focus. He immediately jumps up, coming straight for me and pulling me in for a long kiss.

"Good morning, wife! Grab your coffee and come sit with me. I want to tell you what I've been doing this morning."

"Damn, hubs. How much coffee have you had this morning to have all this energy?" I chuckle, relieved by the hint of normalcy after our explosion last night.

"Probably too much," he admits with a grin that makes my heart melt. "But I've been up for a while doing research." Adam grabs his computer and leads me to the couch.

"What kind of research?"

"I Googled some things about the functions of the male body, if you know what I mean," he says with a wink. "First of all, do not Google 'men getting hard,' because I saw way more than I bargained for."

We both break into laughter as he describes his morning mishap.

"Anyway," he continues, "after I got out of that mess, I found some informational articles. I think my issue might be low testosterone. So I found a clinic that can run some tests and, if that's the issue, recommend some medicine to help." He pauses to let the information settle. "I called and set up an appointment for next week."

I blink, staring at him. This is the effort I've begged for. The kind that makes me feel seen, heard.

"You called and scheduled a doctor's appointment? That's like your seventh circle of Hell."

"Ha. Ha." He laughs dryly, knowing it's true. "Yes, sweetheart, I did. You were right last night. I wasn't doing everything I could to give you what you've been asking for. You told me several times what you needed, and I was too scared to listen. But please understand, if this is the issue, it's not going to improve right away."

"Thank you," I say, setting my mug on the table before leaning in for a deep kiss. "I've never asked for perfection, just effort. Thank you for doing something I know you hate for me. For us."

This time, he pulls me in for another kiss, deeper, surer.

"And look," I start, feeling my cheeks flush, "just because you can't get hard doesn't mean we can't have sexy fun times. There are plenty of things we can do."

Adam stands, holding out a hand to pull me from my chair. "Come show me," he says, his tone playful but full of promise, leading me back toward the bedroom.

As he leads me down the hall, a cautious warmth blooms in my chest. His effort means more than words ever could. For the first time in months, I feel seen, wanted. Not because everything's fixed, but because he's trying.

Chapter 29

1 Year Ago

After Adam's appointment, we learn he does have low testosterone—an actual medical reason for why he struggles to satisfy my need for physical connection.

The doctor's words echo in my mind as we walk out of the clinic. Adam's voice is low, but I can hear the frustration beneath it. "Well, at least we know what's going on now, right?"

I want to say something reassuring, but my throat is tight. Hearing it confirmed makes it real.

Adam's hand slips into mine, but it feels like he's a million miles away. When I glance over, his expression is a mixture of disbelief and quiet sadness. He's trying not to let it bother him, but I know it's eating at him.

A knot forms in my stomach, knowing this will be a long road to get our sexual relationship where I want it to be. He starts on medication right away, but progress is slow.

It's been about a year of patience. A year of being intimate, maybe once a month, while I lie next to him every night, quietly taking care of my own needs.

Sometimes I wonder if he ever notices me beside him, my hand slipping under the covers. If he does, he never says anything. Maybe he's asleep. Or maybe he just doesn't want to know.

What he doesn't know is that when I touch myself, it's not him I'm thinking of. It's Jason, the fantasies we built in words, the feeling of being wanted again.

Adam is a great partner, steady, loving, and endlessly supportive, but even the best relationships have their cracks. I feel emotionally safe with him, but there's still a part of me starving for touch, craving the kind of connection that makes me feel alive.

And I hate myself for it. For knowing his struggle isn't his fault...and still looking to Jason for validation, afraid to cut the final string that keeps him tethered to me. I scroll through my contacts, my thumb hovering over Jason's name.

I tell myself I just want to say hi, just a little conversation to remind me I still exist outside this quiet, controlled life. But the second I type his name, a warmth spreads through my chest, a dangerous mix of comfort and desire. I hesitate, fingers trembling, before typing a simple, innocent message:

Me: Hey...It's been a while. How have you been?

Almost immediately, my heart hammers. I know I shouldn't. I know it's risky. But I need this, just for a moment, just to feel like someone sees me.

Jason: Hey, baby. Yeah, it has. How are you?

And just like that, the wall I've built around my longing feels a little thinner, my guilt a little heavier. I shouldn't feel relief...but I do.

Me: I'm okay. Busy with life, marriage, you know how it is. Adam's great, but...some things are harder than I expected.

Jason: Hard, huh? As he should be.

Me: Not that kind of hard.

Jason: Damn. Baby, he should always be hard for you. I always am.

Me: Yeah... It's not his fault; it's a medical thing. He loves me, takes care of me, but...sometimes I feel like

I'm missing something. I probably shouldn't even be talking about this with you. Sorry.

Jason: I get it. But missing something doesn't make you a bad person, baby. You deserve to feel wanted. And you are wanted, even if it's not always obvious.

Me: I know...I just...It's complicated. I keep thinking maybe it's me.

Jason: Nope. Not you. You've always been full of desire, and it's part of what makes you you. You deserve someone who wants you as much as you want them. Someone who wants to tell you all the dirty things they want to do to you. Is that what you need from me right now?

Me: I'm married.

Jason: I know. And you love him. But...just imagine, if it were me, I'd show you exactly how it's done. Make sure you never feel unwanted again.

Me: I hate you sometimes.

Jason: Just telling you what I know you want and what you deserve. I'm happy to remind you of that whenever you like.

Me: Ooh, maybe we need a sex therapist. Someone to come show hubby how it's done. Is that a thing?

Jason: I can definitely make it a thing if you need a volunteer.

Me: You're trouble.

Why do I still talk to him? I feel the weight of the question, knowing there's no easy answer. If someone asked me if I loved him, I'd say yes. But it's not in the way people typically think of love. It's not romantic love. I wouldn't even say it's love for a friend. It's something deeper, messier, harder to explain. I know he doesn't love me, and I don't expect or really need him to.

I exhale a shaky breath, thinking about the years of pain I've been through and how Jason has been there in his own way, pulling me out of the darkness.

He doesn't know what he did for me. He doesn't know how he saved me. How he saved me from wanting to leave this life when I thought I had lost it all, reminding me that somebody wanted me. That I have something to live for. To hope for. That all of the crazy, messed-up shit in life can lead to something good.

For that, I love him.

And Chad, for that matter. I would not be where I am today if not for the hell he put me through. The self-worth I had to find because of him. I'll be forever grateful—not for him, but for the lessons.

My eyes drift back to the message on the screen, feeling the stirring of both longing and guilt.

Everything in life, every heartbreak, every mistake, has brought me to Adam. Adam is who I want to build a life for. The one I want to bring life into the world with.

But it has been a struggle to conceive, not just because of his low sex drive, but because we also learned his sperm count is almost nonexistent.

I'm standing in front of the mirror, my reflection staring back at me, tired, worn out, and defeated. I'm tired of planning when sex happens, of telling him when it's time to try, when the "best window" is for conception. It feels mechanical, clinical, like a job that's stripped away the intimacy.

And Adam's effort to please me, though admirable, doesn't erase the void inside. I try not to feel guilty for feeling so frustrated for longing for more than he can give.

But there's a voice in my head that keeps whispering: *You deserve more.*

Chapter 30

The weekend activities start on Thursday night with dinner and a movie with my parents. The familiar smell of Mom's roast fills the kitchen as I walk in, the low hum of the TV coming from the living room. She's already wiping her hands on a dish towel, ready to interrogate.

"Adam didn't want to come have dinner with us?" my mother questions as soon as I walk in the door, one eyebrow lifting as she leans against the counter.

"No, his dad is in town, so he is hanging out with him tonight." I drop my keys on the counter, trying to sound casual.

"What are they doing?" she presses, turning back to stir the pot.

"Not sure, actually."

The clink of the spoon against the pot echoes around the room, as if to question my words. "What do you mean you're not sure? They could have come too."

I watch the steam rise from the pot, curling into the air like an unspoken accusation. "I know," I say, trying to keep my tone even. "They talked about going to see a movie tonight. Adam was still working when I left, and his dad wasn't back from running errands yet, so I'm not sure what they decided."

Mom hums under her breath, not satisfied but pretending to be. She turns down the burner, the faint hiss of gas fading as she sets the lid on top with a little more force than necessary.

"What are you two doing this weekend?"

"Saturday, I'm going with some friends to see a musical that a local theater company is putting on."

Again, she raises an eyebrow at me. "Is Adam not going?"

"No, he's staying home to watch football."

Her cooking halts mid-motion, her wooden spoon hovering in the air. Her voice sharpens with accusation. "Are you guys okay?"

"Yeah, why?" I ask, reaching for a glass and turning on the faucet. The rush of water drowns out the uneasy pause that follows. I can feel her eyes on me, studying, waiting for a crack.

"No reason," she says too casually, returning to stir the pot. "You just seem to have a lot of separate plans this weekend."

I take a long sip of water, mostly to buy time and to hide any involuntary twitch of an eye roll. Does she think couples can't have their own interests? She and Dad do different things and go different places all the time. Yes, we are fine. It's just me who is not.

"Yes, Mom, we are fine," I say with slight annoyance, forcing a smile. The audacity of her to pry into our business like this. It's not like I can talk to her about my sex life. That would just be too weird.

"Adam is not a fan of musicals, and I'm not going to force him to go see something we both know he won't enjoy. Besides," I add, setting the glass on the counter with more force than I intended, "tomorrow we have a party we are going to together."

She finally lets the inquisition go, the air in the kitchen softening as we settle into dinner before heading to the movie. When the theater lights dim and the opening credits roll, I let myself sink into the dark, grateful for a few quiet hours where no one expects answers. For a few hours, I get to disappear into someone else's story instead of explaining my own.

By the next night, I'm ready to let loose. The party hums with laughter, music, and the buzz of alcohol-fueled energy. Adam drinks more than usual, and somewhere between what I think is his third or fourth drink, I start to recognize a side of him I haven't seen in a while. The fun, flirty kind of drunk. The slightly inappropriate kind.

He laughs louder, leans closer, and his usual restraint softens. At one point, he wraps an arm around my waist, hand slipping under my shirt. His hand is lingering on the bare skin of my hip in a way that makes my pulse spike. His eyes are playful and mischievous as he leans in to whisper something that makes me giggle and bite my lip, the excitement crawling up my spine.

I step inside for a moment to fix Adam a cup of water and greet the other wives, the mundane task giving me a few seconds to steady myself. When I return outside with his water, the words hit me like a shock: Adam, loud and unfiltered, joking to the group, "Who wants to grab my wife's boobs?" before they all erupt into giggles like schoolgirls.

"Alright, boys," I interject before anyone can answer. "I think it's time to get him to bed." I hand Adam the water as we make our way to the car.

Once he's settled in bed, I retreat to the quiet of the living room and pull out my phone, the impulse to share what just happened overwhelming. Someone needs to know.

With the right people, I'd be down for that. Maybe not with this group of friends, but if he's truly open to that kind of thought, maybe there's hope to bring some of my fantasies to life. My chest tightens with anticipation, a tiny spark reminding me that desire doesn't have to stay buried, even in a marriage filled with love and patience.

I sit on the edge of the couch, phone in hand, thumb hovering over the send button. I hate myself a little for even thinking about it, but the urge to share, to vent, to feel that familiar spark of validation, is too strong.

Me: You will never guess what hubby said tonight.

The weight of my marriage presses down on me, but so does the longing I've been trying to bury. I tell myself it's harmless, a way to release a little tension, but deep down, I wish it could be more.

Jason: Hopefully how fucking sexy you looked. I saw that photo you posted.

Me: No, but he did basically offer me to his friends. Or at least my boobs.

Almost instantly, his reply comes through, teasing, flirty, like it always does.

Jason: *Damn, baby. Bet that got your heart racing. Too bad I wasn't there to volunteer.*

I bite my lip, a mix of guilt and excitement curling through me. I remind myself: Adam is everything I want in a life partner. He's steady. He loves me. He's here for me in ways no one else ever has been.

Me: *Married. Don't make me think about this.*

Jason: *I know. But if he's offering to share...I'd show him exactly how to make sure you never feel unwanted again.*

The screen glows in the dark, my fingers hovering as a flush rises to my cheeks. The familiar pull is there, exciting, forbidden, but so dangerous. My heart hammers, guilt and desire twisting together.

I lean back, letting out a shaky breath. I shouldn't. But a tiny part of me...wants to.

Me: *Oh. And how's that?*

I bite my lip, heat rising to my cheeks as I imagine all the ways this scene could play out with the two of them.

Jason: *Let's give him a show. Letting my hands slowly roam your body, making sure every nerve of your body remembers this moment.*

Me: *Don't tease me.*

Jason: *Only until your body is aching for me. Then I'll throw you onto the bed and show your husband how his wife likes her orgasms.*

Me: *Don't.*

Jason: *Don't what, baby? Stop? Because I don't intend to.*

Me: *You're dangerous.*

I can't stop my hands from drifting south, no matter how hard I try. My reflection on the black screen stares back with something that mirrors a look of regret, but I don't care enough to stop.

Because the idea of having Adam and Jason together sparks something I can't shake.

Jason: *And you are turned on. Are you touching yourself, thinking of your husband watching me fuck you?*

I send the last text as I fall over the edge.

Me: *Yes.*

Chapter 31

The light of Saturday morning filters softly through the curtains. Adam isn't in bed beside me; he must have gotten up earlier.

I stir awake, noticing the muffled noise of the football stream coming from the other room. Stretching lazily, I take a moment to savor the rare stillness, knowing the day ahead will be slow and easy.

Assuming Adam will be occupied for a little while, I take advantage of the empty room to take care of my needs, reimagining last night's conversation. I force myself to stay quiet as I come, something I do a lot to hide the fact that I'm getting myself off.

I feel a presence in the room as I ride out the wave, my back arching off the bed.

Opening my eyes, I see Adam freeze mid-step, eyes widening as they land on me. My chest rises and falls rapidly, cheeks flushed.

"I...uh..." His voice catches.

I sit up a little, trying to cover myself, words tumbling out before I can filter them. "I was just...how long have you been standing there?"

Adam exhales slowly, running a hand down his face, shaking his head slightly. "Lydia...you don't have to hide from me."

"I know," I murmur, avoiding his gaze. "I just...didn't want to make it awkward."

He steps closer, coming to the edge of the bed to stand over me, voice soft and steady. "It's not awkward. I get it...I know you have needs, and I want us to figure this out together. I don't want you feeling like you have to do it alone."

He flips the sheets off of me, eyes widening at the sight of my naked body, toy still vibrating deep inside me. "I actually..." He swallows, hand moving toward the toy. He gently starts moving it in and out, maddeningly slow, as he leans down. "I came in here to wake you up for a little fun." His lips brush against my ear. "But it looks like you already did that."

I grab the back of his neck, pulling him in for a deep kiss. The movement of the vibrator doesn't stop, heightening the need for more. "I never said I was done."

Stepping back, he strips his clothes before moving back to continue fucking me with the vibrator while he strokes his cock. He bends down and brings a nipple into his mouth, adding more torment to his assault. Once he's ready, he positions himself between my legs, removes the vibrator, and settles himself inside me.

He moves at a pace comfortable for him, his face full of concentration, giving nothing away of his enjoyment. He thrusts in a few more times before his orgasm quietly takes over, and he stills his movements.

After a few quiet minutes, Adam pulls back slightly, brushing a strand of hair from my face. We lie there, letting the soft glow of the morning sun fill the room. His kisses are slow, tender, and full of reassurance, each "I love you" settling the restlessness that's been building between us.

Eventually, he starts to dress, the casual rhythm of getting ready grounding the intensity of what just happened. "I know we should do this more often," he murmurs with a grin, slipping into his shirt.

"Yeah, we should definitely be doing that on a daily basis," I murmur, a small, satisfied smile slipping on my lips. I feel lighter, the quiet contentment of a shared morning wrapping around us like a warm blanket. I didn't get the release I needed, but his effort gives me the comfort I need to feel the spark again.

Adam chuckles, shaking his head. "I don't know about daily, but I'm trying to make it more often." He leans down to press a quick, lingering kiss to my forehead before heading back to the living room, remote in hand, leaving me with a warm, contented glow.

The room falls quiet, and my mind begins to race. Tears sting behind my eyes, though I try to blink them back. *He's said that before.* He's explained he doesn't have a recovery period; that's part of why we can go a month or two without sex. Today's five-day window rips a hole in that explanation, and I struggle to know what to believe or how to feel. The confusion twists into something heavier, the feeling that our sex is given out of obligation. *Anxiety is a bitch.*

It's not as if he doesn't know how often I'm thinking about him, wanting him. I'm never shy with the sexual innuendos, the lingering touches, or the "fuck me" eyes I cast his way.

What he doesn't know is how often I think about someone else, how I fantasize about being fucked by him *and* someone else, how I still have explicit conversations with that particular someone.

I feel guilty about wanting these things, though a little less so after the party yesterday and the comments he made. I want him to take me to a sex club and offer to share me because what he gets from me is so good that others need to know. That has been a fantasy for a little while now, only ever a recurring dream.

I would never act on these fantasies. Not without his permission. But the longing, the deep aching need to feel wanted, to feel *desired*… That's something I can't deny.

Dreams and fantasies have some level of psychological truth to them, right? Mine boils down to feeling like I'm wanted, even if it's only in my dreams.

Sometimes I prefer when my mind is blank. There is no hurt. Just nothingness. When I have no plans, it leaves too much time for my brain to run wild.

I stare out the window, a heavy sigh leaving my chest. I feel trapped between two worlds. In one, there's Adam, who is everything I could ever need: stable, loving, reliable. In the other, there's Jason, a reminder of the fire, the passion I'm missing.

It feeds the guilt low in my belly.

I know this isn't a sustainable way to live, and I don't know what that means for my future with Adam. But something has to change before I lose to this tug-of-war forever.

For now, I settle next to Adam on the couch, living my fantasies through a spicy romance novel, adding more fuel to the fire.

Damn, these books put too many fantasies in my head.

Chapter 32

Present Day

I sit on the couch at 9 AM, tears streaming down my face, staring at the coffee table where my untouched mug has gone cold. Morning light filters through the curtains, soft and ordinary, mocking the chaos inside me.

Adam thinks it's because I hate my job. Don't get me wrong, I do hate my job right now. But that's not the real reason I'm in this state. The truth is so much deeper, so much more complicated. But it's easier to let him believe the lie than to tell him how he made me feel rejected again this morning.

"Oh, Lyds. I know you're stressed. Just think how much worse it could be. We'll find something better for you. Just give it time; the right thing will come along." He rubs my shoulders and pulls me into a hug. "You need a break. Maybe take a day off."

His calm sweetness grates on my nerves, and I hate myself even more for lying. He's trying to comfort me with the wrong information. I know he's right, in a way. A break would help. But right now, it's the last thing I want to hear.

I can't tell him the truth. I can't tell him that going to work is the only reprieve from the real reasons I'm crying. I can't explain that it's not my job. It's the constant turmoil inside me. The thoughts that keep me awake until 2 AM, the desires I try to drown out with those spicy romance books he calls smut. How could I tell him without shattering his heart?

Reading those books is probably a terrible idea. But they give me ideas, fantasies, and desires I can't ignore. Fantasies I'll never explore because I'm too afraid. Not afraid of the acts themselves, but of the rejection that would follow if I ask for what I want. The fear that my desires could hurt him, that our relationship could never recover from the truth.

Reading is supposed to be my escape. My fuel. But lately, it feels like torture, the cruelest kind of tease. The more I read, the darker my fantasies grow. Or maybe they've always been that dark, and I'm only just now brave enough to notice.

There are scenes I used to skip. Ones that made my stomach twist with something I couldn't name. Now I seek them out. Reread them. Let them linger in my mind long after I've closed the book. The concept of choking, the sensation of physically losing my breath, suddenly makes something deep inside me flicker to life. I used to hate the idea.

After that incident with Chad, I avoided any hands near my neck. But now, I wonder if I was more afraid of how much I liked it than of the actual danger it represented.

I should be happy. I have a lot to be grateful for: a loving husband, a beautiful home, and a stable job. I'm in love with my best friend. But still, something is missing. Something I can't name without breaking the fragile peace I've built.

I need more. And maybe that makes me selfish. I'm supposed to be content with what I have, with love that's steady and safe. So why does it feel like I'm suffocating under the weight of it all? How do you ask for more when the person beside you has already given everything they can?

I think about asking him for what I want, but saying the words out loud feels impossible. I know he'd try—he always does—but I also know it's temporary. A flicker of effort before everything settles back into the same quiet routine. And I'd be left feeling emptier than before, haunted by the taste of something I can't have.

My mind is a battlefield. One part whispers that his medical issues are to blame, that it's out of his control. But another part—the darker, crueler one—insists it's me. *You're too fat to be wanted. If he really wanted you, he would make it happen.*

The voice drags me back through the years, high school, college, when everyone else was dating, and I was invisible. No one ever really wanted me. I didn't start dating until my twenties, not by choice.

A deeper part of me craves more than affection. I want to be demanded, desired in a way that's urgent and raw. I want him to need me so badly that he can't resist, to look at me like I'm the one thing he can't walk away from, the one thing he has to have.

I can't have that conversation with him again. I know how it will end. We'll both break down but for different reasons. He'll promise to try harder, but it'll be temporary, like always. The same routine.

I envy the women in those books. Yes, it's fiction, but it has to be based on someone's reality. How did they make that their reality? How can I ask for what I want without destroying everything?

Am I being selfish for wanting more? When you love someone, you're supposed to be willing to do anything for them, right? But where does that end? Where's the line you don't cross?

If I truly loved him, shouldn't I suffer quietly for his sake? Shouldn't I protect him from my desires? But if he really loved me, shouldn't he want to fill this void? Or at least be willing to try?

I finally understand the appeal of stories in which women get multiple men. It's not just a fantasy; it's a solution. Each man gives her something the others can't, emotionally and sexually. Together, they make her whole. Maybe it's not about needing someone else involved as much as it is about the freedom to be fully seen, fully satisfied, craved.

I know it's wrong, these fantasies that haunt me. I keep telling myself I'm not asking for much, but deep down, I know I am. *What if I say it out loud and he looks at me like I'm broken?*

It says something about our relationship that I'm willing to break down with him, even if I'm not telling him the full truth. I hate being seen like this. He always says, "We have nothing to be sad about," or "We have a good life," or "I just need you."

All true. But that last one? That one kills me.

I want more than he's been able to give me. And my first thought is to bring someone else into it. God, I'm so fucking selfish. We can't be the only ones struggling like this. How could I even ask that of him? How do other couples handle this?

I want someone who needs me so badly that the second we're alone, they pounce because their need is so intense, so raw, so animalistic.

But right now, I don't feel any of that. I'm not sure I ever have.

Except with Jason. Even if it's not real.

The thought stops me cold. My breath catches, tears still wet on my cheeks. Jason. The one person who's always made me feel like he would devour me. Like I was worth the hunger.

I glance at Adam, still sitting beside me, patient and kind, waiting for me to calm down. And something inside me fractures and shifts. Like a fault line finally giving way.

I can't keep doing this. I can't keep pretending I'm fine when I'm drowning. I can't keep protecting him from the truth when the truth is the only thing that might save us.

I take a deep, shuddering breath, letting the tears dry on their own. For the first time in months, maybe years, a strange clarity settles over me. I know what I want, and more importantly, I know I deserve it. No more half-measures, no more quiet compromises. I can't keep burying these desires, pretending they don't exist.

I will lay it all on the line. Every fantasy, every longing, every part of me that's been waiting in the shadows. It will be selfish. It will be scary.

But sometimes you have to risk burning to become someone new. And I'm finally willing to self-destruct to have it all.

Chapter 33

I've been stalling, running in endless circles in my own head for days, unsure how to even start this conversation with Adam. Every possible opening feels wrong, every word a trap I could fall into.

What if I scare him? What if he hates me for wanting this? What if I ruin everything we've built?

But I can't wait any longer. This has to happen tonight.

I spent the afternoon cooking his favorite dinner, the aroma of garlic and rosemary filling the kitchen, hoping the familiar comfort might soften the blow. The sizzle of the pan, the clink of utensils... everything sounds louder than usual, like the house itself is holding its breath.

The air feels heavy with inevitability. My stomach twists, and my hands tremble slightly as I set the table. The mix of anticipation and fear reminds me I'm teetering on the edge of something I can't take back.

A small, nagging voice in my head whispers: *Maybe this is too much. I'm asking too much. I'm being selfish.* But I know, deep down, I can't let myself turn back. Tonight, the truth comes out.

I hear Adam moving around in the living room, the soft shuffle of his feet, the distant hum of the TV. Each sound twists the knot in my stomach tighter, a reminder that he's out there, expecting a normal evening, while I'm about to unravel everything.

"Hey, hubby," I call from the kitchen. "Dinner's ready."

He comes in from the living room, wrapping his arms around me from behind and pressing a quick kiss to the back of my head. "Mmm, something smells amazing, sweetheart."

"Me or the food?" I tease, letting a small, nervous grin slip past the tension in my chest.

We settle at the table, the quiet clink of silverware filling the space between us. I push food around my plate, trying to find the courage.

After a few minutes of silent eating, I finally speak.

"Adam...we need to talk."

He looks up from his plate, brows knitting in concern, sensing the weight behind my words. "Okay... What's on your mind?"

I take a slow breath, hands clutching the fork as if it might anchor me. Every fiber of me wants to back down, to pretend this is just another minor discussion about schedules or chores. But it's not. This is everything I've been holding in—the fantasies, the desires, the part of me that's never been fully satisfied.

"I've been thinking...about us, about our marriage...about me." I force the words past the lump in my throat. "And I need to be honest. I need to tell you everything I want, everything I've been imagining, because I can't keep pretending anymore."

He sets his fork down slowly, watching me with a mix of apprehension and concern. I can see him bracing for what's coming, but I can't stop now.

"I love you," I start slowly, letting those words sink in. "I love the life we've built together. I'm okay with the fact that we've given up on trying for a baby. I'm happy with where we are..." I pause, searching his eyes. My hands fidget in my lap, twisting the napkin into knots. "...mostly. But...there's a part of me, something I've been holding back, that I can't keep hiding anymore."

"What are you saying, Lydia?" His voice carries a note of alarm, but he stays still, waiting.

My voice falters, and I take a shaky breath. "I have desires...fantasies...things I want that...I don't know how to ask for without risking everything. And I've been afraid, Adam. Afraid of hurting you, afraid you'll see me differently."

I swallow hard, feeling the heat of vulnerability rise in my chest. "I need to tell you what I want, even if it's selfish, even if it's more than you can give me. Because pretending I don't want these things isn't fair to either of us anymore."

"Pretending that I'm enough?" he asks softly, his voice careful.

"No," I whisper, the words catching in my throat. "Pretending that we both don't know we're compatible in every way...except in bed."

Adam leans back slightly, running a hand through his hair, his expression soft but heavy. He takes his time processing what I've said.

"I know..." His voice is quiet. "I've heard this before, and I've tried, you know, I've tried. I just...maybe I can't be everything you need in that way." He swallows, his eyes searching mine. "But I don't want you to stop telling me. Please, keep opening up. I need to understand what you want, even if I can't always give it to you. I love you too much not to try."

His words give me courage and terror all at once. I take another shaky breath, letting the first layer fall away.

"It's...It's more than just wanting to feel close," I whisper. "I want to be *wanted*, Adam. Not just loved, not just cared for, because you do make me feel that. But I want that raw, desperate need. I want to feel like my pleasure is the only thing that matters at that moment. I need to feel you burn for me."

My voice falters, heat rising to my cheeks. "Please don't take this wrong. I can't imagine this life without you. But sometimes I wonder if there's another way to satisfy us both."

I force myself to continue. "I want passion that shakes me, that leaves me breathless...and I want it often. Not planned, not timed around your recovery schedule, or my ovulation. Just...spontaneous. Urgent."

"I'm listening, Lydia," he says quietly. "I'm not making any promises, but I'm open to listening."

I take a breath, my next words coming out in a rush. "Do you know that every night after you fall asleep, I touch myself? Needing to feel the release I've been begging you for?"

I pause, seeing the flicker of hurt in his eyes, but he doesn't look away. He's listening. That's all I need right now.

"No, I didn't," he says softly, hesitant. "What do you think about when you do? Do you think about me?"

"Yes." I swallow hard, the next words even harder to say. "And no. Sometimes it's reimagining scenes from the books I read, sometimes replacing the characters with you. But…" I hesitate, my chest tightening. "Sometimes I create fantasies that involve more than just you. Things that involve other people."

His expression doesn't change, but I see his jaw tighten slightly.

"Like that comment you made the other night," I bring up, hoping he'll recognize this is not just a spontaneous ask. "It's not about cheating," I say quickly. "It's about being wanted, desired, craved in ways I…that I don't get from you. And yes, I know that's selfish. I know it's confusing. I hate myself a little for even thinking about it. But it's there. And I can't ignore it anymore."

Silence stretches between us, thick and heavy. My chest feels tight, my palms clammy, my heart hammering. I've said it. The truth is out.

He reaches across the table, taking my hand in his. His thumb brushes over my knuckles, and his eyes are distant in thought.

"Thank you for telling me," he whispers. "I don't want you to hide any part of yourself from me."

There's a long silence before he speaks again, his voice hesitant but not closed off. "So, are you asking for us to bring someone else into this relationship?"

I press my lips together slowly, my throat tight. "Yeah, I guess I kind of am. But more like...someone to fill in when you've reached your limit. When you can't...when your body can't."

He exhales slowly, his grip on my hand tightening just slightly. "I...I hear your frustration. I want to give you the world, Lydia, but this...this is a lot for me to process." He pauses, searching for the right words.

"I love you, Adam. I love us," I squeak out as tears swell in my eyes. "I just want us both to have what we need—whatever that looks like."

"I want to understand this," he says quietly. "But I'm scared that if I open that door, you'll realize there's nothing in me worth coming back to. I need a little time to think about it, to figure out if I can even begin to meet you halfway here."

I meet his eyes in understanding, swallowing the lump in my throat. "That's never the case, but I get it. This is a lot, and I never expected you to have a response right away. I also want to hear other ideas. But I just needed you to know the things haunting my mind."

It's not the immediate reassurance I crave, but it's something. He's listening. He cares. And for now, that has to be enough.

Chapter 34

The days after my confession feel hollow. Adam asked for time to think, and every silent minute rips at my heart, leaving me terrified of losing him.

He's been gone, silent, for four days.

And for the last four days, I've drifted through our home like a ghost, replaying everything I said over and over, wishing I could take it back, terrified that I've destroyed the best thing I've ever had.

If he walks away, I'll know it's because I asked for too much. Because I finally said out loud what should've stayed inside.

My stomach twists, my hands fidget with nothing, and I can't stop imagining him leaving, taking with him every piece of safety he's built in this marriage.

I pace the living room, unable to settle on the couch or in the kitchen. Each corner of the house reminds me of him: the couch where we curl up together, the counter where he leaves his coffee mug, the bedroom where I'm supposed to feel safe but now feels like glass, so fragile it might shatter if I breathe too hard.

Just when I'm about to call him and beg him to forget everything I said, he comes home. Adam steps into the room, and I freeze.

My throat tightens, my heart hammering so loud I'm sure he can hear it. I can't read him. His expression is terrifyingly calm but serious, like he's both weighing and containing a storm.

I open my mouth to apologize, to take it all back before he even has a chance to speak, but he raises a hand gently, stopping me.

"Lydia...let me speak first," he says softly, his voice steady but heavy with thought.

I swallow hard, waiting, my chest tight with anticipation. The tension coils between us, the silence stretching almost unbearably. I force myself to stay still, giving him the same judgment-free space he gave me.

He takes a slow step toward me, his eyes never leaving mine. "I've thought a lot about what you said," he begins, and I cling to his words, afraid to breathe too loudly in case it shatters the fragile tension. "I hear you.

All of it. And I know…I'm not everything you need in this area."

"But you are…" I try cutting him off, needing him to know he is enough.

He holds up a hand, silently asking me to let him continue. "But I want to try, Lydia. I want to figure out what this means for us. I don't want to lose you."

The relief hits me like a wave, but it's tangled with guilt, fear, and an unsteady spark of hope. I manage a faint, wordless acknowledgement, unable to speak, feeling the weight of everything I've been holding in finally start to shift, even just slightly.

He takes a breath, steadying himself. "I've been sexually distant," he says, his voice thick with emotion and regret. "I know I don't show you enough of how I feel about you—not the way you need me to. I know I should be giving you more through physical intimacy. You've been screaming for it, and I've been ignoring you. That's not fair to you."

Tears stream down my cheeks, blurring his face. Adam steps forward, gently wiping them away with the edge of his shirt.

"I've been hiding behind my medical issues," he continues, his voice cracking slightly. "Telling myself it was noble to protect you from disappointment. But all I was doing was protecting myself. Love isn't supposed to make you feel starved. I'm sorry for starving you."

He pauses, his eyes steady on mine, voice low but firm. "I don't want to lose you. Not over this. I'm willing to try something different if it means keeping our marriage alive."

I blink, my heart thudding hard against my ribs.

He takes a slow breath, choosing his words carefully. "If there are times I can't meet your needs physically, then maybe...we find someone. One person. Someone we both trust, who can step in when I can't, to help fill that space. To...show me how it's done."

The weight of what he's saying presses against me, heavy but not suffocating.

"Our marriage comes first," he continues, voice gentle but unwavering.

I choke back a sob. He's choosing me, choosing us, even as I'm still regretting my own confession, feeling broken and unworthy of any of this.

"Always. You and me. That doesn't change. But if this is what it takes to make sure you feel whole, then I'd rather face it with you than pretend it isn't there."

I stand there, stunned, moved, frightened, and oddly relieved all at once. My chest feels tight, my pulse thrumming in my ears.

The depth of his love hits me like a wave I wasn't ready for, raw and unshakable. Adam isn't giving me away. He's giving me back to myself, trusting that even with this vulnerability, I'll still choose him.

I swallow hard, tasting the salt of my own tears. Relief and guilt twist together in my stomach. Part of me wants to run into his arms, to cling to him and never let go.

But another part freezes, fear filling in the silence. Fear of what this means, fear of the path we just stepped onto.

And yet...there's a spark of hope that maybe I don't have to sacrifice myself to keep our marriage breathing.

He reaches for me, and I let him, letting his hands anchor me while my mind races. The weight of everything

I've held inside starts to shift, just slightly, and for the first time in weeks, years, I think I breathe again.

Chapter 35

I wake up mid-dream, the same dream that has haunted me for months now, my body aching for a release.

The air between us feels heavy, thick with the residue of last night's conversation. Relief? Danger? A mix of both.

Someone. The word keeps circling back in my mind. *Someone we could both trust.* There's only one person I can trust. I'm going to suggest Jason as the partner in this.

The thought feels both reckless and right. He already knows me in ways Adam is trying to. He's seen the parts of me I've tried to hide, helped me explore my desires without shame, and guided me through a side of myself I barely dared to acknowledge.

Memories of our shared history replay through my mind, the way he made me feel seen and wanted when no one else did. He awakened a part of me I had buried, a fire I didn't know I had.

I roll over to face Adam, draping one leg over his as my hand slides along his body. He stirs, pushing me away. But before the disappointment reaches the surface, he's on top of me, lips crashing against mine in a hard, deep kiss. My chest tightens with anticipation and desire.

I gasp slightly against his lips, my hands clutching at his shoulders as he leans into me. There's a hunger in him I haven't felt in a long time, a rawness that makes my pulse hammer. I can feel his warmth, the press of his body, and it's grounding me in a way that's almost dizzying.

He breaks the kiss just enough to breathe, forehead resting against mine. His eyes search mine, intense and questioning. "You know I want you," he murmurs, voice low and rough. "I'm here. Always."

Words fail me as my heart races with a mix of relief and something more dangerous: hope. His arms tighten around me, holding me as if he could keep all the chaos at bay. He takes his time, loving me in the only way he knows how. For the first time in days, I feel like maybe we'll be okay.

After, we lie there, limbs tangled, soaking in each other. "So," he begins, voice low and thoughtful as he stares at the ceiling, "when you have these fantasies...being satisfied by someone else..." He shifts, rolling over so we're face to face. "Who's the someone you think about?"

I hesitate, a flutter of nerves stirring in my chest. "You really want to know?"

"Yes. Honesty is the only way this is going to work," he says, his gaze steady. "No judgment."

I take a slow breath. "An old friend of mine," I answer vaguely, my heart thumping at the admission.

"Why him?"

I lay out my history with Jason. How he's helped me from afar with my struggles in sexual identity, how our conversations once sparked fantasies I'd never shared with anyone else, how he's always made me feel wanted. How he saved my life without even trying.

Adam listens, his eyes searching mine with a mix of curiosity and caution. "Do you think he'd actually be willing to do this with us?"

I chew the inside of my cheek, thinking through logistics. "Assuming he's not in a relationship, I'd say there's a pretty decent chance. Honestly, he's the one I'd want to ask first. He lives a few states away, so that makes it easier to manage. Controlled access, no daily entanglement. It would have to be prescheduled, very intentional, leaving us space to focus on our marriage, and just bring him in from time to time…easing into it."

I pause, sitting up and straddling Adam's lap to search his face, gauging his reaction, wondering if he can imagine this without feeling threatened. "This…isn't about replacing you. It's about filling a space that only exists when I'm with you. I want us first, always, but I need…I think we need this. At least sometimes."

"Okay." His voice is filled with a certainty I didn't expect to hear. "Let's lay out the ground rules, then you can ask him when you feel ready."

I exhale, a mix of relief and nervousness twisting in my stomach. Together, we go through the details, boundaries, limits, the schedule, and how to make sure it's controlled, safe, and centered on us. Every rule we set feels like a lifeline, a way to keep our marriage intact while giving me a chance to feel the desire I've been missing.

When we finish, the room is quiet, the tension softened by shared understanding. The hardest part is done between us. Now I just have to talk to him. Jason.

My pulse quickens just thinking about it. Every fantasy, every conversation we've ever had, every longing I've buried for years...It's all riding on this one moment. And there's no turning back.

I wait until later that evening to talk to Jason while Adam is at the gym. My fingers hover over the screen, hesitating for a heartbeat before finally typing.

Me: Hey.

Jason: Hey, sexy.

Me: You busy?

Jason: Never too busy for you.

I take a deep breath, feeling my heart hammering against my ribs. This isn't just a casual chat. This is everything I've been holding back, everything I've fantasized about admitting for years.

Me: I need to be honest with you, and it may start weird and deep, but bear with it for a minute.

Jason: I'm intrigued.

Me: You've always been...the glue holding me together in ways no one else could. You've shown me what it feels like to be wanted when nobody else did.

There's a pause long enough for me to hear my own pulse in my ears.

Jason: ...Wow. I had no idea. I mean, I knew we had an unconventional relationship, but you saying that...

Me: I'm sorry, I should have told you sooner about the effect you have on my life. It started out as just a game that Emily set in motion, but it somehow became the self-esteem boost, the lifeline I needed.

I stare at the blinking cursor, my fingers trembling slightly.

Me: And you need to know what I'm risking to ask you this.

Jason: Risking?

Me: If this is too much and you want to forget all about me, I risk losing the one person who continuously heals me, saves me, without even trying, without even knowing.

Another pause. He's typing, then stopping, then typing again.

Jason: Okay...I'm listening.

Me: Hubby and I...we've talked about me needing more. About things he can't give me physically. He loves me, and I love him. That hasn't changed. But we agree that there might be a way for someone else to...help fill that gap sometimes.

I can almost feel the shift through the screen, the hesitation, the quiet recalibration in his tone. Or maybe that's just my mind projecting my own insecurities.

Jason:...*and you're asking me?*

Me: *Maybe. I'm not assuming anything. I wanted to talk to you first, explain everything, and see how you feel. This isn't casual. There are rules, boundaries, and everything is about keeping our marriage safe.*

Jason: *What are the rules?*

Me: *Well, here are the basics, but subject to change: 1. Emotional fidelity: our marriage comes first. 2. The third party is there in a purely physical capacity when the married couples agree. 3. Full transparency: there are no secrets, no solo contact that's not discussed first.*

There's a brief silence again. I brace myself for rejection, for judgment, for that gut-punch of loss I've been dreading.

Jason: *Ok.*

Me:...*ok...?*

Jason: *Yes, I'm in.*

Me: *Wait, just like that?*

Jason: *Baby, I was never kidding when I said I would make you feel everything you need. There's clearly* more we need to iron out, but it seems like the basics are there. I've never been a relationship type, so this works for me.

For a moment, I just stare at the message. My pulse stutters, stalling then surging again. Relief, fear, and something dangerously close to excitement ripple through me all at once.

Jason: *On one condition.*

I push to my feet, needing to pace. Sitting suddenly feels impossible.

Me: *What's that?*

Jason: *Change number 3. I want us to go back to our typical conversations. I want your body to remember all the things I can do to it, even when I'm not there.*

My breath catches, half a gasp, half a quiet laugh I can't suppress. Typical conversations. The kind that leaves me flushed and restless, lying awake replaying his words like a pulse under my skin.

Me: *I think we can make that adjustment. However, I will not hide the conversation anymore. If he wants to read it, I'll let him.*

Jason: *Mmm, perfect, let him read so he can see what I do to you.*

Jason: *Give me his number.*

Me: *His number?*

Jason: *Yes. I'm only agreeing to this on the condition that he agrees with it.*

Me: *Would I be laying it all on the line like this without him being on board?*

Jason: *Not at all, baby. I know what you want from me in this, but I want to talk to him about what he wants too. What are his boundaries when it comes to me and you?*

Me: *Right, makes sense. I'll share his contact info.*

Me: *<contact>*

Jason: *Good girl.*

I stare at the glowing words on my phone, feeling the aftershock of everything we've just agreed to. The world feels sharper somehow. The air hums, my skin tingles, and my thoughts blur between guilt and something that feels dangerously close to desire. And just like that, this plan is set in motion.

When Adam returns from the gym, I can't stop watching him. The way he moves, calm and careful, unaware that the ground beneath us has shifted. I wait until we're done cleaning in the kitchen after dinner, my voice low but sure.

"Jason agreed," I tell him, heart pounding. "But he wants to talk with you directly. He said to expect a call."

Adam's expression is unreadable at first then softens into quiet resolve. "Okay," he says finally. "We'll take it one step at a time." His back straightens slightly, almost unnoticeably, before turning toward the living room. His phone rings before he even reaches the couch. I watch as he glances at the screen, takes a breath, and answers, retreating to his office.

Listening to the hum of their conversation, I can't make out the words, but the sound of their muffled voices settles deep in my core. They are talking about me, deciding things with me at the center. It makes me feel claimed in a way I've ached for. A way I've cried for.

Adam knows what I need, and Jason knows how to provide it.

A small smile tugs at my lips before I can stop it. My chest is alive with an energy that's part nerves, part hunger, and part something I can't quite name. The line between fear and excitement blurs, and for the first time...I get to see where it leads.

Chapter 36

Jason and Adam talked off and on for a few days, getting to know each other and ironing out the ground rules. I tried not to eavesdrop, wanting them to bond naturally, but hearing their low voices, calm and deliberate, sometimes tense, sends a strange thrill through me.

When they finally finished the discussions, Adam looked oddly settled, and I knew there was no going back.

"I'm letting you and Jason draft the plan for the first meeting. Y'all can fill me in once it's decided," Adam said, kissing my forehead.

Since the night Adam gave his blessing, Jason and I have been talking more often. Almost daily, actually. At first, it was logistics, like where, when, and how this would even work. But our conversations have taken on a life of their own, settling back into our normal rhythm. Each message sews a new thread of anticipation tighter inside me. I can feel the heat building with every word, every teasing thought that slips between us.

I've stopped being so discreet about the way I talk to Jason, sharing the conversations with Adam. I no longer cover up when I touch myself while lying next to Adam, letting the sound of Jason's words echo in my mind.

And somehow, that honesty, the openness, has sparked something in Adam. Our intimacy has deepened, our touches more urgent, our kisses longer. I wonder if he's turned on by watching it all unfold or if this is out of jealousy.

It's strange how something so risky, so taboo, could make me feel more alive in my marriage than I have in years.

Adam is more involved in the planning than I expected. I thought he'd want distance, to look away from the details, to just let it happen and not think too hard about it. But instead, he's in it with me, asking questions, giving suggestions.

His calmness surprises me, but I can see the flicker of curiosity in his eyes when we talk about it. His eyes flare, lingering on me longer when I mention Jason's name. His breath catches when I read him our conversations.

Part of me hopes that watching Jason give me pleasure might awaken his own kinks. Maybe seeing me wanted, touched, and alive again will stir something that's been dormant in him for far too long. Even if his body can't fully join in, maybe his desires can.

I want this fantasy to come true—for me, yes, but also for us. For Adam. That's why, for his sake, we are starting small. Something contained. Something safe enough to test the edges without crossing too far.

Next week, Jason will arrive, and the plan will morph from theory to reality. And as much as I crave what's coming, a quiet voice keeps whispering in the back of my mind that, after this, nothing will ever be the same.

I just hope our marriage is strong enough to survive it.

I have to have faith that it is.

Chapter 37

Tonight is the night.

I take my time getting ready. Not for vanity, but for control. For confidence. My outfit feels like armor. A black skirt with slits up both sides that stops just shy of indecent, hugging my hips like a dare. My boots climb high, stopping just above my knees, and my top dips low enough to draw the eye without apology.

The mirror catches me off guard for a second. I look like a sexy warrior. How anyone fights in this kind of outfit, I'll never understand, but damn does it make me feel powerful.

And I'll need that power tonight. Because while this is something we've all agreed to, none of us really knows how it's going to feel once it's real.

Adam and I start with dinner. Something that is just the two of us, a quiet attempt to ground ourselves before things shift into something new. The candlelight between us feels both intimate and heavy, the kind of silence that's full of unspoken questions. We talk about normal things like it's any other date night.

But underneath it all, we both know what's waiting on the other side of this meal. It feels strange to break something open to make it feel whole again. But honesty isn't gentle. It's the thing that forces us to see what's left, what's real, when comfort is stripped away.

After dinner, we head to the bar where our friend Stacy works. The plan is simple: a drink or two, a casual hangout. Jason will meet us at the bar so the three of us can talk and confirm that everyone still wants this before taking the next step. If all feels right, he'll take me out on the dance floor for a while, just enough to feel the electricity move between us in public, with Adam watching nearby.

The food sits heavy in my stomach, not from the meal but from what's waiting at the end of this car ride.

The bar is warm and loud, a comfortable mix of laughter, clinking glasses, and low music pulsing through the floor. Stacy spots us from her spot behind the bar and waves us over, her smile bright as ever. I can feel Adam's hand resting gently at the small of my back as we weave through the crowd, a gesture that feels protective, maybe even possessive.

Stacy, well aware that this is happening tonight, immediately places a drink in front of me as we reach the bar. A Devil's Margarita—the moment when the thrill outweighs the consequence. It's smooth, dark, and daring enough to make me forget who's watching.

Jason's already here, standing at the far end of the bar, leaning casually against the counter. His presence feels impossible to miss, tall and toned, like he takes up more space than the room can afford. When his eyes find mine, something deep in my stomach twists—not just attraction, but recognition. That familiar, dangerous energy leaping from text to reality.

I imagined this moment a thousand times, rehearsed every possible reaction. But seeing him now, existing in the same air, feels like standing on the edge of a cliff, ready to jump.

Jason walks over, his eyes never leaving mine, sparking with every conversation that ever burned between us.

"Lydia." My name drips from his tongue, smooth and heavy, while his fingers curl around a strand of my hair, twirling it with a focus that feels like restraint, like he's been waiting years to touch me, yet he's still trying to hold back.

My breath stumbles. Every rehearsed response evaporates. All I manage is a shaky exhale, my pulse fluttering like it's trying to escape.

The guys shake hands, their expressions measured, respectful. Adam keeps his voice steady, but the tightness in his shoulders betrays how nervous he really is, while Jason looks like he's built for this. They talk around me as I sit between the two, caught in the space where adrenaline and anticipation collide.

The longer they talk, the more Jason takes advantage of the slit in my skirt. I take small but frequent sips of my drink to keep my face from giving anything away. The tension builds quickly, like the moment before a match is struck. Jason's hands are drifting higher and higher until he reaches my hip, noticing I'm not wearing anything underneath.

Suddenly removing his hand, Jason comes to stand behind me, leaning in until his breath grazes my ear, sending shivers down my spine. My head tips back instinctively, resting against him, needing to close the distance between us.

"Come dance with me."

My heart skips. I glance at Adam, silently asking permission. His head gestures toward the dance floor, quick and decisive, and that's all I need.

The music hits me the moment we step onto the floor, the deep bass and seductive rhythm, bodies moving too close for it to be innocent. Jason's hand finds my waist, drawing me in until my back is against his chest, barely leaving space to breathe. My body responds, arching into him, letting his confidence guide me.

At first, it's just dancing, movements syncing with the beat, the kind of closeness that would look normal to anyone else. But then his hand drifts higher, tracing along the slit of my skirt, fingertips tracing the inked snake on my bare thigh, reminding me why I got it a few months ago. Something just for me as a dark reminder that transformation is necessary.

Snakes shed their skin to survive, to keep growing: shed or die. I liked the edge of it, the predator beneath the elegance, a quiet vow to shed what no longer serves me, to keep moving, no matter what. Sure, a butterfly is a classic symbol of change, but it is too ostentatious, too cute. I chose the snake over a butterfly for its edge, its predator's stealth, its quiet control. Like it, I want to be hidden, yet powerful, capable of surviving anything and moving forward on my own terms.

Right now, with Jason's touch, I feel that power more than ever. The parts of me weighed down by fear, doubt, and the ghosts of the past…each one shed, each one renewed by his touch.

The music fades into the background; the whole room could disappear, and I wouldn't notice. My skin tingles as his hands travel inward, feeling the heat of my core. His lips find the spot just behind my ear, not a kiss exactly, but the combination of his lips and hand sends a shiver down my spine.

Back at the bar, I can feel eyes on us. I catch Stacy's expression, a mix of curiosity and wonder. She leans toward Adam, whispering something, her eyes flicking between him and Jason. Adam says something back, face wearing nothing but a smirk. His drink sits untouched, his focus locked on us.

When Stacy's eyes find mine, I flash back to the night I unloaded every messy truth onto her, the dream she somehow became a part of. She'd told me then to tell Adam what I really needed. She gives a quick thumbs up, a quiet support without a word spoken.

Eventually, the heat of the moment gives way to exhaustion. Jason presses his forehead to mine for a brief second, then takes my hand, leading me off the floor to where Adam's waiting. No words, just a shared look that somehow says everything and nothing all at once.

We walk out of the bar together. The night air is cool, grounding. Watching Jason and Adam together, calm and polite, feels surreal, almost like they are old friends. These are two parts of my life that were never meant to share the same air, yet here they are, shaping what comes next.

The ride home with Adam is quiet, anticipation thick enough to taste. When we pull into the driveway, my pulse quickens again, because whatever happens next, we've already crossed the line.

The house feels different when we walk in, familiar but tense, like the air itself knows what's coming. Adam locks the door behind us, the soft click echoing louder than it should.

No one speaks at first. The silence is thick, vibrating with everything we've already said and everything we haven't. I set my purse down, trying to steady my breathing, but my body is still humming from the dance, from Jason's hands, from Adam's eyes on us.

Adam's the one to break the quiet. "Drink?" he offers, voice calm but a little too even.

"Sure," Jason answers, settling onto the couch like he's trying not to take up too much space. He glances at me, and there's a question in his eyes. *Are you okay?* I give him a tiny, nervous smile, unable to speak under the weight of his stare as I settle onto the coffee table across from him.

Adam pours three glasses of whiskey and hands them out like a ritual. I take a sip, letting the burn settle my nerves.

Jason's the first to speak again, his tone careful. "I just want to say...Thank you. For trusting me with this. I know it's not small."

Adam's shoulders relax slightly, expression softening. "It's not. But we made this choice together. I meant what I said. We do this openly, honestly. No games. If it doesn't work, we can make it a clean break."

"I can handle that," Jason says, looking me in the eyes.

"So, you are still okay with this, Adam?" I ask timidly. He responds with an answering look, letting his expression do the agreeing.

I look between them—my husband, steady but uncertain, and Jason, confident but dangerous. I feel something shift inside me. It's not guilt exactly, not fear either. It's a realization that what we're doing isn't betrayal. It's about trying to bridge something that's been broken for a long time. And for the first time, the bridge isn't built on apology, but on truth.

For once, I'm not waiting for permission. I'm here because I chose this, because I finally trust myself to want without shame.

I stand, my legs trembling just slightly, and step toward Adam. I wrap my arms around his neck and pull him into a kiss, slow at first then deeper, heavier. I pour everything I can't say into it. The gratitude, the fear, the love, the ache of everything we've been through to get here.

Jason comes up behind me, sliding his hands around my waist while I continue to kiss Adam. He takes his time, feeling my body before sliding his hands under my shirt. The warmth of his hand spreads across my body. He lifts my shirt, causing me to break the kiss with Adam so he can remove it fully.

When I pull back, I hold Adam's eyes as I whisper, "Thank you," the words small but thick with everything I mean and can't quite explain.

Once my shirt is off, I bring my lips back to Adam's, Jason moving in to brush kisses across the back of my neck and across my spine while moving his hands to play with my nipples. The actions cause me to moan into Adam's mouth as their touches send an electric charge through my body.

This is the feeling I was missing. The simple acts by them both are just the beginning of the promise the night holds. They awaken the feeling of being wanted that I craved for so long. Only now, I understand it isn't just about being wanted; it's about being safe inside the wanting.

Still focusing on my connection with Adam, I whimper into his mouth as Jason steps back, the warmth of his body dissipating in the cool air. Adam chuckles as he pulls away. "I don't think our girl likes it when you're not touching her."

My pussy clenches at the use of his phrasing. *Our.* If I had any doubts that Adam wasn't okay with this, that one word shut them down.

It's not long before Jason's hands are back on me. "I think you're right." His deep voice reverberates down my spine. I don't know when he removed his shirt, but the heat of his skin on mine spurs me on.

Reluctantly, Adam pulls away, but there's no hiding that this has made him hard. Adam looks me in the eyes before tilting his chin toward Jason.

"I'm changing the plan."

Chapter 38

My heart drops, worried about what he's going to say next. Did I read everything wrong? To get this worked up only to be let down. I tamp down the tears, not expecting to be this emotional, but the night has my heart racing and adrenaline high.

I search his face, looking for an answer, but his eyes give nothing away. He doesn't sound angry. He sounds certain. Whatever this change is, it's his way of reclaiming control.

Adam's admission does not stop Jason's actions, his hand migrating south as his lips work at my neck, sucking, biting, then licking away the pain. "You're ready to jump to plan B already?" Jason questions between nibbles on my neck, one hand still palming my breast, playing with a nipple as the other slips between the slit of the skirt, reaching for my center

"Wh...shat's plan B?" My voice shakes, but I can't tell if it's from nerves or from how dangerously close Jason's hand is to finding the evidence of my arousal.

"After seeing her like this, hell yes," Adam responds to Jason, both of them ignoring my question.

"What is plan B?" The question comes about breathy and needy instead of the irritation I intended to show.

"Trust me, baby. You'll like plan B," Jason says as he removes both hands from my body. The space between us feels like miles, making me shiver from the loss of body heat from them both.

The plan was for Jason to take the lead, and Adam was going to watch and hopefully take some notes. I try my best to give Adam a questioning look, hoping for more of an explanation but bracing myself for him to call this off. "If plan B is neither of you touching me, I definitely do not like it."

With a slight smirk, Adam cups my cheek and lowers his lips to hover just above mine. "We made a contingency plan," he whispers before diving back into a kiss. This time, the kiss is rougher than anything we have shared before. As if he needs this kiss like he needs air to live.

I barely notice Jason unhooking my bra as Adam deepens his kiss. This has been a recurring fantasy of mine, both of these men working in tandem. The fact that it is now coming to reality has my head spinning, and I no longer care what plan B is, as long as they don't stop.

Adam releases the kiss as Jason's body comes back to mine. My head falls back onto his shoulder, causing my chest to push forward. Adam pulls the straps of the bra from my shoulder, exposing my nipples to the cool air. "Suck," Jason commands from behind as he flattens his hand to my stomach, pulling me flush against his body before returning his attention to my exposed neck.

My body heats quickly with his body pressed to mine as I realize Jason is now completely naked.

I know the difference between being taken and being chosen. Tonight, I'm both, and I let them take willingly.

Reaching behind, I slowly start to stroke his cock as his hand moves to remove my skirt. My mouth falls open as I realize just how massive his size is. The pictures didn't do him justice.

Jason takes the lead, like a puppet master controlling all the limbs. Once he has me fully naked, he tells Adam to follow as he throws me over his shoulder, my brain too satiated to worry if I'm too heavy for him to carry. Bringing me to the bedroom, he tosses me onto the bed, spreading my legs apart without breaking our eye contact.

"I'm starving," he says, licking his lips. "Strip and get on the bed and play with your wife's tits while I taste this perfect pussy. I want to see some bite marks."

I hear Adam move behind me, but I don't see him until he's settled on the bed behind my head.

"Once I get her to come once...no twice, you can fuck your wife," Jason continues. I whimper at the anticipated, at his control, at his command of my pleasure.

He eats like he's starved, working me into a frenzy. Between the pressure of his tongue and the pain of Adam's bites, I'm quickly hovering on the edge of bliss. One nip at my clit pushes me off the edge, my thighs holding Jason in place as he licks me through the orgasm, lapping up the evidence.

He doesn't let me finish before he continues his assault on my clit, adding two fingers to work my G-spot, bringing me to the edge again. I've never had someone else give me one, let alone bring me on the brink of a second orgasm, this quickly. I didn't think two would even be possible, let alone his promise of more to come.

It's not long before I feel an unfamiliar rush of fluid followed by an even more powerful orgasm. The tremor that runs through me isn't just release; it's relief.

Jason kisses his way up my body before plunging his tongue into my mouth. He had always promised to let me have a taste of myself from his lips. The taste is intoxicating, and I need more.

He and Adam switch places. Adam lines up with my entrance as Jason returns his assault to my lips before kissing down my neck to my nipples. Adam fucks me harder than he ever has, and his movements are only intensified by Jason's actions.

When Adam finishes, Jason returns to between my legs before slowly sliding in. We groan in unison at the sensation, at the years of tension built up and finally being let go. It's better than I ever imagined.

He pulls out and flips me over. I notice Adam watching from across the bed, leaning relaxed against the headboard in admiration as Jason pounds from behind as a third orgasm builds. Adam's eyes stay on mine, asking without words if I'm still here. I am.

My head drops to the bed as I lose myself to the feeling of being so full. Pain blooms as Jason's hand suddenly makes contact with my ass with a growl. "Keep your eyes on your husband. Show him how grateful you are that he's letting me give you these orgasms."

My head snaps up, locking onto Adam's gaze as Jason pulls a reaction from deep inside me, my body giving into every movement. Adam's eyes say everything: permission, trust, want. As if he's not just okay with this...he wants it too.

A low sound escapes me, impossible to hold back, my head dropping under the weight of pleasure. When I look back at Adam, I mouth *I love you.* A declaration only meant for him.

"Fuck, this pussy is everything I imagined," Jason growls, thrusting with each word for emphasis.

It's too much. Every thrust. Every boundary crossed. Every selfless action is designed to unravel me.

All of it fuses into a lethal combination that sends me over the edge.

I collapse on the bed, chest rising and falling in uneven breaths. Jason follows, guiding me onto my back before painting my chest, finishing what he started in a way that leaves me trembling.

Adam dips down, retrieving his shirt from the floor, and uses it to wipe my chest clean before getting me comfortable in the center of the bed. Adam pulls me into his side as Jason settles behind me, wrapping an arm around my waist.

"See, Adam," I murmur, a sleepy grin tugging at my lips, "I told you we could fit three people in this bed."

He hums softly, pressing a gentle kiss to my forehead, and I melt into him, feeling the warmth of both him and Jason beside me. My eyes grow heavy, the soft weight of their presence lulling me toward sleep. My pulse eases, my mind settling into a rare, perfect stillness.

I used to mistake the stillness for emptiness, but tonight it feels full. I've never felt more wanted and seen than they've made me feel tonight. If love is a promise, maybe tonight was our way of testing whether it still holds under heat and pressure.

For years, I chased validation like air, but this doesn't feel like chasing. It feels like being home in my own skin. I'm not sure what tomorrow will bring, but for now, I feel seen in a way that terrifies and steadies me all at once.

Chapter 39

I wake slowly, muscles pleasantly sore, a rare, deep sleep finally behind me. The bed is empty. The smell of coffee drifts from the living room, mingling with the low hum of the TV. My chest stills, curiosity and anticipation tangling as I prepare to face the aftermath.

I freshen up quickly, splashing water on my face, then wrap myself in a silk robe and tiptoe toward the living room, pausing before they can see me in the doorway. The sight that meets me makes my pulse stutter. Adam and Jason are on the couch, mugs in hand, their conversation calm, casual, but charged in ways my ears can't ignore.

I hold my breath, not daring to make noise, just to catch snippets of words that make heat rise through me: "I think she would like that…"

Every word, every pause, every shared glance between them fuels the heat building inside me. I know I shouldn't eavesdrop, and yet, I can't stop myself. I need to hear the things they are planning, the care, the thoughtfulness, but now I need to feel the pulse of desire behind their calm voices.

As I round the corner, I'm greeted with a loving smile from Adam and a full head-to-toe eye fucking from Jason.

I make my way over to the couch to give Adam a good-morning kiss as Jason pulls me down on the couch between the two of them in the perfect position to put my head on Adam's lap and my legs across Jason's. He immediately begins rubbing his hands across my bare legs, getting closer to my uncovered core as Adam strokes my hair.

I think I've died and gone to heaven with these two touching me. But I can't let that distract me. The three of us have so much to talk about

I clear my throat, trying to keep my voice steady. "How long are you here for?" I ask Jason, careful not to let anxiety in my chest leak into my words.

We planned for this weekend, but never really talked about how long he would stay. In truth, I didn't want to know. What if we planned for a week, but he left after the first night? I could manage the disappointment if

I only expected him to stay for a day or two. But after last night, I need to know how much time I have left, how many more orgasms I could steal before life goes back to normal.

"Adam and I have been making some plans."

"Without me?" I tease, pretending to be upset but feeling a thrill bubble beneath the surface.

"For you, but you can have veto power," Adam jumps in quickly, piquing my curiosity. For once, I'm not on the outside of my own story. They're talking about me, for me, but I'm allowed to say no. I gesture for one of them to continue.

"I had only planned for the weekend, so I didn't have to take too much time off, but after last night, I'm not ready to leave any time soon," Jason starts, his hand continuing to stroke my legs. "And I don't think you want me to either."

He pauses his words with a hand dangerously close to my core. His eyes darken, pinning me in place. His finger runs along my undoubtedly very wet slit before bringing his finger to his mouth and licking it clean. "Yes, definitely not ready to leave yet." It should make me blush, but it doesn't. Desire doesn't feel like shame anymore; it feels like being known.

"I think he should stay for a while," Adam pipes in with assurance. "You have been telling me for so long what you needed. I heard the words, but I don't think I fully comprehended what you were asking for, what you need, until last night."

"I see now that you were begging for attention and how my denial of that affected you, how it chipped away at your self-esteem, until I saw you come alive last night. You were powerful, uninhibited, and so fucking beautiful." His voice is steady, reverent. "I'm sorry for ever denying that from you. I love you. You are my wife and my best friend. I want you to have everything you could ever need, even if I can't be the one to physically give it to you all the time. I can at least give you him."

I couldn't stop the tears from falling even if I wanted to. I pull up and straddle Adam so I can hold his face in my hand and look him in the eyes.

"You are the most selfless man I have ever met. I love you. You are my husband and my best friend. I can't imagine doing this life without you." I pause because I cannot wait a second longer to kiss him.

"I know we have talked about this already, but at the time, I thought it might end up as a one-time thing. Selfishly, I was willing to take every inch you were willing to give. If you are sure about this, we need our marriage to come first. We need to be open every step of the way. If you say stop, it stops."

"Yes, we had that conversation, and honestly, the few weeks since then have been great for me too. You were less secretive when you masturbated, and watching you kind of turned me on more than I thought. Watching you and Jason last night was probably the hottest thing I've ever seen."

"Ouch!" I gasp with fake offense, hand to my chest.

"What I mean is, the foreplay and the pleasure he gave you, the noises you made, were incredibly sexy. I didn't know sex could be like that until the pressure was off of me to perform. But your eyes told me everything about how you felt at that moment. You felt worshiped. That was what was so sexy. I think I need him here as much as you do, if anything, to learn how to worship you properly, how to make you feel like the goddess I saw last night. If I could give you that 24/7, I would, but I know I physically can't."

For years, I begged him to see me. Now he does, and somehow, he's grateful for it. Staring into his eyes, I can see the love. I am in awe of this man. I didn't think that he could be any more perfect. I'm at a loss for words. All I can do is grab his face in both hands and kiss him again.

Reluctantly breaking the kiss, I pull back slightly, leaving my lips brushing against his. "Thank you. Thank you for needing me enough to share."

Turning to Jason, I have questions for him too. "And you're okay with this? What about work? What happens when you leave? Wha—"

"Baby, stop. I see the gears turning, but let's take it one step at a time. Come here," he says, patting his lap. I move from Adam to straddle Jason, and I can feel his erection straining against his pajama pants, rubbing against my needy center.

"I know you have a lot of questions, and we will have things to work out, but this is what we both want. I'll have to go home soon for work, but while I'm there, I'm going to talk to them about working from home for longer chunks of time so I can be here."

"I told him he can have the extra room. I suspect he'll end up sleeping next to you most nights, but he can use it as an office," Adam confirms.

"You can come back with me some too, and we can plan some vacations together."

"Wow, y'all really have talked through this. Like long-term talk through this," I say, looking between the two of them.

"Yes. I'm your boyfriend; he's your husband," Jason says with a silly smile as if this is the most normal conversation in the world.

"Oh, like we are actually labeling this too? You know, I didn't peg you for the boyfriend-label type."

"No, I never intended to be someone's boyfriend. But being your boyfriend would be an honor."

"Ha, an honor! Since when do you talk like that!"

"You wound me, my lady," he says with a cheeky dramatic flair, and I can't help but laugh, some of the tension finally breaking loose.

"But in all seriousness, you are the only one I want calling me her boyfriend." The word should sound small, but it doesn't. It feels like claiming space I didn't know I was allowed to take from him.

"People will talk."

"Fuck them."

"No thanks. I'd rather fuck you," I tease as I grind down on his lap.

"There she is," Adam chimes in. "Now, wife, stop talking, get on your knees, and suck your boyfriend's cock."

My head snaps to Adam, mouth falling open. "You have never talked to me like that before."

As much as I've wanted him to, he never has, but Jason knows what his demands do to me. He must have done some coaching this morning. They really did talk about a lot already.

"Oh, wife, everything is about to change. Now, open your mouth and get ready."

And I do. Not out of obedience, but trust.

Every yes is mine to give.

Chapter 40

6 months later

I sit on the edge of the hotel bed, my fingers drumming against my thighs, waiting for them to come back.

The room smells faintly of a typical hotel, a mix of cleaned linen and stale air, but it barely registers over the thrum of my heartbeat. I keep thinking back over the last few days, over the subtle signs I tried to ignore: the queasy mornings, the sudden fatigue that left me dragging, the missed period that should have been impossible to overlook. Each one nudges at the edges of my mind, whispering a possibility I've been both craving and fearing.

I've experienced all these before, only to be let down with a negative test and a late period. While the guys were out, I reluctantly ran across the street to the drug store for a test.

When I finally take the pregnancy test, the world narrows to the small white stick in my hands. The silence is almost sacred, the air thick with anticipation. I can feel the weight of the test as if it holds the power to tilt my entire life.

Then it happens. A second line, faint at first, then undeniable. Finally, it happened. After Adam and I had given up hope, after giving myself over to the quiet resignation that it would never happen, the test confirmed it. My chest hammers, and my stomach does a slow, twisting somersault. Time feels like it both stretches and stops.

A flood of emotions crashes through me. Joy, disbelief, a spark of fear, each one competing for space in my chest. My hands tremble slightly, the test slick in my grip, but I won't tell them yet. Not yet. I want to see them first, to watch their faces, to let myself feel the normalcy of this moment before everything changes. Before the world tilts again.

I think back to six weeks ago, remembering exactly what we were doing, how close we were, how alive everything felt in that moment. The memory sharpens everything, makes this real in a way that only the little lines can.

Jason had been to that hotel in the past for a game, finding the room with the best view of the field from the balcony. While he was at the game, he noted that the hotel did a remarkable job of blocking window views into the rooms from the field. Since then, it had been a fantasy of his to fuck me while watching the game.

We got a strange look from the receptionist checking three of us into one room with a king-size bed, but I didn't care.

Adam and Jason took turns playing with my body while pinning me to the window so they could also watch the game. After Adam had his way, for the second time that weekend, which was a lot for him, he sat watching me in awe as I was on my knees, taking my pleasure from the way Jason used my body. Jason even had me on my knees on the balcony for him. He came down my throat as his team hit a home run to win the game.

It was definitely a great game—not that I saw any of it. And the rest of the weekend was just as wild.

They said they'd talked about the details…I hope a baby was part of that conversation too. My nerves are running wild, but it's not fear. It's that electric, jittery kind of anticipation that makes my pulse race and my stomach flutter.

The guys have been gone most of the day, running errands for some surprise they're setting up for me. Over the past six months, they've been bringing my wildest fantasies to life, little scenes ripped straight from my favorite books, sprinkled into our life at least once a month, on top of the mind-blowing orgasms I get almost daily from at least one of them. I can't get enough.

Today, they seem genuinely excited about this one. My heart pounds at the thought of sharing my news tonight. I can hardly wait.

"Wife! We're back."

"Hey, where have y'all been?"

"Clothes shopping." My eyebrow must have been up to my hairline in confusion.

"No questions," Jason commands. "We are leaving in about two hours. Go shower, shave, do all the prepping you need to do to feel your sexiest." He takes a step closer with each command until he is so close that I have to look up to meet his eyes.

"Okay, but…"

Jason cuts me off with his dominating look. "Didn't I say no questions?" His words may pretend to be harsh, but his tone is smooth and seductive. "Your only response should be 'Yes, sir.'"

Oh, so it's going to be that kind of night? "May I ask one question, please, sir?" I say, batting my eyelashes, putting a little brat into the response.

"Fine," he forces out, trying to hide his desire to take me right now in the kitchenette of the hotel, but his eyes betray him.

"Who's gonna come in the shower with me?" I choose my phrasing carefully so he knows what kind of shower I intend to have, whether someone joins me or not.

I watch him swallow hard. Glancing down, I watch his body betray him once again. "No one is coming in the shower." Jason takes another step closer as if there was still room between us, his lips brushing against mine as he speaks. "Including you."

I reach forward and palm his growing cock. "Are you sure about that?"

"Damn, y'all's sexual tension is fucking hot."

"Put your dick away, Adam. No one comes before I say so. Now, be a good girl and go get ready. Stay naked after. We will dress you when you're done."

His commands make me whimper with need, and I feel the wetness pooling between my legs. My bratty side wants to fight more, to make him break until he spanks me. But I get the feeling that he has big plans for us, and I'll need my strength. Reluctantly, I drop my hand from his cock and start to walk off toward the bathroom.

Jason clears his throat before grabbing me by the wrist and spinning me back around to face him. "I gave you instructions." He tries to sound intimidating, but we all know the truth. He's too turned on by this, by me. Jason loves my bratty side, and I've learned that Adam loves watching us in this dynamic. I hold his stare a while, stalling for the two words I know he wants.

Finally, I give in, ready to see where this night will take us. "Yes, sir," I say, adding as much smirk as I can.

"Good girl," he purrs, releasing my wrist and sending me off with a pat on the ass. *This night is going to be fun.*

After I finish with my shower, hair, and makeup, I walk out of the bathroom to both of my guys dressed in black suits. I stand there under their inspecting eyes before Jason kneels down in front of me as he carefully removes a dress from a garment bag. He holds the dress open for me to step into. He kisses up my leg as he brings up the fabric of the dress, pausing for a long time when he reaches my pussy. "God, you smell good," he purrs after a deep inhale before reaching out his tongue and licking at my core. "Tastes perfect."

He continues his torturous kisses up my body before passing the straps of the dress to Adam to secure them at the back of my neck. The dress is a stunning, emerald-green velvet with a halter neck and a slit so high that I worry each step forward will give everyone a peep show. Adam comes around to stand by Jason, both of them eyeing me with approval, and damn, do I feel sexy.

"If you boys are done eye fucking me, is someone going to tell me where we are going?"

"Let's get your shoes on and get you in the car first."

Once in the car heading toward our surprise destination, I ask again. "Okay, so now will one of you tell me where we are going tonight?"

From the backseat, Jason hands me a small bag. "Put this in first." Looking into the bag, I immediately see a remote-controlled vibrator, giving me a strange sense of deja vu. The velvet halter dress, remote toy. I've had this dream before. I shared this dream with Adam and Jason a few months ago.

"Are we going to..."

"The Revel? Yes, baby, we are."

Moving my dress to the side, I slide a few fingers into my needy slit and pull the wetness to my clit to rub a few circles, giving the guys a good little show. I slip in the vibrator and pass Jason the remote before making a show of licking my fingers clean. He growls in jealousy before flicking on the vibrator to the highest setting, making me squirm in my seat, only to abruptly cut it off in retaliation for my little tease.

I've only dreamed of The Red Veil, of being at a sex club with Adam and Jason, showing the guests how they bring me to my knees with pleasure. Guilted by wanting them both there with me. But this… this was the Revel. A real-life version of that fantasy. Full of the same hunger, but the guilt no longer exists.

After checking in, the guys make their way around the room as I follow behind, taking in the scene. By the time I catch up to them, there are already three drinks on the bar in front of them, and Adam is already moving to hand me a glass.

"Your usual, gin. A Basil Gimlet this time."

Shit, I forgot to plan for drinks. "Oh, right, um. You know, I don't think I want gin tonight. Go find our table, and I'll order something else."

"Oh, sorry, guess we should have asked. We have time before the show starts. Order what you want. We will wait, sweetheart."

Scanning the menu, they have an intriguing selection of mocktails. One catches my eye, a black cherry and pomegranate juice mixed with lime juice and a splash of ginger beer, finished with some black edible glitter to fit the name, Obsidian. "I'll take an Obsidian, please."

After glancing at the menu, Jason raises an eyebrow. "You're not drinking tonight? That's not like you. You usually have at least one drink."

"Yeah," I say timidly, looking back and forth between the two of them. "I, uh...I actually can't drink right now." The intensity of their stare causes me to break out in goosebumps.

"Wife?"

I turn to Adam, Jason closing in on my back, wrapping his arm around my waist, laying his hands protectively on my stomach as if he knows what I'm about to say.

I grab Adam's hands to steady my nerves, looking him in the eyes.

"I'm pregnant."

Chapter 41

Adam's eyes flicker to Jason in silent communication—so quickly I almost miss it. Silence hangs between us, thick and heavy, even as the music and chatter hum around us. I can feel Adam's eyes on me, but his expression is unreadable, a mask I can't decipher.

Adam's hand squeezes mine, a tether to reality. The music keeps playing, the laughter continues somewhere in the background, but for me, the world has gone still. My body tenses, a mix of exhilaration and fear swirling together.

Jason's fingers curl around my wrist, breaking my connection with Adam as he pulls me gently but firmly toward a numbered door. I follow, heart hammering, and Adam trails behind, setting the drinks carefully on a small table. The noise of the main room fades as the door is closed, replaced by a hush that feels like it's pressing in on us from all sides.

Jason stops, his eyes dark and unreadable as he studies me. My pulse spikes, my stomach tightening in anticipation and nerves. Adam stands beside him, his gaze flicking between my face and my stomach. Both of them are silent, but the weight of their attention presses on me, and I can't look away.

Everything I've been carrying, every hope and fear, feels exposed in that moment. I draw in a shaky breath, feeling like the next words I speak could change everything. "Someone say something," I manage to force out.

"Strip." Jason's command is harsh, almost strained. The harshness of it makes me jump slightly. Not the gentle reaction I imagined.

"What?" I stutter out. My stomach twists, my pulse spiking.

"You heard me, baby." His harshness fades almost immediately, replaced by a warmth that makes my chest ache. "Strip."

My lips part, trying to force the next words out, but my voice feels fragile, like it might break under the weight of the moment. "I'm sorry, did y'all not hear me?"

A sly smile spreads on Adam's face. "Yes, wife, we heard you. Now listen to the man and strip so we can show you just how happy we are about this."

I take a step back from them, needing space to breathe. "What is happening?"

"Baby, we told you when we started this…we talked through details. This is one of those details we agreed on."

"I'm sorry. Y'all made decisions about my body without consulting me?" Anger begins to bubble to the surface.

"No, baby, but we did agree how the two of us would handle this if you ever did get pregnant."

"Care to clue me in?"

Adam eases forward. "We had been trying to conceive for a while. I know we gave up on trying, but I don't think we ever really let go of wanting to have a baby. One of the things we discussed that morning was what if you got pregnant. I knew if you did, that it would likely be Jason's. Since we had talked about IVF or adoption, Jason said he would be the sperm donor if we ever wanted, and he would just be Uncle J."

I pace the room, unsure of how to take this. "I should have been involved in this."

"Baby," Jason jumps in, "on some level, you knew this would happen. You never started taking birth control and begged me to come in that sweet pussy. I'm actually a little surprised it took us this long to knock you up."

And they are right. None of us ever tried to prevent anything. I pause my pacing and looke at the guys. Really look at them. They look happy about this. My heart melts at the thought of what our life would be like with a little one running around.

"Wife, are you worried about what people are going to say?"

I think about Adam's question. Yes, I'm terrified of how we will handle this, what people will say but I also feel excitement. Happiness.

"Fuck them." Turning and walking toward the sofa, in front of what I assume in a sex club—or hope—is a two-way window, I reach behind to undo my halter. "Now, I believe one of you mentioned something about putting on a celebratory show."

"Fucking beautiful." Adam's is voice rough with desire.

More and more, these men make me feel like I'm not just wanted. I'm chosen. Claimed. Not just out of impulse, but out of intention.

From over my shoulder, I see the guys removing their clothes. Jason's voice comes next, low and certain, "Our girl's going to look so fucking sexy carrying our baby."

The words hit me like a spark, wild and impossible to control, fueling a fire that steals the breath from my lungs.

And I can't wait for them to burn with me.

Epilogue

9 months later

The house is quiet, except for the soft cooing of the baby in my arms. I rock her gently after a late-night feeding, feeling the weight of her warmth settle against my naked chest. Tiny fingers curl around mine as I inhale that newborn smell.

Her features mirror mine, and that scares the hell out of me. If she's anything like me, we will have our hands full.

But her eyes are all Jason, and her nose is all Adam. Somehow, she's a perfect blend of the three of us, proof of how beautifully our lives have woven together.

Jason is asleep on the couch, soft breaths rising and falling in the dim light, while Adam sits nearby, watching us with quiet attentiveness, ready to hand me anything I might need.

For the first time in years, the chaos that once ruled my heart feels distant, like a storm I survived and finally outran.

I think about how impossible it once felt. The guilt for wanting too much, needing too much, feeling divided between worlds and people. And yet, here we are, a life carefully and fully chosen. Every piece falls into its place. I can see it now: the love, the trust, the messy, beautiful truth of our connection. I stopped shrinking. I stopped apologizing for what I wanted.

Some nights, I still wake up wondering how we got here. Then I see them, both of them, and remember I stopped trying to choose.

I simply chose myself.

I used to crave permission to want, but now I understand.

Wanting was never the sin. Forgetting who I was would've been.

And these two men taught me that.

Thank you!

Thank you so much for reading *The Guilt of Wanting*. Your support means everything.

If this story stayed with you, broke you open, or made you feel seen, please consider:

- **Leaving a review** — even a single sentence helps others discover the book.
- **Sharing your favorite quotes** on TikTok or Instagram.
- **Follow me on social media** for updates, behind-the-scenes content, and future releases.

Your voice helps stories like this find their readers.

Connect with me:
Instagram: @rainey_pavo
TikTok: @rainey_pavo
Website: Raineypavo.com
Email: raineypavo@gmail.com

Learn more about Lydia, Jason, and Adam in books two and three of the Guilted Trio.

COMING SOON

The Guilt of Wanting Her: Book 2 in The Guilted Trio

She was the one thing I couldn't have—and the one thing I couldn't let go.

Jason has always been good at keeping secrets—especially from himself—until Lydia walks into his life: quiet, wounded, and hiding a life she refuses to show the world. She's everything he shouldn't touch and everything he can't let go of.

Some desires heal. Others destroy. Jason just hasn't decided which one she'll be.

The Guilt of Wanting Them: Book 3 in The Guilted Trio

Some compromises don't save a marriage. They redefine it.

Adam was the perfect husband in every way—except the one that mattered most. And that one flaw was enough to fracture everything.

Desperate to save their marriage, Adam agrees to try anything she wants. But what she wants is Jason.

Now, Adam must decide which risk to take: preserving the life he's built or surrendering to the desires that threaten to unravel them all.

UNVERIFIED

Siren Biotech Solutions in Marrow Bay.

She lost everything to expose a lie. Now she'll make sure the truth is verified.

When Rowan Mercer accepted a new role as Director of People & Culture at Siren Biotech Solutions in the sleepy, fog-covered town of Marrow Bay, Oregon, she believed she'd joined a company dedicated to saving lives.

But a mysterious phone call and routine credential check unravel everything. She expects chaos, not a cover-up. Now she's out of a job, under threat, and the only thing more dangerous than the company's secrets is the truth she's determined to prove.

ABOUT THE AUTHOR

Rainey Pavo writes at the crossroads of hidden desire, fractured identity, and the quiet battles waged beneath the surface. Whether exploring emotional intimacy or unraveling psychological tension, her work leans into the shadows we rarely name but always feel.

There's no long list of credentials, only an attentiveness to internal conflict and interpersonal dynamics and an understanding of how people rationalize longing, misplace guilt, and learn to live with the choices they make. An interest in human behavior has shaped her perspective, informed by careful observation of the interactions that unfold around her.

Rainey approaches storytelling as a craft in constant evolution, always learning, continually improving. Alongside writing itself, she builds visual and audio aesthetics that deepen the narrative world at work, treating the story as an experience rather than a single format.

Little else is known—and that's by design, letting the story speak for itself.

Her two current works, The Guilt Trio and Unverified, span different genres, each offering its own descent into the complexities of being human.

Even more ideas are in the works! Keep an eye out on my website and social media for upcoming release information.

www.ingramcontent.com/pod-product-compliance
Lightning Source LLC
LaVergne TN
LVHW091618070526
838199LV00044B/847

Ce livre est dédié à mes parents,
Annick Demay et Pierre Roux.

Cet ouvrage a bénéficié
de tous les conseils attentifs
que Monsieur le Professeur Jean Touzot
m'a patiemment donnés durant cinq années.
Qu'il trouve ici l'expression de toute ma gratitude.

Julie Boch, Daniel Lecler et Sandrine Lerou
ont soigneusement relu et annoté le manuscrit,
Emmanuel Bauchet m'a prodigué ses remarques,
Christophe Masson a pris la photographie de couverture,
Nelly Marzet s'est chargée des tableaux et schémas ;
à tous, je tiens à témoigner de ma profonde reconnaissance
pour le travail fourni.

Enfin Émeric Fisset a gracieusement assuré la mise en pages.

Introduction

Parmi les écrivains français nés après la Seconde Guerre mondiale, Patrick Modiano est celui qui a accordé dans ses œuvres la place la plus importante à la mémoire et aux souvenirs liés à cette période historique. De 1968, avec *La Place de l'Étoile*, à 1999, avec sa dernière publication en date, *Des inconnues*, ses romans, nouvelles ou œuvres diverses l'ont établi comme le familier des déambulations nocturnes, dans un Paris livré aux Allemands. Cette fascination pour une époque inconnue, dont l'exploration incessante a fini par constituer aux yeux du public la « marque de fabrique » du romancier, embrasse la totalité de sa création littéraire.

Point de passage obligé pour la compréhension non seulement des écrits, mais également de la personnalité et des motivations profondes du créateur, le thème de l'Occupation a pourtant été relativement peu étudié de façon autonome. Les travaux critiques qui lui ont été jusqu'à présent consacrés ont avant tout retenu l'aspect fonctionnel de ce sujet, toile de fond sur laquelle le romancier aurait projeté des névroses aisément explicables par sa biographie. Sévèrement réductrices, ces interprétations semblent sous-estimer la part fondamentale représentée par les années sombres dans les écrits de Modiano.

Celui-ci est né peu de temps après la capitulation de l'Allemagne d'une actrice flamande, réfugiée en France en 1940, et d'un père juif d'origine italo-égyptienne, effectuant de basses besognes commerciales pour la Gestapo, plusieurs fois arrêté puis relâché à la suite de l'intervention de ses amis. Ce père, absent et mystérieux, disparaîtra de la vie du jeune Modiano et de son jeune frère Rudy peu après la guerre. Élevé par sa mère, avant que de fréquenter nombre de pensionnats du pays, le jeune homme prend très vite la mesure de sa condition d'apatride, dans un pays dont il ne partage que la langue. En 1956, la mort de son petit frère, dont il gardera longtemps le deuil, parachève la solitude du futur écrivain. À ce désarroi vient se mêler la culpabilité sourde d'être, en quelque sorte, un enfant de la Collaboration. De fait, tout se passe comme si le jeune Modiano s'était chargé au cours de ses années d'enfance et d'adolescence de la mémoire et des angoisses familiales. Il tente d'exorciser celles-ci dans un premier roman, rédigé en

1966 et paru en 1968 : *La Place de l'Étoile*. Quatre ouvrages suivront[1], tous articulés autour de l'Occupation, qui mettent en scène les différentes figures de la compromission avec l'ennemi. Privé d'identité réelle, le protagoniste des récits, éternel intrus dans un univers où il s'efforce de pénétrer, apparaît comme le relais d'un romancier qui tente, comme son personnage, de discerner les contours d'un monde qui le fascine, et lui échappe en même temps – et dont il s'efforce de comprendre les mécanismes.

L'œuvre qui s'esquisse montre un jeune créateur soucieux de s'affranchir des spectres d'un passé traumatisant, susceptible toutefois de pourvoir l'écrivain d'une filiation et d'une identité qu'il ne possède pas. Contrairement aux écrivains de sa génération, Français de souche, le romancier ne place pas ses écrits dans une lignée collective, mais la réduit à la dimension de l'individu, celui qu'il eût pu être sous l'Occupation. Paradoxe apparent, et celui-ci nous guidera tout au long de notre travail, que celui qui consiste à chercher l'enracinement tant recherché au sein d'une fratrie et d'une nation qu'il fait siennes, en se rattachant à ce que celles-ci ont produit de pire. L'épigraphe de *La Ronde de nuit* donne toute la dimension du projet : « [s']identifier aux objets mêmes de [sa] compassion ». Quête traumatisante du passé et rejet de l'identification impossible, telles sont les données du paradoxe auquel le créateur est confronté. L'arpentage de l'histoire de l'Occupation, « terroir[2] » de l'écrivain, et les interrogations taraudantes sur l'engagement et la duplicité tissent les fils d'une thématique obsessionnelle.

---

[1] *La Ronde de nuit* 1969 ; *Les Boulevards de ceinture* 1972 ; *La Polka* (théâtre) 1973 et de *Lucien* (scénario) 1974. On peut y rattacher le livre d'entretiens avec Emmanuel Berl de 1976.
Nous désignerons, dans notre étude, les trois premiers romans de l'Occupation par le terme « trilogie » ; les multiples points de rapprochement et ramifications thématiques paraissent justifier une semblable appellation.
[2] Selon les mots de Modiano dans un entretien accordé à J.-C. Tixier de *La Croix*, 9-10 novembre 1969, p. 8.

À partir de *Villa triste* (1975) le ton change cependant. Modiano semble délaisser l'introspection pour une technique de roman plus traditionnelle, et laisse jouer en mineur les thèmes précédemment explorés. Désormais écrivain attitré de la nostalgie des années enfuies, le romancier revient pourtant aux sources de son œuvre avec trois romans complémentaires : *Voyage de noces* (1990), *Fleurs de ruine* (1991) et *Dora Bruder* (1997), qui viennent constituer un second triptyque et donner une nouvelle cohérence à l'œuvre. Quoi qu'il en soit, la thématique de l'Occupation traverse chaque ouvrage des années quatre-vingts comme un courant souterrain. Elle se trouve rattachée directement au passé que scrute et ausculte l'écrivain, passé énigmatique et tragique, qui, dans ses replis et zones d'ombre, détient la clef des origines.

L'attirance pour cette période ainsi expliquée, il reste à montrer comment celle-ci est abordée dans le corps des ouvrages. Il appartient, en effet, de déterminer la place du romancier dans le grand mouvement de relecture historique survenu au début des années soixante-dix, associé à une réhabilitation des écrivains de la Collaboration.

Une première étape d'analyse portera donc sur la peinture des années d'Occupation. La richesse de l'information, mise au service d'une reconstitution très proche des images mentales associées à cette période, constitue une grande force romanesque. Nous opérerons une distinction entre les deux triptyques, qui procèdent par des moyens d'évocation différents. En effet, à la fin des années soixante, le romancier rend volontiers opaque les événements, en présentant « son » Occupation comme un continuum mal défini, échappant aux repères fixes des dates, qu'il s'agit d'intégrer, avant tout, à l'actualité immédiate de la narration. Deux décennies plus tard, la liberté de ton, voire d'invention, laisse la place à une gravité et une solennité plutôt inattendues chez l'auteur de *la Place de l'Étoile* ; le fantasme semble laisser la place à l'ascèse.

Les limites historiques définies, il convient, dans un deuxième temps, d'analyser les procédés narratifs propres au

Modiano de la première période. Perçue comme un abcès de fixation des pires turpitudes du temps, la période de la guerre entraîne un sentiment d'aversion que vient combattre l'indéniable force de la nostalgie qui sourd sous chaque tableau historique. Se trouve ainsi mise en œuvre une esthétique particulière, qui marque le triomphe de l'imaginaire narratif sur la réalité – à l'exception de son dernier ouvrage en date, qui emprunte davantage à l'état-civil qu'au libre jeu de l'imaginaire.

Ce mode d'approche semble conditionner l'échec de la quête identitaire entreprise depuis le premier roman. En effet, nous avons vu que l'écrivain se tournait vers le passé familial afin de dissiper les opacités de sa filiation « morale ». Cette recherche, d'ordre ontologique, s'effectue selon une déclinaison des strates de la mémoire, mise en péril, cependant, par l'aspect fantasque de la peinture de l'Occupation – comme si la reviviscence d'un monde disparu, seul lien véritablement identitaire, mettait en danger, par sa force même, le projet qu'elle entend servir. On peut y ajouter la contradiction suivante : l'écrivain ne peut trouver de réponse à ses demandes et besoins d'enracinement, puisque c'est lui-même qui crée la matière de ses propres souvenirs. Sa date de naissance ne lui a pas permis, en effet, de vivre les événements qu'il relate, et le condamne à ne pouvoir inventorier son passé que par procuration.

La traque de l'identité comme la perception de l'Histoire s'avèrent un échec. Le recours à l'écriture s'impose comme la seule issue possible, celle des récits de la quête vaine, patiente recension du passé qui se dérobe, des êtres qui s'évanouissent et des retrouvailles décevantes. C'est d'ailleurs sous la forme de la mélancolie des rencontres, de la nostalgie poignante, que se trouve psalmodiée, à partir des années quatre-vingts, la mélopée sans fin des interrogations sur le passé. Condamné à se heurter à des obstacles inchangés, Modiano donne la précellence, dans ses dernières œuvres, à l'arpentage de la mémoire plutôt qu'à la résolution de ses questionnements intimes. L'ensemble s'articulera ainsi autour d'un certain désenchantement confronté à la richesse de la mémoire, qui vient prolonger la quête de soi commencée dès *La Place de l'Étoile*. La figure de l'Occupation vient donc s'inscrire en filigrane dans les récits ; les renvois constants qui sont faits à cette période montrent bien que les fantômes du passé n'en finissent pas de mourir dans les œuvres de Modiano.

Première partie :

L'écriture de l'Histoire

Lorsque paraissent, en 1968 et 1969, les deux premiers romans de Patrick Modiano, la France, et tout ce qu'elle compte de penseurs et de créateurs, ausculte avec la plus grande attention les soubresauts de la révolte de mai. En ce temps sont foulées aux pieds les valeurs de la famille, vilipendées les notions d'ordre établi et très volontiers méprisées les recherches historiques ignorant l'apport considérable de la pensée du Grand Timonier dans l'évolution du monde[1]. Dans le domaine des lettres, le « nouveau roman » – alors pourtant en pleine impasse créatrice – ainsi que les théories structuralistes viennent frapper d'anathème toutes les composantes du récit romanesque traditionnel, à savoir l'intrigue, l'idée de personnage – totalement remise en question – ou la narration.

Un jeune écrivain de vingt-trois ans vient pourtant bousculer ce nouvel ordre littéraire en publiant presque coup sur coup deux ouvrages presque entièrement tournés vers le passé, inventoriant l'histoire – très – récente pour mieux cerner son identité. Dès *La Place de l'Étoile*, Modiano fixe ses obsessions : l'Occupation – et la Collaboration, son corollaire naturel –, la quête des ombres et des disparus, le règlement de l'identité juive ainsi que les lentes dérives et errances de la mémoire. Seuls comptent alors les regards tournés vers les années quarante, la lente fusion de l'invention et du souvenir, qui viennent sans cesse recomposer une quête inachevée. Pendant dix ans, le romancier tentera de baliser ce qu'il nomme

---

[1] Nous songeons, en particulier, à la période structuraliste de la revue *Tel Quel*, de la fin des années soixante au milieu de la décennie soixante-dix, années durant lesquelles Philippe Sollers ou Julia Kristeva résistaient difficilement à la citation des doctrines de Mao Tsé-toung dans leurs travaux.

son « paysage naturel[1] », à savoir le Paris nocturne d'Albert Modiano, son père, entre couvre-feu et *Schwerpunkt Aktion*.

Le jeune Modiano ne se reconnaît absolument pas dans la génération de ses pairs, davantage préoccupés par les barricades et les dazibaos que par l'inventaire des années de compromission de la France avec l'envahisseur nazi : « Ils défilaient contre la famille : je n'en avais pas. Ils rejetaient l'histoire de leur nation : je n'étais pas de ce pays [...] les écrivains du nouveau roman, quant à eux, me semblaient des martiens. Je me sentais complètement étranger à leur style et à leurs ambitions littéraires[2]. » Deux réserves s'imposent pourtant, la première concernant le style même de l'écrivain. À première vue, rien ne peut, en effet, apparaître plus éloignés des centres d'intérêt modianiens que les jeux narratifs complexes d'un Sollers ou les expérimentations littéraires d'un Ricardou. Pourtant, l'œuvre qui s'ébauche ne dédaigne pas la reprise de certains procédés du roman nouveau. On se reportera avec intérêt aux deux premières œuvres ; la « narration en étoile » et l'inachèvement volontaire du premier roman, ou l'existence toute virtuelle des compagnons de Swing Troubadour, se situent dans la droite ligne des travaux expérimentaux publiés par les Éditions de Minuit, procédés narratifs inimaginables deux décennies auparavant.

En second lieu, le statut même du jeune écrivain va rapidement évoluer. Si la publication de *La Place de l'Étoile*, en plein Mai 1968, se heurte à l'indifférence du grand public, l'œuvre suivante annonce le mouvement de relecture critique des années d'occupation allemande, qui va passionner les milieux intellectuels et artistiques durant les années soixante-dix. En 1972, *Les Boulevards de ceinture* s'inscrivent pleinement dans la grande entreprise de remise en cause de la vérité officielle. Cette contestation, préparée en partie par la

---

[1] Entretien avec J. Montalbetti, *Magazine littéraire*, novembre 1969, p. 44.
[2] Entretien accordé aux *Inrockuptibles*, juin 1990. À cette époque, Modiano lit essentiellement les écrivains d'avant-guerre, et se déclare fasciné par Céline et Drieu. Bertrand Westphal, dans son article, « Pandore et les Danaïdes, Histoire et temps chez Modiano », *Francofonia*, XIV, 26, printemps 1994, p. 103, écrit à propos du romancier que « [celui-ci] serait un Morand récrivant Robbe-Grillet. »

radicalité des deux premiers romans de Modiano, n'aurait pu prendre place dans les mentalités sans la remise à plat des enseignements politiques inspirée par la révolte de mai. Les premiers écrits de Modiano, pour marginaux qu'ils apparaissent au sein de la production littéraire française, n'en sont pas moins rattachés à un courant artistique dominant, dans lequel le travail de l'écrivain semble naturellement trouver sa place.

Cependant, la vision qu'il propose de l'Occupation ou le traitement de ses intrigues et personnages le distinguent très nettement des autres créateurs de cette époque : le choix des années sombres ne représente en rien un impératif dicté par la mode, mais s'inscrit bien dans une recherche identitaire entamée au moment de la mort du petit frère. Comme nous l'avons déjà vu, Modiano, pour révulsé qu'il soit par les turpitudes qu'il découvre et met en scène, n'hésite pas à considérer ces figures d'une époque honnie comme une parentèle de substitution ; cette optique bien particulière tranche singulièrement sur les motivations d'une partie des créateurs de cette époque. Ces questionnements et interrogations, que la démarche romanesque peut aider à mettre en forme, sinon à comprendre, constitueront le centre de notre étude. Il convient toutefois de ne jamais exclure l'écrivain des projets romanesques tentés par ses contemporains, et surtout du climat général dans lequel ses ouvrages prennent place – contexte artistique et politique dont le rôle mérite d'être signalé et analysé. On pourra mieux ainsi apprécier la valeur et la portée du jeune romancier à la lumière de quelques rappels historiques.

L'Occupation et ses séquelles (1968-1978)

LE DOMAINE POLITIQUE

De la Libération de Paris jusqu'à la mort du général de Gaulle, la France connaît une sorte d'amnésie de son histoire la plus récente. Pendant vingt-cinq années, le pouvoir gaullien et son antagoniste communiste vont s'attacher à minimiser, voire à gommer, les actes de collaboration idéologique avec l'occupant allemand, poursuivant en cela des desseins différents bien que complémentaires. Pour le parti communiste, dont les cadres issus de la Résistance ont été exclus à la suite de campagnes de calomnies, il s'agit de faire allégeance aux ordres de Moscou. La dictature stalinienne s'accommode mal d'un personnel jugé incontrôlable, imposant des hommes dont l'engagement effectif contre les forces occupantes fut des plus timides. On comprend bien que ces nouveaux caciques n'aient nullement souhaité contribuer à un débat qui les eût remis en cause. Pour les gaullistes, la question apparaît plus complexe. Si les mémoires d'Alain Peyrefitte ne mentionnent aucune intervention de l'exécutif destinée à placer sous le boisseau la question des années sombres, il n'en demeure pas moins que celle-ci fut soigneusement occultée durant les deux premières mandatures présidentielles de la Ve République. Il est possible, à cet égard, de hasarder deux hypothèses. La première postule l'idée d'une union nationale voulue par le Général, susceptible de dépasser les clivages doctrinaux et les incompatibilités partisanes afin de donner un nouvel élan au pays, paralysé, selon lui, par une décennie d'administration et de gestion précautionneuses. Dans un second temps, on peut considérer que la vision gaullienne de la politique supposait le pardon des trahisons et des reniements au nom de la synthèse des forces vives, destinées à bâtir la France du futur. À cette fin, le travail de mémoire importait moins que la modernisation indispensable de l'appareil industriel et économique du pays.

Le régime de Vichy apparut ainsi gommé de la conscience collective, tel un épiphénomène honteux contre lequel le silence fournirait un rempart idéal. La collaboration économique et politique ne traduisait tout au plus qu'une errance morale imputable à une minorité d'extrémistes spontanément issus de la défaite, sans aucune appartenance réelle au reste de la communauté nationale. L'historien Henri Rousso, dans son ouvrage *Le Syndrome de Vichy de 1944 à nos jours*[1], distingue trois étapes dans la mise en place de l'idéologie française et l'acceptation des turpitudes.

Au sortir du conflit, le travail de mémoire prend l'aspect d'un deuil inachevé (de 1944 à 1954) : la réconciliation nationale, qui suit les déchirements de cinq années de guerre civile et le souvenir d'une épuration souvent expéditive, forcent au silence sur les années d'Occupation, et explique l'absence de débat. De plus, les événements internationaux de la fin des années quarante – l'affrontement américano-soviétique et le début de la guerre froide, l'affirmation des républiques populaires de l'Est ou les débuts de la crise indochinoise – imposent au pays une union nationale au nom de laquelle le châtiment des dignitaires du régime vichyste paraît sacrifié. Enfin, le gouvernement qui préside aux destinées du pays durant cette décennie ne représente pas la forme de pouvoir investi de la victoire sur l'occupant. En effet, le cabinet constitué par le Général est tombé au bout d'une année, miné par ses dissensions, pour se trouver relayé par une IVe République éclaboussée par les scandales de l'affaire Boutemy et du « cas » Pinay.

Tout concourt ainsi au « refoulement » des quinze années qui suivent l'arrivée au pouvoir du général de Gaulle. Celui-ci ne fera paradoxalement que prolonger, au nom d'une France réconciliée, purgée de ses vieux démons, et travaillant à construire l'expansion économique des années soixante,

---

[1] Le Seuil, 1987.

l'amnésie collective ainsi que la mise sous le boisseau de toute investigation irrévérencieuse. Quelques éléments perturbateurs viennent bien convoquer le souvenir des années sombres, comme la candidature de Jean-Louis Tixier-Vignancour aux présidentielles de 1965, mais sans réellement ébranler le mythe d'une France humiliée mais patriote[1], la figure gaullienne du « père » contribuant à assurer la validité de l'héritage de la lutte nationale.

Les événements de Mai 1968 viennent briser le miroir dans lequel tous les Français étaient invités à se refléter pour mieux s'agréger à la communauté nationale. Henri Rousso[2] écrit ainsi : « Les étudiants de mai s'en prennent à un pouvoir qui se veut et se présente comme l'héritier de la Résistance [...] ; ils [dénoncent] une société réfugiée derrière l'honneur inventé. » François Nourissier semble lui répondre dans *Le Point*[3] : « Le Père est mort, et l'on fait l'inventaire de l'héritage ». On pourrait surtout parler de dépeçage. En l'espace de trois ans, la vision que le Général portait sur l'Histoire vole en éclat sous les assauts critiques et les remises en cause véhémentes de la jeune génération. Le nécessaire travail de reconstruction matérielle et intellectuelle apparaissait cohérent et nécessaire, mais ne pouvait proposer qu'une lecture inexacte du passé proche[4]. Celle-ci, soucieuse de confronter les aventures individuelles à la vérité collective, abolie depuis vingt-cinq ans, va instaurer un mouvement de suspicion légitime concernant les cinq années d'occupation allemande. C'est cette remise à plat d'un quart de siècle de doctrine que nous nous proposons d'analyser à présent.

---

[1] Mythe largement relayé par l'imagerie communiste de la Libération jusqu'à nos jours.
[2] *Op.cit.*, p. 119.
[3] N° du 11 mai 1974.
[4] Colin Nettelbeck, *Getting The Story right in Journal of English Studies*, XV, 1985, p. 90.

UNE NOUVELLE IDÉOLOGIE CRITIQUE

Dans son article *Rétro Satanas* paru dans *Le Débat*[1], au début des années quatre-vingts, Pascal Ory fait le point sur dix années de fascination pour la période de l'Occupation. En 1970, note-t-il, « les enfants de de Gaulle et de Coca-Cola se retrouvèrent orphelins et, avec la mauvaise éducation qui les caractérisait, s'empressèrent d'aller fouiller dans les papiers de famille. » Ils sont soutenus en cela par la parution de deux œuvres clés : *La France de Vichy*, de Robert Paxton, qui paraît à la fin de 1972, et le film de Marcel Ophüls, *Le Chagrin et la pitié*, sorti sur les écrans un peu plus d'un an auparavant. L'ouvrage de l'universitaire américain démontre que « l'image sépia, réconfortante, d'un peuple uni en ses profondeurs dans une même hostilité à l'Allemand et au régime fantoche de Vichy[2] » mérite d'être examinée de nouveau, à la lumière des archives allemandes, en particulier. La profonde passivité du peuple français, ainsi que les nombreuses compromissions ponctuelles ou régulières d'une frange non négligeable de celui-ci sont ainsi mises en évidence. Si la méthode semble aujourd'hui contestable – utilisation quasi exclusive de documents provenant d'archives d'outre-Rhin à l'exactitude et à l'impartialité parfois discutables – le livre n'en contient pas moins nombre de vérités blessantes pour l'orgueil national. La polémique commence dès sa parution ; ce sont moins les erreurs factuelles ou les sources lacunaires qui sont attaquées que l'approche générale de la période – et partant l'esprit critique avec lequel procède l'historien – qui subissent les foudres de nombre de personnalités politiques ou intellectuelles. Toutefois, l'agitation médiatique qui suit la sortie de l'ouvrage paraît bien quiète à côté du tumulte provoqué par l'œuvre de Marcel Ophüls.

En avril 1971, un film de plus de quatre heures, réalisé par le fils de Max Ophüls, en collaboration avec Alain de Sédouy et André Harris sort sur les écrans parisiens. Chronique

---

[1] N° 16, 1981, p. 103-117.
[2] *Ibid.*, p. 109.

de la vie quotidienne durant la guerre à Clermont-Ferrand, ville devenue pour la circonstance « miroir national », le film présente une typologie de Français à l'heure de l'occupation allemande : les notables (représentés en particulier par le pharmacien Verdier, à l'attentisme avéré), les résistants (peu flattés par la figure des frères Grave), les collaborateurs sémillants (la dernière partie s'articule presque exclusivement autour de Christian de La Mazière, ancien Waffen SS) et la masse des anonymes, dont les propos sont souvent infirmés par l'impitoyable Ophüls, au moyen de bandes d'actualité ou de témoignages filmés qui viennent présenter un douloureux contrepoint. Mais, au-delà du témoignage, la spécificité du film réside sans doute dans le rendu très réaliste de l'air du temps et d'une vie quotidienne où les petites lâchetés l'emportent de très loin sur l'idéologie. Le scandale constitué par le film trouve peut-être son origine dans l'approche très empirique de l'Occupation. De fait, l'occupant allemand, l'élément étranger, n'y joue qu'un faible rôle. Henri Rousso peut ainsi écrire dans *Le Syndrome de Vichy*[1] :

> Deux éléments [...] surgissent [...] au premier plan : primo, le régime de Vichy, ses lois, ses actions, ses projets ont obéi à une logique qui ressortit autant à la situation de la défaite et de l'Occupation qu'à une logique interne, propre à l'histoire politique et idéologique de la France ; secundo, la guerre étrangère [...] a moins laissé de traces que la guerre civile, une évidence que rappellent la plupart des non-dits et lapsus des témoins de la base.

Si l'accueil d'une partie de la presse est enthousiaste, un concert de voix discordantes se fait rapidement entendre. Alfred Fabre-Luce s'insurge dans *Le Monde* contre l'antipétainisme des réalisateurs. Il semble gênant, selon lui, que des « survivants [les juifs] accablent un homme [Pétain] auquel ils doivent la vie[2] ». À l'autre bord de l'échiquier politique, Jean-Paul Sartre dénonce, dans *La Cause du peuple*, « l'idéologie dominante » et la « transcription inexacte [du

---

[1] *Op.cit.*, p. 124-125.
[2] *Ibid.*

film]¹ ». Enfin, Claude Mauriac, dans *Le Figaro*, plus mesuré à l'égard de l'œuvre, se désole, pour sa part, de l'absence de la présence gaullienne. Les réactions les plus violentes viendront de la télévision, pour laquelle le film avait été conçu au départ, et partant du pouvoir pompidolien. L'ORTF refuse ainsi d'acquérir les droits de diffusion de l'œuvre, jugée susceptible de diviser les Français, pratiquant de la sorte une sorte de censure passive. Jean-Jacques de Bresson, lui-même ancien résistant, explique devant la commission des Affaires culturelles du Sénat que *Le Chagrin et la pitié* « détruit les mythes dont les Français ont encore besoin² ». Il faudra attendre 1978 pour que le film soit projeté sur le petit écran – sans que la polémique s'apaise.

La parole historique ainsi libérée, une floraison d'ouvrages consacrés à l'Occupation peuvent voir le jour. Durant cette décennie, l'approche bipolaire, après avoir été implicitement érigée en dogme, paraît définitivement condamnée. Cet ébranlement des certitudes ne concerne pas seulement les idéologies vichystes ou leurs zélateurs, plus tard discrètement reconvertis au sein du personnel politique de la IVe République, mais la validité même de la transmission du passé et de la mémoire. On citera, à titre d'exemple, *Les Pousse-au-jouir du maréchal Pétain*³, ouvrage dans lequel le psychanalyste Gérard Miller se livre à une lecture toute freudienne du régime de Vichy. Pour ludique et irrévérencieux qu'il soit, le livre dissèque les fondements idéologiques et les représentations mentales de ce gouvernement dans une optique historicisante, dont les conclusions paraissent assez peu éloignées de celles de Paxton. L'aspect volontiers provocateur et corrosif, et par conséquent excessif, de la démonstration eût sans doute rendu difficile sa publication sans la préparation effectuée par cet historien. Celui-ci trouve un émule dans la personne de Pascal Ory qui, dans *Les Collaborateurs*⁴, inventorie sans concession les itinéraires collectifs ou

---

¹ *Ibid.*
² *Ibid.*, p. 131.
³ Paris, Le Seuil, 1975.
⁴ *Ibid.*, p. 131.

individuels qui conduisirent à l'apologie de l'« Europe nouvelle » et de la politique de collaboration entre la France et l'Allemagne. L'historien s'y fait l'analyste minutieux des idéologues tentés par l'aventure totalitaire. Sa démarche s'inscrit dans un cadre naturellement beaucoup plus rigoureux – et forcément moins polémique – que celui de Paxton, sans aucune volonté d'identification d'un régime politique à l'ensemble de la conscience nationale.

Ces quatre œuvres ne constituent pas les seules études sur l'Occupation, bien entendu, mais représentent par leur diversité d'approche autant de perspectives analytiques d'une période éminemment controversée[1]. On ajoutera à ce propos que les intellectuels susnommés procèdent moins en censeurs véhéments d'un régime – que nul d'ailleurs n'entend plus louer – qu'en pourfendeurs d'une logique manichéenne que la prise en considération des aspirations individuelles eût rendu inopérante. Ces remises en cause, ces interrogations répétées et approfondies semblaient devoir se cantonner au cercle étroit des passeurs d'idées. La désillusion qui suit l'euphorie de Mai, la pesanteur du régime pompidolien, ainsi que l'évolution de l'intérêt collectif vont donner aux recherches sur l'Occupation une dimension proche du débat national, relayé et alimenté par des œuvres littéraires et cinématographiques. L'Occupation devient dès lors un sujet « grand public ».

LA MODE « RETRO »

Durant la décennie soixante-dix, vrais créateurs et faux penseurs inventorient à leur manière les recoins obscurs de l'âme sous les années d'Occupation. La mode, et tout ce qu'elle compte de publicistes patentés – producteurs en quête d'idées, auteurs peu ambitieux ou créateurs avides d'exploiter un créneau jusqu'alors ignoré – va décliner à l'envi le thème de la France occupée, au gré des différents moyens d'expression

---

[1] Paris, Le Seuil, 1975.

dont elle dispose. À cette époque, note Pascal Ory[1], « l'on considère que tout devient dicible et donc montrable [...] ; les années soixante-dix nag[ent] au fil d'une imagerie populaire bien spécifique, où les photos Agfa de Pierre Zucca[2] répond[ent] en harmoniques à la voix veloutée de Zarah Leander. » De 1974 à 1978, le nombre de films consacrés ou inspirés par la Seconde Guerre mondiale en France augmente brusquement. Henri Rousso estime leur nombre à quarante-cinq, soit plus que durant toute la décennie précédente. « En 1976, avec onze films au moins, on retrouve un taux de 7 % de la production totale, la même qu'en 1946 [...]. Le phénomène du miroir brisé a une réalité dans le cinéma français, d'autant que beaucoup de ces films traitent directement de l'Occupation comme sujet, et non comme simple arrière-plan[3]. » La fin des certitudes réveille les souvenirs des anciens réprouvés...

Dans le domaine du roman, on peut distinguer deux types d'approche de la face sombre de l'Occupation, à savoir l'évocation[4] et la justification. La première catégorie concerne les écrivains trop jeunes pour avoir connu l'occupant, mais qui ont approché les principaux acteurs de la période. Deux récits retiennent l'attention, celui de Marie Chaix, *Les Lauriers du lac de Constance*, et *La Guerre à neuf ans*, de Pascal Jardin. Le premier confie sur un ton feutré les impressions d'enfance d'une femme qui vécut la collaboration politique de très près, puisque son père était un doriotiste patenté. Dans le second, le fils du directeur de cabinet de Pierre Laval livre lui aussi ses souvenirs de jeunesse, animé par un souci polémique : il s'agit moins d'évoquer la vie quotidienne à Vichy, du point de vue forcément parcellaire d'un enfant, que de nuancer les jugements négatifs prononcés contre la politique du régime de Pétain, conduite au nom de la défense des intérêts de la nation :

---

[1] Article cité.
[2] *Les Années quarante ; Le Journal de la France.*
[3] Henri Rousso, *op.cit.*, chapitre « Vecteurs du syndrome », p. 267.
[4] Nous nous référons, pour une partie importante de cette étude, à un article d'Alan Morris, *Attack on Gaullist Myth in French Literature since 1969*, in *Forum for Modern Language Studies* n° 21, 1985, p. 71-83.

> Si la collaboration qui se faisait là était indispensable à la survie économique de la France, elle se révèle, après-coup, intolérable au regard de l'histoire. Pourtant, dans un pays occupé, noyauté par la fantastique infrastructure militaire et policière du Troisième Reich, collaborer, c'était la raison. Résister, c'était l'espérance. De toute manière, Vichy a perdu. En politique, c'est plus qu'une faute, c'est un crime[1] !

Alan Morris, dans son article consacré à l'image artistique de Vichy, dans les œuvres des années soixante-dix, ajoute à la suite de ces lignes[2] :

> Cette défense de Vichy conduit à la réhabilitation du père [...]. Celui-ci se révèle un oppresseur, un tyran et un dominateur, c'est la vérité, mais ne possède aucune des caractéristiques démoniaques attribuées fréquemment aux collaborateurs par le mythe [...]. Plusieurs commentateurs notaient à cette époque que cette réhabilitation marquait « la rentrée en grâce de tout le passé qui s'insinue d'un air de rien ».

Parallèlement aux écrits « de l'enfance », paraissent – ou sont de nouveau publiés – nombre d'ouvrages écrits par des « collaborateurs engagés qui plaident leur cause sans remords[3] ». Jean-Jacques Pauvert réédite ainsi, en 1972, *Mémoires d'un fasciste* et *Les Deux Étendards* de Rebatet, qui voisinent en librairie avec les derniers écrits de Drieu, de nouveau disponibles[4] : on compte, au début des années soixante-dix, huit rééditions en moins de trois ans des ouvrages de cet écrivain. Paul Wernie, autre ténor de la collaboration, fait paraître deux romans en 1970 et 72 : *La Souille* et sa suite : *Les Chiens aveugles*[5]. Alan Morris note, horrifié, que « ces livres montrent que leur auteur tire encore gloire de ses actes

---

[1] *Op.cit.*, p. 87.
[2] C'est nous qui traduisons.
[3] Article cité, p. 79.
[4] Son journal ne sera publié qu'en 1992, à la suite de dispositions testamentaires.
[5] Éditions Mercure de France.

antérieurs, en dépit de son isolement actuel ». Il cite, pour confirmer ses propos, le passage suivant :

> On est les rebuts, nous, les rebuts de l'humanité, des détritus, les rescapés du grand naufrage, ceux qu'on appelle les salauds, ceux qui ont cru, ceux qui n'ont pas su se retourner à temps, qui auraient eu honte de faire machine arrière, de retourner leur veste, comme il y en a eu tant[1].

Le critique remarque, à la suite :

> Wernie défend l'idée que le sort des « collabos » ne peut se comprendre que par l'infortune – il n'existe pas d'idée absolue du bon ou du mauvais ou du bien et du mal pour lui ; seules comptent la justification des actes des vainqueurs et la condamnation de ceux des vaincus.

Le public accorde un certain intérêt aux essais de ces représentants de la compromission politique et intellectuelle avec l'occupant, peut-être davantage qu'aux témoignages de résistants. Le relatif attrait qu'exercent ces œuvres ne doit pas s'interpréter comme une « fascisation » de la société française, nostalgique de l'ordre vichyste, mais comme une marque de défiance à l'égard des idées véhiculées par la IVe République et les douze années de gaullisme qui suivirent. La suspicion légitime qui frappe alors les enseignements reçus conduit à une certaine empathie pour les figures des collaborateurs. L'esprit de provocation conduit ainsi à majorer les excès de l'Épuration, à trouver un certain panache dans le parcours intellectuel et politique d'un Céline ou d'un Brasillach, et à ne juger chaque personnalité qu'à l'aune de sa conduite pendant la première moitié des années quarante.

L'Occupation devient ainsi un climat, un lieu de rêverie propice à l'inscription d'histoires. *Le Point* du 11 mars 1974 consacre un dossier d'une dizaine de pages à cette « mode rétro », relayé en cela deux mois plus tard, mais de façon beaucoup plus conceptuelle et idéologique, par *Les Cahiers du cinéma*. Ces deux revues articulent leur réflexion autour de

---

[1] *Op.cit.*, p. 19.

Lacombe Lucien, le film de Louis Malle, sorti peu de temps auparavant. Avant d'examiner la réflexion critique qu'une revue d'extrême gauche – à cette époque, *Les Cahiers du cinéma* semblent pétrifiés dans un freudo-marxisme virulent et militant–, il paraît intéressant d'étudier le commentaire d'un magazine grand public sur ce phénomène de mode. François Nourissier, que nous avons déjà cité, écrit ainsi :

> Ce qui intéresse aujourd'hui, ce n'est pas l'exemplaire, c'est l'authentique. [...] Bref, pas le mythe, mais la réalité [...]. Les Français croient reconnaître dans la France des années soixante-dix certains stigmates des années quarante : l'asservissement aux préoccupations matérielles, la domination des nouveaux riches, la peur de l'engagement. Il y a là ni procès de la Résistance ni réhabilitation de la Collaboration, mais la dénonciation d'une France sans passion ni idéal, mal remise encore d'être orpheline de de Gaulle, comme elle avait mal supporté naguère d'avoir deux pères, l'un à Londres, l'autre à Vichy.

Le film de Louis Malle, qui réunit au début de l'année près de quatre cent mille spectateurs, en trois semaines, prend l'allure d'un phénomène de société, révélateur à ce titre des obsessions de la mémoire collective.

Interrogé, Patrick Modiano déclare : « Ce n'est pas vraiment l'Occupation qui me fascine. Elle me fournit un climat idéal, un peu trouble, une lumière un peu bizarre, l'image démesurément grossie de ce qui se passe aujourd'hui[1]. » Du côté des théoriciens, on se révèle beaucoup plus véhément ; la démarche rétro ne paraît pas soluble dans le matérialisme dialectique, et ne peut que détourner le révolutionnaire de ses desseins idéologiques. *Les Cahiers du cinéma*, soucieux d'ausculter les moindres convulsions du corps social, consacrent un numéro entier[2] à la nouvelle tendance, mouvement de mode auquel vient faire écho, dans la livraison suivante, un long article de Michel Foucault sur les

---

[1] *Le Point*, numéro cité.
[2] N° 250, mai 1974.

idéologies véhiculées par la représentation de l'histoire immédiate au cinéma.

Disséqué par Pascal Bonitzer, dans l'article « Histoire de sparadrap », qui voit dans l'œuvre les ferments d'une pensée profondément réactionnaire, le film s'attire les foudres des rédacteurs. Pour eux, c'est l'Histoire et ses oppositions de blocs idéologiques qui portent le sens du film, et non le personnage de Lucien – qui apporte pourtant à celle-ci toute sa complexité et son ambiguïté. Malle et son scénariste auraient perverti la vérité afin de mieux la travestir, et de la réincarner dans un ludion privé de toute conscience politique : « [la] vérité de Lucien n'est pas dans le réel, l'Histoire n'est qu'apparence et les étiquettes ne sont que des étiquettes. Tout ce qui se déroule dans le réel, l'Histoire, est frappé de contingence, de futilité et d'irréalité. »

Au-delà de son analyse, Bonitzer renvoie à toute la culture « rétro », sollicitée de façon pernicieuse, et délestée de toute mise en perspective historique. Selon lui, si « Lucien est attachant, c'est qu'en dernière instance l'Histoire assume sa bêtise[1]. » Dans le numéro suivant, Michel Foucault prolonge ce raisonnement pour réfléchir sur les formes de représentation à l'écran de l'histoire contemporaine, du *Cuirassé Potemkine* à la guerre d'Algérie. Prenant également l'exemple de *Lacombe Lucien*, qu'il rapproche du film de Liliana Cavani, *Portier de nuit*, sorti peu de temps auparavant, le philosophe démontre que les mécanismes propres à illustrer les parcours mentaux des personnages s'appliquent à rendre compte également du sens de l'Histoire. La mode rétro, qui exploite les déviances et forfaits de figures compromises avec l'occupant, se révélerait coupable de trahison intellectuelle de la logique et du sens de l'Histoire. Michel Foucault déclare à ce sujet[2] : « Comment l'Histoire en est-elle arrivée à tenir le discours qu'elle tient et à récupérer ce qui s'est passé, sinon par un procédé qui était celui de l'épopée, c'est-à-dire en se racontant comme une histoire de héros ? » Dès lors, il ne peut exister de représentation innocente de l'Histoire dans la fiction, puisque

---

[1] Article cité, p. 42-47.
[2] Article cité.

celle-ci n'est constituée que de la somme des oppositions entre les différentes entités projetées sur l'écran.

La remise en question des cadres et des normes par les artistes des années soixante-dix aura donc eu lieu grâce à l'exploitation de la guerre et de l'Occupation, qui leur permet de représenter leur désarroi. La fin de la décennie, marquée par les prémices de la crise économique, met rapidement fin à cette fascination, liée selon l'historien Marc Ferro « à la grande remise en cause des idées et des certitudes qui est la marque de notre temps[1]. » Les romans de Modiano paraissent trouver tout naturellement leur place dans le courant dit « rétro », mais cette mise en perspective mérite d'être relativisée.

MODIANO RATTRAPÉ ?

Nombre de critiques s'exaspèrent de l'obsession de ce romancier, lors de la publication des *Boulevards de ceinture*, à l'automne 1972. On accuse l'écrivain de creuser le même sillon, et d'exploiter le mouvement de mode alors en plein essor. Le grand public, qui prend connaissance de l'écrivain, le place alors sur le même plan que l'Olivier Todd de *L'Année du crabe* ou le Jacques Laurent des *Bêtises*. C'était oublier que le manuscrit de *La Place de l'Étoile* avait été déposé au début de 1967[2], bien avant que la nostalgie apparût comme une valeur éminemment commerciale dans le domaine littéraire, et que l'ouvrage incriminé constituait le dernier tome de la trilogie de l'Occupation, commencée une demi-douzaine d'années auparavant. Pourtant, les lecteurs qui découvrent à cette époque *Les Boulevards de ceinture*, à la faveur du Grand Prix de l'Académie française, ne distinguent pas forcément ce récit

---

[1] *Les Cahiers du cinéma*, mai-juin 1975, n° 257.
[2] La parution du livre fut repoussée d'un an en raison de la « Guerre des six jours », afin de ne pas heurter la sensibilité israélienne. Publié peu de semaines avant les événements de Mai 1968, le roman, bien qu'il eût été salué par Queneau et Aragon, passa relativement inaperçu. C'est seulement avec *La Ronde de nuit* que l'écrivain commença à se faire connaître du grand public.

onirique du roman de Pascal Jardin, également articulé autour de la figure paternelle. De fait, le premier roman apparaît comme une entreprise cathartique rendue nécessaire par vingt années d'interrogations. L'œuvre tient à la fois du manifeste, contre les antisémites ou les réactionnaires, et de la proclamation identitaire. L'écriture – et la réflexion sur la langue – semblent représenter la seule planche de salut pour le jeune homme, qui voit dans l'acte narratif l'unique recours contre les angoisses :

> C'est vrai que je n'ai jamais considéré la langue française comme mon monde [...] mais je voulais utiliser le français pour qu'il se retourne contre lui-même de l'intérieur. J'avais beaucoup lu les écrivains antisémites du début du siècle. Je me suis dit qu'un Juif pouvait très bien utiliser leur manière d'écrire le français, très filée, un français très clair. [...] Et c'est pour cela qu'il y a cette espèce d'ambiguïté. Eux, c'étaient les phares de la culture française d'avant-guerre. [...] L'antisémitisme détruit en même temps que l'harmonie avec les autres, avec le monde ambiant, l'harmonie avec la parole[1].

Les deux romans suivants poursuivent cette dénonciation, en plongeant directement dans les abîmes de la Collaboration économique et intellectuelle. Le malentendu persiste avec *Lacombe Lucien*. Modiano et Malle exploiteraient la mode rétro, cultivant le scandale par simple opportunisme. Rares sont les comptes rendus mentionnant l'activité antérieure du romancier et son travail sur la restitution de la mémoire « vive » des années sombres. L'écrivain paraît ainsi à la remorque d'un mouvement dont il fut involontairement l'initiateur[2]. Ses trois romans, son scénario et sa pièce, écrits

---

[1] Propos recueillis par Julien Brunn, *Libération*, 22 septembre 1975.
[2] Pierre Daprini, dans son article sur la restitution du climat de l'Occupation dans les romans de Modiano écrit à ce propos : « Quelques années plus tard, on assimilera cet auteur aux tenants de la mode "rétro", à ceux qui cultivent nostalgiquement le temps de l'Occupation, comme si le surgissement d'une authentique écriture (au demeurant sur le mode pamphlétaire) pouvait vraiment laisser à un écrivain le choix de sa parole et de l'émotion qui

entre 1967 et 1974, ont certes bénéficié d'un écho grandissant au fur et à mesure que les thèmes de la guerre et de l'Occupation devenaient des centres d'intérêt largement relayés par les médias, mais l'écrivain n'aurait pas moins poursuivi son investigation personnelle – et littéraire – si la réception des œuvres était restée confidentielle.

La confrontation avec le père, encore en vie au moment où commence à paraître la trilogie – mais depuis longtemps absent de l'univers de son fils –, l'évocation de la clandestinité ou des méandres de la collaboration économique et politique ou la peinture onirique d'un Paris voué à la rapine et à la débauche : tous les thèmes de *La Place de l'Étoile* et des romans suivants ne cesseront de jouer en majeur ou en basse continue dans l'œuvre de Modiano. Cette plongée dans un univers angoissant et fascinant tout à la fois, qui rend possible l'exorcisme des démons surgis du passé, s'effectue sur un mode narratif oscillant entre l'authenticité et le fantasme, constitutif du ton modianien du début des années soixante-dix. Cette approche doit sa spécificité à l'alliance de deux principes de récit, en apparence contradictoires, que constituent la rêverie et l'anecdote. Le romancier parvient à construire une narration qui prend appui sur une restitution pratiquement parfaite du cadre historique qu'il vient briser, en interrompant la linéarité du récit ou en faisant intervenir des éléments totalement extérieurs à l'histoire (en particulier les personnages de Coco Lacour et Esmeralda dans *La Ronde de nuit*).

L'apport modianien essentiel à la restitution de l'Occupation réside dans cette association insolite de la pure spéculation et du soin presque policier apporté aux détails, de sorte que la fresque gagne en force évocatrice ce qu'elle perd en valeur testimoniale. Une étude détaillée de cette peinture paraît nécessaire à la compréhension de l'ambition romanesque de Modiano. On sera alors en mesure d'en apprécier toute l'originalité, eu égard notamment aux écrivains de cette période.

---

l'ébranle en lui ». *In Australian Journal for French Studies*, XXVI, 1989, p. 194-205.

Une vision subjective des années d'Occupation

Les romans de la première trilogie de l'Occupation ou de la seconde[1] ne visent en aucun cas la restitution de la guerre, dans tous ses détails et particularités. La recomposition mentale à laquelle se livre l'écrivain interdit en effet tout exercice de précision historique, mais ne pourrait prendre corps toutefois sans une totale imprégnation de l'esprit de l'époque. Il semble donc légitime de procéder à un repérage des êtres, événements et lieux mis en scène, avec plus ou moins d'exactitude, par le romancier. Il sera alors possible de prendre une première mesure du travail littéraire effectué.

LE PAYSAGE TEMPOREL

Si l'écrivain fait preuve d'une totale liberté dans sa façon d'agencer le cours de son récit ou de mettre en scène les personnages, sa conduite de la narration repose sur des éléments historiques réels et des situations avérées. Ce postulat posé, il convient de reconnaître que c'est l'Histoire qui paraît mise au service du romancier dans cette recomposition onirique des années sombres. La Seconde Guerre mondiale n'intéresse pas l'écrivain pour ce qu'elle fut, mais pour l'éclosion spontanée d'êtres – et de comportements – qui, sans elle, ne se seraient jamais révélés. Modiano s'est exprimé sur le sujet à de nombreuses reprises, insistant avant tout sur la face obscure des êtres brusquement plongés dans la lumière de l'Occupation. Il déclarait ainsi à Françoise Jaudel[2] : « Je suis attiré par l'Occupation, par ce genre d'époque, ces atmosphères troubles et équivoques. J'imagine qu'il devait y avoir la même

---
[1] *Remise de peine*, *Voyage de noces* et *Fleurs de ruine*.
[2] *L'Arche*, octobre-novembre 1972, p. 61.
Dans une tonalité semblable, il déclare également à Claudine Jardin, du *Figaro littéraire*, (le 8 octobre 1969) : « l'Occupation me fascine, mais j'aurais tout aussi bien pu prendre le Directoire pour ses incertitudes et ses ambiguïtés. »

atmosphère à Shanghai durant la guerre d'Indochine. J'aime observer les gens qui se salissent, qui n'ont pas peur des pires compromissions. » Dans le même registre, il affirmait, dans une interview au *Monde*[1], vouloir « glorifier Joanovici ».

Les débuts de la guerre et les souffrances des populations civiles n'interviennent que peu dans les récits, à l'exception près du chapitre IV de *Livret de famille*, consacré à l'arrivée de Louisa Colpeyn, la mère du narrateur, à Paris, après l'invasion de la Belgique par les forces de l'Axe en 1940. Seuls l'intéressent la « décomposition morale[2] » et le vacillement des repères propres à la seconde partie de la guerre, au moment où la victoire de l'Allemagne paraît chaque jour moins certaine – instants qui voient les exactions et forfaits des séides de la Gestapo ou de la Milice gagner en intensité.

Modiano semble avant tout préoccupé par la restitution d'un climat particulièrement propre aux derniers mois du conflit, cet « entre chien et loup » de l'Histoire, où l'engagement prolongé aux côtés du régime nazi ou vichyste s'apparente à un sacrifice volontaire et consenti. L'écrivain ne fait pas pour autant des héros des agioteurs, tortionnaires ou courtisanes qu'il met en scène ; privés de tout sens moral, incarnant le mal dans ses aspects les plus systématiques et mécaniques, ces êtres constituent, avant tout, les objets mêmes de « [s]on horreur et de [s]a compassion[3] », trop longtemps fréquentés par son père durant ses années de clandestinité. Circonscrits aux derniers mois de l'Occupation, les romans n'offrent, d'autre part, aucun point de vue extérieur sur la situation. Fondamentalement subjective, la narration épouse la vision interne du protagoniste, qui expose de façon lapidaire les actes des collaborateurs. Le récit s'articule autour de ce personnage central qui, par faiblesse ou intérêt, se trouve obligé de côtoyer les plus abjectes figures du Paris de l'époque

---

[1] Interview accordée à Josyane Duranteau, le 11 novembre 1972.
[2] Ce mot intervient comme un *leitmotiv* tout au long de *La Ronde de nuit*, de même que la formule : « une époque aux relents de rastaquouérisme et d'assassinats ».
[3] Épigraphe de *La Ronde de nuit*.

(Raphaël Schlemilovitch dans *La Place de l'Étoile*, Swing Troubadour dans *La Ronde de nuit* ou Serge Alexandre dans *Les Boulevards de ceinture*). L'histoire et son récit se trouvent donc constitués par la somme de leurs remarques et impressions, sans qu'aucune voix extérieure vienne se mêler à cette monodie. Rien de plus étranger à cette reconstitution que l'intimisme de la fresque d'Elsa Triolet du *Premier Accroc coûte deux cents francs* ou de la chronique minutieuse de *Drôle de jeu* de Roger Vailland. Ces deux ouvrages, proposent chacun une vision très personnelle du Paris – et de la France – de l'Occupation[1], sur lesquels viennent trancher les focalisations internes de Modiano.

La restriction du champ de vision permet au roman de gagner en intensité ce qu'il perd en humanité. Dans les deux œuvres précédemment citées, et en particulier les quatre récits d'Elsa Triolet, les résistants, les attentistes ou les collaborateurs représentent des êtres à part entière, êtres de désirs, de haine ou de passions, aux motivations toujours identifiables. Chez Modiano, peu de personnages de chair et de sang, mais des abstractions ou modèles correspondant avant tout à des caractères et figures historiques.

Cette stylisation volontaire semble moins imputable à l'inexpérience du jeune romancier qu'à un choix purement esthétique, puisqu'il s'agit pour lui de restituer une ambiance générale, et non de développer une narration classique organisée autour du Paris occupé de la Seconde Guerre mondiale. À partir de celle-ci, l'écrivain fait évoluer des personnages qui n'ont d'autre fonction que de mettre en valeur le récitant, figure déléguée de l'écrivain à la recherche d'un point d'ancrage dans le passé. À cette faible caractérisation des personnages fait écho la discrétion relative aux événements mentionnés. Si l'on excepte *La Place de l'Étoile*, premier roman atypique, l'on cherchera vainement dans les romans ultérieurs des références directes au contexte historique évoqué. L'écrivain procède avant tout par allusions dans l'évocation des années sombres. Les vocables « Seconde

---

[1] Mais assortis d'une pluralité de voix narratives pour le premier et d'un très grand souci de réalisme pour le second.

Guerre mondiale », « antisémitisme », « déportation », « Occupation » ou « Collaboration » paraissent rarement employés, le corps du texte se limitant à des notations plutôt vagues sur les événements, privilégiant l'imprécision :

> Tous ces personnages [...] avaient brusquement surgi du black-out, d'une période de désespoir et de misère, par un phénomène analogue à celui de la génération spontanée[1].

D'autre part, le drame de la guerre est évoqué sur le mode de la rêverie, dans laquelle les drames humains paraissent mis à distance :

> Le monde mourait de consomption. Une très douce, très lente agonie. Les sirènes, pour annoncer un bombardement, sanglotaient. Ensuite, je ne percevais qu'un roulement de tambour étouffé. Cela durait deux ou trois heures. Des bombes au phosphore[2].

> Des gens comme vous et moi risquent de se faire arrêter à chaque coin de rue. Il ne se passe pas un jour sans que des rafles se produisent à la sortie des gares, des cinémas et des restaurants[3].

Dans le domaine des idées, les prises de position se caractérisent par une certaine indistinction ; le lecteur doit procéder seul au décryptage idéologique des propos tenus par les personnages des *Boulevards de ceinture* :

> En somme, on lui reprochait de prendre parti à une époque ou la plupart des gens se « vautraient dans l'attentisme ». Lui, au moins, proclamait ses opinions. Noir sur blanc. Il était jusqu'à présent du bon côté du manche, mais la situation évoluerait peut-être dans un sens défavorable pour lui et ses amis[4].

La guerre, et son cortège de souffrances et de persécutions apparaissent en filigrane sous le récit, évoqués par

---

[1] *Ibid.*, p. 140
[2] *Ibid.*, p. 140.
[3] *Les Boulevards de ceinture*, p. 112.
[4] *Ibid.*, p. 134.

les renvois et remarques discrètes concernant les « événements ». L'antisémitisme se trouve évoqué de façon indirecte, non par ses victimes mais ses fourriers (la mention du « tennis juif » au cours d'une conversation entre Gerbère et Lestandi, dans *Les Boulevards de ceinture*, en constitue un bon exemple). Modiano se montrera beaucoup plus explicite dans ses œuvres ultérieures, où il revient sur les thèmes et situations déjà esquissés dans les romans de la trilogie, mais assortis, à ce moment, de dates et de notations claires.

Ainsi, l'épisode récurrent de l'arrestation du père – scène centrale, presque « primitive » de l'œuvre de Modiano –, s'enrichit à chaque fois d'informations et de détails significatifs. Ainsi nous comparerons six moments :

Son père à lui connaissait aussi Frédo le Gestapiste. Il en avait parlé pendant leur séjour à Bordeaux. Le 16 juillet 1942, Frédo avait fait monter Schlemilovitch père dans une traction noire : « Que dirais-tu, mon colon, d'une vérification d'identité rue Lauriston et d'un petit tour au Vél d'Hiv ? Puis, contemplant le costume bleu Nil de Schlemilovitch père [...], Frédo avait ajouté : Un vrai dandy ! Vous ferez fureur à Auschwitz ! »

Schlemilovitch fils avait oublié comment Schlemilovitch père s'arracha des mains de ce brave homme[1].

On rappellera qu'Albert Modiano, après avoir été appréhendé en 1941 par la police, rue Marignan, fut réellement arrêté par celle-ci en 1942. Sa libération presque immédiate, par un ami, collaborateur actif et proche de l'occupant, n'a jamais cessé de hanter l'écrivain, qui la représente à de nombreuses reprises dans son œuvre. Le premier roman de Modiano, qui constitue l'exorcisme des interrogations angoissées du jeune créateur, se devait de faire figurer cet épisode – qui vient s'ajouter à tous les traumatismes traités sur le mode de la dérision ; il s'inscrit parfaitement dans la tonalité d'ensemble du récit, à l'irrévérence et au cynisme accomplis. L'écrivain, pour lequel la question de l'identité demeure à cette

---

[1] *La Place de l'Étoile*, p. 96.

époque insoluble, se réfugie derrière le paravent « Schlemilovitch » ; il n'ose pas se confronter avec l'horreur de la scène, qu'il évacue grâce au sarcasme, seul recours contre l'innommable.

Cinq ans plus tard, Modiano tente l'affrontement direct avec les années sombres, qu'il investit de sa présence dans *Les Boulevards de ceinture*. Entièrement articulé autour de la figure paternelle, ce roman marque une sorte de rétrécissement très net du centre d'intérêt. À la relecture iconoclaste d'un demi-siècle d'histoire française – et au développement d'un de ses pires chapitres avec *La Ronde de nuit* – vient succéder la focalisation sur la question majeure : comment puis-je penser l'idée de ma filiation, et me reconnaître dans la figure d'un homme velléitaire et aboulique ? Il s'ensuit un long travail d'empathie, qui semble rejeter le contexte historique à l'arrière-plan :

> Vous ne les avez pas entendu approcher. [...]
> – On voulait filer en Belgique, sans nous prévenir ?
> Il arrache la doublure de votre veste, compte les billets avec application, les empoche [...]. Il vous gifle [...].
> – Vous m'embarquez cette racaille [...].
> Le panier à salade stationne un peu plus haut [...] je vous accompagnerai jusqu'au bout[1].

La scène se trouve beaucoup plus développée que dans le premier roman. À la figure paternelle se joint la présence filiale, dans une confusion de voix qui vise à donner à l'épisode toute la portée et la dimension requises. On peut également déceler, dans cette évocation de l'arrestation, unissant dans une même épreuve un père et son fils né trois ans après, un artifice dramatique indispensable à la mise à distance l'événement et du traumatisme généré par celui-ci.

Une demi-décennie plus tard, l'épisode est de nouveau mis en scène au chapitre IX de *Livret de famille* :

> Une nuit de mars 1942, un homme de trente ans à peine, grand, l'air d'un Américain du Sud, se trouvait au

---

[1] *Les Boulevards de ceinture*, p. 180-82.

Saint-Moritz. [...] C'était mon père. Une jeune femme l'accompagnait, du nom de Hella Hartwich. [...] Un groupe de policiers français en civil entrent dans le restaurant et bloquent toutes les issues. Puis ils commencent à vérifier l'identité des clients. Mon père et son amie n'ont aucun papier. Les policiers français les poussent dans le panier à salade avec une dizaine d'autres personnes pour une vérification plus scrupuleuse rue Greffühle, au siège de la Police des Questions juives[1].

Cette fois-ci, Modiano ne rejette plus dans l'ombre les lieux et les dates, afin de prendre en considération la seule intensité émotionnelle de la scène. L'emploi de la troisième personne, la neutralité et l'exactitude des notations associées à la concision du récit montrent que l'écrivain n'aborde plus cette période comme le traumatisme douloureusement ineffable des premiers romans. L'évocation rend compte des moindres circonstances du drame, comme si, après avoir refoulé et camouflé l'événement, durant des années, le romancier tentait de l'envisager dans son caractère brut, sans l'interférence d'un système narratif original et complexe.

Après une décennie durant laquelle le romancier délaisse les vertiges de la Collaboration pour le malaise de la guerre d'Algérie[2], la première « autobiographie fictive » – ou

---

[1] *Livret de famille*, p. 127.
[2] L'angoisse relative à ces deux guerres, dont l'une pourtant précédait sa naissance, emprunte des voies identiques : angoisse de la dénonciation – en particulier les toutes premières pages de *Villa triste* –, obsession de la fuite, avec *Une jeunesse* ou interrogation sur l'identité, comme dans *Un cirque passe*. Chaque agression caractérisée contre les lieux de retraite, réels ou imaginaires, semble de fait entraîner les mêmes réactions. On pensera ainsi aux sentiments de Modiano à l'annonce de l'invasion d'Israël, au début de la Guerre des Six Jours, au chapitre VI de *Livret de famille* : « Ce soir-là, j'ai senti que quelque chose touchait à sa fin [...]. J'avais la certitude que plus rien ne serait comme avant et je peux indiquer la minute précise où tout a changé pour moi [...]. Mais sans doute beaucoup de gens, à la même heure, ont-ils éprouvé la même angoisse que moi... »

autofiction[1] –, *Remise de peine*, rejoint dans sa dernière partie la trace douloureuse de Modiano, celle de l'Occupation et de l'arrestation du père. Le texte, dans lequel l'Occupation ne constitue pas un rôle fondamental, annonce par son ton plus feutré et plus recueilli l'évolution ultérieure du romancier. Errant à la lisière du XVIIe et de Levallois, le narrateur se rappelle son père et un passé plus lointain qui le hante. Modiano reprend le récit de la rafle opérée rue Marignan[2] :

> Il avait été arrêté un soir de février dans un restaurant de la rue de Marignan. Il n'avait pas de papiers sur lui. La police opérait des contrôles à cause d'une nouvelle ordonnance allemande : interdiction aux Juifs de se trouver dans les lieux publics après vingt heures.

Le récit se poursuit après quelques paragraphes :

> L'année suivante, on l'avait appréhendé à son domicile. On l'avait conduit au Dépôt, puis dans une annexe du camp de Drancy, à Paris, quai de la Gare [...]. Une nuit, quelqu'un était venu en voiture [...], et avait fait libérer mon père. Je m'imaginais – à tort ou à raison – que c'était un certain Louis Pagnon qu'on appelait « Eddy », fusillé à la Libération avec les membres de la bande de la rue Lauriston dont il faisait partie[3].

Le caractère presque exhaustif du récit et sa valeur solennelle paraissent bien loin de la recomposition fantasmatique de *La Place de l'Étoile*. Les circonstances précises de l'arrestation ainsi que la minutie apportée à l'exposé des lieux et des dates montrent que Modiano ne travestit plus l'Histoire afin de s'en détourner, et semble accepter dans son intégralité la part d'ambiguïté qui demeure

---

[1] Notion définie par Thierry Laurent dans sa thèse de doctorat : *L'Autofiction dans les romans de Patrick Modiano*, thèse soutenue à Paris-IV Sorbonne, en février 1995, et publiée sous le titre suivant, *Patrick Modiano : une autofiction*, aux Presses Universitaires de Lyon, en 1997.
[2] Article cité.
[3] *Remise de peine*, p. 116-117.

attachée aux agissements et aux énigmatiques relations et accointances du père pendant le conflit.

L'avant-dernière mention de l'épisode se situe à la page 112 de *Fleurs de ruine*, deuxième volet du nouveau triptyque consacré à l'Occupation. Modiano y adopte une forme plus concise, traitant la scène de façon dépouillée et informative :

> À quoi correspond ce rêve de la vie réelle ? Au souvenir de mon père qui, sous l'Occupation, avait vécu une situation ambiguë elle aussi : arrêté dans une rafle par des policiers français, sans savoir de quoi il était coupable, et libéré par un membre de la bande de la rue Lauriston ? [...] Quelle étrange impression de sortir du « trou » – comme disait mon père – et de se retrouver dans l'une de ces voitures au parfum de cuir qui traverse lentement Paris en direction de la Rive droite après le couvre-feu... Mais, un jour ou l'autre, il faudra rendre des comptes[1].

Enfin, en 1997, *Dora Bruder* insère l'épisode dans une réflexion d'ensemble sur le destin de la jeune fille qui donne son nom au roman. Internée en février 1942 à la prison des Tourelles, boulevard Mortier, à la suite d'une interpellation par les forces de l'ordre, elle sera alors conduite au camp de Drancy. L'écrivain place en perspective ces arrestations concomitantes et s'attarde ensuite sur l'histoire familiale[2]. L'épisode reprend les données précédentes pour les exposer avec une certaine tendresse :

> Ce mois de février, le soir de l'entrée en vigueur de l'ordonnance allemande, mon père avait été pris dans une rafle, aux Champs-Élysées. Des inspecteurs de la Police des questions juives avaient bloqué les accès

---

[1] *Fleurs de ruine*, p. 67.
[2] Il évoque, en effet, une autre arrestation, quelque peu sordide celle-là, qui mit aux prises le fils et son père en 1963. Conduits tous deux dans un « panier à salade », au poste de police de la rue de l'Abbaye, dans le sixième arrondissement, parce qu'Albert Modiano refusait de payer la pension alimentaire de son enfant, les deux hommes n'échangent aucune parole. Le futur romancier médite alors sur les deux voyages de son père en voiture cellulaire, à deux époques distinctes.

d'un restaurant de la rue Marignan où il dînait avec une amie[1].

Cette fois-ci, et il s'agit d'une information importante, à laquelle Modiano accorde une place prépondérante dans son texte. Les circonstances de la narration de cette histoire se trouvent mentionnées avec une grande précision :

> Mon père avait fait à peine mention de cette jeune fille lorsqu'il m'avait raconté sa mésaventure pour la première et la dernière fois de sa vie, un soir de juin 1963 où nous étions dans un restaurant des Champs-Élysées, presque en face de celui où il avait été appréhendé vingt ans auparavant[2].

En l'espace de vingt-cinq ans, le fantasme de la recomposition mentale a laissé la place à une approche moins infantile du traumatisme ; l'Histoire, qui intervenait comme toile de fond, reprend ses droits, et les impressions qui lui demeurent attachées témoignent de sa légitimation par le romancier, comme si ce dernier avait dû se déprendre de l'aspect destructeur de l'Occupation pour mieux l'accepter. Nous verrons, par la suite, comment le débordement juvénile des premiers romans consacrés à cette période laisse la place à une lecture plus sereine de l'époque. À cet égard, *Dora Bruder* prend l'aspect d'une véritable enquête policière ; l'écrivain multiplie les travaux d'investigation et les recoupements historiques susceptibles de reconstituer les derniers mois de la jeune fugueuse.

Les exemples développés marquent clairement cette décantation de l'angoisse qui ne pouvait être circonvenue que par la dérision ou la mise à distance des faits : dans les premiers ouvrages, les dénonciations et tortures semblaient représenter les éléments banals du quotidien – acceptés comme les inévitables corollaires des turpitudes et compromissions de Raphaël et de Swing Troubadour. Ce dernier personnage paraît ainsi incapable de distinguer les infamies commises par le groupe d'agioteurs, auquel il s'est agrégé, de la répétition

---

[1] *Dora Bruder*, p. 64.
[2] *Ibid.*, p. 65.

systématique et mécanique d'actes condamnables dans leur globalité – démarche qui aboutit à placer sur le même plan la confiscation de biens juifs et la mise à mort d'un résistant. Le brouillard apathique dans lequel il évolue à la fin du récit correspond, sur le plan romanesque, à ce refus de la confrontation avec la part la plus inhumaine de la Collaboration – que la figure paternelle semble avoir inscrit en lui.

C'est pourtant cette faiblesse psychologique qui constitue la force évocatrice des romans de Modiano, puisque l'horreur, qui n'intervient pas dans la narration, s'inscrit dans les liaisons et enchaînements qu'élabore l'esprit du lecteur. Nous retiendrons comme exemple l'un des derniers séjours du protagoniste de *La Ronde de nuit* dans l'hôtel particulier du 3 bis square Cimarosa[1], qui voit jouer de façon contrapuntique une séance de torture et une expérience de chiromancie :

> Il levait la tête. Une tache rouge sur le tapis de la Savonnerie, à l'endroit où son front reposait [...] Le Khédive le giflait trois fois de suite. [...]
> – Tout ce sang, balbutiait la baronne Lydia Stahl. Son front reposait de nouveau contre le tapis de la Savonnerie [...]. Quelques minutes plus tard, Tony Breton annonçait d'une voix sourde : « Il est mort, il est mort sans parler ».[...] Simone Bouquereau retouchait son maquillage devant le grand miroir de Venise. Ivanoff examinait gravement la main gauche de la baronne Lydia Stahl.

Le chroniqueur n'établit aucune hiérarchie entre les informations, qu'il place toutes sur le même plan, sans que soit exprimé le moindre sentiment. Ce refus d'acceptation de l'horreur, qui exploite toutes les ressources de la suggestion pour atteindre le plus haut degré de force romanesque, fonctionne sur le mode de l'euphémisme, procédé qui avait été déjà longuement utilisé dans le roman antérieur, en particulier dans la peinture des camps de concentration, assimilés à de géants « luna-parks » – provocation délibérée, non contre le

---

[1] P. 133-34.

peuple juif, pour lequel le romancier a toujours exprimé toute son empathie[1], mais contre les angoisses profondes rendant le sarcasme nécessaire afin que l'innommable pût être exprimé :

> Vous voyez Hilda, lui expliquai-je, les foires sont horriblement tristes [...]. Les bennes des montagnes russes déraillent systématiquement et vous vous fracassez la colonne vertébrale. Autour du manège, les archers forment une ronde et vous transpercent l'épine dorsale au moyen de petites fléchettes empoisonnées. [...] J'oubliais de vous parler des pochettes surprises que l'on vend dans les stands de confiserie : l'acheteur y trouve toujours quelques cristaux bleu améthyste de cyanure, avec leur mode d'emploi : « Na ! friss schon ! » Des pochettes de cyanure pour tout le monde ! Six millions ! Nous sommes heureux à Therensienstadt[2].

C'est à la suite de ce processus de maturation, entériné par la mort du père, tout juste avant la parution de *Rue des boutiques obscures*, que l'écrivain pourra enfin mettre à distance ses émotions, de façon à pouvoir parler presque sereinement des années sombres, sans recourir pour cela au procédé sécurisant d'une Histoire privée de sa substance. Après avoir analysé les relations qu'il entretient avec les événements,

---

[1] Dans son entretien accordé à J.-C. Texier, Patrick Modiano faisait le point sur ses sentiments à l'égard de ce peuple : « Je ne suis pas hostile à Israël, ce serait monstrueux. Je suis triste [...]. C'est la fin d'un génie d'inquiétude. » Vingt-cinq ans plus tard, il rend compte, dans *Libération* du 25 novembre 1994, d'un ouvrage de Serge Klarsfeld, *Mémorial de la déportation des Juifs de France* : « Son mémorial m'a révélé ce que je n'osais pas regarder vraiment en face, et la raison d'un malaise que je ne parvenais pas à exprimer. J'avais écrit trop jeune un premier livre où je rusais avec l'essentiel, en tâchant de répondre de manière désinvolte aux journalistes antisémites de l'Occupation, mais c'était comme pour me rassurer, comme pour faire le malin quand on a peur et que l'on parle très fort dans le noir. Après la parution du mémorial de Serge Klarsfeld, je me suis senti quelqu'un d'autre. Je savais maintenant quel genre de malaise j'éprouvais ».
Cette déclaration confirme nos remarques à propos de l'évolution des sentiments de l'écrivain concernant l'acceptation de la *Shoah*. Il faut sans nul doute mettre sur le compte de cette maturité la révision des pages les plus violentes et provocatrices de *La Place de l'Étoile* pour la réédition de 1985.
[2] *Op.cit.*, p. 112-113.

il paraît important, à ce stade, d'étudier plus en détail les éléments informatifs que le romancier communique au lecteur. On sera alors en mesure d'estimer la place de l'anecdote dans la recomposition romanesque de l'Occupation. Le romancier se montre en effet très attentif à la reconstitution du climat politique, des lieux et des personnages, qui constituent des indications essentielles pour la compréhension de la vision portée.

LE PAYSAGE POLITIQUE ; VOYAGE EN TERRE DE HAINE

De 1966 au milieu des années soixante-dix, le jeune Modiano entend répondre à la violence antisémite de la nation française, qui semblait avoir atteint toute sa virulence pendant la guerre. Des groupes d'individus, intellectuels, artistes ou industriels ont désigné le juif comme bouc émissaire de la débâcle de 1940, puis participé, de façon plus ou moins directe, à sa déportation. L'écrivain voit dans cette collusion entre l'intérêt particulier et le service de l'État l'une des formes les plus achevées de l'abjection.

On chercherait difficilement un discours idéologique articulé autour d'une idée politique bien affirmée, dans les romans de Modiano. Les deux forces antagonistes de l'Occupation – les collaborateurs ou les membres du RCO – semblent bien incapables de conceptualiser leur action, cette impéritie paraissant liée à la totale absence de « chair » romanesque qui les caractérise. Réduits à des silhouettes abstraites, les personnages n'accèdent que rarement à une existence autonome, indépendante de leur statut d'archétype ; tout se passe en fait comme si Modiano considérait que l'appartenance à un groupe pouvait à elle seule donner corps et épaisseur à un être.

Cette notion de noyau constitué autour d'une idée ou d'un centre d'intérêt représente un aspect fondamental, non seulement des romans consacrés à l'Occupation, mais également de l'ensemble de l'œuvre. De fait, chaque récit présente une communauté, plus ou moins importante, à laquelle un individu tente de s'agréger – et qui entraînera ainsi sa perte. Séparé très tôt de son frère, délaissé par une mère et un père absents, Modiano semble donner toute son importance à l'idée de fratrie, seules instances capables de dispenser l'identité tant recherchée. Cette constante prend toute sa valeur au moment de l'étude des groupes représentés dans chacun des ouvrages.

Le protagoniste ne semble se définir que par le rapport qu'il entretient avec le groupe dont il fait partie (les œuvres de la trilogie, *Lacombe Lucien*, ou les couples inséparables de *Villa triste*, d'*Une jeunesse* ou d'*Un cirque passe*) ou auxquels il a appartenu, comme l'amnésique de *Rue des boutiques obscures*, Jean Dekker dans *Quartier perdu*, le narrateur de *Dimanches d'août* ou celui de *Voyage de noces*. Dans l'univers modianien, le personnage a fort peu de chances d'accéder au statut de figure romanesque s'il n'adhère pas à une communauté par laquelle, ou contre laquelle, il se définit. Contrairement à nombre de romans consacrés à la période de l'Occupation, qui rapportent la validité, voire la légitimité, de l'action à une stricte échelle de valeurs individuelles, les ouvrages de Modiano paraissent essentiellement articulés autour de la façon de comprendre, puis de s'approprier, le sentiment collectif. Le meilleur exemple demeure celui de *La Place de l'Étoile* : un jeune homme dépourvu d'histoire pénètre au cœur même de celle-ci (les conseils de rédaction de *Je suis partout* ou les « thés » de Brinon), et multiplie, à cette fin, les points d'entrée.

La recréation du Paris de la débâcle, puis de l'Occupation, vient dessiner une géographie mentale bien différente des récits qui la prenaient pour toile de fond. Le paysage urbain, historique, est perçu sous la forme d'une coalition de groupes distincts prenant l'aspect d'un conglomérat de forces attaché à la destruction de l'individualité. Le protagoniste n'a d'autres chances de survie que l'agrégation – forcée – ou la fuite – impossible. À cet égard, il convient de noter que celui-ci n'envisage jamais d'avoir recours à une lutte ouverte contre les « forces du mal », et n'entrevoit d'autre solution que la compromission avec l'ennemi abhorré. Qu'il soit choisi par l'un des membres du groupe (*La Ronde de nuit* ou *Lacombe Lucien*) ou qu'il force son admission (*Les Boulevards de ceinture*[1]), les conséquences demeurent identiques : le héros finit anéanti par les forces qu'il a provoquées, monades indépendantes les unes des autres, dont les caractères particuliers peinent à se détacher. On notera, enfin, que ces clans fonctionnent en vase clos ; le narrateur décompose la somme des différentes personnalités sous la seule forme de fiches signalétiques. Il paraît ainsi impossible de rompre le cortège de la « ronde de nuit » :

> Rastas, avorteurs, chevaliers d'industrie, journalistes véreux, avocats et comptables marrons qui gravitaient autour du Khédive et de monsieur Philibert. À quoi venait s'ajouter un bataillon de demi-mondaines, danseuses de genre, morphinomanes […]. Mes deux patrons m'introduisaient dans ce monde interlope. Champs-Élysées. On appelait ainsi le séjour des ombres vertueuses et héroïques […]. J'y vois des ombres, mais ce sont celles de Monsieur Philibert, du Khédive et de leurs acolytes[2].

De fait, contrairement à nombre de films ou de romans pour lesquels l'Occupation constitue un cadre propice à l'affrontement des idées ou des personnalités ou à la révélation progressive d'une nouvelle identité − au terme d'un parcours moral riche d'enseignements sur soi-même[3] −, l'écrivain associe à l'occupation allemande l'idée d'une nébuleuse de factions souterraines, contre lesquelles l'individu paraît entièrement désarmé. Celui-ci n'a d'autre solution que de rejoindre une faction antagoniste (comme le pitoyable RCO de

---

[1] Le cas de *La Place de l'Étoile* paraît différent, qui associe quatre groupes distincts aux quatre strates historico-sociologiques que le protagoniste visite : les idéologues du premier chapitre, les khâgneux bordelais, la province profonde (les amis du colonel Aravis et le « clan » Fougeire-Jusquiames) et enfin les phalanges de l'occupation juive puis allemande, renvoyées dos à dos, dans le dernier chapitre. On notera que les stratégies d'accès paraissent semblables à celles qui étaient évoquées précédemment.
[2] *La Ronde de nuit*, p. 88-89.
[3] Nous songeons en particulier à *L'Armée des ombres*, de Joseph Kessel.

La Ronde de nuit) ou de s'associer très étroitement, et de façon irrévocable, à un cercle de collaborateurs, afin de se forger un semblant d'identité – on pensera ainsi à Raphaël dans la première partie de *La Place de l'Étoile* ou à *Lacombe Lucien*, dans le film éponyme. Il peut également se réfugier (Swing Troubadour) ou sauver son père, ou à tout le moins l'image de celui-ci, comme Serge Alexandre dans *Les Boulevards de ceinture*.

Être seul, telle est la véritable angoisse du héros modianien. Livré à lui-même, le personnage se retrouve confronté à sa vacuité existentielle, ce qui ne fait que renforcer sa déchirure ; en effet, si le rapport des forces paraît bien inégal entre le groupe et l'individu conduit par son instinct grégaire, cette démarche constitue le seul moyen d'accès au monde extérieur. Les protagonistes semblent émerger des limbes dans lesquels ils se morfondaient, même s'ils quittent ce monde pour l'enfer de la Collaboration. Leur véritable expérience de l'identité commence lorsqu'ils décident de rejoindre le cercle qui les accueillera. Après avoir été fils prodigue, maître chanteur, surveillant d'internat ou paysan, les personnages modianiens n'accèdent à l'existence réelle qu'à l'instant où ils décident de mettre la leur en danger. Ils sont ainsi conduits à prendre connaissance des divers aspects de l'idéologie française et du paysage politique des années 1940-1944.

Les références à la « Révolution nationale » et les réflexions sur le climat strictement politique de l'Occupation s'estompent au fur et à mesure des romans. Seule *La Place de l'Étoile* s'appesantit sur les réflexes conservateurs et réactionnaires que flatte la doctrine du Maréchal, brocardée dans la première partie de l'œuvre. Les multiples facettes du nationalisme et du patriotisme figurent des déviations de la raison et sont, à ce titre, combattues par un recours systématique à la dérision et à la caricature.

Le premier courant représenté est celui de l'institution militaire. Ses plus hauts cadres paraissent fournir à Modiano des caricatures idéales de personnages réactionnaires. Le colonel Aravis, rencontré à T.[1], au bord du lac d'Annecy, constitue ainsi un exemple révélateur de l'imagerie mentale de l'écrivain : l'officier en retraite devient la figure attitrée d'un certain esprit français, pétri de conservatisme et de xénophobie :

> Chaque petit Français possède, au fond de la province, un grand-père de cet acabit. Il en a honte [...].
> – Des Essarts, me disait Aravis, soyez chasseur alpin, nom d'une pipe [...]. Mon petit, s'il te plaît, la tête haute. Une poignée de main énergique. Surtout, évite de ricaner bêtement. Nous en avons assez de voir la race française dégénérée. Nous voulons de la pureté[2].

La réduction caricaturale ne s'embarrasse que rarement de nuance en ce qui concerne la complexité psychologique. Nous songerons, par exemple, à la fausse biographie de Jacob X, manifeste publié par Raphaël dans les journaux de gauche. Pour Modiano, il s'agit d'esquisser le portrait-charge d'une famille corsetée dans la tradition militaire :

> Confession de Jacob X [...] parut dans un hebdomadaire parisien : Jacob X avait été recueilli par une famille française dont il tenait à préserver l'anonymat. [...]
> Cette famille habitait Paray-le-Monial et Jacob X passa son enfance à l'ombre de la basilique. Les portraits de Gallieni, de Foch, de Joffre, la croix militaire du colonel X et plusieurs francisques vichyssoises ornaient les murs du salon[3].

L'écrivain recourt au cliché, inscrit dans la pensée collective, dont l'excès invalide tout réalisme. En effet, il ne cherche pas à restituer l'image d'un corps de la société française à un moment précis, et procède, à cette fin, par inflation de détails convergents ; la famille d'officiers patriote à l'excès devient l'exemple même du conservatisme militaire à

---

[1] *La Place de l'Étoile*, p. 70.
[2] *Ibid.*, p. 74-75.
[3] *Ibid.*, p. 17.

la française, de même que la marquise de Fougeire-Jusquiames incarne l'essence de l'aristocratie tarée – autre spécialité française... On songera ainsi à cet extrait de *La Place de l'Étoile* :

> Crois-tu vraiment que Fougeire-Jusquiames soit le « cadre d'un roman, un paysage imaginaire ? » Un bordel, entends-tu, le château a toujours été un bordel de luxe ! Très couru sous l'occupation allemande ! Mon défunt père, Charles de Fougeire-Jusquiames, servait d'entremetteur aux intellectuels français collabos. Statues d'Arno Breker, jeunes aviateurs de la *Luftwaffe*, SS, *Hitlerjugend*, tout était mis en œuvre pour satisfaire les goûts de ces messieurs[1].

Peu épargnés sous la plume du romancier, les assises de l'ordre établi que constituent l'armée et la noblesse rejoignent les représentants de la compromission intellectuelle, par l'intermédiaire des portraits outranciers qu'en brosse l'écrivain. Dans ce dernier domaine, Modiano use à la fois de la déformation caricaturale des idéologies par le recours à des figures tutélaires et une libre recomposition historique. Ainsi, Adrien Debigorre, professeur de littérature en classe d'hypokhâgne à Bordeaux, est représenté selon les lois du premier système. Les convictions politiques, à l'extrême-droite de celles de Maurice Bardèche, ainsi que la personne, pitoyable et ridicule, chargée de les véhiculer – le vieillard est obsédé par le complot judéo-maçonnique – n'échappent pas au genre du portrait-charge, si souvent utilisé dans le roman :

> Notre professeur de lettres portait une barbe imposante, une redingote noire, et son pied bot lui valait les sarcasmes des lycéens. Ce curieux personnage avait été l'ami de Maurras, de Paul Chack et de Mgr Mayol de Lupé ; les auditeurs français se souviennent certainement des « Causeries au coin de feu » que Debigorre prononçait à Radio-Vichy. En 1942, il fait partie de l'entourage d'Abel Bonheur [...]. Debigorre tente de grouper autour de lui des commandos de pêcheurs pour résister aux Anglais [...]. Il avait

---

[1] *Ibid.*, p. 95.

entretenu, pendant l'Occupation, une volumineuse correspondance avec Paul Chack, dont il nous lisait des passages[1].

Les incarnations de la haine du narrateur-écrivain, Aravis, la marquise ou Debigorre, interviennent dans la partie du roman située durant la période contemporaine. Elles constituent autant de témoignages d'un état d'esprit, d'une mentalité, que la débâcle du Reich n'a en rien modifié ; la réaction, qu'elle provienne des corps armés, de l'Université ou du terroir, semble toujours en germe, et demeure l'une des valeurs pérennes d'un pays attaché viscéralement à ses traditions.

Dans la partie « fantasmée » du roman, les incursions de Raphaël au sein des sphères parisiennes de la Collaboration idéologique mettent en scène des personnages authentiques, et non de grotesques caricatures, qui viennent exprimer toutes les tendances des doctrines vichystes ou fascistes. L'ensemble dessine l'image d'une France pétrifiée par l'admiration qu'elle porte à un envahisseur auquel elle n'offre que veulerie et soumission – tout en exaltant chez ce dernier la pugnacité et l'esprit de combat qu'elle dénonce chez les résistants. Les Brinon, Luchaire ou Darquier de Pellepoix dont le protagoniste fait la rencontre, représentent, à ses yeux, un versant particulier d'une nation qui se dérobe à ses désirs d'adoption. À cette fin, il embrasse les idéologies les plus conservatrices – celles qui fondent l'identité de la nation dans le droit du sang et la pureté de la race – et devient l'ami de leurs porte-parole, dans le chimérique espoir de conquérir un semblant d'identité française. Pour l'écrivain, qui projette sur le héros de son œuvre ses interrogations existentielles, ces personnages viennent illustrer la permanence d'une xénophobie institutionnelle, qui a retardé son désir d'enracinement :

> Juin 1940. Je quitte la petite bande de *Je suis partout* en regrettant nos rendez-vous place Denfert-Rochereau. Je me suis lassé du journalisme et caresse des ambitions politiques […]. [Je] cultive

---

[1] *Ibid.*, p. 56.

soigneusement l'amitié de Brinon [...]. Il me semble absurde de supprimer 500 000 juifs français, quand il suffirait d'un lavage de cerveau pour qu'ils éprouvent de meilleurs sentiments vis-à-vis de l'Allemagne. [...] Doriot ne me plaît pas beaucoup à cause de son passé communiste et de ses bretelles. Je flaire en Déat l'instituteur radical-socialiste[1].

Raphaël ne choisit pas de fréquenter les réformateurs situés à l'aile gauche de l'échiquier politique, puisque ceux-ci ne paraissent pas s'inscrire dans la longue tradition réactionnaire qui, à ses yeux, représente le génie français. Le pays apparaît ainsi comme un vivier de patriotes véhéments et de nationalistes rancis, confits dans les idées d'un autre siècle, et à ce titre totalement imperméables à l'idée d'évolution. Modiano charge à dessein le portrait qu'il brosse afin d'exprimer, avec toute la violence de la post-adolescence, le désarroi d'un être réduit à sa seule personne, incapable de s'intégrer à un groupe constitué, qu'il s'agisse d'un cercle d'amis, d'un parti, et *a fortiori* d'une nation.

L'ANTISÉMITISME

Le conservatisme allié au patriotisme le plus réactionnaire se nourrit de la peur du changement et de la croyance en un esprit corrupteur, qui pervertirait le génie national. La hantise de l'altérité, de l'extranéité, trouve rapidement un corollaire naturel dans un antisémitisme culturel, voire instinctif, pour lequel le Juif incarne par essence une menace d'ordre interne – cet être apatride qui ne peut adhérer à une communauté sans autre intention que celle de la phagocyter. Nous consacrerons ultérieurement un long développement à cette question cruciale, mais il paraît essentiel de noter, dès à présent, l'importance du martyrologe du peuple juif dans l'œuvre modianienne.

---

[1] *Ibid.*, p. 25-26.

Le premier roman s'articule exclusivement autour des notions connexes de la judéité et de l'identité personnelle. L'écrivain ne cesse d'interroger la mémoire de ses origines pour la confronter à l'horreur du XXᵉ siècle ; la partition du narrateur prend l'aspect d'un cri de douleur, retenu pendant des années, et dissimulé derrière les protections élémentaires de la dérision et du cynisme. L'ensemble s'inscrit dans une perspective historique qui fait la part belle aux compromissions et aux atrocités. Celles-ci peuvent être simplement mentionnées au détour d'une anecdote, d'un portrait de personnage, ou donner lieu à un développement plus important. On songera ainsi à la discrète mention de la rafle du Vél d'Hiv[1], que Modiano ne cite pas de façon précise, ou encore au jeu de mots de l'épigraphe[2]. Le créateur se montre plus disert, en revanche, sur le système concentrationnaire nazi ou sioniste – même si l'essentiel de la vision relève du pur fantasme.

Le deuxième volet de la trilogie fonctionne de manière différente. En effet, l'écrivain délègue sa parole à un être dénué de toute consistance intellectuelle et physique, pour lequel la question de la judéité ne semble pas se poser. Enfin, *Les Boulevards de ceinture* reprennent de façon beaucoup plus apaisée les interrogations et émois du premier ouvrage. Le personnage de Gerbère, qui expose les règles de son « tennis juif » avec délectation, et appelle à la purgation totale de tous les « enjuivés », renvoie aux vaticinations antisémites de Robert Brasillach dans *Je suis partout* – même si ce dernier hebdomadaire offrait une tenue intellectuelle sans comparaison avec les ragots colportés par Jean Murraille et ses collaborateurs[3]. Cependant, la revue fasciste ne répugnait pas,

---

[1] « Un panier à salade, semblable à ceux que la police française utilisa pour la grande rafle des 16 et 17 juillet 1942, était arrêté au coin d'une rue. » *Ibid.*, p. 124.
[2] « Au mois de juin 1942, un officier allemand s'avance vers un jeune homme et lui dit :
"Pardon monsieur, où se trouve la Place de l'Étoile ?"
Le jeune homme désigne le côté gauche de sa poitrine. »
(Histoire juive)
[3] De fait, la revue de Murraille renvoie au magazine de Luchaire, *Toute la vie*.

elle aussi, à mentionner les noms et adresses de personnalités israélites dont la liberté de mouvement paraissait scandaleuse. On peut également citer, afin de compléter ce tableau de l'abjection, les propos tenus par Georges Lestandi[1], qui prépare « une série d'échos », « s'apprête à citer des noms », en exhortant « les autorités compétentes à intervenir ».

On retrouve les brimades et angoisses quotidiennes des juifs français ou étrangers dans *Lacombe Lucien*, *Voyage de noces* et surtout *Livret de famille*. Le chapitre XIV de ce dernier ouvrage s'articule, en particulier, autour du père de l'écrivain, Albert Modiano. Celui-ci travailla durant la guerre pour le compte de la Gestapo, comme nous l'avons déjà vu, et multiplia les identités et faux papiers afin d'éviter la déportation. L'écrivain raconte de façon précise, dans cette première autofiction, l'existence recluse de cet homme, condamné à la clandestinité :

> [Il] se cachait dans un manège du bois de Boulogne dont l'écuyer était l'un de ses amis d'enfance [...]. Elle se rappelait que mon père s'était caché pendant un mois 14, rue Chalgrin, sans sortir une seule fois de la maison, parce qu'il n'avait aucun papier et qu'il craignait les rafles [...]. La peur le gagnait, comme en cette fin d'après-midi de l'été 43. Une pluie d'orage tombait et il était sous les arcades de la rue de Rivoli. [...] Un jour, à l'aube, le téléphone sonna et une voix inconnue appela mon père par son véritable nom. On raccrocha aussitôt. Ce fut ce jour-là qu'il décida de fuir Paris[2].

Ce climat d'incertitude et de confusion caractérise les dernières pages de *Rue des boutiques obscures* ; l'errance du narrateur, qui parcourt au hasard un paysage recouvert par la neige, illustre la vulnérabilité d'un homme exposé aux hasards de l'existence, sans le moindre repère. Les autres ouvrages évoqués s'attachent, avant tout, à la restitution d'une atmosphère, d'un climat – d'ordre presque mental –, où l'appréhension et l'anxiété dominent. À cette fin, le roman

---

[1] Le nom de ce journaliste renvoie à la figure de Jean Lestandi de Villani, directeur de l'hebdomadaire antisémite et antimaçonnique *Au pilori*.
[2] *Livret de famille*, p. 202-208.

privilégie les notations subjectives ; le point de vue des acteurs du récit ainsi que leur perception des événements offrent, à ses yeux, des perspectives narratives beaucoup plus intéressantes qu'une vision globalisante provenant de l'extérieur. On retiendra ainsi la longue déambulation d'Ingrid Theyrsen, jeune juive réfugiée à Paris avec son père, dans les rues de la capitale à l'heure du couvre-feu, en novembre 1942. La scène tout entière s'organise à partir du regard et des sentiments de la jeune fille ; le caractère subjectif du récit permet au lecteur de partager les émotions de celle-ci :

> Elle n'avait plus beaucoup de temps devant elle pour rejoindre son père dans l'hôtel du boulevard Ornano où ils habitaient depuis le début de l'automne [...]. Elle suit le boulevard de Rochechouart sur le trottoir de gauche, celui du neuvième arrondissement. De temps en temps, elle jette un regard sur le trottoir opposé qui marque la limite du couvre-feu et où il fait plus sombre, bien que l'heure ne soit pas encore sonnée : encore quinze minutes avant que la frontière ne se referme, et si elle ne la franchit pas d'ici là, elle ne pourra plus rejoindre son père à l'hôtel[1].

Cet extrait offre un exemple remarquable du style de Modiano. L'écrivain parvient à retranscrire, avec une réelle économie de moyens stylistiques, servis par une écriture minimaliste, l'atmosphère oppressante de l'Occupation parisienne et la déréliction des êtres les plus faibles. Ingrid représente, seule, ce quartier coupé du reste de la ville et du monde des vivants. Son statut de juive semi-clandestine, qui choisit de transgresser la règle de l'oppresseur, et d'échapper au sort fatal qui attendra son père – figuré par la mort symbolique du périmètre soumis au couvre-feu, et partant plongé dans l'obscurité – donne toute sa portée à l'épisode[2]. Il convient de noter que ce dernier roman fut écrit en 1989, après

---

[1] *Voyage de noces*, p. 125-27.
[2] L'errance d'Ingrid rejoint les parcours nocturnes d'un autre personnage clandestin et marginal, replié aux côtés des êtres les plus redoutables, à savoir le Swing Troubadour de *La Ronde de nuit*.

que Modiano eut été bouleversé par la lecture d'un entrefilet, paru en son temps dans *Paris-Soir*, le 31 décembre 1941 :

> Paris
> On recherche une jeune fille, Dora Bruder, 15 ans, 1 m 55, visage ovale, yeux gris marron, manteau sport gris, pull-over bordeaux, jupe et chapeau bleu marine, chaussures sport marron. Adresser toutes indications à M. et Mme Bruder, 41 boulevard Ornano, Paris[1].

Pendant plusieurs mois, le romancier tentera de reconstituer la vie ainsi que la personnalité de la jeune juive, qu'il livrera près d'une décennie plus tard dans le récit éponyme ; en effet, Dora Bruder incarne, à ses yeux, la figure de la suppliciée, paradigme de la jeunesse broyée par la machine totalitaire. D'autre part, son parcours lui semble recouper certains aspects de la biographie de son père, voire de sa propre adolescence parisienne. Parvenant difficilement à fondre tous ces éléments dans une seule unité narrative, l'écrivain se consacrera au seul récit fictif de *Voyage de noces*, dont l'héroïne renvoie directement à Dora :

> Il me semblait que je ne parviendrais jamais à retrouver la moindre trace de Dora Bruder. Alors le manque que j'éprouvais m'a poussé à l'écriture d'un roman, *Voyage de noces*, un moyen comme un autre pour continuer à concentrer mon attention sur Dora Bruder, et peut-être, me disais-je, pour élucider ou deviner quelque chose d'elle, un lieu où elle était passée, un détail de sa vie [...].
> Je pensais, en écrivant ce roman, à certaines femmes que j'avais connues dans les années soixante [...]. Je me rends compte aujourd'hui qu'il m'a fallu deux cents pages pour capter, inconsciemment, un vague reflet de la réalité[2].

---

[1] *Dora Bruder*, p. 9.
[2] *Ibid.*, p. 55-56.

Le texte de 1997 renonce aux principes formels du roman pour présenter une sorte de rapport d'investigation[1], qui voit l'écrivain Modiano inventorier les lieux et recomposer les événements avec une exactitude dévouée à l'expression de sa douleur. Dès lors, la fiction paraît dérisoire face à l'horreur, que le romancier avait tenté de transcender par la provocation farcesque des premiers écrits.

Les formes de la Collaboration

La confrontation renouvelée avec l'angoisse primitive, démultipliée parce que recréée et vécue sur le seul mode de l'imaginaire, constitue un des enjeux fondamentaux de l'œuvre de Patrick Modiano. Il est ainsi loisible de discerner, dans le double mouvement d'acceptation et de déni de l'identité juive, le motif romanesque essentiel des romans de la trilogie de l'Occupation et de *Lacombe Lucien*. Chaque protagoniste se trouve confronté à un choix impossible à effectuer : la reconnaissance de la judéité, qui délivre une identité ainsi qu'un certain enracinement dans une histoire collective, mais conduit à une mort inéluctable – eu égard au climat des années d'Occupation – ou le pacte avec l'ennemi. Cette dernière solution offre une sécurité, toute provisoire, mais prive l'individu d'un statut défini, susceptible de le situer dans l'espace et le temps.

Ce dilemme constant renvoie bien évidemment à l'itinéraire du père de l'écrivain, Albert Modiano, dont les cinq années de guerre ont rejeté l'existence dans une zone indistincte, proche du « non-être » ; composant avec la clandestinité et les tractations commerciales, celui-ci se condamnait à une réclusion dans un royaume des limbes, qui

---

[1] Modiano s'efforce de comprendre et de démonter les mécanismes de la répression antisémite à Paris. Le récit s'apparente en cela à un dossier de police, riche en informations présentées de la façon la plus brute. L'écrivain détaille les procédures d'arrestation, le fonctionnement de l'organe représentatif des institutions juives, l'UGIF, ou énumère les *curriculum vitae* des jeunes filles internées en même temps que Dora à la prison des Tourelles – précautions historiques absentes des premiers textes, où la personnalité des héros primait le témoignage.

accueillait toutes les figures de la marginalité, refusant, elles aussi, de trancher la question de la survie ou de l'identité.

Les trois premières œuvres romanesques de Modiano, ainsi que la pièce et le scénario, restituent l'atmosphère des milieux interlopes de la Collaboration mondaine et économique, avec une outrance et une démesure assumées, qui, paradoxalement, ne servent que mieux la peinture de l'Occupation. Malgré des apparences trompeuses, l'écrivain a effectué un méticuleux travail de documentation, et ne laisse que peu de fois à son imagination le soin de recomposer, à son gré, l'ambiance délétère des sphères et des réseaux associés à la Gestapo ou au Reich. Le romancier pourrait faire siens les propos de Swing Troubadour, qui justifie de la sorte ses comptes rendus : « Je rapporte ce que j'ai vu, ce que j'ai vécu. Sans aucune fioriture. Je n'invente rien. Toutes les personnes dont je parle ont existé. Je pousse même la rigueur jusqu'à les désigner sous leurs véritables noms[1]. » En effet, le jeune écrivain suscite l'admiration de la critique, dès la parution de ses deux premiers ouvrages, pour sa connaissance stupéfiante de la « petite histoire » des faits et méfaits des acteurs de la Collaboration[2].

Afin d'apprécier toute la portée de la reconstitution romanesque du Paris des années sombres, nous nous attacherons, tout d'abord, à la recension et à l'étude des visages convoqués dans les romans. Ces personnages semblent peu dissociables des lieux qu'ils hantent, et auxquels ils communiquent leur présence. Le portrait original d'une ville

---

[1] *La Ronde de nuit*, p. 131. On verra ultérieurement que cette dernière sentence ne peut caractériser de façon pertinente le projet romanesque de Modiano ; celui-ci se contente d'allusions à des personnes ayant réellement existé, modifie les patronymes ou change les attributions ou activités, et ce afin d'éviter les poursuites judiciaires – *La Ronde de nuit* fut publiée moins de vingt-cinq ans après la capitulation de l'Allemagne.

[2] Bernard Pivot écrit ainsi dans *Le Figaro littéraire* du 24 avril 1968, au moment de la parution de *La Place de l'Étoile* : « Patrick Modiano a lu tous les témoignages sur l'Occupation […]. Il va hanter le siège de la Gestapo, rue Lauriston ; attiré par l'horreur, fasciné par le cauchemar qu'il a chaque fois la sensation de revivre, il se rend au 93 de la rue Lauriston comme s'il retournait sur les lieux de son propre crime, étant l'assassin et sa victime, la Gestapo et tout le peuple juif. »

livrée à la rapine et aux exactions, légitimées et approuvées par le pouvoir, occupe une place prépondérante dans les œuvres de la trilogie.

Deux formes particulières de Collaboration sont à distinguer dans les quatre premiers textes de Modiano. On séparera, en effet, le partenariat avec l'ennemi, source d'enrichissement personnel et sans réelle préoccupation idéologique, d'une politique de collaboration articulée autour d'une certaine idée de la France. Celle-ci est représentée par le premier et le quatrième ouvrage, qui encadrent les deux autres aspects, évoqués dans *La Ronde de nuit* et *Les Boulevards de ceinture*. Cette vue d'ensemble permettra de mieux apprécier le traitement romanesque de cette époque. En effet, pour Modiano, elle constitue le nadir de l'histoire française, et a permis de donner libre cours aux plus déplorables aspects de l'espèce humaine. Objet d'un court chapitre du premier roman de Modiano et thème exclusif du scénario qu'il cosigne avec Louis Malle, l'idée d'un rapprochement politique avec l'Allemagne constitue un premier volet de la coopération souhaitée par le Reich.

On distinguera, en premier lieu, les sectateurs de l'idéologie nazie, représentés dans *La Place de l'Étoile* – intellectuels et hommes politiques, réels ou fictifs – des exécuteurs des basses œuvres de la Gestapo, auxquels Lucien vient s'agréger. Ces deux composantes paraissent toutefois, à des niveaux certes totalement différents, l'illustration d'un relais idéologique identique – celui dont ont pu bénéficier les forces allemandes.

LA PLACE DE L'ÉTOILE : PRECIS DE REACTION

Parcours moral et cognitif en quatre étapes, le premier roman de Modiano propose, dans son premier volet, un voyage dans les contrées du conservatisme français, sur fond de rêverie et de désir d'union à un pays hostile. Le narrateur passe ainsi des figures de la littérature traditionaliste aux notables xénophobes et antisémites, côtoyant également les hérauts de la politique de collaboration franco-allemande. L'ensemble vient constituer une sorte de cartographie de la France réactionnaire, une approche de l'âme d'un pays.

La provocation prend toute sa mesure lorsqu'elle se pare des déclarations antisémites du protagoniste-narrateur ; celui-ci espère ainsi trouver la clé de la mentalité française et rejoindre la communauté de cette nation. De fait, avec ce premier roman de la prématurité, tant dans sa conception que son écriture, Modiano entend inventorier les diverses strates et composantes de l'identité française, clamant, par la même occasion, son désarroi de juif apatride, tout à la fois désireux de trouver un enracinement et de rejeter les images que son pays d'adoption lui renvoie. Le pays qu'il dépeint ne semble pas avoir purgé ses démons de l'avant-guerre ; il se plaît encore à discerner une gangrène morale dans le « Juif », et stigmatise la figure de la République avec conviction.

Le jeune Modiano voit dans ce fonds idéologique, qui fut représenté par Boulanger et Pétain, non seulement la pérennité de valeurs dérivées d'un nationalisme caricatural, mais également la cause du comportement des Français durant la Seconde Guerre mondiale. On pensera ainsi à l'allocution prononcée par le professeur de lettres du protagoniste, Adrien Debigorre – dont le nom constitue déjà tout un programme –, figure totalisante des idéologues de Vichy :

> Ah ! Raphaël, j'aurais voulu que vous fussiez à Bordeaux, juin 1940 ! Le beau spectacle ! Imaginez ! un ballet effréné ! Des messieurs avec barbes et redingotes noires ! des universitaires ! Ce pauvre Léon Brunschwicg, par exemple ! des ministres de la RÉ-PU-BLIQUE, Mandel, Herriot, Reynaud, Blum ! Ils papotent ! Ils font de grands gestes ! [...]. La patronne de l'établissement, qui s'appelle Marianne, court de-ci de-là. Pousse de petits cris ! C'est une vieille putain ! LA GUEUSE[1] !

---

[1] *La Place de l'Étoile*, p. 60.

L'adhésion à la politique de rapprochement franco-allemand, prônée par le Reich, apparaît comme le corrélat naturel de l'idéologie antidreyfusarde et antiparlementariste, qui constitue un prolongement de la réaction contre-révolutionnaire de 1789. La peur de l'altérité ou la compromission avec toutes les forces de la réaction dessinent un parcours rectiligne qui commence au Moyen Âge, avec la maison Fougeire-Jusquiames, pour s'achever dans une officine de la Gestapo. Selon Modiano, le Reich n'a fait que ressusciter les vieux démons de la revanche auprès d'une catégorie sociale pétrifiée dans sa frustration politique depuis 1870, en décalage total avec l'évolution des mentalités et l'ouverture sur le monde extérieur. Le gouvernement de Vichy apparaît donc comme une réincarnation toute naturelle d'une France du XIXe siècle, désireuse de purger le pays d'un mondialisme nocif et corrupteur.

LACOMBE LUCIEN : LES EXECUTANTS

Peu d'idéologie politique chez les familiers de l'« Hôtel des Grottes », mais un minutieux travail de dénonciation et de torture, effectué dans tous ses aspects mécaniques, sans la moindre justification théorique. Loin des discours sur une France nouvelle et une Europe impériale, Tonin, Lucienne, Jean-Bernard ou Aubert représentent les relais indispensables de la politique nazie, à l'échelon le plus bas. Contrairement aux agioteurs du square Cimarosa et de la bande du « Clos-Foucré », qui voient dans les « événements » un moyen de donner libre cours à un hédonisme revendiqué, ces nervis de la Gestapo se livrent à leurs exactions avec l'assurance et la satisfaction d'une besogne justement accomplie. La lecture de *Mein Kampf* n'a pas constitué leur activité de prédilection avant-guerre, et leur conscience politique vaut ce que valent les lettres de délation qu'ils reçoivent.

Ils constituent des auxiliaires de choix d'un pouvoir incapable de se maintenir sans ces maillons, appliquant sur le terrain la politique décidée par le pouvoir central. Celui-ci leur confère, en retour, une importance sociale qu'ils n'auraient jamais osé escompter en temps de paix. Ainsi, les nouvelles prérogatives de Faure lui permettent d'exercer un micro-pouvoir, susceptible de lui donner l'avantage sur ses anciens supérieurs dans la hiérarchie sociale : « C'est drôle, je n'ai jamais aimé les instituteurs[1] », déclare-t-il peu avant de torturer Peyssac.

Bras armé d'un système politique qui, en offrant une légitimité à ses rouages inférieurs, s'assure de leur absolue dévotion, ces hommes et femmes paraissent condamnés au sort des janissaires de la « Police allemande », eu égard à leur total manque de sens historique. Trop maladroits pour composer avec les événements ou tenter de se ménager des amitiés utiles, ces mercenaires de l'ordre nouveau sont incapables de prendre la moindre distance avec leur action. Brusquement promus agents privilégiés de l'envahisseur, ces commis du nazisme, qui ont engrangé le bénéfice de quatre années de distinction sociale, perdraient tout brevet d'existence en n'exécutant pas à la lettre les instructions de leurs chefs, ou en remettant leur autorité en cause.

On verra comment le personnage de Lucien traduit cette tension entre la responsabilité esquivée et le nécessaire octroi d'une identité ; analyse que l'on aura peine à appliquer aux collaborateurs parisiens, représentants de la forme la plus dégradée de l'idéologie nazie.

LA COLLABORATION MAFIEUSE

La trilogie de l'Occupation offre peu d'occasions au lecteur de s'identifier aux personnages des récits. Ces derniers s'ingénient, en effet, à dessiner les contours d'un monde offert aux spéculateurs, tortionnaires et autres affidés de la collaboration allemande, créatures « surgi[e]s du black-out, d'une période de désespoir et de misère, par un phénomène

---

[1] *Ibid.*, p. 33.

analogue à celui de la génération spontanée[1] », dont il convient à présent de dresser la typologie – tout en sachant que les figures évoquées dans les romans empruntent leurs traits à chacune des spécialités susmentionnées, dans le vacillement général des valeurs présenté par l'écrivain. La mise en place de la politique d'entente commerciale entre la zone occupée et le Reich nécessite le recours à des intermédiaires et à la création d'officines, chargées de contrôler les importations et exportations de toutes les denrées et marchandises destinées à être écoulées au marché noir en France, ou fournies à l'Allemagne, en vertu des lois du marché.

Le romancier retient de cette collaboration d'État les aspects les plus choquants, sans jamais expliciter, de façon détaillée, les tenants et aboutissants des échanges financiers entre les différents organismes d'achats, nationaux ou transfrontaliers. Même si la documentation dont il dispose lui permet d'évoquer de façon suggestive, comme nous allons le voir, les silhouettes les plus représentatives de la collaboration économique souterraine, son but réside dans la reconstitution d'une atmosphère générale de corruption et de dégénérescence institutionnalisées, permettant au lecteur de saisir l'essence de l'abjection – au-delà de tout jugement de valeur – à l'aide du truchement des protagonistes.

QUELQUES COLLABORATEURS

La débâcle des armées françaises, le repli du gouvernement de Pétain à Vichy, et surtout la volonté du Reich de contrôler l'approvisionnement du pays, ont permis à un système d'économie parallèle de se mettre en place, et ce avec la bénédiction des forces d'Occupation. Dès la fin de 1940, un réseau efficace de centrales d'achat, de vente et de distribution voit le jour. Pascal Ory, dans l'ouvrage qu'il a consacré à cette

---

[1] *La Ronde de nuit*, p. 127.

période¹, présente ainsi le fonctionnement d'un de ces organismes commerciaux :

> Sur un capital à cent pour cent allemand, la participation d'autochtones passifs [...] tisse des liens, dont on devine la solidité, entre les milieux les plus louches de toutes les collaborations possibles [...] La grande mine à profits est représentée par les organismes d'achat officiels des trois armées allemandes, et plus encore par les bureaux d'achat plus ou moins avoués qui, sans s'encombrer de beaucoup de prétextes légaux, se conduisent en vraies officines de marché noir, avec filiales, sous-traitants et réseau de courtiers-rabatteurs-maîtres chanteurs².

On peut reconnaître dans la bande du 3 bis square Cimarosa les principaux composants de l'organisation décrite par Pascal Ory. Les figures majeures de l'officine dirigée par M. Philibert et le Khédive apparaissent déjà dans le cortège maléfique du dernier chapitre de *La Place de l'Étoile*, qui entraîne Raphaël dans son sillage, avant de le mettre à mort au son d'une chanson de Charles Trénet³. Jacques Delarue, dans son ouvrage *Crimes et trafics sous l'Occupation*⁴, rend compte de l'itinéraire de cet homme au premier chapitre :

> Otto [est le pseudonyme] d'Herman Brandl, né en 1896 en Bavière. Agent de l'Abwehr (Service de

---

¹ *Les Collaborateurs*, Paris, Seuil, 1976.
² *Les Collaborateurs*, p. 47. L'universitaire ajoute : « On comptera jusqu'à deux cents de ces bureaux clandestins, le plus connu étant le "bureau Otto" (trente officines satellites) de Brandl et Radecke, couvert par l'Abwehr et le SD. En vingt mois d'activités, Otto aurait ainsi acheté pour cinquante milliards de produits les plus variés, du cuir vert aux tableaux impressionnistes. » *Op.cit.*, p. 47-48.
³ « Ils furent aussitôt rejoints par un groupe de fêtards qui leur tapèrent allégrement sur l'épaule. [...]
– Je viens de vendre cinquante mille paires de chaussettes à la Wehrmacht, annonça Jean-Farouk de Mérode quand ils furent attablés.
– Et moi, dix mille pots de peinture à la Kriegsmarine, dit Otto da Silva.
– Savez-vous que les boy-scouts de Radio-Londres m'ont condamné à mort ? dit Paulo Hayakawa. Ils m'appellent le bootlegger nazi du cognac ! » *La Place de l'Étoile*, p. 141.
⁴ Paris, Fayard, 1968.

Renseignement allemand constituant une section du Grand État-Major de l'Armée), [...] il était en relation avec la Gestapo pour laquelle il travaille dès 1941 [...] contrairement à la séparation des services qui existait alors en Allemagne[1].

Il en précise le portrait psychologique dans la suite du livre :

[Il] achetait très cher des tableaux de maître, de l'argenterie ancienne, des tapisseries des Gobelins, des collections de timbres rares, des bijoux, de l'or, des devises étrangères « solides ». Grand amateur de femmes, de bonne chère et de grands vins, il fréquentait les meilleurs restaurants et les boîtes de nuit, y amenait ses collaborateurs, ses amis, et parfois aussi ses meilleurs fournisseurs[2].

Évoluant entre marché noir et œuvres de basse besogne pour les polices allemande et française, le groupe constitue le point d'ancrage du narrateur de *La Ronde de nuit*[3]. On se gardera toutefois de simplifications hâtives, qui tendraient à ne proposer qu'un modèle unique pour l'organisme ainsi présenté. De fait, Modiano semble avoir fusionné les identités et les lieux, pourtant soigneusement cloisonnés, afin de mettre en scène des figures archétypales, plutôt que de faire œuvre strictement historique, en présentant des personnages calqués sur leurs modèles exacts. Il est ainsi possible de proposer plusieurs pistes pour chacun des personnages. En premier lieu, la bande du square Cimarosa paraît constituer un mixte de celle de Berger, au 180, rue de la Pompe, et de celle de l'ancien inspecteur Pierre Bonny et de son affidé, Henri Chamberlin, dit

---

[1] *Op.cit.*, p. 28 et 39.
[2] *Op.cit.*, p. 93.
[3] « Les femmes sont beaucoup trop fardées. Les hommes portent des habits acides. Lionel de Zieff est vêtu d'un complet orange et d'une chemise à rayures ocre, Pols de Helder d'une veste jaune et d'un pantalon bleu ciel, le comte Baruzzi d'un smoking vert cendré. Quelques couples se forment. Costachesco danse avec Jean-Farouk de Méthode, Gaëtan de Lussatz avec Odicharvi, Simone Bouquereau avec Irène de Tranzé. » *La Ronde de nuit*, p. 14.

« Lafont », au 93 de la rue Lauriston[1]. Celui-là constitue presque indiscutablement le modèle direct de Philibert, honoré par le Khédive de « premier flic de France » – empruntant les propos du ministre Chéron qui, au début des années trente, avait présenté ainsi cet inspecteur principal, révoqué peu après, à la suite du scandale de l'affaire Stavisky[2]. Philibert est le jouet de son acolyte, qui clame sa soif de respectabilité, et dont les exactions paraissent orientées dans le seul but d'imposer ses *desiderata* aux puissants – auxquels il rend de grands services, et qui seront plus tard, du moins l'espère-t-il, ses obligés. Afin de mieux restituer la part que l'atmosphère évoquée dans les romans de Patrick Modiano doit à la réalité, il semble opportun de s'attarder sur ces deux officines – qui ont marqué de leur noire empreinte les années d'Occupation.

Le groupe Berger.

Né en Saxe en 1911, Friedrich Berger avait été recruté par l'Abwehr en 1933 et infiltré en France comme émigrant, avec mission de s'engager dans la Légion étrangère – ce qu'il fit en 1934. Réformé trois ans plus tard, il revient en Allemagne et se trouve chargé, après l'armistice, de retourner

---

[1] On peut également songer au groupe d'individus gravitant autour d'un certain Bernard, dont les bureaux furent situés rue Pétrarque avant de connaître une relative extension à Neuilly. Ses missions consistaient à rechercher les immeubles susceptibles d'être réquisitionnés, et de surveiller les locaux du bureau Otto, ainsi que les transports de fonds, (auxquels s'associait un certain Serge de Lenz). Venaient s'y ajouter la récupération de l'or et des devises étrangères (en particulier les métaux fins cachés chez les particuliers) et la recherche des opposants (résistants ou réfractaires au STO). Bernard avait emprunté à Masuy le système de la baignoire dont il se flattait d'être l'inventeur.
[2] Jacques Benoist-Méchin note à son sujet, à la page 400 du tome II de *À l'épreuve du temps*, Paris, Plon, 1980 : « En 1933, Robert Bony [sic], alors inspecteur de la Sûreté, avait été chargé par le parquet d'enquêter sur l'affaire Stavisky. Il avait si bien maquillé en suicide l'assassinat du conseiller Prince que M. Henri Chéron, alors Garde des Sceaux, l'avait publiquement félicité de son zèle. Ce scandale avait abouti à la fusillade de la place de la Concorde le 6 février 1934. »

en France, afin de s'infiltrer près du Deuxième bureau français, à Vichy. Démasqué presque immédiatement, puis condamné à mort, il est transféré à la prison d'Oran. Réclamé par les Allemands, il leur est rendu le 31 mai 1942. À cette époque, il s'installe à Paris et vit de marché noir, emménageant le 17 avril 1944 au 180, rue de la Pompe, avec l'équipe de rabatteurs qu'il avait constituée. Jacques Delarue, dans un numéro d'*Historia* consacré à la Gestapo[1], donne la fiche signalétique des mercenaires de Berger, sur un mode proche de la liste de *La Ronde de nuit* :

> Il y avait là le « trio Guicciardi » père et fils, Italiens naturalisés ; un Iranien, Rachid Zulgadar, ancien chauffeur de taxi que sa force herculéenne avait fait surnommer « King-Kong » et qui devint le spécialiste de la baignoire ; Théo Leclerc, ancien tourneur chez Citroën, parti volontairement en Allemagne ; Zimmer, dit « Le Prof », Luxembourgeois et pianiste amateur de talent ; un Caucasien, Tcherbinia, dit « Manu » ; Fouchet dit « Raoul le Tatoué » ; Roger dit « Cri-Cri » ; Favriot, spécialiste des tortures infligées aux femmes, et quelques autres[2].

La disposition des pièces de l'appartement, la concomitance des fêtes et des actes de torture et, de façon générale, l'ambiance du 180, rue de la Pompe semblent avoir inspiré Modiano pour son évocation du square Cimarosa :

> Les personnes arrêtées étaient amenées dans le grand salon violet. [...] on les faisait déshabiller complètement. [...] Puis, on les traînait à la salle de bains et on les plongeait dans l'eau glacée. King-Kong leur maintenait la tête dans l'eau jusqu'à suffocation. On les frappait à coups de nerf de bœuf, on leur entaillait la plante des pieds et on salait les coupures, on les faisait marcher pieds nus sur des pointes de tapissier [...].
> Au milieu de ces scènes d'horreur, on continuait à trafiquer [...]. Zimmer jouait du piano pendant que

---

[1] « La Gestapo en France », *Historia*, hors-série n° 26, vol. I, 1972.
[2] *Op. cit.*, p. 60-61.

Kley, interprète allemand de Berger, faisait une conférence sur les beautés de la Collaboration[1].

Au moment de la libération de Paris, les satellites de Berger prirent la route de l'Est. Berger fut arrêté à Milan le 7 mai 1945, par les Anglais. Il parvint à s'échapper lors d'un transfert, en février 1947, fut condamné à mort par contumace, mais ne fut jamais arrêté. Il mourut d'une maladie du foie, le 10 février 1960, à Munich.

« Monsieur Henri ».

Né en 1902, Henri Chamberlin connaît une enfance et une adolescence tumultueuse, avant d'être condamné pour proxénétisme, au début des années vingt. Il semble suspendre ses activités au moment de son mariage et de la naissance de ses enfants, mais la fuite de son épouse, qui disparaît brutalement avec la caisse du magasin qui l'employait, le conduit à changer son nom pour celui de Lafont, et à connaître de nouveau la clandestinité[2]. Emprisonné pour insoumission en

---

[1] J. Delarue, *ibid.*
[2] La confession que le Khédive livre à Swing Troubadour, lorsqu'il lui relate les heurs et malheurs de son existence, s'inspire très largement de la biographie de Lafont :
« Enfant, à la colonie pénitentiaire d'Eysses. Puis au bat' d'Af' et à la prison de Fresnes. Désignant le portrait de Monsieur de Bel-Respiro, il m'énumérait toutes les médailles que l'on pouvait voir sur la poitrine de cet homme. "Il suffira de remplacer sa tête par la mienne. Trouvez-moi un peintre habile. À partir d'aujourd'hui, je m'appelle Henri de Bel-Respiro". Il répétait, émerveillé : "Monsieur le Préfet de police Henri de Bel-Respiro." » , *La Ronde de nuit*, p. 134-135. Ce désir de reconnaissance, qui fournit une parfaite illustration de complexe d'infériorité sublimé en désir d'asservissement, s'inspire directement des déclarations du personnage, citées par Fabrice Laroche dans son article : « Henri Lafont, pape de la Gestapo française », *Historia*, numéro cité, p. 67 : « Tu vois, petit, confie-t-il à l'un de ses adjoints, ce qui compte dans l'existence, ce n'est pas ce que l'on fait, c'est le rang que l'on occupe. Honnête ou pas, si tu es au bas de l'échelle, personne ne s'intéresse à toi. » On notera la suprême revanche qui consiste, pour Normand, l'orphelin, à imposer son pouvoir à une société dont il a éprouvé toute la violence. Personnage important d'un monde parallèle qui tend à dicter ses lois au reste du pays, il occupe la place laissée vacante par les

mai 1940, il est transféré au camp de Cépoy, duquel il parvient à s'évader. Deux Allemands de l'Abwehr l'accompagnent, qui lui proposent la gestion d'un « bureau d'achat », rue Tiquetonne. Il opère, à cette époque, sous les faux noms de Georges Rigaud et de Chaise, avant d'opter définitivement pour celui de Lafont, jusqu'en 1944.

> Il achète, pour le compte de la Wehrmacht, des produits [...] de toutes sortes. [...] Très vite, il attire l'attention de deux personnages qui font partie du « Tout-Paris germanique » [...] Lafont, qui a très vite vu le parti qu'il pouvait tirer de ses fréquentations, joue les utilités. [...]
> En l'espace de quelques semaines, le magasin de la rue Tiquetonne devient trop étroit [...]. C'est [enfin] l'installation dans un grand immeuble cossu, où l'ancien petit voyou des Halles va prendre ses aises. Une adresse qui va devenir légendaire : 93, rue Lauriston[1].

Dans *La Place de l'Étoile*, l'immeuble du square Cimarosa représente une bonne synthèse des deux « bureaux » de Berger et Lafont, même si les parentés avec le 93 de la rue Lauriston sont les plus nombreuses. Ces officines associaient le commerce à la politique, ainsi que toutes les entreprises susceptibles de permettre de fructueuses plus-values. L'aspect caricatural et outré du roman n'apparaît guère comme une enflure de style, et semble constituer un bon témoignage de la vie quotidienne des caudataires du nazisme, au moment de la Collaboration triomphante – époque où les valeurs et la morale se trouvaient sacrifiées au Moloch du Grand Reich :

> Mes patrons étaient [...] un ancien repris de justice [...] et un inspecteur principal révoqué. [...] À partir d'aujourd'hui notre « agence » va connaître – paraît-il –

---

dignitaires de l'ancien ordre – à savoir les ors et lambris de l'hôtel particulier du square Cimarosa.
Pour la petite histoire, on notera que le souhait du Khédive-Lafont se voit rapidement réalisé, puisque ce dernier se voit présenter Bonny par le préfet de police Amédée Bussière, qu'il appelle par son prénom et méprise ouvertement.

[1] Article cité, p. 67.

une extension considérable. [...] Le « Service du square Cimarosa » cumulera deux fonctions : celles d'un organisme policier et d'un « bureau d'achat » stockant les articles et matières premières introuvables depuis quelque temps. [...] Affairistes, morphinomanes, charlatans, demi-mondaines comme on en voit grouiller aux « époques troubles ». [...] Il semblait même que [...] Henri Normand, dictât ses volontés au cabinet du préfet de police et au parquet de la Seine[1].

Assuré d'une impunité totale, Lafont va multiplier, jusqu'à l'été 1944, les arrestations et tortures, assisté dans cette tâche par un groupe d'individus, le plus souvent d'anciens « droits communs », totalement acquis à sa personne. Nous consacrerons ultérieurement un développement aux différentes recrues du Khédive-Lafont. Auparavant, il paraît intéressant d'évoquer en détail la vie du 93, rue Lauriston, avant de montrer comment cette atmosphère a pu être restituée dans le deuxième ouvrage de Modiano.

La « bande de Lafont » exerçait essentiellement ses activités dans les domaines du marché noir et de la répression des trafiquants, susceptibles de menacer son empire, ou des résistants. Les victimes étaient torturées rue Lauriston, ou le plus souvent sur les lieux mêmes de leur arrestation. Dans son *Histoire de la Gestapo*, citée par Fabrice Laroche, Jacques Delarue détaille les souffrances et les humiliations que les mercenaires de Lafont infligeaient à leurs victimes :

> Les procédés employés étaient toujours les mêmes. Pour les faire parler, on obligeait les personnes interrogées à s'agenouiller sur une règle triangulaire pendant qu'un tortionnaire montait sur leurs épaules ; on les suspendait par les bras ramenés en arrière, jusqu'à l'évanouissement. [...]
> Le supplice de la baignoire d'eau glacée consistait à plonger le patient, menottes aux mains ramenées dans le dos, et à lui maintenir la tête sous l'eau jusqu'à suffocation presque complète. On le ramenait à la

---

[1] *La Ronde de nuit*, p. 89-90, 107, 112 et 113.

surface en le tirant par les cheveux ; s'il refusait de parler, on le replongeait immédiatement dans l'eau[1].

Ces exactions ne perturbaient en rien les activités mondaines de Lafont, dont le salon était l'un des plus recherché de Paris. Selon Georges Prade, ancien vice-président du Conseil municipal de Paris et ancien administrateur de *Paris-Soir*, le 93, rue Lauriston était

> une adresse très courue, un genre de talisman que les initiés se transmettaient de bouche à oreille. On voyait là des quémandeurs d'*Ausweis* et de permis de circulation, des parents et amis de prisonniers, des candidats à l'exemption du STO, des contrevenants du marché noir [...]. Le Tout-Paris intriguait pour s'assurer un tour de faveur. Les gardes du corps, sentinelles grasseyantes, devenaient des personnalités. C'était une garantie de pouvoir tutoyer Lulu, Eddy, Michel, Gaby, et, grâce à leur complicité, de pouvoir grimper quatre à quatre, sans trop attendre, l'escalier qui menait au bureau du Patron[2].

De nombreuses personnalités de l'Occupation composent un cercle d'habitués, dont Patrick Modiano s'inspire pour illustrer sa galerie de convives au square Cimarosa : le préfet de police Bussière, dont il a déjà été question, Jean Luchaire, directeur des *Nouveaux Temps* et officieux patron de la presse parisienne[3], Lionel de Wiet, l'actrice Yvette Lebon et sa fille, le comte Grafkreuz, le baron von Tauber, le pseudo-prophète bulgare Popov – que Modiano met en scène sous les traits du mage Ivanoff –, ainsi qu'un

---

[1] Article cité, p. 71.
[2] *Ibid.*, p. 73.
[3] Dans une lettre adressée à Thierry Laurent, et publiée en tête de l'édition de sa thèse, Patrick Modiano fait état de ses sentiments à l'égard de ce personnage : « [Son] aventure n'avait rien à voir avec celle d'un Rebatet ou d'un Brasillach. Luchaire venait de la gauche (destins contradictoires : Luchaire avait créé une revue avant la guerre, *Notre Temps*, où écrivaient ses amis Pierre Brossolette, Jean Prévost et Mendès-France), il n'était absolument pas antisémite, du joueur qui mise tout sur une mauvaise carte... [...] Luchaire me semble tout à fait représentatif d'une certaine atmosphère et d'un certain monde troubles du Paris de l'Occupation. »

certain nombre d'hommes de lettres, de médecins, de banquiers, d'administrateurs et d'artistes.

Lafont continuera ses activités jusqu'à la Libération de Paris, avant d'être dénoncé par Joanovici, et fusillé le 26 décembre 1944. Selon Fabrice Laroche, ses dernières paroles furent les suivantes :

> Se moquant de Bonny, qui se traîne devant le peloton d'exécution, Lafont, très détendu, fait des plaisanteries et des jeux de mots. [...] Il s'adresse à son avocate, maître Drieu, qui plaide pour lui au côté de maître Floriot :
> – Je ne regrette rien, madame. Quatre années au milieu des orchidées, des dahlias et des Bentley, ça se paie ! J'ai vécu dix fois plus vite, voilà tout. Dites à mon fils qu'il ne faut jamais fréquenter les « caves ». Qu'il soit un homme, comme son père[1].

Le cynisme du personnage annonce celui des amis de Murraille évoquant leurs *ultima verba* lors du mariage de sa nièce. L'esprit de jouissance et la frivolité hédoniste, qui annihilent toute idée de responsabilité, sont les autres caractéristiques qui viennent compléter la typologie du « collaborateur mondain ».

« Un rastaquouérisme à relents de trahisons et d'assassinats ».

L'entourage immédiat des acteurs principaux du deuxième roman se compose de « rastas, avorteurs, chevaliers d'industrie, journalistes véreux, avocats et comptables marrons[2]. » L'écrivain réunit en un lieu unique un exemple caractéristique de chaque figure associée par l'imaginaire collectif aux milieux troubles, mêlant, à cette fin, la pure fantaisie aux exactes qualités des personnages. Ces derniers sont passés trois fois en revue par le narrateur au cours du récit.

---

[1] Article cité, p. 79.
[2] *La Ronde de nuit*, p. 88.

Si cette liste s'enrichit de quelques individus nouveaux lors de chaque évocation, le noyau du 3 bis square Cimarosa ne semble guère varier, présentant régulièrement les mêmes affairistes et agioteurs, que le cerveau troublé de Swing Troubadour convoque dans l'incessant tumulte d'une sarabande nocturne :

> Rictus du baron de Lussatz ; regard cruel d'Odicharvi ; la perfidie des frères Chapochnikoff ; Frau Sultana faisant saillir la veine de son bras gauche à l'aide d'une courroie et s'injectant de l'héroïne ; Zieff, sa vulgarité, son chronomètre en or, ses mains grasses couvertes de bagues ; Ivanoff et ses séances de paneurythmie sexuélo-divine ; Costachesco, Jean-Farouk de Méthode, Rachid von Rosenheim parlant de leurs faillites frauduleuses ; et la cohorte des gangsters que le Khédive recrutait en qualité d'hommes de main : Armand le fou, Jo Reocreux, Tony Breton, Vital-Léca, Robert le Pâle, Gouari, Danos, Codébo[1].

De façon générale, Modiano emprunte largement la composante de ce groupe au cercle des individus qui gravitaient non seulement autour de Lafont, mais également, comme nous allons le voir, de Joseph Joanovici et de Michel Szolnikoff. Le point de vue unique, qui privilégie frénésie et dérèglement de la raison, symboles du désordre de l'époque, donne un caractère hallucinatoire à cette restitution, que le bouleversement mental du protagoniste vient renforcer[2]. La recension des figures originelles dessine les contours d'un monde à peine plus rationnel.

Juif russe, Michel Szolnikoff, *alias* « Monsieur Michel » fournit le patronyme et l'activité des frères Chapochnikoff (l'orthographe hésite d'ailleurs constamment entre cette dernière désinence francisée et le *Chapochnikov* aux résonances slaves davantage marquées). Ces Dioscures du courtage, sans « fonction bien définie et virevolt[ant] de-ci de-

---

[1] *Ibid.*, p. 96.
[2] « J'écoutais, j'observais tous ces forcenés. Leurs visages, sous les lustres, dégoulinaient de sueur. Leur débit s'accélérait. Ristournes... courtages... commissions, stocks... wagons... marges bénéficiaires... » *Ibid.*, p. 130.

là[1] » voient leur raison sociale calquée sur celle de leur modèle historique.

> [Celui-ci] est l'un des fournisseurs attitrés de Brandl. Il traite parfois directement avec la Kriegsmarine, et c'est ainsi qu'il est présenté, en mars 1941, par le Hauptmann Klauss à une Allemande, réfugiée en France depuis près de dix ans. Szolnikoff l'épouse, et fait d'Elfrieda, rebaptisée Hélène, la femme la plus riche et la plus élégante de Paris [...]. Brandl, Füchs et Lüttcher comptent parmi les habitués[2].

De fait, Szolnikoff constitue l'une des figures les plus marquantes de la Collaboration. Protégé par le *Hauptsturmführer* SS Fritz Engelke, envoyé spécial du WVHA[3], il parvient à amasser une fortune colossale en travaillant, entre autres, pour le service Otto, jusqu'à la fermeture des bureaux d'achats au début de 1943. Après quelques démêlés avec les autorités allemandes, eu égard aux origines juives de Michel Szkolnikoff, le couple se réfugie en Espagne. Le trafiquant y trouve la mort le 20 juin 1945, dans des circonstances mystérieuses.

Il est également possible de voir dans le patronyme *Chapochnikov* une réminiscence lointaine du nom de la deuxième épouse de Lafont, Natacha Kolnikov, une

> comtesse russe [qui] n'a pas encore atteint la retraite. Fort belle, elle a fait, avant-guerre, un peu de cinéma avant de séduire un riche industriel brésilien. Revenue à Paris en 1941, elle tombe sous le charme de « Monsieur Henri ». Mais celui-ci est volage. Après quelques mois de liaison, il décide de rompre avec cet être envahissant pour l'abandonner à son chauffeur. La troisième amie de Lafont, Jeanne-Claire-Marguerite d'Audengen, n'est pas sa maîtresse, bien qu'elle se soit

---

[1] *Ibid.*, p. 128.
[2] Hervé Le Boterf, *La Vie parisienne sous l'Occupation*, Paris, France-Empire, 1974.
[3] *Wirtschaftsverwaltungshauptamt* : Service central de l'Administration économique.

livrée avec le mage Popov[1] et quelques autres personnes à de curieuses séances « sexuélo-divines »[2].

Le nom « Jean-Farouk de Méthode » revient souvent dans le roman, et désigne Rudy de Mérode, pseudonyme de Frédéric Martin, né en 1905 en Moselle, ancien entrepreneur de travaux publics à Metz – il avait également adopté les noms de Rudi von Mérode ou Rudi von Montaigne. Travaillant à la construction de la ligne Maginot, il avait livré des plans de défense aux Allemands, et fut à ce titre repéré par « Otto », qui l'engagea à la fin de 1940. Il remplissait quatre fonctions principales au sein de ce bureau : réquisitionner les immeubles vides, surveiller les transports de fonds, récupérer l'or et les devises étrangères, et questionner les individus suspects d'activités anti-allemandes. Intéressé par le marché noir, il quitta en mars 1941 l'immeuble de la rue Pétrarque où il résidait avec deux associés, Van Houten et Bernard, pour s'installer avec ces derniers dans un hôtel particulier à Neuilly. Le climat y était assez proche des soirées décrites par Modiano : des commerçants venaient traiter des affaires dans des pièces où se trouvaient des hommes enchaînés, au visage marqué de coups, dont on avait abandonné l'interrogatoire pour conclure une transaction importante. En 1943, chargé d'installer en Espagne un réseau radio clandestin, il installa son quartier général à Saint-Jean de Luz, d'où il put gagner Madrid, dès que la situation politique changea en France. Il y fut condamné à mort par contumace, le 18 novembre 1945, mais ne fut jamais arrêté. À la fin de la guerre, il s'installe de façon permanente à Madrid, et fréquente les bars de la *Gran Via*, sous le nom de « prince de Mérode ». Installé dans un appartement de la *Residencia Rio*, il fréquente d'anciens nazis et collaborateurs, continuant ses activités commerciales. En 1953, il quitte Madrid pour s'installer dans un village, à une soixantaine de kilomètres au nord, où il fait racheter, par un

---

[1] « Ivanoff », dans *La Ronde de nuit*.
[2] *Ibid.*, p. 35. Cette dernière information est à mettre en relation avec les « séances de paneurythmie sexuélo-divine » organisées par le « mage » précédemment cité.

prête-nom, une briqueterie-tuilerie. Les informations sur Frédéric Martin cessent totalement à partir de ce moment.

Il ne semble pas exagéré de voir dans ce personnage l'archétype des agioteurs de l'Occupation présentés dans la trilogie romanesque – et pour Modiano l'un des hommes pour lesquels son père dut travailler pendant la guerre –, même si l'écrivain n'associe pas à son nom les activités pour lesquelles il fut connu pendant la période : « [...] propriétaire du cirque d'automne et de "L'Heure mauve", proxénète, interdit de séjour dans tout le Commonwealth » – pour reprendre les termes de la fiche signalétique présentée dans *La Ronde de nuit*. L'invention littéraire se joue des simples détails historiques, afin de rêver sur l'onomastique, et associer au patronyme des activités bien plus romanesques que la fréquentation des sièges sociaux.

Dernier personnage d'envergure cité dans *La Place de l'Étoile*[1], Joseph Joanovici, dit « Monsieur Joseph », a sa place aux côtés des ténors de la Collaboration du square Cimarosa, pour lesquels il a, sans nul doute, prêté son histoire[2]. Ce juif né en Bessarabie en 1902, citoyen soviétique d'adoption, arrive à Paris en 1921. Il crée avant-guerre une prospère société qui fait de lui le ferrailleur le plus important de la région parisienne. Hermann Brandl, auquel il est présenté par son ami Krasnik, discerne rapidement chez cet ancien chiffonnier des aptitudes exceptionnelles pour le négoce. « Monsieur Joseph » touche, à cette époque, un franc par kilo de métaux non ferreux procuré à l'ennemi – mais doit rétrocéder discrètement la moitié de cette commission.

Il étend son entreprise à tous les métaux neufs et à l'outillage, devenant le plus important fournisseur d'Otto dans

---

[1] « Je me sentis plus à l'aise en compagnie de Pierre Bonny, d'Henri Chamberlin-Lafont et de leurs acolytes. Et puis je retrouvai, rue Lauriston, mon professeur de morale, Joseph Joanovici. » *La Place de l'Étoile*, p. 117.

[2] Son nom apparaît, de façon plaisante, au milieu d'une liste d'ouvrages qui ont pour thème commun la dissimulation et la duplicité dans l'Histoire : « Quelques livres : *Anthologie des traîtres, d'Alcibiade au capitaine Dreyfus, Joanovici tel qu'il fut, Les Mystères du chevalier d'Éon, Frégoli, l'homme de nulle part*, m'éclairèrent sur mon compte. » *La Ronde de nuit*, p. 109.

ce secteur, livrant selon les estimations du « service des confiscations des profits illicites » les trois quarts, et peut-être les quatre-cinquièmes de ces approvisionnements. Au cours du premier semestre 1942, il réussit à se procurer dix-huit mille tonnes de cuivre, d'aluminium et d'étain. Il peut ainsi mener grande vie dans son appartement somptueux du boulevard Malesherbes, dans lequel il accueille les fonctionnaires allemands chargés des questions économiques – ce qui ne l'empêchait pas de transporter ses cent vingt millions de courtage mensuels, prélevés dans les bureaux d'achats allemands, dans de vieux sacs de pommes de terre. De fait, la force – et la quasi-impunité – de Joanovici proviennent de la profonde sagacité du personnage, qui cultive les amitiés dans les deux camps opposés :

> En 1943-1944, sa puissance est considérable. Est-il passé entièrement du côté de la Gestapo ? [...] Répondre affirmativement serait méconnaître le bonhomme. Ce n'est sans doute pas par hasard que Monsieur Joseph finance largement l'une des organisations de Résistance [...]. Il remet les fonds de la main à la main au commissaire André Fournet, chef en titre de cette organisation, à l'inspecteur Piednoir [...] ou encore à Yves Bayet, dit « Bouchet », ancien commissaire de police à Nantes, mêlé aux affaires de la brigade de répression du communisme, mais fils d'Albert Bayet, alors président de la Fédération nationale de la presse clandestine[1].

Au moment de la Libération, Joanovici devient l'un des principaux bailleurs de fonds des organisations résistantes et de la presse « postclandestine ». Reçu et félicité par le préfet Luizet, il obtient un diplôme d'honneur de « combattant sans uniforme », signé du commissaire Fournet, d'« Honneur de la Police » et de Robert Lecourt, chef du mouvement « Résistance » et futur garde des Sceaux. Le 29 août 1944, il se rend quai de Gesvres pour dénoncer à l'inspecteur Morin (qu'il a tiré des mains de la Gestapo) ses deux anciens amis Bonny et

---

[1] André Brissaud : « Ce bon Monsieur Joseph », *Historia*, numéro cité, p. 105.

Lafont. Son existence s'annonce calme et prospère, l'enrichissement des années sombres paraissant miraculeusement oublié – le contrôleur principal des services du Contrôle économique, où se trouve un épais dossier sur les activités de Joanovici, n'est autre que le mari de la secrétaire du ferrailleur...

Toutefois, le 17 mars 1947, le ministre de l'Intérieur Depreux décide d'ouvrir une information contre le milliardaire, qui prend la fuite aussitôt. Réfugié dans un camp de « personnes déplacées », en Bavière, il est retrouvé huit mois plus tard. Le procès s'ouvre le 6 juillet 1949, et tourne très vite à la farce. Lacunaire, l'accusation laisse une large place aux témoins à décharge, et omet la plupart des faits. De fait, l'instruction cherche à dissimuler les relations de ce personnage encombrant avec les dignitaires de la IVe République balbutiante, minimisant, de façon systématique, les faits et méfaits du « bon Monsieur Joseph » :

> [Il est normal] de prêter [des] camions à [...] Bonny et Lafont pour que des Nord-Africains puissent traquer quelques maquisards du côté de Limoges. [...] Ces « détails » ne sont pas sérieusement discutés à l'audience. Le procureur Robert y fait allusion avec beaucoup de réticences, comme à des choses sans importance. Mieux, les « visites » de Monsieur Joseph à la Gestapo de l'avenue Foch ou de la rue Lauriston ne sont pas niées et mises au compte de « la courtoisie et du bon voisinage »[1].

La mascarade inspirera Marcel Aymé qui, dans *La Tête des autres*, représentée pour la première fois en février 1952, met en scène le représentant du Ministère public sous les traits du procureur Maillard. « Monsieur Joseph » devient Alessandrovici, homme d'affaires richissime qui dicte ses volontés à un gouvernement soumis et corrompu :

> Qu'est-ce qui m'a foutu des goinfres pareils, qu'ils sont toujours à sangloter dans mon gilet, ces cochons goitreux ! Vous savez ce que ça coûterait tout ce que vous me demandez ! [...] un milliard à la République

---

[1] *Ibid.*, p. 111.

poldave et la République, c'est moi ! Quand je pense à ce que j'ai déjà fait pour vous, chiens que vous êtes [...] ! Et vous voilà encore à vous plaindre et à réclamer. Le préfet, il veut être gouverneur, l'administrateur, il veut l'ambassade et le sous-directeur veut coller au cul de l'Excellence, la directrice de l'OHB devenir archiprésidente de l'OSTU[1].

Assigné à résidence pendant cinq ans à Mende, Joanovici continue sereinement ses activités. Il quitte la France en 1957 pour s'établir en Israël, d'où il sera extradé quelques années plus tard. Il s'éteint à Clichy, en 1965, « avant que soient réglés ses démêlés avec la Justice et l'Administration des Finances[2] ». Ce personnage est brièvement évoqué dans *Un héros très discret*, film de Jacques Audiard, réalisé en 1995. Il y apparaît au crépuscule de sa carrière de collaborateur, peu de jours avant son entrée dans la « Résistance ». À cette époque, son chiffre d'affaires était estimé à quatre milliards. Jacques Delarue note à ce propos : « [Ce nom] est demeuré chargé d'une valeur symbolique pour ceux qui ont vécu l'occupation de la France. On en a fait le synonyme de "trafiquant", bien qu'il ait été dépassé en cela par Szolnikoff[3] ».

Les capitaines d'industrie et nervis des services commerciaux allemands, que Modiano met en scène, empruntent tous leurs traits à ces figures presque légendaires, au caractère éminemment romanesque – eu égard à leur origine, leur enrichissement soudain et leur fin précipitée. Ainsi, les réceptions que donne le couple Szolnikoff, à cette époque, trouvent leur répondant parodique dans l'évocation des soirées au 3 bis square Cimarosa :

> Les habituels commensaux étaient tous des fournisseurs [...]. Trois frères corses, recherchés par le Parquet de Marseille pour diverses histoires louches [...], vendant un peu de tout ; une Alsacienne, « Joséphine », qui trustait les parfums dont les dames

---

[1] *La Tête des autres*, Livre de poche, p. 154-155.
[2] André Brissaud, *ibid.*
[3] Jacques Delarue, *op.cit.*, p. 88.

étaient friandes ; un Antillais qui vendait des gâteaux secs par tonnes et le gruyère par wagons [...]. Ajoutons à ces habitués, allemands et français, quelques étrangers « de marque », un marquis espagnol, membre de l'ambassade ; un personnage étrange, se disant Turc et attaché consulaire, quelques femmes aux nationalités variables, quelques hommes d'affaires, notaires et agents immobiliers[1].

En 1942, date la plus vraisemblable de l'action du roman, les gentilshommes de fortune paraissent au faîte de leur puissance, grâce à la *Schwerpunkt Aktion*, mentionnée au cours d'une conversation. Le terme désigne une campagne destinée à fournir des articles « sociaux » aux travailleurs allemands des usines d'armement. Lancée par Goering au début de 1942, elle avait pour but d'augmenter les achats du Reich en France[2], et s'acheva en novembre 1943. Compte tenu de la quantité impressionnante de commandes auxquelles l'entreprise donnait lieu, de nombreuses fortunes s'édifièrent rapidement :

– On a noté une hausse sur le wolfram, déclare Baruzzi. Je peux vous en procurer à des prix intéressants. Je suis en cheville avec Guy Max, du bureau d'achat de la rue Villejuif.
– Je croyais qu'il s'occupait uniquement de textiles, dit Monsieur Philibert [...]
– Que diriez-vous de 36 000 jeux de cartes que je vous livre dès demain matin ? Vous pourriez les revendre au prix fort. C'est le moment. Ils ont entamé la Schwerpunkt Aktion depuis le début du mois[3].

---

[1] Jacques Delarue, *op.cit.*, p. 99-100.
[2] « C'est l'organisation Munimin-Pimetex, désignée par le délégué du "plan de quatre ans", c'est-à-dire Hermann Goering, qui fut chargée d'acheter des pipes (plus de trente-cinq mille), des porte-cigarettes, des stylos (quarante-six mille), des crayons, des calepins, des peignes, près de trois cent cinquante mille miroirs, du savon à barbe, des lames de rasoir [...] et huit cent soixante-dix-sept mille jeux de cartes ». *Op.cit.*, p. 70. On ajoutera que cet inventaire « à la Prévert » trouve son écho dans la nomenclature des articles que s'engagent à fournir les agioteurs du square Cimarosa, dans *La Ronde de nuit*.
[3] *La Ronde de nuit*, p. 31.

Pour mémoire, le narrateur recense, à plusieurs reprises, le pedigree des sicaires du Khédive et de Monsieur Philibert, énumérant une suite d'activités où la caricature vient servir l'effet de réel. Cette nauséeuse galerie de portraits donne l'impression au lecteur que la lie de l'humanité est venue se déposer au 3 bis square Cimarosa. Nous renvoyons, pour cette étude, à la dernière des trois présentations des hommes de main du Khédive, de la page 126 à la page 129 de notre édition de référence.

On citera ainsi « Mickey de Voisins, la "soubrette", prostitué homosexuel », que l'on pourrait rapprocher de Guy de Voisins, ami intime de Corinne Luchaire, dont il va bientôt être question, « l'ex-commandant d'aviation Costantini », que Modiano désigne sous son véritable nom, familier de la Collaboration parisienne ou « Jean Le Houleux, journaliste, ancien trésorier du Club du Pavois et maître chanteur » ; le romancier associe deux occurrences distinctes, que nous allons tenter d'expliciter.

« Le Houleux » est le nom qu'il donne au caricaturiste de *C'est la vie* dans *Les Boulevards de ceinture*. Le « Cercle du grand pavois », fondé par Bertrand de Jouvenel et Suarez, constituait un satellite du comité France-Allemagne, fondé le 22 novembre 1935. Dirigée par Jean Lestandi de Villani, futur directeur de *Au pilori*, dont il a déjà été question, cette association se veut un relais entre la France et l'Allemagne hitlérienne. Pascal Ory[1] note à ce sujet :

> Au moment de la crise de Munich, son parti pris plus encore proallemand que pacifiste est devenu si flagrant que les activités s'interrompent moins du fait des autorités françaises que de la désaffection progressive de ceux de ses membres qui, tel Henri du Moulin, étaient restés fidèles aux valeurs du nationalisme français.

Les figures féminines « historiques » sont très présentes dans *La Ronde de nuit*, et apparaissent, le plus souvent, sous

---

[1] *Op. cit.*, p. 20.

leur véritable nom[1]. Modiano cite volontiers Violette Moriss et Magda d'Andurian, qui fréquentèrent, de façon assidue, le 93 de la rue Lauriston.

Ancienne championne de France féminine des poids et haltères, Violette Moriss se joint dès 1941 à la bande de Lafont, mais ne dédaigne pas non plus la compagnie d'une autre figure marquante de l'Occupation : « Jo la Terreur ». Elle participe, de façon active, aux actes de torture commis sur les résistantes, en plaçant des cigarettes allumées sur la poitrine des victimes. Cette cruauté particulière devait sans doute constituer un acte de compensation, puisque cette adepte du saphisme s'était fait sectionner les deux seins avant-guerre, afin de gagner en puissance en haltérophilie. L'ancienne amie d'Yvonne de Bray (dont la péniche avait reçu les visites de Jean Marais et de Jean Cocteau, à la fin des années trente) acquit très rapidement une réputation épouvantable, et fut abattue par la Résistance à la fin de 1943.

Surnommée « la comtesse de la Gestapo », Magda d'Andurian – de son véritable nom Magda Fontanges – prétendait avoir été la maîtresse de Mussolini. Elle participait fréquemment aux agapes de la rue Lauriston, en compagnie de Violette Moriss, bien sûr, mais également de trois « piliers » du 93 : la marquise d'Abrantès, épouse divorcée d'un descendant de Junot, Marie Doufflot, Danièle David et Marie Burguière. Elle finit étranglée sur son yacht, le *Sapho*, pour des motifs sans doute totalement étrangers à la guerre.

En ce qui concerne le reste du personnel, janissaires de Monsieur Philibert et du Khédive, Modiano mêle fiction et réalité, à partir de patronymes authentiques ou recomposés, le plus souvent empruntés aux hommes de main de Lafont. On

---

[1] « Quelques femmes : Lucie Onstein, dite "Frau Sultana", jadis danseuse de genre au *Rigolett's* ; Magda d'Andurian, directrice à Palmyre d'un hôtel "mondain et discret" ; Violette Moriss, championne de poids et haltère, portait toujours des costumes d'homme ; Emprosine Marousi [de son vrai nom Sonia Boukami], princesse byzantine, toxicomane et lesbienne ; Simone Bouquereau et Irène de Tranzé, ex-pensionnaires du One-two-two ; la baronne Lydia Stahl, qui aimait le champagne et les fleurs fraîches. » *La Ronde de nuit*, p. 127.

n'oubliera pas de citer les membres du personnel affectés aux opérations strictement policières : Tony Breton, bellâtre, sous-off de la Légion et tortionnaire avisé ; Jo Reocreux, tenancier de maison close ; Vital-Léca dit « Gueule d'Or », tueur à gages ; Armand le Fou : « Je vais les buter, les buter, tous les buter » ; Codébo et Robert le Pâle, relégables, utilisés comme portiers et gardes du corps ; Danos « le mammouth » ou « Gros Bill » ; Gouari, « l'Américain », braqueur, travaillant à la pige... Le Khédive régnait sur ce joyeux petit monde que les chroniqueurs judiciaires appelleraient plus tard « la bande du square Cimarosa »[1].

« Armand le fou » renvoie à un authentique tueur, d'origine pied-noir, familier de la rue Lauriston, « Danos, "le mammouth" ou "Gros Bill" » renvoie à Albert Danos, dit « Le Danois » ou « le bel Abel », habitué des officines de collaboration économique franco-allemande, sur lequel nous allons nous attarder.

Il figure parmi les vingt-cinq détenus que Lafont fit libérer de Fresnes, au début d'août 1940, pour recruter le personnel de son premier « bureau d'achat ». Il s'associe très rapidement avec deux autres prisonniers, Jean-Michel Chaves dit « Nez-de-braise » et Adrien Estebéteguy dit « Adrien le Basque », avec lesquels il forme un redoutable trio, pillant, dénonçant et torturant tous ceux qui semblent vouloir faire entrave à l'ascension de « Monsieur Henri ». Après la Libération, il se terre durant quelques années, et échappe à la répression. Il est pourtant appréhendé sur la plate-forme arrière d'un autobus, après avoir tenté de cambrioler une chambre de bonne. Il est fusillé peu de temps après. José Giovanni lui a consacré un roman, adapté au cinéma en 1960 par Claude Sautet : *Classe tous risques*[2].

---

[1] *La Ronde de nuit*, p. 129.
[2] Le film constitue une variation pathétique sur les derniers jours du personnage, trahi par les siens, et ne fait pratiquement pas référence à la période de l'Occupation.

De façon générale, les états-civils des sicaires de M. Philibert et du Khédive constituent autant de variations savoureuses sur l'identité et les activités des affidés de Lafont :

> Dès les premiers mois de l'année 1941, la « bande de la rue Lauriston » est à peu près au complet. C'est un curieux mélange de petits fonctionnaires ratés, d'artistes en goguette et de truands. La plupart portent des surnoms pittoresques.
> Par l'intermédiaire de Danos, on voit arriver rue Lauriston d'autres « caïds » : « Jo le Corse », tireur d'élite et tueur à gages ; le cambrioleur « Feu-Feu » ; Mohamed Begdane, dit « Jean le Manchot » [...] Il y a encore René Mâle, dit « Riri l'Américain », François Lorand et son adjoint, Charles Blénot, l'Arménien Georges Kaïdijian, Pierre Sibert [...] etc.[1].

L'écrivain entremêle ainsi le « mensonge historique » à la « vérité romanesque », en associant à chacune des figures une activité quelque peu singulière ; la réunion de chacune détourne cet inventaire de la veulerie et de l'ignominie vers une sorte de dérision systématique :

> La plupart d'entre eux occupaient un poste au sein de la « Société Intercommerciale de Paris-Berlin-Monte-Carlo[2] ». Zieff, Méthode et Helder dirigeaient le département des cuirs. [...] Costachesco, Hayakawa et Rosenheim avaient choisi les métaux, les matières grasses et huiles minérales. L'ex commandant Costantini opérait dans un secteur plus restreint mais rentable : verrerie, parfumerie, peaux de chamois, gâteaux secs, vis et boulons[3].

Figures à la fois monstrueuses et pathétiques, ces personnages n'ont rien de commun avec les militants de la cause nazie, aux motivations exclusivement idéologiques – pour lesquels la destruction de l'ennemi, juif, communiste ou homosexuel constitue un impératif catégorique, une nécessité

---

[1] Fabrice Laroche, article cité, p. 68-69.
[2] Dénomination plaisante d'un bureau d'achats, fonctionnant de façon similaire à celui qui fut placé sous la responsabilité de Hermann Brandl.
[3] *La Ronde de nuit*, p. 127-128.

d'ordre historique, venant s'inscrire dans le cadre d'une purgation et d'un salut collectifs. Les affairistes du 3 bis, surgis des ténèbres de l'avant-guerre, agissent, avant tout, dans leur intérêt personnel, l'enrichissement individuel constituant la seule fin avérée et revendiquée de leurs exactions.

Cette « génération spontanée » peut trouver sa place, *mutatis mutandis*, aux côtés des sociétés parallèles décrites par le Sue des *Mystères de Paris* ou le Balzac de *Splendeurs et misères des courtisanes*. L'agglomérat de figures interlopes présenté dans ces œuvres, contrôlant une activité souterraine, aux lois et aux statuts qui reproduisent ceux de l'économie officielle, semble la préfiguration des barons de la finance clandestine qui virent le jour pendant les riches heures de la Collaboration – poursuivant avec l'occupant les règles du libéralisme économique, fondé sur la libre circulation des capitaux et marchandises.

Il semblerait ainsi légitime de discerner, dans la présence de ces « chevaliers d'industrie », la résurgence d'une constante presque historique, celle qui voit les représentants des marges de la société se mettre au service d'une puissance venant renverser l'ordre établi, et établir sa domination. Liés de façon très étroite au nouveau pouvoir mis en place, auquel ils doivent leur réussite, et dont la force économique dépend entièrement de leur concours, ces prédateurs sont associés à sa progression, avant de le suivre dans sa chute. On pensera, à titre d'exemple, à la façon dont les empereurs romains se servaient d'une certaine partie de la plèbe pour fomenter leurs coups d'état, puis asseoir leur pouvoir, ou aux septembriseurs de la Révolution, recrutés aux plus bas échelons de la société[1]. Plus près de nous, il est possible d'imaginer que les sectateurs du Khédive eussent ainsi tout aussi bien pu mettre leurs activités

---

[1] Au cours d'une émission qui lui était consacrée, en 1992, Louis Malle expliqua qu'il avait pensé au départ, à situer le motif de l'intrigue de *Lacombe Lucien* au Mexique, sous le gouvernement de Diaz. Il entendait montrer comment un péon pouvait choisir de servir la dictature, dès l'instant où celle-ci reconnaissait et valorisait son existence. Compte tenu de certaines difficultés inhérentes aux conditions de production, il choisit de se tourner vers la période de l'Occupation, et demanda, alors, la collaboration de Patrick Modiano.

au service de l'Italie fasciste de Mussolini que de la Russie stalinienne.

L'intérêt que le romancier porte à l'Occupation réside, pour une part importante, dans les personnages équivoques et les atmosphères troubles que les événements génèrent. Les figures qu'il place sur la scène de ses souvenirs recomposés semblent investies d'une seule fonction illustrative ; en effet, le principe romanesque de Modiano ne réside pas dans une « concurrence à l'état civil », au nom d'une dénonciation véhémente de la France occupée, mais dans l'élucidation – au sens étymologique – des recoins les plus obscurs de l'âme humaine.

C'est un système de valeurs identique qui prévaut pour l'évocation de la collaboration dite intellectuelle, dans *La Place de l'Étoile* et *Les Boulevards de ceinture*, notion que nous étudierons après avoir apporté une réserve importante à ce qui vient d'être démontré.

Le cas de *Lacombe Lucien*.

L'étude du scénario que Louis Malle porta à l'écran en 1973 vient quelque peu nuancer les propos concernant la caractérisation des personnages. Cette fois-ci, le behaviourisme propre aux figures des romans, difficilement transposable à l'écran, se trouve abandonné au profit d'une caractérisation beaucoup plus précise des personnages et de leur psychologie – même si, dans cette œuvre cinématographique, c'est avant tout l'aspect mécanique, presque professionnel, des exactions commises par les miliciens qui paraît le plus important. Confronté à la difficulté de donner une existence véritable à des êtres représentés sur un écran, et non pas saisis au travers du prisme déformant que sont l'imagination et la sensibilité du lecteur, le romancier opte pour une approche minimaliste des personnages, susceptible de cerner les comportements individuels avec exactitude et précision.

Cette vision de l'Occupation, beaucoup plus schématique et réductrice que celle des romans, répond tout autant aux nécessités de l'écriture cinématographique qu'à un souci de clarté. Les personnages de l'histoire appartiennent à une Occupation qui semble plus familière au spectateur que les fantasmes mis en scène dans les œuvres de la trilogie. On retrouve, certes, les thèmes chers à l'écrivain[1], en particulier la relative inconscience des personnages, qui semble oblitérer l'idée de responsabilité individuelle[2], mais cette fois marquée au coin d'un certain vérisme – préoccupation qui, jusqu'alors, ne constituait pas l'un des signes distinctifs de l'écriture de Modiano. Celui-ci, ainsi que son coscénariste, a constitué un inventaire presque exhaustif des figures exemplaires de l'imagerie de l'Occupation, véhiculées par le roman ou le cinéma.

L'ensemble se caractérise par un aspect délibérément utilitaire. Le caractère fonctionnel des personnages, des lieux et des situations constitue une certaine déviation de l'esprit de l'écrivain, quelque peu trahi par la restitution de son univers à l'écran. Les figures principales du film représentent à peu près toutes les catégories sociales et morales que le spectateur moyen peut associer à la collaboration crapuleuse en province. On trouve ainsi un jeune dandy parisien égaré, Jean-Bernard de Voisins, un champion cycliste déchu, Henri Aubert, une femme de tête en relation avec les caciques du marché noir, Madame Georges, un policier révoqué, Tonin[3], un idéologue nazi fanatique, Faure, et – sans doute pour compléter le quota national – un Martiniquais, Hippolyte.

Ces figures obligées balisent le parcours de scènes inévitables, comme l'incontournable supplice de la baignoire (à la seizième séquence du film) ou l'intrusion chez des résistants (dix-huitième séquence). L'ensemble fonctionne à la façon de vignettes, dont le caractère prévisible constitue la principale faiblesse de l'œuvre, l'univers modianien ne s'accommodant

---

[1] Qui expliquent, sans doute, le choix de Modiano par Louis Malle, soucieux, à l'évidence, de faire œuvre de provocation.
[2] À cet égard, Betty Beaulieu, qui n'entretient aucune distance critique avec les événements, semble la sœur de lait d'Annie Murraille, telle qu'elle apparaît dans *Les Boulevards de ceinture*.
[3] Qui semble, de fait, contrôler l'ensemble du groupe, à la façon de Monsieur Philibert régentant le 3 bis, square Cimarosa.

que fort médiocrement de la simple restitution d'images mentales sur grand écran[1]. Nous ne souscrivons qu'avec difficulté au jugement que Colin Nettelbeck et de Penelope Hueston[2] portent sur la profonde originalité du parti pris esthétique :

> On reconnaît ici la manière dont Modiano met en lumière l'insolite plutôt que l'attendu, modifiant ainsi notre perspective habituelle [...]. Tout au long de ce film, on retrouve cette même tendance à nuancer les idées reçues et les souvenirs familiers [...]. On retrouve certes les images habituelles de l'Occupation : les queues devant le boulanger, les patrouilles allemandes, la famille juive qui se cache [...]. C'est l'optique de Modiano qui empêche ces images de se figer, ou plutôt qui les ranime, qui les tire de la fixité à laquelle la mémoire collective les avait trop vite condamnées[3].

Nous infirmerons ces propos en mettant en regard deux scènes de torture, l'une présentée dans *La Ronde de nuit*, l'autre dans *Lacombe Lucien*. On pourra certes objecter que les supports narratifs diffèrent, et que l'écriture cinématographique possède des exigences qui paraissent éloignées de celles du roman, mais il semble intéressant de considérer la seule force évocatrice de ces épisodes, indépendamment des moyens d'expression.

Les séances de torture infligées au 3 bis, square Cimarosa reviennent de façon récurrente dans le roman. Noyées dans le maelström des pensées de Swing Troubadour, qui relate de façon identique et systématique tous les événements survenus dans ce lieu, elles gagnent en banalité insoutenable ce qu'elles perdent en sensationnel. L'apathie du narrateur donne ainsi une force supplémentaire à ce *topos* de l'Occupation ; la violence ne surgit pas de l'évocation

---

[1] C'est sans aucun doute ce qui peut expliquer l'échec artistique – et commercial – du film tiré d'*Une Jeunesse* par Moshe Mizrahi, en 1982.
[2] *Patrick Modiano : écrire l'entretemps*, Paris, Archives des lettres modernes-Minard, 1986.
[3] *Op. cit.*, p. 57-59.

proprement dite, mais du décalage entre l'événement exposé et la voix qui énonce le message :

> – Nous venons d'épingler quelqu'un, Henri. Distribution de tracts. Nous l'avons pris sur le fait. Breton et Reocreux s'occupent de lui à la cave.
> Les autres sont encore étourdis par la valse. Ils ne disent mot et demeurent immobiles à l'endroit où la musique les a laissés [...]. Un hurlement. Puis deux. Puis trois. Extrêmement aigus. [...]
> – Tu es la plus belle, déclare Paulo Hayakawa à la baronne Lydia en lui tendant une coupe de champagne[1].

Dans le cas de *Lacombe Lucien*, on assiste à une certaine dramatisation (au sens étymologique) de l'événement, peu exempte d'une certaine pesanteur, sous couvert, cependant, d'une volonté de distanciation – puisque la séquence filmique n'excède pas trois minutes :

> On entend un gémissement, une plainte, très faible. [Lucien] s'approche et jette un coup d'œil par l'entrebâillement de la porte. Une grande salle de bains, avec lavabo double et baignoire. On y a rajouté une table, sur laquelle est posée une machine à écrire et un canapé [...]. Jean-Bernard, en manches de chemises, tient la tête d'un prisonnier enfoncée dans l'eau de la baignoire. [...] Jean-Bernard relève la tête de l'homme [qui] suffoque bruyamment, essayant de reprendre son souffle. [...]
> Faure (off) : Tu vas parler, salopard !
> Il a l'air d'aimer ça, ma parole[2] !

La scène, telle qu'elle a été écrite, ne peut être comprise par le spectateur que s'il partage les références des scénaristes – à savoir la plupart des clichés littéraires ou cinématographiques concernant la période, véhiculés dans les années cinquante ou soixante ; de fait, l'ensemble fonctionne, d'une certaine manière, sur le mode de la démonstration illustrative. Une grande partie du film s'articule, en effet,

---
[1] *La Ronde de nuit*, p. 36-37.
[2] *Lacombe Lucien*, p. 56-57.

autour d'invariants historiques qui paraissent moins s'inscrire dans la logique du récit que dans une certaine volonté de connivence avec le spectateur. Il peut donc sembler légitime de parler de « connotation autonymique[1] » à propos de l'image de l'Occupation, telle qu'elle est présentée dans l'œuvre. Là où Modiano réinventait une Occupation fantasmée, créant un monde cohérent, assujetti aux seules règles de la narration romanesque, le scénario de *Lacombe Lucien* se présente comme un discours critique et réflexif sur les « lieux communs » de l'Occupation. L'intrigue y cède le pas à la tentation de l'inventaire ; à cet égard, le film transforme en poncifs des comportements ou des réactions qui, parfaitement assimilés par le sens commun, ont perdu l'audace et l'aspect corrosif qui les caractérisait quelques années auparavant.

On pourrait donc considérer *Lacombe Lucien* comme un *vade-mecum* de l'imagerie de la France collaboratrice, qui aurait parfaitement assimilé les enseignements du *Chagrin et la pitié*, pour les intégrer à son propre discours. L'anticonformisme de *La Place de l'Étoile* ou des *Boulevards de ceinture* s'est institutionnalisé, donnant à l'irrévérence un caractère didactique. Les thèmes et situations de base de la trilogie de l'Occupation sont relayés par un discours balisé, qui évacue entièrement toute la subtilité que les commentaires volontairement ingénus du narrateur laissaient supposer.

Le regard dédoublé (celui de Lucien, observateur indiscret, et partant celui du spectateur) sur la torture de Peyssac, le résistant, apparaît comme une redondance, qui alourdit considérablement la portée de la scène, et l'inscrit dans une logique didactique – comme si cette unique caution d'ordre historique pouvait donner sa seule légitimité à l'histoire. Une semblable analyse, qui ne porterait plus sur des actes mais sur des propos dont le caractère dogmatique surprend le spectateur de la fin des années quatre-vingt-dix, serait légitime. La comparaison montrerait également la supériorité des romans publiés avant l'écriture du scénario. Nous pensons ainsi aux

---

[1] Ce procédé discursif ou narratif vise à faire de l'instance ou du procédé d'énonciation le véritable enjeu du message écrit, parlé ou filmé.

tractations commerciales et aux basses besognes de marché noir pratiquées dans la région de Cahors :

> Aubert est au téléphone, près du bar. À côté de lui, Mme Georges, un carnet à la main.
> Aubert : Allô... Reoyo[1] ? C'est Henri...Oui... Oui.
> [...]
> Aubert (mettant la main sur l'écouteur) : Il y a deux wagons de chaussures à la frontière espagnole...
> Mme Georges : Wagon de chaussures ? Et ce bon de déblocage ?
> Aubert : Il peut l'avoir par Guy Max, contre le wolfram.
> Mme Georges : Dites-lui que c'est d'accord[2].

Cet épisode du film est le seul à présenter les aspects économiques de la Collaboration ; il se borne à remplir, à ce titre, le rôle d'une simple notice illustrative – puisque c'est la seule occurrence de cette activité, et qu'elle n'apparaît pas à d'autres moments du film. La scène appartient donc à la catégorie de la citation, justifiable uniquement par volonté d'« effet de réel ». Elle n'accède pas à une autonomie qui lui ferait quitter le cadre des références obligées – on songera ainsi à l'inévitable file de ravitaillement, à la lecture à haute voix de sordides lettres de dénonciation ou à l'audition d'un poste de TSF : autant d'indications qui, loin de concourir à la mise en place d'un certain climat, n'en font qu'exhiber les artifices. Seule la seconde partie de l'histoire trouve réellement son rythme et son équilibre, au moment où Lucien et la famille de France paraissent, en quelque sorte, livrés à eux mêmes, loin de la tutelle d'une atmosphère reconstituée de façon factice.

Lacombe Lucien n'en reste pas moins un film essentiel, dont les imperfections peuvent s'expliquer par l'« esprit du temps » – et dont il a déjà été question dans un développement antérieur. Les milieux artistiques multipliaient, à cette époque, les signes de provocation, souvent gratuits, à l'égard du

---

[1] Ce nom constitue une réminiscence d'une filiale d'« Otto », le « Bureau Marcias-Reoyo ».
[2] *Lacombe Lucien*, p. 53.

pouvoir pompidolien, qui semblait poursuivre le travail d'amnésie commencé par le général de Gaulle.

On notera toutefois que Patrick Modiano avait montré beaucoup plus de subtilité et de pénétration dans sa peinture de la collaboration dite « intellectuelle » dans *Les Boulevards de ceinture*.

LA COLLABORATION ARTISTIQUE

Pour son troisième roman, Modiano choisit les personnages de Jean Luchaire et de sa fille Corinne pour représenter les milieux du journalisme engagés aux côtés du vainqueur, durant la guerre. Les personnages que l'écrivain met en scène constituent les principales figures d'une sorte de cénacle, équivalant pour le monde des « idées » à la bande du square Cimarosa pour ce qui concernait le négoce. Les trois années qui se sont écoulées – à ce jour le plus long intervalle entre deux publications de Modiano – ont permis l'affinement du style. L'écrivain poursuit, si l'on ose le mot, l'épuration narrative commencée avec *La Ronde de nuit*. La provocation, dont on percevait encore quelques traces dans le deuxième ouvrage, fait place à un récit articulé autour d'une quête de filiation et de reconnaissance d'identité, sur fond de guerre finissante. Là où les épisodes de *La Ronde de nuit* n'offraient que peu de prise à une analyse rigoureuse de la situation, les personnages et lieux des *Boulevards de ceinture* marquent le roman au coin d'une certaine vraisemblance. Il convient de noter, tout de même, que les acteurs du récit se caractérisent – et c'est peut-être en cela que les trois premières œuvres de Modiano présentent une certaine unité – par un schématisme qui fait encore obstacle à la complexité psychologique. De ce point de vue, la faune interlope de la collaboration dite « intellectuelle » (avec toutes les précautions d'emploi attachées à l'usage des guillemets) paraît aussi peu ménagée que son homologue du square Cimarosa.

L'ambiance générale paraît moins importer que l'exactitude des notations anecdotiques – qui permettent, par exemple, de situer l'action du roman avec précision. On pensera, par exemple, à la reprise de *Forfaiture* en avril 1944, avec Sessue Hayakawa[1], à « L'Ambigu », mentionnée au cours de la description générale du « Clos-Foucré ». Le romancier semble effectuer, dans ce dernier ouvrage, une sorte de synthèse des constituants narratifs de ses deux livres précédents ; il parvient, en effet, à unir dans un même ensemble l'esprit de nomenclature, à l'œuvre dans *La Place de l'Étoile*, et le soin apporté à la caractérisation des personnages de *La Ronde de nuit*. Enfin, le changement le plus important semble le statut du narrateur. Muni d'une identité légale – le drame pour Modiano, en 1972, est qu'elle se limite au statut administratif – et d'un passé (évoqué sous forme d'anamnèse cohérente), Serge Alexandre relate une histoire ignorante des méandres de la pure imagination, et adoptant une forme narrative plus proche du récit traditionnel.

Se trouvent donc convoqués un patron de presse volontiers porté sur le chantage par journal interposé, une cohorte de demi-mondaines fort opportunément ralliées au nouvel ordre, un légionnaire déraciné et un capitaine d'industrie. Tous ces personnages reçoivent, comme dans le roman précédent, une fiche signalétique retraçant, sur le mode policier, leur histoire d'avant-guerre. L'écrivain se plaît, en cette occasion, à composer une galerie purement illustrative, susceptible de mettre en relief le seul personnage complexe, et à ce titre réellement intéressant de l'histoire, à savoir le « baron » Chalva Deyckecaire, figure déléguée du père du narrateur. Pour les autres, il faut se contenter d'une caractérisation sommaire.

Jean Luchaire et sa fille Corinne prêtent leur identité à Jean Murraille et à sa nièce. Le sort malheureux de cette dernière, victime de son hédonisme revendiqué, qui la rend peu exigeante sur le choix de ses fréquentations, en fait une

---

[1] Il sera longuement question de l'acteur à la fin de *Livret de famille*, lors d'une conversation entre une amie des parents du narrateur-écrivain, Flo Nardus, et ce dernier.

homologue de la Betty Beaulieu de *Lacombe Lucien*[1]. Ainsi, c'est moins par idéologie que par souci de poursuivre son mode de vie d'avant-guerre qu'elle s'agrège aux fidèles du « Clos-Foucré » :

> Annie Murraille avait vingt-deux ans. Une blonde diaphane. Était-elle vraiment la nièce de Jean Murraille ? Je n'ai jamais pu l'éclaircir. Elle voulait faire une grande carrière au cinéma [...]. Après avoir tourné quelques petits rôles, elle fut la vedette de *Nuits de rafles*, un film aujourd'hui bien oublié [...]. Elle éprouvait pour son oncle (l'était-il vraiment ?) une affection sans limites. S'il se trouve encore quelques personnes qui se souviennent d'Annie Murraille, ils auront gardé d'elle l'image d'une jeune actrice malchanceuse mais si émouvante... Elle voulait profiter de la vie[2]...

Née en 1921, l'actrice Corinne Luchaire débute au cinéma sous la direction d'Yves Allégret, en 1935, avec *Les Beaux Jours*. Elle enchaîne les films mineurs, avec des réalisateurs comme Léonide Moguy et Raymond Bernard, qui seront interdits sous Vichy, en raison de leur judéité. On peut citer *Prison sans barreaux* (œuvre dans laquelle elle fait preuve d'une « extraordinaire présence », selon Jean Tulard[3]), *Le Déserteur* ou *Cavalcade d'amour*. Contrairement à ses incarnations romanesques, elle ne tournera pas sous l'Occupation, et semble peu se soucier d'idéologie. Hervé Le Boterf écrit à son propos[4] : « Corinne Luchaire, la fille du directeur des *Nouveaux Temps*, ne tient pas tellement à se

---

[1] Identification renforcée par la présence de *Nuit de rafles* dans leurs courtes filmographies respectives – c'est le seul titre de gloire de Betty dans *Lacombe Lucien*. Le titre du film est totalement imaginaire.
[2] *Les Boulevards de ceinture*, p. 73. La commisération dont fait preuve l'écrivain se trouve confirmée par les propos qu'il tient à Thierry Laurent, dans la lettre que nous avons citée : « Dans un certain sens, [Corinne Luchaire] a été victime de l'aventure dans laquelle s'était fourvoyé son père entre 1940 et 1944 – aventure qui n'avait rien à voir avec celle d'un Rebatet ou d'un Brasillach. »
[3] *Dictionnaire du cinéma*, t. II : « *Les acteurs* », Paris, Robert Laffont, 1984.
[4] *Op. cit.*, p. 12.

mêler au groupe constitué par son père. Elle fait bande à part, entourée de comédiens et de chanteurs, avant de consacrer l'exclusivité de ses soirées tour à tour à Guy de Voisins [qui prête certains de ses traits à Marcheret[1]], puis au capitaine autrichien Gerlach, les deux derniers hommes qu'elle ait aimés. » Le journaliste, qui minore dans son ouvrage les activités de nombre de collaborateurs, omet de mentionner qu'elle fréquentait l'ambassade d'Allemagne très régulièrement, avec ses amis. Elle fait paraître un livre de mémoires, après la mort de son père : *Ma drôle de vie*[2], demeuré confidentiel, et meurt peu après, de tuberculose, en 1951.

Murraille, pour ce qui le concerne, tire l'essentiel de ses caractéristiques de Jean Luchaire, président de la Corporation nationale de la presse française – instance créée par ce dernier, au mépris de la législation vichyssoise, avant d'être habilitée en 1942. Né en 1901, auteur en 1929 d'*Une génération réaliste*, directeur avant-guerre de *Notre Temps*, hebdomadaire prônant l'apaisement[3], et dont Abetz épousa la secrétaire, il était l'interlocuteur privilégié du *Militärbefehlshaber im Frankreich*. Le pouvoir de la Corporation résidait essentiellement dans le règlement des œuvres sociales et surtout les départs au STO. Ce modèle du « Groupement corporatif de la presse parisienne »[4] permettait d'exercer un contrôle certain sur la conformité idéologique des publications de la zone Nord, tout en élargissant, selon Vidal de La Blache[5], les intérêts pécuniaires du « gang Luchaire[6] ».

---

[1] On retrouve le couple formé par Corinne Luchaire et Guy de Voisins avec Betty Beaulieu et Jean-Bernard de Voisins (*sic*) dans *Lacombe Lucien*.
[2] Paris, Sun, 1949.
[3] Bertrand de Jouvenel et Pierre Brossolette collaborent à ce mensuel, aux sympathies radicales revendiquées, mis au service d'Aristide Briand, puis du Quai d'Orsay de façon systématique.
[4] *Les Boulevards de ceinture*, p. 145.
[5] Journaliste à *Paris-Soir*.
[6] Le commissaire du gouvernement chargé de contrôler la gestion de la CNPF n'était autre que Luchaire lui-même, lorsque Laval revint au pouvoir. Selon Pascal Ory, « les créatures et complices du président accapareront sans peine les fauteuils présidentiels des groupements corporatifs mis en place petit à petit à la suite de celui de la presse parisienne : presse de province, presse

Appelé par Bunau-Varilla à la rédaction en chef du *Matin*, à l'été 1940, il accepte, à l'automne, de diriger un grand quotidien du soir, *Les Nouveaux Temps* – dont il abandonnera progressivement la ligne politique à un ami d'avant-guerre, Crouzet, en contact permanent avec l'Ambassade d'Allemagne[1]. Il crée *Toute la vie* en 1941 ; cet hebdomadaire, concurrent de *La Semaine*, lancée une année auparavant, aux articles courts illustrés par d'abondantes photographies, constitue le modèle de *C'est la vie*, pour lequel Modiano reprend les noms déformés d'hommes de presse proches de Luchaire.

On pensera ainsi à Eugène Gerber – François Gerbère dans *Les Boulevards de ceinture* –, propriétaire des Éditions Théophraste-Renaudot, placé à la tête de *Paris-Soir* en novembre 1940, dramaturge passionné, dont les pièces ne dépassaient jamais les premières représentations, et qui préférera faire jouer sa dernière œuvre à Nuremberg plutôt que de la laisser sans public. Modiano plaque également la figure de Robert Brasillach – directeur de *Je suis partout* jusqu'au début de 1943, journal dont s'inspire également le romancier pour la publication de Murraille – sur ce personnage, en lui donnant un aspect ridicule et presque pathétique :

> Gerbère appartenait à cette catégorie de garçons hypernerveux qui zézaient et jouent volontiers les pasionarias ou les fascistes de choc [...]. Il était resté fidèle à l'esprit – très provincial – de la rue d'Ulm et

---

périodique générale, agences françaises de presse. La presse Luchaire fournira de même le vice-président, le secrétaire général et le trésorier général de la Corporation. Cette position prédominante fait de Luchaire le pivot du nouveau Tout-Paris. » *Op. cit.*, p. 78. Céline, dans *D'un château l'autre*, évoque le séjour de ce personnage à Sigmaringen, dans les derniers mois de la guerre.

[1] Stipendié par les Allemands, Luchaire avait déclaré une guerre sans merci au marché noir dans les colonnes de ses journaux, combat auquel il se gardait d'adhérer lorsqu'il s'agissait de son propre ravitaillement. Hervé Le Boterf raconte, à titre d'exemple, un de ses retours de Belgique : « Le directeur de la Presse française rentre le 22 juillet 1942 avec vingt kilos de beurre, quatre douzaines d'œufs, six livres de crème et pour près de mille francs de viande dans ses bagages [...]. Interpellé par le contrôle économique, il est immédiatement relâché. » *Op. cit.*, p. 12-13.

l'on s'étonnait de ce que ce khâgneux de presque trente-huit ans pût se montrer aussi féroce [...]. Ses yeux se sont appesantis sur moi [...] :
— C'est fou comme vous ressemblez à Albert Préjean [...]. Vous me rappelez aussi mon meilleur ami de l'École, un garçon superbe. Il est mort en 36, chez les franquistes [...]. Je me sens si seul[1].

Le directeur de l'hebdomadaire *Au pilori*, Jean Lestandi, donne son patronyme à l'un des collaborateurs principaux de Murraille – ainsi que le ton de sa revue. Cette dernière, spécialisée dans l'hystérie délatrice, tenait tout autant de la feuille de chantage illustrée que de la publication journalistique[2], et représentait le versant populaire de *Je suis partout*, débarrassé de toute prétention intellectuelle. Viennent s'ajouter à cette galaxie José Germain[3], ancien président de la Société des gens de lettres, qui stigmatisait le caractère efféminé et démoralisant de la littérature de l'entre-deux-guerres, ou Alain Laubreaux[4], cacique officieux de *Je suis partout* jusqu'à l'arrivée de Brasillach, responsable de la rubrique théâtrale de cette revue, et dramaturge raté[5].

---

[1] *Les Boulevards de ceinture*, p. 171-172. Au moment de la parution de l'ouvrage, Modiano avouait s'être directement inspiré de Brasillach et de son beau-frère Maurice Bardèche pour les personnages de Gerbère et Lestandi.
[2] Les hebdomadaires *France-Révolution*, consacrée à la « défense et à l'illustration de la race française », *France-Europe*, journal corse de Paris, appelant à l'épuration des cadres de l'État français, et dans une moindre mesure *Signal* et *Actu*, servent de modèles, à des titres divers, à la revue de Murraille.
[3] « Ce mystérieux Jo-Germain, qui signe en première page une chronique consacrée au renouveau et au printemps. Écrite dans un français cosmétiqué, elle se termine par une injonction : "Soyez gais !" » *Les Boulevards de ceinture*, p. 34-35.
On notera le penchant de Modiano pour la critique parodique ; l'idéologue intransigeant devient journaliste frivole et primesautier, célébrant la belle saison. Comme dans *La Place de l'Étoile*, le romancier s'ingénie à effectuer des associations incongrues, instillant une certaine distance à l'aide de l'ingénuité du protagoniste-narrateur.
[4] « Alin-Laubreaux » dans l'ouvrage.
[5] Critique enthousiaste d'une pièce sur Stavisky, qu'il avait écrite sous le pseudonyme de Daxiat, il se fit rosser d'importance en public par Jean Marais, après la parution d'un article vipérin et diffamatoire qu'il avait publié

On peut enfin établir des rapprochements entre les collaborateurs du magazine, dont la liste est donnée au début des *Boulevards de ceinture*, et certaines personnalités des milieux politiques de l'Occupation. « Suaraize » évoque Georges Suarez, directeur du quotidien *Aujourd'hui*, biographe de Clemenceau et de Briand, nègre de Jean Chiappe et pamphlétaire anti-allemand durant la « drôle de guerre ». C'est à ce conservateur qu'échoit la responsabilité de reprendre la direction du journal, après l'éviction de Henri Jeanson, qui s'était refusé à célébrer l'entrevue de Montoire. Sous la tutelle de Suarez, le quotidien adoptera un ton feutré de publication acquise à la cause du Reich. « Sayzille » (pour le capitaine Paul Sézille) fut le rédacteur en chef du mensuel antisémite *Les Cahiers jaunes*[1], et le directeur de l'Institut d'étude des questions juives, entre Xavier Vallat et Louis Darquier de Pellepoix. Il fut, à ce titre, l'organisateur de l'exposition « Le Juif et la France » en septembre 1941, au palais Berlitz, pour le compte du Reich, commanditaire officieux de la manifestation. « Malou Guérin » est sans doute la déformation du docteur Paul Guérin, membre du comité de rédaction de *Je suis partout* avant-guerre, et personnage éminent du PPF.

Modiano conclut son énumération par la mention de figures réelles ; le docteur Maulaz était expert en économie pour les services SS de l'avenue Foch, et Zeitschel attaché pour les affaires juives à l'ambassade d'Allemagne. Pierre Costantini, né en 1889, ressorti invalide à cent pour cent de la Grande Guerre, et ancien commandant, en 1940, de la base aéronautique d'état-major de Coulommiers, vécut la débâcle comme un deuil personnel, et ne cessa de vaticiner jusqu'à son internement après la guerre, dans une maison de santé. Prêchant, notamment dans *L'Appel*, l'anéantissement des Juifs, des Anglais – après Mers el-Kébir – et des francs-maçons, pour

---

sur *Les Parents terribles* de Jean Cocteau. Cet épisode est repris dans une scène du *Dernier Métro*, qui voit l'acteur Bernard Granger, interprété par Gérard Depardieu, rouer de coups le critique Daxiat, à la sortie du théâtre.
[1] Publication « concurrente » de *L'Action antijuive* et de *La Question juive en France*, plus scientifique et moins populaire que *Les Cahiers jaunes*. Ces trois revues, émanant de l'Institut, étaient placées sous le contrôle étroit de la *Propagandastaffel*.

lesquels il préconisait le port du brassard, cet ancien aviateur constituait une sorte de tribun délirant, vitupérant les forces occultes tout au long de l'Occupation – en particulier au sein de la Ligue française d'épuration. Jean Boissel, architecte diplômé des Arts décoratifs, héros de la Première Guerre mondiale, fut le président fondateur du Front franc[1], organisation qui rassemblait quelques dizaines de sectateurs fanatiques des thèses ethno-raciales de Gobineau. Enfin, le « professeur d'anthropologie Montandon », auteur, en 1940, de *Comment reconnaître le Juif?* avait été nommé en 1933 à l'École d'anthropologie, et fut le principal théoricien de l'Institut des questions juives sous Xavier Vallat.

L'incorporation à la fiction de ces trois névropathes avérés donne la mesure de l'outrance irrévérencieuse qui caractérise le troisième roman de Modiano – et partant le degré de dégénérescence intellectuelle des fidèles du « Clos-Foucré ». Est-ce pour cette raison que Robert Poulet accusait le jeune écrivain de « piétiner des cadavres », dans sa critique de *Rivarol*[2] ? De fait, le mélange d'êtres de papier et de figures historiques rapproche ce procédé du parti pris esthétique adopté par Woody Allen pour son film *Zelig*, en 1983. À l'aide de l'insertion de documents et de bandes d'actualité d'époque, le cinéaste parvenait à unir de façon très étroite les deux sphères de l'Histoire et du récit fictif. Patrick Modiano procède de façon semblable, en faisant voisiner les hérauts de la Collaboration, précédemment évoqués, avec des personnages manifestement inventés – déjà présents, pour certains, dans ses deux livres précédents. À cet égard, l'évocation du sommaire de *C'est la vie*, dont il vient d'être question, se montre particulièrement révélatrice du projet romanesque de Modiano. Celui-ci entend brasser le réel et l'imaginaire dans une même entité, qui appartiendrait à la fois aux domaines de la vérité et de la fiction afin d'exprimer à la fois l'ambiguïté d'une époque et son caractère irrationnel :

---

[1] Qui déclara au moment de Montoire, dans le périodique publié par son parti, *Le Réveil du peuple*, que « ce serrement était un serment ».
[2] Numéro du 7 décembre 1972, p. 15.

> Parmi les autres « personnalités » que cite « Monsieur Tout-Paris » on trouve la comtesse Tchernicheff, Mag Fontanges, Maulaz, Violette Morris ; l'écrivain Boissel, auteur des *Croix de sang*, l'as de l'aviation Costantini, Delvale et Lionel de Wiet, directeurs de théâtre[1] [...].

On peut déjà retrouver des silhouettes esquissées dans les romans précédents ; figurent ainsi, au rang des personnages de fiction, la princesse Chericheff-Deborazoff, déjà évoquée dans *La Place de l'Étoile*, Violette Morris ou Lionel de Wiet – que l'on peut rapprocher de son paronyme Lionel de Zieff dans *La Ronde de nuit*. En ce qui concerne les figures historiques, on reconnaîtra Costantini, évoqué au roman précédent[2] et Darquier de Pellepoix, commissaire à l'« Institut d'études des questions juives et ethno-raciales[3] » – du départ de Vallat (fin 1942) à 1944 – sous l'égide de Montandon. Modiano semble particulièrement affectionner ce personnage, puisqu'il est le seul à apparaître dans tous les romans de la trilogie, puis dans *Livret de famille*. On le trouve sous son identité véritable dans *La Place de l'Étoile* et *Les Boulevards de ceinture*, et sous les traits d'un personnage de fiction dans *La Ronde de nuit*. Il est désigné en effet, dans cette dernière œuvre, par la mention « Darquier dit "de Pellepoix", avocat marron ».

Ce dernier, né en 1897, d'origine gasconne, ancien combattant de la Grande Guerre et blessé durant les manifestations du 6 février 1934, s'était rendu célèbre avant la guerre par la violence de ses propos antisémites. Faux gentilhomme et vrai collaborateur, créateur, en 1937, du Rassemblement antijuif de France, directeur, à cette époque, de *La France enchaînée*, il était conseiller municipal du quartier des Ternes, et bénéficiait de l'entier soutien de l'Action

---

[1] *Les Boulevards de ceinture*, p. 36.
[2] Membre de la cohorte nocturne du square Cimarosa, il est présenté ainsi : « L'ex-commandant d'aviation Costantini opérait dans un secteur plus restreint mais rentable : verrerie, parfumerie, peaux de chamois, gâteaux secs, vis et boulons. » *Ibid.*, p. 128.
[3] Successeur de l « Institut d'étude des questions juives », dirigé par Vallat et Sézille.

Française. Darquier donnera, durant ses deux années à la direction de l'Institut des questions juives, une orientation particulièrement agressive et odieuse à la propagande. Il créa, à cette occasion, l'Union française de la défense de la race, qui s'attachait à intensifier le conditionnement psychologique de la population par les articles de journaux, les actualités cinématographiques ou les brochures spécialisées. Comme dans le cas de Costantini, le détournement de l'identité véritable du personnage, par l'attribution de fausses activités, constitue une bonne illustration de l'entreprise de dérision à laquelle se livre l'écrivain.

Le dernier nom de la liste que nous examinerons est celui de Maulaz, qui semble avoir joué un rôle important dans la vie mondaine sous l'Occupation, si l'on en croit Hervé Le Boterf[1] :

> « Maxim's » est le rendez-vous d'élection du Tout-Paris de la Collaboration et de vieux soiristes d'avant-guerre, tels que le comte de La Rochefoucauld, le marquis de Castellane ou le marquis de Polignac [...]. Un certain Maulaz, attaché à la section financière du SD, devient un peu le maître-Jacques des festivités de l'endroit. Le privilège lui revient d'organiser des dîners entre Allemands et « collaborateurs économiques » français.

Dans son roman, *Drôle de jeu*, Roger Vailland évoque la rencontre de deux journalistes de la Collaboration, alors au crépuscule de leur puissance, avec le protagoniste du roman, François Lamballe[2]. La scène se passe dans un restaurant de marché noir, et annonce l'atmosphère du mariage de Marcheret et d'Annie Murraille. L'angoisse de l'avenir, face au renversement des forces, se traduit par un déchaînement de hargne et de fiel, semblable à celui de Gerbère ou de Lestandi :

> « Tiens, tiens, Lamballe est remonté à Paris...

---

[1] *Op.cit.*, p. 187.
[2] On se souvient de l'identité forgée de façon fantasmatique par Swing Troubadour, la « princesse de Lamballe ».

– Ils viennent tour à tour respirer l'odeur de nos futurs cadavres !

– Les cadavres ne se portent pas trop mal, reprend l'autre [...].

Je tiens [...] mon écho : 'L'ex-journaliste enjuivé François Lamballe, créature de l'immonde Lecache, continue à tenir le haut du pavé dans les restaurants de marché noir. [...]

– Tu vas le faire foutre en taule.

– Ça en fera un de moins. [...] J'ai encore reçu ce matin trente-deux lettres de menace, je les ai comptées[1] ... »

Admirable prescience partagée par Murraille, qui déclarait, pour sa part : « Nous aussi, figure-toi, nous allons bientôt quitter la compétition, avec l'article 75[2] et douze balles dans la peau[3]. »

Sauf erreur de notre part, Modiano ne fera plus allusion à des figures historiques travesties dans ses romans suivants. Une œuvre comme *Livret de famille*[4] constitue la seule exception, qui évoque de façon détournée le journaliste Robert Courtine – présenté sous le paronyme de Xavier Curtine – et Darquier de Pellepoix[5], présentateurs d'une émission musicale sur Radio-Lausanne. La fiction et la réalité sont ici étroitement imbriquées, puisque, dans le récit, cet homme est un haut dignitaire de la Gestapo, ancien persécuteur du père de Modiano :

> Cette tête qui se détachait du mur avec netteté était celle de D., le personnage le plus hideux du Paris de l'Occupation ; D. que je savais s'être réfugié à Madrid puis en Suisse, et qui *habitait sous un faux nom à Genève et avait trouvé un travail à la radio*[6]. [...] Un visage plat, sans arête. Une bouche à la lèvre supérieure ourlée et tombante, à la minuscule lèvre inférieure [...],

---

[1] Roger Vailland, *Drôle de jeu*, Paris, Plon, 1945, p. 67-68.
[2] Qui condamnait à mort les coupables de haute trahison.
[3] *Les Boulevards de ceinture*, p. 174.
[4] P. 134-137.
[5] Présenté sous le pseudonyme de Robert Gerbauld.
[6] En italiques dans le texte.

tel m'apparut, cette nuit-là, D., celui qui se déplaçait dans les restaurants de marché noir de l'Occupation entouré d'une cohorte [...] qu'on appelait curieusement « les gants gris[1] ».

Modiano brouille les dates et les lieux, en faisant naître Gerbauld/Darquier le 23 mars 1901, à Cahors, et lui invente une biographie relativement imaginaire – du modèle de celle qu'il avait élaborée pour Maurice Sachs dans son premier ouvrage :

> Ainsi, tout près de moi, était assis l'homme qui avait été responsable de quelques milliers de déportations de 40 à 44, celui qui dirigeait les « équipes » de la rue Greffulhe auxquelles mon père échappa par miracle... Je connaissais son pedigree. Petit avocat besogneux avant la guerre puis conseiller municipal, il avait rajouté une particule à son nom et créé le Rassemblement antijuif. À la Libération, il s'était réfugié à Madrid, où, sous le nom d'Estève, il avait enseigné le français.

Il crée un personnage composite à partir de la vie de Darquier, qu'il se plaît à voir survivre aux événements, et lui forge une existence proche de celle du personnage observé par le narrateur de *Vestiaire de l'enfance*, à Majorque :

> Sa maigreur et sa peau bronzée lui donnent l'aspect d'un grand insecte. Ses cheveux blancs sont coupés en frange et son long visage osseux taillé dans un bois mat qu'une hache n'entaillerait pas [...]. Lui aussi, à la rigueur, pourrait me replonger dans le passé à cause de l'un de ses ouvrages : *Chant funèbre pour Karl Heinz Bremer*. Une photo illustre le livre. On y reconnaît l'auteur en compagnie de ce Karl Heinz Bremer et de tout un groupe d'écrivains français de l'époque [...]. Ils ont choisi de se rendre à un congrès de littérateurs européens à Weimar[2].

L'écrivain excelle dans la recomposition romanesque des existences brisées. Leur évocation constitue l'une de ses

---

[1] *Livret de famille*, p. 127-128.
[2] *Vestiaire de l'enfance*, p. 16-38.

constantes thématiques ; il n'existe rien de plus poignant, pour l'artiste, qu'une vie au scénario gâché, qu'il s'agisse de celle d'un garagiste, dans *Villa triste*, d'une grande bourgeoise condamnée à la gérance d'un hôtel meublé, dans *De si braves garçons*, et bien évidemment la longue liste des collaborateurs qui se voient contraints de mener une existence obscure et recluse après la Libération. Ce dernier aspect sera développé ultérieurement, dans la dernière partie de ce travail, qui se trouve consacrée à la part de nostalgie que l'Occupation semble receler de façon naturelle. Enfin, il reste à noter que, dans ce dernier cas, la pitié de l'écrivain l'emporte sur le ressentiment de l'homme Modiano, censeur impitoyable des actes commis par les acteurs principaux de cette période.

En ce qui concerne le patronyme de l'acolyte de Gerbauld, il s'agit d'un renvoi à Robert Courtine, journaliste gastronomique, antisémite notoire, collaborateur du *Réveil du peuple*, *La France au travail*, *Au pilori* ou du *Bulletin d'information antimaçonnique*[1], qui continua sa carrière après la Libération, comme critique gastronomique au *Monde* sous le pseudonyme de La Reynière. Il meurt le 14 avril 1998.

L'écrivain s'inspire d'un climat particulier ou de la consonance de certains patronymes afin de mieux restituer toutes les ambiguïtés de l'époque. Il ne cherche pas à citer les faits et méfaits des héros ou sans-grade de la Collaboration d'une façon particulièrement scrupuleuse, mais s'attache à rendre l'atmosphère et la couleur des années d'Occupation. Le lecteur peut ainsi bâtir son propre univers à partir des informations que Modiano délivre. Dans cet esprit, le jeu sur l'onomastique, dont nous avons pu étudier les nombreuses variations, ressortit à l'emploi de la fonction poétique du langage, théorisée par Roman Jakobson. Selon ce linguiste, le message, dans ce cadre précis, importe moins que les moyens phonético-acoustiques qu'il mobilise. Ainsi, la déformation de patronymes ou leur mélange de façon exotique (« Paulo

---

[1] Pierre Assouline rapporte, dans sa biographie de Combelle, que celui-ci refusa ses articles pour sa *Révolution nationale*, *Le Fleuve Combelle*, Paris, Calmann-Lévy, 1997.

Hayakawa » ou « Otto da Silva ») contribuent à la création d'un monde en demi-teintes, qui voit vaciller toutes les certitudes du temps de paix.

Ce jeu se trouve relayé par la libre association de personnages de fiction et de figures réelles, qui vient rendre difficile la démarcation entre l'univers de la rêverie et celui de l'Histoire. C'est une perspective d'approche semblable qui vient régir l'évocation des lieux dans les romans de Modiano.

Le « paysage naturel » de l'Occupation

Modiano apparaît comme un romancier de la ville ; ses œuvres inventorient les événements à la lumière des pérégrinations de ses narrateurs. Le paysage cadastral devient l'équivalent du parcours moral des protagonistes. Si l'on fait exception de la seule œuvre écrite en collaboration, le scénario de *Lacombe Lucien*, dont l'action se passe dans une bourgade du Lot, on s'apercevra que la totalité, ou peu s'en faut, des romans de Modiano possède un décor urbain comme toile de fond. De surcroît, l'exploration des zones troubles et de la faune interlope de l'Occupation requiert le choix de la capitale, non seulement d'un point de vue dramatique, mais également historique, puisque c'est dans cette ville que le père de l'écrivain vécut la guerre.

Un système raisonné de correspondance entre le paysage historique et le déchiffrage de l'espace vient ainsi se mettre en place. Afin de montrer comment l'écrivain associe pleinement la force des lieux à l'intensité de l'histoire et des personnages qui leur sont associés, il convient de définir, en premier lieu, la notion de « paysage naturel », avant de s'attacher de façon précise à l'étude du « lieu modianien ».

UN ARPENTAGE DU MONDE

Les personnages des romans apparaissent comme des êtres mobiles, mais cette appréciation se doit d'être nuancée rapidement. Si leurs déplacements dans le temps trouvent leurs répondants dans un espace qu'ils balisent au fur et à mesure de leurs pérégrinations, ces derniers se voient limités à un périmètre restreint. Le voyage réel, souvent désiré, dépasse rarement le domaine de l'intention[1], et l'arpentage répété d'un même territoire constitue l'un des aspects les plus notables des récits. Le personnage ne semble exister que pour (et par) un lieu précis, qui vient légitimer son existence, à un moment particulier.

Les œuvres consacrées de façon spécifique à l'Occupation s'articulent essentiellement autour d'un lieu unique, délimité de façon presque mentale – à cet égard, ce n'est sans doute pas un hasard si le repaire des collaborateurs de *C'est la vie* s'appelle le « Clos Foucré ». Chaque roman vient mettre en scène un lieu, un théâtre, sur lequel les actions viennent prendre place : les quatre moments de *La Place de l'Étoile*[2], le salon des Bel-Respiro, l'auberge du village de Seine et Marne (certainement Barbizon, d'après les informations que Modiano communique) et l'« Hôtel des Grottes » (et ses alentours immédiats) dans *Lacombe Lucien*.

Ces espaces circonscrits représentent une certaine projection de l'univers intérieur des personnages principaux, hantés à la fois par la crainte du vide et l'angoisse de la culpabilité. Ils trouvent, dans des endroits aussi anonymes que des salons ou des halls d'hôtel[3], l'exacte traduction de leur

---

[1] *Une Jeunesse* et *Du plus loin de l'oubli* constituent deux exceptions notables – et également, à notre sens, les deux romans les plus faibles de Modiano. Dans les autres œuvres, le changement de pays reste à l'état de projet : l'Angleterre, dans *Villa triste*, l'Italie dans *Rue des boutiques obscures*, *Dimanches d'août* ou *Un cirque passe*, et l'Amérique du Sud dans *Voyage de noces*. Aucune de ces destinations ne sera atteinte, les personnages devant se contenter des seules virtualités du voyage à défaut d'un déplacement effectif.
[2] L'hôtel des Bergues de la première partie, Bordeaux dans la deuxième, puis la province française (la Savoie et la Normandie) et l'Israël des *kibboutzim*, rapproché du Paris de l'Occupation.
[3] On notera la fascination que ces derniers endroits exercent sur l'écrivain, et ce depuis son premier roman. Le caractère anonyme des lieux semble constituer un refuge idéal pour des narrateurs privés d'identité.

absence totale de consistance. Des endroits à la « présence » plus forte paraîtraient inadaptés, puisque les protagonistes éprouveraient le plus grand mal à y imposer leur inanité. La ville, et son enceinte symboliquement forclose dans l'imaginaire des personnages, vient figurer l'espace ultime dans lesquels ces derniers se trouvent habilités à exister. Lieu d'oppression physique et morale, l'espace urbain, mentalement géométrisé et cadastré, transcrit leurs obsessions de façon géographique.

Nous verrons, tout au long de ce développement, comment l'arpentage des lieux (et) de la cité se trouve en totale correspondance avec l'état d'esprit du héros. Filatures, dénonciations, traques et retraites : le climat de l'Occupation nourrit l'imaginaire du romancier ; la ville constitue donc pour celui-ci l'espace idéal – voire le seul lieu possible – pour l'inscription des errances de ses personnages.

UNE OBSESSION URBAINE

À l'exception du cadre rural du Lot, où se déroulent l'action de *Lacombe Lucien*, et la fuite dans l'obscurité nivale de *Rue des boutiques obscures*[1], Paris constitue le cadre d'élection des œuvres articulées autour de l'Occupation. Comme nous l'avons montré précédemment, la capitale représente la scène naturelle des rêveries et des angoisses de l'écrivain, né – à Boulogne – de parents qui, pour des raisons diverses, avaient choisi de se fixer à Paris. Bercé par les souvenirs et influencé par la charge symbolique des lieux, le romancier trouve dans cette ville son « terroir » d'élection.

Livret de famille, qui joue un peu le rôle de *Urtext* modianien, en présentant une sorte d'inventaire des scènes

---

[1] L'errance dans l'immensité blanche des Alpes, qui marque le dernier souvenir du narrateur, est à la fois le symbole de son amnésie et celui des ténèbres « mentales » de l'Occupation ; le voile de la neige s'apparenterait ainsi au silence et à l'oubli collectifs qui suivirent cette période, du moins dans l'imaginaire de l'écrivain.

fondatrices, rend compte de la nécessaire fascination du romancier pour son paysage naturel. Outre l'évocation de la rencontre de ses parents durant la guerre, il consacre un long chapitre à l'appartement qu'il occupait dans son enfance, et qui vient se rappeler à sa mémoire quelque quinze ans plus tard, et ce de façon fortuite :

> En feuilletant un journal, mes yeux s'étaient posés par hasard à la page des annonces immobilières [...]. Cet appartement m'évoquait des souvenirs plus lointains : les quelques années qui comptent tant pour moi, bien qu'elles aient précédé ma naissance [...].
> Il n'osait pas parler de sa peur. Lui et ma mère étaient deux déracinés, sans la moindre attache d'aucune sorte, deux papillons dans cette nuit du Paris de l'Occupation où l'on passait si rapidement de l'ombre à une lumière trop crue et de la lumière à l'ombre[1].

Les scènes et situations dont l'écrivain nourrit ses premiers romans constituent autant de questions sur une époque, certes inconnue, mais au souvenir douloureux. Le traumatisme demeure, indissociablement attaché à des lieux qui sont les dépositaires de la mémoire : « Pourquoi ici plus que dans n'importe quel autre endroit, ai-je senti l'odeur vénéneuse de l'Occupation, ce terreau dont je suis issu[2] ? »

Dans *Un cirque passe*, publié quinze ans plus tard, puis dans *Dora Bruder*, en 1997, Modiano avoue que l'appartement avait été occupé auparavant par Maurice Sachs, dont il a déjà été question précédemment[3]. On serait presque tenté de voir une sorte de déterminisme dans les rapports qui unissent les personnages aux lieux qu'ils habitent. Le romancier peut ainsi noter la coïncidence entre l'existence des Modiano et celle du locataire de l'appartement :

---

[1] *Livret de famille*, p. 195, 200 et 208.
[2] *Ibid.*, p. 202.
[3] Les lieux et événements semblent toujours suivre un parcours cyclique chez Modiano.

[...] Ma chambre d'enfant était l'une des deux pièces qui donnaient sur la cour. Maurice Sachs raconte qu'il avait prêté ces deux pièces à un certain Albert, surnommé « le Zébu ». Celui-ci y recevait toute une bande de jeunes comédiens qui rêvaient de former une troupe [...]. Ce « Zébu », Albert Sciaky, portait le même prénom que mon père et appartenait lui aussi à une famille italienne de Salonique. Et comme moi, exactement trente ans plus tard, au même âge, il avait publié à vingt et un ans, en 1938, chez Gallimard, un premier roman[1] [...].

Les liens entre les êtres et les lieux qui les abritent mettent en évidence la complémentarité et les échanges naturels qui constituent l'une des constantes de l'univers modianien.

Prisonniers de leurs traumatismes, les narrateurs trouvent une sorte de correspondance entre les méandres de leur esprit et les espaces clos qu'ils se trouvent contraints d'arpenter. *La Ronde de nuit* constitue, à cet égard, l'exemple le plus remarquable de la dimension symbolique de l'espace urbain. Le maillage des rues vient ainsi figurer la solitude affective et morale de Swing Troubadour, homme privé de toute attache familiale, et confronté à la totale vacuité de son existence. Cette illustration se trouve développée sur les deux axes synchronique et diachronique du texte.

La traduction du vacillement moral et l'impossibilité d'effectuer un choix se trouvent figurées, dans la synchronie du texte, par les traversées quotidiennes de la Seine, solution de continuité entre le Passy de la Collaboration et le quinzième arrondissement du RCO. La « bipartition » d'une zone de Paris en secteur résistant et collaborateur témoigne de la faculté du héros-narrateur à projeter des catégories psychologico-morales sur des espaces théoriquement neutres, comme si la géographie pouvait servir de repère dans une quête de sens, au sein d'une capitale livrée tout entière au cynisme et à la rapine. L'ensemble vient dessiner les contours d'un monde dans lequel l'éthique ainsi que la responsabilité intellectuelle semblent des

---

[1] *Dora Bruder*, p. 100-101.

valeurs immuables, et cela en parfaite opposition avec la corruption du 3 bis, square Cimarosa :

> Calme, préservé, le quartier de Vaugirard [paraissait] une petite ville de province. Le nom même de « Vaugirard » évoquait les feuillages, le lierre, un ruisseau bordé de mousse [...]. Le métro s'est arrêté sur le pont de Paris. Je souhaitais qu'il ne reparte jamais plus et que personne ne vienne m'arracher à ce *no man's land* entre les deux rives[1].

La seule manière de dépasser la contradiction, d'échapper à l'enfermement dans l'espace forclos d'une ville asphyxiante, réside dans la fuite libératrice, contée par la diachronie. Contrairement à ce que de nombreux critiques ont cru voir dans le roman, la cohérence de *La Ronde de nuit* ne réside en rien dans l'ajointement achronique de scènes disparates, mais dans la confrontation des indicateurs spatiaux. Au cours de cette soirée, Swing Troubadour passera de l'aliénation morale attachée à la Place de l'Étoile[2] aux grands espaces de la banlieue. L'arrachement progressif à l'univers délétère de la Collaboration se trouve balisé par les différentes stations du parcours parisien : les Champs-Élysées, la rue de Rivoli, le Châtelet et la gare d'Austerlitz. La réalité toponymique prend alors le pas sur la cohérence de l'anamnèse, substituant la logique de la géographie à l'ordre chronologique. Les deux axes finissent pourtant par se recouper à la fin du roman, lorsque le héros parvient enfin à laisser derrière lui la capitale.

> Avenue Kléber. Ils klaxonnent, leurs bras se tendent à l'extérieur des portières, s'agitent, battent l'air [...].
> Place du Châtelet. Le café Zelly's où le lieutenant et Saint-Georges doivent me retrouver à minuit [...]. Je me retrouve gare d'Austerlitz en été. Je marche vers l'ouest de Paris. Châtelet. Palais-Royal. Place de la Concorde. [...] Les jardins des Champs-Élysées ressemblent à une

---

[1] *Ibid.*, p. 111-115.
[2] « L'enfer commence à la lisière du bois : boulevard Lannes, boulevard Flandrin, avenue Henri-Martin. Ce quartier résidentiel est l'un des plus redoutables de Paris. » *La Ronde de nuit*, p. 38.

station thermale. Avenue Kléber. Je tourne à gauche. Square Cimarosa. *Une place calme comme il y en a dans le XVIe arrondissement*[1].

La Ronde de nuit est un roman situé à la croisée de l'inspiration d'un Modiano quelque peu hésitant sur l'orientation qu'il entend donner à sa carrière littéraire. Située entre le bouillonnement juvénile de *La Place de l'Étoile* et l'écriture beaucoup plus traditionnelle des *Boulevards de ceinture*, cette œuvre prend appui sur un compromis narratif qui tente d'unir l'éclatement logique du premier texte à un témoignage plus direct sur l'atmosphère de l'Occupation dans la capitale. Le chaos narratif de ce roman, qui combine les techniques de la prolepse, de l'analepse et du chevauchement des strates temporelles, s'ordonne de façon logique dès que l'on cesse d'observer la succession des scènes pour ne plus considérer que le seul point de vue, ambulatoire, du personnage central.

Un développement ultérieur traitera plus spécifiquement de la structure temporelle du roman. Pour le moment, il importe de remarquer la confusion établie par l'écrivain entre l'instant de la narration et celui de l'énonciation, à savoir le parcours réel du protagoniste, de retour sur le « lieu du drame » après un certain nombre d'années, et l'évocation proprement dite des instants tragiques :

> Le mois d'août à Paris provoque l'afflux des souvenirs. Le soleil, les avenues vides, le bruissement des marronniers... Je m'assieds sur un banc et contemple la façade de briques et de pierres. Les volets sont fermés depuis longtemps. Au troisième étage se trouvaient les chambres de Coco Lacour et d'Esméralda. J'occupais la mansarde de gauche[2].

Ainsi, le narrateur va projeter son univers mental sur les lieux qu'il parcourt, ces derniers paraissant moins découverts que reconnus et avérés par le regard. Le héros convoque, de la sorte, nombre d'images et de réminiscences qui vont nourrir

---
[1] *La Ronde de nuit*, p. 56-57 et 76.
[2] *Ibid.*, p. 77.

son esprit, et surtout apporter leur propre code de référence. La confusion qui s'établit alors renforce le chaos ambiant :

> Les arcades de la rue de Rivoli. Il se passait quelque chose de grave. J'avais remarqué des files ininterrompues de voitures le long des boulevards extérieurs. On fuyait Paris. La guerre sans doute. Un cataclysme imprévu[1].

Loin de constituer un simple artifice de style, le déchiffrage d'une époque confuse par une conscience perturbée, ordonnée autour d'une marche solitaire et nocturne, vient se mettre au rang des stratégies narratives de Modiano – qui visent à déplacer ou à permuter l'élément essentiel afin d'en diminuer la charge affective et traumatisante. La fuite de Swing Troubadour semble prendre fin dans le village des *Boulevards de ceinture*, dont la configuration générale se limite à un périmètre de quelques centaines de mètres englobant une villa et une auberge de campagne. Le talent de Modiano semble résider dans l'exploitation de ces contraintes et de leur dimension symbolique. La décomposition morale, réduite à un unique quartier de la capitale – laissant donc au narrateur la possibilité de « changer de rive » – se concentre en un seul territoire, le village de peintres et sa réduction synecdochique, à savoir le « Clos-Foucré », synthèse des exactions et turpitudes de la France collaboratrice. Les déambulations dans le village se trouvent très vite réduites aux allers et retours entre la villa Mektoub et l'auberge, et exceptionnellement à une visite aux haras voisins.

Le caractère oppressant du village communique au protagoniste une sorte de délire obsidional. Le jeune homme se trouve rapidement sommé de choisir entre l'obligation morale de protéger son père et le désir de fuite que lui inspire l'aspect presque concentrationnaire de l'endroit. La solution retenue, qui propose la fusion des deux aspirations – le narrateur fuit les lieux en compagnie de Chalva –, signera la perte des deux hommes, puisqu'elle suppose un retour dans le Paris mortifère du roman précédent.

---

[1] *Ibid.*, p. 97.

L'importance conférée à l'espace et au marquage topographique constitue un des aspects essentiels du travail effectué par l'écrivain. Cette présence physique du lieu, qui constitue symboliquement la transcription géographique d'un espace mental, participe directement de l'« inquiétante étrangeté » produite par la restitution romanesque de la France de l'Occupation. La présence de l'envahisseur, la modification des rapports entre les êtres et l'angoisse diffuse liée aux bouleversements survenus depuis le début des années quarante ont remis en cause le sentiment de confiance et de sécurité que l'individu pouvait éprouver à l'égard d'un endroit familier. Les rues et bâtiments deviennent les dépositaires et relais des déchirures morales. Dès lors, une sorte de correspondance insidieuse vient s'établir entre l'univers intérieur et l'univers extérieur du héros-narrateur, qui répercute et renforce les traumatismes nés de la guerre et de ses désarrois. On remarquera enfin que l'importance conférée à l'espace et la croyance en leur pouvoir conservatoire trouvent leur aboutissement logique dans l'avant-dernier texte en date de Modiano. Celui-ci se trouve consacré à la communion indirecte avec un être par le contact avec les lieux qui l'ont vu évoluer.

LE CAS DE *DORA BRUDER*

L'exploration du Paris des années soixante ou de la fin du siècle permet de remonter le temps, puisque les lieux conservent la trace des souvenirs enfuis et des êtres disparus. D'autre part, la symbiose qui s'opère entre ces représentations d'un monde révolu et la sensibilité de Modiano facilitent le contact ou la sympathie entre le passé insaisissable et un présent silencieux. Aussi le Modiano des années quatre-vingt-dix attache-t-il une importance considérable à l'arpentage de la capitale, dans l'espoir de partager l'esprit d'un lieu, et partant les sentiments de ses occupants.

L'obsession cadastrale, déjà présente dans les romans précédents, prend toute son ampleur dans le troisième volet de la seconde trilogie de l'Occupation, *Dora Bruder*. Profondément marqué par la figure d'une jeune juive, dont le drame entretient – d'après lui – nombre de résonances avec l'histoire des Modiano, l'écrivain entreprend d'inventorier toutes les stations de son chemin de croix. Il arpente, plus de cinquante ans après les faits, la plupart des lieux qui jalonnèrent son itinéraire funeste : l'appartement du boulevard Ornano, l'internat religieux du Saint-Cœur-de-Marie ou la prison des Tourelles. Les déambulations du romancier sont soigneusement consignées sous la forme d'un rapport de détective, offrant autant de renseignements sur la jeune fille qu'il lève d'énigmes sur la personnalité de l'enquêteur.

Celui-ci prend toute la mesure du sort fatal de la jeune Dora, et tente, dans un récit qui essaie de « dire l'absence, la rendre présente[1] », de se faire gardien de mémoire. La démarche géographique permet, en effet, de lire le passé dans les restes d'un présent décomposé – Modiano note avec la plus grande méticulosité les changements architecturaux et urbains survenus en cinquante ans[2] ; d'autre part, le romancier se plaît à noter une sorte de déterminisme, qui inscrirait sa rencontre avec Dora dans un espace prédéfini. L'empathie qu'il éprouve pour la jeune fille ne serait pas le fruit du hasard mais d'une nécessité d'ordre spatial :

> En 1965, je ne savais rien de Dora Bruder. Mais aujourd'hui, trente ans après, il me semble que ces longues attentes dans les cafés du carrefour Ornano, ces itinéraires toujours les mêmes – je suivais la rue du Mont-Cenis pour rejoindre les hôtels de la Butte Montmartre : l'hôtel Roma, l'Alsina ou le Terass, rue Caulaincourt – [...] tout cela n'était pas dû simplement au hasard[3].

---

[1] Pierre Lepape, *in Le Monde des livres*, p. II, vendredi 4 avril 1997.
[2] « L'urbanisation elle-même devient une opération de nettoyage de la mémoire. Il y a dans *Dora Bruder* des pages simples et magnifiques sur le Paris d'aujourd'hui, qui essaie d'effacer jusqu'aux dernières traces du Paris d'hier pour gommer de son paysage jusqu'à l'écho des voix de ces enfants aux noms polonais "et qui étaient si parisiens qu'ils se confondaient avec les façades des immeubles" ». Pierre Lepape, *ibid.*
[3] *Dora Bruder*, p. 12.

On ajoutera, pour tempérer ces propos, qu'un journaliste du *Figaro Magazine*, Bertrand de Saint Vincent, publia le récit de ses déambulations sur les traces de Modiano – qui suivait lui-même l'itinéraire de la jeune Bruder –, peu de temps après la parution de l'ouvrage. Il notait, à cette occasion, les nombreuses inexactitudes du compte rendu de l'écrivain, sans doute rattrapé, malgré qu'il en eût, par sa vocation de romancier :

> [Le 41 du boulevard Ornano] était un hôtel, ainsi que le 39. Aujourd'hui, c'est « *un immeuble de cinq étages [...] indiquant le nom de son architecte, un certain Pierrefeu* ». J'ai longuement observé la façade [...]. Le nom qui y figure est Richefeu [...]. J'ai suivi le boulevard Barbès jusqu'à la rue Polonceau [...]. Quand Dora Bruder y habitait, il y avait deux hôtels, l'un au 49, le second au 32 : « *Ces deux hôtels ne portaient pas de nom*, affirme Modiano. *Aujourd'hui, ils n'existent plus* ». Au n° 32, sur la façade d'un établissement discret, j'ai pourtant lu : « *Café vins Polonceau-Hôtel* ». Juste en face, au n° 29, une affiche signale la présence d'un autre hôtel[1].

Ces rectifications remettent moins en cause la validité du travail de l'écrivain qu'elles montrent la nécessaire interprétation de la réalité, et ce dans le cadre d'un témoignage. Celui-ci tire toute sa force non d'une scrupuleuse recension de faits et de constatations irréfutables mais d'une vision globale – à savoir la disparition de l'« univers du drame », à tout jamais hors de portée. Elle scelle, de la sorte, l'oubli définitif dans lequel seront précipités les personnages, puisque leur présence ne subsiste que dans les lieux investis de leur présence.

LES COMPOSANTS DU « PAYSAGE NATUREL »

Attachés à des repères précis, les personnages se définissent par les endroits qu'ils ont pris l'habitude de hanter.

---

[1] Le *Figaro Magazine*, p. 122-123, vendredi 28 mars 1997.

De fait, la méticulosité avec laquelle le romancier établit la nomenclature des lieux que les acteurs du récit fréquentent – ou ont fréquenté – poursuit le travail entrepris sur les ressources de l'onomastique[1]. L'écrivain, qui recompose une période sublimée par les inflexions de sa mémoire, tente, de la sorte, d'unir vérité contrefaite et fiction réaliste, dans une semblable continuité de style, utilisant à cette fin toutes les ressources offertes par l'espace et le temps.

Nous nous intéresserons principalement aux lieux de fête et de plaisir des soirées parisiennes, havres dans lesquels les « oiseaux de nuit » viennent se poser durant un moment. Dénués de toute envergure morale et psychologique, ceux-ci viennent tromper leur vacuité dans ces lieux anonymes, avec lesquels ils finissent parfois par être confondus, comme en une étrange osmose. Les protagonistes et leurs comparses se trouvent naturellement à leur place dans ces bars ou cabarets, qui représentent des refuges tout indiqués pour ces êtres venus de nulle part. La plupart des rencontres déterminantes se nouent dans ces lieux. En effet, Raphaël fait la connaissance de Lévy-Vendôme au « Dubern », restaurant bordelais ; Swing Troubadour est recruté par le Khédive au « Royal-Villiers » ; « Le Clos-Foucré » abrite la plupart des entrevues de Serge Alexandre avec Murraille et les rédacteurs de *C'est la vie* ; l'action de *Lacombe Lucien* prend place essentiellement autour de « l'Hôtel-restaurant des Grottes » ; Ingrid Thyrsen se réfugie dans un café du neuvième arrondissement, au moment du couvre-feu, et fait ainsi la rencontre de Rigaud. On pourrait multiplier les exemples[2].

Angoissé par l'idée de laisser des traces identifiables, le narrateur des romans affectionne ces lieux dans lesquels son absence totale d'identité ne risque pas de le distinguer du reste

---

[1] À savoir la mobilisation de la fonction poétique du langage dans la création des patronymes.
[2] Notamment dans les romans dont l'occupation ne constitue pas le thème central. Ainsi, l'action de *Villa triste* se limite à la chambre d'hôtel occupée par Chmara et sa compagne. Les cafés de la rue de Tournon et de la rue Dante constituent, par exemple, les indispensables points de rencontre des personnages d'*Un cirque passe* et de *Du plus loin de l'oubli*.

de ses semblables, fugaces[1] et insignifiants. On peut suivre ainsi Annie Murraille à la trace, introuvable promise égarée dans quelque cabaret à la mode, où elle se consacre au divertissement, afin de mieux fuir le néant de sa propre existence :

> Sylviane Quimphe consultait son agenda [...] : « Chez Tonton », Trinité 87-42. « Au Bosphore », Richelieu 94-03. « El Garron », Vintimille 30-54, « L'Étincelle » [...]. On lui avait signalé le passage d'Annie, vers onze heures, au « Monte-Cristo ». Avec un peu de chance, on la « coincerait » chez « Djiguite » ou à « L'Armorial »[2].

L'écrivain établit la recension des établissements dédiés à la nuit, comme il énumère les garages dans *Remise de peine*. Le numéro de téléphone qui les suit relève tout autant de l'« effet de réel » que du plaisir, presque sensuel, que l'écrivain éprouve à citer, comme en une longue litanie, les anciens indicatifs téléphoniques – qui constituent les seules traces d'un continent englouti, et porteurs donc d'une grande force nostalgique[3]. On retrouve, encore une fois, l'usage de la fonction poétique du langage, associé de façon étroite aux rêveries sur le passé dans les romans de Modiano ; le détail importe moins que sa forme phonique, riche en puissance nostalgique.

Le romancier, d'autre part, ne travestit que rarement les noms, et la plupart des établissements cités semblent avoir réellement existé. La consultation de sources d'informations telles que les annuaires de l'époque ou les conversations familiales – rappelons qu'Albert Modiano n'accordait ses rendez-vous d'affaire que dans les cafés et cabarets fréquentés par la Gestapo – aura permis à l'écrivain de faire preuve d'une réelle exactitude dans sa peinture de l'Occupation frivole. À la

---

[1] Au sens étymologique du terme.
[2] *Les Boulevards de ceinture*, p. 137-138.
[3] Patrick Modiano n'a jamais caché sa passion de collectionneur d'annuaires périmés. À ce titre, les propos de Hutte, au début de *Rue des boutiques obscures*, sur le caractère presque tragique des informations contenues dans le bottin, pourraient être les siens.

suite de ces cabarets, Hervé Le Boterf ajoute dans son ouvrage[1] une liste de « points chauds que la presse allemande recommandait tout particulièrement à ses lecteurs : « Chez Elle », le « Ciro's », le « Danube », le « Grand Jeu », « Don Juan », « Ève », « Paris-Paris », « le Jockey », le « Liberty's », « Château-Bagatelle », « L'Impératrice », « Le Lido », « Shéhérazade » et le « Tabarin ». En ce qui concerne « l'événement mondain le plus « parisien » du mois, rapporté par « Monsieur Tout-Paris[2] » dans le numéro 57 de *C'est la vie*, à savoir la réouverture du cabaret « Jane Stick », rue de Ponthieu, Hervé Le Boterf indique, dans une notule qui suit cette recension des lieux de plaisir :

> Roland Toutain avec la complicité de Jimmy Gaillard, lance dans [ce] cabaret la mode d'un ballet de remplacement. Le jeu consiste à faire valser des assiettes en direction d'une victime préalablement consentante et qui doit éviter, par des réflexes plus ou moins conditionnés, de les recevoir en pleine figure. [...] Ainsi on peut, dès 1941, classer les boîtes de nuit en deux catégories : celles qui reçoivent leur pratique avec ou sans spectacle de neuf heures du soir à minuit, et celles qui leur offrent asile jusqu'à l'aube[3].

Les établissements cités par Modiano appartiennent bien évidemment à cette seconde catégorie. Les maisons closes et leurs réguliers arrivages de nouvelles pensionnaires constituaient également les délices des soirées parisiennes. L'un des collaborateurs intervenant à la fin de *La Place de l'Étoile* fait ainsi état d'un goût partagé par la plupart des acteurs de la Collaboration :

> Voulez-vous que nous allions au « One-Two-Two » me propose Paulo Hayakawa. Il y a là-bas des filles sensationnelles. Pas besoin de payer ! Il suffit que je montre ma carte de la Gestapo française[4].

---

[1] *Op.cit.*, p. 205.
[2] *Les Boulevards de ceinture*, p. 36.
[3] Hervé Le Boterf, *op.cit.*, p. 207.
[4] *La Place de l'Étoile*, p. 145.

Endroit particulièrement prisé, cette maison « de luxe de la rue de Provence »[1] recevait régulièrement la visite de Henri Lafont – et de ses nombreux amis – lorsqu'il paraissait las de donner des réceptions dans sa maison. C'est dans cet endroit que Rodrigue, l'un des personnages principaux de *Drôle de jeu*, propose de combler une après-midi de fin mars 1944 :

> « Viens au bordel avec nous, proposa-t-il. Ça te changera les idées. Les filles du *one-two-two* sont bien stylées et évitent les trivialités qui effraient les jeunes gens. C'est oui[2] ? »

Si Patrick Modiano ne se pose pas en historien dans ses premières œuvres concernant l'Occupation, recomposant à son gré les personnages et situations selon sa lecture personnelle de la période, il n'en demeure pas moins vrai que son travail romanesque s'appuie sur une solide connaissance de la « petite histoire » de Paris à l'heure allemande. Si cette reviviscence du passé ne constitue pas une fin en soi, et sert de substance, pour une part essentielle, à une recomposition de l'Histoire, elle participe très nettement à la création d'un climat particulier mis au service de l'« effet de réel » et de la vraisemblance romanesque. Lorsqu'il n'éprouvera plus le besoin de travestir ses interrogations et angoisses derrière les oripeaux de la fiction, dans les années quatre-vingt-dix, l'écrivain en délaissera les artifices pour ne plus tendre que vers un traitement de la période, privilégiant l'épure et le dépouillement.

LIBERTE HISTORIQUE ET VERITE DE L'IMAGINAIRE : UNE APPROCHE DE L'AUTOFICTION

Les œuvres de Modiano qui prennent appui sur la période de l'Occupation abondent en notations et en détails

---

[1] Hervé Le Boterf, *op.cit.*, p. 32.
[2] Roger Vailland, *op.cit.*, p. 183.

susceptibles de donner des gages de vérité à cette évocation. On rappellera que le romancier ne se présente pas comme historien et en (re)-créateur d'une époque, qui l'intéresse moins par le charme nostalgique dont elle serait le dépositaire que pour les obsessions familiales – et personnelles – qu'il peut y projeter. Ainsi, la figure de Lacombe Lucien, qui choqua terriblement les esprits lors de la sortie du film, ne représente qu'une variation cinématographique de la nullité existentielle d'un Swing Troubadour, déjà illustrée dans *La Ronde de nuit*. En effet, d'un point de vue strictement historique, il paraissait difficilement crédible de montrer la totale relativité des engagements dans le Lot de juin 1944, tant semblaient tranchées les positions politiques et idéologiques dans cette région. Le sort des combats était scellé depuis déjà quelques semaines, et seul un attachement viscéral à la cause nazie pouvait justifier l'agrégation à la « Police allemande » ou à la Milice – ce qui n'est absolument pas le cas du jeune Lucien.

Modiano n'ambitionne nullement de brosser une fresque convaincante de la France des années noires, mais explore, en essayant de respecter autant que possible l'atmosphère d'une époque, les sentiments des êtres qu'il choisit de mettre en scène. Ces derniers incarnent des figures déléguées qui viennent illustrer « le malaise que [son père] avait éprouvé sous l'Occupation »[1], ainsi que l'incapacité absolue de se repérer en fonction d'une norme morale. Bernard Pivot pouvait ainsi noter dans *Le Figaro littéraire* du 8 octobre 1969, au moment de la parution de *La Ronde de nuit* :

> Le jeune romancier semble mettre l'histoire à distance : la tour Eiffel prend des libertés avec le « black-out », et la présentation de touristes anglais dans un théâtre à l'époque est saugrenue. L'Occupation n'a pas, de fait, de valeur réaliste mais obsessionnelle. Ce qui touche [Modiano] dans le Paris de cette époque-là, ce n'est pas sa signification politique ou historique, mais sa valeur de « dernière en date » des figures dangereuses et héroïques des *Mystères de Paris*, avec ses maquisards et ses mohicans. C'est le Paris de

---

[1] *Dora Bruder*, p. 72.

l'ombre qui enveloppe cette *Ronde* et sa valeur d'obsession qui explique les retours et les répétitions presque cycliques du récit qui semble parfois, comme dans une ronde, revenir sur ses pas.

Cette mise à distance de la réalité représente un des enjeux majeurs de l'œuvre du jeune Modiano, qui recompose l'histoire de ses origines, gardées secrètes durant nombre d'années, à l'aide des seules ressources de la création romanesque.

Une vingtaine d'années plus tard, l'écrivain parcourt de nouveau le champ de ses interrogations existentielles, liées de façon intrinsèque à la période des années sombres. Pendant cet intervalle, il a quelque peu délaissé la peinture du Paris de la guerre pour explorer d'autres thèmes. Cette période, qui couvre la quasi-totalité des années quatre-vingts et le milieu de la décennie suivante, nous paraît la moins intéressante de cet auteur, incapable de développer de façon convaincante des récits n'entretenant que peu de rapports avec son histoire personnelle. La fiction semble se nourrir d'elle-même, tournant à vide, et exhibant les aspects les plus caricaturaux d'une écriture qui présente son propre pastiche[1].

Conscient de l'impasse romanesque dans laquelle il se fourvoyait, ou peut-être taraudé par des questions restées sans réponse, Modiano développe une nouvelle trilogie de l'Occupation, qui prend l'exact contre-pied du système narratif du premier triptyque. Le roman cède progressivement le pas à une sorte d'autofiction qui gagne en émotion ce qu'elle perd en inventivité romanesque. Il convient de remarquer, à cet égard, que seul *Voyage de noces* porte la mention « roman », *Fleurs de ruine* et *Dora Bruder* (qui joue essentiellement le rôle

---

[1] Nous pensons notamment à l'écriture blanche de romans tels qu'*Une jeunesse*, *Vestiaire de l'enfance*, *Un cirque passe* et surtout *Du plus loin de l'oubli*. À l'exception du deuxième, ces textes racontent, d'une façon de plus en plus maladroite, une histoire identique, celle de la jeunesse corrompue par l'expérience adulte ; des jeunes gens sont, malgré eux, entraînés dans de confuses affaires plus ou moins commerciales, totalement illicites, qui auront raison de leur innocence originelle.

d'apostille au premier) ne comportant aucune information particulière sur la nature du texte. De fait, ces deux derniers écrits paraissent fonctionner sur le mode de l'autocritique, ou à tout le moins du commentaire *a posteriori* sur l'histoire de leur composition.

L'écrivain, bouleversé par la lecture du *Mémorial* établi par Serge Klarsfeld, récuse l'approche ludique de ses premiers romans, qu'il juge infantile – c'est à cette époque qu'il propose une version revue et corrigée de *La Place de l'Étoile* en collection de poche, dans laquelle les aspects les plus provocateurs et scabreux de l'œuvre sont gommés.

> J'avais découvert dans [l]a bibliothèque de mon père, quelques années auparavant, certains ouvrages d'auteurs antisémites parus dans les années quarante qu'il avait achetés à l'époque, sans doute pour essayer de comprendre ce que ces gens-là lui reprochaient. [...] Moi, je voulais dans mon premier livre répondre à tous ces gens dont les insultes m'avaient blessé à cause de mon père. Et, sur le terrain de la prose française, leur river une bonne fois pour toutes leur clou. Je sens bien aujourd'hui la naïveté enfantine de mon projet [...]. Oui, malheureusement, je venais trop tard[1].

On mesure très précisément le clivage qui vient s'établir entre l'irrévérence juvénile de la fin des années soixante et la sérénité critique qui lui fait pendant, trente années plus tard. À partir de ce moment, l'écrivain reprend les principaux aspects de ses premières œuvres, qu'il traitera selon une symétrie inverse – en particulier dans son avant-dernier ouvrage en date. À la fascination mêlée de répulsion pour les collaborateurs et autres dignitaires de l'ordre nouveau répond la compassion véritable – et non dérisoire, comme celle éprouvée pour les fantoches Coco Lacour et Esmeralda – pour les victimes de l'Occupation, les Ingrid Theyrsen et autres Dora Bruder. Le personnage du père, pathétique et ridicule dans le premier et le troisième roman, vient prendre sa réelle dimension de réprouvé

---

[1] *Dora Bruder*, p. 72-73.

impitoyable[1]. Enfin, la disposition et la composition du récit subissent les conséquences de cette évolution ; les derniers textes semblent constitués de vignettes qui n'entretiennent entre elles que des rapports de contiguïté temporelle ou locale, sans l'appui d'une histoire solidement charpentée.

On pourra objecter que *La Place de l'Étoile* ne pouvait que très difficilement être qualifiée de « roman », mais l'emploi des temps ainsi que la présence de personnages récurrents donnaient au texte une apparence de récit fictif, qui paraît absente des deux derniers ouvrages de la seconde trilogie. La fiction impensable et l'autobiographie impossible laissent ainsi la place à un témoignage où l'émotion mesurée sert de relais à la violence contenue des premiers textes, qui pratiquaient, avec une certaine jubilation, le jeu des masques et le travestissement de la réalité.

Afin de comprendre comment l'écrivain a pu, au fur et à mesure des années, accepter puis dépasser le choc traumatisant de l'Occupation – pour évoluer vers le dépouillement de *Fleurs de ruine* et de *Dora Bruder*, il paraît important de réfléchir sur les procédés narratifs des œuvres de jeunesse. Ces derniers, qui donnaient toute son alacrité au récit, en esquivant de ce fait le contact direct avec la période, refoulaient les angoisses sans permettre à l'écrivain de les sublimer. Il appartient, à présent, d'en analyser les procédés.

---

[1] Il dénonce son fils à la police ou tente de l'enrôler de force dans l'armée, après lui avoir subtilisé ses papiers militaires.

Deuxième partie :

L'Occupation : une réalité fantasmée ; étude des procédés.

1940-1945 : ces six années représentent la période clé de l'histoire de Modiano, ce « centre du mystère, [son] obsession [et sa] raison d'être écrivain[1] ». Né au terme de la demi-décennie la plus dramatique de l'histoire contemporaine, le romancier entretient avec celle-ci les rapports les plus ambigus.

Hasards des destinées, l'Occupation voit en effet la rencontre d'un juif, agioteur opérant pour des officines et des centrales d'achats affiliées à la Gestapo, et condamné à une totale clandestinité, avec une jeune première hollandaise, Louisa Colpeyn, qui avait fui l'invasion nazie de son pays. La nature de la relation entre ses deux futurs parents, et surtout les activités de son père, tour à tour protégé et menacé par ses relations d'affaire, ne laisseront d'exercer une trouble attirance sur le jeune homme. Concerné par les années sombres au plus profond de son être, incapable de prendre ses distances avec une période qui lui semble beaucoup plus proche que les menées pseudo-révolutionnaires de la fin des années soixante, ce dernier ne peut aborder ces événements avec recul et détachement.

La part la plus intime de l'écrivain se trouve ainsi convoquée sur l'autel de la création, au même titre que les scènes et personnages issus de ses fantasmes. La recomposition de l'histoire va prendre chez lui la dimension d'une révision de la réalité, envisagée du point de vue de l'héritage familial et non du témoin, même indirect. Les œuvres s'articuleront autour d'un point de vue délibérément subjectif, de sorte que Modiano puisse accepter, dans un premier temps, sa lecture personnelle de l'Occupation, avant d'en assumer toutes les implications.

L'objet de ce présent développement réside dans la mise au jour de l'autonomie absolue du thème, inlassablement

---

[1] Pierre Lepape, article cité.

inventorié et exploré dans les premiers textes du romancier. Fondée sur une totale « dé-réalisation » de l'Histoire, l'écriture va progressivement rendre difficile la distinction entre un travestissement désiré et la croyance involontaire en celui-ci.

À cette fin, si nous ne pratiquons pas l'identification systématique de l'écrivain au protagoniste des récits, il semble par trop tentant, en revanche, de rapprocher la situation du jeune Modiano, au début des années soixante, avec la déréliction de ses personnages. On ne songerait guère à opérer une semblable projection[1] si la narration de *La Place de l'Étoile*, *La Ronde de nuit* ou des *Boulevards de ceinture* ne semblait revêtir l'apparence d'une entreprise cathartique, dont le but serait la purgation des angoisses, confrontant, de la sorte, le romancier aux démons et spectres de son passé – ou, à tout le moins, celui qu'il reconnaît comme sien. Le procédé va trouver ses obstacles naturels dans les contraintes mêmes du genre littéraire ; l'emploi ludique des instances d'énonciation ou des temps du récit révèle rapidement les limites du projet : si celui-ci emporte l'intérêt de l'exégète, il se heurte, en revanche, au scepticisme du critique, pour lequel une narration doit trouver du sens dans sa finalité, et non dans l'exhibition de ses moyens.

Notre analyse s'efforcera de mettre en évidence l'émiettement de la réalité historique ; celle-ci vient prendre appui sur une mobilisation de toutes les ressources de la mémoire et de la nostalgie, son corollaire naturel. Loin d'abolir la distance entre l'objet et le sujet créateur, cette dernière va, au contraire, constituer un écran entre le héros-narrateur et le monde. Auparavant, un inventaire nécessaire des instances de récit, ainsi que du personnel romanesque aura permis une première approche de l'univers modianien.

---

[1] Celle-ci, d'un strict point de vue méthodologique, consisterait à rapprocher systématiquement l'écrivain et sa créature, ce qui représenterait une démarche condamnée d'avance par la logique.

Le statut des personnages : de l'archétype au stéréotype

Loin de livrer concurrence à un quelconque « état-civil » – du moins dans ses premières œuvres[1] –, le romancier cultive volontiers la caricature dans ses textes de jeunesse. Les acteurs des récits paraissent réduits à un simple statut archétypal, qui les met davantage au service d'une démonstration d'ensemble que d'une narration fictive. Le protagoniste lui-même n'échappe pas à cette règle, selon laquelle toute complexité psychologique constitue un obstacle au projet romanesque, qui adopte la logique de la tragédie pour rendre compte du climat délétère de l'Occupation.

Le « nouveau roman » semble avoir exercé sur Modiano une influence plus profonde qu'il n'y paraît. Si le schéma narratif de ses textes, fragmentés et brisés de façon presque systématique, le rattache directement à ce courant, la conception de ses personnages n'est pas sans rappeler celle de ses devanciers, Michel Butor ou Nathalie Sarraute[2].

Le rôle exclusivement fonctionnel du personnel romanesque constitue l'un des aspects saillants des premiers récits. Essentiellement préoccupé par la vision d'ensemble de

---

[1] Nous avons vu, en effet, que l'évolution naturelle de Modiano l'avait conduit à une épure et à une économie de moyens, qui lui faisaient délaisser la fiction pour des témoignages concrets, voire des extraits de fichiers administratifs.

[2] Anne-Marie Obajtek-Kirkwood note, dans son article consacré à Raphaël Schlemilovitch, « [que] la personnalité ne se définit que par ses fonctions, puisqu'elle repose sur un vide originel. La foi en un univers stable et cohérent n'est plus. » Elle cite, à ce propos, le texte fondamental de Nathalie Sarraute, *L'Ère du soupçon* (p. 71-72, dans la collection « Bibliothèque des idées », chez Gallimard) : « Depuis les temps heureux d'*Eugénie Grandet* [...] [le personnage de roman] n'a cessé de perdre successivement ses attributs et prérogatives. [...] Il a, peu à peu, tout perdu : ses ancêtres, sa maison soigneusement bâtie, bourrée de la cave au grenier d'objets de toute espèce [...], et surtout, ce bien précieux entre tous, son caractère qui n'appartient qu'à lui, et souvent jusqu'à son nom. » A.-M. Obajtek-Kirkwood, « Simplement un homme ? Le Protagoniste de *La Ronde de nuit* », in *Französisch heute*, XXVII, 1996, p. 189.

ses romans – la dénonciation des totalitarismes légitimés par les forces vives de la réaction, pour *La Place de l'Étoile*, ou le tableau de l'abjection de *La Ronde de nuit* –, Modiano se soucie peu de la psychologie la plus élémentaire ou de la caractérisation individuelle. À cet égard, l'écrivain apparaît dans une situation plutôt inconfortable, à la croisée de deux tendances irréconciliables ; d'un côté, un roman traditionnel qui s'épuise à renouveler ses formes, tentant d'adapter les canons classiques du récit aux nouvelles préoccupations de son lectorat, et de l'autre une écriture soucieuse de « modernité », qui depuis la fin de la guerre, interroge à chaque instant ses formes d'expression, pour se heurter aux limites mêmes de la communication[1].

Il faudra attendre *Villa triste*, en 1975, pour que la « petite musique de Modiano[2] » parvienne enfin à s'imposer, alors qu'un contemporain comme Le Clézio avait plus rapidement évolué vers une approche plus traditionnelle de la narration, après *Le Procès verbal*, en 1966[3]. Hésitant à franchir le pas, Modiano réduira encore longtemps les interprètes de ses récits à de simples schémas intellectuels, comme s'il n'avait pu dépasser la période de transition contemporaine de ses premiers romans.

Si l'absence de caractérisation leste ses dernières créations d'une certaine pesanteur narrative, ce parti pris se justifie pleinement dans les ouvrages consacrés à l'Occupation. Articulés autour de cette période, et de l'acceptation de celle-ci – qui donnerait à l'écrivain sa légitimité –, les textes échappent difficilement à la caricature. Seules les réactions individuelles,

---

[1] On notera, ainsi, qu'au moment de la publication de *La Place de l'Étoile*, Aragon publiait *Blanche ou l'oubli*, Mauriac, *Un adolescent d'autrefois* et Sollers, *Drame* ; témoignage, s'il en est, de l'aspect protéiforme du roman à cette époque.
[2] Il est difficile de trouver une critique d'un roman de Modiano qui fasse l'économie de cette épithète presque homérique.
[3] On remarquera que ces écrivains de même âge, présentés en leur temps comme les espoirs du roman français, manifestent vers la cinquantaine un intérêt particulier pour les victimes de la *Shoah*. Par exemple, entre *Voyage de noces* et *Dora Bruder*, Le Clézio publie *Onitsha* et *Étoile errante* (1990 et 1991).

déterminées par les conditions matérielles ou idéologiques – et non par les passions humaines – importent à Modiano. Celui-ci paraît beaucoup plus enclin à multiplier les classifications et typologies réductrices qu'à attacher de l'importance aux créatures de chair et de sang qui les constituent.

L'idéal littéraire ne serait pas à chercher du côté du roman balzacien[1], mais de la fiche signalétique extraite d'un rapport de police – en cela, son dernier ouvrage, *Dora Bruder*, remplit parfaitement son objectif, puisque les personnages de l'histoire appartiennent à la réalité, et ne sont évoqués qu'à partir des notes et témoignages des témoins ou registres officiels. Le romancier apparaît comme un enquêteur sur les traces d'un passé qu'il s'approprie, au fur et à mesure de ses découvertes, semblable en cela au Swing Troubadour de *La Ronde de nuit*, qui présentait à trois reprises les *curriculum vitae* des habitués du square Cimarosa, ou au Serge Alexandre des *Boulevards de ceinture*, qui procédait de façon identique, afin d'évoquer l'itinéraire social et matériel des sectateurs de Murraille. C'est d'ailleurs cette dernière présentation, particulièrement abrupte, qui marque le lecteur de l'ouvrage, comme si le parcours de chacun des collaborateurs pouvait se réduire à une série d'anecdotes, nullement insérées par l'écrivain dans le corpus narratif, mais reléguées dans un exposé permettant de se débarrasser d'informations nécessaires mais fastidieuses. On songera ainsi au portrait de Sylviane Quimphe :

> Je [l'ai] mieux connue [...]. Milieu modeste. Son père occupait un poste de veilleur de nuit aux anciennes usines Samson. Elle passa toute son adolescence dans un quadrilatère limité au nord par l'avenue Daumesnil, au sud par les quais de la Rapée et de Bercy [...]. Dans ce décor ingrat, il existe pourtant une zone privilégiée

---

[1] Les deux romanciers marquent pourtant des pauses à certains moments du récit, afin de détailler l'origine et l'histoire des forces en présence – on pensera notamment à *Un début dans la vie* ou *Une ténébreuse affaire* ; mais quand l'auteur de *La Comédie humaine* rebâtit toute une généalogie embrassant des siècles d'histoire de France, consacrant nombre de pages à la dissection des motivations de ses personnages, Modiano se contente d'allusions et d'exposés quelque peu schématiques.

qui aimante les rêves : la gare de Lyon. C'est devant elle qu'échouait toujours Sylviane Quimphe[1].

Adepte d'une croyance en un certain déterminisme social, voire idéologique, Modiano réduit la plupart du temps le comportement de ses personnages à une explication par le milieu, à l'image du conditionnement maternel qui conduisit Marcheret à la Légion étrangère[2]. De fait, Modiano semble adapter la fiche au personnage – qui devient ainsi une simple exemplification – sans ménager de zone d'ombre dans les biographies. Il n'en reste pas moins relativement éloigné des simples vignettes illustratives, et semble soucieux de présenter des caractères originaux[3] ; cependant, il n'en utilise pas leur complexité ou leur potentiel romanesque, puisque ces êtres restent limités à de simples silhouettes fugitives, entraperçues le temps de quelques lignes suggestives : seule la place symbolique qu'ils occupent dans son système narratif paraît le préoccuper.

LE PROTAGONISTE DES ROMANS

À l'exception d'*Une jeunesse*, tous les romans de Modiano sont écrits à la première personne. Témoin et interprète d'un passé qui vient brusquement effleurer la quiétude de son existence, et dont il tente de remonter la piste, le narrateur assume la totale subjectivité des récits. Cette

---

[1] *Les Boulevards de ceinture*, p. 74.
[2] « Sa mère, veuve d'un colonel, avait essayé de l'élever le mieux possible. Cette femme, vieillie prématurément, se sentait menacée par le monde extérieur. Elle aurait souhaité que son fils entrât dans les ordres. Là, au moins, il ne risquerait rien. Marcheret, dès l'âge de quinze ans, n'eut qu'une idée : quitter le plus vite possible leur minuscule appartement de la rue Saussier-Leroy, où le maréchal Lyautey, dans son cadre, semblait l'épier d'un regard très doux. » *Ibid.*, p. 69-70. On se trouve bien proche de l'environnement familial de Jacob X.
[3] Comme le mage Ivanoff, spécialiste de paneurythmie sexuélo-divine, « bulgare charlatan, tatoueur officiel des églises coptes ».

coïncidence entre le nynégocentrisme[1] de l'instance narrative et le « je » de l'écrivain rend aisé le rapprochement et l'identification du créateur avec sa figure déléguée. Si une semblable lecture peut se justifier, à la rigueur, dans les premiers romans, il paraît beaucoup plus contestable d'appliquer cette analyse aux œuvres de la maturité, qui placent l'écrivain Modiano en situation d'observateur, voire d'enquêteur.

Raphaël Schlemilovitch, Swing Troubadour et Serge Alexandre semblent partager nombre de traits avec le jeune Modiano, à savoir la timidité, la haute stature – « le hasard m'avait fait naître dans un pays de culs-bas » déclare Raphaël, lorsqu'il relate ses démêlés avec les khâgneux bordelais – et la jeunesse. Cette dernière mention revient à intervalles réguliers dans les romans de la trilogie ; les protagonistes y font état d'une dépravation qui forme un contraste saisissant avec l'innocence de leur visage juvénile. Porte-parole du romancier, ils illustrent le désarroi d'un homme qui ne trouve pas sa place dans la France des années soixante ; leur caractère falot est la seule réponse qu'ils puissent apporter à l'agression du monde extérieur, faiblesse qui rendra beaucoup plus faciles les différentes compromissions avec les forces du mal. S'ils éprouvent des remords aigus liés à leur totale absence de sens éthique, ils justifient celle-ci au nom d'une forme de veulerie congénitale :

> Ne me sentant aucune vocation particulière, j'attendais de mes aînés qu'ils me choisissent un emploi. À eux de savoir sous quel aspect ils me préféraient […]. Le plus curieux avec les garçons de mon espèce : ils peuvent aussi bien finir au Panthéon qu'au cimetière de Thiais, carré des fusillés. On en fait des héros. Ou des salauds. On ignorera qu'ils ont été entraînés dans une sale histoire à leur corps défendant[2].

---

[1] On appelle phénomène de nynégocentrisme, en narratologie, toute action ou tout événement perçu et retranscrit par le seul point de vue du narrateur. Celui-ci réfère la situation à sa seule perception *hic et nunc*.
[2] *La Ronde de nuit*, p. 92.

Frère de sang de Swing Troubadour, Lacombe Lucien illustre à la perfection ces aphorismes – à la seule différence près que les activités de celui-là ne lui confèrent pas la moindre distinction sociale, contrairement à son jumeau cinématographique. Le jeune Parisien éprouve, en effet, un profond mépris pour ses employeurs, sentiment qu'il change en apitoiement sur lui-même dès que l'occasion lui en est offerte.

En tout état de cause, ces différentes voix battent en brèche tous les discours romanesques sur l'Occupation, qui ont volontiers tranché la nécessaire ambiguïté de l'engagement en une dichotomie des plus réconfortantes pour l'esprit. Dans ses œuvres, Modiano désamorce jusqu'à l'idée même d'une voix narrative cohérente[1], qui vient redoubler celle de la disparition du héros. Les premiers romans se veulent, avant tout, des réponses à l'argument sartrien, illustré dans ses romans et pièces de théâtre, selon lequel l'humanité s'articulait autour des seules catégories du « héros » et du « salaud ». Modiano, comme la plupart des auteurs de sa génération, interroge la notion d'acte – idée qui sous-tendait la catégorisation de Sartre – en partant du postulat de la passivité et de l'indolence.

Les protagonistes apparaissent comme des ombres évoluant dans un royaume de limbes, et sont les jouets des événements ou des personnages extérieurs. Il ne s'agit plus, dès lors, de s'interroger sur la nature de l'action, mais sur la validité proprement dite de celle-ci, sérieusement remise en cause dans le premier texte. L'être, eu égard à son passé ou à sa condition d'apatride, ne peut s'intégrer à un groupe qui lui donne le loisir ou le choix de penser pour ou contre celui-ci. Cantonné, de ce fait, à un simple statut d'observateur, il paraît contraint à se réfugier dans la provocation – *La Place de l'Étoile* – ou la déréliction – Swing Toubadour ou, dans une moindre mesure, Serge Alexandre : autant de variations sur le thème de l'individu livré seul aux passions d'un monde qu'il ne reconnaît pas comme sien.

---

[1] On note, en effet, une absence totale de logique narrative dans *La Place de l'Étoile*. *La Ronde de nuit* est régie par le principe de la paralepse, et *Les Boulevards de ceinture* se caractérisent par de nombreuses invraisemblances.

LE TRAGIQUE DE L'OCCUPATION

Protagoniste ou simples acteurs des drames qui se jouent dans les romans, tous les personnages semblent promis à un destin qui paraît pour le moins prévisible – et qu'ils n'excluent pas de leurs pensées journalières –, usant d'un cynisme achevé ou d'une relative résignation. Il ne faudrait pas pour autant voir dans chaque collaborateur un condamné à mort en puissance, puisque les œuvres consacrées à l'Occupation mentionnent un certain nombre de dignitaires de la cause nazie ayant échappé aux fourches caudines de l'Épuration.

Il n'en demeure pas moins vrai que la menace, évidente, pèse sur chacun d'eux, mais, comme le *fatum* de la tragédie antique, n'empêche pas les personnages d'aller jusqu'au bout de leur destin. À cet égard, les pedigrees fournis par Modiano semblent annoncer et justifier le caractère inéluctable et prévisible de leurs actes. Ainsi, les séides du Reich constituent, avant tout, un système de figures déterminées par leur existence passée à endosser un rôle. L'exercice de cette fonction ne s'inscrit pas dans une quelconque optique finaliste, susceptible de donner un sens idéologique ou existentiel à leur action[1], mais dans la logique de leurs personnalités et comportements.

Si tous se savent condamnés d'avance par une intervention judiciaire inéluctable, dont l'action pourrait être rapprochée de la justice immanente de la tragédie, aucun ne tente d'infléchir le cours des fatals enchaînements d'exactions – dans lequel on serait tenté de voir l'*hubris* des héros de la scène tragique, violence exercée tout autant contre la puissance divine que sur soi-même, et ce dans une provocation identique de l'inexorable accomplissement du destin. Les personnages

---

[1] À une exception près, et de taille, celle de Lacombe Lucien. Celui voit dans ses exactions, commises au nom de la « Police allemande », une réelle validation de son existence, jugée jusque-là inutile. Il est, d'autre part, le seul personnage dont la mort, et les circonstances de celle-ci, soient clairement indiquées. Faut-il y voir la sanction de l'engagement ou une concession au spectateur, susceptible d'être désarmé par une fin « trop » ouverte ?

des romans n'inscrivent pas leur action, qui, rappelons-le, vaut pour eux brevet d'existence, dans une durée susceptible de représenter un total bouleversement de leur existence. Dotés de l'infaillible prescience des sursitaires, ils n'en dévient pas moins d'une conduite qu'ils savent pertinemment répréhensible, mais qui, elle seule, et c'est en cela que réside tout le paradoxe de la notion, peut octroyer tout le sens qui avait, jusqu'à cette période, fait défaut à leur vie.

L'Occupation permet donc d'actualiser pleinement toutes les virtualités du caractère, faisant ainsi prendre conscience à l'individu de sa véritable dimension – toute néfaste et nuisible qu'elle semble ; la thématique mise en évidence rejoint encore une fois la logique de la tragédie, qui associe à la démarche, au sens propre, « fatale » des héros une révélation ontologique, qui se fait d'autant plus prégnante que la vie du protagoniste touche à sa fin. C'est ce même type de dévoilement identitaire qui se trouve mis en œuvre dans les romans de Modiano consacrés à l'Occupation ; les chimères que nourrit Henri Normand semblent contenir en elles-mêmes, dans la dérisoire constance qui caractérise leur culte, la vanité et l'échec des ambitions du Khédive. Celui-ci ne sera jamais préfet de police, pas plus qu'Annie Murraille ou Betty Beaulieu ne connaîtront la gloire de l'écran ; toutefois l'exercice d'un pouvoir relatif, ou l'accès à des sphères sociales demeurées jusqu'alors hors d'atteinte, aura légitimé leurs actes et révélé leur personnalité profonde. L'occupation allemande représente un moment unique et privilégié, proche du *kairos* grec, qui vient soudainement mobiliser les instincts et traits de caractère condamnés par l'ordre social défunt – ce qui constituait l'obstacle majeur aux ambitions de ces hommes et de ces femmes.

Les pouvoirs totalitaires et dictatoriaux ont toujours utilisé, pour leur plus grand profit, les services de ces personnages frustrés de reconnaissance, immanquablement reconnaissants et attachés de façon indéfectible au régime qui leur octroyait la liberté de donner libre cours à leurs penchants. Exécuteurs fidèles de toutes les basses besognes – pour le compte d'une instance qui les sacrifiera en cas de nécessité afin d'assurer sa survie –, les janissaires de l'ordre constituent un inestimable vivier de forces obscures qui s'estime souvent en deçà des attentes du pouvoir. Pasolini, dans sa dernière œuvre, *Salo ou les cent vingt jours de Sodome*, montrait de façon convaincante comment le bras armé de tout régime totalitaire constitue son auxiliaire indispensable, en s'érigeant comme force de relais dans les moindres parties du corps social, en donnant au plus infime exécutant une importance considérable. Ainsi, le GI Lévy du *kibboutz* disciplinaire ou, dans un autre contexte, Ferdinand Poupet, Maud Gallas ou Tonin Luciaga[1] viennent échanger leur concours ponctuel contre la reconnaissance existentielle octroyée par le Léviathan, incarné par Israël ou Vichy, et dont la IIIe République, dans le second cas, les avait privés.

S'il se garde de faire l'apologie de ces nervis patentés, Modiano ne porte sur ces derniers que des jugements moraux de convenance. Il semble beaucoup plus intéressé par la nature des comportements et leur observation méthodique que par leur stricte condamnation. L'écrivain s'efforce, avant toute chose, d'élucider les mécanismes mentaux susceptibles de conduire à l'abomination et à la barbarie. Cette obsession trouve son corollaire dans l'intérêt manifesté pour le reniement des convictions et la trahison des principes.

« Tu trahiras sans vergogne. »

Le Paris de Modiano se trouve approximativement scindé en deux groupes de forces antagonistes. Intermédiaire, dans le meilleur des cas, ou agent double dans la plupart des situations, le narrateur vient se mettre au service des deux entités, gommant les traits saillants de sa personnalité afin de

---

[1] Personnages qui apparaissent dans les quatre premières œuvres respectives de Modiano.

mieux diluer son absence d'identité dans l'accomplissement de sa tâche.

D'abord traître moral à sa patrie, en ne choisissant pas d'emblée le camp de la Résistance, le protagoniste double cette lâcheté de la systématique inconsistance de ses choix. Piètre idéologue, ses revirements n'ont rien à voir avec les palinodies que l'on pourrait associer à des remises en cause, et apparaissent plus simplement liés à une profonde débilité de caractère. Jouet des événements, désireux de ne mécontenter personne, épousant spontanément les opinions de son interlocuteur, le narrateur se retrouve obligé de trahir, par simple faiblesse d'âme plutôt que par impératif moral. Paradoxalement, cette pusillanimité le libère de toute partialité, et Raphaël, Swing Troubadour ou Serge Alexandre représentent les seules personnes capables de porter un jugement totalement dépassionné sur les situations auxquelles ils sont confrontés – loin de toute idéologie ou de toute revendication partisanes. Totalement lucides en ce qui concerne leurs faiblesses et lacunes, ils ne souffrent que davantage de leur passivité, quelquefois criminelle. En effet, quiconque se contenterait d'observer les réquisitions auxquelles procède, scrupuleusement, le protagoniste de *La Ronde de nuit*, conclurait à la totale désincarnation du personnage, simple mécanique exécutant fidèlement des instructions monstrueuses. Pourtant, c'est avant tout dans les confins du non-être que le héros modianien trouve sa légitimité existentielle. Œuvrant de façon systématique pour un groupe qui aliène toute sa liberté de pensée – donc qui le délivre de ses angoisses les plus profondes –, il peut ainsi échapper à la taraudante question de l'identité. De façon générale, c'est l'ensemble des personnages de Modiano qui paraissent habités par une langueur et une apathie réconfortantes, seul rempart contre le traumatisme causé par les événements. Ce trait de caractère ne concerne donc pas seulement les acteurs des récits consacrés à l'Occupation, mais également les Jean Dekker ou les Victor Chmara – dont on ne peut savoir quel eût été leur comportement durant les années noires.

Enfin, il faut peut-être se reporter à la figure du père, ce personnage dont l'auteur relate les faits et méfaits (trafics commerciaux, vols dans les usines[1] ou délation de son propre fils), en excusant *a posteriori* les exactions accomplies par celui-ci, les mettant sur le compte d'un nécessaire instinct de survie dans un milieu hostile. L'acte de trahison quitte ainsi le domaine de l'idéologie pour investir celui de la psychologie.

De fait, l'inertie des figures déléguées de l'écrivain, associée à une absence totale de considération d'ordre moral, constitue le principe de base de son fonctionnement affectif et mental – sans que cette carence, comme nous l'avons vu, puisse se justifier par une quelconque rétribution gratifiante. À l'inverse du Genet du *Journal du voleur* ou de *Notre-Dame des fleurs*[2], qui trouve la légitimation de son existence dans la décadence de l'Occupation – celle-ci lui paraît représenter d'un point de vue politique sa perversion et son amoralisme –, le héros modianien ne tire aucun plaisir de ses méfaits. Tout se passe, en effet, comme si son apathie ne pouvait trouver d'autre fin que sa propre réactivation ; la lâcheté d'un Swing Troubadour, par exemple, enferme celui-ci dans un réseau de culpabilité et d'angoisse, qui vient atrophier, en quelque sorte, sa personnalité – bien loin de la jouissance libertaire et solaire ressentie par Genet dans son errance parisienne.

Le protagoniste modianien, hanté par l'idée de déplaire à son entourage, ne peut même pas imaginer un comportement offensif, qui impliquerait son être tout entier, et le ferait passer, presque de force, à un âge adulte qu'il semble redouter plus

---

[1] «Mon père aussi, en 1942, avec des complices, avait pillé les stocks de roulements à billes de la société SKF avenue de la Grande-Armée, et ils avaient chargé la marchandise sur des camions, pour l'apporter jusqu'à leur officine de marché noir, avenue Hoche. Les ordonnances allemandes, les lois de Vichy, les articles de journaux ne leur accordaient qu'un statut de pestiférés et de droit commun, alors il était légitime qu'ils se conduisent comme des hors-la-loi afin de survivre. » *Dora Bruder*, p. 119.

[2] «Après Proust, les deux écrivains français du XXe siècle dont la lecture m'a le plus impressionné du temps de mon adolescence, sont Céline (*Voyage au bout de la nuit, Mort à crédit*) et Jean Genet, celui de *Notre-Dame des fleurs* et de *Miracle de la rose*... » Lettre de Modiano à Thierry Laurent, *op. cit.*, p. 7.

que tout au monde. Réfugié dans une sorte de néant existentiel, qui le place à l'abri des questions sur son identité, le représentant du romancier se condamne à une aboulie presque totale, qui demeure la seule manifestation d'une conscience anéantie par l'absence de tout engagement réel. Encore une fois, nous serions tenté de voir dans cette anesthésie l'image renvoyée par Albert Modiano, sans doute dénoncé puis libéré par les mêmes individus, et qui semble avoir traversé les années d'Occupation dans une semi-inconscience. Toutefois, l'assimilation présente ses limites dans le fait que la seule « traîtrise » réside dans la collaboration d'un juif avec les représentants d'un pouvoir foncièrement antisémite, et non point dans une quelconque allégeance à l'idéologie défendue par celui-ci. En fait, en forçant quelque peu le trait, il serait possible de discerner dans l'atonie des protagonistes modianiens le désarroi du jeune romancier, confronté d'un côté aux vertiges de l'histoire familiale, et d'autre part aux démons de son pays d'adoption.

Il apparaîtrait alors pertinent de distinguer deux mouvements dans la carrière littéraire de Modiano durant les années soixante-dix. Jusqu'en 1978, les personnages centraux se caractérisent par une totale absence de volonté, qui semble paralyser tout esprit de décision. Ballottés au gré des événements, Raphaël, Swing Troubadour ou Victor Chmara laissent à leurs compagnons de rencontre le soin de régir leur destinée. Avec le tournant autofictif de *Livret de famille*, l'écrivain semble considérer le monde sous un nouvel aspect ; l'amnésie succède à l'apathie, de façon presque systématique. On pensera, ainsi, au passé refoulé de Pedro Mc Evoy dans *Rue des boutiques obscures*, à la confusion des souvenirs de Jean Dekker – dont le seul nom demeure son pseudonyme d'écrivain – ou à celle du narrateur de *Dimanches d'août*. Après avoir fait montre d'une irrésistible passivité, le héros annihile le souvenir en le refoulant, de sorte que l'objet même du roman devient le long inventaire de la mémoire. Là où un Serge Alexandre osait une timide riposte face à l'adversité, quitte à laisser son père seul arbitre de la situation, Pedro Mc Evoy ou Jean Dekker semblent nier toute idée de réalité, eu égard à leur absence de contact avec le monde contemporain.

Le réel ne se présente plus que sous l'aspect d'une déclinaison possible de la mémoire, qui vient oblitérer, *ipso facto*, la validité de l'expérience vécue. Très rapidement, le narrateur se trouve confronté à la prégnance du souvenir, qui impose au « réel » son propre code de lecture. Les réminiscences de *Rue des boutiques obscures* viennent rapidement se fondre dans l'évocation de la quête de Mc Evoy, de sorte qu'il devient difficile d'effectuer le départ entre la recension des souvenirs et le libre épanchement de ces derniers au sein de l'existence. À cet égard, l'épisode hautement symbolique de la fuite dans la montagne vient figurer à la fois le refuge – réel – face à l'adversité et l'immersion dans la nuit apaisante de l'amnésie. Seule l'entrée de l'écrivain « en autofiction », à partir de *Remise de peine*, inversera la tendance du repli vers l'imaginaire pour une confrontation directe – et douloureuse – avec l'existence véritable.

La trahison du pays ou des origines semble moins une affaire de conscience que de totale absence de conscience. Privés d'une certaine part d'humanité, les héros modianiens, en laissant aux figures de rencontre la direction de leur existence, paraissent faire preuve d'une certaine forme d'autisme, qui se traduit par un repli sur soi et par la négation de l'idée même de communication – et de « soumission » à l'événement. Seuls les êtres de traverse semblent imposer un contact direct avec la réalité, comme si le protagoniste n'entrait que dans une part mineure de la composition du drame. De fait, son existence se limite à un contact strictement superficiel avec le monde, puisque la notion d'acte lui est presque totalement étrangère.

Swing Troubadour pourrait ainsi faire siennes les paroles d'un autre étranger au monde, Meursault, qui ne parvient pas, lui non plus, à donner à l'existence une autre dimension que celle d'un enchaînement mécanique de faits et d'impressions :

> Quand Raymond m'a donné son revolver, le soleil a glissé dessus. Pourtant, nous sommes restés encore immobiles comme si tout s'était refermé autour de nous.

> Nous nous regardions sans baisser les yeux et tout s'arrêtait ici entre la mer, le sable et le soleil, le double silence de la flûte et de l'eau. J'ai pensé à ce moment qu'on pouvait tirer ou ne pas tirer. Mais brusquement les Arabes, à reculons, se sont coulés derrière le rocher[1].

L'idée d'acte impliquant la personne, il paraît donc impossible, pour les personnages de Modiano comme pour Meursault, de donner une quelconque validité à leur action, puisque celle-ci ne s'inscrit pas dans l'acceptation préalable de l'existence – et donc du réel. Dans les premiers romans de la trilogie, les protagonistes ne semblent jamais s'investir dans une démarche qui leur conférerait une certaine légitimité en tant qu'êtres humains. Les récits se trouvent placés sous le signe de la contemplation distanciée des actes, sans que leur auteur se sente engagé, ou s'investisse, dans leur accomplissement.

On pourrait objecter que toutes les actions du jeune Schlemilovitch – l'attaque contre Val-Suzon, le rapt de la jeune Loïtia ou l'évasion du kibboutz disciplinaire – ou de Serge Alexandre – à savoir la recherche active de son père, au péril de sa vie – contredisent cette idée de langueur et d'apathie dans le rapport au monde ; en fait, la soumission à une autorité supérieure (en l'occurrence Adrien Debigorre, le comte Lévy-Vendôme ou la jeune Rebecca) ou la dévotion – apitoyée – à la figure du père ne peuvent être assimilées à de convaincantes manifestations d'autonomie : celles-ci impliquent, en effet, une autonomie aussi bien morale qu'existentielle.

Rien ne paraît plus étranger au personnage modianien que la transgression de l'ordre – politique, moral, social ou idéologique – ou la contestation du cadre juridique cité. Peu convaincus de leur appartenance au monde adulte, les héros confient la transparence de leur personnage aux représentants du pouvoir. Ces derniers se voient investis, par une instance supérieure, d'une sorte de puissance. Celle-ci leur permet de combler leur vide existentiel, pourvoyant à la sécurité du

---

[1] Albert Camus, *L'Étranger*, édition Folio, p. 90-91.

protagoniste dans le monde mortifère de l'Occupation. On peut donc difficilement appliquer le concept de trahison à cette soumission – garantie d'un certain confort de l'âme – qui apparaît comme une totale anesthésie de la conscience.

Il n'en demeure pas moins vrai que les héros-narrateurs sont des êtres doués d'intelligence, aptes à analyser avec la plus grande clairvoyance l'ordre des événements auxquels ils sont confrontés, sans paraître toutefois capables de mobiliser, de façon effective, leur énergie intellectuelle, afin d'estimer la situation délicate dans laquelle ils se trouvent. Il semble plus rassurant, en effet, de demeurer en retrait des actes (de résistance ou de collaboration, comme les membres du « Clos-Foucré ») plutôt que de risquer une sécurité mentale acquise au prix d'un certain renoncement à l'existence. Le héros peut être alors habilité à justifier ses actes en déclarant :

> Pourtant je n'ai pas le goût des situations morbides.
> « Un petit village
> Un vieux clocher »
> combleraient mes ambitions. Je me trouvais, malheureusement, dans une ville, sorte d'immense Luna Park où le Khédive et Monsieur Philibert me ballottaient de stands de tir en montagnes russes, de Grand-Guignol en chenilles « Sirocco ». À la fin, je m'allongeais sur un banc. Je n'étais pas fait pour tout ça. Je n'avais rien demandé à personne. On était venu me chercher[1].

Une semblable éthopée renouvelle les clichés traditionnellement associés à l'image du félon, qui trouve dans le mal une source de puissance gratifiante et porteuse de jouissance – valorisant toute ou certaine partie du « moi ». Chez Modiano, nulle possibilité d'expliquer en ces termes le comportement du renégat ; le traître n'est pas condamnable, non pas parce qu'il trahit, mais parce qu'il n'*est* pas.

Son tort unique réside, sans doute, dans une quête éperdue de la sécurité presque maternelle – et partant dans une recherche de protecteurs – qu'il espère trouver dans les pères

---
[1] *La Ronde de nuit*, p. 94-95.

de rencontre, ces figures échappées des enfers, qui, pour un bref instant, viennent peupler l'imaginaire de l'écrivain.

LES FIGURES RECURRENTES

Le romancier éprouve une fascination, teintée de répulsion, pour les personnages nocturnes, les êtres qui évoluent dans l'« entre chien et loup » de l'Occupation ; ces créatures semblent des intermédiaires entre le monde des ténèbres et la clarté diurne du quotidien.

La galaxie des personnages modianiens est riche d'une multitude de figures énigmatiques, qui hantent les récits de leur présence intangible et mystérieuse. Ces passeurs permettent aux héros de franchir, par leur seule présence, les rives du Léthé, et d'accéder, pour un bref instant, au temps révolu de l'Occupation.

Situés à mi-chemin des figures récurrentes de *La Comédie humaine* et du personnage « occasionnel », ces individus méritent une étude particulière, puisqu'ils représentent, pour Modiano, des points de contact précieux avec un monde disparu – qu'ils ne tarderont sans doute pas à rejoindre. Un statut indéfini s'attache à ces êtres, et celui-ci est rendu plus opaque par le traitement romanesque. En effet, l'écrivain dote d'un nom identique des personnages dont la psychologie et le statut diffèrent d'un roman à l'autre – comme s'il était seulement intéressé par leur aspect paradigmatique.

L'incohérence des repères, la confusion volontaire des identités, ainsi que la confusion finale qui en résulte, forment une partie intégrante de l'univers modianien, participant à la reconstitution délibérément floue du passé. La multiplication des fausses balises, qui cernent tous les méandres de la mémoire, constitue l'un des principes mêmes du projet romanesque – celui-ci tend à démontrer, par ses moyens narratifs, l'impossibilité de saisir la globalité du passé et celle d'une histoire familiale tourmentée, et à en prendre toute la mesure – de façon à s'acquitter définitivement de son poids.

Nous retiendrons deux figures essentielles dans notre exposé des personnages récurrents. Ces dernières se trouvent situées au point de jonction de deux mondes, à savoir Eddy Pagnon et Philippe de Pacheco ; ces êtres traversent les histoires recomposées de l'Occupation, des *Boulevards de ceinture* à *Fleurs de ruine*. Afin de mieux pénétrer cette esthétique de l'équivoque, nous essaierons d'établir une fiche généalogique pour chacun de ces personnages, puis nous tenterons de recouper les informations dépouillées. Il sera alors possible de mettre en évidence le parcours erratique de la mémoire, élaboré de roman en roman.

Eddy Pagnon est au cœur de l'une des scènes « primitives » de l'univers modianien ; celle-ci recoupe à la fois la fiction et la réalité historique, et constitue l'un des rares épisodes de l'Occupation, évoqués dans les œuvres de jeunesse, à ne pas être travesti. Il s'agit de l'arrestation du père, pendant l'hiver 1943, de son internement et de sa libération presque immédiate par un membre « de ce que l'on a nommé plus tard la bande de la rue Lauriston[1] ». Cette scène a déjà été évoquée dans le développement précédent ; seuls avaient été étudiés les faits et les variations de l'évocation. Il importe, à présent, d'en préciser le contenu informatif.

Le premier personnage apparaît dans *Les Boulevards de ceinture*, au cours d'une conversation dans le silence nocturne du « Clos Foucré » :

> Sylviane profite du silence pour raconter qu'un certain Eddy Pagnon, dans un cabaret où elle se trouvait en sa compagnie, a brandi un revolver d'enfant devant les clients terrifiés. Eddy Pagnon… Encore un nom qui court dans ma mémoire[2].

Et qui attendra près de quinze ans pour être analysé, après une longue période de décantation, durant laquelle Modiano ne traite pas, ou seulement peu, de l'Occupation. *Remise de peine* constitue le premier ouvrage depuis *Rue des*

---

[1] *Fleurs de ruine*, p. 48.
[2] *Les Boulevards de ceinture*, p. 52-53.

boutiques obscures à aborder le thème de manière frontale. Eddy Pagnon constitue, à ce moment, l'enjeu d'un chapitre[1], et Modiano délivre sa fiche signalétique :

> Il était né à Paris dans le Xe arrondissement, entre la République et le canal Saint-Martin [...]. De 1937 à 1939, il avait été employé de garage dans le XVIIe arrondissement. Il avait connu un certain Henri[2] [...] et un nommé Edmond Delehaye. [...] Ces mauvais garçons [...] ont glissé peu à peu dans l'engrenage : des affaires de marché noir, ils se sont laissé entraîner par les Allemands dans des besognes de basse police [...]. Quand mon père avait-il connu Pagnon ? Au moment de l'affaire des chaussettes de Biarritz-Luisait[3] ?

Comme à l'accoutumée, il paraît difficile d'effectuer le départ entre la réalité des faits et leur recomposition romanesque. Ainsi, outre le nom que Modiano a pu être conduit à changer, et ce pour d'évidentes raisons de discrétion, une partie de l'existence évoquée ne peut-elle pas être le fruit de la seule imagination de l'écrivain ? Si tout ce qui se rapporte au père reprend, sans aucun doute, les propos de ce dernier – de toute façon, cet épisode paraît trop poignant pour avoir été inventé –, que penser du *curriculum vitae* ainsi présenté ? Celui-ci est beaucoup plus succinct dans *Fleurs de ruine*, et se borne à compléter les aspects peu développés dans *Remise de peine* :

> Détenu à la Santé. Libéré par Chamberlin *alias* « Henri ». Entre à son service, rue Lauriston. Quitte la bande de la rue Lauriston trois mois avant la Libération. Se retire à Barbizon avec sa maîtresse, la marquise d'A. Il était possesseur d'un cheval de course et d'une auto.

---

[1] Le personnage se trouve mentionné lors d'une conversation entre le narrateur de *De si braves garçons* et la mère d'un de ses anciens amis : « Une photo plus petite : elle, à cheval, en compagnie d'un autre cavalier.
– Ça c'était avec Pagnon, un ami d'Asnières. Il travaillait pour les Allemands... Il nous a fait libérer quand nous avons été arrêtés, le père de Christian et moi... » *De si braves garçons*, p. 148.
[2] Il s'agit, sans doute, de Henri Chamberlin, dit « Lafont », qui sert de modèle à Henri Normand, dit « le Khédive », dans *Les Boulevards de ceinture*.
[3] *Remise de peine*, p. 119-120.

SE TROUVE UNE PLACE DE CHAUFFEUR SUR UN CAMION POUR LE TRANSPORT DE VINS DE BORDEAUX A PARIS[1].

Controuvée ou bien réelle, l'exposition des activités de Pagnon recoupe, dans sa globalité, les itinéraires des principaux acteurs de la Collaboration, tels qu'ils apparaissent dans les romans de la trilogie, en particulier *Les Boulevards de ceinture*[2]. Ces personnages ont surgi du chaos, au début de la guerre, pour retourner, dès la fin de celle-ci, à leur néant originel. En 1972, Modiano déclarait à leur propos : « [Ces êtres], ce n'est pas de gaieté de cœur que je donne leur pedigree. Je me penche sur ces marginaux, ces déclassés, pour retrouver, à travers eux, l'image fuyante de mon père[3]. »

En effet, au-delà de la reconstitution à la fois minutieuse et fantasmatique de la période, c'est bien la figure paternelle qui est interrogée, riche en évocations, celles des hasards et des rencontres : « A la sortie des Magasins généraux, je me demande quel chemin a suivi mon père dans le black-out[4].

Beaucoup plus fournies sont les indications concernant Philippe de Pacheco ; celles-ci apparaissent délibérément orientées du côté de la fiction – Modiano ayant composé avec ce personnage un agrégat de différentes figures réelles, qui évoluaient dans le Paris de l'Occupation.

Le nom du personnage apparaît, de façon incidente, dans *Rue des boutiques obscures* – cité parmi les membres d'un

---

[1] *Fleurs de ruine*, p. 49.
[2] On notera d'ailleurs que Barbizon, où se réfugie le personnage à la fin de la guerre, constitue sans doute le cadre de ce dernier roman.
[3] *Liberté dimanche* (Fribourg), 4 novembre 1972.
[4] *Fleurs de ruine*, p. 49. On lira également les remarques suggestives de Bertrand Westphal, dans son article consacré aux rapports entre l'Histoire et l'écriture, sur la fonction romanesque de ce personnage : « [Eddy Pagnon] semble le comparse d'une Histoire qui, de roman en roman, se profile sans se révéler, une histoire aux fragments épars, sous lesquels on devine l'existence d'un fil conducteur. Si tous les romans de Modiano finissent par se ressembler, n'est-ce pas parce qu'ils participent d'un même projet : hausser un destin dévoilé par avancées infinitésimales au niveau de l'Histoire ? » Article cité, p. 107.

groupe, pendant la guerre – et *Une jeunesse*, où le patronyme est mentionné dans un sommier de police[1]. Dans *Voyage de noces*, au moment de la fuite d'Ingrid et de Rigaud, le portrait se précise[2]. Enfin, Pacheco est à l'origine de la plus grande partie de *Fleurs de ruine* : rencontré par le narrateur à la Cité universitaire, il devient l'objet d'investigations, qui précisent la généalogie esquissée dans l'ouvrage précédent :

> Mon père était péruvien [...]. Ma mère était moitié belge, moitié française. Et, par elle, je suis un descendant du maréchal Victor [...]. [Celui-ci] était un maréchal du Premier Empire. Napoléon l'avait fait duc de Bellune [...]. Quand j'étais plus jeune, je me faisais appeler Philippe de Bellune, mais je n'avais aucun droit à ce titre.
>
> Ainsi son prénom était Philippe. Nous avions pris l'habitude de l'appeler « Pacheco » et, pour nous, « Pacheco » tenait à la fois lieu de nom et de prénom[3].

On notera que le patronyme « Bellune » a déjà été utilisé dans deux œuvres presque concomitantes, *Memory lane* et *Une jeunesse*, toutes deux publiées en 1981. Le personnage, Georges Bellune, présent dans les deux romans, est un ancien compositeur viennois, de son vrai nom « Bluene », qui fuit le nazisme pour venir travailler en France. Il ne semble pas qu'il faille établir d'autres liens qu'un simple effet de récurrence entre les deux termes.

---

[1] « L'intéressée était la maîtresse de Pacheco durant l'Occupation », *op.cit.*, p. 46.
[2] « [Il] porte un costume gris clair. Le visage poupin contraste avec la dureté du regard et de la bouche aux lèvres minces. Ce qui rend le regard dur et fixe, c'est une grande tache à l'œil droit. Les cheveux blonds sont ramenés en arrière », *op.cit.*, p. 130.
Le portrait se trouve complété quelques pages plus loin : « Il tutoyait Rigaud. Ils s'étaient connus, enfants, dans les petites classes du pensionnat de Passy et il aurait voulu évoquer plus longtemps cette période de leur vie [...]. Le blond gagnait beaucoup d'argent grâce à des combines de marché noir [...]. Il jouait à l'homme du monde et indiquait d'un ton faussement détaché qu'il avait pour ancêtre un maréchal d'Empire. Rigaud l'appelait tout simplement Pacheco. » *Voyage de noces*, p. 138-139.
[3] *Fleurs de ruine*, p. 60-61.

L'autofiction *Fleurs de ruine* s'articule, de fait, autour du personnage de Pacheco, individu énigmatique auquel le protagoniste va attribuer de nombreux méfaits :

> Le hasard avait voulu que, dans un lot de vieux journaux des années 1946 et 1948, je tombe sur deux entrefilets. Le premier faisait état d'une liste de personnes recherchées à cause de leurs activités pendant l'Occupation. Parmi celles-ci figurait « Philippe de Bellune », dit « de Pacheco », qui serait mort l'année dernière des suites de son internement à Dachau. Mais on exprimait des doutes sur cette mort[1].

En fait, le dénommé Pacheco a usurpé l'identité du véritable « Philippe de Bellune », fils de Mario Riclos y Perez de Pacheco et de Éliane Werry de Hults[2]. Ses nom et prénom véritables sont Charles Lombard, ancien garçon de café figurant aux côtés de deux couples, sur la photographie qui ouvre le récit – celui-ci, comme *Les Boulevards de ceinture*, commence par une rêverie sur un instantané.

Le véritable Pacheco a fréquenté les milieux troubles de l'Occupation – sans que l'on apprenne en quoi consistaient ses activités véritables – et a eu maille à partir avec les autorités : on cite le mandat d'amener délivré contre lui, en 1946, et une audience à laquelle il ne s'est pas présenté, deux ans plus tard.

Le personnage central du texte ne renvoie donc qu'indirectement à la Collaboration, qu'il désigne nominalement, sans pour autant entretenir de liens étroits avec elle. Lombard *représente* Pacheco, comme la pièce, le jeton, désigne de façon symbolique une valeur monétaire sans la constituer. Contrairement à la première trilogie, dans laquelle la force de l'Occupation subvertissait la narration, entraînant le narrateur dans un jeu halluciné avec les images du passé

---

[1] *Ibid.*, p. 66.
[2] *Fleurs de ruine*, p. 74. On remarquera que cette dernière filiation correspond, à peu de choses près, à celle de Modiano ; dans les deux cas, un apatride (italo-égyptien pour Modiano, péruvien pour Pacheco) épouse une Belge. De cette union naît un fils, marqué par la période de l'Occupation. On notera le vif intérêt que porte Modiano à de semblables croisements.

portées à reviviscence, le second triptyque prend ses distances, et assourdit considérablement le tumulte : *Voyage de noces* est un roman écrit par défaut, une suture entre la violence de l'Histoire et l'impuissance du témoin, *Dora Bruder* prend l'aspect d'un long repentir, et *Fleurs de ruine* multiplie les efflorescences narratives pour masquer la vacuité des personnages.

Lombard est un imposteur, qui, par maladresse, adopte l'identité d'un collaborateur, sans entretenir lui-même la moindre relation avec le passé tant redouté par le narrateur-écrivain. Comme dans *Rue des boutiques obscures*, l'identité réelle de Pacheco reste discutable – l'œuvre s'achève par l'évocation très ambiguë du personnage – et c'est la période tout entière qui se trouve dès lors frappée de soupçon. La précision des informations – fiches signalétiques, mains courantes, coupures de presse, dans *Fleurs de ruine* et *Dora Bruder* – ne change rien à la confusion de l'esprit, puisque ce sont les figures tutélaires, les présences testimoniales qui se trouvent remises en cause. Lombard figure, avant tout, une forme « désignatrice », réduite à sa pure fonction de signe, marquant la perte de valeur du personnage – et partant de l'Occupation, en tant que période fondatrice.

Il ne s'agit pas de déclarer que celle-ci a perdu de sa pertinence ; bien au contraire, l'écrivain lui consacre la totalité de son dernier ouvrage en date. L'Histoire ne véhicule plus les angoisses, elle se substitue à une identité défaillante. Le temps de la mémoire devient alors celui du recueillement et de la compassion pour les victimes. Auparavant, Modiano avait dû dépasser le règlement de l'identité par l'intermédiaire du roman. Il recrée à cette fin, dans ses premières œuvres, une Occupation qui doit beaucoup plus aux lois de l'imaginaire qu'à celles de la vérité historique.

L'Occupation constitue une représentation mentale

Modiano forge la pâture de sa mémoire à partir des sources historiques avérées et des souvenirs racontés par les témoins de cette époque. Nous avons vu précédemment qu'il paraissait difficile d'effectuer le départ entre l'invention pure et la reconstitution minutieuse, qui caractérisent l'Occupation de Modiano, recomposée au gré des inflexions de sa mémoire. Les lieux, les époques ou les personnages sont comme filtrés par le prisme d'une conscience qui adapterait, plierait, la réalité à sa nécessité – afin de nourrir une œuvre et, de façon concomitante, de mettre en règle cette conscience avec un héritage difficile à assumer.

Paradoxalement, c'est en prenant ses distances avec la réalité, en inscrivant le traumatisme au cœur de l'imaginaire, chargé d'en moduler toutes les tonalités affectives ou objectives, que l'écrivain va toucher au plus près du drame primitif; celui-ci eût sans doute été occulté par une approche plus rationnelle de la réalité.

Dans la première partie de son œuvre, le romancier va ainsi multiplier les angles d'attaque, demeurant fidèle à une seule stratégie, celle de la résurrection d'un passé demeuré inconnu, porté au point d'incandescence du souvenir, grâce à une confusion volontaire entre l'invention et le réel. Loin de se borner à un questionnement du passé, le créateur recentre, au fur et à mesure des romans, l'investigation sur ses origines – interrogation qui trouvera sa réponse la plus apaisée dans *Livret de famille*. La démarche de l'écrivain empruntera des chemins de traverse, dans une lecture résolument non-linéaire de l'histoire familiale, associée, de façon connexe, à la France, et surtout au Paris de l'Occupation. Cette période se trouve ainsi douée d'une totale autonomie, perdant son statut historique, et devient une sorte de lieu de confrontation entre le silence du passé et la voix de la fiction. Ainsi, le fait de porter certains épisodes douloureux à reviviscence, en y incorporant nombre d'éléments fictifs, constitue moins une déformation du passé qu'une façon de comprendre la période – comme si la vérité subjective semblait aussi pertinente que la stricte objectivité de l'Histoire.

Le romancier prend néanmoins le risque de conférer à cette recomposition, aux confins de la rêverie et de la réalité, une indépendance, difficilement mise à mal par la raison, qui viendrait constituer la seule évocation littéraire recevable de l'Occupation. Ainsi définis, les éléments nécessaires à l'écriture du passé peuvent prendre place dans l'ordre du récit. L'interaction entre chacun d'eux constitue la part prééminente de l'interrogation concernant le statut propre du passé, recréé par l'écrivain.

La présence de l'Occupation dépasse largement le cadre de l'évocation historique, de l'anecdote, pour s'ériger en constituant narratif fondamental. Dès son premier ouvrage, le romancier donne un tel poids à ce moment que ce dernier acquiert une autonomie, étant placé au premier plan du récit, loin devant les personnages et les actions narrées. L'ensemble représente, chez l'écrivain, l'enjeu d'une tension entre des forces antagonistes, qui voit s'affronter deux processus narratifs, à savoir la transcription fidèle de la réalité et la restitution, plus ou moins fantasmée, de celle-ci. Si la supériorité du premier s'affirme au fur et à mesure des romans, il convient de noter que l'évocation de la Seconde guerre mondiale semble régie par des lois qui lui sont propres. Comme nous l'avons déjà vu, l'Occupation se vide d'une partie de sa substance au profit d'une relativisation de l'horreur, qui donne à l'imaginaire la précellence sur le réel.

Modiano ne peint pas la réalité telle qu'elle fut, mais telle qu'elle eût pu l'être, en l'investissant, de surcroît, de toutes les angoisses qu'elle a suscitées, et génère encore en lui. Le héros-narrateur perd, de la sorte, une grande part de ses prérogatives pour devenir un personnage-relais, autour duquel l'Occupation vient prendre place, dans toute sa violence.

Tout se passe comme si se produisait un « épanchement de l'Occupation dans la vie réelle »... La fiction et les personnages véhiculent, en effet, tant de questions – et endossent tant d'inquiétudes – que la période devient l'un des actants du récit, imposant à la narration son propre code d'évaluation et de validité des actes. D'abord zone-écran entre la rationalité du réel et l'imaginaire pur, l'Occupation vient subvertir jusqu'aux lois mêmes de l'ordre temporel logique. On assiste, ainsi, à un triomphe du passé qui, intriqué dans les plis et replis du présent, vient prendre possession de celui-ci, en rendant de ce fait impossible toute agrégation à l'ordre du réel.

Le romancier, en laissant jouer sur la scène de son théâtre mental les figures de son angoisse, devient prisonnier des chimères enfantées. Toutefois, on notera que ce sentiment d'échec mérite d'être relativisé, puisque c'est cette stratégie de rupture – à savoir le jeu constant pratiqué sur les temporalités ou la dispersion et confusion des voix et des personnages – qui permet, elle seule, de mettre l'événement central à jour, ce point nodal que chaque œuvre recèle dans les plis de son histoire. Reposant sur une exploration minutieuse des textes de l'écrivain, ces axes d'étude paraissent représenter un faisceau convergent, capable de rendre compte du traitement spécifique de l'Occupation.

Le traitement spécifique de la Seconde Guerre mondiale en France conduit l'écrivain à articuler non seulement l'action, mais également l'ensemble du personnel romanesque autour de celle-ci. Il s'établit, de la sorte, une barrière entre le créateur et le monde qui l'entoure. Obstacle presque épistémologique, la reconstitution littéraire de l'Occupation témoigne d'une construction originale – d'un point de vue stylistique –, qui se manifeste dans la façon même dont est rendue la confrontation entre le narrateur-écrivain et la temporalité évoquée.

Modiano met alors en place une esthétique de subversion temporelle, introduisant un « récit poétique[1] » au sein de la narration. Ce procédé traduit, sur le plan du rapport logique entre le temps et les actions, la même entreprise de transgression de certaines données historiques – stratégie d'évocation que nous avions analysé dans la première partie de ce travail.

Dès *La Place de l'Étoile*, Modiano fait surgir la rêverie au sein d'un récit, qui débute pourtant d'une façon des plus classiques : « C'était au temps où je dissipais mon héritage vénézuélien ». Rapidement, toutefois, les ruptures temporelles, les invraisemblances (la rencontre avec Maurice Sachs ou

---

[1] Nous employons ce terme dans le sens que lui donne Jean-Yves Tadié dans son ouvrage, *Le Récit poétique*, Paris, PUF, 1972.

l'affaire Jacob X) et les provocations outrancières viennent donner à l'histoire le sens d'une farce tragique, savamment « déconstruite ». Le processus prend toute son ampleur lorsque l'écrivain aborde les années d'Occupation, adoptant un type de narration bien particulier, qui se traduit par l'abandon de toute cohérence dans l'exposé des actions ou l'organisation de la chronologie – séquences peu logiques ou emploi peu orthodoxe des temps du récit. Nous avons déjà remarqué que la restitution littéraire de l'Occupation procédait, chez Modiano, de l'imagerie mentale. Cette dernière, en faisant abstraction des limites posées par la raison aux débordements de l'imagination, infléchit le cours de l'histoire vers la sphère de la poésie, et non plus de la simple fiction.

Dans *Le Récit poétique*, Jean-Yves Tadié définit l'objet de son étude dans les termes suivants : « Le récit poétique est un récit qui reprend, en prose, les moyens du poème, et définit un univers privilégié ». Les premiers romans de Modiano, s'ils n'entretiennent évidemment aucun rapport, dans leur contenu, avec un discours poétique au sens strict du terme, empruntent certains procédés proches des mécanismes du poème en prose. La diffraction du temps, l'éparpillement de la narration ou la variation des formes verbales constituent, à cet égard, des exemples patents ; ce choix ne doit rien au hasard.

Nous avons déjà montré ce que les œuvres de jeunesse témoignaient de fascination, mêlée d'une mise à distance angoissée, pour les années sombres. La narration dite « classique », qui suppose une certaine linéarité dans le récit, ainsi qu'une relative maîtrise de l'action et des personnages, apparaît peu satisfaisante lorsqu'on l'applique à la transcription des doutes et inhibitions. En revanche, les procédés du poème en prose, s'ils contribuent à rendre le récit plus opaque – en dressant une sorte de barrière entre le cadre formel et les événements narrés – semblent cependant adéquats pour restituer l'anomie et la confusion d'une époque. L'écrivain n'adoptera sa célèbre « transparence » langagière qu'après avoir entièrement expurgé ses démons et ses incertitudes, si présents dans son écriture des jeunes années.

De fait, la dénomination de « roman », qui figure sur chacun des titres de la trilogie, paraît bien loin de la forme d'expression associée à ce vocable par la tradition. Si, comme l'écrit Paul Ricœur dans *Temps et récit*[1], « une structure discontinue convient aux romans d'aventure, une structure linéaire plus continue au roman d'apprentissage [...], tandis qu'une chronologie brisée, interrompue par des sautes, des anticipations et des retours en arrière, bref une configuration délibérément pluridimensionnelle, à une vision du temps privée de toute capacité de cohésion interne[2] », la figure narrative que Modiano emploie dans ses romans fournit une illustration parfaite de ses propos – et s'inscrit de plain-pied dans la définition, donnée par Jean-Yves Tadié, du discours poétique.

La première évocation du monde de la Collaboration dans *La Place de l'Étoile* constitue un bon exemple de subversion des catégories logiques attachées à la narration. L'extrait que nous retenons débute à la page 25 du roman (« Juin 1940. Je quitte la petite bande de *Je suis partout*... ») et s'achève page 26 : « Je me fais abattre par un GI nommé Lévy qui me ressemble comme un frère. »). L'ensemble se présente comme un résumé des cinq années d'une des existences possibles de Raphaël Schlemilovitch durant la Seconde Guerre mondiale. Il constitue, d'une part, un condensé des représentations fantasmatiques de la période pour le narrateur-écrivain – qui tente de pénétrer les événements de l'intérieur, adoptant, à cet effet, l'itinéraire politico-moral d'un collaborateur anonyme –, et d'autre part une application des principes de Ricœur.

Dans son ouvrage, celui-ci distingue, en effet, le temps du récit (*Erzählzeit*) de celui de l'histoire (*Erzähltezeit*). La « vie imaginaire » de Raphaël est rédigée au présent, dans un ensemble romanesque orienté – par sa première phrase – vers le passé. Ce jeu entre le temps du narrateur et le temps raconté se complique avec les ruptures permanentes que Modiano établit à l'intérieur de l'*Erzähltezeit* (lorsqu'il s'agit d'aborder au plus près la période de l'Occupation). À ce moment,

---

[1] Paris, Seuil, 1972, 1974-1975. (trois volumes).
[2] *Op.cit.*, p. 45.

certaines séquences narratives paraissent échapper à toute cohérence chronologique.

Le procédé de la libre utilisation des temps – qui constitue l'une des ressources majeures de la poésie en prose, comme *Les Chants de Maldoror*, par exemple – caractérise les ouvrages du jeune Modiano. L'anarchie apparente dans l'emploi des catégories temporelles représente, sur un plan formel, l'équivalent du chaos mental du protagoniste, plongé au cœur de la tourmente. À ce titre, l'action de *La Ronde de nuit*, condensée en une seule et même soirée, semble s'étirer sur une durée bien plus importante, et cela grâce au jeu des analepses et des emboîtements temporels – que nous mettrons en évidence ultérieurement.

L'écrivain fait se juxtaposer, puis s'interpénétrer, des réseaux temporels et des strates narratives qui atomisent la narration en une multitude d'îlots ; ceux-ci ne trouvent leur continuité que dans l'unicité du point de vue, celui que Swing Troubadour porte sur eux. De nouveau, la fragmentation du récit semble obéir à une logique de « désubstantialisation » du thème exposé. En rendant impossible toute perception globale de celui-ci, ce procédé évite à l'écrivain, encore fragilisé par ses angoisses, une confrontation directe avec l'objet de ses craintes.

Loin de se limiter à un traitement anecdotique, l'évocation des années sombres se livre en creux, dans les changements de points de vue ou les permutations temporelles, comme s'il existait une isomorphie totale entre la perception de cette période et sa restitution littéraire. « La narration s'accorde parfaitement avec cette philosophie du temps », écrit Jean-Yves Tadié. « La brièveté générale du récit, son découpage en fragments très courts ne suffisent pas. On peut noter la rareté des subordonnées, des coordonnants ou des adjectifs, les temps simples des verbes ou domine le présent[1]. » Ces lignes, qui rendent compte de l'écriture poétique, dans ses aspects formels les plus généraux, caractérisent de façon convaincante la structure narrative de *La Place de l'Étoile* et de *La Ronde de*

---

[1] J.-Y. Tadié, *op.cit.*, p. 71.

nuit, récits poétiques par excellence, « faits de ces rythmes qui sont des systèmes d'instants[1] », et, dans une moindre mesure, des *Boulevards de ceinture*.

De fait, au fur et à mesure que l'écrivain avance en âge, la perception, et surtout la transcription de l'Occupation, perdent en recherche stylistique ce qu'elles gagnent en évidence et limpidité. Tout se passe comme si le créateur avait dû, en premier lieu, se frayer une piste dans le brouillard d'une conscience rétive à un semblable cheminement. Le travestissement des voix et des temps, mêlé aux provocations permanentes, fera place – comme nous le montrerons par la suite – à la sérénité lucide de la seconde trilogie.

FONCTIONNEMENT DE CE SYSTEME ORIGINAL : LA STYLISTIQUE DES TEMPS

Modiano procède à la reconstitution de l'Occupation, « son » Occupation, non seulement par le détournement des faits et de la réalité, mais également à l'aide d'un jeu très subtil, portant sur les rapports hiérarchiques entre les grandes catégories temporelles et leurs sous-classes. Une certaine composition se met ainsi en place – puisque, par-delà l'Occupation, c'est un temps fondateur que l'écrivain souhaite retrouver[2] – obéissant à des lois complexes d'organisation narrative. Le récit élaboré neutralise les oppositions entre le passé et le présent, redessinant, de la sorte, les contours mentaux de sa mémoire.

Les premiers récits de Modiano ne procèdent pas, comme la plupart des romans classiques, par succession d'événements et de péripéties orientés vers une résolution finale, délivrant une réponse à chaque interrogation suscitée par le cours de la narration. Bien au contraire, les premiers

---

[1] *Op.cit.*, p. 75.
[2] « La raison principale est que le récit poétique, s'il organise le temps, veut également en triompher. Il ne reconstruit ni la vie, ni l'histoire, mais en délivre ». *Ibid.*

textes obscurcissent à plaisir une intrigue, qui perd une grande partie de sa consistance au cours du récit, et surtout s'attarde sur la notion même d'événement – pour en explorer toutes les modalités, ou en repenser la définition. Le temps s'échappe hors de ses cadres, rendant inopérantes les tentatives de rationalisation. Les premières œuvres apparaissent très difficiles à résumer de façon satisfaisante ; le principe même de l'écriture repose sur la succession de scènes, dont la somme donne au récit son atmosphère et sa portée. Inexistante ou étouffée par les jeux formels, la narration se compose d'actes, qui n'entretiennent que fort peu de rapports entre eux – constituant des sortes de monades, indépendantes les unes des autres.

Cette impression de pesanteur dépasse le stade de l'écrit pour investir sa représentation cinématographique. Ainsi, le film de Louis Malle se présente comme une succession de séquences, certes chronologiques, mais qui semblent beaucoup plus ajointées qu'unies dans une même continuité narrative. Comme dans *La Ronde de nuit*, les scènes composent des sortes de tableaux autonomes, qui viennent rendre compte d'un climat et d'un état d'esprit particuliers, en négligeant quelque peu les impératifs de la tension dramatique.

De *La Place de l'Étoile* à *Lacombe Lucien*, les événements apparaissent comme autant de situations virtuelles, qui ne prennent corps que selon le bon vouloir de la conscience organisant la narration. Présentant des actions ramassées, ou extraordinairement dilatées, chaque ouvrage de la première trilogie subordonne le réel aux lois de l'aperception.

Comme nous venons de le voir, *La Ronde de nuit* n'excède pas la durée d'une longue soirée. *Les Boulevards de ceinture*, en dépit des multiples analepses qui structurent le récit – et semblent en accentuer la durée interne –, s'inscrivent dans l'espace d'un printemps. L'action de *La Place de l'Étoile*, quant à elle, se réduit à une durée nulle : constituée essentiellement de rêveries accolées les unes aux autres, selon un principe de contiguïté historique, l'histoire se situe en dehors d'un temps, logique et historique, dont elle remet en cause les principes fondamentaux – puisque le texte n'a pas d'autre fonction que de montrer l'impossibilité d'accéder à l'existence, dans la sphère temporelle dévolue au protagoniste et à l'écrivain.

Dans son deuxième *opus*, Modiano installe un « véritable » personnage dans une durée définie – celle de la déambulation dans le Paris de l'après-guerre, d'une part, et celle de l'anamnèse, qui constitue la plus grande partie de la narration –, mais qui très rapidement, d'associations confuses en brouillages narratifs, laisse la place à un continuum mal défini – censé traduire de façon romanesque le désarroi d'un homme confronté aux ambiguïtés de l'époque[1]. L'histoire se développe sur trois plans narratifs, sur lesquels viennent se greffer les lieux de l'action (l'extérieur, l'appartement des chevaliers du RCO et le repaire du Khédive), sans réelle suture. Ainsi, les scènes concernant les résistants peuvent suivre ou précéder un développement consacré à la rêverie parisienne, et ce sans aucune incidence sur la cohérence interne du récit. En effet, c'est autour de sa déambulation, et uniquement de celle-ci, que viennent prendre place les événements, de façon presque simultanée.

De fait, nous serions tenté de discerner, dans le principe narratif de *La Ronde de nuit*, un déplacement semblable à celui induit par l'expression métaphorique – obtenue, d'après Roman Jakobson, par une translation de repère. C'est, en effet, du glissement de la parole de l'axe syntagmatique sur l'axe

---

[1] Shounong Feng, dans sa thèse *La Problématique de l'identité chez Patrick Modiano*, 347 pages, Université de Besançon, 1996, écrit : « Dans *La Ronde de nuit*, Modiano utilise une structure en spirale à laquelle il avait déjà fait appel dans *La Place de l'Étoile*. Cette composition circulaire du roman épouse la trajectoire d'un personnage que se disputent plusieurs identités contradictoires. [...] Topographiquement parlant, *La Place de l'Étoile* devient le centre de la ville, et *Les Boulevards de ceinture* le contour de Paris, où la police fait la "ronde de nuit". Sur le plan du temps, l'année 1942, la plus noire de l'Occupation, constitue le centre de la drôle d'époque (l'action des deux premiers romans se passe à cette date), tandis que l'année 1944, veille de la Libération nationale, ressemble à la lisière de l'Occupation. » *Op.cit.*, p. 307-308.

paradigmatique que naîtrait la métaphore ; la logique de la consécution laisserait la place à celle de l'association. Dans le texte de Modiano, ce sont les lieux, chargés de mémoire, qui semblent porter la matière même du déroulement fictionnel. Les épisodes semblent se chevaucher de façon systématique, créant une difficulté de repérage pour le lecteur – et le critique. Shounong Feng ne relève pas moins de six plans temporels, lors de la méditation à laquelle se livre Swing Troubadour, dans le salon des Bel-Respiro :

> Dans les tiroirs, deux ou trois photos jaunies, de vieilles lettres. Un bouquet de fleurs séchées sur le secrétaire de Madame de Bel-Respiro. À l'intérieur d'une malle qu'elle n'avait pas emportée, plusieurs robes de chez Worth [plan 1 : 1942 ; milieu de soirée]. Une nuit, j'ai revêtu la plus belle : en poult-de-soie bleu avec tulle-illusion et guirlande de volubilis roses [plan 2 : 1942 ; quelques semaines avant la soirée évoquée]. Je n'éprouve pas le moindre goût pour le travesti [plan 3 : présent gnomique][1].

Pour cet exégète, la composition du roman s'apparente à une spirale temporelle, chargée de représenter la trajectoire erratique d'un personnage que se disputent plusieurs identités contradictoires – nous reviendrons sur cet aspect dans l'étude particulière de l'œuvre, à la fin de ce développement. Pour l'heure, nous noterons la totale coïncidence des principes de l'écriture poétique avec le postulat narratif de ce texte. Celui-ci se présente comme une promenade nocturne (axe de la continuité syntagmatique) autour de laquelle viennent se décliner les actes associés à un lieu précis (axe de la substitution paradigmatique). Le récit ainsi constitué s'articule autour d'une autre caractéristique du langage poétique, à savoir l'absence de lien logique dans la chaîne parlée. Le sens réside moins dans la consécutivité des lexies que dans les relations

---

[1] *La Ronde de nuit*, p. 80-81. Pour des raisons de droit, nous ne pouvons citer plus de huit lignes du texte de Patrick Modiano utilisé par Shounong Feng dans son travail. Nous invitons le lecteur à se référer à la suite de l'analyse du critique, un résumé ne présentant aucun intérêt sans la mention de la partie narrative correspondante.

entre celles-ci. La reconstitution schématique du passage où le héros convoque des souvenirs, qui jalonnent son parcours, confirme cette observation :

> Nous remontions l'avenue Kléber. Coco Lacour bâillait. Esmeralda s'était endormie et sa petite tête avait basculé contre mon épaule [...]. Une humanité assez molle se trouvait collée autour des tables de velours rouge et sur les tabourets, devant le bar [...].
> – Nous vous emmenons à notre nouveau quartier général, décida Monsieur Philibert. C'est un hôtel particulier, 3 bis square Cimarosa [...]. Quand j'entrai dans le salon, la phrase mystérieuse me revint à la mémoire : « un rastaquouérisme à relents de trahisons et d'assassinats » [...]. Avenue Kléber. Esmeralda parle dans son sommeil[1].

La succession des événements peut se formaliser comme suit :

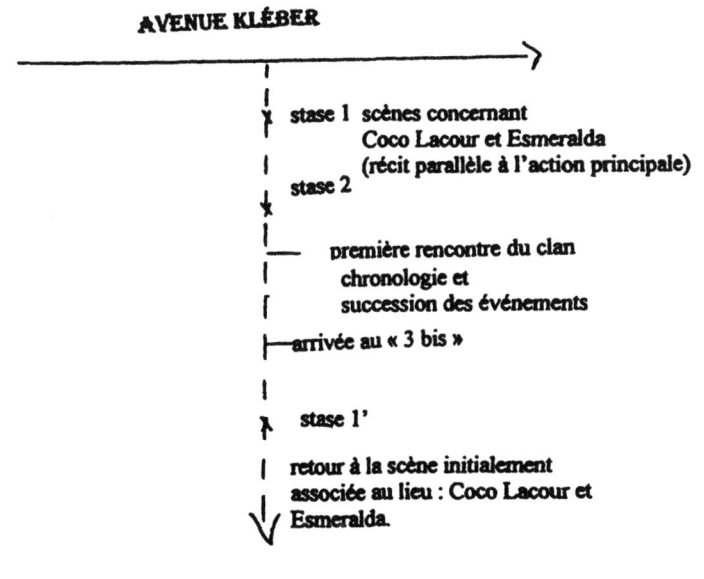

---

[1] *Ibid.*, p. 41-46.

À l'image du langage poétique, qui, selon les travaux de Roman Jakobson, transpose sur l'axe de la succession des éléments relevant de l'axe de la sélection, l'organisation narrative de *La Ronde de nuit* propose un récit régi par les seules lois de la synchronie. La statigraphie que nous venons de proposer constitue un bon exemple de l'utilisation des coordonnées du temps et de l'espace mobilisées par Modiano : à chaque étape parisienne correspond un certain nombre de moments et d'événements, plus ou moins traumatisants, que le roman associe librement, selon les libres inflexions de la mémoire ordonnatrice. C'est à ce titre que le texte semble s'inscrire dans un cadre chronologique, susceptible de rendre compte d'un délabrement moral, alors que le seul principe narratologique valide est celui de la précellence de la sphère topographique érigée au rang d'espace romanesque.

Cette décomposition paradigmatique constitue un aspect essentiel de la logique narrative de *La Ronde de nuit*. Les actes n'ont d'autre existence ou validité que celle qui leur est octroyée par la reviviscence de la mémoire. Leur enchaînement ne doit rien à une quelconque chronologie, inexistante dans le texte, mais à un rapport de contiguïté spatiale – comme si le traumatisme provoqué par l'Occupation avait rendu impossible la perception du temps, au bénéfice des seuls lieux.

Peu de critiques, lors de la sortie de l'ouvrage, ont insisté sur son aspect particulièrement novateur, qui rendait compte des bouleversements de l'Histoire dans le langage des grands poèmes en prose. L'écriture minimaliste, aux antipodes du foisonnement de *La Place de l'Étoile*, permettait à Modiano de radicaliser sa démarche. À l'image de la compartimentation des activités – seul y échappe Swing Troubadour, dont la situation dramatique réside dans l'impossibilité de trouver sa place au sein d'un cadre précis – sous l'Occupation, Modiano substitue au principe de successivité des actes un système de stases dont la somme constitue le récit. La diffraction de celui-ci en unités autonomes, apparemment dépourvues de rapports entre elles, traduit ainsi le chaos mental du narrateur-écrivain – lié à la confusion née de l'époque – et renouvelle des principes romanesques qui, loin de stériliser le récit, selon les théories du « nouveau roman », lui communiquent une force indéniable.

    Cette remise en cause de l'ordonnance logique des actions – qui n'est pas sans rappeler, *mutatis mutandis*, les interrogations des cubistes à propos de l'idée même de représentation – conduit le récit vers une sorte d'atemporalité. Le système élaboré dans le texte, qui semble abolir jusqu'aux valeurs de passé et de présent, sous-tend un code esthétique qui donne une place de premier plan à l'Occupation – prééminence qu'une narration traditionnelle remettrait particulièrement en cause.

UNE ESTHETIQUE DE L'ACHRONIE

    Dans ses premiers textes, Modiano mobilise des moyens d'expression qui servent sa vision particulière des années noires, sa *Weltanschauung*. Afin de montrer toute l'importance de la subversion temporelle à laquelle cette écriture procède, nous nous attacherons à étudier l'alternance et la variation des temps verbaux. Sous la plume de l'écrivain, ceux-ci paraissent neutraliser leurs oppositions. Le présent d'« omnitemporalité », ainsi mis en place, et dissimulé au cœur d'un passé perdu et recherché, permet à l'Occupation de prendre possession du narrateur-écrivain.

    Les romans marquants des années soixante ont montré que le rapport au temps s'accommodait mal des trois unités classiques. S'il réprouve la démarche radicale d'un Butor ou d'un Simon, Modiano réfléchit lui aussi à une nouvelle approche du réel, qui dépasserait le cadre étroit des catégories augustiniennes. Incapables de se situer dans une époque précise, les créatures modianiennes tendent à se confondre, à faire corps, avec la période qu'ils visitent, échappant, de la sorte, à un choix douloureux, celui qui consisterait à s'ancrer dans une temporalité déterminée et établie. Les protagonistes semblent, en effet, inaptes à la préhension de la réalité autrement qu'en position de spectateurs ; ils peuvent quelquefois être impliqués dans l'action, mais se trouvent, le plus souvent, en retrait de celle-ci.

Raphaël et Swing Troubadour, à deux échelles différentes, se laissent chacun entraîner dans un mouvement régressif, qui les conduit de la fin des années soixante au Paris de l'Occupation. Nous illustrerons notre propos par deux exemples tirés de *La Place de l'Étoile*.

Le premier chapitre, qui explore les voies d'incursion dans le Paris littéraire de la Collaboration, se caractérise par le « feuilleté temporel » mis en place. Le héros évoque au présent sa rencontre avec Maurice Sachs, puis, par le biais d'une étude sur Robert Brasillach, se retrouve au milieu des journalistes de *Je suis partout*. Ce récit est rapporté au passé :

> J'ai connu Robert Brasillach à l'École Normale Supérieure. Il m'appelait affectueusement « son bon Moïse » ou « son bon juif ». Nous découvrions ensemble les bars de Pierre Corneille et de René Clair[1].

En explorant le passé, le narrateur rejoint le monde qu'il se trouve en train d'évoquer. Ce faisant, il s'immerge totalement, au cours d'un passage écrit au présent, dans les milieux du journalisme d'extrême-droite, avant-guerre. À ce moment, le héros-narrateur semble avoir « spirituellement » assimilé l'époque qu'il décrit, et fait corps avec elle :

> Je quitte la petite bande de *Je suis partout* […]. Je me lance d'abord dans la collaboration mondaine[2].

Ce travestissement a partie liée avec le changement d'identité qui s'opère à cette occasion :

> Je suis le seul bon juif, le bon juif de la Collaboration[3].

Le procédé revient à de nombreuses reprises au cours du roman, sous forme de variation dans les pronoms – ces derniers se trouvant associés à une modification des catégories

---

[1] *La Place de l'Étoile*, p. 23.
[2] *Ibid.*, p. 26.
[3] *Ibid.*

temporelles. Nous retiendrons, parmi de nombreuses occurrences, les événements qui prennent place avant le voyage de Tel-Aviv, au quatrième chapitre, ainsi que la fin des amours de Raphaël avec la marquise de Fougeire-Jusquiames. À cet effet, nous introduisons le concept de « métaphore temporelle », emprunté à Harald Weinrich, dans son ouvrage *Temps et récit*[1].

Dans ces passages, l'auteur adopte un point de vue différent sur l'action, en faisant intervenir une voix qui se pose sur celle du narrateur, cette fois-ci omniscient – vision en rupture avec la perspective narrative générale (auto et homodiégétique). L'extrait que nous retenons débute page 115 : « Des deux femmes de ton harem, de ces deux gentilles putains, Yasmine fut bientôt la favorite ». La narration se poursuit de la sorte jusqu'à la fin de la section : « Voilà, tu avais achevé ton itinéraire de Paris à Jérusalem » (page 116).

L'emploi de pronoms de la deuxième personne – ou de la troisième – marque une rupture évidente avec le reste du texte, rédigé, lui, à la première personne. Ce changement de repère énonciatif suspend, d'une certaine manière, le point de vue adopté, en notifiant, pour un temps, l'absence d'adhésion du narrateur à la réalité évoquée. En effet, à la différence du pronom de la première personne, qui oriente la narration vers la confession autobiographique, les autres formes marquent, de façon claire, l'entrée du récit dans la fiction. C'est ce changement brutal que Harald Weinrich nomme « métaphore temporelle » :

> [Cette figure de style] se définit comme signe linguistique pris dans un contexte inattendu, surprenant, contre-déterminant, et tout autant, de notre actuel point de vue, comme signe pris dans une transition hétérogène inattendue[2].

On observe un écart similaire dans le récit des amours finissantes de Raphaël et de la marquise. Surpris dans son

---

[1] *Ibid.*, p. 26.
[2] *Ibid.*, p. 226.

« idylle aux champs » par le vicomte Lévy-Vendôme, le jeune homme livre le récit suivant :

> Toutes les amours sont éphémères. La marquise costumée en Aliénor d'Aquitaine s'abandonnera, mais le bruit d'une voiture interrompra nos effusions. Les freins crisseront [...] je reconnaîtrai le vicomte [...].

L'hapax réside dans l'emploi du futur, nullement motivé, puisque l'ensemble du chapitre est une recension de souvenirs. Le concept de « métaphore temporelle » prend ainsi tout son sens. Cette liberté dans l'emploi des pronoms et des temps obéit moins à une volonté de provocation qu'au désir d'abolition, de la façon la plus efficace, les distances séparant le narrateur-écrivain de la période évoquée. Si une part de ludisme intervient dans cette approche, Modiano ne fait pas pour autant litière de l'authenticité. En effet, l'exhibition du code et des moyens narratifs, loin de reléguer les actes à l'arrière-plan du récit, leur donne, comme par ricochet, toute leur importance.

Enfin, le romancier recourt également à un autre procédé, qui, à l'instar de la « métaphore temporelle », permet de saisir l'événement et d'en restituer toute la violence – tout en le conservant suffisamment à distance. Celui-ci réside dans l'annulation des oppositions logiques entre les sphères du présent et du passé.

Dans ses deux premières œuvres, Modiano s'ingénie à dépasser nombre d'antinomies – politiques, historiques, et, dans le cas qui nous intéresse, formelles. Les marques logiques dévolues au présent et au passé se trouvent abolies, à de nombreuses reprises, comme si le narrateur-écrivain cherchait à rendre les événements évoqués contemporains du temps de l'écriture. Un vaste mouvement de régression temporelle s'amorce, créé par la suppression des oppositions entre les deux périodes.

Le romancier se trouve entraîné au cœur du moment qu'il met en scène. C'est ce que figurent métaphoriquement l'arrestation de Raphaël à la fin de *La Place de l'Étoile* par le groupe de collaborateurs, la traque sans fin de Swing Troubadour ou la déportation annoncée du père et du fils à la fin des *Boulevards de ceinture*. Pour l'écrivain, le travail de mémoire, qui consiste à plonger une figure déléguée au sein d'un monde hostile et redouté, ne peut trouver son juste dénouement que dans le maelström de l'Occupation.

Le passé, privé de sa substance propre (qui inclut, pour une bonne part, l'éloignement du moment d'énonciation), semble communiquer celle-ci à un présent incapable de rendre compte de la « perception immédiate de la réalité ». Cette libre communication – on serait tenté de parler d'osmose – entre les deux instances entraîne une totale liberté dans l'usage des temps – en particulier dans la première œuvre, qui fait alterner des emplois narrativement non motivés du présent de narration et du futur. Bien qu'atténué, ce procédé se retrouve dans les deux textes suivants. Ainsi, dans *La Ronde de nuit*, la structure complexe du récit conduit à juxtaposer des strates temporelles distinctes, en les fondant dans une continuité de surface. Le dernier texte du triptyque, à la structure beaucoup plus claire[1], invite pourtant le lecteur à effectuer le départ entre les différents plans du récit : présent historique[2], présent gnomique[3], présent de narration[4], passé proche[5], passé éloigné[6] et temps fantasmatique[7].

---

[1] Colin Nettelbeck parle, à ce propos, de « [forme] narrative devenant progressivement plus linéaire ». Il ajoute quelques lignes plus loin : « Ce principe de linéarité, qui deviendra l'un des aspects essentiels de l'œuvre future de Modiano, dépend du déblocage du matériau historique particulier, et préfigure, ainsi, la démarche historique, conduite durant la même période, qui gagne en clarté et cohérence ». Colin Nettelbeck, « Getting the Story Right », in *Journal of English Studies*, XV, 1985, p. 77-116.
[2] Par exemple, le *curriculum vitae* des personnages, détaillé des p. 66-77.
[3] L'évocation « intemporelle » du village et des activités des énigmatiques occupants de l'auberge, pages 28 à 33.
[4] Les scènes situées au bar du « Clos-Foucré ».
[5] Le premier dîner à la villa Mektoub.
[6] La relation de l'existence menée par le père et le fils durant l'adolescence de celui-ci et le récit de la tentative de meurtre à la station George-V. Nous établissons une distinction entre deux types de passé : celui du récit, qui correspond à un emploi que l'on pourrait qualifier de « classique », et celui, plus lointain, appliqué à la convocation des souvenirs de Serge Alexandre – qui relate les activités paternelles, durant son adolescence.

D'autre part, l'ensemble de l'histoire fonctionne comme une sorte d'épanadiplose, encadrée par deux scènes liminaire et ultime – la rêverie sur la photographie –, de sorte que le récit prend l'aspect d'une analepse de cent quatre-vingts pages. Comme le roman précédent, le texte se clôt par une paralepse – puisque les narrateurs ne peuvent revenir d'entre les morts pour narrer leurs aventures – venant estomper un peu plus les strictes déterminations des catégories temporelles.

Cette confusion, parfaitement maîtrisée, apparaît comme la traduction formelle des desseins littéraires de Modiano. L'écrivain se rapproche mentalement de la période évoquée, en gommant tous les éléments susceptibles de constituer une entrave à la fusion des époques – celle de la rédaction, d'une part, et celle de l'Occupation. Enfin, la fragmentation des temps, en une multitude de sous-ensembles, facilite paradoxalement un contact avec les années noires, trop difficiles à aborder de front.

L'originalité de l'écriture est à chercher du côté de la thérapie ; la première trilogie ne peut fonctionner que sur le mode de la diffraction et de l'éparpillement. Cette stratégie est rendue nécessaire par la force d'un passé toujours prêt à déborder de son cadre pour menacer une conscience encore fragile.

DE QUELQUES VACILLEMENTS ; ETUDE D'UN
TEMPS : LE PRESENT

Avant que l'évocation des images et des souvenirs parentaux ne surgisse, de façon claire et apaisée, dans les trois chapitres de *Livret de famille* consacrés à l'Occupation[1], il aura

---

[7] Le présent, temps non marqué, des pages 145 et 146, où le fils imagine ce qu'eût pu être la vie avec son père, dans la maison que celui-ci s'est arrogée.
[1] Respectivement aux chapitres IV – la fuite de la mère –, IX – avec l'évocation de Robert Gerbauld – et la visite de l'appartement, quai Conti, où les parents du narrateur vécurent la fin de la guerre, racontée au chapitre XIV.

fallu se livrer au pénible travail de la digestion des années de guerre – qui se trouvent à l'origine de la trilogie. Dans cet ensemble d'œuvres, le passé n'est jamais ressenti comme définitivement absent, mais ranimé par un écrivain qui ne choisit jamais de présenter ses récits sur le mode de la simple rétrospection[1]. Chez Modiano, en effet, le temps ne résulte que de la « somme » des zones d'ombre et des opacités chronologiques qui la composent.

Ainsi, aucun de ces trois romans n'indique avec clarté le point précis d'énonciation à partir duquel le texte s'organise. Le premier chapitre de *La Place de l'Étoile*, par exemple, fait suivre un *incipit* des plus classiques de prolepses fallacieuses – la rencontre avec Sachs – ou d'affabulations, comme l'odyssée de Raphaël dans le Paris de l'Occupation. Le récit se voit rapidement frappé de nullité historique, puisque ces épisodes invalident les prémisses de la narration. L'achronie qui s'installe semble dictée par la conscience même du narrateur : il s'agit moins d'une plongée au cœur du passé, afin de se ressourcer, que d'établissement de liens avec un présent, peu à peu vidé de sa véritable valeur énonciative.

Nous nous proposons de conduire une étude sur les valeurs du présent, comme exemple de la liberté dans l'emploi des temps. Cette analyse sera conduite à partir des travaux de Kate Hambürger, consacrés au présent de narration, dans une section de *Logique des genres littéraires*[2]. Pour cette linguiste,

> le présent de narration n'a pas pour fonction d'actualiser, au sens temporel du terme, mais bien au sens fictionnel. Les personnages apparaissent plus nettement dans leur fonction et statut d'agent autonome que ce n'est le cas avec le prétérit ; ils sont montrés dans l'accomplissement de leur action, alors que, dans

---

[1] On trouvera également une analyse des temps du récit chez Modiano, dans l'article de Gerhard Gerhardi, « Topographie et histoire : Paris et l'Occupation dans l'œuvre de Patrick Modiano, actes du troisième colloque des Universités d'Orléans et de Siegen, Heidelberg, 1995, p. 114-121. Le critique analyse, en particulier, le glissement temporel entre la contemplation de la photographie, qui ouvre *Les Boulevards de ceinture*, et les premières lignes de l'intrigue proprement dite.
[2] Paris, Seuil, 1972.

un compte rendu de la réalité, l'imparfait sert plutôt à marquer les actions accomplies, à les donner pour faites[1].

Si on les applique aux procédés narratifs de Modiano, les éléments de cette analyse semblent conduire au paradoxe suivant : le passé, celui de l'Occupation, ne joue pas un rôle particulier, puisque c'est le présent de narration qui inscrit l'action dans l'orbite de celui-ci. Il n'est jamais plus « présent » à l'esprit que lorsqu'il réussit à instiller sa substance aux valeurs temporelles et logiques, véhiculées par le présent.

Nous avons déjà signalé l'emploi particulier de ce temps dans le *curriculum vitae* de Raphaël, aux pages 25 et 26 du premier roman. Dans cet extrait, l'existence fictive du protagoniste n'est pas relatée au passé, comme toute évocation historique, mais au présent, délesté de ses valeurs traditionnelles[2], pour venir transcrire le passé. On retrouve ce même procédé dans *La Ronde de nuit*, où les différentes rencontres avec le Khédive se trouvent relatées au présent[3], ou dans les scènes fantasmatiques des *Boulevards de ceinture*. Serge Alexandre infère, à partir des objets qui ornent le salon où il se tient avec son père, la vie qu'il aurait pu connaître, dans une demeure semblable :

> Vous êtes exploitant forestier et moi, votre fils, officier d'active. Je viens passer mes permes dans notre chère bonne vieille maison [...]. Les rideaux sont tirés. Le feu crépite doucement. Bavardons en vieux complices[4].

Dans les deux cas, l'emploi du présent se trouve lié aux scènes itératives. Privé de son aspect essentiel, ce temps indique simplement, de la façon la plus neutre, que

---

[1] *Ibid.*, p. 102.
[2] « Le présent désigne un événement actuel, marquant la contemporanéité entre l'acte d'énonciation du syntagme verbal et le procès qu'il vise. » M. Grévisse, *Le Bon Usage*, Duculot, 1992.
[3] « Il sifflote le refrain de la chanson, bat la mesure en hochant la tête [...]. Le Khédive propose que nous sablions le champagne et sort une bouteille de la poche gauche de sa veste... » *La Ronde de nuit*, p. 100-101.
[4] *Les Boulevards de ceinture*, p. 146.

l'événement évoqué ne prend sens que dans la succession et la répétition de l'acte. Insérées entre deux épisodes au passé, comme les évocations du Khédive comprises entre les mentions au passé des soirées au 3 bis, square Cimarosa, ces séquences acquièrent, *de facto*, les valeurs du passé, fournies par le contexte. Ces exemples viennent illustrer l'un des nombreux procédés employés par l'écrivain, dans sa stratégie d'abolition des oppositions temporelles. Le passé, en apparence évacué, s'immisce au sein de la forme narrative la plus neutre. Une semblable subversion ne se limite pas seulement au présent dit « historique », mais gagne également les autres temps du récit.

À titre d'exemple, nous analyserons un passage de *La Ronde de nuit*, dans lequel le narrateur relate sa déambulation dans les rues de la capitale. Ce récit confond les trois catégories temporelles principales dans une sorte de lacis qui marque, incidemment, la faiblesse de deux d'entre elles, et ce au profit du seul passé, sans que les occurrences de cette dernière catégorie soient supérieures en nombre :

> C'*est* la saison des feux d'artifice. Tout un monde prêt à disparaître *jetait* ses derniers éclats sous les feuillages et les lanternes vénitiennes. Les gens *se bousculaient, parlaient* fort, *riaient, se pinçaient* nerveusement. On *entendait* les verres se briser, des portières claquer. L'exode *commençait*. [...] Quand ils *seront partis*, des ombres *surgiront* et *formeront* une ronde autour de moi. Je *reconnaîtrai* quelques visages. Les femmes *sont* beaucoup trop fardées, les hommes *ont* une élégance nègre[1].

Ce passage paraît représentatif de la liberté qui réside dans l'emploi des temps chez Modiano. Deux temps du futur – le futur et le futur antérieur – un temps du passé – l'imparfait – et le présent sont utilisés. Bien qu'apparaissant dans des proportions égales à celles des autres temps, le passé semble décider de l'orientation temporelle globale, comme si le futur et le présent revêtaient la seule fonction de temps de contact avec la principale orientation temporelle. Privés de leurs statuts

---

[1] *La Ronde de nuit*, p. 23.

respectifs, ils apparaissent, avant tout, comme les ramifications d'un passé omniprésent.

Le présent d'évocation « immédiate » sert la rétrospection, et, de fait, se pose comme présent « historique ». Le futur, temps de la prévisibilité, prend une valeur prospective, perçue, encore une fois, à partir du seul passé. Cette redisposition des catégories logico-temporelles constitue autant d'hypostases d'une scène primitive, celle de la débâcle de juin 1940. Modiano ne peut l'aborder de façon frontale, et contourne l'obstacle par le recours aux images mentales d'un homme, taraudé par les spectres de l'Occupation.

Nous proposons, à titre d'illustration, le schéma narratif du roman, qui offre le mérite de restituer de façon claire un cheminement romanesque pour le moins confus – et sert, de la sorte, le dessein du créateur, pour lequel le bouleversement né de la guerre doit présider à l'organisation du récit.

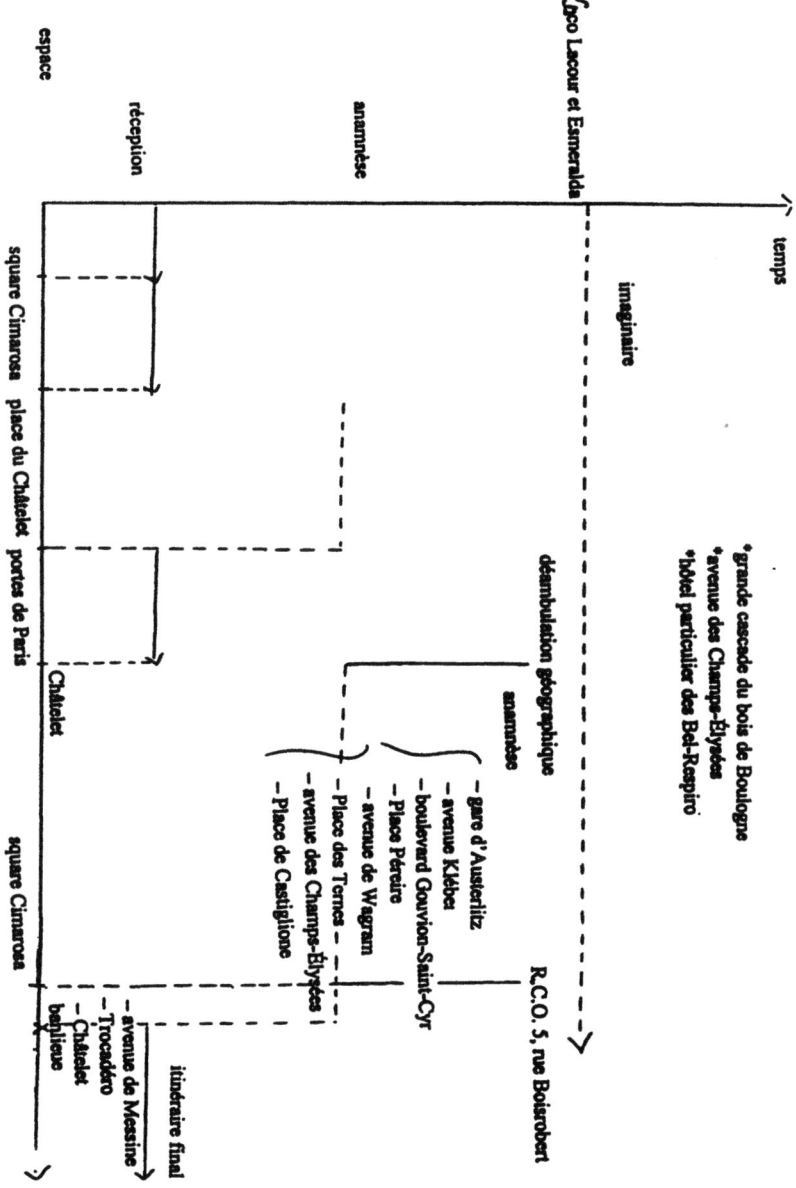

Cette représentation appelle plusieurs commentaires, que nous empruntons, pour la plupart, à Shounong Feng[1]. Celui-ci replace la démarche modianienne dans une perspective taoïste, et accorde, à cette fin, une attention toute particulière aux formes et éléments. Pour ce critique, le sens naît de la structure, et réside, pour ce roman, dans sa construction en spirale – qui finit par abolir très rapidement les distinctions entre le passé et le présent, ou si l'on préfère, entre le traumatisme et son évocation.

L'exégète propose ainsi de distinguer deux grandes parties dans le récit, l'une subdivisée en quatre sous-catégories, l'autre se voyant dotée d'un fonctionnement pratiquement autonome, marquant la neutralisation des oppositions temporelles. L'ensemble peut se représenter comme suit :

Temps / Pages	Présent	Passé
p. 13-19 (7p.)	↓	
p. 20-27 (7p.)		⇓
p. 27-38 (11p.)	↓	
p. 38-48 (8p.)		⇓

[1] *Op. cit.*

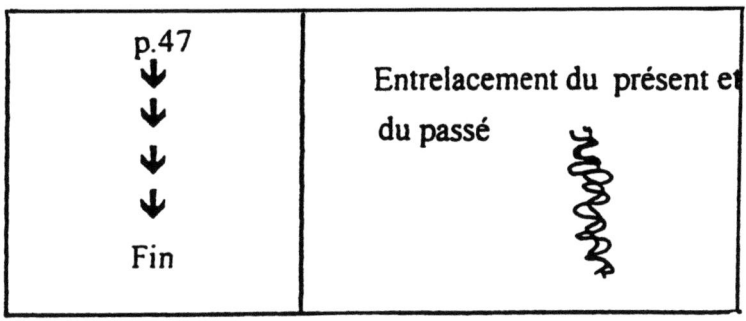

Les deux instances des temps alternent et les deux actions se succèdent par intervalle. Les deux premières séquences du récit sont construites de façon symétrique (sept pages). À partir de la page 46, les deux temps s'entrelacent :

présent 1   passé 1   présent 2   passé 2   présent 3 et
                                                    passé 3

⊢-------⊣------⊣-------------⊣-------⊢---→
p.13   p.20   p.27   p.38   p.46

Au présent menaçant de l'Occupation se trouve superposé un autre « maintenant », qui est celui du temps de la narration. D'autre part, cette structure en spirale [...] épouse la trajectoire d'un homme que se disputent plusieurs identités contradictoires[1].

La douleur née du chaos se trouve quelque peu atténuée par la diffraction des réseaux « temporels », mais l'évocation se trouve marquée du sceau du refoulement. Si, dans ses jeunes années, l'écrivain entreprend un ouvrage plongeant au cœur même du traumatisme, il apparaît que l'exorcisme peut se révéler pire que le mal. L'immersion au sein de l'Histoire devait effacer les distances avec le passé ; elle ne fait qu'abolir

---

[1] Shounong Feng, *op.cit.*, p. 308-311.

la sécurité offerte par l'écoulement du temps. La zone de « médiation », représentée par l'écriture, se voit contaminée par les chimères, de sorte que l'Occupation gagne une force inespérée, grâce à la libre recomposition des temps. Pire encore, ces techniques de récit se trouvent réintroduire les distances que l'écrivain entendait supprimer. À la fin de la première trilogie, les angoisses et inhibitions paraissent décuplées ; les points de fracture avec le réel sont multipliés, et la force destructrice des événements réinstaurée.

L'OCCUPATION DESSINE UN PARCOURS REGRESSIF

Il semble pertinent de conclure ce développement par une approche des tentatives effectuées par Modiano dans le but de parvenir au plus près du temps fondateur, cette période disparue qui détient les réponses aux interrogations sur l'origine et la filiation. Deux lignes stratégiques se mettent ainsi en place : une rupture savamment concertée avec la réalité – multipliant les points d'approche d'un réel fragmenté – et le désir de fusion avec un passé tour à tour désiré et redouté. Dans la première trilogie, l'évocation de l'Occupation conduit à transformer, de l'intérieur, une époque – selon l'image mentale de l'auteur.

Outre les procédés de recréation, déjà largement analysés, il convient d'insister sur deux procédés narratifs concernant directement l'interrogation du temps, à savoir l'organisation des récits autour d'un point nodal et la fragmentation de ces derniers, sous la forme d'un « feuilleté » temporel.
Le jeu à l'œuvre dans les textes, entre un passé prompt à resurgir et un présent qui se délite, sous les assauts de l'imaginaire, fait apparaître un point central constitutif de l'enjeu de la narration. Inséré dans le désordre apparent de l'histoire – comme l'« image dans le tapis » de la nouvelle de James – cet événement central, qui donne sa forme au texte,

détermine un point de passage, à la suite duquel le roman connaît une autre orientation. Chaque récit est ainsi traversé par une frontière, une brisure, interne, qui vient séparer deux pôles distincts, relatifs à l'expérience du narrateur, en un « avant » – qui renvoie à une période précédant le début de l'histoire – et un « après » constituant l'enjeu même de la narration. Dans *La Place de l'Étoile*, ce moment est, sans doute, la révélation de l'identité juive. Dans *La Ronde de nuit*, il s'agit de la rencontre avec le Khédive – cette dernière est bien à l'origine du récit, mais ne prend place qu'à la page 85[1]. C'est en vertu de ce principe de retardement que la tentative d'assassinat, évoquée dans *Les Boulevards de ceinture*, n'est mentionnée qu'en milieu de roman. Dans le scénario de *Lacombe Lucien*, l'événement dit « nodal » est plus clairement identifiable, et surtout vient prendre place dès le début du film : il s'agit du refus de l'ancien instituteur, qui s'oppose à l'engagement du jeune homme aux côtés de la Résistance.

Difficilement isolable au sein du réseau des temporalités croisées et des jeux d'annonce ou de retardement d'événements, le point central tire toute sa force de cet enfouissement. La démarche de Modiano tend à son exorcisme ou à son exhibition, sans pour autant le mettre en valeur. De fait, comme tout élément relatif au passé, sa charge traumatique se trouve aussitôt refoulée, et ce afin de sortir de l'impasse temporelle qui préside généralement aux premières pages des romans. Cet instant remarquable détermine l'essentiel de la narration, marquant une limite en deçà de laquelle le passé à reconstruire, à « rentoiler » – pour employer un terme du vocabulaire proustien –, se situe. Ce projet littéraire – si l'on fait abstraction de l'ampleur d'*À la recherche du temps perdu* – présente nombre de similitudes, dans ses intentions, avec l'œuvre proustienne. Dans les deux cas, il s'agit de mettre à jour un élément, ou une sensation, appartenant au passé, et

---

[1] « Le soir, pendant la belle saison, je m'asseyais à la terrasse du Royal-Villiers. Quelqu'un qui occupait la table voisine m'a souri. Cigarette ? Il m'a tendu un paquet de Khédives, et nous avons engagé la conversation. Il dirigeait une agence de police privée, avec un ami. Tous deux m'ont proposé d'entrer à leur service. »

susceptible de redonner du sens au moment de l'évocation. L'on pourrait ainsi appliquer aux romans de Modiano l'analyse que Gérard Genette donne de l'œuvre de Proust :

> L'importance du récit « anachronique » dans *La Recherche* est évidemment liée au caractère rétrospectivement synthétique du récit proustien, à chaque instant tout entier présent à lui-même dans l'esprit du narrateur qui – depuis le jour où il en a perçu en extase la signification unifiante – ne cesse d'en tirer les fils à la fois[1].

Si l'anamnèse proustienne ne motive qu'un chapitre d'une trentaine de pages environ, au milieu de *Du côté de chez Swann* et à la fin du *Temps retrouvé*, celle des récits modianiens constitue à elle seule l'ensemble du roman. Celui-ci offre, dans son éparpillement, le parcours heuristique d'un narrateur qui, à partir du choc représenté par l'Occupation, tentera de reconstituer son passé. Il adoptera, à cet effet, la forme éclatée, offerte par le travail de la mémoire.

Avec *Livret de famille*, le procédé narratif se modifie quelque peu. Il y a bien éclatement de l'histoire, dans les quinze chapitres du récit – qui se trouvent correspondre aux quinze pages du document administratif –, mais ceux-ci paraissent constituer, à chaque fois, une approche différente de l'identité, plutôt qu'une diffraction de celle-ci. La voix d'un narrateur délégué cède la place à un récit autofictif, où le « je » ne vient plus désigner un être de papier. Pour la première fois, l'Occupation ne représente que trois chapitres sur l'ensemble, comme si, à partir de cet ouvrage, les questions posées par l'Occupation se trouvaient incluses dans la totalité des interrogations identitaires. Les ouvrages ultérieurs adoptent un cheminement plus linéaire, délaissant la narration « en étoile[2] » pour un récit fonctionnant sur le mode de l'élucidation introspective. Une œuvre comme *Voyage de noces*, par exemple, approche l'événement nodal à rebours – à savoir la fuite d'Ingrid dans le Paris hivernal de 1942. Seul un lent

---

[1] *Nouveau Discours du récit*, Paris, Seuil, 1983.
[2] Nous empruntons cette expression à Aragon, utilisée par celui-ci à propos de *La Mise à mort*.

dévoilement, procédant par une série de retours en arrière, qui atteignent à chaque fois un point plus reculé dans le temps, permet l'approche du point fondateur, particulièrement douloureux. Ce dernier roman constitue également une excellente illustration d'un autre procédé modianien, celui de la narration sous forme de strates.

La composition des dernières œuvres de Modiano, si elle ne se résout pas à développer un récit organisé de façon strictement chronologique, s'articule autour d'une construction beaucoup plus claire que celle des premiers textes. Toutefois, la limpidité – toute relative – de l'enchaînement narratif ne doit pas occulter l'extrême attention accordée par l'écrivain aux emboîtements temporels et à l'arrangement entre ces derniers. Nous fonderons ce développement sur l'étude de *Fleurs de ruine*, en empruntant quelques remarques à l'article que Jacques Almira a consacré à cette œuvre[1].

Fleurs de ruine se présente comme une histoire fictive, mâtinée d'autobiographie romancée. L'œuvre se caractérise, avant tout, par ses diverses couches temporelles qui, loin de s'assembler comme les kaléidoscopes narratifs de la première trilogie, s'incluent les unes dans les autres, à la façon de figures gigognes ; le point nodal est constitué par l'arrestation du père du narrateur. Nous distinguerons ainsi plusieurs axes dans cette autofiction. Celle-ci débute par une évocation attendrie, dans le Paris de 1990, de cette ville dans les années soixante. Puis s'effectue un retour au temps contemporain de l'écriture, qui conduit à une réflexion sur une photographie prise en 1933. Le romancier revient, alors, au Paris de 1960, en relatant une série de rencontres avec un homme, Philippe de Pacheco, imposteur dont le nom véritable est Lombard, qui s'avère un « témoin » du drame survenu en 1933.

Cette construction suit un *crescendo* conduisant, par rétrospection, de 1990 à l'Occupation, évoquée de la page 66 à la page 76, puis, de façon inverse, de celle-ci à l'époque contemporaine. Tout se passe comme si ce jeu de strates avait pour seul but de faire reculer le moment d'approche de

---

[1] « Toute vie peut être un sujet de roman », *in La Revue des deux mondes*, juin 1991, p. 153-157.

l'Occupation, instant isolé et enfoui au plus profond de la mémoire. Jacques Almira écrit, à propos de ce dispositif :

> [L']écriture permet, dirait-on, d'appréhender le temps comme tissu continu de la vie où passé et présent ne font forcément qu'un [...]. Cette mémoire se rappelle le passé, et enregistre le présent au fur et à mesure qu'il devient le passé à son tour [...]. Le passé subsiste sous le présent, intimement mêlé à lui comme un palimpseste [...]. Trois temps, au moins se superposent, interfèrent, se confondent parfois. [...] L'Occupation, comme un film en noir et blanc [...] continue de jouer sur le temps d'aujourd'hui par le rêve[1].

Cette imbrication des temps et des époques, au-delà de la fragmentation de la réalité qu'elle suggère, marque la précellence du passé sur tout autre mode de perception et de restitution de cette même réalité. De *La Place de l'Étoile* à *Dora Bruder*, les récits de Modiano n'en finissent pas de dessiner, au passé, les contours indistincts du paradis de la mémoire perdue, vers lequel tend l'essentiel des narrations.

Le parcours temporel tracé par les romans de Modiano constitue un voyage sans cesse renouvelé aux confins du souvenir, de la mémoire évanouie et de l'angoisse liée à la fuite du temps. Un instant privilégié, traumatisant et tentateur s'est estompé. L'ensemble du récit, par le recours aux nuances verbales et à une grande liberté dans l'usage des temps, n'illustre rien d'autre que la gravitation d'une conscience autour de cet archipel enseveli.

Le désir sans cesse renouvelé de retrouver l'instant parfait et insaisissable d'un temps révolu détermine l'ensemble des choix narratifs de l'écrivain – ce qui explique, peut-être, l'inconsistance de l'univers romanesque recréé. Celui-ci n'existe que dans la mesure où il incarne les images mentales de la conscience, et celui-ci subordonne l'ensemble du récit à son évocation. Ainsi, chaque roman constitue pour Modiano l'occasion d'une fusion avec l'époque convoquée.

---

[1] Article cité.

Les romans de Modiano donnent de l'Occupation l'image d'une capitale déserte, au crépuscule, à l'heure où se croisent de rares silhouettes d'agents doubles, ou d'une campagne (la Seine-et-Marne ou le Lot), livrées aux caprices du temps : soleil écrasant pour *Les Boulevards de ceinture* et *Lacombe Lucien*, tapis de neige pour *Voyage de noces*. Les revendications politiques et idéologiques sont évacuées au profit de « la trace de l'instant », à savoir les disques ou la radio, qui égrènent leurs rengaines surannées, ou bien le charme d'un rire perdu dans l'or du soir, pendant que se tournent les pages d'une revue d'avant-guerre. En passant sous silence les angoisses liées aux événements, le lecteur pourrait se croire plongé au milieu des parfums nostalgiques de *Comme le temps passe*, de Robert Brasillach.

L'histoire de l'Occupation incarne, avant tout, la somme des moments éphémères qui contiennent en eux toute la plénitude des instants rares – et qui évoquent beaucoup mieux le temps perdu, auquel ils demeurent associés, que les ouvrages historiques :

> Temps troubles. Rencontres inattendues. Par quel hasard mes parents passèrent-ils le réveillon 1942 au Beaulieu, en compagnie de l'acteur Sessue Hayakawa et de sa femme, Flo Nardus ? [...] À la fin d'une journée de juin 1942, par un crépuscule aussi doux que celui d'aujourd'hui, un vélo-taxi s'arrête, en bas, dans le renfoncement du quai Conti, qui sépare la Monnaie de l'Institut. Une jeune fille descend du vélo-taxi. C'est ma mère[1].

Si ce moment évoque les persécutions antisémites, les étranges amitiés paternelles et l'incertitude, l'image qu'en garde (et en donne) Modiano est celle d'une époque isolée, au fonctionnement autonome et presque dissocié de la marche de l'Histoire, où l'amnésique peut espérer trouver sa place – puisque l'Occupation semble réunir tous les déracinés, les victimes aussi bien que leurs oppresseurs, dans une sorte de « thébaïde » commune.

---

[1] *Livret de famille*, p. 200.

La totalité des ouvrages de Modiano se présente comme une tentative de ralliement d'un temps disparu, au moyen de personnages témoins[1], de méditation sur des lieux précis – on songera, notamment, à l'évocation d'Aimos, dans l'ancienne guinguette des bords de Marne[2] – ou d'un abandon total à la force du souvenir, en particulier dans les œuvres de jeunesse. La conscience de l'écrivain se fond entièrement dans la brume apaisante du temps recréé. Le passé n'a pas d'autre substance que celle délivrée par la nostalgie, ce désir de retour aux origines, que le poids du réel n'a pu encore entacher. Sans la prégnance de ces images, le passé ne constituerait rien d'autre qu'un flou historique indistinct. Idéalisé – au sens strict du terme –, le souvenir vient anéantir non seulement les frontières de sa sphère et celles du présent, mais également ôter à celui-ci ses prérogatives, à savoir le contact avec la réalité, la – relative – rationalité de la vision du monde ou encore le plaisir de l'instant.

Le parcours régressif dessiné par l'orientation narrative de chaque œuvre de Modiano – à l'exception de *Lacombe Lucien*, scénario de film, forme narrative dont la cohérence linéaire se doit, généralement, d'être respectée – vient bouleverser les règles de ses deux genres de prédilection : le roman traditionnel (qui n'aurait pas connu la « suspicion » sarrautienne) et l'autobiographie. Ainsi, *Fleurs de ruine* constitue un excellent exemple de récit personnel détourné de son cours – et de son sens – par les multiples incursions de la

---

[1] « Elle avait ensuite travaillé chez le couturier J.F. 32, rue La Boétie, en qualité de mannequin ; puis elle se serait associée avec un certain Van Allen, sujet hollandais, qui créa en avril 1941 une maison de couture, 6, square de l'Opéra à Paris (9e). Celle-ci eut une existence éphémère et ferma en janvier 1945. Mlle Coudreuse aurait disparu au cours d'une tentative de passage clandestin de la frontière franco-suisse, en février 1943. » *Rue des boutiques obscures*, p. 150-151.
[2] « Ces bords de Marne ont toujours été mal fréquentés... surtout pendant la guerre... Je vous ai parlé de ce pauvre Aimos... mon mari l'aimait beaucoup... Aimos habitait à Chennevières... il est mort sur les barricades, pendant la libération de Paris... [...] Il entendait leurs conversations dans les auberges du coin. » *Dimanches d'août*, p. 153-154.

mémoire dans la rêverie sur l'usure du temps[1] et par l'irruption de l'Occupation dans l'existence des personnages. De reculs en avancées temporelles, l'écrivain subordonne le récit de ce qui devait être, au départ, une méditation sur le passage de l'adolescence à l'âge adulte au souvenir d'une nuit passée, par son père, au dépôt :

> Par quel enchaînement de circonstances avait-il [Philippe de Pacheco] été entraîné dans cette situation contradictoire ? Je pensais à mon père qui avait vécu toutes les incohérences de la période de l'Occupation et qui ne m'en avait rien dit avant que nous nous quittions pour toujours[2].

Toutefois, à la fin des années soixante-dix, la perspective se modifie quelque peu, puisque, contrairement aux premiers ouvrages, un texte comme *Livret de famille* se clôt par une réflexion sur la mémoire. Celle-ci vient prendre directement appui sur le socle de la réalité – notamment lorsque l'écrivain fait référence à la naissance de sa fille :

> Je me souviens de tout. Je décolle les affiches placardées par couches successives depuis cinquante ans pour retrouver les lambeaux des plus anciennes [...]. J'avais pris ma fille dans mes bras et elle dormait, la tête renversée sur mon épaule. Rien ne troublait son sommeil.
> Elle n'avait pas encore de mémoire[3].

Les ouvrages postérieurs reviennent systématiquement sur l'époque contemporaine, comme si le voyage au centre de la mémoire et du passé devait prendre fin pour que l'écrivain pût réfléchir et s'interroger sur les possibilités – et les origines – de sa création :

---

[1] « Vingt ans ont passé. Et, sur la grande pelouse, Pacheco nous montrait ses photos du Maroc [...]. Il portait un polo bleu marine, des lunettes de soleil, et ses cheveux coupés très court le rajeunissaient encore plus. Je finissais par douter que la date de naissance de cet homme fût le 22 janvier 1918. » *Fleurs de ruine*, p. 76.
[2] *Fleurs de ruine*, p. 67.
[3] *Livret de famille*, p. 214-215.

> Le printemps est précoce cette année. Il a fait très chaud ces 18 et 19 mars 1990. Du jour au lendemain, les bourgeons sont devenus des feuilles aux marronniers du Luxembourg. Devant l'entrée du jardin, rue Guynemer, s'arrêtent des cars multicolores d'où descendent des touristes japonais [...]. J'ai eu envie de les suivre par cette matinée radieuse qui annonçait le printemps [...]. Sans doute aurais-je retrouvé une ville que j'avais perdue et, à travers ses avenues, la sensation de légèreté et d'insouciance que j'éprouvais autrefois[1].

Extrait des dernières pages de l'autofiction, ce passage marque un retour épanoui à la réalité, à cette périphérie de la mémoire, après une centaine de pages consacrées à l'arpentage de celle-ci. Il convient de noter que l'immersion salvatrice au cœur d'un passé édénique ne constitue plus, à ce moment, la seule voie d'accès à l'identité.

Les œuvres des années quatre-vingts ont quelque peu abandonné, en effet, les interrogations sur ce thème, de sorte que la quête du temps perdu se voit délestée de l'aspect compulsionnel qui était le sien dans les premières œuvres du romancier.

Ces remarques sur la spécificité de l'écriture modianienne tendent à montrer que le romancier ne dresse jamais, à ses yeux, un rempart suffisamment efficace contre le déferlement des souvenirs, cette mémoire de « seconde main », dont la charge affective semble encore le désarçonner, et ce malgré la distance des années. En effet, le créateur ne parvient pas à exprimer le lancinant traumatisme né de l'Occupation et de ses drames, et choisit d'en anesthésier la douleur dans les incertitudes et circonvolutions de sa narration.

Le travestissement du passé, la confusion volontaire entretenue entre une réalité parfaitement connue, mais souvent remodelée pour les besoins du récit, et une version fantasmatique des faits, lestent d'un poids affectif l'évocation des années noires. Les événements refoulés sous les différentes strates d'un passé, qui se dérobe à tout entendement, prennent une résonance plus forte lorsque le lecteur parvient à les

---

[1] *Fleurs de ruine*, p. 140-141.

décrypter et à les disposer dans un ordre fonctionnant à rebours de la logique personnelle[1].

Modiano entretient, à ce titre, une relation étroite avec le Nerval de *Sylvie*, cette autre aventure de la mémoire, qui tente de recomposer les fragments d'un passé enfui. Le poète n'apparaît jamais plus présent que dans l'enchevêtrement des dates et des lieux, qui constitue, en apparence, le principe ordonnateur de la nouvelle. Les faits s'y succèdent selon un principe de contiguïté, voire de condensation[2] – la simple lecture d'un programme de festivités champêtres conduit le souvenir à une scène d'enfance, puis aux personnages associés à cette époque, avant que le déplacement de la mémoire devienne voyage effectif –, cheminement que le décrypteur du récit suit pas à pas, en épousant les inflexions de la pensée, participant, de la sorte, à l'œuvre désordonnée de la mémoire.

Parvenu à la fin de *Sylvie* ou de *La Ronde de nuit*, le lecteur ne reçoit aucune information déterminante susceptible de légitimer le récit et justifier, *a posteriori*, son parcours erratique. Ainsi, l'enfance du narrateur de *Sylvie* ou les comptes rendus sur les officines de la Gestapo n'ont guère plus d'importance que celle de simple support narratif. L'anecdote ne sert jamais qu'à illustrer le parcours mental d'un être en quête de son essence. La recension des souvenirs devient donc démarche ontologique, impliquant, *in fine*, une reprise de contact définitive – et douloureuse – avec le monde réel, hors des turbulences de la mémoire.

---

[1] On lira avec intérêt l'article de Bertrand Westphal. Celui-ci écrit, à propos de la confusion entretenue entre l'Histoire authentique et sa réécriture fantasmée : « À force d'entrelacer actualité et passé, on s'expose au risque de ne plus être en mesure de définir clairement les niveaux temporels. [...] À force d'emmêler la chronologie, on transforme l'Histoire en une image manquant de profondeur et de vérité – comme il advient dans ce qu'on appelle le postmodernisme. [...] L'histoire n'est plus une identité collective ; en d'autres termes, elle perd son homogénéité. Du reste, si elle est au bout d'une anamnèse, autant dire qu'elle s'est déjà estompée. » Article cité, p. 103.
[2] Qui annonce, *mutatis mutandis*, certains procédés d'écriture de *La Place de l'Étoile*.

En effet, l'anamnèse révèle, dans les deux cas, une trace douloureuse, les flétrissures du temps chez Nerval ou la mise à mort chez Modiano, comme s'il était nécessaire de se confronter au deuil – du passé chez celui-là et de l'existence chez celui-ci – pour renouer avec le monde, au terme d'une sorte d'odyssée de l'âme. Les réminiscences provenant du « plus loin de l'oubli », après de longs détours par toutes les étapes de la conscience, viennent toucher l'être d'une façon durable, inespérée. Cette plongée dans la matrice obscure des souvenirs vient révéler toutes les fêlures et fragilités du narrateur, certes, mais un refoulement du souvenir eût sans doute été cause d'une lente consomption de celui-ci.

De fait, l'œuvre modianienne se fait l'illustration du principe du témoignage. Chaque texte constitue le procès-verbal d'une série d'événements délivrés par la mémoire, de façon inopinée[1]. Dans les ouvrages de jeunesse, c'est la forme – à savoir la démarche introspective entreprise par le narrateur – qui porte le sens de l'ouvrage. L'acte d'écriture devient le principal enjeu du texte, qui subordonne l'objet narratif – l'Occupation et ses corollaires – à la réussite du parcours mémoriel. Au terme de celui-ci, l'écrivain sera en mesure d'accéder à son identité, recherche qui motivait l'essentiel de la démarche. Auparavant, il aura fallu prendre toute la mesure des difficultés liées à cette entreprise, comme si, à chaque instant, le narrateur-écrivain courait le risque de s'abîmer dans les vertiges de la nostalgie.

Une certaine esthétique du passé

En s'éloignant toujours davantage du point initial, l'observateur n'en perçoit plus que les reflets effacés ou les échos assourdis. L'image de l'Occupation, dans l'œuvre de Modiano, procède d'un cheminement identique. Un continent

---

[1] On pensera, notamment, à l'intrigue et aux conditions de narration de *Quartier perdu*, *Dimanches d'août*, *Chien de printemps* ou *Du plus loin de l'oubli*. Dans chaque récit, le passé survient sous la forme d'une rencontre inattendue avec un personnage, qui révèle au protagoniste une part obscure de son existence.

englouti jette ses dernières lueurs, recueillies par un homme que leur extinction bouleverse : ce monde constituait, en effet, son point d'attache unique avec l'existence. Il n'en restera plus qu'un souvenir confus, dernier lien avec un passé dont ne subsistent plus que les répliques – stade ultime de l'affadissement d'une époque, remplacée par des simulacres.

Ainsi, c'est l'ensemble de l'œuvre qui apparaît hantée par un jeu souterrain de forces contraires. L'écrivain ne cesse d'interroger les sources de la mémoire afin de fonder ses propres souvenirs, et vient se heurter à sa force destructrice. Sans passé, le narrateur amnésique ne peut trouver sa place dans une époque façonnée par des années de guerre, qui ont laissé leur trace indélébile sur tous les personnages de rencontre. Les débuts de la Ve République, caractérisés par l'occultation des heures les plus sombres de la Collaboration, ont enterré une mémoire que l'écrivain estime nécessaire à sa survie. Afin de s'approprier de nouveau ce continent englouti, Modiano tentera de forcer les barrières temporelles et logiques qui le séparent de cette « période matrice ». Les travestissements narratifs, la pochade, la réécriture amusée de l'Histoire ou l'enfouissement d'un événement, sous des strates de récit artificiellement ajoîntées, seront mobilisés pour retrouver l'esprit d'un lieu ou d'une époque – loin de leur artificielle duplication, dans les années soixante.

Il paraît ainsi pertinent de montrer comment l'écriture de la nostalgie participe des processus de détournement étudiés antérieurement. L'Occupation représente, dans les romans de Modiano, un monde recomposé par le rêve, dont les pires aspects viennent trouver place dans un ordre gouverné par la nostalgie. Après avoir montré que l'originalité de l'écriture réside dans cette tension entre un passé idéalisé et un présent désespérément silencieux, nous pourrons analyser avec précision les procédés d'édification de la mémoire, sélective et infidèle. Celle-ci vient choisir, avec une totale liberté, les éléments destinés à former les contours d'un « nouveau passé », cette Occupation pétrifiée dans le souvenir et délibérément hors d'atteinte.

Inlassable arpenteur d'un passé qui se dérobe[1], l'écrivain compulse, avec toute la précision du hasard, des galeries de spectres auprès desquels il choisit de s'attarder. Simples présences, ou détenteurs d'un savoir, ces derniers représentent les seuls points de contact avec un univers disparu[2].

L'œuvre convoque toutes les formes de la mémoire, du simple regret à l'obsession douloureuse, née d'une étrange fascination pour un instant ou une image. Nous nous attacherons, dans ce développement liminaire, à préciser les contours de cette étude. Il semble important, en effet, de restreindre l'extension du concept à sa signification dans l'œuvre. Pour le romancier, la nostalgie diffuse, qui affleure sous ses récits, évoque moins la douleur que le vide. Celui-ci fait prendre conscience à l'être de sa béance et de sa totale insignifiance. Nous tenterons ainsi une approche raisonnée de la notion, à l'aide de réflexions d'écrivains et de théoriciens de la mémoire, afin de montrer l'originalité de la voie tracée par le créateur de *Rue des boutiques obscures*.

Point de départ d'une recherche qui pousse ses ramifications au plus profond de l'être, l'évocation nostalgique représente, le plus souvent, une méditation mélancolique sur le caractère labile des êtres et des choses. Selon l'étymologie, cet état est celui de la souffrance (le retour ou *nostos*, associé à l'idée de douleur, ou *algos*), indicible et lancinante. Ce sentiment de manque résulte de l'impossible conjonction entre deux états de conscience, susceptible d'annihiler l'instant de la pensée pour lui substituer la réitération de l'acte ou du fait

---

[1] « La sensibilité nostalgique de celui qui est le plus beau, le plus singulier, le plus modeste, et sans doute le plus doué des jeunes écrivains français. » Gilles Pudlowski : « Modiano le magnifique » *in Les Nouvelles littéraires*, numéro du 12 au 19 février 1981, p. 28.
[2] Sur la question de la nostalgie, on se reportera à la thèse de Françoise Davidovits, *L'Écriture de la nostalgie chez Patrick Modiano*, dirigée par Jacqueline Levi-Valensi, Université d'Amiens, 1993.

regrettés. Dans *L'Irréversible et la nostalgie*[1], Vladimir Jankelevitch propose une formulation convaincante de ce paradoxe :

> La nostalgie est une mélancolie humaine rendue possible par la conscience, qui est conscience de quelque chose d'autre, conscience d'un ailleurs, conscience d'un contraste entre passé et présent, entre présent et futur. Cette conscience soucieuse est l'inquiétude du nostalgique. Le nostalgique est en même temps ici et là-bas, ni ici ni là, présent et absent, deux fois présent et deux fois absent[2].

Le statut des narrateurs modianiens, et particulièrement ceux de la première trilogie, semble le reflet d'une prédisposition naturelle à l'errance aux confins du temps. Raphaël parcourt trente ans d'histoire en spectateur immobile, Swing Troubadour, qui retourne après guerre square Cimarosa, se laisse submerger par le poids du passé. Enfin, Serge Alexandre représente, avant tout, la figure symbolique de l'écrivain désireux de renouer le contact perdu avec le père. La forme même des textes donne toute son importance à un « entretemps », situé à mi-chemin entre l'évocation du passé et l'acceptation de ses conséquences. Ainsi, le récit n'apparaît à aucun moment exonéré du regard porté sur l'Histoire, bien longtemps après le dénouement des faits relatés. Au cours des années quatre-vingts, lorsque la narration gagne en linéarité, le principe du regard rétrospectif, appliqué jusqu'alors de façon formelle, évolue sensiblement, et devient l'un des enjeux mêmes du récit.

Le protagoniste se voit confronté à des silhouettes ou des situations surgies du passé – Lafaure, dans *De si braves garçons*, Villecourt, dans *Dimanches d'août*, ou l'hôtel milanais de *Voyage de noces*[3] – qui le renvoient directement à

---

[1] Paris, Flammarion, 1972.
[2] *Op.cit.*, p. 280-281.
[3] De façon générale, les romans de Modiano sont riches en personnages chargés d'incarner un pays, un régime politique, ou simplement un « temps insouciant », sans que leur caractère prenne le pas sur la fonction de

une période lointaine de son existence. Le présent met brusquement à jour des sentiments enfouis au plus profond de l'être, de sorte que, dans le vacillement des temps qui se crée – fût-ce de façon particulièrement fugace –, le protagoniste se trouve suspendu, hésitant, entre deux mondes distincts, sans qu'il appartienne réellement à aucun. L'instant mis entre parenthèses reflète ainsi le vide et l'évanescence du personnage. Pour Daniel Parrochia, qui consacre un chapitre à l'écriture de l'« entretemps », dans son ouvrage sur la caractérisation du personnage modianien[1], le concept de nostalgie réside essentiellement dans cette idée de suspension :

> Philosophiquement, ce que suggèrent les romans de Modiano, et qui contribue à créer le charme troublant de leur atmosphère, c'est une sorte de superposition des temps, qui fait [...] que le passé peut toujours faire irruption dans le présent, pour dessiner soudain un avenir inaperçu où tout paraît possible[2].

Le philosophe cite le passage suivant, extrait de *Vestiaire de l'enfance*, comme illustration de ses propos :

> J'ai ouvert la fenêtre. Il faisait encore jour [...]. C'était la même lumière de fin de jour, en été, lorsque je

---

représentation qui est la leur. On songera, ainsi, au « Gros », à savoir l'ex-roi Farouk dans *Livret de famille*, Carpentieri, dans *Quartier perdu*, qui arpente les avenues, à la nuit tombée, afin de suivre celui qu'il estime réincarner l'ami disparu depuis vingt ans, ou encore Georges Bellune, dans *Une jeunesse*, réfugié autrichien, au moment de l'Anschluss, que le regret de son pays finit par tuer. C'est la perte de l'identité, dans ce dernier cas, qui explique le suicide du personnage.
Rêverie infinie sur la douleur d'un temps disparu, la souffrance engendrée par la nostalgie, conduit souvent au désespoir. Les personnages des romans de la deuxième période peinent à s'inscrire dans la réalité. On se souviendra des propos tenus par le narrateur de *Voyage de noces* : « Depuis longtemps déjà [...], l'été est une saison qui provoque chez moi une sensation de vide et d'absence et me ramène au passé. Est-ce la lumière trop brutale, le silence des rues, ces contrastes d'ombre et de soleil couchant ? [...] Le passé et le présent se mêlent dans mon esprit – par un phénomène de surimpression. Le malaise vient de là, sans doute. » *Voyage de noces*, p. 26.
[1] Daniel Parrochia, *Ontologie fantôme (essai sur l'œuvre de Patrick Modiano)*, Encre marine, Fougère, 1996.
[2] *Op. cit.*, p. 35-36.

surveillais, de la fenêtre de chez ma mère, la petite qui faisait rebondir son ballon sur le trottoir de l'avenue Junot.

Tout se confondait par un phénomène de surimpression – oui, tout se confondait et devenait d'une si pure et si implacable transparence... la transparence du temps, aurait dit Carlos Sirvent[1].

La nostalgie apparaît ainsi comme un instant de vertige, de concomitance déstabilisante, et non comme un douloureux état de prostration angoissée. Nous serions tenté de rapprocher cette démarche de la définition du *desiderium* latin ; la douleur qui naît du regret tire moins son origine d'un élément déterminé, d'un référent précis, que de la posture mentale suscitée par le sentiment.

L'Occupation se révèle et se présente à la mémoire par le contact brusque établi avec les traces ou les témoins du passé, qui demeurent les seuls intermédiaires avec la période. L'écrivain, qui ne peut aborder de front la période de l'Occupation, n'envisage d'autre mode d'évocation qu'une libre variation romanesque autour des personnages et des situations avérées – démarche illustrée par les ouvrages de la première trilogie – ou l'enquête minutieuse sur les victimes du passé, qui devient l'objet principal de la narration (on songera à *Fleurs de ruine* et surtout à *Dora Bruder*). Ces deux approches, que tout semble opposer, paraissent sous-tendues par un désir identique d'abolition du temps. Cette entreprise permettrait le retour à l'époque fondatrice, en facilitant l'immersion au sein de l'Histoire – loin de la sécheresse de la reconstitution. L'ensemble s'inscrit dans une démarche nostalgique *lato sensu*, en ce sens que la quête du passé ne s'articule pas autour d'un regret objectivé, mais se caractérise par l'adoption d'une posture mentale. Le manque et le désir deviennent ainsi la matière même d'une existence – et partant d'un récit – qui ne peut fonder sa légitimité que dans le travail, et surtout dans l'ordonnance de la mémoire. Dans la plupart

---

[1] *Op. cit.*, p. 144-145.

des autres œuvres de Modiano, la démarche nostalgique se heurte à une limite logique. Le passé sur lequel vient s'attarder la rêverie ne représente pas le temps irénique, représentatif d'un bonheur perdu, mais bien au contraire une géhenne surgie des pires cauchemars – que l'auteur n'a pas connue. Si celui-ci s'attarde sur les bords de ce continent englouti, c'est moins pour retrouver la plénitude d'un moment parfait que pour tenter de donner corps à une mémoire qui « précèd[e] sa naissance[1] » et s'avère indispensable pour affronter les années d'après-guerre.

Nous sommes donc en présence d'une nostalgie indirecte, concentrée sur les seuls signes et vestiges d'un temps qui apparaît comme l'unique dépositaire de sens. Le présent demeure silencieux, incapable de fournir un semblant de cohérence à l'existence du personnage :

> Et voilà maintenant que j'arrive devant ce cinéma que l'on a transformé en magasin [...]. Le café du rez-de-chaussée, dont elle m'avait parlé, n'existe plus. [...]
>
> Peu importent les circonstances et le décor. Ce sentiment de vide et de remords vous submerge, un jour. Puis, comme une marée, il se retire et disparaît. Mais il finit par revenir en force et elle ne pouvait pas s'en débarrasser. Moi non plus[2].

Dans le meilleur des cas, la réalité ne délivre que des simulacres, ou, bien pire encore, anéantit la substance même de la mémoire. Les œuvres de Modiano paraissent rongées par la lèpre du temps ; *Rue des boutiques obscures* constitue, à cet égard, l'exemple le plus flagrant. Pedro Mc Evoy devient, malgré lui, l'arpenteur involontaire d'un territoire dévasté par le passé, cheminant de décombres en galeries de spectres[3].

---

[1] *Livret de famille*, p. 115.
[2] *Voyage de noces*, p. 157-158.
[3] Ces dernières offrent nombre de ressemblances avec les fantômes de la fin du *Temps retrouvé*, usés et ravagés par le passage des années. On songera, notamment, au portrait de Charlus, lors de sa dernière rencontre avec le narrateur : « Je fis arrêter la voiture et j'allais m'apprêter à descendre pour faire quelques pas à pied quand je fus frappé par le spectacle d'une voiture qui était en train de s'arrêter aussi. Un homme, les yeux fixes, la taille voûtée,

À l'image de ses devanciers, Nerval et Proust, l'auteur de *La Place de l'Étoile* excelle dans la peinture de la décomposition. Rongés par le temps, les êtres – comme le pianiste Blunt, exsangue et désespéré – ou leurs demeures – le château de la famille de Luz, dont le spectacle de ruines pétrifiées n'est pas sans rappeler les vestiges de Mortefontaine, dans *Sylvie* – s'abîment et se meurent dans une silencieuse agonie. Réduits à la seule fonction de présence testimoniale d'un temps disparu – et du caractère à proprement parler mortifère du souvenir –, ils incitent à la fuite et au refuge dans une sphère protégée de l'emprise temporelle, celle de la rêverie mélancolique.

L'EVOCATION DE LA GUERRE : AUX SOURCES DU SOUVENIR

Les textes de Modiano s'articulent autour de la seule figure d'un protagoniste omniprésent, soucieux de gommer les aspérités de son récit. Ils se caractérisent par leur aspect « lisse », ne s'écartant jamais d'une certaine idée d'un roman intellectualisé, et ce même dans les passages violemment polémiques et provocateurs.

Cette conception de l'écriture, qui donne peut-être la clef de l'univers modianien, est particulièrement remarquable,

---

était posé plutôt qu'assis dans le fond, et faisait pour se tenir droit les efforts qu'aurait faits un enfant à qui on aurait recommandé d'être sage. Mais son chapeau de paille laissait voir une forêt indomptée de cheveux entièrement blancs ; une barbe blanche, comme celle que la neige fait aux statues des fleuves dans les jardins publics, coulait de son menton. [...] Les yeux n'étaient pas restés en dehors de cette convulsion totale, de cette altération métallurgique de la tête, mais, par un phénomène inverse, ils avaient perdu tout leur éclat. [...] Quand Jupien eut aidé le baron à descendre et que j'eus salué celui-ci, il me parla très vite, d'une voix si imperceptible que je ne pus distinguer ce qu'il me disait, ce qui lui arracha, quand pour la troisième fois je le fis répéter, un geste d'impatience qui m'étonna par l'impassibilité qu'avait d'abord montrée le visage et qui était due sans doute à un reste de paralysie. » *Le Temps retrouvé*, Bibliothèque de la Pléiade, tome III, p. 859-861, édition de Pierre Clarac et André Ferré.

puisqu'elle définit une esthétique du récit – et du style – unique dans l'histoire de la littérature de l'après-guerre. Afin de montrer l'originalité de ces histoires contées par des narrateurs aux yeux « mi-clos », nous nous attarderons sur l'étude des modalités de ces récits rêvés. Aussi nous intéresserons-nous, dans un premier temps, aux personnages créés par le romancier, puis aux lieux parcourus dans les textes.

Modiano ne propose pas la peinture de personnages, mais polit des romans dans lesquels la restitution des ambiances ou des atmosphères l'emporte sur toute autre considération narrative. Cette littérature se méfie des corps, qui lestent les récits de leur trivialité prévisible et fastidieuse. À cette fin, l'écrivain évacue de son univers tous les éléments qui ne lui semblent pas indispensables à la stricte caractérisation d'un personnage.

Celui-ci n'accède à l'existence romanesque que par la mention d'un détail particulier, qui vaudra description exhaustive : le regard du Saint-Cyrien, responsable du RCO, les costumes de Schlemilovitch père ou la marque des cigarettes de Henri Normand. Chez Modiano, la figure de la synecdoque régit souvent l'ensemble du dispositif descriptif – la mention d'un élément vaut représentation de l'être ou de l'objet dans sa globalité –, comme si l'écrivain se méfiait d'une attention trop exclusive accordée à une stylisation qui le détournerait de l'idéalisation du personnage. Ce dernier n'a pas d'autre fonction que la fusion dans un tableau où nulle aspérité ou accident d'exécution ne pourraient trouver leur place. L'écrivain privilégie le cercle, la « ronde », puisque le nombre élevé de figures lui permet de ciseler la composition de son morceau de bravoure : l'évocation du temps suspendu, au cours d'une réunion ou d'un dîner. De fait, tout se passe comme si le créateur ne s'intéressait qu'à la somme des éléments réunis et non aux spécificités de chacun d'eux.

Le refus de la matérialisation des idées et de l'autonomie réelle d'un personnage donne aux œuvres un aspect aussi peu terrien que possible. Comme nous le verrons ultérieurement, le romancier ne semble jamais aussi libre de ses moyens et maître de son art que lorsqu'il nie le caractère particulier pour se réfugier dans une globalité indistincte. À cet égard, les personnages de *La Ronde de nuit* n'ont guère plus de consistance que les deux créatures chimériques, Coco Lacour et Esmeralda, ces deux anges égarés dans le dernier cercle infernal. La guerre, et ce jusque dans ses pires aspects, n'impose jamais sa gravité et ses abominations chez Modiano. Son monde est peuplé de silhouettes immobiles, qui hantent des immeubles vidés de leurs habitants, le long d'avenues désertes – à la façon d'un minuscule théâtre d'ombres reproduisant, après la mort, le spectacle du monde.

Ce récit sans corps entraîne *ipso facto* la disparition du corps du récit. Jusqu'en 1978 avec *Rue des boutiques obscures*, et surtout 1981, avec *Une jeunesse*, Modiano semble à proprement parler incapable de raconter une histoire. Si l'on ausculte ces figures privées de récit, on s'aperçoit que de suites de fantasmes en constructions analeptiques les œuvres se révèlent incapables de présenter une narration. Les textes se composent de suites d'instants, de moments plus ou moins longs, plus ou moins agréables, que l'écrivain s'efforce de réunir.

Villa triste ne propose, par exemple, qu'une continuité de séquences, sans progression dramatique ni approfondissement psychologique. Le choix du tableau, plutôt que de la scène, qui permettrait aux corps déniés de s'animer, participe de cette esthétique du vide, de « dessubstantialisation ». Cette approche constitue la meilleure garantie contre les attaques et ravages du temps, comme le note fort justement Daniel Parrochia :

> Il n'y a que le fantôme qui puisse *vraiment* durer. Car c'est là tout le secret : seul le plus fugitif a la capacité de rester vivant [...]. Pour Modiano, le seul moyen d'accéder à l'immortalité, ou, à tout le moins de se mettre hors d'atteinte du temps, est précisément de n'être rien, de ne pas laisser de trace, d'être un fantôme. Les lieux, les objets seuls ont une permanence. Mais les

êtres qui les hantent, ceux qui les possèdent, n'en ont point[1].

Le philosophe voit dans la recherche de la « grégarité[2] », dans le caractère translucide de l'être modianien, son seul et unique principe de conservation. Il cite, à ce propos, les nombreux passages de *Dimanches d'août*, qui abordent le thème de l'anonymat et de l'immersion au sein de la foule. Ce dernier état représente un refuge satisfaisant contre les dangers et agressions du monde – et il faut sans doute discerner, dans cette recherche constante de sécurité, la présence du père et le repli de celui-ci au sein de la capitale, auprès de ceux qui préconisaient l'anéantissement de sa race.

> L'angoisse [...] ne se dissipe [et encore, provisoirement] que dans ces « dimanches d'août » où le couple, dans une station balnéaire océane, confondu avec les estivants, ne sera plus qu'un parmi d'autres, accédant ainsi à cette invisibilité fantomatique qui, un instant, le sauve[3].

Ce commentaire renvoie au passage suivant du roman de Modiano :

> Il faisait très chaud cet été-là et nous avions la certitude que l'on ne nous retrouverait jamais ici [...]. Jamais nous n'avons été aussi heureux qu'à ces moments-là, perdus dans la foule au parfum d'ambre solaire. Nous étions comme tout le monde, rien ne nous distinguait des autres, ces dimanches d'août[4].

Daniel Parrochia ajoute aux propos précédents les remarques suivantes :

> Le paradoxe, on l'a dit, veut que ce soit celui qui n'est rien qui reste, ou plutôt revient, c'est-à-dire vit, par l'intermédiaire des autres, l'éternité sous forme de retour [...]. La mort, en effet, est toujours du côté du singulier et celui-ci, en tant que non-universel, est

---

[1] D. Parrochia, *op.cit.*, p. 40.
[2] *Ibid.*
[3] *Op.cit.*, p. 40-41.
[4] *Dimanches d'août*, p. 160-161.

> inéchangeable et impossible à reproduire. Dépourvus de ces particularités qui permettent une « identification », les fantômes, au contraire, n'ont pas d'épaisseur, ils sont imperceptibles [...]. Être ainsi en état d'empiétement [...] oui, à coup sûr, c'est cela, être éternel[1].

Si les œuvres n'apparaissent jamais dérangeantes, au sens fort du mot, c'est sans doute parce qu'elles évacuent entièrement cette représentation frontale de l'être. Les contours de celui-ci sont estompés, les facettes intimes de sa personnalité, ses imperfections et faiblesses passées sous silence : le lecteur ne peut s'attacher à ces créatures – et ce n'est assurément pas le but de l'écrivain, qui se contente de désigner les protagonistes des derniers romans par un prénom fonctionnel et transparent, Jean, voire le pronom personnel de la première personne[2]. Cette négation du corps rend à proprement parler « imprésentable » le héros modianien, créature incorporelle, dont l'existence semble limitée au seul stade de l'idée. Il ne fait ainsi aucun doute que l'échec des adaptations cinématographiques soit imputable, pour une bonne part, à l'impossibilité de figurer *physiquement* l'abstraction – c'est-à-dire de donner corps à une création intellectuelle, sur écran. Le dernier film en date, *Le Parfum d'Yvonne*, de Patrice Leconte, échoue justement dans la restitution de l'histoire, qui compense l'absence apparente d'intrigue en multipliant les scènes d'intimité – comme si l'unique chance de « donner corps » au récit résidait dans l'exhibition de celui-ci.

La démarche esthétique de Modiano se trouve trahie par la survalorisation du couple et l'aspect physique de la relation. En revanche, l'unique moment du livre où le corps se trouve magnifié – l'épisode de la remise de la coupe Houligant, lorsque Meinthe saute avec grâce par-dessus la portière de la

---

[1] D. Parrochia, *op.cit.*, p. 41.
[2] La question de la dénomination est au centre d'une œuvre comme *Rue des boutiques obscures*, puisque l'amnésique ne peut indiquer aux personnages de rencontre le « moyen » de le désigner. Il évoluera donc d'identités fluctuantes en patronymes précaires, sans que le mystère de son identité soit levé à la fin de l'ouvrage.

voiture, dans un mouvement de morgue et de détachement – se trouve gommé du film. La restitution de l'Occupation obéit à des principes identiques. L'écrivain rêve son époque en images sépia, se laissant bercer par un extrait de dialogue ou l'aspect lugubre d'une pièce. On ajoutera que, dans les textes consacrés à cette période, le temps le plus fréquemment utilisé est l'imparfait, dont la valeur descriptive et itérative semble peu adaptée à la narration d'actes « singulatifs » par définition. De fait, l'emploi de ce temps sert le dessein de l'écrivain, lequel s'attache à aplanir les événements, en fondant les années de guerre dans une continuité indistincte, et se gardant bien de préciser les dates et la durée interne des épisodes, de façon à éviter un « effet de réel » capable de donner quelque consistance au personnage.

La primauté accordée au flou narratif et la mobilisation de toutes les ressources romanesques pour insuffler la vie à des photographies mentales permettent de « déréaliser » la période des années noires. La connaissance presque parfaite des figures marquantes de la corruption, appliquée à un travail consciencieux sur les *topoï* de la Collaboration (à titre d'exemple, les agapes des trafiquants dont les rires couvrent les voix des résistants torturés, ou les marchandages sordides entre les agioteurs du square Cimarosa), donne un étrange statut aux tableaux de la guerre. La connaissance historique, qui permet d'avérer la réalité des événements narrés, est le seul élément interdisant de voir, dans cette évocation, une rêverie spéculative sur la période – en effet, comme nous l'avons vu, les récits des témoins attestent le caractère hallucinatoire des soirées des bandes Berger et Bonny-Lafont. Les effets de style ôtent à cette peinture ses côtés insoutenables pour tirer le récit vers le romanesque, au sens littéral du terme.

Enfin, le talent de l'écrivain tend à imposer au lecteur cette vision particulière de l'Occupation, à l'exception de toute autre, à savoir un dialogue réduit au strict minimum entre des entités réduites à leur principe idéel – cinématographiquement parlant, les Straub eussent été de bien meilleurs adaptateurs de *Villa triste* que Leconte –, entrecoupé de quelques gestes et déplacements, saisis de façon fugitive.

En plaçant la rêverie au cœur de l'Occupation, Modiano tranchait de façon singulière sur la production littéraire des années soixante et soixante-dix. Les romans de cette époque s'attachaient à heurter le lecteur par le recours à l'émotion facile. Le jeune Modiano travaille, lui, dans un registre différent : il ne refuse pas l'émotion, mais la détourne. Elle prendra sa source non dans l'évocation de l'abjection quotidienne, mais dans le souvenir de celle-ci. En effet, le jeu original avec la temporalité, étudié dans les chapitres précédents, contribue à supprimer tout principe de proximité avec l'événement. Celui-ci, au moment même où il se trouve évoqué, paraît surgir du plus profond de la mémoire – de sorte que son pouvoir de suggestion, duquel naît l'émotion, se voit réduit à néant.

Pourtant, les romans de la première trilogie constituent, sans aucun doute, les meilleurs ouvrages de fiction consacrés à l'Occupation. L'aspect poignant – absolument indéniable – des récits provient d'une substitution thématique. Le caractère aseptisé de l'Occupation, auquel vient s'ajouter la neutralité des observations formulées à l'imparfait, vient figer le texte dans une posture nostalgique, qui finit par se prendre elle-même pour objet. Cette ruse narrative se verrait frappée de nullité si les personnages semblaient régis par des sentiments, c'est-à-dire s'ils habitaient réellement des corps. Reniés, évacués du récit[1], afin d'offrir au narrateur-écrivain la sécurité

---

[1] À la fin de *La Place de l'Étoile*, lors du voyage de Tel-Aviv, les colons menacent Schlemilovitch des pires sévices s'il refuse l'acclimatation imposée :
« Bientôt on se servira de toi pour faire des savonnettes. N'est-ce pas, Saül ?
– De ton sang on fera du jus de viande, lui dit Saül.
– De tes os des allumettes, lui dit Isaac.
– De ta peau des abat-jour, lui dit Isaïe. »
Il ne faut pourtant pas voir un retour au corps, qui retrouverait droit de cité avec ce rappel des tortures infligées aux juifs dans les camps d'extermination, mais un *topos* historique prenant place dans la parodie – et l'écriture de l'inversion – du quatrième chapitre. Cette menace, qui prend le corps pour objet, s'avère en réalité purement abstraite et fonctionnelle, puisqu'elle est reformulée quelque temps après par Raphaël, dans le kibboutz disciplinaire :
« Oui, mon général ! De mon sang il fera du jus de viande, de mes os des

à laquelle il aspire, ces derniers ne prendront place dans les romans qu'à partir d'*Une jeunesse,* au moment où l'écrivain délaisse l'Histoire pour débusquer les spectres d'un passé beaucoup plus proche du moment de l'écriture. Le lecteur conservera le souvenir d'une Occupation marquée par l'apathie des protagonistes. L'angoisse, la menace, la révolte ou la haine ne lui parviennent que de façon assourdie, comme s'ils étaient filtrés par les héros du récit, êtres apathiques errant à la lisière de la réalité.

Quelque vingt-cinq ans plus tard, Modiano proposera une démarche radicalement différente, en replaçant le personnage au cœur du texte. *Dora Bruder* marque le retour au corps, mais un corps ravi à jamais par l'Histoire, rayé de la mémoire, qui vient habiter chaque page de sa douloureuse absence. Le « désir d'écriture » n'a pas d'autre origine que cette lutte perdue d'avance, visant à installer de nouveau l'être dans son existence et à contrer les effets de l'oubli. La reconnaissance – au sens militaire du terme – des quartiers et des lieux (le couvent du Saint-Cœur-de-Marie ou la prison des Tourelles) ou la recherche de traces, scripturales ou autres (les fichiers ou les témoignages oraux) tentent de suppléer à la disparition du corps, en plaçant ses manifestations et traces au cœur de la conscience. Cette démarche, nostalgique par excellence, n'a pourtant que peu à voir avec la langueur dont font preuve les narrateurs des œuvres de jeunesse.

Le lecteur assiste bel et bien à une entreprise vouée à l'échec – mais hautement significative –, qui consiste à combler le vide par l'activité de la quête[1]. Tout se passe

---

allumettes, de ma peau des abat-jour. » À ce moment, le rappel du corps meurtri fonctionne comme une sorte d'antienne qui ponctue le récit. Cette reprise constitue surtout un commentaire métalinguistique de la première déclaration, un retour réflexif sur l'écriture même de l'abomination, et non un échange d'information dans le cadre de la fonction dénotative du langage. En définitive, ce n'est pas le corps qui se trouve au centre de l'échange, mais bien la question de la représentation de l'Histoire par le roman.

[1] « Le Jadis de la nostalgie est, comme le charme, infiniment lointain, incomplet et cryptique ; et bien plus encore ! car il faut le retrouver non pas dans l'espace, mais dans le temps irréversible, et sans aucune chance de réitération. L'homme nostalgique voudrait redonner vie au fantôme du

comme si les résultats de la démarche importaient moins que sa mise en œuvre – de sorte que c'est le livre, *in fine*, qui devient « corps parlant ». En effet, non content d'inscrire le personnage éponyme au cœur même de la matière textuelle, l'ouvrage, cette couture de traces et de pistes, se trouve entièrement habité par la présence toute virtuelle de la jeune fille – afin de « faire corps » avec celle-ci et de triompher de la destruction. Le contact avec les lieux, pour décevant et infructueux qu'il soit, reste ainsi l'unique recours contre la lancinante absence de l'être recherché. Ces derniers demeurent, en effet, les seuls dépositaires de la mémoire, jouant le rôle de passeurs, d'intermédiaires entre le monde perdu et la réalité, terne et muette.

Si l'écriture modianienne tend à ôter aux êtres leur caractère humain, elle s'attache, en revanche, à spécifier – de manière particulièrement scrupuleuse – les contours des souvenirs liés aux endroits visités et parcourus. Les descriptions empruntent leur exactitude au cadastre, et il n'est pas un immeuble ou un square qui ne reçoivent une localisation précise.

L'espace ainsi mesuré, la toponymie soigneusement vérifiée, l'écrivain peut laisser flâner une imagination qui se plaît à agencer les scènes du passé selon les libres inflexions des associations d'idées :

> Au bas de l'hôtel du 41 boulevard Ornano, le café Marchal avait un téléphone : Montmartre 44-74, mais j'ignore si ce café communiquait avec l'immeuble et si Marchal était aussi le patron de l'hôtel. Le pensionnat du Saint-Cœur-de-Marie ne figurait pas dans l'annuaire de l'époque. J'ai retrouvé une autre adresse des Sœurs des Écoles chrétiennes de la Miséricorde qui devait être en 1942 une annexe du pensionnat : 64 rue Saint-Maur. Dora l'a-t-elle fréquentée[1] ?

---

souvenir, compléter cette insuffisance, ressusciter la présence en chair et en os. » V. Jankelevitch, *op.cit.*, p. 303.
[1] *Dora Bruder*, p. 61.

Cette géométrisation policière du cadastre ne s'oppose pas à la liberté que procure la rêverie, bien au contraire. Celle-ci se trouve circonscrite dans des limites strictes, et reçoit ainsi toute latitude pour se déployer. Deux siècles plus tard, le caractère maniaque de la recension – les adresses et numéros de téléphone soigneusement conservés, la disposition d'un groupe d'immeubles ou la notation systématique des changements survenus au cours des années – rappelle, *mutatis mutandis*, la minutie d'arpenteur dont faisait preuve Restif de la Bretonne dans ses *Nuits de Paris*.

Les deux écrivains se caractérisent, en effet, par leur propension à installer l'étrange au cœur des lieux les mieux connus, faisant surgir l'inattendu au cœur de leur évocation personnelle des endroits que balise l'imaginaire du lecteur. C'est, sans doute, en accordant la plus grande attention à ces lieux maintes fois arpentés que les écrivains parviennent à isoler le détail qui donnera à leur récit un contour mystérieux, né d'un léger dérèglement du regard porté sur le monde quotidien. On se livrera ainsi à une étude comparée de deux tableaux nocturnes de Paris, à savoir un extrait de la cent quarante-sixième *Nuit de Paris*, sous-titré *La Fille qu'on promène la nuit*, dans lequel Restif de la Bretonne découvre brusquement un aspect ignoré de la capitale – et se trouve entraîné, comme cela lui arrive fréquemment, dans une aventure surprenante – avec un passage extrait du deuxième ouvrage de Modiano :

> Je voulus rompre, à mon retour, l'habitude trop douce de repasser par la Nouvelle Halle. Pour me distraire, je suivis la rue du Temple, et je pris le boulevard Saint-Antoine, afin de venir à la porte, qui subsistait encore. Là, je pris la rue de la Roquette, et je m'éloignai au hasard, dans le silence profond de la nuit. Je me trouvai vis-à-vis Sainte-Marguerite. Un chien vint à moi, et par ses aboiements hardis, m'annonça que son maître n'était pas loin. – Qui va là ? (me dit-on) : retirez-vous. – Qui que vous soyez, qui me dites, de me retirer, sachez que je ne suis pas un homme dangereux. Le hasard m'a conduit dans ce quartier solitaire, et qui ne m'est pas connu. Je vous prie de m'aider à en sortir,

en me faisant retrouver la grand'rue du faubourg Saint-Antoine ! À ces mots, un jeune homme en robe de chambre vint à moi, avec une jeune personne qui me parut enceinte, et très avancée[1].

Après avoir implicitement accepté de jouer un double jeu, et dénoncé au Khédive l'identité et les activités des hommes du RCO, Swing Troubadour se trouve en proie à un profond désarroi. Les éléments du décor se trouvent alors en totale correspondance avec son état d'esprit :

> À ma droite, si proche, le faisceau lumineux de la tour Eiffel. Je revenais de la rue Boisrobert. Le métro s'est arrêté sur le pont de Passy. Je souhaitais qu'il ne reparte jamais plus et que personne ne vienne m'arracher à ce *no man's land* entre les deux rives. Plus un geste. Plus un bruit. Le calme enfin. [...] Ma peur faisait place à une sorte d'engourdissement. J'accompagnais du regard le faisceau lumineux. Il tournait, tournait comme un veilleur poursuivant sa ronde de nuit. Avec lassitude. Sa clarté s'affaiblissait à mesure. Bientôt il ne resterait qu'un filet de lumière presque imperceptible. Et moi aussi, après des rondes et des rondes, mille et mille allées et venues je finirais par me perdre dans les ténèbres[2].

S'il peut paraître surprenant de rapprocher deux écritures – et deux genres littéraires – qui semblent offrir peu d'aspects communs, il semble intéressant d'insister sur les liens de parenté qui les unissent. Dans les deux extraits, la nuit modifie la perception du cadre urbain, qui apparaît sous une perspective entièrement nouvelle. Les sensations et le jugement s'ordonnent autour d'une autre logique, qui délaisse la rationalité du jour pour laisser libre cours à l'inattendu. Cette rencontre avec la banalité du quotidien, brusquement transcendée par le regard de l'« oiseau de nuit[3] », n'est pas sans rappeler la démarche surréaliste, selon laquelle le plus

---

[1] *Les Nuits de Paris*, édition de J. Varloot et M. Delon, « Folio », p. 183-184.
[2] *La Ronde de nuit*, p. 111-112.
[3] Restif de la Bretonne se surnomme le « hibou », dans ses *Nuits de Paris*.

grand plaisir des sens et de l'esprit pouvait naître de la simple réévaluation de l'objet le plus dérisoire.

La force de l'écriture modianienne réside justement dans l'attention constante portée aux détails les plus insignifiants – comme si leur présence devenait brusquement signifiante, riche de virtualités jusqu'alors inaperçues ou inexploitées. La disparition d'un café, la démolition d'une maison ou, au contraire, l'immutabilité d'un lieu fonctionnent comme des signes métonymiques, et se révèlent les impitoyables indicateurs de la marche des années.

L'attitude nostalgique prend l'aspect d'une réaction désespérée contre les atteintes du temps[1], traduite concrètement par la quête de traces et de vestiges testimoniaux. L'errance et les déambulations le long des avenues ou des bâtiments délaissés donnent lieu à un rapport consciencieux sur les changements survenus au cours du temps. Ainsi, le présent se résume à la somme des modifications affectant les lieux chargés d'histoire. On serait tenté de voir, chez les héros modianiens, une démarche proche de celle de Pedro Mc Evoy, l'enquêteur de *Rue des boutiques obscures*. Le protagoniste des romans devient, comme ce dernier, l'inspecteur du quotidien, trouvant la justification de son existence dans cet inventaire du déclin.

Pour Modiano, le drame réside dans la précarité des éléments. L'univers idéal serait celui où les lieux et les êtres conserveraient un caractère pérenne, susceptible, à ce titre, de les mettre à l'abri des altérations – dramatiques – causées par le temps[2]. Nous rejoignons ici ce que nous énoncions

---

[1] « Le temps, chez Modiano, cache une force entropique qui use les objets, qui estompe les traces du passé, qui vieillit les gens […]. Pour Modiano, c'est à cause de la guerre que le temps est devenu nuisible. L'irréversibilité de celui-ci se manifeste par son pouvoir de décomposition, de corrosion, de dégradation de l'être humain. » Shounong Feng, *op.cit.*, p. 284.
[2] Publié l'année même des *Boulevards de ceinture*, le bel ouvrage de Jankelevitch propose un grand nombre d'élucidations philosophiques de postures nostalgiques, si familières aux héros de Modiano : « C'est pour les mathématiciens que tout lieu en vaut un autre ; et c'est au contraire pour un cœur nostalgique qu'il existe un espace concret diversifié par des sites qualitativement hétérogènes. […] Aussi peut-on parler d'une espèce de

précédemment à propos des personnages : le roman de Modiano rêve d'une immortalité illusoire capable de pétrifier l'existence en une sorte d'instant éternel – loin des désastres du changement, de la dégradation.

Figure centrale du théâtre de ses souvenirs, le narrateur-écrivain en ordonne scrupuleusement le sanctuaire. La lente régression mentale qui consiste à se retrancher dans le monde clos de la mémoire traduit généralement, chez les personnes âgées, une volonté d'enfermement fondée sur un désir de sécurité. On imagine aisément la signification qu'une semblable attitude prend chez un jeune écrivain, pour lequel la modification de son univers équivaut à l'agression de son espace intime. Cette angoisse trouve sa correspondance formelle dans la facture traditionnelle des romans. À l'exception du premier ouvrage, ces derniers se caractérisent par leur esthétique fondée sur une fluidité du récit et la transparence de l'écriture – les moyens propres à l'évocation de la mémoire ne devant pas représenter un obstacle à l'expression de celle-ci. Jeune vieillard, Modiano s'est toujours attaché à la qualité du style[1], cherchant ses modèles du côté des romanciers de la « clarté », les Larbaud, Alain-Fournier ou Aragon. L'émotion ne peut naître du chaos, et seule une manière (au sens pictural du terme) classique permet à l'écriture d'« endiguer l'oubli, [de] retrouver le temps perdu, et de redonner vie à une « silhouette claire » [...]. Par l'écriture, on peut regarder le temps écoulé, et résister au temps qui passe[2]. »

---

topographie mystique dont la seule toponymie, par sa force évocatrice, met déjà en branle le travail de la réminiscence et de l'imagination. » *Op. cit.*, p. 276-277.

[1] « La langue française, pour moi, c'est un peu une amarre... Sinon tout fout le camp. Tout se dissout s'il n'y a pas la phrase avec le sujet, le verbe, le complément. Évidemment ceux qui lisent, ils n'en ont rien à foutre. Ils disent, c'est du Paul Bourget. Je me suis dit qu'au fond je pouvais très bien utiliser leur manière d'écrire le français, très filée, un français très clair. Je me suis dit que ce serait bien comme arme... » Interview recueillie par J. Brunn, citée par C. Wardi dans « Mémoire et écriture dans l'œuvre de Modiano », *in Les Nouveaux Cahiers 80*, printemps 1985, p. 40-48.
[2] Shounong Feng, *op.cit.*, p. 285.

L'EDIFICATION DE LA MEMOIRE

L'une des particularités de l'œuvre de Modiano réside dans la présentation des événements. Ces derniers apparaissent comme inscrits dans le souvenir, au moment même où ils surviennent, comme s'ils n'avaient jamais cessé de faire corps avec celui-ci. Le temps, la logique ou les rapports avec les autres ne paraissent pas exister par eux-mêmes, mais uniquement grâce à la façon dont ils s'inscrivent dans le processus de réminiscence.

L'univers tout entier semble se réduire au principe unique de la mémoire. De ce fait, l'expérience a moins de valeur que la trace conservée (ou non). Cette attitude trouve sa justification chez un écrivain comme Marcel Proust, hanté justement par la disparition de ces traces –, qui bâtit son œuvre, voire son existence, sur la mise en forme de celles-ci – créateur auquel nous consacrerons le second moment de ce développement. Auparavant, nous nous serons interrogé sur l'incongruité apparente du système modianien, qui tend à ériger une période historique inconnue en moment fondateur de l'existence.

Le passé ignoré peut-il représenter la seule source de légitimité ? Ôte-t-il toute validité aux souvenirs avérés ? À quelques nuances près, ces principes semblent régir, en effet, la plupart des romans de Modiano. Leurs héros apparaissent en quête permanente d'une vérité enfouie au plus profond de l'oubli. Le présent ou le passé identifiables ne leur sont d'aucune utilité pour l'édification ou le recouvrement de leur identité. La « révélation » réside au cœur des ténèbres d'une mémoire qui se dérobe, et cela en raison d'une loi de consécution logique – né en 1945, Modiano n'a aucune connaissance directe de la période qu'il relate –, d'une cause psychologique – l'amnésie du supposé Pedro Mc Evoy – ou d'un refoulement choisi : le départ de Jean Dekker pour Londres, après le dénouement tragique de son séjour à Paris.

Les souvenirs survalorisés, parce qu'inaccessibles, deviennent très vite les objets d'une recherche impérieuse. Le narrateur va tenter de compenser, de façon physique, l'impossibilité de se mouvoir librement dans le temps[1]. L'accès à l'identité semble impossible sans la confrontation avec ce passé intangible. À cette fin, l'enquêteur privilégiera les témoignages, les comptes rendus ou les expériences indirectes. *Livret de famille* se révèle, à cet égard, un exemple particulièrement éclairant de la reconstitution *a posteriori* d'une mémoire, grâce à la fusion des époques et des voix. L'ensemble de ces dispositifs psychologiques favorise l'accès à la période qui, sans le recours de l'écriture, demeurerait hors d'atteinte.

> Cette œuvre « s'affirme [...] comme un récit à caractère autobiographique, véritable entreprise de reconstruction de l'histoire mystérieuse de la famille du scripteur/narrateur, dont le point de départ est l'inscription de la naissance de sa fille dans son livret de famille[2]. »

En effet, l'ouvrage est un texte charnière, fonctionnant sur le mode du legs : celui de la mémoire, que Modiano désirerait transmettre à sa fille, au moment de son entrée dans l'existence – mémoire authentifiée, dont il n'a pas la jouissance. Chacun des quinze chapitres apparaît comme une lutte contre l'entreprise désastreuse de l'amnésie. Tous ont pour vocation d'inscrire l'écrivain au sein de la réalité, par la relation d'une expérience, validée par des témoins, concernant l'inscription dans le Temps. L'œuvre s'ouvre et se ferme avec le personnage de la petite fille – constat de stabilité –, dont le rôle est de servir de rempart contre les transgressions opérées par la mémoire ; celle-ci tend, en effet, à estomper les quelques limites claires établies par le présent.

---

[1] On songera également aux promenades hallucinées dans le Paris de *La Ronde de nuit*, dans la période de l'après-guerre, aux multiples déplacements en province, puis à l'étranger, dans *Rue des boutiques obscures* ou à la scrupuleuse recherche topologique à l'œuvre dans *Dora Bruder*.

[2] D. Perramond, « *Livret de famille* : grandeur et misère de la mémoire », *in French Review*, n° 56, p. 70.

L'écrivain multiplie les points d'approche du passé, en donnant des résonances personnelles aux récits des tiers[1] – en particulier lorsqu'il s'agit de l'Occupation – et en inscrivant la « quotidienneté » dans l'expérience collective de ces témoins. L'ensemble se doit de donner une certaine cohérence au passé, même si celle-ci se borne au simple arrangement de zones d'ombre, de sorte que l'enfant ne se voie pas confrontée, parvenue à l'âge adulte, au silence effrayant d'un passé énigmatique.

Si les expériences personnelles du narrateur sont quantitativement plus nombreuses que les récits indirects, il semble que ces derniers soient dotés d'une importance excédant largement leur volume. Le souvenir, qui s'est agrégé à la réalité, et semble l'avoir en partie phagocytée, transforme insensiblement le réel en histoire. Une partie de chasse en Sologne évoque l'insurrection du ghetto de Varsovie, la guerre de Corée convoque les heures douloureuses de l'Occupation – et nécessite l'obtention d'un certificat de baptême – et celle du Kippour, enfin, se voit associée au génocide du peuple juif dans les camps allemands.

Le texte marque cependant la fin de la première manière du narrateur, qui ne pouvait concevoir l'évocation des années sombres sous une forme différente de la relation dialectique entre l'oubli et le refoulement – cet anéantissement de la mémoire, prédominant dans l'inconscient collectif après 1945. Le romancier ne cessera de cesse de recadrer sa démarche,

---

[1] Nous songeons notamment au personnage de Korominé, présent dans deux chapitres de l'ouvrage. Dans son article, *La Trace douloureuse*, paru en juillet 1991, dans *L'École des lettres*, Norbert Czarny écrit à ce propos : « [...] la présence [...] [du plus vieil ami de son père] n'est pas indifférente. S'il n'a pas assisté au mariage de ses parents, il sait du moins dans quelles circonstances ils se sont mariés, à Megève, en 1944. Et pourrait expliquer le mystère de sa naissance : "Sans cette époque, sans les rencontres hasardeuses et contradictoires qu'elle provoquait, je ne serais jamais né." C'est pourquoi les substituts du père, qu'ils soient amis, frères ou autres, viennent expliquer pour une part le mystère de sa vie entre 1940 et 1945. Qu'il s'agisse de Marignan, l'aventurier qui a disparu de l'état-civil en 45, de l'oncle qui n'est de "nulle part" ou de Henri Dressel [...], tous les héros masculins sont des êtres incertains que le narrateur côtoie avec l'espoir d'apprendre qui il est. » (p. 72-73).

distinguant son existence de celle de ses protagonistes. Dès lors, l'œuvre devient témoignage, comme si les dix années d'une écriture expérimentale – qui bouleversait les catégories de l'imaginaire et de la fiction – constituaient une première phase, indispensable à l'assimilation d'un passé rendu « maîtrisable ». Avant d'analyser, dans l'ultime développement de ce travail, les répercussions qu'une semblable évolution entraîne dans l'édification de l'identité, il semble pertinent de commenter les recherches de Proust, grand devancier de Modiano dans l'écriture de la nostalgie.

Les premiers romans de Modiano se présentent comme des autobiographies – au sens générique du terme, puisque nous verrons que les œuvres semblent régies par les lois propres à l'autofiction – rédigées par un homme parvenu au terme de son parcours, plaçant dans la confession le solde de sa mémoire. Contrairement aux grands écrivains du XX⁰ siècle, qui ont fait de leur existence ou d'un élément fondamental de celle-ci, la matière même de leur œuvre littéraire – nous pensons à Proust, Céline ou Claude Simon – Modiano ordonne son corpus autour d'une époque disparue, inconnue, en inversant les rapports entre l'écriture et le souvenir.

Le roman proustien ou célinien constituait la somme des expériences d'une vie, modelées et transformées par l'acte narratif. Chez l'auteur de *La Place de l'Étoile*, nous assistons à un changement complet de perspective : c'est l'écriture, elle-même, qui semble donner à l'existence sa légitimité, inscrivant pleinement le protagoniste-romancier dans le siècle. Quand un Claude Simon revient à trois reprises sur un épisode traumatique de la Débâcle – celle-ci se trouve mise en fiction dans *La Route des Flandres*, romancée de façon « autofictionnelle » dans *L'Acacia* et théorisée dans le livre testament de son auteur, *Le Jardin des plantes* – qui a marqué à jamais son parcours d'homme adulte, Modiano multiplie les témoignages fictifs concernant une période dont il n'a pu prendre connaissance que de façon indirecte. À ce titre, son premier texte constitue une tentative intéressante de captation de la mémoire, celle d'une nation, passée au tamis de la critique par l'adoption de la *Zeitgeist* des années sombres, qui apparaît comme le véhicule d'un certain antisémitisme culturel repris à son compte par le protagoniste. Cette adhésion aux valeurs collectives – ou supposées telles – a pour but son insertion dans la collectivité, indéniablement réactionnaire[1].

L'écrivain se trouve donc confronté à un travail d'enquêteur et de rédacteur, puisqu'il s'agit de revisiter les moments les plus épouvantables d'un pays, en en conservant les épisodes les plus représentatifs – susceptibles de donner quelque validité à son existence. À cette fin, l'écriture demeure l'unique moyen de plonger dans les heures sombres d'une mémoire qu'il convient de façonner[2]. C'est sans doute de ce décalage constant – et obligé – entre ce que Marja Warehime a nommé dans son article[3] « le signe et le référent de l'Occupation » que naît l'absence de linéarité dans le récit. Ce dernier oscille entre les incohérences d'un passé reconstitué et le sentiment de vide devant le présent.

Comme nous l'avons vu précédemment, les romans de Modiano sont nostalgiques par essence, articulés qu'ils sont autour de l'idée de retour. Le *nostos*, cette expérience du même, s'inscrit au cœur de la narration de façon explicite – dans la forme du texte, qui voit l'Occupation revisitée de façon scripturale, puisque la somme littéraire qu'elle représente permet à l'écrivain de se bâtir une mémoire. Toutefois, sa puissance ne permet guère de contrer la dispersion du « moi ».

Il existe, en effet, une différence fondamentale entre l'entreprise proustienne et la démarche de Modiano, qui réside

---

[1] C'est, en tout cas, le projet qui préside à l'écriture de ce premier roman. Très rapidement, l'assimilation de l'apatride aux valeurs françaises – strictement nationalistes – ou juives – qui déplacent ce nationalisme en plein désert du Sinaï – se révèle impossible. Modiano ne saurait être français ou juif, et encore moins « juif français », cette dernière synthèse reposant, selon lui, sur des termes strictement antinomiques.
[2] « Modiano croit que l'écriture, elle seule, peut endiguer l'oubli, retrouver le temps perdu et redonner vie à une "silhouette claire". [...] Par l'écriture, on peut regarder le temps écoulé, et résister au temps qui passe. » S. Feng, *op. cit.*, p. 302.
[3] Article cité, p. 342.

dans l'utilisation personnelle et très particulière du souvenir. Chez Proust, dans des conditions certes exceptionnelles, il apparaît possible de retrouver l'essence du temps disparu, et ce par la convocation de l'ancien « moi », enfoui au plus profond de l'être, sous les couches successives déposées par le temps[1]. Ora Avni, sur les travaux de laquelle nous fondons une partie de cette étude, met particulièrement bien en valeur les différences entre les deux romanciers. Pour elle, les romans de Patrick Modiano, privés d'une réelle conscience organisatrice, et habités par un sujet qui se dérobe à la pensée, marquent une date importante dans l'histoire de la littérature. Pour la première fois, la narration doit se prendre elle-même pour objet, puisque le « je » parlant s'avère une forme vide, et se dérobe à toute tentative de constitution.

Quand Proust pouvait faire corps avec son passé, en « fais[ant] abstraction de son milieu ambiant, se confin[ant] en lui-même et s'adonn[ant] à un solipsisme sans réserve[2] », Modiano peut à peine ancrer son protagoniste dans la réalité. Dépourvu d'attache avec le présent, réduit à la convocation d'une mémoire de « seconde main », le héros modianien se trouve bien incapable de retrouver un « moi » disparu, étant donné que celui-ci n'a jamais réussi à effleurer la surface délicate de la conscience.

Modiano – et ses personnages – ne peuvent se réfugier au cœur d'un passé qui se dérobe à leur prise, puisque leur état d'apesanteur – physique et sociale – les oblige à créer ce temps de toutes pièces ; à l'image du sujet-scripteur, celui-ci se trouve dépourvu de toute substance, et se révèle incapable de procurer au héros la plénitude éprouvée par le narrateur proustien.

Le passé devient ainsi un espace à réinventer, au même titre que le présent – bien que celui-ci ne puisse bénéficier de

---

[1] « Il fallait qu'il n'y eût pas eu de discontinuité, que je n'eusse pas un instant cessé d'exister, de penser, d'avoir conscience de moi, puisque cet instant ancien tenait encore à moi, que je pouvais encore retourner jusqu'à lui rien qu'en descendant plus profondément en moi. » Extrait du *Temps retrouvé*, p. 352, édition de J.-Y. Tadié, collection « Pléiade », Gallimard 1990. Cité par O. Avni, *Patrick Modiano, aux portes de l'histoire*, Paris, L'Harmattan, 1997, p. 28.
[2] Ora Avni, *op. cit.*, p. 29.

l'aura, du nimbe, entourant chaque acte ou chaque évocation de ce temps élaboré par la rêverie. Les propos suivants de Shounong Feng[1] semblent, à cet égard, particulièrement pertinents :

> Le passé est considéré comme un point de départ, un point d'inspiration que l'on peut [...] compléter. L'auteur peut donc imaginer un passé dans le but de refaçonner une identité à ses héros et de proposer une existence ou des existences possibles que ses personnages peuvent identifier à leur passé.
> Le monde retrouvé par l'illumination proustienne avait une épaisseur, une cohérence, une consistance qui se dessinaient progressivement. Le passé, non pas tout à fait retrouvé mais évoqué [...] est un fantôme inconsistant, évanescent, comme les ombres et les silhouettes qui traversent les romans.

Le décryptage du passé ne donne donc jamais lieu aux épiphanies proustiennes, puisqu'il ne saurait y avoir, par essence, de concordance entre le temps disparu et la réalité. Si le narrateur vit parfois un instant privilégié, en ressentant au plus profond de son être la coïncidence entre deux époques, ces moments semblent rares et l'authenticité du passé suspecte :

> Alors une sorte de déclic s'est produit en moi. La vue qui s'offrait de cette chambre me causait un sentiment d'inquiétude, une impression, que j'avais déjà connus. Ces façades, cette rue déserte, ces silhouettes en faction dans le crépuscule me troublaient de la même manière insidieuse qu'une chanson ou un parfum familiers. Et j'étais sûr que, souvent, à la même heure, je m'étais tenu là immobile, sans même oser allumer une lampe[2].

Les textes sont riches de ces flots brusques de mémoire, qui viennent donner au protagoniste l'impression d'avoir, un jour, *été* :

---

[1] *Op. cit.*, p. 303.
[2] *Rue des boutiques obscures*, p. 103.

> Enfant, j'avais dû faire ici des parties de cache-cache en compagnie de mon grand-père ou d'amis de mon âge, et au milieu de ce dédale magique qui sentait le troène et le pin, j'avais sans doute connu les plus beaux moments de ma vie. Quand nous sortîmes du labyrinthe, je ne pus m'empêcher de dire à mon guide :
> – C'est drôle... Ce labyrinthe me rappelle quelque chose[1].

La plupart de ces souvenirs, forgés par l'inconscient, devront s'effacer devant les révisions déchirantes imposées par la réalité. C'est alors l'intégralité du processus qui se trouve entaché de suspicion, condamnant l'être à l'incertitude, et ce jusqu'au terme du récit :

> Voilà, c'était clair, je ne m'appelais pas Freddie Howard de Luz. [...] Je ne m'étais jamais promené le long de cette pelouse, au bras d'une grand-mère américaine. Je n'avais jamais joué, enfant, dans le « labyrinthe ». Ce portique rouillé, avec ses balançoires, n'avait pas été dressé pour moi. Dommage[2].

Le protagoniste ne peut avoir accès au temps fondateur de son existence. Contrairement au narrateur proustien, il ne parvient jamais à rassembler les différentes composantes d'un « moi » caractérisé par sa discontinuité. Or, sans ce passé, l'individu ne peut se bâtir une identité susceptible de lui donner accès au monde dans lequel il se trouve contraint de vivre. Cette tension paraît gouverner un grand nombre de romans de la première période, et constitue leur principal enjeu.

---

[1] *Ibid.*, p. 76.
[2] *Ibid.*, p. 77.

Troisième partie :

L'identité au miroir de l'Occupation.

Modiano déclare volontiers que l'Occupation représente le terroir, la province, où il fit jouer les premières scènes de son histoire personnelle, à la façon d'un François Mauriac, avec la Guyenne, ou un Alain-Fournier pour la Sologne. Cette période, qui représente le seul domaine que l'écrivain puisse – et désire – aborder, va très rapidement constituer son héritage naturel, le dotant de racines et de référents auxquels il puisse se reporter. Jusqu'au milieu des années soixante-dix, c'est-à-dire lors de son entrée dans le monde adulte – littérairement parlant –, les années noires vont prendre la place des figures associées à l'histoire familiale.

En effet, le silence de sa mère, l'absence de son père, puis la mort de ce dernier, rendent très difficile l'inventaire des origines et la connaissance du « lignage ». La rencontre d'Albert Modiano, juif d'origine italienne, avec la jeune Hollandaise Louisa Colpeyn n'eût sans doute jamais eu lieu sans les contraintes et nécessités de la vie sous l'Occupation. Parce qu'il ignore à peu près tout de ses origines, Modiano procède, dès sa première œuvre, à un rapprochement qui opère par relation de contiguïté, en inversant les données : les conditions de cette rencontre – à savoir les lieux et le climat particuliers de ces années – seront non seulement les seuls témoins de cette union presque impensable entre l'actrice et le trafiquant, mais surtout les seuls dépositaires de la mémoire. L'acte narratif joue, à cet égard, un rôle fondamental. Il faut lire les œuvres de la première trilogie comme les témoignages d'une identité en quête d'elle-même, recherche que seule l'écriture romanesque peut conduire à terme.

Avant d'aborder l'étude du questionnement identitaire auquel se livre l'écrivain, il paraît intéressant de préciser les enjeux de ses récits, à la lumière des analyses de Marthe

Robert, dans *Roman des origines et origines du roman*[1]. Publié la même année que *Les Boulevards de ceinture*, l'essai propose une nouvelle façon d'aborder l'idée de narration ; si elles ne s'appuient jamais sur les deux premiers romans de Modiano, les thèses de la critique n'en donnent pas moins nombre de clés pour saisir une grande partie de leur sens.

L'acte d'écriture n'est jamais gratuit et ne procède pas du seul désir de raconter une histoire. Celui-ci paraît lié aux interrogations que l'enfant peut formuler sur son origine et son statut dans le monde – et dans sa famille. Vers l'âge de cinq ans, ce dernier bâtit ses premières défenses contre les agressions de l'univers extérieur ou de la structure parentale, en mobilisant toutes les ressources de son imaginaire. Ainsi, face à une situation de crise ou un simple traumatisme, l'enfant peut s'inventer une parentèle de substitution – un de ses parents n'est pas le sien, et il est donc possible de rêver sur le tiers absent, en mettant en place une autre « famille » : il s'agit du modèle du « Bâtard » – ou, de façon plus générale, reconstruire le monde à sa fantaisie, pour trouver la place qu'il estime être la sienne – c'est le modèle de l'« Enfant trouvé ». Cette réaction, que Freud désigne par le vocable de « roman familial », représente un point de passage obligé dans l'édification du psychisme. Selon Marthe Robert, les romanciers ne font que prolonger, à l'âge adulte, ce processus de mise en fiction de la réalité, refoulé durant la période de latence, et exploité inconsciemment dans la création littéraire. Patrick Modiano se situe donc, selon la typologie de la critique, du côté de l'« Enfant trouvé ». Le monde qu'il évoque n'est pas celui de la réalité – c'est ce que nous avons démontré dans les développements antérieurs. Il s'agit plutôt de la reconstitution mentale d'une époque dans laquelle le personnage pourra se fondre, afin de retrouver la clef de ses origines et, d'autre part, imposer sa marque et ses lois – c'est-à-dire surmonter ses angoisses en feignant d'en être l'organisateur.

---

[1] Paris, Grasset, 1972.

Le père a disparu, la mère est absente : il paraît donc indispensable d'écrire le roman des origines. L'écriture devient ainsi l'unique voie de compréhension et de connaissance de l'histoire d'un pays et d'une lignée – juive – auxquelles il demeure étranger. Les dates peuvent être changées, les époques se confondre, les fantasmes trouver place aux côtés des événements de la vie réelle : ce monde est un univers sans loi, dont les pères ont été chassés. L'« Enfant trouvé » devient, de la sorte, le grand ordonnateur d'une société, d'un microcosme, qu'il organise selon les règles de son espace mental. À cet égard, les personnages de la première trilogie semblent entretenir certains liens de parenté avec les figures évoquées par Marthe Robert – *Don Quichotte* ou les personnages créés par les romantiques allemands tels que Jean-Paul ou Tieck, nommés « phantastes » par la critique –, qui s'ingénient à plier la réalité aux règles de leur « roman familial ». Inconsciemment, le récit réinstalle un ordre disparu, propose une nouvelle logique, dont la cohérence se lit dans l'agencement des épisodes. Dans le cas de Modiano, le traumatisme se trouve provoqué par ce que l'écrivain ressent au mieux comme un abandon – on songera au passage de *La Ronde de nuit* dans lequel Swing Troubadour présente Stavisky comme son père, bel exemple de réécriture des origines pour compenser la douleur de l'absence –, au pire comme un forfait. Dans le roman suivant, l'abandon devient un meurtre, comme si le narrateur incarnait la mauvaise conscience, le côté sombre du père, que celui-ci tentait de sublimer : c'est l'épisode du métro George-V. De fait, les trois premiers romans se trouvent construits de façon cyclique, comme s'ils proposaient, chacun, une résolution provisoire de la question complexe de l'identité. *La Place de l'Étoile* représenterait le chaos originel, à partir duquel Modiano tenterait de mettre en place la fiction de l'origine ou, si l'on préfère, proposerait la matrice de l'œuvre à venir. Ce roman constituerait ainsi le point de départ tout aussi bien historique – les racines de l'antisémitisme et du nationalisme exposées dans les deux premiers chapitres – que psychologique : la négation du père, dont la présentation bouffonne constitue une réaction de compensation face à l'angoisse de l'abandon.

Au risque de caricaturer quelque peu les thèses de Marthe Robert, on pourrait affirmer que la totale désorganisation de l'Histoire, qui est l'une des figures centrales du roman, représente l'équivalent sociologique et politique d'un psychisme immature, justifié et expliqué par le refus du père. Systématiquement humiliée et néantisée en raison de son aspect grotesque – la représentation théâtrale ou l'épisode de l'hôtel Continental –, la figure paternelle se révèle inapte, en effet, à jouer le rôle de « sur-moi » et à assurer un développement équilibré à l'enfant.

Dans l'œuvre suivante, celui-ci change de comportement à l'égard de son père. Le « phantaste » tente d'égaler cette figure, après avoir pu constater que son annihilation entraînait une totale aliénation à la période des années sombres. Le père se trouve ainsi « magnifié » ; le clown stupide devient Serge Alexandre, paradigme de la duplicité et de la trahison – c'est-à-dire, à peu de choses près, le personnage de Swing Troubadour, qui légitime ses exactions par une hérédité chargée. Le texte ne semble pas avoir d'autre objectif que la « réinstallation » du père dans son rôle psychanalytique, à savoir une position susceptible de valoriser son personnage, et de favoriser le rapprochement avec son fils – loin du comique et de la dérision du premier roman. Avec celui-ci, les relations se trouvent entièrement modifiées. L'écriture permet d'inverser entièrement les rôles, de sorte que le fils devient la Loi – incarnant l'ordre et la raison – et peut ainsi tenter de sauver son père, en le tirant des griffes de Murraille et de ses acolytes. D'un point de vue symbolique, ce retournement opère à deux niveaux.

Dans un premier temps, la démarche permet au jeune homme de trouver sa place dans le lignage et l'héritage familial que représente la reconnaissance du père. D'autre part, l'acte prend valeur de dédouanement : Serge Alexandre[1] absout son

---

[1] On notera que, dans le troisième *opus*, l'adoption du patronyme du père dans *La Ronde de nuit* vaut adoption de la fonction symbolique de celui-ci. Dans *La Place de l'Étoile*, Raphaël tente d'être lui-même, son père, la France,

père de ses compromissions et atermoiements, en acceptant de prendre place dans l'« histoire » de celui-ci – au sens familial, bien sûr, et surtout au sens littéral, puisqu'il choisit de le suivre jusque dans la mort. D'autre part, ce renversement de la raison permet au récit de s'inscrire pleinement dans la logique organisatrice de l'« Enfant trouvé » puisque tout se passe comme si l'enfant, à proprement parler, acceptait de reconnaître psychologiquement et presque administrativement son père, loin de toute soumission à l'ordre historique. Le sauvetage inespéré – qui s'achève d'ailleurs sur un échec, mais cette question ne concerne pas directement notre champ d'interrogation – n'a pas d'autre raison d'être que l'affirmation de la toute-puissance du jeune homme, qui vaut brevet d'existence. Il semble indéniable que, sans cette ruse de la raison, Serge Alexandre n'eût jamais pu prétendre à la reconnaissance de son identité. En sauvant le père, le protagoniste légitime sa position dans le monde, et peut ainsi pleinement justifier son existence. Symboliquement, le retournement lève l'hypothèque qui pesait jusqu'à ce moment sur le héros-scripteur. Il ne faut pas oublier que celui-ci – par le jeu de l'analepse – transpose sur des épisodes situés en 1944 la culpabilité de l'âge adulte relative à la période de l'Occupation[1].

L'incursion miraculeuse dans l'Histoire, ce fantasme romanesque de l'« Enfant trouvé », n'a pas d'autre but que l'expiation de cette faute inconnue. Tout se passe comme si, par l'effet du paradoxe temporel, le narrateur pouvait modifier le temps et les événements et suspendre le cours des

---

l'Occupation et Israël en une seule et même personne – position insoutenable s'il en est. Au terme du parcours, il accepte sa défaite et lave la figure du père de toute accusation. Mieux, il endosse la fonction psychique de ce dernier, en inversant le cours de l'histoire.
[1] « Je sais bien qu'il ne s'agit que d'un répit. Plus tard, on me demandera des comptes. J'éprouve un vague sentiment de culpabilité dont l'objet demeure vague : un crime auquel j'ai participé en qualité de complice ou de témoin, je ne pourrais pas vraiment le dire. Et j'espère que cette ambiguïté m'évitera le châtiment. À quoi correspond ce rêve dans la vie réelle ? Au souvenir de mon père qui, sous l'Occupation, avait vécu une situation ambiguë elle aussi ? [...] ». *Fleurs de ruine*, p. 112.

événements, rendant impossible le processus d'édification de cette « mémoire qui précède la naissance », gouffre aux chimères et aux fantasmes.

Au terme de ce rapide survol, nous pouvons avancer l'idée que la faillite du monde dont Modiano dresse le constat (monde de l'Occupation et des années d'après-guerre) provient de l'incapacité des *pères* – c'est-à-dire des représentants de la loi, des figures de l'ordre – à assumer et à jouer pleinement leur rôle de garants contre les agressions extérieures. Une société sans père se révèle incapable d'assurer aux enfants un développement équilibré, et leur interdit de trouver leur place dans l'univers des adultes.

Tant que la précellence paternelle se trouve niée ou remise en cause, les enfants paraissent condamnés à se mouvoir dans un vortex temporel et psychique – on pensera à *La Place de l'Étoile* – ou dans les limbes : *La Ronde de nuit*[1]. Il faut attendre le dernier volet pour que les tentatives de l'« Enfant trouvé » prennent leur justification, le père devenant enfin, à son corps défendant, la principale puissance opératrice – jouant le rôle de « sur-moi » indispensable à l'épanouissement intellectuel du fils : il s'agit de la première œuvre dans laquelle le narrateur se révèle doué d'une intelligence conceptuelle, qui le rend apte à penser ses actes et à analyser ses émotions. Toutefois, cette légitimité retrouvée se paie au prix fort, puisque pour être accepté et reconnu par son père, Serge Alexandre doit suivre ce dernier jusque dans la mort.

L'histoire personnelle de Modiano rendait inéluctable cette confrontation avec les démons du passé. L'Occupation représente, comme le Moyen Âge des *Märchen* pour Novalis, la seule période capable d'accueillir les tourments de l'« Enfant trouvé » et de leur offrir une sublimation narrative, satisfaisante pour l'esprit. Cette conjonction du roman familial et de l'histoire nationale constitue l'un des éléments

---

[1] Ces deux premières œuvres, créations de l'« Enfant trouvé », sont des « romans familiaux » inexorablement voués à l'échec, puisque fondés sur la négation du père.

fondamentaux de l'écriture modianienne. Celle-ci doit sa spécificité au choix original de l'écrivain, qui adopte le point de vue d'un être trouvant sa seule légitimité dans les turpitudes du pays d'adoption. Les acceptations et dénis successifs des heurs et malheurs de l'Histoire, tour à tour convoqués dans la réflexion polémique sur l'engagement ou la passivité, scelleront l'échec de la démarche – fondée sur une transparence identitaire qui se révélera rapidement un leurre. L'écrivain, en masquant ses interrogations angoissées derrière la provocation hallucinée des deux premiers ouvrages, ne parvient pas à leur donner la cohérence nécessaire à leur résolution. Il faut attendre la maturité dont fait preuve Modiano dans la seconde trilogie pour que les deux traumatismes de l'identité introuvable et du martyre juif soient pleinement acceptés, compris et surtout dépassés.

Il paraît donc nécessaire de distinguer deux étapes dans l'évolution de cette quête identitaire. Nous nous attarderons, dans un premier temps, sur les romans de jeunesse. Ces derniers exposent, de façon schématique, le drame de la vacuité existentielle, qui résulte de la tension entre une identité dissimulée au cœur de l'Occupation et l'aspect insignifiant du héros-narrateur – incapable d'appréhender la réalité historique sans la dénaturer, recourant, à cette fin, à d'invraisemblables figures déléguées, ignorant tout de la limite entre la réalité et le fantasme. L'ultime artifice prend sa place au cœur même des principes narratifs : Modiano adopte les lois de l'autofiction afin de mettre à distance les démons du passé qu'il a eu l'imprudence de convoquer. Il se heurtera, toutefois, à une difficulté de taille. Le travestissement du réel, s'il constitue un rempart efficace contre les angoisses les moins supportables, s'oppose à une recherche ontologique qui doit prendre appui sur un récit conduit de façon rationnelle. L'imagination du romancier prend le pas sur le souci de vérité – pourtant dominant dans l'évocation des lieux et des décors, c'est-à-dire l'aspect le moins déstabilisant de la recréation historique – et conduit à la négation de l'idée même d'identité. Enfin, les figures et les événements mis en récit, loin d'apporter à l'écrivain le réconfort d'une Histoire qu'il pourrait faire sienne, renforcent, bien au contraire, le malaise, en mettant à jour la culpabilité dont il a été question précédemment – et qui se trouve constituer un autre obstacle à la connaissance de soi.

En se fondant sur l'unique point de vue d'un romancier désireux de trouver sa place au sein d'un univers encore très proche de celui de l'après-guerre, force nous est de reconnaître que l'entreprise littéraire des premières années aboutit à une impasse. L'écriture romanesque ne peut apporter de réponse définitive aux interrogations fondamentales, ni aider à affronter les tourments de l'existence. Après la première esquisse d'autobiographie, *Livret de famille*, en 1977, il faut attendre *Voyage de noces* pour que Modiano reprenne un contact direct avec ses angoisses primitives. Ce sera d'ailleurs le dernier roman consacré à cette période, puisque les œuvres suivantes s'articuleront, avant tout, autour d'un récit de la création (celle de la mémoire avec *Fleurs de ruine*, d'un traumatisme avec *Un cirque passe* et surtout *Du plus loin de l'oubli*, et enfin d'un corps, avec *Dora Bruder*, en 1997), et non plus de la création d'un récit.

Ce retour au thème fondamental, au début des années quatre-vingt-dix, s'effectue sous un mode d'approche radicalement opposé à celui des années antérieures : la précision presque clinique de *Dora Bruder* tranche singulièrement avec les vertiges et les rêveries de *La Ronde de nuit*. À cinquante ans, l'écrivain semble apaisé, de sorte qu'il lui est possible de reprendre posément le questionnement sur l'identité juive, la culpabilité paternelle ou l'occultation du passé par une certaine partie du peuple français. Déjà placées au centre des récits de jeunesse, ces questions vont prendre une nouvelle acuité, et se verront prolongées par une réflexion sur la mémoire collective – et la crainte d'une possible altération de celle-ci.

Une identité inscrite au cœur de l'Occupation

Les années de plomb recèleraient, inscrit au plus profond d'elles-mêmes, le mystère des origines, et permettraient de lever les ambiguïtés concernant l'être profond. La convocation des figures de l'Occupation, ainsi que la plongée romanesque[1] au cœur de ses ténèbres, sont les seules voies d'accès à une époque qui détient tous les secrets – supposés – de l'existence. Il s'agit de montrer que cette quête de l'identité passe avant tout par une recréation de l'Histoire à l'aide de la mémoire, qui change la vision attendue des événements. Nous nous attacherons à étudier, dans un premier temps, l'obsession revendiquée de l'enracinement, au sein d'un lieu ou d'une époque, avant d'analyser, de façon systématique, le statut de chaque protagoniste. On pourra alors apprécier toute l'originalité de la démarche modianienne.

UNE RECHERCHE DE LA LIGNEE

L'individu, chez Modiano, semble moins le dépositaire d'une culture ou d'une tradition familiales[2] que le produit d'un certain nombre de rencontres ou de confrontations avec certains êtres modelés par l'Histoire – et le temps. Ses origines se perdent dans les brumes de la diaspora (Raphaël Schlemilovitch, le narrateur de *Livret de famille* ou, dans une moindre mesure, Serge Alexandre) ou le néant total (Swing Troubadour). Le seul être capable de fournir les renseignements désirés sur l'identité, le père tour à tour nié et convoqué dans les romans, s'avère un clown pathétique – dans le premier ouvrage –, un être inaccessible (dans *Les Boulevards de ceinture*) ou purement symbolique (Alexandre Stavisky dans *La Ronde de nuit*). Dès lors, le héros se trouve réduit à effectuer des recoupements hypothétiques ou à se perdre dans

---

[1] Dont le chaos stylistique représente les bouleversements de l'époque.
[2] Susceptibles de lui octroyer, par hérédité, une place déterminée au sein d'un groupe, d'une fratrie.

la rêverie afin de trouver sa place au sein d'un groupe constitué.

Le héros modianien ne peut se contenter de sa seule personnalité – totalement insignifiante – pour tenter de survivre dans un univers hostile. En effet, il paraît beaucoup plus facile d'opposer une attitude déterminée par une culture ou une idéologie que d'imposer un comportement dicté par des lois strictement individuelles, fondées sur la valeur de l'expérience. Si l'on ajoute à cela un caractère indolent joint à une rare pusillanimité, on comprendra aisément la nature des angoisses du narrateur-écrivain.

Ses créatures, êtres exilés et apatrides, recherchent vainement – et cette remarque vaut pour les œuvres qui ne choisissent pas l'Occupation comme thème essentiel – un lieu d'attache dans l'espace et un point fixe dans leur passé. Ainsi, le seul argument narratif de *La Place de l'Étoile* réside dans les incursions au sein de communautés. Imaginant qu'il partage – ou doit partager – certains points avec celles-ci, Schlemilovitch tente de se plier à leur démarche intellectuelle et d'adopter leur mode de fonctionnement, sans jamais devenir membre à part entière. Cette tâche se trouve rendue plus difficile encore par la crispation d'ordre névrotique autour du seul héritage connu, la judéité. De fait, il semble pratiquement impossible de concilier cette volonté d'enracinement avec les siècles d'errance et de persécutions subies par le peuple juif. La tension qui en résulte constitue le principe même du roman, et donnera lieu à de multiples tentatives de dépassement[1], qui tenteront de conserver l'essence de l'élément « dépassé » en s'opposant à lui. Toutes se solderont par un échec.

Dans ce sens, l'amitié nouée avec Des Essarts, les rencontres avec les journalistes de *Je suis partout*, la fréquentation du colonel Aravis, la dévotion pour la marquise de Fougeire-Jusquiames ou le « retour à Sion » s'inscrivent

---

[1] Au sens hégélien de *Aufhebung*, c'est-à-dire en conservant les oppositions sans les exclure du travail de la pensée, selon une démarche dialectique susceptible de conduire à un nouvel état.

dans une volonté d'agrégation à un système socialement et idéologiquement défini. Les rapports que le héros modianien entretient avec le clan ou l'institution paraissent, à chaque fois, marqués par l'ambivalence entre une adhésion recherchée et une identification refusée. De fait, Raphaël refuse *in fine* l'assimilation qu'il appelait de ses vœux, comme si son « moi » profond s'opposait violemment au reniement de la conscience juive. L'alternative – que la première trilogie ne permettra pas de résoudre – est la suivante : si l'individu accepte d'appartenir à un groupe, il doit en accepter les valeurs – fussent-elles des plus critiquables et abjectes. Celles-ci seront très rapidement intégrées par une conscience vide, en état de permanente élaboration, puis brusquement rejetées par un « sur-moi » refusant des schèmes de pensée nationalistes et antisémites, hostiles par essence à un enfant de la diaspora. Ce dernier ne se trouve pas en mesure de dédaigner les identifications proposées ; tout odieuses qu'elles sont, celles-ci garantissent au héros une protection contre les dangers du monde extérieur, en lui octroyant une identité éphémère.

Le premier ouvrage n'a pas d'autre substance narrative que l'intégration des existences recomposées – selon la nature des fréquentations – à la forme vide de la conscience. L'hallucination et le fantasme demeurent les seuls recours contre cette tension constante entre la vacuité et la volonté d'enracinement. Le héros se trouve partagé entre l'inanité de son être et les pièges de la recomposition existentielle issue du fantasme, à savoir – selon Shinong Feng – « l'identité sociale et l'identité de l'ego, l'identité extérieure et l'identité intérieure, autrement dit l'identité réelle et l'identité imaginaire[1] ». Ce hiatus permet donc de mieux comprendre la prédilection éprouvée par le juif Schlemilovitch lorsqu'il s'agit de s'identifier à ses persécuteurs et bourreaux. Il peut non seulement inverser les rôles, mais surtout recevoir une forme d'identité qui, à tout prendre, apparaît plus sécurisante que le constat de sa « béance » fondamentale. Le critique conclut ainsi son développement :

---

[1] *Op.cit.*, p. 95.

L'hallucination fait surgir un effet dramatique : le rien devient tout et *vice versa* ; l'irréel se transforme en authentique ; le faux en vrai. Dans l'hallucination, par le renversement des rôles, Raphaël pourrait atteindre l'égalité ou l'équilibre mental. C'est le phénomène de « surcompensation psychologique[1] »

Livré à lui-même, privé de repères, l'être modianien n'a guère d'autre choix que cette opération de substitution identitaire. Nous verrons ultérieurement que cette stratégie s'avère illusoire, entraînant la destruction du personnage romanesque « première manière ». Dans les œuvres du début, celui-ci se caractérise par son aspect fonctionnel et inconsistant. Afin d'apprécier exactement la dimension de cette figure déléguée, il convient d'étudier chacune de ses incarnations dans la première trilogie.

Un caractere superficiel

Dépourvu d'attaches et indépendant par nécessité, le narrateur semble un « pur[2] » esprit, perdu au cœur des ténèbres. Si la plongée dans les turpitudes et l'abjection paraît nécessaire à cet homme fragile, elle provoquera, du même coup, son anéantissement programmé.

Une perspective globale ne nous paraissant pas rendre justice à l'originalité de chaque figure romanesque, il importe d'étudier séparément les protagonistes. Il sera alors possible de montrer que l'appartenance à un groupe, et la reconnaissance que l'être tire de celle-ci peuvent, elles seules, l'inscrire au sein de la communauté des vivants.

Les trois romans de jeunesse sont écrits à la première personne, et entretiennent, avec le narrateur, une relation à la fois autodiégétique et homodiégétique – à quelques nuances

---

[1] *Ibid.*, p. 98.
[2] Au sens où l'entendait Gide, avec l'idée de complétude et de cohérence attachée à ce vocable.

près[1]. La subjectivité de l'énoncé présente l'avantage de laisser pratiquement inexplorées les multiples zones d'ombre et de mystère qui entourent chacun des protagonistes. Ces derniers ne fournissent qu'un minimum d'informations sur leur histoire – qu'ils ne connaissent d'ailleurs pas véritablement – et laissent au narrataire le soin de se forger un jugement sur les actes ou la psychologie de la principale instance de récit. L'aspect éminemment parcellaire des informations s'inscrit dans le projet romanesque de l'écrivain, lequel s'efforce d'associer le lecteur à la quête identitaire de ses créatures.

D'autre part, les noms mêmes de ces personnages ne semblent pouvoir définir des êtres réels, comme dans les romans de facture classique. On montrera, dès lors, que l'Occupation représente la seule composante capable de transformer un néant originel en existence certes fragile – et particulièrement destructrice –, mais susceptible de calmer, durant quelques moments, les angoisses relatives à l'identité.

Raphaël Schlemilovitch : de la nuée au néant.

De nombreux critiques et universitaires[2] ont réfléchi sur la création originale représentée par le personnage de

---

[1] Les œuvres de la trilogie sont régies par des principes narratifs d'une apparente simplicité, en dépit des multiples entorses à la logique traditionnelle des récits. Outre la condensation du temps et des lieux de *La Place de l'Étoile*, on remarquera la paralepse finale de *La Ronde de nuit* : le récit ne peut être raconté par un être destiné à trouver la mort dans les minutes qui suivent la fin de l'exposé narratif. On pensera, enfin, à l'analepse centrale, elle-même subdivisée en de multiples sous-analepses, dans *Les Boulevards de ceinture*.

[2] Jacqueline Chassenet-Smirgel, *Pour une psychanalyse de l'art*, Paris, Payot, 1971, Jean-Marie Maignan, « Drame de l'identité chez Patrick Modiano », *Sud*, n° 28-29, hiver 1978-1979, p. 181-185, Charlotte Wardi, « Mémoire et identité dans *La Place de l'Étoile* et *Rue des boutiques obscures* », *Yod*, n° 147, février 1982, p. 87-95, Olivier Tardy, *La Quête de l'identité chez Patrick Modiano*, thèse de troisième cycle, sous la direction de Michel Malicet, Université de Besançon, 1984, Charlotte Wardi, « Mémoire et écriture chez Patrick Modiano », *Les Nouveaux Cahiers*, n° 80, 1985 et Thierry Laurent, *op.cit.*, 1995.

Schlemilovitch, être de néant, qui constitue la somme des interrogations du jeune Modiano sur la question juive, l'appartenance à une communauté ou sur la persistance de la xénophobie. Chacun d'eux s'est ingénié à démonter le jeu onomastique de ce patronyme original – dont la surcharge de sonorités caricaturalement juives fait figure de provocation.

Le nom provient de l'union de *Schlemihl* et du suffixe *ovitch*, plaisante référence à la finale d'une importante catégorie de noms hébraïques, employée avec dérision de façon générique. L'origine du substantif proviendrait, selon les sources, de la formation yiddish de *schlimm* (mauvais) et *mazel* (chance), donnant l'adjectif *schlimazl* – que l'on pourrait traduire en français par *porte-guigne*. Une autre étymologie donne *shlelu-nual*, mot hébraïque signifiant « qui ne vaut rien ». La tradition historique et littéraire fait du *schlemihl* un être malheureux, victime et naïf, en butte continuelle à la risée du monde. Enzo Traverso, dans son ouvrage, *Les Juifs et l'Allemagne*[1], écrit à propos de ce *topos* de l'histoire et de la littérature juives :

> Figure simple et comique, chargée d'ironie et de mélancolie à la fois, il n'est cependant pas un malheureux mais, tout au contraire, se fait porteur d'une sagesse profonde qui échappe à la rationalité bornée du monde dont il n'accepte ni l'ordre ni les hiérarchies. Imprégné de valeurs spirituelles, le *schlemihl* n'arrive pas à s'adapter à une société dominée par des valeurs purement matérielles.

Modiano emploie ce patronyme de façon distancée, en reprenant le nom rendu célèbre par Chamisso, en 1824, avec *Peter Schlemihl ou l'homme qui a perdu son ombre*, conte fantastique démarqué du mythe de Faust, et repris par Balzac pour son *Melmoth réconcilié*. Ultime clin d'œil, le prénom associé à la longue suite d'échecs annoncés est Raphaël, dont la signification hébraïque est « Dieu qui guérit » – prénom antiprogrammatif, en quelque sorte, puisque le protagoniste du

---

[1] La Découverte, 1992, p. 45.

roman donne la mort à Des Essarts, en sciant les freins de sa voiture, et provoque le suicide de sa compagne Tania, à l'aide de lames de rasoir savamment disposées autour de cette candidate au suicide.

Les analystes s'accordent pour insister sur l'identité déchirée de Raphaël, qui s'approprie le livret de famille de Des Essarts[1], ou sur sa volonté éperdue d'enracinement, désespérée et critique tout à la fois, mais n'accordent pas une place suffisante à la caractéristique essentielle de cet être, à savoir son aspect résolument spirituel et idéel – qui en fait un non-personnage par excellence.

Présent en tout temps, en tout lieu (à tout le moins l'Europe, de la Grande Guerre à 1966), marqué par une certaine schizophrénie dans son comportement et ses réactions, Raphaël semble, avant tout, un ludion permettant au romancier d'inventorier cinquante ans de nationalisme et d'antisémitisme, avec une liberté totale. Reprenant les thèses de Nathalie Sarraute, défendues dans *L'Ère du soupçon*, Modiano entérine non seulement la mort du personnage, mais également celle de la narration – qui se trouve rapportée aux intermittences de l'être et aux libres variations de celui-ci. Le roman ne représente plus qu'une somme de sensations et de considérations intellectuelles, qui échappent à toute rationalité critique. En somme, les multiples incarnations de Schlemilovitch permettent de donner au « rien » sa pleine dimension. Afin de plonger dans le gouffre de l'Occupation, en en explorant méthodiquement les aspects et prémisses, l'écrivain a convoqué une forme vide, ductile et facilement adaptable, susceptible de représenter toutes les figures de la Collaboration ou de la *Shoah*.

Les multiples identités de Raphaël (de Jacob X à Des Essarts, en passant par le Schlemilovitch collaborateur,

---

[1] À cette occasion, on remarquera que le romancier donne à ce personnage sa propre date de naissance, le 30 juillet 1945. Il est intéressant de noter que ce transfert vient redoubler l'autre substitution d'identité à l'œuvre dans le roman. Ainsi, le créateur d'un personnage apatride, qui décide de ravir la personnalité d'un ami noble, s'approprie au second degré cette assimilation.

fugitivement réincarné en docteur Petiot) constituent autant de voyages « ontologiques » dans l'histoire mentale de la France du XXe siècle. Cette odyssée immobile fonctionne sous la forme de déclinaisons synchroniques d'une conscience, venant se modeler sur les simulacres qu'elle entend représenter. À cet effet, nous renvoyons à la thèse de Shounong Feng, qui applique à l'œuvre de Modiano les principes de la philosophie chinoise traditionnelle.

Le chercheur cite, dans son travail, un texte de Lao Tseu, qui semble particulièrement riche d'enseignements sur l'option thématique choisie par l'écrivain. Les premiers romans seraient ainsi placés sous le double signe du combat entre être et non-être et de la relation personnelle, affective, que le créateur entretient avec cette dernière instance :

> Non-être et être sortant d'un fond unique
> Ne se différencient que par leurs noms.
> Ce fond unique s'appelle obscurité.
> Obscurcir cette obscurité
> Voilà la porte de toutes les merveilles[1].

Le troisième et le quatrième vers semblent rendre compte, de façon convaincante, du projet narratif de *La Place de l'Étoile*. Il convient toutefois de nuancer le parallèle, en notant que les « merveilles » prennent dans l'ouvrage l'aspect d'une consultation chez Freud, c'est-à-dire, selon la symbolique modianienne, d'un retour aux sources vives de la mémoire – donc bien avant l'éclosion de l'être, ce qui aboutit à une certaine évacuation de la question.

Nous remarquerons enfin que cette négation de l'idée d'identité constitue le principal centre d'intérêt du texte, qui ne saurait se résumer au simple exposé de stratégies d'approche du « génie français ». Modiano-Raphaël ne désire jamais tant posséder une *essence* que lorsqu'il constate l'impossibilité matérielle et physique d'accéder à une existence qui ne soit pas limitée à une carte d'identité ou à un nom sur un livret de famille. En effet, le combat contre l'entropie, que représente la

---

[1] S. Feng, *op.cit.*, p. 70.

période de l'Occupation – lutte morale qui fournit l'argument implicite du premier roman –, apparaît dans chaque tentative du protagoniste. Ce dernier n'a pas d'autre choix que le recours à l'altérité, au moyen de l'annexion d'expériences et d'identités allogènes. On peut classer dans cette catégorie les différentes défroques déjà évoquées (l'adoption du patronyme « Des Essarts », en particulier) et surtout les différentes postures mentales empruntées à des paradigmes : le « Juif-aux-champs », façon Marcel Proust, lors du séjour chez la marquise ou le nationalisme réactionnaire, dans la « khâgne » bordelaise. On pourrait appliquer sans difficulté cette analyse au héros du roman suivant, dont la vacuité *essentielle* – au sens premier de l'adjectif – se trouve masquée par l'aspect *bifrons* du personnage et une aptitude à endosser, presque simultanément, deux identités opposées – eu égard à sa qualité d'agent double.

Si la somme de ces incarnations n'aboutit qu'à une multiplication de quantités nulles, il n'en demeure pas moins vrai que c'est ce seul produit qui peut assurer quelque validité à la démarche. La volonté désespérée d'accéder à l'identité constitue, en effet, une sorte de préalable à son acquisition. D'autre part, l'acte d'écriture accorde au narrateur la possibilité de considérer les cinquante dernières années comme les pages d'un livre : l'ensemble des acteurs, à l'image de la conscience organisatrice, vient de fait participer à cette déréalisation. Dans *La Place de l'Étoile*, nulle créature ne peut se prévaloir d'une existence avérée et établie, et les figures « réelles » sont placées sur un plan identique à celui des êtres de pure fiction. L'usage de la parodie, du pastiche littéraire, ainsi que les références fort nombreuses aux écrivains du XXe siècle – auxquelles vient s'ajouter la rêverie proustienne autour du nom de Fougeire-Jusquiames – donnent à l'ouvrage un aspect ludique, comme si Modiano avait livré, pour son premier essai, le « roman d'un roman » de l'Occupation, qui se trouve réduite à la fonction de texte feuilleté.

Le drame de Raphaël réside donc dans l'accès indirect à cette période, par l'unique intermédiaire des textes et documents mis à la disposition de sa génération – à cet égard, il est particulièrement révélateur que l'*incipit* de l'œuvre soit consacré à une réécriture de *Bagatelles pour un massacre*.

La fable a été jouée ; seules subsistent les traces écrites du drame. L'unique moyen de comprendre le passé est de le vider de sa substance et de le considérer sous le seul angle de l'*idée*. Les êtres et événements semblent réductibles à un ensemble de schèmes, et paraissent justiciables d'un traitement presque uniquement spéculatif.

Cette opération s'inscrit dans le processus mental régissant l'écriture des trois premiers livres. Modiano procède à une réification de la réalité – afin de la purger de sa charge traumatisante. Il peut ainsi maîtriser ses angoisses, et aborder presque sereinement le continent ténébreux de l'Occupation. Le procédé se révélerait satisfaisant si l'écrivain ne demandait pas à cette réalité, vidée de sa substance, de lui fournir une raison d'exister – cet octroi de l'identité qui justifie l'acte romanesque.

Ayant réduit l'essence du réel à un objet purement littéraire, le romancier ne peut que se heurter à la désincarnation de l'univers recréé. Il ne lui reste plus alors qu'à se perdre dans les vertiges du mal pour tenter de pénétrer de l'intérieur un monde qui lui échappe[1].

---

[1] Au terme de son article, « Topographie et histoire », Gerhard Gerhardi formule les constatations suivantes sur les personnages modianiens : « Au contraire du héros sartrien, qui s'engage en toute connaissance de cause pour tel mouvement politique porteur d'un meilleur avenir, le héros de Modiano semble incapable de mesurer la portée historique de ses actes et même de les accepter comme siens. L'Occupation est vécue non comme un esclavage transitoire qui incite à la révolte, mais comme un destin – comme le symbole de la condition humaine. [...] Le moi n'est pas une manière brute qu'on façonne par les actes, mais une donnée mystérieuse dont on essaie de reconstruire les origines. » Article cité, p. 120.

Swing Troubadour : un esprit au royaume des ombres.

Le narrateur de *La Ronde de nuit* possède à peine plus de réalité physique que celui de *La Place de l'Étoile*. Plongé presque malgré lui dans l'obscurité délétère de la collaboration mafieuse, il choisit rapidement l'annihilation de son être, afin de pouvoir supporter une réalité qui le terrifie. Nous nous attacherons, tout d'abord, à analyser la psychologie du personnage, avant d'étudier les figures du vide dans le roman. Il sera alors possible de mettre en évidence les liens que l'œuvre entretient avec le premier volet du triptyque.

Le héros de *La Ronde de nuit* est un personnage sans nom. Ses divers patronymes (Swing Troubadour ou Princesse de Lamballe) appartiennent à une chanson – *Seul depuis toujours*, créée d'ailleurs par Charles Trénet en 1946, soit quatre ans après les événements relatés, preuve s'il en est de la mise à distance de l'Occupation – ou à l'histoire de la France. On rappellera que la princesse de Lamballe était la surintendante de la maison de Marie-Antoinette. Née en 1749, elle refusa de trahir la monarchie et fut guillotinée en 1792. Sa tête fut, en cette occasion, brandie au bout d'une pique sous les fenêtres de la prison royale. On pourrait voir dans l'appropriation de cette figure historique un référent susceptible de donner quelque pesanteur au personnage ; loin de cela, il semble que cette femme partage avec le « Swing Troubadour » du roman et celui de la chanson de Trénet[1] une semblable destinée tragique, à la fois connue et redoutée, sans recours possible contre le joug de la fatalité.

Le héros le répète à l'envi tout au long de l'ouvrage : il n'est rien, et se voit réduit aux identités d'emprunt qui lui procurent une fugace sensation d'existence. Il doit impérativement adopter la personnalité des êtres qu'il côtoie,

---

[1] « Tout est fini, plus de promenade
Plus de printemps, Swing Troubadour
Ton destin Swing Troubadour […].» *La Ronde de nuit*, p. 75.

afin de combler sa profonde vacuité. À l'image de la cire molle de Descartes, conscience qui devait recevoir l'empreinte de la pensée afin de prendre forme, son esprit adopte la marque de figures qu'il choisit brièvement pour modèle. Il sera tour à tour collaborateur ou résistant, incapable de trouver au sein de son engagement une compensation à sa nullité fondamentale. Il passera successivement d'un camp à l'autre, sans s'investir personnellement dans l'expérience, comme si l'échec rencontré dans la quête de l'identité invalidait tout investissement personnel dans les événements vécus. On notera enfin que Modiano s'inspire très largement, pour la personnalité et la psychologie de cette créature, du narrateur de la nouvelle *L'Agent double*, publiée dans le recueil *Histoires déplaisantes*, de Drieu La Rochelle. Ballotté d'un camp politique à l'autre – comme le personnage de Drieu dans la Russie de 1917 –, il se distingue de celui-ci par l'apathie dont il fait preuve. Il est impossible, en effet, de l'imaginer revendiquer le caractère particulier de son existence avec la virulence caractérisant le discours du récitant :

> Dès lors, je pouvais vivre entièrement dans deux univers. Je passais de l'un à l'autre sans gêne ni bafouillage ; je glissais en une seconde de l'un dans l'autre – la vie des communistes, la pensée des orthodoxes. [...]
> Je me meus dans un ordre de problèmes qui n'est pas le vôtre, dans un labyrinthe où vous n'avez jamais mis les pieds. Je suis avec les femmes, les enfants, les vieillards, les plantes contre vos spécifications. Je ne suis pas dans la société, je suis dans la nature[1].

Contrairement à Raphaël, ou au personnage dont nous venons de citer les propos, Swing Troubadour a conscience des enjeux, mais semble incapable de leur donner la moindre importance. En effet, les événements ne franchissent jamais le seuil d'une conscience en permanente élaboration, de sorte que le héros demeure un être instinctif, pratiquement incapable de

---

[1] *L'Agent double in Histoires déplaisantes*, Gallimard, 1963 (édition posthume), p. 117-122.

jugement et de réflexion. Comme la plupart des créatures modianiennes, il est une figure « angélique », incorporelle, qui n'appartient pas à la réalité, et n'en partage ni les codes ni les devoirs – désespérée de ne pouvoir « éclore » au monde :

> Lui dire la vérité ? Laquelle au juste ? Agent double ? ou triple ? Je ne savais plus qui j'étais. Mon lieutenant, JE N'EXISTE PAS[1].

En vertu de ce principe, le protagoniste peut dès lors se présenter comme le fils de Stavisky ou du marquis de Bel-Respiro – rêvant son existence dans l'hôtel particulier du square Cimarosa[2] –, ou encore comme Marcel Petiot en personne, à la faveur d'un *analogon* :

> Je m'appelais Marcel Petiot. Seul au milieu de tous ces bagages. Inutile d'attendre. Le train ne viendrait pas. J'étais un garçon sans avenir. Qu'avais-je fait de ma jeunesse ? Les jours se succédaient aux jours et je les entassais dans le plus grand désordre[3].

C'est l'appartenance au monde des vivants qui se trouve placée sous un sceau de suspicion identique à celui de la conscience. Swing Troubadour peut, de la sorte, faire jouer sur la scène de son désarroi deux figures sorties de son imagination et auxquelles il accorde le statut d'êtres : Coco Lacour et Esmeralda. La plupart des critiques refusent le statut de personnages à ces deux incarnations, dont l'unique fonction semble l'objectivation des pulsions morales d'un narrateur à la recherche d'une norme susceptible de pallier son absence d'identité. Pour Shounong Feng, les deux êtres trouvent leur légitimité du côté du tableau qui donne – en partie – son titre au roman :

---

[1] *Ibid.*, p. 117.
[2] « La maîtresse de maison souriait. J'étais son fils, le lieutenant de vaisseau Maxime de Bel-Respiro, en permission, et j'assistais à l'une de ces soirées qui réunissaient au 3 bis les artistes et les hommes politiques : Ida Rubinstein, Gaston Calmette, Frédéric de Madrazzo, Louis Barthou, Gauthier-Villars, Armande Cassive, Bouffé de Saint-Blaise, Franck Le Harivel, José de Strada, Mery Laurent, Mademoiselle Mylo d'Arcille. Ma mère jouait au piano *Le Rondel de l'Adieu.* » *Ibid.*, p. 78-79.
[3] *Ibid.*, p. 146.

> Dans cette toile se trouve un être tout à fait étincelant qui se trouve à gauche du capitaine au premier plan, dans une ronde claire. Eugène Fromentin parle à son propos d'une petite personne à mine de sorcière, enfantine et vieillotte, contenant une sorte de phosphorescence extraordinairement bizarre [...]. Cet être imaginaire appartient plus au monde intérieur du peintre qu'à la réalité qu'il est chargé de représenter[1].

Ainsi, Coco Lacour et Esmeralda[2] partageraient avec cette silhouette la particularité de représenter un monde intérieur, celui de leur créateur, qui les investirait d'une présence symbolique. D'un strict point de vue littéral, ces êtres semblent, de toute façon, partager avec le protagoniste une existence placée à la frontière poreuse de la vie et du néant, et située au-delà du bien et du mal pour ce qui concerne l'éthique. La guerre, et les engagements personnels qu'elle postule, ne font que rendre plus aiguë la douleur d'un homme incapable non seulement d'effectuer un choix, mais surtout de parvenir au degré de conscience nécessaire à la réalisation de celui-ci :

> Le Bien, la Justice, le Bonheur, la Liberté, le Progrès exigeaient beaucoup trop d'efforts et des esprits plus chimériques que le mien, n'est-ce pas[3] ?

---

[1] S. Feng, *op.cit.*, p. 157.
[2] Dans sa thèse, *La Métaphysique chez Modiano*, rédigée sous la direction de Marc-Matthieu Munch, Université de Metz, 1994, Pierre Srour formule, en page 166, les remarques suivantes à propos de ce dernier personnage : « Empruntée à Victor Hugo, dans *Notre-Dame de Paris*, [Esmeralda a] toujours besoin du héros de *La Ronde de nuit* pour la protéger et la défendre, comme l'ont fait bien avant lui Phoebus et Quasimodo. [...] À la fin du roman, le narrateur affirme qu'Esmeralda n'existait pas [et qu'ils ne forment qu'une seule et même personne]. C'est parce que Swing Troubadour voit peser sur lui cette fatalité métaphysique du destin tragique et de la mort qu'il supprime en lui – symboliquement – l'autre face de son existence en l'abandonnant. [...] Coco Lacour, lui, ser[t] de décor. Il n'est autre que le symbole du destin qui accompagne l'intrigue romanesque de l'auteur et de son protagoniste [...]. Le récit et le personnage ne sont qu'un prétexte à partir duquel Modiano crée – sur le plan stylistique et thématique – un tableau riche et complexe dont les couleurs suggestives et allusives [...] prêtent à des interprétations diverses au sein de la période de l'Occupation. »
[3] *Ibid.*, p. 81.

Enfin, un comportement déterminé, qui surmonterait les ambiguïtés, forcerait Swing Troubadour à renoncer à la moitié des personnes qui lui permettent d'entretenir un rapport avec le monde. La fragilité du protagoniste est telle qu'un conflit le renverrait définitivement dans cette zone du non-être qu'il redoute plus que tout. L'Occupation va donc servir de révélateur d'identité, grâce (ou malgré) aux choix qu'elle impose. Là encore, le héros et le romancier ignorent les véritables enjeux, puisque loin de favoriser une « épiphanie » identitaire, la dichotomie mentale – créée par les événements – n'aboutit qu'à un chaos spirituel. Modiano n'a d'ailleurs jamais caché cet aspect de sa relation avec les années de plomb :

> Ce n'est pas l'Occupation pour elle-même qui me fascine, mais tout autre chose, à savoir la façon dont tous les problèmes se posaient de façon tranchée, dans ce monde crépusculaire. Si je recours à l'Occupation, c'est parce qu'elle me fournit un climat idéal, un peu trouble, cette lumière un peu bizarre[1]. Modiano affinera encore son questionnement, en recentrant la quête sur le personnage du père, à l'occasion d'un voyage au cœur même de la turpitude. Le personnage central n'en gagnera que présence et épaisseur romanesques.

Serge Alexandre : l'identification mortifère.

Centré sur la figure du père, le troisième roman s'affranchit des libertés et transgressions narratives qui caractérisaient le premier et le deuxième roman de la trilogie. L'argument romanesque ne réside plus, à ce moment, dans la levée des questionnements ontologiques – comment être ou ne pas être juif ? La trahison est-elle consubstantiellement attachée à l'espèce humaine ? Suis-je ou ne suis-je pas un traître ? –, mais dans la remontée du temps.

Pour comprendre comment son père a pu non seulement collaborer avec les tortionnaires de son peuple, mais également

---
[1] Cité par Jean-Louis de Rambures, *Comment travaillent les écrivains*, Paris, Flammarion, 1978, p. 128.

renier son fils, le narrateur-écrivain se plonge dans l'atmosphère vénéneuse des derniers jours de l'Occupation. L'empathie et la magnanimité doivent, en théorie, aider à comprendre les actes de l'être énigmatique que représente le père, et permettre ainsi au romancier de retrouver une place dans une lignée qui est la sienne, légitimée par la figure paternelle. Cette dernière a toujours constitué pour le fils un objet de fascination et d'angoisse – et la plupart des traumatismes du jeune écrivain n'ont pas d'autre origine. Albert Modiano sortira de la vie de ce dernier en 1965, et mourra, sans que son fils l'ait revu, en 1978[1].

Nous tâcherons de définir les modalités de cette rencontre, avant de nous attarder sur les constantes thématiques de l'écrivain. Il sera alors possible de prendre pleinement conscience des enjeux du troisième moment de la trilogie.

Les Boulevards de ceinture s'inspire très largement des activités du père de Modiano, qui joua pendant la guerre un rôle de relais entre les fournisseurs de matières premières et les caciques du marché noir, étroitement contrôlés par la Gestapo. De confession israélite, il opéra dans ce milieu sans jamais porter l'étoile jaune, ni éprouver le moindre remords à propos de la collaboration avec les ennemis de ses coreligionnaires. Nous avons vu comment il échappa, à deux reprises, à la déportation.

Modiano ne juge pas son père et ne tente pas davantage de pardonner[2], mais essaie, à une époque où Albert Modiano ne constituait plus qu'un souvenir, de comprendre l'enchaînement des causes rendant possible le renoncement à soi. Le père de Serge Alexandre apparaît comme un être privé de sentiment, impénétrable – l'unique moyen de communication que trouve le narrateur est de partager la mort

---

[1] *Rue des boutiques obscures* lui est alors dédié.
[2] « Ces gens-là n'étaient pas recommandables, mais c'étaient avant tout des truands. Ils auraient pu faire du trafic aussi bien avec les Américains qu'avec les Allemands. […] C'était une époque tellement trouble. Aujourd'hui, on la juge d'après notre époque, alors, évidemment, on ne peut pas très bien comprendre les compromis et les compromissions avec ces gens. » Entretien avec Jean-François Josselin, *in Le Nouvel Observateur*, 8-14 janvier 1988, p. 88.

avec lui – et dépourvu d'amour-propre : on se souvient de l'humiliation qu'il subit de la part des invités de Murraille.

Modiano, pour cette deuxième évocation du père, renonce à l'esprit de démesure et de provocation qui caractérisait son premier ouvrage. Schlemilovitch père y prenait l'aspect d'un clown pathétique et grotesque – notamment dans la représentation théâtrale organisée par son fils, ou dans ses habits de représentant en kaléidoscopes –, mais capable d'humour : lors de l'Exposition sur les Juifs, au Grand Palais, il n'avait pas hésité à se placer sous une photo qui le représentait, et avait pris la foule à partie. Six années plus tard, le père n'est plus cet objet de moquerie, mais un instrument entre les mains d'agioteurs, qui semblent avoir anesthésié toute forme de pensée chez cet homme. Cette mécanique froide et butée correspond sans doute davantage à l'idée que le romancier se faisait d'Albert Modiano, à cette époque de son existence. Il confiera à Jean-Louis de Rambures que ce roman, qui recourait volontiers à l'excès – en particulier l'évocation de la tentative d'assassinat dans le métro –, tentait de traduire l'hostilité sourde que le futur écrivain pouvait ressentir de la part de son géniteur, durant son enfance. On sait qu'il passa sa jeunesse chez des amis de ses parents – cette période se trouve évoquée dans *Remise de peine* – avant de partir dans nombre de pensionnats, sans jamais recevoir de nouvelles de son père.

L'écriture des *Boulevards de ceinture* constitue un moyen romanesque d'exprimer des émotions qui, sans cela, eussent été refoulées. Le romancier procède, à cette fin, par un jeu de translation logique, en remontant à la période précédant sa naissance afin d'y replacer le type de rapports qu'il entretenait avec son père, durant les années cinquante. Il se produit donc un double mouvement, temporel et psychologique, au cours duquel le fils fait preuve de la plus grande abnégation, et ce dans le but de comprendre les raisons de cet abandon. Le roman peut se lire comme l'exact contrepoint du *Chemin des écoliers*, roman de Marcel Aymé publié un quart de siècle auparavant, dans lequel deux pères, Michaud et Lolivier, se trouvent confrontés à l'évolution de leurs enfants. Les deux fils du premier s'adonnent respectivement au marché noir et à des actes de résistance, l'unique enfant du second s'avère un criminel. L'intérêt de l'ouvrage réside dans la quête psychologique conduite par les deux hommes, désireux de comprendre des comportements imprévisibles, à rebours des préceptes éducatifs inculqués depuis l'enfance. La brutale remise en cause de leurs certitudes et valeurs fondatrices les invite à une revue critique de la pertinence de leurs principes moraux.

Vingt années plus tard, la perspective se trouve totalement modifiée. Les œuvres des années 1960 font état d'une crise d'identité, qui concerne cette fois-ci les enfants et non les géniteurs. Ceux-là endossent le rôle jusqu'alors dévolu à l'autorité parentale, et interrogent le comportement de leurs aînés. Contrairement aux insurgés de Mai 1968, les enfants de la Collaboration ne tentent pas de nier ou de renverser l'autorité paternelle. Bien au contraire, ils donnent la primauté aux pères, en leur consacrant des volumes entiers. Au moment où Modiano présente au public *Les Boulevards de ceinture*, Pascal Jardin a publié *La Guerre à neuf ans*, réhabilitation de son père, proche de Laval, et Marie Chaix prépare *Les Lauriers du lac de Constance*, œuvre dans laquelle la fille de l'adjoint de Doriot – Beugras – livre la chronique des activités de son père. Chacun de ces ouvrages tente de clarifier les rapports avec l'image parentale, en reconstituant le cadre historique pour y inscrire les actes supposés du père. Cette démarche est rendue plus complexe encore par Modiano, qui la situe délibérément du côté de la fiction.

Le troisième *opus* ne se situe pas en complète rupture avec les romans qui précèdent. Les procédés de mise à distance sont conservés pour l'essentiel, sans doute au titre de barrières protectrices contre les doutes et les angoisses. La trilogie se trouve ainsi placée sous l'égide de Stavisky, associé volontiers par le romancier à la figure de son père. Cet homme partage, en effet, un certain nombre de traits avec Albert Modiano : issu d'une famille israélite vivant en Ukraine, il quitte son pays pour se faire naturaliser français, en 1910. Conduisant des affaires à un niveau bien plus élevé que le père de l'écrivain, qui représente le versant pauvre de la mystification en affaires, il incarne aux yeux de Patrick Modiano la légèreté – et le vide – des êtres vivant à l'écart des normes sociales. Le milieu dans lequel ils évoluent leur est naturellement hostile, et ils ne pourront trouver d'autre légitimité que celle de leurs exactions.

La relation entretenue avec Stavisky évolue au cours des romans. Dans *La Place de l'Étoile*, Schlemilovitch père est le secrétaire de Stavisky. Dans *La Ronde de nuit*, ce dernier devient le père du narrateur :

> Une telle soif de respectabilité me bouleversait car je l'avais déjà remarqué chez mon père, Alexandre Stavisky. Je garde sur moi la lettre qu'il écrivit à maman avant de se suicider : « Ce que je te demande surtout, c'est d'élever notre fils dans le sentiment de l'honneur et de la probité ; et, lorsqu'il aura atteint l'âge ingrat de la quinzième année, de surveiller ses fréquentations pour qu'il soit bien guidé dans la vie et qu'il devienne un honnête homme. » Lui-même, je crois, aurait aimé finir ses jours dans une petite ville de province[1].

Enfin, l'opération de transfert se trouve achevée dans le dernier ouvrage, puisque le protagoniste *est* Stavisky, ou plutôt son pseudonyme, Serge Alexandre. Ce glissement s'explique, en partie, par le recentrage historique effectué dans l'œuvre : l'une des composantes de l'Occupation est abordée de front, à savoir la collaboration dite intellectuelle, avec ses relents mafieux. L'adoption d'un patronyme lourd de la charge symbolique que nous venons d'évoquer rendra ainsi l'assimilation plus aisée.

Lacombe Lucien : une identité conditionnelle.

Le jeune Lacombe n'accède véritablement à un statut accordant une réelle valeur sociale – du moins à ses yeux – qu'à partir du moment où il se trouve inclus dans un groupe. En effet, livré à lui-même, le héros ne possède ni attaches ni moyens d'identification – il est proche en cela de ses

---

[1] *La Ronde de nuit*, p. 135. On notera, bien évidemment, la dérision et l'ironie qui s'attachent à cette évocation.

devanciers, Raphaël ou Swing Troubadour, pour lesquels les repères moraux et les codes sociaux semblent inexistants. Le début et la fin du film illustrent une thèse identique : sans la structure et la stabilité apportées par le groupe, l'individu se trouve condamné à l'errance physique – et partant morale.

Dans les premières scènes, Lucien prend acte des changements qui affectent son environnement – à savoir l'installation de Laborit et des ouvriers dans la ferme paternelle – sans parvenir à trouver sa place dans un monde transformé. Sa déréliction conditionne des déplacements incessants – la partie de chasse, la visite à la jeune bergère, puis à l'instituteur – qui ne cesseront qu'après la rencontre avec les amis de Tonin. Incapable de se situer précisément dans le nouvel ordre politique et relationnel, Lucien cherche éperdument la justification de son existence. Il sera comblé, au-delà de ses attentes, par les besognes dont le chargeront ses nouveaux amis.

La fin du film signe l'arrêt de mort intellectuel du personnage, en offrant un brouillage narratif total : les repères temporels et géographiques s'estompent, l'imprécision s'installe – puisque la communauté a disparu, et ne peut plus, de ce fait, légitimer les actes, en leur offrant une cohérence susceptible d'assurer l'équilibre mental. Tout se passe comme si le personnage surgi de nulle part, au début du film, rejoignait ses limbes originels, selon un processus régressif. Les indications du scénario sont en cela riches d'enseignements :

> À partir de là, il n'y aura plus de suite chronologique, mais des moments très longs. [...] On aura l'impression d'être hors du temps, de l'histoire (plus aucune allusion à la guerre), dans une sorte d'éternité où les activités les plus essentielles de la vie se répètent de manière monotone[1].

Ce repli, presque infantile, dans le confort de l'« achronie » s'inscrit directement dans la continuité thématique de l'œuvre modianienne. Les trois ouvrages précédents s'achevaient par une fuite – mentale dans *La Place*

---

[1] *Lacombe Lucien*, p. 139.

de l'Étoile, physique dans les deux livres suivants – qui traduisait, de manière symbolique, le retour à la vie intra-utérine, loin des agressions du monde adulte. De fait, de sa première œuvre jusqu'à *Une jeunesse*, Modiano aura décliné, de façon obsessionnelle, un thème unique, celui de la nécessaire – et anxiogène – confrontation avec le réel. Le seul repli acceptable réside dans sa négation ou son refoulement : la fuite, la cellule protectrice (l'hôtel, dans *Villa triste*) ou l'amnésie, dans *Rue des boutiques obscures*.

Au début de sa carrière littéraire, Modiano projette la rationalité du réel au sein de l'Occupation, selon une logique d'inversion – puisque c'est le fantasme qui, présidant à la restitution historique, devient réalité. Placés devant la nécessité d'accéder à un statut susceptible d'octroyer l'identité, les personnages doivent être confrontés avec ce qu'ils estiment représenter le réel, afin de prendre leur place dans le monde, et d'exister véritablement. Cette démarche suppose l'adoption d'une discipline enseignée par les personnages de rencontre. Dans *Lacombe Lucien*, ce sont les tortionnaires et les collaborateurs qui se font les instructeurs ordinaires du héros. Sous leur conduite, celui-ci parvient à s'approprier les codes qui lui échappaient, au tout début :

> Émile (toujours souriant) : [...] Va voir le patron, il t'expliquera... [...]
> Lucien (à Thérèse, agressif) : Et les autres, qu'est-ce qu'ils font des noms ?
> [...]
> Thérèse (sans le regarder) : Ils aident M. Laborit. Je leur ai laissé la maison...
> Lucien (regardant Laborit) : Y en a du changement ici...
> Laborit (agacé) : Il faut bien faire le travail ! Ton père est prisonnier, Joseph est parti...
> Lucien : Ah bon[1] !

Quelque six mois plus tard, Lucien s'est parfaitement adapté à l'ordre nouveau, dont la remise en cause signera sa

---

[1] *Ibid.*, p. 12-13.

perte. À l'image des romans antérieurs, l'œuvre doit être lue comme une tentative d'adaptation au monde extérieur, sanctionnée par le retour à l'univers « matriciel », et caractérisée par une aboulie que l'on pourrait qualifier de prénatale. Par la suite, nous verrons comment cette logique symbolique pourra se trouver affinée – notamment dans les ouvrages des années quatre-vingts.

Dans la première trilogie, l'Occupation joue un rôle fondateur ; ses figures – au sens de silhouettes entrevues ou de faces changeantes de la réalité historique – permettent de valider l'existence des êtres, grâce à l'ordre mis en place – même si celui-ci trouve sa légitimation dans les pires instincts de l'être humain. Les nouvelles conditions paraissent ainsi susceptibles de combler, momentanément, le vide existentiel du héros, dans chaque récit.

L'infime pouvoir concédé par les auxiliaires de la Gestapo procure sécurité et reconnaissance sociale. L'être tout entier se trouve valorisé, exerçant une autorité légitimée par le nouveau pouvoir. Rangé du côté des puissants, passant de l'obscurité à la pleine lumière de la force, Lucien délaisse la virtualité de son existence pour tenter de pénétrer le monde réel. Dans l'article qu'il consacrait au film[1], Pascal Bonitzer critiquait l'approche essentiellement individualiste de l'œuvre qui, selon lui, évacuait l'Histoire et la dédramatisait, afin de se fixer sur l'unique personnage de Lucien. Le référent historique se trouvait ainsi escamoté, afin de mieux servir une approche purement psychologique, voire behaviouriste des événements – ce qui représentait un crime pour ce critique postmarxiste et maoïste, attaché à l'étude des masses et du matérialisme historique :

> Le film repose sur un système bien particulier : il s'agit d'aveugler, de borner, de troubler la dénotation du comportement de Lucien, de telle sorte que ce comportement dénote bien le fascisme, mais connote tout autre chose, en principe indéfinissable (la *psyché* de Lucien) qui emporte en dernière instance le sens. […]

---

[1] « Histoire de sparadrap », *Les Cahiers du cinéma*, mai 1974, n° 250, p. 42-47.

La vérité de Lucien n'est pas dans le réel, puisque l'Histoire n'est qu'apparence et que les étiquettes ne sont que des étiquettes. Tout ce qui se déroule dans le réel, l'Histoire, est frappé de contingence, de futilité et d'irréalité.

Incidemment, Pascal Bonitzer définit, de façon très satisfaisante, l'esthétique globale de Modiano, de *La Place de l'Étoile* jusqu'au scénario commenté. Depuis 1966, l'écrivain ne fait qu'interroger le sens et la validité de l'Histoire afin de trouver un enracinement, et de combler sa vacuité existentielle. Cette démarche, qui est celle de ses personnages avant d'être la sienne, semble suivie, dans ses grandes lignes, par Louis Malle. Avec l'aide de son coscénariste, ce dernier privilégie la symbolique au détriment de l'analyse, comme si les circonstances importaient moins que les réactions et comportement qu'elles suscitent et déterminent[1].

À titre d'exemple, nous retiendrons un passage du film, dans lequel la dichotomie fondamentale entre l'engagement au côté de l'occupant nazi et la résistance contre celui-ci se trouve réduite à un unique symptôme, celui de la confrontation entre deux hommes qui appartiennent au camp idéologique opposé :

> Le prisonnier : Tu n'as pas l'air d'un voyou !... (persuasif) Écoute, je vais te donner une chance : tu m'enlèves les menottes et tu pars avec moi... Compris ? [...] Mais réponds-moi, nom d'un chien ! C'est ta dernière chance...
> Lucien ne le laisse pas continuer : il a coupé un morceau de sparadrap et le colle au travers de la bouche du prisonnier.
> Lucien : J'aime pas qu'on me tutoie[2].

L'antithèse représentée par cette réunion trouve sa portée singulièrement limitée par la réduction immédiate à

---

[1] On rappelle qu'avant la rencontre avec Modiano, le cinéaste entendait situer son film au Mexique, montrant comment un simple péon pouvait servir d'auxiliaire aux forces armées, diligentées par les gros propriétaires, afin de réprimer les émeutes de paysans.
[2] *Lacombe Lucien*, p. 132-133.

laquelle procèdent Lucien – et les scénaristes, oserait-on écrire. Le protagoniste refuse de s'inscrire dans l'Histoire (« Si Lucien délivre le prisonnier, il passe du côté de la Résistance ; s'il ne le délivre pas, il se marque du côté de la Gestapo[1] ») pour se borner à la simple énonciation, considérant que le signe vaut l'objet ou la pensée représentés. L'engagement se retrouve entièrement dévalorisé, puisque suspendu au choix d'un pronom, comme auparavant à la réaction d'un instituteur[2]. Désémantisée, l'Histoire n'est plus envisagée comme un processus, déterminé par un certain nombre de lois humaines, et dirigée vers une fin qui lui donnera son sens – et l'on comprend fort bien les oppositions d'un jeune marxiste à une semblable conception –, mais comme une somme d'accidents imprévisibles. L'ensemble se trouve donc rapporté à la seule subjectivité de l'individu, qui tente de se situer dans une série apparemment irrationnelle de faits. La passivité et l'indolence des créatures modianiennes, réduites à un état larvaire – qui leur interdit la moindre prise sur les événements – s'expliquent par leur incapacité à dépasser le signe, l'empire de la forme, pour en pénétrer les significations essentielles.

Lorsqu'il est pris à partie par le résistant, Lucien, bercé par la jouissance que lui procure sa nouvelle identité, qui le valorise et lui donne confiance en lui[3], ne songe pas une seule seconde à laisser de côté le signifiant du message pour accéder à son sens premier – son signifié. Le prisonnier, qui fait appel à

---

[1] Pascal Bonitzer, article cité, p. 45.
[2] On pourra également songer au personnage de Swing Troubadour, dont la complicité avec la bande du Khédive tient à une rencontre fortuite avec celui-ci, à la terrasse du « Royal-Villiers ».
[3] Ce changement est lié à son appartenance à la « Police allemande ». Ces deux mots fonctionnent comme un *credo*, qui vient légitimer l'existence du jeune homme et conférer une grande puissance, garantie par l'ordre nouveau, à chacun de ses actes. Lucien, là encore, ne peut déchiffrer correctement le réel, puisqu'il se limite aux apparences. Il ne perçoit pas l'incongruité qui réside dans le martèlement du vocable avec l'accent rocailleux du Lot – ce qui imposerait, pour tout esprit équilibré, une mise à distance immédiate du référent (la « Police allemande ») par rapport au locuteur. Pour celui-ci, ce sésame devient une manifestation d'ordre ontologique, constituant la justification de son être. Il lui paraîtrait proprement impensable de remettre en cause la caution de sa nouvelle existence, en s'interrogeant sur sa validité.

la capacité de réflexion de son bourreau, en postulant que celui-ci agit au mieux par faiblesse, au pire par idéologie, ne peut espérer atteindre le milicien, lequel se situe, à chaque instant de ses actes, en dehors de l'Histoire – et ne dépasse jamais le « degré zéro » de la signification des paroles ou des actes[1]. Loin de replacer les déclarations du résistant dans un sens qui postulerait une analyse critique de l'Histoire, Lucien ne retient que l'emploi de la fonction conative du langage – qui se trouve remettre brutalement en cause son nouveau statut. Il choisit de clore la communication, au sens figuré comme au sens propre, par l'obstruction, au moyen d'une phrase défensive – « J'aime pas qu'on me tutoie », dont l'aspect gnomique installe le nouveau statut dans la durée, et lui confère une sorte de pérennité – et, plus concrètement, par l'emploi d'un morceau de ruban adhésif, appliqué sur la bouche du prisonnier. Dans son article, Pascal Bonitzer analyse ainsi la situation :

> En tutoyant Lucien, le résistant réitère l'erreur de l'instituteur et renouvelle, sans le savoir, l'humiliation initiale de Lucien. [...] [Celui-ci] répondra au seul niveau de l'énonciation : « Pourquoi me tutoyez-vous ? » Ainsi se trouve esquivée la fonctionnalité du sens, sa transparence, c'est-à-dire la dénotation[2].

Lucien se situe dans la droite ligne des Schlemilovitch et Swing Troubadour, demeurant un être réduit à ses uniques virtualités. Son existence se trouve ramenée à la production de signes dont le déchiffrage n'obéit pas aux lois logiques – et sociales – en vigueur. Il serait inexact de parler d'une absence de conscience, puisque la notion même d'éthique ou de réflexion morale semble totalement inadaptée au cas de Lucien. Ce dernier n'appartient pas au monde, comme nous l'avons vu,

---

[1] « Le prisonnier : Ne fais pas le malin !... Tu sais qu'on va te fusiller ? [...] Écoute, je vais te donner une chance ; tu m'enlèves les menottes et tu pars avec moi... Compris ? [...] Mais réponds-moi, nom d'un chien ! C'est ta dernière chance. » *Lacombe Lucien*, p. 132.
[2] Article cité, p. 46.

et n'entretient que des rapports de surface, presque accidentels, avec celui-ci.

Le contexte très particulier de l'occupation allemande lui aura permis de prendre un bref contact avec ses « potentialités d'existence », malheureusement tributaires de son appartenance à la bande de l'« Hôtel des Grottes ». Il convient d'ajouter que Lucien n'a pas la moindre affinité intellectuelle ou idéologique avec le groupe de Tonin – pas plus qu'il n'en aurait eu avec les amis de Peyssac s'il eût épousé la cause de la Résistance. Pour le jeune homme, seule importe la confiance que les représentants d'un ordre ou d'un pouvoir établis placent en lui[1]. La relative réussite artistique du film réside dans l'observation behaviouriste du personnage central, enregistrant les faits et les actes sans chercher à restituer des liens de causalité inexistants, ou à rendre vraisemblable, selon les canons de la logique, le comportement de chacun – ce qui reviendrait à trahir l'esprit de Modiano.

La critique cinématographique loua ou condamna le film pour de mauvaises raisons, puisqu'elle n'entrevoyait pas les relations de cette œuvre avec les romans précédents. En effet, il s'agissait moins, pour Malle et Modiano, de proposer une réflexion démystificatrice sur la relativité de tout engagement – à partir d'un archétype – que de livrer une étude presque clinique – proche de l'entomologie – d'un être difficilement réductible à un paradigme. Le voisinage du *Chagrin et la pitié* ou de *Portier de nuit*, films qui usaient de la provocation pour mieux bousculer les dogmes, assura le succès de l'œuvre, mais contribua à en affaiblir le sens et la portée. Les deux auteurs ignoraient en fait, dans leur création, le didactisme propre au film de Liliana Cavani[2], et inscrivaient la réflexion dans le

---

[1] « Le plus curieux avec les garçons de mon espèce : ils peuvent aussi bien finir au Panthéon qu'au cimetière de Thiais, carré des fusillés. On en fait des héros. Ou des salauds. » *La Ronde de nuit*, p. 92.
[2] Cette réalisatrice partait de la confrontation de la femme juive et de son ancien tortionnaire pour développer une parabole sur l'aliénation désirée, et légitimée, d'une victime à son bourreau par la nécessaire soumission amoureuse régissant les rapports de couple. Dans ce sens, le recours à l'Occupation donnait une acuité supplémentaire au propos, sans constituer un

cadre général d'une méditation sur l'identité, au miroir de l'Occupation.

L'être modianien, eu égard à sa fragilité, exerce une étrange attraction sur les forces du mal. Ces dernières exploitent son besoin de reconnaissance en l'associant à leurs basses besognes – et, plus tard, à leur naufrage. Deux raisons fondamentales l'empêchent d'adhérer à l'orthodoxie morale, représentée par les chevaliers du RCO ou les amis de Peyssac qui tentent de surnager dans la débâcle des valeurs foulées au pied par la Collaboration. Dans un premier temps, l'exercice du droit moral, nécessitant l'adoption de principes rigoureux, suppose une réflexion minimale sur le monde. En outre, le choix de la Résistance implique une certaine transgression de l'ordre établi, de sorte que l'individu les rapporte à sa seule norme – dans un système autoréférent – ce qui semble impossible pour un Swing Troubadour ou un Lacombe Lucien[1]. En second lieu, leur débilité de jugement semble les renvoyer à des êtres qu'ils estiment proches d'eux, dépourvus de censure morale. Les protagonistes commettent en cela une erreur d'appréciation, puisque loin de se battre pour survivre dans un milieu hostile, les affairistes du square Cimarosa ou les miliciens de l'« Hôtel des Grottes » sont les organisateurs, ou les principaux bénéficiaires, du chaos. Les héros n'en demeurent pas moins attirés par ces ombres, avec lesquels ils partagent une certaine faiblesse d'âme :

Maman me disait : « On a les amis qu'on mérite[2]. »

L'un des paradoxes du personnage modianien réside dans le mélange de sa nullité existentielle, qui expliquerait sa

---

élément intrinsèque du message. De fait, sa place était davantage du côté du *Dernier Tango à Paris* que de *Lacombe Lucien*.

[1] Ces derniers n'arrivant déjà pas à exister à leurs propres yeux, on voit mal comment ils seraient capables d'adopter une position critique sur un monde dans lequel ils peinent à trouver leur place : « Le Bien, la Justice, le Bonheur, la Liberté, le Progrès exigeaient beaucoup trop d'efforts et des esprits plus chimériques que le mien, n'est-ce pas ? » *La Ronde de nuit*, p. 81.

[2] *La Ronde de nuit*, p. 39.

lente plongée vers l'abîme[1], et l'intelligence critique qui lui permettrait de juger ses compagnons, en pointant leurs travers avec une acerbe minutie. Le héros semble donc moins victime de ses fréquentations que prisonnier d'une apathie dont il assume pleinement les conséquences, sans être pour autant en mesure de modifier le cours des événements. Afin de montrer que cet état de fait représente un thème récurrent chez Modiano, nous nous attarderons sur les différentes manifestations de l'être dans ses romans. Celles-ci viennent dessiner les contours d'une œuvre placée sous le signe de la perte et de la reconquête de *l'essence*.

GLISSEMENTS PERMANENTS DE L'IDENTITE

L'ensemble formé par les romans de Modiano peut être considéré comme le récit d'une quête de soi, dont l'Occupation – seuil primitif de l'être – constituerait le point de passage obligé. Tout se passe comme si le but ultime de l'écrivain était de fournir un corps au « je » omniprésent des récits, lui donnant une enveloppe charnelle, afin qu'il ne soit plus limité au statut de simple énonciateur du discours romanesque. On serait alors tenté de suivre la progression de l'être selon une gamme évolutive, qui partirait du néant halluciné de *La Place de l'Étoile* pour s'achever – provisoirement – par l'abandon du roman, avec *Dora Bruder*.

Deux grandes parties peuvent être ainsi distinguées, qui correspondent, *mutatis mutandis*, à un regroupement décennal. Durant les années soixante-dix, Modiano tente de s'approcher

---

[1] « [...] On doit débuter dans la vie [...]. Elle finit par vous envoyer ses sergents recruteurs : en l'occurrence le Khédive et Monsieur Philibert. Un autre soir, sans doute, je serais tombé sur des personnages plus honorables qui m'auraient conseillé l'industrie des textiles ou la littérature. Ne me sentant aucune vocation particulière, j'attendais de mes aînés qu'ils me choisissent un emploi. À eux de savoir sous quels aspects ils me préféraient. » *La Ronde de nuit*, p. 92. Nous sommes proches du début de *Lacombe Lucien*, lorsque le jeune homme se trouve devant le choix forcé de la Collaboration, après le refus de l'instituteur de le prendre à ses côtés.

au plus près de la réalité de l'Occupation, grâce au fantasme et à la rêverie – moyens détournés mais efficaces d'immersion dans le climat d'une époque – afin d'y trouver un lignage, un enracinement. L'entreprise échoue, mais la quête se referme sur l'apaisement de *Livret de famille*, autofiction qui voit l'écrivain accepter, voire revendiquer – la plupart des portraits renvoient à des êtres déracinés – sa condition d'apatride. Après *Rue des boutiques obscures*, qui marque l'abandon du « roman de l'être », et partant de l'Occupation, une longue parenthèse romanesque s'ouvre. Patrick Modiano endosse, à ce moment, l'identité de l'écrivain français traditionnel, livrant des ouvrages d'une facture classique, qui semblent esquiver les spéculations sur l'être. Le retour à l'Occupation, au début de la décennie suivante, entérine la mort de la fiction. Il paraît désormais impossible de raconter cette époque à l'aide des artifices du roman – en ce sens, le dernier ouvrage qui adopte les lois du genre, *Voyage de noces*, paraît savamment déconstruit. Après trente ans de dissimulations et de travestissements, l'écrivain peut non seulement affronter l'Histoire sous forme de récits, de témoignages ou d'enquêtes, mais surtout sa propre identité – sans recourir, à cette fin, à la mise en scène littéraire du vide. Ce rappel du parcours « formel » de Modiano nous permettra de mieux replacer la première partie de l'œuvre dans l'esthétique globale du romancier.

Les personnages des premiers romans ne se définissent que par les liens qui les unissent à l'Occupation. Raphaël, Swing Troubadour, Serge Alexandre ou Lucien en constituent les produits, dépositaires de l'angoisse et des interrogations concernant la période – la fréquentation des figures du mal apparaissant comme un pis-aller au néant. Sans la guerre, ces héros ne sont rien, puisque tous les événements antérieurs à celle-ci ne s'articulent qu'autour de ce continuum temporel. Ils sont placés devant la nécessité de pénétrer le cœur de l'Occupation, afin d'obtenir l'élucidation des énigmes ou la levée partielle des angoisses.

Ainsi, les divers épisodes de *La Place de l'Étoile* doivent moins être lus de façon diachronique que sous la forme d'une coupe stratifiée, déclinant les différents moments de la guerre : la préparation idéologique avec les réactionnaires et nationalistes (Debigorre, Aravis ou *Je suis partout*), les persécutions antisémites (Tania) ou l'épilogue de celles-ci, à savoir la fondation de l'État hébreu. À l'intérieur de ce vortex, Schlemilovitch n'acquerra sa véritable dimension de personnage qu'à partir du moment où il se trouvera aux prises avec les dignitaires ou les trafiquants du marché noir. De la même façon, la créature informe de Swing Troubadour s'anime au seul moment où elle se trouve contrainte de réfléchir sur son existence, à la lumière de son expérience d'agent double. Un constat identique s'applique à Serge Alexandre et à Lucien, avec pour l'un la recherche du père, et pour le second l'inclusion dans un groupe de collaborateurs.

Ce sont avant tout les silences, les doutes ou les ombres de l'Occupation qui valident l'existence des individus – tout se passe comme s'il leur était impossible d'accéder à la vérité de leur être sans le secours de cette période. Généralement, celle-ci se trouve perdue dans un passé brumeux, et ne surgit, dans toute sa violence, qu'après de nombreuses évocations – au sens étymologique du terme. À cet égard, la disposition des chapitres de *Livret de famille* paraît particulièrement révélatrice, qui concentre en un même écrin – c'est-à-dire au cœur de l'ouvrage – les données essentielles concernant le narrateur, à savoir la rencontre d'Albert Modiano et de Louisa Colpeyn, pendant la guerre. Les autres pièces du dossier ne prennent leur sens qu'à partir de cet épisode nodal, fondateur.

Dans la première partie de l'œuvre romanesque, le dispositif narratif semblait ne tendre qu'à la convocation du passé le plus lointain, le plus « refoulé », lourd d'angoisses. L'exemple le plus frappant est sans doute celui de la composition de *Rue des boutiques obscures*, organisé autour d'un parcours mental régressif. Comme dans les textes précédents, l'objet de la narration réside dans l'obtention de l'identité ; il convient toutefois de noter qu'il s'agit de la première œuvre à présenter cette quête de façon aussi explicite.

Les déambulations physiques et mentales aboutissent à une inversion, presque définitive, des polarités. Le roman s'ouvre par un constat de nullité – qui eût pu être formulé par tous les héros de la première trilogie –, le « je ne suis rien » fondateur, qui laissera progressivement la place à une sorte d'épiphanie identitaire, consacrée par l'anamnèse finale, à savoir le passage de la frontière, moment à partir duquel commence l'oubli. Toutes proportions gardées, on pourrait dire que la démarche de Pedro Mc Evoy entretient un certain rapport de similarité avec le *cogito* cartésien. Si la recherche ne débouche pas sur une conclusion définitive – le « blanc » des années 1944-1955 ne peut être comblé –, sans doute impensable, celle-ci demeure, de toute façon, plus importante que le résultat proprement dit. En effet, comme chez Descartes, c'est la démarche active qui donne sa valeur identitaire à l'être. La vérité finale devient dès lors accessoire, puisque c'est le processus heuristique qui donne tout son sens à la question posée.

Ainsi, Patrick Modiano aura présenté, pour ses douze premières années de création littéraire, une approche identique de l'Occupation, dans des œuvres marquées par nombre de différences formelles. La période marque le moment fondateur par excellence, dont l'importance s'accroît en raison des multiples obstacles qui s'opposent à sa révélation. Privé de contact avec cette « drôle d'époque[1] », l'être n'est qu'une forme vide, entretenant un rapport des plus superficiels avec la réalité, cette « buée qui recouvr[e] les vitres, cette buée tenace qu'on ne parvient pas à effacer avec la main[2]. » Seule la rencontre décisive avec l'Occupation permet de combler le néant, offrant à l'individu la sécurité d'une réelle pesanteur.

Le rôle fondamental de l'Occupation dans l'édification de la personnalité se trouve confirmé, s'il en était besoin, par la déréliction des créatures marquées par cette époque, et qui connurent leur apogée au début des années quarante. On ne

---

[1] Le terme revient de façon récurrente dans les œuvres pour caractériser l'Occupation. On dénombre une bonne dizaine d'occurrences dans *La Ronde de nuit* ou *Rue des boutiques obscures*.
[2] *Rue des boutiques obscures*, p. 184.

compte plus les figures spectrales rencontrées dans une gare ou un café, qui semblent davantage survivre à leur souvenir que mener une existence digne de ce nom. Nous verrons, dans l'ultime développement de ce travail, comment la combinaison de la liberté ambiguë et de l'incertitude permanente représenta, durant la guerre, la période d'élection qui permit l'épanouissement de ces êtres. Ces derniers semblent d'ailleurs renaître à son seul souvenir, derniers représentants d'un univers englouti. On pensera, ainsi, au René Meinthe du début de *Villa triste*, à la cohorte de spectres croisée dans *Rue des boutiques obscures*, au suicide de Georges Bellune, dans *Une jeunesse* ou à Arlette d'Alwyn, gloire éteinte, dans *De si braves garçons* :

> Elle lui avait expliqué qu'elle était mariée à un officier aviateur dont elle ne recevait plus de nouvelles, depuis le début de la guerre [...]. Un soir, il était arrivé quelques instants avant elle et il avait fouillé au hasard le tiroir d'une commode où il trouva un reçu du crédit municipal de la rue Pierre-Charron. Il apprit ainsi qu'elle avait mis en gage une bague, des boucles d'oreille, un clip et, pour la première fois, il sentit un léger parfum de naufrage dans cet appartement, un peu comme dans celui de sa grand-mère. Était-ce l'odeur opiacée qui imprégnait les meubles, le lit, le pick-up, les étagères vides et la photo du prétendu aviateur, entourée de cuir grenat[1] ?

Livrés à eux-mêmes, à la fin de la guerre, les êtres apparaissent incapables de s'adapter à la société nouvelle, privés de l'égide protectrice de l'Occupation parisienne, au sein de laquelle ils paraissaient vivre en parfaite symbiose. Vingt ou trente ans plus tard, leur transparence n'est pas sans rappeler l'inconsistance des deux créatures chimériques de *La Ronde de nuit*. Cette traversée d'un univers régi par l'évanescence donne une bonne part de son originalité à l'univers de Modiano. Selon lui, les apparences constituent la seule réalité acceptable.

---

[1] *Op. cit.*, p. 120.

Une ontologie fantôme

De traces effacées en existences précaires, le monde labile du romancier semble hanté par la figure du vide, omniprésente dans son œuvre. Les deux thèmes de la fugacité et du vacillement sont régulièrement illustrés par des êtres, ou des époques, qui se limitent à un simple passage dans le monde – cette apparition semblant la principale justification de leur existence. Afin de montrer comment la recherche de l'identité peut, paradoxalement, prendre appui sur cette fragilité, nous approfondirons la notion en la liant au concept de durée.

Peu de romanciers auront fait preuve de la cohérence thématique et formelle de Modiano. Fasciné et horrifié par l'idée de dissipation, celui-ci réfléchit particulièrement à la notion de passage. Schématiquement, le monde se trouve constitué d'un agrégat de fantômes[1], évoluant dans une infraréalité représentant la seule garantie de survie. Peu d'analystes de l'œuvre ont noté l'angélisme[2] des créatures ou leur caractère asexué ; tout se passe, dans les œuvres, comme si le corps constituait un élément adventice dans la représentation de l'individu. De fait, l'enveloppe charnelle ne peut représenter une preuve convaincante de l'existence ou un gage d'appartenance à la communauté humaine. En effet, il s'en faut de peu pour que celle-ci ne vacille pas en même temps que l'être qu'elle est censée protéger :

> Drôles de gens. De ceux qui ne laissent sur leur passage qu'une buée vite dissipée. [...] Ainsi Hutte me citait-il en exemple un individu qu'il appelait l'« homme des plages ». Cet homme avait passé quarante ans sur des plages ou au bord de piscines. [...] Dans les coins et à l'arrière-plan de milliers de photos de vacances, il

---

[1] À ce titre, il est donc possible de composer une œuvre telle que *La Place de l'Étoile*, totalement désubstantialisée, dans laquelle les personnages se limitent à l'idée de leur propre corps ou incarnation, sans accès possible à la matière.
[2] Au sens psychanalytique du terme, c'est-à-dire l'association du corps et de ses fonctions à l'idée de dégradation.

figure en maillot de bain au milieu de groupes joyeux, mais personne ne pourrait dire son nom et pourquoi il se trouve là. Et personne ne remarqua qu'un jour il avait disparu des photographies[1].

La plupart des personnages modianiens sont des « hommes des plages », victimes d'un temps trop rapidement enfui, qu'ils eussent aimé fixer à jamais. L'entreprise s'avère totalement illusoire, puisque, selon Daniel Parrochia, « le fantôme [est] en réalité l'unique solution du problème ontologique. [...] Contrairement à ce que pensait Hegel, ce n'est pas l'être qui est néant. Il faut retourner la formule : c'est le néant – que nous sommes et qui nous constitue – qui est la seule forme possible d'être[2]. » Dès lors, il n'est plus guère possible que d'accéder à de brefs instants de révélation existentielle, en utilisant justement la force de ce vide pour une sorte de sursaut de l'être, qui donnera à l'existence un sens presque véritable. Le plus souvent, cette victoire sur le néant achoppe sur la toute-puissance que le temps oppose à la fragilité humaine.

Le fantôme ne disparaît pas, il se contente d'une existence marginale, liminaire, dans une sorte de nébuleuse. Sans parvenir toutefois à s'accommoder de ce mode d'appartenance au monde, les individus doivent se contenter de cette condition, qui offre l'incomparable avantage de protéger leur vulnérabilité. D'autre part, leur enfermement – plus ou moins volontaire – dans la sphère des souvenirs, les rend moins sensibles au passage du temps – puisqu'ils paraissent déjà claustrés dans celui-ci. On pourrait ainsi – en ne modifiant que certains aspects propres au personnage – appliquer aux personnages du roman les remarques sur Emmanuel Berl[3] :

> Une question me brûle les lèvres : comment s'y est-il pris pour déjouer le temps et éviter tous les pièges dont le siècle était semé ? [...] Avant de connaître Berl, j'ai cru que ceux qui « duraient » c'était par avarice

---

[1] *Rue des boutiques obscures*, p. 60.
[2] Daniel Parrochia, *op.cit.*, p. 16.
[3] Au début de l'ouvrage que Modiano a consacré à l'écrivain, en 1976 : *Emmanuel Berl, interrogatoire*.

d'eux-mêmes, sécheresse de cœur ou indifférence. Berl m'a appris [...] que le secret de la « durée » ne consistait pas à se ménager ou à s'endurcir[1]...

Ces êtres « d'outre-temps » n'ont aucune raison de sortir du silence, puisque c'est la discrétion, englobée dans la mémoire, qui assure leur pérennité. Ils semblent ainsi destinés à tenir le seul rôle qu'ils puissent endosser, celui de vestiges d'une époque révolue :

> La « pâte légère » [du temps] a l'impondérabilité des événements : du reste, elle ne semble pas avoir d'existence ou de substantialité en dehors du fantôme qui l'éprouve, c'est-à-dire perçoit et, dans le même temps, indissociablement se remémore, puisque son devenir est un revenir. Il ne s'agit donc pas ici d'une structuration indépendante des fantômes : elle est leur milieu, sinon leur substance[2].

Quelques rares personnages parviennent à briser cette chape, en revendiquant une existence réelle – qu'ils perdront de ce fait. L'unique moyen d'échapper à l'apathie, à la condition de fantôme, est l'affirmation de la singularité. Bien entendu, cette rupture place l'être dans une position périlleuse, puisqu'il perd, de ce fait, la sécurité que son retrait et son effacement lui dispensaient. Pour caractériser ce processus, nous retiendrons le terme de « révélation ontologique », moment au cours duquel l'être s'affirme brutalement. Cet accès à la connaissance ne permet pas, toutefois, de passer à un état supérieur. La cassure vient détruire l'édifice protecteur que le temps et l'oubli avaient érigé autour de l'individu.

Ainsi, lorsque Swing Troubadour et Serge Alexandre s'écrient respectivement : « Je suis la princesse de Lamballe » et « C'est mon père », ils acquièrent, pour la première et unique fois de leur vie, leur véritable stature humaine, passant brusquement du néant à la clarté de l'existence. En ce qui concerne Swing Troubadour, son affirmation vient justifier *a posteriori* la veulerie et la bassesse de son comportement,

---
[1] *Ibid.*, p. 10.
[2] D. Parrochia, *op.cit.*, p. 38.

puisque grâce à ce transfert d'identité, tous ses actes se trouvent légitimés. Il gagne ainsi une image de grand homme, toutefois limitée à la satisfaction de son amour-propre :

> Les gangsters et les vendus qui tiennent, en ce moment, le haut du pavé, LAMBALLE ne les épargnera pas. LAMBALLE frappe vite et fort. Nous obéirons à LAMBALLE les yeux fermés. LAMBALLE ne se trompe jamais. LAMBALLE est un type admirable. LAMBALLE, notre seul espoir[1]...

On peut raisonnablement parler de révélation ou d'« épiphanie » : le verbe *être* constitue, en effet, le noyau central des deux affirmations identitaires précédemment citées. Il renvoie tout aussi bien à la nature profonde des personnages – tout à la fois désignée et façonnée par la profération des paroles – qu'à leur nouvel état : l'espion affiche sa duplicité, et le feuilletoniste sa judéité. Par ces mots, ils anéantissent, en un instant, l'immunité qui les protégeait des agressions du monde extérieur – l'un se fait prendre en chasse, le second suit son père vers la déportation –, sans que l'on puisse parler, pour autant, de sacrifice volontaire. Il s'agit, avant tout, de l'ultime sursaut d'une conscience, ignorant les conséquences de cette manifestation ontologique – puisque la révélation est suivie d'une mise à mort –, mais soucieuse de clamer et de justifier son existence.

Il est remarquable que la revendication de l'ipséité se situe, dans les premières œuvres de Modiano, au moment où celui-ci liait l'introspection à l'exploration des années noires. Seule cette plongée au cœur des ténèbres permet aux protagonistes – et par là même à l'écrivain – de prendre la véritable mesure de leur identité. En effet, nous rappellerons qu'à cette époque le romancier projetait la plupart de ses inquiétudes et désarrois sur les êtres qu'il mettait en scène, dans le Paris de l'Occupation. Les origines familiales fournissent une parfaite justification de cette démarche : Modiano se sert du cadre historique afin d'exposer, par l'intermédiaire de ses héros, les deux points qui lui paraissent

---
[1] *La Ronde de nuit*, p. 122.

fondamentaux, à savoir la revendication de l'identité et le pardon accordé au père. Les deux « épiphanies » que nous venons d'étudier s'inscrivent ainsi pleinement dans la construction progressive d'un être confiant à ses livres la tâche délicate de l'insérer dans le monde (des) adulte(s).

L'œuvre va progressivement multiplier les notations personnelles et détails autobiographiques – délaissant les hallucinations et projections fantasmatiques – pour dessiner les contours d'une autofiction maîtrisée. Celle-ci témoigne de la maturité d'un créateur, capable d'affronter son passé, sans éprouver la nécessité de combattre les angoisses par la provocation.

Vers une autofiction ?

Trente années d'écriture auront dessiné l'évolution particulière d'une création polie par des moyens d'expression sans cesse renouvelés. L'affinement du style passe par l'abandon de la dérision, au bénéfice d'une émotion réelle. Modiano ne renonce pas pour autant à son projet – la compréhension du monde et la place qui doit être la sienne, à l'intérieur de celui-ci –, mais modifie sa perspective d'étude. Les éléments authentiques de sa biographie vont occuper une place plus importante, sans toutefois prendre le pas sur les ressources de l'imaginaire, formant un ensemble que l'on peut rattacher à la catégorie de l'autofiction. Si ce terme ne nous semble pas le plus adéquat pour caractériser les premières œuvres, il s'applique, de façon convaincante, à des textes comme *Livret de famille*, *De si braves garçons*, *Remise de peine*, *Fleurs de ruine*, *Chien de printemps* et, dans une moindre mesure, *Dora Bruder*.

Pour des raisons de commodité méthodologique, nous emploierons le terme *lato sensu*, à propos de la première trilogie[1], pour le réserver *stricto sensu* à la seconde. Ainsi, après avoir défini cette notion, et estimé sa pertinence pour la compréhension des textes de Modiano, nous pourrons montrer

---

[1] Nous suivons en cela la démarche de Thierry Laurent, *op.cit.*

que ce type de narration se révèle des plus satisfaisants pour la conquête de l'identité.

UNE OCCUPATION REVUE PAR LES LOIS DE L'AUTOFICTION

L'appellation est employée pour la première fois par Serge Doubrovsky, en 1977, pour caractériser son roman, *Fils*. Il s'agissait d'une fiction, d'événements et de faits strictement réels :

> si l'on veut, autofiction, d'avoir confié le langage d'une aventure à l'aventure du langage, hors sagesse et hors syntaxe du roman, traditionnel ou nouveau. Rencontre, fils des mots, allitérations, assonances, dissonances[1].

Deux conditions doivent être remplies pour que le texte satisfasse aux critères de l'autofiction : « le livre doit être clairement désigné comme « roman », c'est-à-dire comme histoire feinte ou fictive, et le même nom, de préférence conforme à l'état-civil, doit désigner l'auteur, le narrateur, le protagoniste[2]. » Publié la même année que *Fils*, *Livret de famille* répond parfaitement à ces principes de composition :

> Patrick Modiano [...] sait rendre indispensables les souvenirs imaginaires et les références administratives. S'il dit détester l'autobiographie, il n'en écrit pas moins, sur une musique de Pierre Loti ou de Georges Simenon, un subtil quatuor d'autofictions avec *Livret de famille*, *De si braves garçons*, *Remise de peine*, *Fleurs de ruine*[3].

---

[1] Serge Doubrovsky, *Fils*, Grasset, 1977. Cette définition se trouve sur le quatrième de couverture. Trois autres autofictions suivront : *Un amour de soi*, 1982, *Le Livre brisé*, 1989 et *L'Après-vivre*, 1994. Tous ces ouvrages sont publiés aux éditions Grasset.
[2] Jacques Lecarme, *Le Monde des livres*, vendredi 24 janvier 1997, p. VI.
[3] *Ibid.*

Thierry Laurent, dans son travail sur Modiano, inclut les premières œuvres de la trilogie. Ce classement trouve sa justification, selon lui, dans le fait que le romancier s'investit directement dans ses écrits, multipliant les identités transparentes pour relater des fictions proches de l'histoire familiale. Pourtant, la ténuité de l'intrigue et les identités fluctuantes ne permettent pas de tenir les deux premiers écrits pour des romans véritables, et l'on souscrirait plutôt à la dénomination d'« autofiction en mineur ». L'essentiel demeure cependant de réfléchir sur les apports du concept à l'étude de l'Occupation et à sa place dans la création littéraire. À cette fin, nous rappellerons quelques principes essentiels pour la compréhension des œuvres. Chacune des périodes romanesques de l'écrivain représente une version différente du même roman familial. Le recours à l'autofiction – au sens strict du terme – témoigne de l'évolution psychologique d'un homme, qui n'hésite plus à croiser les éléments de son histoire personnelle avec des faits inventés. La mise en fiction de la réalité, succédant à l'illusion romanesque, régissant les principes de l'histoire, selon les lois de la vraisemblance et de la réalité – plaisamment démystifiée dans les deux premiers ouvrages –, participe d'un seul et même projet littéraire : celui conduit et ordonné par l'« Enfant trouvé », comme nous avons pu le voir précédemment.

Jusqu'à *Fleurs de ruine*, chaque acte créatif a trouvé place dans ce système d'investigation de l'univers extérieur, qu'il fût familial, psychologique ou historique – et les trois aspects ont été souvent mêlés chez Modiano. Il semble intéressant de noter que c'est avec *Dora Bruder* – premier ouvrage depuis *Livret de famille* à ne pas se voir attribuer d'identification générique par l'auteur[1] – que l'écrivain s'affranchit pour la première fois des contraintes inhérentes au roman pour livrer ses émotions – ce texte se présente essentiellement comme une alternance de recherches et de spéculations sur le personnage de Dora, qui offrent la possibilité au narrateur d'évoquer ses expériences personnelles.

---

[1] Nous pensons aux catégories définies par l'histoire littéraire : « récit », « roman », « témoignage » etc.

Modiano n'a plus à recourir aux lois de la narration, puisqu'il peut, d'une part, affronter directement l'Histoire, et en second lieu revivre les angoisses de l'Occupation, par personnage interposé.

Auparavant, il aura fallu trente ans d'approches qui auront balayé tout le spectre de la narration romanesque, de l'hallucination à l'autofiction, afin de prendre toute la mesure d'une époque dominée par l'irrationalité. Ainsi, le dernier mode de récit que nous venons de citer marque moins un changement d'expression qu'un acte de maturité de l'écrivain. De *La Place de l'Étoile* jusqu'à *Fleurs de ruine*, les œuvres n'ont cessé de s'inscrire dans un cadre unique, celui d'une écriture thérapeutique, fondée sur l'idée de maîtrise des démons intérieurs. Il ne s'agit pas d'une autre réalité que celle des lois du roman, définies par Marthe Robert :

> Quels que soient ses visions du monde, ses présupposés idéologiques et ses partis pris esthétiques, le roman se résout en une entreprise essentiellement donquichottesque qui, tout en n'ayant que la réalité de ses chimères, n'en vise pas moins à peindre et à favoriser l'apprentissage de la vie[1].

Les différences entre les deux trilogies apparaissent donc comme des écarts superficiels, puisqu'elles ne modifient en rien le projet initial. Certes, quand l'écrivain quinquagénaire se réfère à des expériences précises, qui pour appartenir à l'espace romanesque renvoient bien souvent au vécu – on songera notamment à la rencontre avec Philippe de Pacheco, dans *Fleurs de ruine* –, le jeune Modiano ne dissocie pas le fantasme vraisemblable de la réalité explicitement controuvée : la visite du père à Bordeaux, dans *La Place de l'Étoile* ou *Les Boulevards de ceinture*, conduit presque immédiatement à un égarement de la raison. Pourtant, le traumatisme n'est en rien atténué dans les dernières œuvres. Il se trouve au contraire renforcé par l'épure stylistique et la sécheresse des notations. Il faut en effet attendre la fin de *Fleurs de ruine* pour trouver la mention explicite du malaise et de la culpabilité liés à

---

[1] *Op.cit.*, p. 67-68.

l'Occupation ; cette confession suit la dernière évocation de l'arrestation du père, et n'aurait pu trouver sa place dans la provocation jubilatoire de la première trilogie.

Le recours à l'autofiction apparaît moins comme une révolution narrative qu'une modification d'approche[1]. Dans les œuvres de jeunesse, c'était les éléments biographiques qui déterminaient le récit ; l'écrivain se projetait dans les personnages qu'il créait – ses figures déléguées – chargées de sonder le passé et d'en inventorier les spectres. À partir de *Livret de famille*, ces références ne se trouvent pas à l'origine de l'ouvrage, mais incluses dans le corps de celui-ci. Elles peuvent, de la sorte, devenir beaucoup plus précises : la rencontre – non romancée – de ses parents, la solitude du père dans le Paris nocturne de l'Occupation ou le baptême, au moment de la guerre de Corée – qui éveillait les échos douloureux du précédent conflit. Le livre suivant, loin d'appartenir à la catégorie de l'autofiction, constitue, sans doute, le roman le plus « classique » de Modiano, mais contient des informations reprises par le troisième texte « autofictif », *Remise de peine*. Dix ans avant la publication de cette seconde esquisse d'autobiographie, l'écrivain livrait au lecteur de la fiction un élément du décor de son enfance. On comparera ainsi les deux passages :

> Cette avenue ombragée d'arbres et qui monte en pente douce lui rappelle la rue de Jouy-en-Josas, qu'elle habitait quand elle était enfant. Elle revoit la maison, au coin de la rue du Docteur-Kurzenne, le saule pleureur,

---

[1] Dans un article consacré au caractère « autofictionnel » de *Remise de peine*, Jean-Michel Adam livre cette remarque, particulièrement éclairante pour la compréhension de l'œuvre modianienne : « La méthode de composition de Modiano déplace la relation vrai/faux dans l'autobiographie. Modiano « invente » un dépassement du souci autobiographique fondé, selon Michel Leiris, sur le refus de laisser travailler les faits par l'imagination et donc sur le refus du roman. Avec Modiano, l'imagination travaille la mémoire jusqu'à ce que survienne le roman [...]. » Jean-Michel Adam, « L'Autofiction dans *Remise de peine* », in *Autofictions et compagnie, Cahiers de recherches interdisciplinaires sur les textes modernes*, Université de Nanterre, n° 6, 1994, p. 55.

la barrière blanche, le temple protestant, en face, et tout en bas l'auberge Robin des Bois[1].

Dans *Remise de peine*, l'évocation est reprise presque mot pour mot – seule la rue retrouve son appellation véritable. Au moment où il fait paraître l'ouvrage lauréat du Goncourt, en 1978, l'auteur n'est pas encore tout à fait prêt à se confronter avec les heures mystérieuses et douloureuses de son enfance, et les intègre à une trame romanesque – qui l'expose beaucoup moins en tant que scripteur :

> La rue du Docteur-Dordaine avait un aspect villageois, surtout à son extrémité. [...] En face de la maison, une avenue en pente douce. Elle était bordée, à droite, par le temple protestant [...] ; à gauche, par une demeure longue et blanche à fronton, avec un grand jardin et un saule pleureur. Plus bas, mitoyenne de ce jardin, l'auberge Robin des Bois[2].

À la fin des années quatre-vingts, les ouvrages laissent une place de plus en plus importante à l'épanchement du « moi », qui vient se mêler au « je » de la fiction. Une production résolument autofictive telle que *Fleurs de ruine*, qui relate l'arrestation du père ou les débuts de l'écrivain dans la carrière littéraire, sur un mode narratif proche du documentaire, se présente sous la forme d'un témoignage. L'instance énonciatrice est proche de celle d'*Un cirque passe* et de *Du plus loin de l'oubli*, deux œuvres qui reçoivent la dénomination de « roman ». Lorsque l'on connaît l'adolescence de Modiano, il paraît difficile de ne pas voir un rappel autobiographique dans cette phrase du deuxième chapitre :

> J'ai presque oublié les visages de mes parents. J'avais habité quelque temps encore dans leur appartement, puis abandonné mes études et je gagnais de l'argent en vendant des livres anciens[3].

---

[1] *Rue des boutiques obscures*, p. 156.
[2] *Remise de peine*, p. 12-13.
[3] *Du plus loin de l'oubli*, p. 16.

Cette période précède de peu l'écriture de *La Place de l'Étoile*. Elle prend place entre le moment où le père dénonce son fils à la police – épisode relaté dans *Dora Bruder* – et son voyage à Vienne, évoqué dans *Voyage de noces* et *Dora Bruder*, qui fournira la trame du troisième chapitre de *La Place de l'Étoile*. Comme on le voit, l'écrivain réduit la distance qui le sépare de la réalité, pour l'intégrer à ses récits, en lui donnant une importance qu'elle n'avait jamais eue auparavant.

Il est intéressant de noter que les groupements d'œuvres fonctionnent sur un mode ternaire, chez Modiano. Nous avons déjà parlé des deux trilogies, qui obéissent à des principes savamment concertés. La première se caractérise par son aspect centrifuge : l'écrivain cherche à abolir la proximité d'une Occupation traumatisante – symboliquement, le départ, ou plutôt la fuite du « Clos-Foucré » marque la volonté de mettre à distance une période redoutée, et redoutable. La seconde trilogie est interrompue par un cycle de trois textes : un roman, un récit – *Chien de printemps* – et un roman. Le second triptyque se caractérise également par une idée de fuite, qui concerne cette fois-ci la forme – fuite du roman, cet ajointement d'épisodes mensongers, pour rejoindre l'ascèse, l'expression de l'ineffable – et non le contenu des ouvrages. En abandonnant – peut-être provisoirement – le roman, Modiano renonce à certains procédés convenus, qui offraient le mérite d'évacuer certaines interrogations trop personnelles, et de les escamoter derrière les facilités de la fiction, pour privilégier une démarche introspective, dont le prétexte est un tiers.

Si nous hésitons, d'ailleurs, à classer *Dora Bruder* dans une catégorie générique précise, c'est parce que l'ouvrage invalide toute typologie textuelle. Certes, il s'apparente à un journal, mais n'évite pas certains artifices de l'imaginaire, lorsque le narrateur évoque la détention de la jeune fille à la prison des Tourelles :

> À Drancy, dans la cohue, Dora retrouve son père, interné là depuis mars[1].

---

[1] *Dora Bruder*, p. 144.

Le père et sa fille n'ayant laissé aucun témoignage – le texte abonde en regrets sur la pauvreté des archives et le silence entourant la disparition de la jeune Dora –, cette mention s'apparente à une paralipse[1], objet de la spéculation romanesque de l'auteur. D'autre part, la focalisation sur des faits concrets, nullement réfutables, et dont l'accumulation tente de se substituer à la quête du néant, détourne l'ouvrage de l'autofiction, car l'on ne peut considérer que cet agrégat de dates constitue une *histoire* :

> La neige était tombée pour la première fois le 6 novembre 1941. L'hiver avait commencé par un froid vif, le 22 décembre. Le 29 décembre, la température avait encore baissé et les carreaux des fenêtres étaient couverts d'une légère couche de glace. À partir du 13 janvier, le froid était devenu sibérien[2].

De fait, il est possible de considérer que, sans prolonger le procédé de mise en abyme qui caractérisait *Le Journal des « Faux-Monnayeurs »*, l'œuvre joue le rôle du « journal » de *Voyage de noces*. Il présente l'écrivain, le motif de la rédaction[3], et le jugement rétrospectif : « Je me rends compte, aujourd'hui, qu'il m'a fallu écrire deux cents pages pour capter, inconsciemment, un vague reflet de la réalité[4]. » À l'époque, la peinture romanesque de l'Occupation se distinguait par le soin accordé au style – nulles considérations météorologiques, mais un récit de fuite, dans le crépuscule hivernal, particulièrement ciselé –, et surtout par l'absence de notations personnelles[5]. Après la lecture du *Mémorial*,

---

[1] Il s'agit d'un élément du récit, ou de la composition de celui-ci, qui, passé sous silence, altère le sens ou la compréhension de la narration.
[2] *Dora Bruder*, p. 91.
[3] Après la lecture du *Mémorial*, de Serge Klarsfeld, Modiano avait décidé d'entreprendre un roman pour réagir contre « la nuit, l'inconnu, l'oubli, le néant tout autour [de Dora]. » *Ibid.*, p. 54.
[4] *Ibid.*, p. 55.
[5] À cet égard, le dénouement de *Fleurs de ruine* fonctionne selon un procédé inverse, avec un retour à la réalité, marqué par l'emploi du « je » auctorial : « Le printemps est précoce, cette année. Il a fait très chaud ces 18 et 19 mars 1990. [...] Tout à l'heure, j'étais assis sur un banc, à proximité [d'une] statue. » *Fleurs de ruine*, p. 140.

Modiano se trouvait dans l'impossibilité de ne pas dissocier les deux plans de la réalité et de la fiction, comme il sera capable de le faire dans l'autofiction suivante.

Chez l'écrivain, l'autofiction joue davantage le rôle d'un révélateur que celui d'un instrument de l'imagination, abusant du réel pour le placer sous l'autorité du récit. La remarque suivante de Thierry Laurent[1] caractérise bien l'originalité du projet modianien :

> L'histoire d'une vie ne peut être de l'ordre de la copie conforme, car son sens n'existe nulle part et doit être inventé, construit. L'« implant fictif » que l'expérience analytique propose au sujet comme sa biographie véridique est vrai quand il « marche », c'est-à-dire s'il permet à l'être de mieux vivre ; inexact ou incomplet, voire nocif, il est rejeté. Ainsi, l'autofiction postanalytique n'est pas forcément plus vraie que l'autoportrait classique, mais plus riche, plus féconde.

Valable pour la plupart des œuvres qui appartiennent à la catégorie de l'autofiction, cette analyse convient tout particulièrement aux deux premières, *Livret de famille* et *De si braves garçons*. Les chapitres, relativement autonomes – même si l'on peut considérer que la petite fille, évoquée dans le chapitre d'ouverture et de clôture, assure la continuité d'un cycle – dessinent en creux un itinéraire personnel, grâce au chevauchement de la rêverie et de la vérité apprêtée. Les trois autofictions suivantes affinent ce processus : c'est moins le désir de se raconter qui importe que la découverte de sentiments profonds. Cette évolution constitue l'aspect le plus remarquable du second ensemble.

Construire l'identité.

Les premiers textes de Modiano recherchaient une fusion presque totale entre le scripteur et le personnage. Celui-ci, véritable coquille vide, n'avait pas d'autre fonction que celle

---

[1] *Op.cit.*, p. 33.

de héraut, chargé de relayer les colères et les doutes. Le protagoniste évoluait dans un monde qui empruntait à l'Histoire ses éléments les plus importants pour mieux les recomposer – selon les inflexions libres d'une sensibilité exacerbée. Le mélange des lieux ou des époques tendait à la restitution subjective de l'Occupation et des années postérieures. Cette peinture très particulière entraînait la dilution de l'autobiographie dans la pure fantaisie ; l'Occupation devenait une sorte de zone-écran, s'interposant entre l'écrivain et le monde, pour constituer un obstacle à l'élaboration de l'identité. L'échec de cette projection se traduisait par la disparition symbolique du héros, vaincu par les forces qu'il avait convoquées, à la fin des ouvrages.

La pause romanesque, qui marque un effacement relatif de l'Occupation – de *Villa triste* à *Vestiaire de l'enfance* – permet au créateur d'explorer d'autres voies, sans perdre pour autant le contact avec la période. Le recul, qu'explique peut-être l'expérience de l'âge adulte, favorise un renouvellement complet de l'approche. *Remise de peine*, qui établit une sorte de pont entre les romans précédents et la seconde trilogie, va ainsi essayer de retrouver l'atmosphère ambiguë et les premières interrogations liées à l'évocation des années sombres – dans la perspective mise en évidence par Thierry Laurent :

> « Andrée fréquentait la bande de la rue Lauriston. » Cette phrase m'avait frappé. [...] Cette femme qui nous intimidait, mon frère et moi, avec sa frange, ses taches de son, ses yeux verts, ses cigarettes et ses mystérieux coups de téléphone, elle me semblait plus proche de nous, brusquement. Roger Vincent et la petite Hélène avaient l'air de bien connaître aussi cette « bande de la rue Lauriston ». Par la suite, j'ai surpris encore ce nom dans leur conversation, et je me suis habitué à sa sonorité. Quelques années plus tard, je l'ai entendu dans la bouche de mon père, mais j'ignorais que « la bande de la rue Lauriston » me hanterait si longtemps[1].

Cette anamnèse précède de peu un autre souvenir, celui de l'arrestation et de la libération du père, par Eddy Pagnon. La

---

[1] *Remise de peine*, p. 87-88.

fiche de renseignements que Modiano joint à la suite – et qui annonce les investigations « policières » de *Dora Bruder* –, constitue la somme d'informations la plus importante sur l'épisode – déjà évoqué deux fois avant cette mention. On y apprend par le menu les différentes activités du personnage, avant que la forme narrative ne reprenne ses droits, sans pour autant se mettre au service de l'histoire. Celle-ci se trouve suspendue afin que l'écrivain expose le *curriculum vitae* de l'ancien collaborateur de son père. Nous quittons, à ce moment, le domaine de l'autofiction proprement dite : le romancier entre de plain-pied dans le récit, afin d'établir un point de contact entre les périodes :

> À l'époque où j'habitais square de Graisivaudan, je voulais élucider cette énigme, en essayant de retrouver les traces de Pagnon [...]. De 1937 à 1939, il avait été employé de garage dans le XVIIIe arrondissement [...].
>
> J'avais traîné du côté de la Porte des Lilas, dans l'espoir qu'on se souvenait encore d'un agent des automobiles Simca qui habitait par là, vers 1939. [...] Et le garage du XVIIIe arrondissement où travaillait Pagnon ? Si je parvenais à le découvrir, [...] je saurais enfin tout ce qu'il fallait savoir, et que mon père savait, lui[1].

Modiano énumère ensuite une trentaine de garages – procédé qui traduit un changement notable de perspective. La rêverie s'efface devant l'exposé des faits. Seule la vérité et l'approche sereine de l'Occupation paraissent susceptibles de lever les craintes et inhibitions. L'écrivain semble annoncer les procédés de *Dora Bruder* : le scripteur livre l'état des recherches préparatoires au récit, de sorte que celui-ci devient l'histoire de son écriture. En y ajoutant toutes ses impressions et sensations, il atteint ainsi à l'émotion, qui lui permet ainsi un contact direct avec l'Occupation. D'autre part, cette approche heuristique favorise la sympathie[2] avec l'être dont on suit la

---

[1] *Remise de peine*, p. 118-121.
[2] Au sens étymologique de « participation aux sentiments, à la souffrance d'autrui. »

piste, puisque c'est de la rencontre avec le témoin, qu'il s'agisse d'un être, d'un lieu ou d'un objet, que naît la compréhension de l'époque à laquelle ils sont associés.

Les œuvres de la seconde trilogie réserveront également une large place aux témoignages de l'auteur, qui réunira les deux plans historiques – Occupation et période contemporaine – grâce à la connexion assurée par des sensations et des impressions communes. Dans le dernier ouvrage en date, Modiano recourt fréquemment à ce procédé, mettant en parallèle les désarrois de la jeune fille avec ses tourments d'adolescent. Ainsi, la fuite de Dora se trouve immédiatement associée au souvenir d'une des fugues du jeune homme :

> Qu'est-ce qui nous décide à faire une fugue ? Je me souviens de la mienne le 18 janvier 1960, à une époque qui n'avait pas la noirceur de décembre 1941. [...] Il semble que ce qui vous pousse brusquement à la fugue, c'est un jour de froid et de grisaille qui vous rend encore plus vive la solitude et vous fait sentir encore plus fort qu'un étau se resserre[1].

Nul égocentrisme dans ces lignes, mais l'unique souci de « comprendre » – au sens claudélien de « prendre avec », de réunir l'autre, son être ou ses passions, avec soi –, sans que les expériences se trouvent placées sur un plan identique. L'arpentage des vestiges participe de la même posture, à la fois intellectuelle et sentimentale, qu'il s'agisse d'errer à la lisière du périphérique pour recenser les garages, ou de rechercher les appartements occupés par un témoin[2], un garant du passé, capable de rendre celui-ci un peu moins brumeux.

La « com-préhension » de l'Occupation passerait donc par la fréquentation de ses incertaines reliques, capables de provoquer une « coïncidence d'âmes » : nous sommes loin des rodomontades d'un Schlemilovitch, dont les déclarations, et surtout le rôle joué dans le récit, rendaient plus opaque la perception de la réalité. En 1997, Patrick Modiano clôt le cycle commencé trente ans plus tôt, qui jetait les bases d'une

---

[1] *Dora Bruder*, p. 59.
[2] Par exemple, l'ancien domicile de Rigaud, dans *Voyage de noces*.

interrogation sur la faute paternelle, la culpabilité familiale et personnelle et l'identité juive. L'étude systématique de ces trois questions complétera le portrait de l'écrivain.

L'Occupation : de l'interrogation à l'interrogatoire.

Poids de la faute paternelle, responsabilité individuelle et ambivalence de la relation avec Israël : ces trois thèmes reviennent, de façon lancinante, dans une œuvre dont ils constituent la basse continue. Leur exposé adoptera toutes les modulations de la forme narrative, sans qu'ils perdent jamais de leur acuité ; en effet, on les retrouve tels quels dans la première et la dernière œuvre du romancier.

Il paraît intéressant de montrer comment la construction de l'identité s'appuie presque uniquement sur ces trois aspects du passé. À cette fin, ils peuvent être vidés de leur signification ou, au contraire, survalorisés, sans qu'ils perdent jamais de leur pertinence. Le statut particulier octroyé par l'histoire familiale – de façon abrupte : comment *être* un écrivain juif, fils d'un collaborateur, fruit de l'union clandestine d'un juif italo-égyptien et d'une réfugiée hollandaise ? – implique, en effet, le contrôle de sa légitimité. Au début de sa carrière, Modiano pratique cette expertise de façon délibérément choquante, afin de mieux se protéger contre la violence qu'elle génère[1].

---

[1] Le livre d'entretiens avec Emmanuel Berl devient ainsi un « interrogatoire », qui dicte sa forme à l'ouvrage :
« Emmanuel Berl : – Mais...je...
– Inutile de nier, j'ai fait mon enquête. » *Op.cit.*, p. 52.
La postface de l'ouvrage commence par ces phrases : « C'est le moment où l'on arrête l'interrogatoire parce qu'on note chez l'inculpé des signes de nervosité et de lassitude. [...] Une déposition d'environ deux cents pages :

L'inventaire des origines est un préalable à la connaissance de soi, même si « l'on éprouve une sorte de doute : un interrogatoire ne suffit pas à rendre compte des méandres d'une vie[1]. »

Les origines juives : de la bouffonnerie à l'acceptation.

Selon les lois de Nuremberg, Patrick Modiano n'est pas juif, puisque la transmission de la « judéité » passe par la mère. Cette précision d'ordre administratif n'a jamais modifié son jugement. Modiano se sent juif, et proclame ses origines. Si les œuvres de jeunesse paraissent aussi peu clémentes à l'égard de ses coreligionnaires, cette acrimonie est à mettre en rapport avec la déception éprouvée face au radicalisme des sionistes. Tout au long de ses romans, l'écrivain va retenir d'autres aspects de l'identité juive, qui vont peu à peu se substituer à la vision caricaturale de *La Place de l'Étoile*. En trente années d'écriture, il aura ainsi appris à accepter son lignage, en excluant la farce.

Nous nous proposons d'examiner cette question complexe en cinq temps. Nous nous intéresserons, tout d'abord, au statut du juif et aux persécutions subies durant la guerre – dont l'évocation nécessitera un développement de fond sur l'idée de fuite et de protection –, puis aux diverses stratégies de survie adoptées par les victimes. De fait, c'est l'itinéraire du père qui se trouve évoqué en creux – attitude qui fut violemment condamnée, dans les premiers écrits de Modiano. Les romans postérieurs doivent être lus comme autant de tentatives pour comprendre le personnage, actes de

---

j'aimerais savoir combien il faut de temps, rue des Saussaies ou quai des Orfèvres, pour en venir à bout. » *Ibid.*, p. 133.
Bien évidemment, ces notations sont à prendre au second degré, mais n'en paraissent pas moins révélatrices de l'état d'esprit de Modiano, lorsqu'il tâche de comprendre comment un juif cultivé a pu tenir la plume du Maréchal et écrire des maximes telles que « La terre, elle, ne ment pas » – ce qui ne manque pas de saveur, lorsque l'on sait que Berl n'avait jamais que fort rarement quitté Neuilly ou la capitale avant la guerre.
[1] *Ibid.*

tendresse qui semblent, d'autre part, indispensables à la connaissance de soi.

Le seul témoignage direct que le romancier ait pu obtenir à propos des lois raciales et de l'oppression des juifs, pendant l'Occupation, est celui de son père – traqué à Paris, réfugié dans un manège près du bois de Boulogne, il n'en continua pas moins ses activités commerciales, et surtout se refusa à porter l'étoile jaune. Plusieurs fois arrêté puis libéré par la Gestapo, il survécut d'expédients jusqu'à la Libération.

L'évocation de ce climat d'angoisse et de menaces sourdes, qui impose une stricte réduction des déplacements, a particulièrement marqué le jeune Modiano. Celui-ci semble voir, dans le contrôle des mouvements, la traduction physique de la dictature. Le Paris qu'il décrit, à l'espace arbitrairement géométrisé par les différents secteurs et zones – quadrillage qui évolue au fil des attentats et des mesures de rétorsion –, est une capitale dans laquelle il paraît presque impossible de se mouvoir. Ainsi, à l'exclusion des deux premiers textes, où les déplacements incessants des deux héros apparaissent comme une projection de leur instabilité psychique – « trajet » purement virtuel pour le premier, et erratique pour le second[1] – , les romans présentent des personnages pétrifiés, enserrés dans le maillage policier de la ville, devenue brusquement étrangère. Cette oppression morale trouve corrélativement son équivalence dans la rigueur du climat. Les traques et les fugues ont lieu en hiver, dans une solitude glacée. La neige rend les déplacements difficiles ; une pesanteur s'installe, qui accentue la menace et rend la disparition indispensable ; la ville si familière change d'aspect, devenant un espace mortifère qu'il convient de quitter au plus tôt.

---

[1] Swing Troubadour n'est pas juif, ou à tout le moins ne revendique pas sa judéité.

Un corps en fuite

Dans l'œuvre de Modiano, l'idée de fuite représente une constante, un invariant caractéristique. Épié par une puissance occulte, par des forces souterraines, insinuantes[1], le clandestin doit quitter son cadre familier pour garantir sa sécurité. Dès lors, l'idée d'un refuge situé loin de Paris, à proximité d'une frontière, devient l'unique pensée. Le lieu désiré se trouve à l'écart du monde, réservé aux seuls êtres traqués, qui pourront ainsi recouvrer une identité qui leur était déniée, jusqu'à ce moment. De fait cette obsession de l'espace forclos, abritant un petit nombre d'élus, s'inscrit dans la configuration mentale qui postule l'agrégation à un groupe comme l'unique possibilité de survie.

Pour l'écrivain – et ses personnages –, l'Occupation est vécue sur le mode du déchirement intérieur. Celle-ci, tout en permettant un contact direct avec l'identité profonde, détruit, dans le même temps, toutes les protections que l'individu avait érigées contre les agressions du monde. Les persécutions renvoient ainsi le juif à sa nature primitive, puisque le propre d'un génocide est de programmer la destruction d'un individu au nom de son essence, de sorte que l'interrogation identitaire se trouve momentanément levée, mais ont pour effet d'exclure celui-ci d'une communauté extérieure, dans laquelle il tentait de se fondre. De façon lapidaire, nous pourrions formuler cette question complexe comme suit : l'être modianien se trouve réduit à une vie infraliminaire, désespérant de s'agréger à un cercle susceptible de valider cette existence. La guerre apparaît alors comme le moment décisif, où l'être sort de son néant originel pour prendre place aux côtés des vivants – puisque l'angoisse conduit inéluctablement à la reviviscence. Pourtant, celle-ci sera de courte durée, car cette mise à jour de l'être

---

[1] On se reportera au passage suivant, qui nous paraît particulièrement représentatif de ce climat d'angoisse diffuse : « Un jour, à l'aube, le téléphone sonna et une voix inconnue appela mon père par son véritable nom. On raccrocha aussitôt. Ce fut ce jour-là qu'il décida de fuir Paris. » *Livret de famille*, p. 208.

révèle *ipso facto* sa fragilité. Poursuivi, pris en chasse, il n'aura plus d'autre désir que de retrouver l'obscurité qu'il entendait combattre.

À l'exception d'*Une jeunesse*, récit narré à la troisième personne – qui implique donc une mise à distance de l'histoire et des personnages –, l'intégralité de l'œuvre s'inscrit, d'un point de vue structurel, dans le schème que nous venons d'exposer. L'acquisition de l'identité implique la reconnaissance des racines juives – et partant le côté le plus tragique de l'histoire de ce peuple : les pogromes et les persécutions – et met conséquemment l'individu en situation de danger.

Chez Modiano, l'interrogation sur l'être et le non-être ne donne lieu à aucune résolution : l'existence précédant la révélation de l'identité est purement végétative, proche de celle qui suit la connaissance de la nature profonde, cette judéité source de tous les maux. Chaque texte de Modiano propose ainsi le même cheminement. Sorti des ténèbres, de sa nullité primitives, le personnage prend place dans une communauté (Raphaël, bien sûr, mais également Swing Troubadour, Serge Alexandre, Lacombe Lucien ou les narrateurs de *Quartier perdu, Dimanches d'août, Un cirque passe* ou *Du plus loin de l'oubli*) ; rapidement poursuivi pour ce qu'il est (dans les textes de la trilogie) ou ce qu'il fait (dans les autres romans), il n'a d'autre ressource que la fuite et l'oubli. Un grand nombre de critiques ont noté l'aspect filandreux du dénouement des intrigues. Les romans s'achèvent, en effet, sur un aveu d'ignorance – *Rue des boutiques obscures* –, de désarroi suite à un abandon – *Villa triste* ou *Dimanches d'août* – ou de mélancolie profonde : *Quartier perdu, Voyage de noces, Un cirque passe* ou *Du plus loin de l'oubli*. La plupart des œuvres adoptant une narration rétrospective, il convient de remarquer que l'histoire est contée par un narrateur-fantôme, renvoyé, après les événements, dans les limbes qu'il s'était efforcé de quitter. Le meilleur exemple demeure celui du narrateur de *Vestiaire de l'enfance*, anesthésié par la bienfaisante apathie des journées éternellement recommencées de l'île dans laquelle il travaille – qui semble décrite sur le modèle de Palma de Majorque.

Les textes concernant l'Occupation prennent place dans cette configuration, privilégiant l'idée d'enfermement. Après la révélation traumatisante de l'identité, le personnage n'aura de cesse de vouloir se mettre à couvert ; la fuite du corps conduit à un corps en fuite. L'être trouvera son refuge en province (Cannes, dans *Voyage de noces*, ou la campagne profonde abritant les amours de Lucien et de France, à la fin de *Lacombe Lucien*), à l'étranger (la Suisse de *Rue des boutiques obscures* ou l'Autriche, à la fin de *La Place de l'Étoile*) ou dans les espaces protégés de la capitale : l'hôtel des *Boulevards de ceinture* ou les appartements dans lesquels le père vient se tapir, dans *Livret de famille* :

> Il s'était terré pendant un mois 14 rue Chalgrin, sans oser sortir une seule fois de la maison, parce qu'il n'avait aucun papier et qu'il craignait les rafles[1].

L'essentiel demeure de se mettre à couvert, d'accepter la claustration comme la garantie d'une existence minimale, au sein de l'*amnion*, la cavité protectrice qui préserve l'intégrité. On se reportera avec intérêt à deux extraits de *Voyage de noces*. Le premier évoque le repli d'Ingrid et de Rigaud, dans leur maison au bord de la mer :

> « Au début, ils tenaient beaucoup à nous inviter à leurs fêtes, a-t-elle dit. Alors nous éteignions toutes les lumières du bungalow et nous faisions comme si nous étions absents.
> – Nous restions dans le noir. Une fois, ils sont venus pour nous chercher. Nous nous étions réfugiés sous les pins, à côté... »
> [...]
> «Le danger est passé, a-t-il dit. Il vaut mieux rester dans le noir. Ils risqueraient de voir la lumière, de la plage. » [...]
> Nous sommes restés un long moment silencieux, sur nos transats, dans l'obscurité, comme si nous nous cachions[2].

---

[1] *Op.cit.*, p. 202.

Ce comportement reproduit celui que le couple avait adopté, vingt années auparavant, au moment des rafles, dans les hôtels de la Côte d'Azur :

> Des hommes guidés par la tache sombre pénétraient dans le hall et ils allaient se livrer à une descente de police. [...] Il serrait le passe-partout dans sa main. Dès qu'il les entendrait ouvrir la porte de la chambre voisine de la leur, il réveillerait Ingrid et ils se glisseraient dans la chambre suivante. Et ce jeu du chat et de la souris se poursuivrait à travers toutes les chambres de l'étage. Les autres n'avaient vraiment aucune chance de les retrouver, car ils seraient blottis tous les deux au fond des ténèbres du « Provençal[1] ».

S'il s'extrait de ce cocon, le personnage s'expose immédiatement aux regards et à la violence des autres. Serge Alexandre, qui clame sa filiation, ou Dora Bruder, qui s'enfuit du Saint-Cœur-de-Marie, perdent immédiatement le bénéfice de leur enfermement « amniotique ». La jeune Dora peut alors faire l'expérience de l'adversité – à laquelle elle s'était jusqu'à ce moment soustraite, comme la plupart des personnages de Modiano :

> Cette ville de décembre 1941, son couvre-feu, ses soldats, sa police, tout lui était hostile et voulait sa perte. À seize ans, elle avait le monde entier contre elle, sans qu'elle sache pourquoi[2].

Jusqu'à l'ouvrage consacré à la jeune Bruder, l'acharnement policier ou l'évocation de la précarité de l'individu, sous l'Occupation, relevaient essentiellement de la narration romanesque. Modiano parlait certes de rafles ou de persécutions, mais celles-ci s'inscrivaient, avant tout, dans une atmosphère générale d'anxiété diffuse. Avec *Dora Bruder*, œuvre dans laquelle l'écrivain proclame sa compassion pour

---

[2] *Voyage de noces*, p. 41-43.
[1] *Ibid.*, p. 78-79.
[2] *Dora Bruder*, p. 80.

les martyrs du nazisme, l'horreur quotidienne se trouve restituée avec la sèche minutie du chroniqueur :

> Ce dernier mois de l'année fut la période la plus noire, la plus étouffante que Paris ait connue depuis le début de l'Occupation. [...] Il y eut la rafle de sept cents juifs français le 12 décembre ; le 15 décembre, l'amende de un milliard de francs imposée aux juifs. [...]. Leur changement de domicile devait être déclaré au commissariat dans les vingt-quatre heures, et il leur était désormais interdit de se déplacer hors du département de la Seine.
>
> Dès le 1ᵉʳ décembre, les Allemands avaient prescrit un couvre-feu dans le XVIIIᵉ arrondissement. Plus personne n'y pouvait pénétrer après six heures du soir[1].

Le lyrisme rageur des débuts a laissé la place à un méticuleux recensement de faits. Bouleversé par la lecture du *Mémorial*[2], qui met l'écrivain au « contact » de la jeune Dora, Modiano donne une nouvelle orientation à ses écrits. La forme romanesque semble un support peu adapté à l'épanchement de l'émotion, lorsqu'on se trouve confronté à l'horreur. Seul un travail analytique, fondé sur la mémoire, apparaît recevable. Plus de deux ans avant la parution de ce livre, dans un article à valeur programmatique, Modiano indiquait le tour nouveau qu'il entendait donner aux ouvrages à venir :

> Après la parution du [livre] de Serge Klarsfeld, je me suis senti quelqu'un d'autre. Je savais maintenant quel genre de malaise j'éprouvais.
>
> Et d'abord, j'ai douté de la littérature [...]. J'ai voulu suivre l'exemple que m'avait donné Serge Klarsfeld. [...] Ces parents et cette jeune fille qui se sont perdus la veille du jour de l'an 1942, et qui plus

---

[1] *Ibid.*, p. 57-58. La dernière indication est reprise telle quelle dans *Voyage de noces*. Ces circonstances décideront de la fugue d'Ingrid.

[2] « Des noms, des prénoms, des dates de naissance. Parfois, la ville de cette naissance était indiquée. Rien de plus. Et cela pour quatre-vingt mille hommes, femmes, enfants. C'était le *Mémorial de la déportation des Juifs de France*, qu'avait publié Serge Klarsfeld, en 1978. Il l'avait dressé tout seul, en déchiffrant souvent avec peine des listes sur du papier pelure. » Article cité, paru dans *Libération*, 15 novembre 1994.

tard, disparaissaient tous les trois dans les convois vers Auschwitz, ne cessent de me hanter.

Grâce à Serge Klarsfeld, je saurai peut-être quelque chose de Dora Bruder[1].

La suspicion dans laquelle Modiano tient le roman, inapte à transmettre un témoignage, invalide, en grande partie, la démarche commencée avec *La Place de l'Étoile*. L'implant de la fiction se révélait décevant, puisque le maelström de l'Histoire n'était qu'un auxiliaire du récit. Avec *Dora Bruder*, l'écrivain entame une nouvelle période littéraire, se servant de l'autofiction, l'annexant à son projet, fondé sur la restitution de la mémoire – postulant l'abandon du mode nostalgique, quelque peu systématique[2] – pour privilégier le réalisme et la sincérité[3].

Enfin, il lui a sans doute paru sacrilège de construire un récit fictif à partir des informations qu'il recueillait. À l'époque de *Voyage de noces*, il pouvait spéculer sur le comportement et les réactions de la jeune Dora, et faire de sa fugue le point de départ d'un roman – en donnant à celle-ci un dénouement heureux. Quatre années plus tard, après avoir pris connaissance de la déportation des Bruder, le créateur se trouve rejoint par l'Histoire, qui rend impossible, par sa violence, l'idée même de narration. « La terrible sensation de vide[4] », qui suit la contemplation de chaque photographie insérée entre les colonnes de noms, est purement et simplement indicible. Après la lecture du *Mémorial*, l'écrivain se trouvait confronté à la question posée à chaque artiste désireux de *témoigner* de

---

[1] *Ibid.*
[2] Procédé entériné par la presse dite « grand public », qui a promu le style sous le cliché facile de « petite-musique-de-Modiano », réduction publicitaire particulièrement peu pertinente pour rendre compte du travail de l'écrivain.
[3] Il faut sans doute attribuer la désaffection du public pour cette dernière œuvre au radicalisme de Modiano. Malgré un accueil critique fort chaleureux, *Dora Bruder* est le premier ouvrage de l'auteur à ne pas être entré sur la liste des meilleures ventes.
[4] *Ibid.*

l'innommable[1]. De fait, comment l'anéantissement d'un peuple – destruction qui, par nature, échappe aux lois de la raison – pourrait-il trouver sa place dans un processus codifié, fût-il celui de la logique narrative ? Ce constat se trouvait déjà implicitement accepté par le jeune Modiano : *La Place de l'Étoile*, seul ouvrage entièrement articulé autour de la *Shoah*, est un texte totalement irréductible à un principe narratif cohérent – et à ce titre étranger à toute idée d'ordre romanesque. L'horreur ne peut se raconter sur fond de « petite musique ». Deux évocations paraissent, seules, acceptables[2] : une écriture furieuse – au sens premier –, plongeant au cœur du chaos pour en adopter la forme, ou la mise à distance de l'impensable, au moyen de l'ascèse. La mise en correspondance du personnage de Dora avec celui du jeune Modiano, qui, sans connaître son destin tragique, a vécu des expériences semblables à celle de la jeune juive, au cœur de la même ville, constitue, à notre sens, la dernière étape de son parcours identitaire.

« COMMENT PEUT-ON ETRE JUIF ? »

Les romans de Modiano peuvent être considérés comme les jalons d'un parcours houleux avec le judaïsme et l'identité juive. Dès les premières œuvres – qui font état de l'impossibilité d'effectuer un choix entre l'identité française et l'héritage juif – à la longue plainte de *Dora Bruder*, chaque roman pose la question de l'acceptation des origines. Nous nous proposons d'ordonner notre réflexion autour de deux axes principaux. Dans un premier temps, nous nous intéresserons au Modiano lecteur du Sartre de *Réflexions sur la question juive* ;

---

[1] Nous pensons notamment à Samuel Fuller, cinéaste œuvrant pour l'armée américaine, en 1945. Celui-ci s'était longuement interrogé sur le droit moral de filmer la libération des camps, et surtout sur la validité d'un tel acte. Son document cinématographique exclut finalement toute prise de vue directe d'Auschwitz et de Buchenwald.
[2] Elles constituent, au moment où nous écrivons ces lignes, les deux termes de l'œuvre.

nous pourrons alors examiner les différentes façons de régler cette lancinante interrogation.

La Place de l'Étoile consacre une place importante à la position de Sartre sur l'identité juive. Selon le philosophe, le juif n'existe pas, à proprement parler, et représente, avant tout, la somme des regards et des idées antisémites projetés sur lui :

> Ce sont nos yeux qui lui [au juif] renvoient l'image inacceptable qu'il veut se dissimuler. Ce sont nos paroles et nos gestes – toutes nos paroles et tous nos gestes, notre antisémitisme, mais tout aussi bien notre libéralisme condescendant – qui l'ont empoisonné jusqu'aux moelles ; c'est nous qui le contraignons à se choisir juif, soit qu'il se fuie, soit qu'il se revendique, c'est nous qui l'avons acculé au dilemme de l'inauthenticité ou de l'authenticité juive[1].

Cette assertion critique se trouve proférée par Freud, à la fin du roman. Ce personnage, qui assimile les revendications de l'identité juive à un délire à caractère hallucinatoire – puisque « LE JUIF N'EXISTE PAS[2] » – entérine le « non-choix » du narrateur-écrivain. Ce dernier se résigne au *status quo*, refusant de trancher la question, au terme d'une minutieuse exploration des formes de la judéité, dans le temps et dans l'espace, entre l'appartenance à une communauté martyre et l'immersion au sein de la nation française.

Auparavant, Schlemilovitch a fait l'expérience de toutes les formes de persécutions et outrages qui ponctuent deux mille ans d'histoire. La récusation de Sartre – cité par Freud, qui postule l'oubli, sinon l'amnésie [sic] dans un souci de paix de l'âme – représente une sorte de coda dérisoire à la longue mélopée, clamée tout au long du roman, qui recense toutes les atteintes à l'intégrité du juif en tant que représentant d'une race, d'une *essence*, et non comme représentation de la haine antisémite. Les exils et les génocides, bien réels, concernaient, selon Modiano, des individus tout aussi réels, subissant les meurtrissures dans leur chair et leur sang, au nom de préceptes

---

[1] *Op.cit.*, p. 164-165.
[2] *La Place de l'Étoile*, p. 150.

religieux et politiques aussi peu virtuels que possible. La recherche des fondements d'une identité juive, floue et difficilement cernable, n'équivaut pas à sa négation, mais bien à la quête d'une légitimité, indispensable à l'élaboration d'une conscience.

Une grande partie de l'œuvre prend l'aspect d'un bréviaire antisartrien, dans lequel le romancier prend systématiquement le contre-pied du philosophe, par l'usage de la parodie, le renversement des propositions ou le recours à la dérision. Le personnage du père constitue ainsi un démenti formel à la thèse du regard d'autrui, seul créateur de la figure du juif. Selon Raphaël, le goût du spectacle et du nomadisme paraît – malheureusement – consubstantiel à l'« ethnie ». Son père, qui en représente la synthèse remarquable, fournit un excellent exemple, affichant une certaine dilection pour les étoffes bariolées et le « funambulisme[1] » cosmopolite :

> Mon père portait un complet d'alpaga bleu Nil, une chemise à raies vertes, une cravate rouge et des chaussures d'astrakan. [...] Nous allâmes boire quelques gin-fizz au « Fouquet's », au « Relais Plaza », au bar du « Meurice », du «Saint-James et d'Albany », de l'« Élysée-Park », du « George V », du « Lancaster ». C'était ses provinces à lui [...]. Né à Caracas, d'une famille juive sefarad, il quitta précipitamment l'Amérique pour échapper aux policiers du dictateur des îles Galapagos, dont il avait séduit la fille[2].

Ce portrait, qui correspond aux pires caricatures, présente la fourberie et la duplicité comme des composants organiques de la race, intrinsèquement liés à chaque enfant d'Israël. Âgé de vingt ans, Modiano renvoie alors aux antisémites l'image volontairement provocante d'un être dont la nature et le comportement sont déterminés par l'origine. De fait, l'évocation renvoie dos à dos les conceptions défendues par les théoriciens situés des deux extrémités de l'échiquier politique, puisque le fait même de penser la question juive – fût-ce pour soutenir la cause de ce peuple – exclut déjà

---

[1] *Ibid.*, p. 40.
[2] *Ibid.*, p. 39-41.

l'israélite du champ de la normalité. En premier lieu, le juif ne constitue pas seulement une vue de l'esprit, puisqu'il semble programmé pour l'exhibition et la rapine – n'en déplaise à Sartre, il existe donc bien un *caractère* juif. D'autre part, la conformité immédiate du personnage au paradigme forgé par les nationalistes invalide, par son outrance, l'idée même de déterminisme attaché à l'origine. Toute démarche proposant une approche intellectuelle du problème juif ne peut, eu égard à ses fondements théoriques, que désigner le juif comme une altérité – justiciable donc d'un traitement particulier –, avec les conséquences historiques que l'on connaît.

La nécessité de varier les aspects de la démonstration peut conduire le romancier à adopter la thèse adverse. Dans ce cas, le développement prend la forme d'une réduction par l'absurde – entérinant la position de Modiano. Ainsi, Raphaël, lors de son séjour chez la Marquise, instruite par des siècles d'antisémitisme culturel, se voit immédiatement associé au stéréotype du Levantin naturellement pervers et concupiscent, « rêvant de ruiner toute la paysannerie française et d'enjuiver le Cantal[1] » –, et, à ce titre, apte à satisfaire les perversions de cette femme :

> Vous êtes juif ? Bon, parfait ! Je suppose que vous aimeriez violer une reine de France. J'ai, dans mon grenier, toute une série de costumes[2].

Le « je suppose » renvoie immédiatement à l'image de l'oriental suborneur, agent infectieux d'une race pure – qu'il entend conduire à la dégénérescence. Le caractère implicite de la formulation rappelle la logorrhée des écrivains antisémites, celle de Henri Béraud ou du Céline de *Bagatelles pour un massacre*[3]. Cette position dénie au juif toute possibilité

---

[1] *Ibid.*, p. 35.
[2] *Ibid.*, p. 95.
[3] « Les pamphlets de Céline m'ont moins choqué que certaines pages de Rebatet : à vingt ans, je les trouvais délirants, puisqu'il disait que Racine était juif. Mais je n'ai vraiment pas envie de les relire. Et je regrette pour lui qu'il les ait écrits. », lettre citée de Patrick Modiano à Thierry Laurent, page 7. Vingt années auparavant, le romancier se montrait beaucoup plus primesautier à l'égard de cet auteur : « En lisant l'œuvre [de Céline], j'ai été

d'existence autonome – ce qui, encore une fois, rejoint par des voies détournées la théorie sartrienne : créé par la pensée de l'autre, le juif est *ipso facto* un être différent. Au cours de l'épisode, Schlemilovitch adopte en tous points cette dernière posture intellectuelle. Toutefois, l'aspect farcesque vient invalider la portée de l'ensemble. Dans son ouvrage consacré à l'identité juive chez Modiano, Ora Avni formule ainsi les enjeux :

> [...] qu'on le déplore [Sartre], ou qu'on s'en réjouisse [les antisémites], le fait est que les juifs doivent leur identité collective au mépris dans lequel ils baignent [...]. Dans l'épisode de Fougeire-Jusquiames, l'échec décisif de Schlemilovitch se fait l'écho, voire la dramatisation, de l'échec de Sartre dont l'analyse achoppe évidemment sur l'importance de l'histoire juive dans la constitution du sujet juif [...] ; tous les moments où fonctionne la réduction par l'absurde sont autant de parodies de son analyse[1].

En effet, lorsque Raphaël se plie aux exigences de la marquise – en transposant symboliquement dans le domaine de l'acte ce qui relève de l'idée –, il procède avec une lucidité de chaque instant, qui rappelle l'acteur de théâtre[2] ; la multiplicité des déguisements utilisés constitue d'ailleurs une sorte de dispositif scénique :

> La semaine qui suivit fut vraiment idyllique : la marquise changeait sans cesse de costume pour réveiller ses désirs. Exception faite des reines de France, il viola

---

frappé par le caractère assez juif de son esprit et de son style, de même que par son côté marginal et le sentiment d'une malédiction qui pesait sur lui. D'ailleurs, Céline avoue lui-même dans *Bagatelles* : « Dans le fond, mon œuvre est assez juive. [...] Au fond, le plus grand écrivain juif par le style, le ton, n'est pas juif... Il est même antisémite. » Propos recueillis par Julien Brunn, article cité.

[1] *Op.cit.*, p. 96.
[2] « Cette situation consiste tout bonnement à se soumettre au regard de l'antisémite, c'est-à-dire à se reconnaître dans l'image de lui-même projetée par l'antisémite [...] : le moi se définit sous le regard de l'autre. » *Ibid.*, p. 93-94.

Madame de Chevreuse, la duchesse de Berry, le chevalier d'Éon [...]¹.

L'illustration philosophique tourne à la pochade, au moment de l'entrée du vicomte Lévy-Vendôme. Celui-ci se présente d'emblée comme une figure irréductible à l'analyse ontologique, puisque tout son être est tendu vers sa condition d'objet regardé :

> Vous ne m'avez jamais vu dans mon interprétation du juif Süss ? [...] Je viens de tuer la marquise, de boire son sang comme tout vampire qui se respecte [...]. Maintenant, je déploie mes ailes de vautour².

En vidant l'analyse sartrienne de sa substance, en la traitant par la dérision – tout être qui existe sous le regard de l'autre constitue, par définition, un spectacle : il apparaît donc logique que le juif Schlemilovitch devienne un bouffon dans une pantalonnade – Modiano affirme, de nouveau, la primauté du passé dans la constitution de l'identité juive. Cette dernière ne représente pas une durée objective, et ne peut, de fait, se réduire à un concept actualisé. Selon le romancier, ce sont l'errance et le martyre de la communauté qui fondent l'appartenance de l'individu à celle-ci. L'œuvre explore ainsi tous les « états », toutes les phases de la judéité, sans la moindre complaisance pour ceux qui, à l'époque, justifiaient l'oppression des Palestiniens par les souffrances séculaires de leur peuple.

Si cette identité paraît rétive à la formalisation, c'est peut-être parce qu'elle ne prend tout son sens que dans le passé et la mémoire – inconvocables et intangibles par essence³. La plongée au cœur de l'Occupation permet ainsi de remonter le cours du temps, de s'immiscer au cœur de l'Histoire, non seulement afin de comprendre le traumatisme, mais surtout

---

[1] *La Place de l'Étoile*, p. 95.
[2] *Ibid.*, p. 100.
[3] Cette « carence » ne doit pas être confondue avec le vide existentiel postulé par Sartre, puisque, selon Modiano, le juif peut prendre conscience de son identité indépendamment du regard de l'autre.

d'accéder à un moment fondateur – parce qu'indicible – de la judéité.

Une identité introuvable ?

L'accès à la conscience juive passe par l'expérience de la symbiose littéraire avec les victimes des persécutions. Au début de sa carrière, Modiano se réincarne, à proprement parler, dans les figures suppliciées de ce peuple ; celles-ci avaient pour nom Schlemilovitch, Albert Modiano ou Pedro Mc Stern – *alias* Pedro Mc Evoy, dans *Rue des boutiques obscures*. En portant l'angoisse fondatrice à reviviscence, celle de la rafle ou de la dénonciation, l'écrivain recrée les conditions qui firent prendre *conscience* de leur être profond à des millions d'hommes et de femmes.

Voyage à l'intérieur d'une identité façonnée par l'Histoire – malgré elle, serions-nous tenté d'écrire –, *La Place de l'Étoile* se double, dans le même temps, d'une volonté d'élucidation, dont la réussite se mesure, avant tout, à la somme des efforts déployés pour comprendre l'impensable. Adoptant une démarche contraire à celle des romans de la maturité, l'écrivain va adapter, le plus souvent, le point de vue du persécuteur, renversant ainsi les perspectives de l'étude.

Serge Alexandre, Swing Troubadour – qui certes n'est pas juif, mais dont sa parenté affichée avec Stavisky favorise le rapprochement – et surtout Raphaël Schlemilovitch vont vivre l'Occupation dans le camp des bourreaux, de sorte que la réflexion sur l'identité empruntera une voie détournée, celle de l'hallucination spéculaire. Ce procédé répond à deux exigences complémentaires, à savoir la plongée dans les tréfonds de l'âme humaine – afin de saisir les mécanismes du mal – et surtout la lucidité, procurée par la mise à distance de l'objet d'étude. Le recours à ce type de recherche, qui met la dystopie et l'achronie au service de l'élucidation identitaire – ainsi, Schlemilovitch combat aux côtés de la division Charlemagne, dans les plaines de Poméranie, ou se trouve interné, en Israël, dans un camp d'extermination commandé par des juifs – illustre le désarroi d'un jeune créateur, trop sensible à la souffrance pour ne pas l'exorciser de façon outrancière.

Dans ce renversement des pôles de la logique de la rationalité, celui-ci espère trouver un sens à l'histoire de sa communauté, de la diaspora au génocide, puisque cette Histoire n'a pas de sens, et que l'esprit se refuse à penser Auschwitz. Toutefois, cette stratégie, qui joue sur l'achoppement de la raison, signera l'échec de la quête de Schlemilovitch-Modiano, car ce chaos se retrouve au cœur d'Israël, transformé en vitrine d'un régime fascisant. Il apparaît nécessaire, à présent, de clarifier le fonctionnement d'une pensée, rendue peut-être opaque par ses multiples ramifications.

Nous avons vu que Modiano refusait catégoriquement les postulats sartriens de l'existence du juif. Celui-ci trouverait sa vérité première, selon le romancier, dans une histoire collective, fondatrice de l'identité. Il suffirait donc de vivre celle-ci « de l'intérieur » – avec toute l'anomie et l'irrationalité narratives que cela suppose – pour retrouver un lignage susceptible d'inclure l'être dans la réalité, en lui fournissant un cadre précis d'existence. Or, l'illustre philosophe semble avoir perverti les pionniers du jeune état hébreu. Ces derniers ont si bien lu Sartre qu'ils ont poussé ses analyses jusqu'à leurs conséquences ultimes, anéantissant vingt siècles de traditions et de culture au nom de la sécurité de l'être, et imposant un régime dupliquant les principes des régimes totalitaires – préconisant le racisme biologique et la création d'un Surhomme national :

> – Alors, écoutez-moi : vous vous trouvez maintenant dans un pays jeune, vigoureux, dynamique. De Tel-Aviv à la mer Morte, de Haïfa à Eilat, l'inquiétude, la fièvre, les larmes, la POISSE juives n'intéressent plus personne ! [...]
> Moi, je vous ferai lire de bons ouvrages ! J'en possède une grande armoire en langue française : avez-vous lu *L'Art d'être chef* par Courtois ? *Restauration familiale et Révolution nationale* par Sauvage ? *Le*

Beau Jeu de ma vie par Guy de Larigaudie ? *Le Manuel du père de famille* par le vice-amiral de Penfentenyo[1] ?

On rappellera enfin que les menées militaires du jeune état représentaient la négation même de ses principes – de sorte que plus rien ne le distinguait des autres nations. La violence du jeune Modiano serait à la mesure de sa déception. En suivant sa logique toute paradoxale, les *Sabras* deviendront auxiliaires du Reich, et une parcelle du Sinaï accueillera un kibboutz disciplinaire. Cette dénonciation précède de peu le dénouement de l'épopée, et marque la fin des illusions. Si l'identité juive existe, des décennies d'assimilation forcée ont corrompu sa substance :

> Je vous signale que nous avons fait récemment un autodafé sur la grand-place de Tel-Aviv : les ouvrages de Proust, Kafka et consorts, les reproductions de Soutine, Modigliani et autres invertébrés, ont été brûlés par notre jeunesse, des gars et des filles qui n'ont rien à envier aux Hitlerjugend : blonds, l'œil bleu, larges d'épaules, la démarche assurée, aimant l'action et la bagarre ! (Il poussa un gémissement). Pendant que vous cultiviez vos névroses, ils se musclaient. Pendant que vous vous lamentiez, ils travaillaient dans les kibboutzim[2].

Une approche plus réductrice tend à ne considérer l'œuvre que d'un point de vue individuel, en limitant la portée de l'ouvrage au seul personnage de Raphaël Schlemilovitch. Ainsi, dans son ouvrage, *Pour une psychanalyse de l'art et de la créativité*[3], Jacqueline Chasseguet-Smirgel – reprise par Shounong Feng, dans sa thèse – voit dans cette assimilation de l'état hébreu à l'Allemagne hitlérienne – et, de façon plus générale, dans la confusion totale des lieux, des époques et des idéologies – un phénomène de compensation de l'instabilité psychique par le rêve, selon les modalités de la condensation et du déplacement. L'identification du persécuté au persécuteur –

---

[1] *La Place de l'Étoile*, p. 133-134.
[2] *Ibid.*, p. 133.
[3] *Op.cit.*

comme nous l'avons vu, Raphaël participe activement à la politique de Collaboration – participerait de la même démarche : il s'agirait moins de conquérir l'identité que d'opposer une défense aux agressions du monde. Celle-ci serait organisée à l'aide des ressources du psychisme et des principes de la *Traumdeutung* freudienne :

> Il s'agit alors de renier le juif en soi, en adoptant le rôle du persécuteur en tant que *surmoi* contre le juif en soi, c'est-à-dire en tant qu'instance interdisant au juif de se manifester *en tant que tel* (c'est-à-dire aux pulsions dont il est le représentant) et non [...] d'intégrer une partie de soi[1].

Une semblable analyse se révèle opératoire si elle se limite à proposer une autre approche de l'œuvre, renouvelée par la lecture psychanalytique. En revanche, nous ne souscrivons que difficilement aux remarques suivantes de Shounong Feng, qui ne relie que très partiellement le personnage de Raphaël aux interrogations de Modiano sur l'existence d'une identité juive. Ce chercheur semble exclure de son champ d'étude les autres figures illustrant le choix épistémologique consistant à adopter le point de vue du tortionnaire :

> Cette identification [du persécuté au persécuteur] est une objectivation de ses pulsions agressives internes inconscientes [...]. Pour Modiano, il existe deux sortes d'identité, l'identité sociale et l'identité de l'ego, ou bien l'identité extérieure et l'identité intérieure, autrement dit l'identité réelle et l'identité imaginaire. L'identité sociale du juif, c'est sa situation réelle dans le monde (il n'est rien). L'identité de son ego existe dans l'imaginaire ou dans l'hallucination. Il veut être le tout pour changer sa situation dérisoire et il pourrait tout pour se venger de sa persécution (d'où viennent les thèmes de la violence et de la folie) : le personnage désire inverser les rôles[2].

---

[1] *Ibid.*, p. 240.
[2] *Op.cit.*, p. 95.

Recevable en tant que tel, ce commentaire trouve sa portée limitée par les œuvres ultérieures, qui s'articulent autour d'êtres marqués par leur néant fondateur – et dont les actes dénotent clairement l'absence de conscience « regardante ». Leurs trahisons et reniements semblent, en effet, les errements d'un esprit totalement malléable, qu'aucune structure n'a jamais pu ordonner. Les deux analystes précédemment cités, qui distinguent Schlemilovitch de ses congénères – régis par des principes mentaux identiques –, commettent, à notre sens, une erreur d'appréciation. L'ensemble des ouvrages consacrés à la période de l'Occupation se révèle, comme nous l'avons montré, d'une grande cohérence. Privés du sentiment d'appartenance à une collectivité – puisque, depuis la fin de *La Place de l'Étoile*, Israël ne constitue plus un modèle susceptible de conférer un enracinement ou une identité –, les héros projettent l'image de leur fragilité sur le monde qui les entoure et leur renvoie son chaos – dans lequel la personnalité des héros est appelée à se dissoudre. Raphaël ne tente pas plus de gagner sa survie, en adoptant l'idéologie des tortionnaires de sa race, que Swing Troubadour et Serge Alexandre ne collaborent avec conviction. Tous trois illustrent les états d'une conscience privée de repères, dont l'élaboration passe par l'adoption des postures qui s'offrent à elle :

> Un autre soir, sans doute, je serais tombé sur des personnages plus honorables qui m'auraient conseillé l'industrie des textiles ou la littérature. Ne me sentant aucune vocation particulière, j'attendais de mes aînés qu'ils me choisissent un emploi. À eux de savoir sous quels aspects ils me préféraient. Je leur laissais l'initiative. Boy-scout ? Fleuriste ? Tennisman ? Non : Employé d'une pseudo-agence de police[1].

Nous avons vu que l'insertion dans le monde passait, dans le cas de Raphaël Schlemilovitch, par l'essai de toutes les positions fantasmatiques susceptibles d'être adoptées par un juif français. On ajoutera qu'au terme de son parcours le personnage se révèle incapable d'être l'un ou l'autre – comme

---

[1] *La Ronde de nuit*, p. 91-92.

ses frères en déréliction. Ora Avni propose une synthèse convaincante de ces itinéraires mentaux :

> Trois fois de suite, Modiano aura infligé un choix impossible à son personnage et à son roman. Et trois fois de suite, acculé à cette impossibilité, il aura laissé la question en suspens, n'aura fourni à son roman ni la catharsis de rigueur après un conflit tragique, ni un dénouement[1].

La seconde trilogie marque un infléchissement très net de cette position. La question de l'identité s'y révèle beaucoup moins cruciale, puisque résolue par l'écriture romanesque. Ni juif, ni français, Modiano se veut avant tout écrivain, et accorde, à ce titre, une place prépondérante aux personnages. Ces derniers ne représentent plus des figures déléguées, mais des êtres qui ont à présent leur place dans l'Histoire, et auxquels le romancier entend rendre hommage.

L'EFFACEMENT DU CREATEUR

Le second triptyque représente un complet changement d'orientation par rapport aux œuvres de jeunesse. L'écrivain délaisse la confession par personnage interposé ; la fiction laisse la place au journal, grâce à un subtil dégradé, qui permet de passer insensiblement d'une forme d'expression à l'autre. *Voyage de noces* est le dernier roman en date consacré à l'Occupation. Son codicille, *Fleurs de ruine*, reprend le thème dans une visée illustrative. Seule semble importer l'enquête conduite par le héros-récitant – de sorte que l'ensemble se place encore dans le domaine de la fiction. Six années plus tard, *Dora Bruder* reprend la forme de l'investigation, mais sans support fictionnel – qu'il importe d'abolir, afin de saisir le personnage dans toute sa vérité, dans son « essence ». L'unique entorse à la règle sera la recréation de ses sentiments, par un phénomène d'empathie, afin de saisir au plus près la réalité de

---

[1] Ora Avni, *op.cit.*, p. 142.

l'héroïne, et de se pénétrer de son angoisse. L'Occupation qui est recréée n'emprunte plus rien au fantasme, et recherche l'exacte restitution historique, grâce à la caution indirecte d'un personnage n'appartenant pas au domaine de la fiction.

Cette seconde période délaisse presque entièrement les préoccupations identitaires. Là où la première trilogie rusait avec l'Histoire, l'ornait des dépouilles du nouveau roman – afin de mieux circonvenir l'angoisse –, le dernier texte refuse toutes les facilités offertes par la fiction. Tout se passe, en effet, comme si le fait de ne plus s'interroger sur soi permettait une approche directe de la réalité. La violence des débuts cède la place à une sincère compassion pour les victimes de l'Holocauste, sans que les interrogations sur la conscience juive viennent interférer avec le travail d'enquêteur. C'est le moment où l'écrivain, en paix avec ses démons, expurge *La Place de l'Étoile* de toutes les scories et aspérités juvéniles. Les tableaux les moins soutenables et les images les plus crues se trouvent retranchés de l'édition « revue et corrigée » de 1985. La question juive, qui se pose avec beaucoup moins d'acuité que vingt-cinq années auparavant, ne paraît plus justifier le discours passionné des années soixante. L'expression de la douleur laisse place à l'analyse et à la réflexion. À près de cinquante ans, l'écrivain comblé d'honneurs, digne représentant de la littérature française contemporaine, ne doute plus de son identité – ou, du moins, ne place plus les questionnements sur cette dernière au centre de son œuvre. Sans voir nécessairement une prise de distance par rapport au thème dans cette opération de réécriture, il semble légitime de noter l'infléchissement du propos – qui ne se doit plus de compenser, par sa violence, le malaise et l'anxiété.

Ainsi, les mentions injurieuses ou les remarques cyniques se trouvent purement et simplement supprimées. On pensera notamment à l'évocation des activités particulières pratiquées, à la Libération, dans le château des Fougeire-Jusquiames :

> Les intellectuelles de gauche affluaient. Elles réclamaient du nègre, de l'Arabe, du juif, du prolétaire ! Simone et Marguerite étaient les plus enragées.

Ce passage, que l'on trouve à la page 95 de notre édition de référence – en collection NRF – disparaît de l'édition de la même collection en 1985. Dans un autre domaine, Modiano a considérablement allégé la charge antisioniste de l'ouvrage, en l'expurgeant des remarques les plus acerbes. Ainsi, l'assimilation des colons juifs aux SS fonctionnait, en 1966, sur le mode de l'équivalence systématique. Le voyage en Terre promise se présente, de fait, comme un déplacement temporel entraînant le protagoniste dans un parcours régressif – le conduisant, de façon naturelle, au cœur du Paris de l'Occupation, en raison de l'analogie fonctionnelle établie entre les nazis et les sionistes. L'itinéraire *physique*, qui devait permettre à l'apatride de retrouver ses racines, donne lieu à la confrontation du héros-narrateur avec les ennemis du passé. Pour détruire la mémoire, les Israéliens recourent ainsi aux pratiques – éprouvées – des camps d'extermination :

> – Tu saignes, Marcel : ça veut dire que tu es encore vivant. [Mais bientôt on se servira de toi pour faire des savonnettes. N'est-ce pas Saül ?
> – De ton sang on fera du jus de viande, lui dit Saül.
> – De tes os des allumettes, lui dit Isaac.
> – De ta peau des abat-jour, lui dit Isaïe[1].]

Le passage entre crochets est retiré de l'édition de 1985. La référence à cet extrait de l'entretien avec le général israélien demeure toutefois dans toutes les éditions. La partie manquante affaiblit la portée du texte, et annule l'effet comique de réitération de la menace, reformulée par Raphaël – nous avons analysé ce procédé dans la deuxième partie de notre travail.

L'équation entre la France occupée et l'Israël des années soixante s'inscrivait parfaitement dans la logique du jeune écrivain. Pour celui-ci, la revendication ou la négation de la judéité paraissaient toutes deux impossibles, dans la mesure où elles engageaient la mémoire d'un peuple, meurtri par l'Histoire. Ce dernier semblait renier ses origines fondatrices,

---

[1] *La Place de l'Étoile*, NRF, Gallimard, 1968.

en employant contre ses ennemis des méthodes assimilées – abusivement, sans doute – à la barbarie du Reich.

Il semble peu probable que l'opinion du romancier quinquagénaire soit conforme à celle de ses jeunes années, marquées par un certain nihilisme de fond – toute forme d'organisation sociale et politique[1] devenant un moyen potentiel d'oppression. À cet égard, *Livret de famille* représente une évolution sensible dans les rapports de l'écrivain avec Israël. Le ton se fait particulièrement solennel pour relater l'annonce du conflit de 1973 :

> Un samedi, à sept heures. Dans la librairie de la rue de Marivaux où je me trouvais, on avait allumé une radio. La musique s'est interrompue brusquement et on a annoncé que la guerre avait repris, au Proche-Orient, contre les Juifs[2].

La juxtaposition de phrases courtes, chargées d'émotion, confère à l'événement un caractère d'exceptionnelle gravité. Nulle suspicion à l'égard d'Israël ou de relativisation des faits : la sympathie du narrateur paraît entièrement acquise au peuple hébreu. Nous nous intéresserons, en particulier, à l'usage de la majuscule employée dans le dernier mot, présentant les Israéliens comme les victimes d'une agression – arabe – commise au nom de la race et non de la nation. La formulation, particulièrement favorable au camp hébreu, ne laisse pas d'étonner, puisqu'elle est le fait d'un homme qui, moins de dix ans auparavant, établissait une analogie fonctionnelle entre les colons du Sinaï et les gestapistes parisiens.

Enfin, on ajoutera que cette lecture des événements souffre d'une certaine partialité ; à de rares débordements près, les Palestiniens n'ont jamais considéré les Israéliens comme les représentants d'une religion ou d'une essence, dont ils souhaitaient l'anéantissement, mais bien comme des ennemis politiques, qui les avaient spoliés d'une partie de leur territoire. L'emploi de la majuscule marque donc un contresens historique, puisqu'au moment de la guerre du Kippour – qui se

---

[1] Au sens étymologique du terme.
[2] *Op.cit.*, p. 86.

voulait une revanche du monde arabe sur la défaite de la guerre des « six jours » – le conflit israélo-palestinien se cristallisait autour de la reconquête de la péninsule du Sinaï, de la bande de Gaza, de la Cisjordanie et des hauteurs du Golan, occupées depuis 1967. L'assimilation des Arabes aux persécuteurs historiques des Juifs paraît donc tout aussi abusive que celle des sionistes aux nazis.

Tout se passe comme si Modiano, en 1977, au moment de l'achèvement de son premier cycle thématique, acceptait avec quiétude l'exil intérieur dans le pays qui l'a vu naître « par hasard », et se trouvait enfin disponible pour l'inventaire et la reconnaissance de son lignage. On constatera, à cet effet, que l'abandon de la forme romanesque – du moins sous son aspect classique, puisque *Livret de famille* se trouve essentiellement constitué de microrécits – traduit le détachement de l'écrivain, lequel n'éprouve plus le besoin de vider la réalité de sa force, en soumettant celle-ci aux lois du roman.

Dès lors, Modiano cessera toute mise à distance de l'Histoire, au moyen de la dérision et de l'humour, et adoptera un ton grave, adulte – oserait-on écrire – afin d'évoquer le martyre subi par les juifs[1]. *Dora Bruder* représente le terme de cette évolution. Pour l'écrivain commence le temps du remords, celui d'avoir concédé à la facilité de certains artifices

---

[1] On notera qu'à la même époque, avec *W ou le souvenir d'enfance*, Georges Perec avait choisi le recours à l'équivalence symbolique pour l'évocation de la réalité concentrationnaire. L'ouvrage se compose de deux récits : l'un expose les lois et règlements sportifs qui régissent l'île de W, l'autre met en scène les années d'enfance de Perec, dominées par la disparition de ses parents dans les camps de déportation et le traumatisme né de cette absence. Une relation d'ordre dialogique finit par s'établir entre les deux textes : la recension des articles relatifs au fonctionnement juridique de W fait rapidement surgir l'image de l'institution nazie, soucieuse de perpétrer l'éradication d'un peuple de la façon la plus méthodique. Modiano voyait dans Theresienstadt un « Luna park » aux mains de déments ; chez Perec, l'idée d'extermination procède, au contraire, d'une logique et rigoureuse élaboration. C'est sans doute ce dernier aspect, fort éloigné de l'hystérie macabre de *La Place de l'Étoile*, qui rend si poignantes les dernières pages de *W*.

narratifs, sans toujours donner aux victimes la dignité qu'elles méritaient[1].

Nous allons voir que cette évolution s'applique également à la réflexion sur la figure paternelle, objet de trente années de passions, de violences, puis de repentirs.

L'INTERROGATION SUR LE PERE : UN QUESTIONNEMENT PERMANENT

Les sentiments que Patrick Modiano a éprouvés pour son père se sont toujours caractérisés par leur ambivalence. Du mépris teinté de pitié, dans les premières années, à la déclaration d'amour du dernier texte, les représentations d'Albert Modiano n'ont cessé d'évoluer.

L'acte d'écriture représente pour le fils un besoin profond d'élucidation des origines. Il le conduit à convoquer, à cette fin, les figures les plus marquantes de son histoire personnelle. Si l'écrivain n'évoque sa mère qu'à de rares reprises – les années de jeunesse, dans deux chapitres de *Livret de famille*, et l'activité théâtrale dans *Vestiaire de l'enfance*, en 1989 –, et ne rompt le silence sur son frère, Rudy, qu'en 1988,

---

[1] On se reportera, à cet effet, à l'article consacré à la découverte du *Mémorial*. Il est vrai qu'avant le personnage d'Ingrid Theyrsen, héroïne de fiction créée à partir de Dora, les représentations de la pureté sacrifiée ont occupé une place des plus marginales dans l'œuvre du romancier. Les figures positives, dans les premiers textes, apparaissaient avant tout comme des victimes consentantes – et se trouvaient, de toute façon, en nombre réduit. Tania, dans *La Place de l'Étoile*, ou France, dans *Lacombe Lucien*, sont les exemples représentatifs de ce choix thématique.

Dans un autre domaine, Coco Lacour et Esmeralda sont, avant tout, des vues de l'esprit, et ne peuvent prétendre à un statut de « personnages réels ». Les rares figures qui refusent la compromission – comme les « chevaliers du RCO » – sont beaucoup trop floues pour retenir l'attention. Ainsi, jusqu'à la fin des années soixante-dix, le narrateur ne peut envisager l'immixtion dans la société humaine sous la forme de l'adhésion à l'éthique ou la morale « traditionnelles », puisque, selon lui, seuls triomphent les êtres dépourvus de « conscience » – ce dernier terme est à prendre dans ses deux acceptions, au sens de morale et d'identité.

dans *Remise de peine*, il met en scène son père beaucoup plus régulièrement. Cette figure paraît indissociable des premiers écrits, étant donné que c'est par rapport à elle – donc aux pôles inconciliables de la judéité et de la Collaboration – que s'ordonnent les textes de jeunesse.

La première trilogie ne cessera de tourner autour de la transmission de l'héritage, filial et historique, accepté avec réticence ou refusé à regret, sans que l'écrivain paraisse en mesure d'effectuer un choix définitif. *La Place de l'Étoile* multiplie les sarcasmes, mêlant le burlesque à la cruauté, déniant, de ce fait, toute légitimité au personnage[1]. *La Ronde de nuit* montre le danger d'une telle négation : privé de la censure permettant à l'enfant de trouver ses repères affectifs et intellectuels – totalement inexistants chez Swing Troubadour, être inconsistant, organiquement pusillanime et velléitaire –, le héros délègue la représentation de l'autorité à des substituts de l'instance paternelle, qui le conduiront aux pires compromissions. Il sera temps, alors, de se ressourcer auprès de la seule figure pertinente, celle du père, réinstallé dans ses fonctions – et reconnu comme tel par son fils. À cette fin, soucieux de favoriser l'épanouissement d'une conscience identitaire encore embryonnaire, le romancier inversera les rapports, en prenant le relais de la représentation défaillante de la Loi – au sens psychanalytique de ce terme –, dans *Les Boulevards de ceinture*.

De fait, seules ces recherches paraissent susceptibles de conférer au héros un statut dans l'existence – si précaire fût-il. Lévy-Vendôme, les protagonistes des récits de jeunesse et quelques personnages fugacement entrevus se doivent d'entretenir quelques rapports de similitude avec le père de l'écrivain – ou tout du moins avec l'image que Modiano en

---

[1] « Mon père s'épongeait le front avec sa cravate de daim rose. J'ai rassuré ce gentil clown [...]. Schlemilovitch père est un gros monsieur qui s'habille de costumes multicolores, Schlemilovitch fils ne pense qu'à ridiculiser Schlemilovitch père [...]. [Ils] ne se ressemblent pas : le premier traîne un physique de poussah abyssin, au second le costume de SS sied à ravir. Il le porte souvent, tandis que Schlemilovitch père se déguise en rabbin. » *La Place de l'Étoile*, p. 49-53.

donne, c'est-à-dire qu'ils doivent joindre la bassesse à la fragilité, chacune des deux composantes entrant en proportion variable dans la composition de la personnalité. Ces figures déléguées assurent l'intercession avec la période de l'Occupation, à laquelle ils se trouvent liés – du point de vue de la diégèse ou, lorsque l'action est contemporaine, par leur aventure personnelle. À des degrés divers, chacun porte en lui la blessure d'un passé rendu particulièrement douloureux par la question de l'identité juive.

Si l'on excepte le vicomte Lévy-Vendôme, dont le tiret qui sépare les deux termes du patronyme indique la suture réussie entre la composante juive et la composante française, les personnages de rencontre témoignent de la difficulté de s'adapter à un monde auquel ils demeurent étrangers. On songera ainsi à Georges Bellune, le compositeur viennois exilé à Paris, qui se suicide au début d'*Une jeunesse*, ou à Georges Rollner, le metteur en scène de *Captain Van Mers du Sud*, dont la seule préoccupation est d'affirmer que l'on « peut être juif et être un as de l'aviation[1]. »

Ces êtres constituent des variations autour de la figure d'Albert Modiano, qui délègue indirectement sa fonction paternelle aux figures évoquées. Celles-ci représentent le versant digne de la judéité ; restées en marge, elles semblent condamner à mener une existence pénible, faisant d'elles des personnages nostalgiques par excellence. Nulle ambivalence chez ces victimes qui, contrairement au vicomte, ou au Chalva des *Boulevards de ceinture*, ne mettent pas leur extranéité au service de la corruption.

Cette « galaxie paternelle » permet de présenter en creux un portrait complet de Modiano père, être protéiforme, difficilement réductible à sa caricature. Le poids des années et le décès de celui-ci entrent pour une part importante dans le

---

[1] *Livret de famille*, p. 99. On remarquera que, chez Modiano, la judéité s'inscrit dans un système d'opposition. Le vicomte montre que l'on peut être juif et français, Bellune, que l'on peut se trouver à Vienne en 1938 et écrire des opérettes légères, et Rollner que l'idéologie prime la raison, dans l'inconscient collectif.

pardon accordé. Cette absolution vaut acceptation non seulement des origines, mais aussi du passé honteux – la Collaboration.

Dans ses premières œuvres, Modiano dissociait entièrement l'identité juive des autres aspects de l'existence ou de la personnalité, comme l'enracinement dans un pays ou, dans un autre domaine, la trahison des siens. Pour lui, la judéité apparaissait comme une monade, dont l'autonomie et l'intégrité eussent été remises en cause par le contact avec l'extérieur. Si *La Place de l'Étoile* est un ouvrage poignant, c'est sans doute parce qu'il porte, inscrit au cœur de son schéma narratif, l'idée de l'impossibilité du contact avec autrui. Enfant de la diaspora, le juif ne peut trouver de fondement identitaire dans sa seule judéité – qui postule l'errance et le déracinement – et se trouve dans l'incapacité d'adopter les valeurs et la culture du pays d'adoption sans dénaturer celles-ci, ni perdre le contact avec le judaïsme, le seul lien qu'il conserve avec lui-même. Il se condamne ainsi à une solitude qui le conduit à stigmatiser ceux qui transgressent ce principe. Chaque personnage qui tente l'intégration se trouve symboliquement rejeté, au nom de la trahison de l'esprit juif, et présenté de façon caricaturale et grotesque.

Il en est ainsi de Sartre, qui, selon Schlemilovitch, renierait ses origines – lointaines –, en déclarant que le juif n'existe pas. On pensera également à Freud, préconisant une véritable anesthésie de la judéité, à Proust, renégat qui dilue cette dernière dans des rêveries aristocratiques, ou à une famille comme les Rothschild[1], tardivement rattachée à la noblesse française[2]. Toutes ces figures sont frappées

---

[1] Cette famille est représentée par Lévy-Vendôme, dans le texte. Selon Modiano, l'agrégation à l'histoire d'un pays ne peut reposer que sur la mystification et la duplicité.

[2] Il paraît intéressant de rapprocher les précisions historiques données par Huguette David, à propos du dreyfusisme de Swann, pourtant bien intégré dans l'aristocratie parisienne, avec la réflexion de Modiano sur l'agrégation d'une partie de la bourgeoisie juive à cette même aristocratie, au XIXe siècle : « [Ce siècle] voit se célébrer un nombre considérable de mariages entre [celle-là] et la noblesse française chrétienne. Cent ans après la Révolution, l'émancipation de la minorité juive a abouti à une certaine intégration dans la

d'opprobre – certes, à des degrés divers –, se voyant reprocher une existence trop quiète pour ne pas avoir refoulé les interrogations liées à l'identité juive. Suivant ce postulat, tout juif écrivain se doit d'être collaborateur, comme Maurice Sachs, ou juif honteux – et converti – comme Montaigne, et tout juif prospère un escroc. La figure paternelle s'inscrit, par défaut, dans cet ensemble, en ce sens que son entreprise de kaléidoscopes s'avère un échec – fiasco prévisible à partir du moment où le personnage se trouvait présenté comme le paradigme de la judéité :

> [...] vous êtes juif, par conséquent vous n'avez pas le sens du commerce ni des affaires. Il faut laisser ce privilège aux Français[1].

À ce moment, l'interrogation ne s'est pas encore déplacée sur la conduite du père pendant la guerre. Ce dernier, présenté durant un bref moment comme modèle potentiel, ne verra sa personnalité explorée que dans le texte suivant – dans lequel le vide constitutif de *Swing Troubadour* représente la lâcheté d'Albert Modiano. Celle-ci sera confirmée dans *Les Boulevards de ceinture* – comme s'il avait fallu deux galops d'essai pour que Modiano pût aborder, de façon directe, la double trahison du père. En effet, celui-ci renie les principes les plus élémentaires de la morale juive, et s'associe aux partisans de l'élimination de sa race. L'échec des retrouvailles, entériné par l'indifférence du père et l'arrestation des personnages, se veut une parabole sur l'impossibilité de communication entre deux générations. À ce moment, il paraît inenvisageable de comprendre la duplicité du géniteur et de l'exonérer de ses responsabilités.

Il faudra une autre figure symbolique du père, à savoir un intercesseur, pour que l'écrivain puisse dépasser des

---

société française. » Huguette David, *Le Judaïsme de Proust*, thèse de doctorat, Université de Nanterre, 1991. Citée par Pierre Srour, *op.cit.*, p. 147. Celui-ci ajoute : « L'avilissement de Raphaël fournit une perspective non seulement pessimiste mais volontairement subversive de tout ce qui pourrait concourir à une réconciliation du juif et du français. »
[1] *La Place de l'Étoile*, p. 39.

contradictions qu'il jugeait inconciliables. C'est Emmanuel Berl, pourtant d'une génération antérieure à celle d'Albert Modiano, qui jouera ce rôle de passeur. Dans l'ouvrage d'entretiens accordés à Modiano, le vieil homme affirme qu'il est des choix rendus nécessaires par les circonstances. On peut ainsi, sans contorsions mentales, expliquer, sinon justifier, le fait de rédiger les discours du Maréchal, lorsque l'on se trouve exilé, malgré soi, à Vichy. Le romancier découvre une situation morale beaucoup plus complexe que ce que son intransigeance juvénile pouvait imaginer :

> E.B. – Quand je « revois » le deuxième discours de Pétain, le 22 juin, il y a au moins quatre-vingt-dix-neuf pour cent de Français pour Pétain.
> – Vous lui avez fait dire quoi ?
> E.B. – « Je hais les mensonges qui vous ont fait tant de mal » et « La terre, elle, ne ment pas ».
> – C'est quand même bizarre pour un juif...
> E.B. – Rétrospectivement peut-être... [...] Mais je vous assure que, sur le moment, ces formules n'avaient pas le cachet « révolution nationale » qu'elles ont pris par la suite[1].

Il apprend que Jean Luchaire était un « garçon très charmant[2] », Drieu un être d'une « grande générosité[3] » et Laval un maire socialiste, soucieux que les familles d'ouvriers fussent « mieux logées, mieux nourries [et] qu'on leur donn[ât] les assurances sociales auxquelles il travaillait[4]. »

La judéité ne trouve donc pas forcément sa limite dans l'adhésion à une communauté, voire dans la « compromission ». *Livret de famille* illustre, l'année suivante, ce bouleversement. Pour la première fois, Modiano procède en historien de ses origines, exposant les faits avec objectivité – proche en cela d'un Berl répondant avec sérénité aux objections de son cadet. Un déplacement de regard se produit. Les romans ne porteront plus sur la culpabilité – avec les

---

[1] *Emmanuel Berl, interrogatoire*, p. 87-88.
[2] *Ibid.*, p. 92.
[3] *Ibid.*, p. 97.
[4] *Ibid.*, p. 96.

questions bien connues : comment porter le poids du judaïsme ? comment peut-on trahir les siens ? –, mais sur la souffrance. La position égocentrique, qui plaçait la transmission de l'héritage juif – par le père – au centre des œuvres, cède la place à une interrogation plus large sur l'Occupation et ses victimes. Albert Modiano acquiert alors sa véritable dimension, celle d'un homme pour lequel la Collaboration constituait la seule possibilité de survie, dans un monde où les repères moraux tendaient à s'effacer ou à perdre de leur pertinence[1]. Après avoir tué symboliquement son géniteur, sous la défroque d'un clown commerçant ou d'un chevalier de fortune, l'écrivain le fait renaître sous les traits d'une victime des circonstances – cette « drôle d'époque » dont la confusion invalide les jugements normatifs et les préjugés.

L'écrivain reprend à son compte, dans les œuvres postérieures à sa première autofiction, le désarroi, la solitude – morale et affective – des personnages livrés à eux-mêmes. Il ne s'agit pas pour lui de se confondre avec les êtres dont il relate l'existence, mais bien de prendre toute la mesure de la douleur, de l'angoisse, que ceux-ci ont pu éprouver.

LA PEUR OU LE FONDEMENT DE L'IDENTITE

Le pardon tardif accordé au père fut donc précédé de deux décennies marquées par une culpabilité que l'écrivain avait reprise à son compte. Fils d'un homme qui avait passé les cinq années de la guerre dans la clandestinité, habité par la terreur de la dénonciation et de l'arrestation, Modiano – dont l'identité « vacillante » interdisait le moindre recul par rapport aux événements – ne pouvait faire autrement que de laisser les tourments paternels envahir sa conscience.

L'œuvre du romancier est traversée par la crainte, la peur presque primitive, qui semble peut-être l'unique instance

---

[1] C'est ce qui explique que Patrick et Rudy Modiano aient été confiés, dans les années cinquante, aux bons soins d'une jeune femme, Annie, familière de la rue Lauriston.

susceptible de combattre le vide ontologique. Il paraît donc pertinent de conclure ce développement, consacré à la question identitaire, par une réflexion sur cette terreur fondatrice.

Dans les œuvres de Modiano, l'individu ne présente pas d'autre qualité[1] que la certitude de son inconsistance et de sa vacuité fondamentales – rendues plus vives par les choix – ou non-choix – qu'il se trouve contraint d'effectuer ; tous s'avèrent générateurs d'angoisse. Avant d'explorer les manifestations de celle-ci chez ses héroïnes, l'écrivain en fait le principe *essentiel* de ses héros-narrateurs. Ces derniers ne prennent conscience de leur appartenance au monde qu'en proportion de la peur que celui-ci leur communique. Si cette crainte permanente, non objectivée, semble annihiler les facultés strictement intellectuelles de l'être, elle sert, en tout cas, d'« indice » de leur identité.

De fait, c'est la peur omniprésente de Swing Troubadour qui lui vaut brevet d'existence – cette terreur consubstantielle, renforcée par les incertitudes liées à la guerre. Dans le roman, le mot revient pratiquement à chaque page, justifiant, de façon abusive, les exactions ainsi que le comportement velléitaire du protagoniste. Ce sentiment constitue la projection des doutes et inquiétudes du jeune Modiano, incapable de trancher entre l'identification à une nation, à laquelle il demeure étranger, et la reconnaissance d'un père au passé mystérieux. Dans les deux cas, c'est l'Occupation qui fournit la connexion, de sorte que l'histoire personnelle du romancier paraît inséparable de cette période.

Le meilleur exemple demeure l'argument du chapitre V de *Livret de famille* ; une chasse à courre, dans une propriété de Sologne, devient le théâtre symbolique de la résistance juive contre l'oppression nazie, et réactive une angoisse sourde, enfouie, depuis toujours semble-t-il, au plus profond des deux êtres menacés, à savoir Albert Modiano et son fils. On ajoutera que rien dans le comportement des hôtes n'indique, de façon objective, la moindre hostilité à l'égard des deux visiteurs. En

---

[1] Nous employons ce terme dans le sens que Philippe Jacottet donne à *Eigenschaften*, dans sa traduction de *L'Homme sans qualités*, de Robert Musil, Le Seuil, 1954.

fait, l'enfant ne peut percevoir qu'une menace diffuse dans cet environnement ; sensible à la servilité et à l'obséquiosité affichées par le père – qui paraît déplacé et inadapté dans un milieu aristocratique dont il ignore les codes –, prompt à déceler du dédain chez des êtres qui ne prêtent pas attention à lui, le jeune Modiano transpose cette angoisse dans le cadre historique de l'Occupation. Les relations d'affaires du père deviennent les doubles des agioteurs du square Cimarosa ; ce jeu de correspondances affectives – qui convoquent les heures les plus sombres de l'Histoire – donne à la campagne solognote l'aspect d'un ghetto au moment de l'insurrection :

> Les choses étaient beaucoup plus graves et plus tragiques qu'il ne le croyait [...]. Tout commencerait par les fanfares d'attaque. Que ferait la meute ? Il ne fallait pas trembler. Et d'abord, essayer de viser juste [...]. Alors tous les autres arriveraient avec leurs chiens et leurs piqueurs, et bien qu'on se trouvât au cœur de la France, en Sologne, ce serait comme à Varsovie[1].

Cette scène fantasmatique semble particulièrement révélatrice d'un état de conscience tourmenté et traumatisé par les souvenirs indirects de la guerre, portés à reviviscence par la présence paternelle. Celle-ci joue le rôle d'un véritable principe réactif, en convoquant les scènes les plus pénibles d'un passé – pourtant inconnu – que l'écrivain entrevoit dans le personnage d'Albert Modiano. On notera que ce dernier adopte dans les situations de menace, réelle ou imaginaire, un détachement identique à celui dont il faisait preuve dans *Les Boulevards de ceinture*. Tout se passe comme si le fils devenait le seul dépositaire d'une angoisse refusée – ou refoulée – par l'auteur de ses jours.

À l'exception des récits concernant son évasion ou sa vie clandestine, le père n'aborde jamais la question de l'Occupation de manière frontale. L'instance paternelle s'est défaussée de cette encombrante succession sur son fils, qui mettra des années à assumer ce refus – le malaise transparaît, en particulier, dans l'usage des *leitmotive* de la série « Il faudra

---

[1] *Livret de famille*, p. 85.

rendre des comptes ». Cet esprit bouleversé détectera les symptômes de l'antisémitisme ou de la résurgence du nazisme dans les situations les moins ambiguës – l'épisode de la chasse ou celui du conducteur de taxi, à Bordeaux, qui semble conduire *naturellement* le père et le fils de l'hôtel Splendid au siège de la Milice –, attitude qui forme un contraste singulier avec l'indolence d'Albert Modiano.

Ce dernier semble incapable d'établir la moindre association entre des faits marqués par un étroit rapport de consonance historique. Amnésique volontaire, le père a entièrement refoulé un passé anxiogène, dont l'enfant porte, seul, les séquelles. On pensera notamment aux trajets que les deux personnages effectuent en estafette de gendarmerie, après qu'Albert Modiano eut dénoncé son fils aux autorités :

> J'ai pensé que c'était la première fois de ma vie que je faisais une telle expérience. Mon père, lui, l'avait déjà connue, il y avait vingt ans [...].
> [...] j'étais étonné que mon père, qui avait vécu pendant l'Occupation ce qu'il avait vécu, n'eût pas manifesté la moindre réticence à me laisser emmener dans un panier à salade. [...] Et cela me semblait d'autant plus injuste que j'avais commencé un livre [...] où je prenais à mon compte le malaise qu'il avait éprouvé pendant l'Occupation[1].

Modiano ne pourra jamais se défaire de cette angoisse diffuse et lancinante. L'anecdote rapportée ne représente qu'un épiphénomène dans la continuité de la névrose, née de cette néantisation du père par l'enfant. Celle-ci ne sera formulée comme telle que dans les ouvrages de la maturité. Au milieu des années soixante, elle se décline plutôt sur les modes de la culpabilité et de l'expiation, son prolongement naturel. L'écriture, obsessionnelle, du premier texte, puis la série des œuvres consacrées – indirectement – à la jeunesse du père prenaient, à ce moment, une dimension piaculaire, comme si l'écrivain se devait d'accepter, sans bénéfice d'inventaire, le passé paternel – et payer le prix moral d'une telle charge.

---

[1] *Dora Bruder*, p. 71-72.

Jusqu'en 1978, l'angoisse et l'inquiétude ne cesseront de hanter Modiano. Cette réaction contre un danger incertain, qui plonge le créateur dans l'atmosphère de l'Occupation, met rapidement en branle des mécanismes de défense, légitimés par les souffrances subies par le père.

Contrairement à celui-ci, les narrateurs choisiront la fuite – comme nous l'avons vu. Les événements qui n'entretiennent qu'un lointain rapport de similarité avec les années d'Occupation prennent alors des résonances dramatiques, convoquant instantanément le spectre des années noires. Nous pensons, en particulier, à l'action de *Villa triste*, située en pleine guerre d'Algérie. Le refuge dans l'hôtel traduit la volonté de se mettre à couvert d'une situation instable, susceptible de donner lieu à des mesures d'exception, de sinistre mémoire. On ajoutera qu'à ce moment, le père de Modiano avait confisqué les papiers militaires de son fils et tenté de l'enrôler de force dans l'armée, ce qui donnait un aspect encore plus angoissant à la période évoquée dans le roman.

Dans un domaine semblable, l'annonce de la guerre du Kippour vient rayer trente années de relative quiétude, installant de nouveau le « climat de rafles et d'expectative[1] » relaté par le père, en rappelant que l'oppression ne connaîtra jamais de trêve :

> Ce soir-là, j'ai senti que quelque chose touchait à sa fin. Ma jeunesse ? J'avais la certitude que plus rien ne serait comme avant […]. Mais sans doute beaucoup de gens, à la même heure, ont-ils éprouvé la même angoisse que moi[2].

Après ce dernier ouvrage, l'écrivain va quelque peu délaisser les thèmes de la faute et de la culpabilité, et tenter de renouveler son approche du récit. Durant les années quatre-vingts, il explorera les contrées de la nostalgie et de la rêverie sur le passé, plus proche en cela de Valery Larbaud ou d'Alain-

---

[1] *Ibid.*, p. 91.
[2] *Livret de famille*, p. 86.

Fournier que de Jean-Marc Roberts, romancier qui a rêvé sur des sujets semblables.

De fait, après la mort d'Albert Modiano, l'écrivain semble délivré de la nécessité d'une autojustification permanente – à laquelle chacun de ses textes était jusqu'alors consacré. *Rue des boutiques obscures* constitue, à cet égard, une sorte de roman charnière, qui reprend chacun des thèmes exposés depuis *La Place de l'Étoile* pour leur donner une autre résonance, ou les exploiter différemment. La conquête de l'identité laisse ainsi la place à celle de la mémoire, désormais défaillante – alors que celle-ci avait imposé sa domination, ravivant, à chaque instant, les angoisses liées à l'Occupation.

Celle-ci n'est plus vécue à la façon d'un drame personnel, d'un travail de deuil inachevé – et inachevable –, porté par la seule force de l'écriture, et vient s'effacer au bénéfice d'une douce mélancolie. La douleur du passé se fond dans la nostalgie diffuse d'un monde perdu qui, au-delà des traumatismes qu'il générait, représentait le seul cadre naturel de l'écrivain. L'exercice de la mémoire semble prendre pour seul but l'insertion dans le monde contemporain, au moyen du témoignage et de la déambulation, loin du fracas des premiers écrits. Le travail de l'écriture devient alors, pour reprendre le titre d'un roman de Pavèse, le « métier de vivre ».

Conclusion

Dans ses ouvrages, Modiano livre beaucoup plus que le cadastre mental d'une âme hantée par ses démons. Novice en la matière, le jeune écrivain se révélera très rapidement doué pour converser librement avec ses souvenirs de contrebande, dans la langue imagée de l'Occupation. « [Sa] mémoire précède [sa] naissance » ; difficile d'y échapper : les récits d'une capitale envahie, puis tenue par les troupes allemandes n'ont jamais laissé la place, dans l'inconscient, aux images de la Libération. Jusqu'au milieu des années soixante-dix, trente années d'occupation spirituelle semblent avoir imposé leur domination sur le psychisme du romancier, jusqu'à l'obsession, la névrose, qu'il ne parviendra que très difficilement à surmonter.

De fait, toutes les facultés intellectuelles et morales semblent avoir été mobilisées afin de circonvenir la fascination éprouvée pour les années sombres. Ironie, distanciation cruelle ou moquerie cinglante : la plupart des ressources de l'esprit furent utilisées, et n'aboutirent qu'à renforcer la dépendance à l'égard du passé tentateur. Les premières années d'écriture sont consacrées à la mise en place de l'univers quotidien d'une abjection, que le créateur estime sienne – et qui ne pouvait que confirmer l'idée de souillure originelle, interdisant au jeune écrivain de se forger une identité solide. Il faudra attendre l'exorcisme représenté par la mort du père – précédé une année auparavant de l'inventaire des origines – pour que le romancier ne se donne plus les années sombres pour seul repère mental et point fondateur de son existence.

Afin d'estimer avec précision l'apport de Modiano à la compréhension de l'Occupation – et sa place dans la littérature de la fin du XXe siècle –, nous proposerons, dans un premier temps, un bilan des analyses conduites dans ce travail, avant d'étudier les ensembles formels qui composent l'œuvre. L'origine des premiers romans de la trilogie – qui fournira ensuite les thèmes joués en sourdine, dans les ouvrages des années soixante-dix – est sans doute l'obsession de la rencontre avec le père, dont l'absence explique la plupart des traumatismes de l'écrivain, ainsi que son incapacité d'adaptation au monde contemporain. Les ouvrages de jeunesse s'ordonneront donc exclusivement autour de cette figure. Dans chaque cas, le recours à l'écriture apparaît comme un moyen de compensation.

La Place de l'Étoile tente ainsi de conjurer l'angoisse par la caricature, *La Ronde de nuit* multiplie les grotesques équivalents d'une figure paternelle absente, et *Lacombe Lucien* trouve son argument dans la désertion symbolique du père – schématiquement parlant, si Lucien ne peut s'intégrer dans les lieux qui lui conviendraient « naturellement » (la ferme et le maquis), c'est sans doute parce que la fonction de régulation morale, traditionnellement assumée par le père ne se trouve plus assurée. Prisonnier de guerre, cet homme laisse une place vacante – concrètement et psychanalytiquement parlant –, comblée par les premières figures paternelles de substitution désireuses d'offrir à Lucien la reconnaissance affective attendue. Enfin, le dernier ouvrage de la trilogie renverse le mouvement – et donne encore plus de valeur à la fonction paternelle – puisque c'est le fils qui, en désespoir de cause, part à la recherche du père, en légitimant ses actes et en l'absolvant de ses fautes. Rejoignant l'Histoire, il espère trouver un statut susceptible de lui conférer une identité – ce qui ne sera pas le cas. Devant cet échec, l'écrivain renoncera à une approche directe de l'Occupation, et délaissera le roman pour une mise à distance des événements, au moyen de l'autobiographie, et surtout de l'autofiction.

La démarche adoptée se complique encore par le fait que l'écrivain reconnaît l'Occupation pour son seul univers naturel. La survalorisation de l'instance paternelle donne à la période une importance considérable, et fait de celle-ci l'élément fondateur de la quête identitaire – la clef des origines se trouverait, selon Modiano, dans le silence et les mystères du Paris occupé, qui abrita les secrets du père durant toutes ces années. En fait, dans ses œuvres de jeunesse, l'écrivain semble prisonnier de l'univers recréé, et cela pour deux raisons.

Dans un premier temps, le recours à des figures de papier, dont l'inconsistance et l'apathie sont censées refléter le désarroi du narrateur – mais rendent l'identification impossible –, signe l'échec attendu de l'entreprise. Le romancier s'obstinera à trouver les réponses à son questionnement – et partant à chercher le « sens » de l'Occupation – dans des marionnettes de fiction, sur lesquelles il projette toutes ses angoisses. Le néant de ces personnages contribuera à l'enliser encore davantage dans celles-ci.

En second lieu, Modiano ne cessera d'hésiter, dans les premières années, entre la négation de la raison et la conformité à l'Histoire. Nous avons vu que les vertiges narratifs, élaborés afin de rendre compte du chaos de l'époque, ne remettaient que très rarement en cause la véracité historique. Les enquêtes minutieuses sur les faits, les hommes et les dates servent ainsi la restitution d'un univers autoréférencé, dans lequel la déconstruction savante des lois du récit se trouve mise au service de la quête de soi. L'écrivain refusera *in fine* l'emprise de cette irrationalité, voulue et créée par ses soins, et demandera à d'autres formes narratives de répondre aux interrogations identitaires.

Il faudra en effet deux décennies – à savoir la seconde trilogie – pour que Modiano cesse de considérer la fiction comme la seule réponse possible – et souhaitable – à ses attentes. En effet, l'Occupation évoquée par ses soins paraît, avant tout, un lieu de sécurité et de conforts mentaux, régi par les seules lois du récit – et radicalement différent du monde contemporain, dont il refusait l'agressive contrainte. L'écriture, envisagée comme moyen de compensation, offrait le double avantage de proposer une alternative à la société extérieure, et surtout de gouverner un ensemble de figures peu offensives, puisque dénuées de toute vie.

Certes, dans les romans de la première trilogie, l'on torture, l'on « commissionne », mais cette écume d'existence apparaît étouffée par la torpeur de la voix narrative. La vacuité de Swing Troubadour ou de Serge Alexandre oblige l'écrivain à prendre en charge – affectivement parlant – les incertitudes et les angoisses des êtres, mais ces quelques désagréments sont beaucoup moins déstabilisants que la confrontation avec la réalité et le quotidien, évacués du travail romanesque. Rues désertes, protagonistes désincarnés jusqu'à la caricature et dénués de toute existence réelle : le monde de l'Occupation ne peut représenter de menace effective. Seuls les tableaux de Delvaux, dans lesquels les objets paraissent souvent plus vivants que les êtres humains, constituent les équivalents visuels de la narration modianienne. En effet, les archétypes, les idées, ne peuvent déstabiliser profondément celui qui les mobilise. Si la fiction se révèle inapte à répondre au désarroi, elle permet au moins de *dévitaliser* – au sens clinique du terme – l'univers de la fiction.

Sous l'apparence d'un retour au roman traditionnel, qu'il vide de toute substance, Modiano radicalise sans doute la démarche entreprise par les écrivains du « nouveau roman ». Ces derniers rejetaient l'idée de personnage, qui, selon eux, fossilisait le récit, et constituait un rempart contre le travail de la forme narrative – qui permettait un renouvellement des moyens d'expression du réel. Chez Modiano, c'est le réel tout entier – pourtant présenté comme unique source de validité et de légitimité de l'existence – qui se voit désubstantialisé.

Afin d'approfondir cette notion, et de mettre en évidence les autres caractéristiques formelles de l'écriture, nous allons nous attarder sur l'idée d'existence et de dualité chez Modiano. Il sera alors possible de réfléchir sur le sens profond de la continuité romanesque, jalonnée par les deux trilogies.

Romancier du vide, l'auteur de *La Place de l'Étoile* est sans doute l'un des premiers écrivains à avoir réservé à l'idée de néant et de vacuité une place fondamentale dans ses œuvres – en particulier celles de jeunesse. Ces dernières s'ordonnent autour d'une interrogation, sans cesse renouvelée, autour de l'idée d'existence. Les questions taraudantes, qui se posent à l'écrivain, concernent l'inscription dans la communauté humaine. Chaque roman prend ainsi un personnage à l'état larvaire, et le confronte à l'adversité du monde. Dans les premiers textes, celle-ci se trouve presque entièrement escamotée ; réduit à un principe d'existence purement virtuel, l'être ne peut, en aucun cas, entretenir de relations avec l'univers qui l'entoure. À la fin des années soixante-dix et au début des années quatre-vingts, l'écriture du vide cède la place à celle de la nostalgie – qui constitue, à sa manière, une autre forme de néantisation, puisque le héros-narrateur se voit condamné à errer dans un « entretemps », qui n'est autre que l'absence de concordance entre un passé révéré, et disparu, et un présent qui se voit dénier toute légitimité.

Observateur consciencieux du théâtre de ses souvenirs, Modiano, de *Rue des boutiques obscures* à *Vestiaire de l'enfance*, va ordonner, avec méthode et révérence, le sanctuaire d'une nostalgie sécurisante. La forme laconique et minimaliste du style entérine le processus de désincarnation des personnages. Le recyclage nostalgique des lieux ou des êtres commence dès que plus rien ne semble constituer un obstacle à la toute-puissance de l'Idée : idée de Paris, idée de l'Occupation ou idée de la femme – puisque celle-ci apparaît aussi fonctionnelle et absente que dans les romans de Julien Gracq. Le mouvement de régression psychique, commencé depuis le premier ouvrage, se poursuit sous un aspect différent. Il ne s'agit plus de nier les manifestations physiques – et partant les postulats d'existence – de l'être par la destruction des catégories logico-temporelles, mais d'empêcher leur épanouissement par le recours permanent au passé et aux souvenirs.

Le monde de Modiano est rêvé avant que d'être retranscrit par une écriture blanche, qui installe la nostalgie au cœur même du récit, et l'érige en unique principe de préhension du monde. L'écriture de ce romancier, tout en entretenant certains rapports de contiguïté avec celle de Larbaud ou du Brasillach de *Comme le temps passe*, semble plus proche de *Sylvie*. Nerval et Modiano ne convoquent pas le passé dans leurs narrations ; c'est la matière même des souvenirs qui gouverne, qui crée, la perception du réel, de façon à ce que l'obsession nostalgique devienne l'unique justification de l'existence, et forme ainsi un écran avec l'univers extérieur. Contrairement à un roman articulé autour de l'idée de nostalgie, comme *Le Grand Meaulnes*, dans lequel l'assomption du souvenir, succédant à la monotonie de jours semblables et monotones, représente le seul principe de réalité – pétrifiant le protagoniste dans une adolescence éternelle, rendant de la sorte très difficile le contact avec les autres –, l'univers de Modiano condamne, par principe, la réalité, pour imposer d'emblée l'unique langage de la mémoire. La félicité et le contentement, qui résident dans les retrouvailles avec un passé enfui, sont impensables, car la nostalgie s'oppose à toute sensation ou à tout sentiment – dont la manifestation marquerait le rattachement du héros au genre humain.

De *La Place de l'Étoile* à *Du plus loin de l'oubli*, l'écrivain part d'un principe unique, qui transcende les différences de forme : celui de l'organisation. Le point de départ de chaque œuvre réside dans un constat d'échec – pourquoi ne puis-je trouver ma place dans l'existence ? pourquoi n'ai-je jamais pu communiquer avec mon père – ou d'ignorance – pourquoi ai-je été trahi par les miens[1] ? – auquel l'acte scriptural se doit d'apporter une justification.

Il est possible d'affirmer que chacun des textes se trouve construit autour d'un jeu d'oppositions entre le temps de l'écriture et le temps de la narration – qui fournit l'argument du récit. Celui-ci va alors s'ingénier à remettre en place les éléments dispersés par la mémoire, et à proposer un ordre nouveau, susceptible de légitimer les actes du héros-narrateur. De fait, s'il est impossible d'abolir la distinction entre les deux sphères du présent et du passé – c'est ce postulat que le Modiano de la première trilogie refuse d'admettre –, il s'avère intéressant, pour le créateur, d'utiliser toutes les ressources romanesques offertes par ce hiatus. Les œuvres de la seconde trilogie, en particulier, tireront toutes les conséquences littéraires de cet état de fait. Placées sous le signe de l'ambivalence, elles offrent l'avantage de poursuivre les interrogations des débuts sous une forme renouvelée, en préservant la sécurité de l'écrivain.

Cette alliance des contraires passe ainsi par des choix narratifs capables de dépasser les antagonismes, et de constituer un ensemble satisfaisant pour l'esprit. Nous en proposerons deux illustrations – mais les exemples pourraient être multipliés. Ainsi, les deux premiers romans de la trilogie

---

[1] On pensera, en particulier, aux romans de la deuxième période comme *Quartier perdu*, *Dimanches d'août* ou, auparavant, *Villa triste*.

parviennent à surmonter l'abîme séparant le temps de la Collaboration et celui de l'écriture – afin de montrer que l'Occupation n'a rien perdu de sa virulence – grâce à la neutralisation des valeurs grammaticales et logiques. Le temps de l'Occupation laisse ainsi la place à une occupation des temps.

Dans *Voyage de noces*, le témoignage personnel, réduit à l'anecdote, s'efface devant une évocation de l'Occupation respectueuse des lois du récit romanesque. Sept années plus tard, c'est le commentaire de l'écrivain sur lui-même qui obéit à ce mode de narration, alors que la peinture de l'Occupation se trouve limitée à une succession de remarques anecdotiques. *Voyage de noces* s'articulait autour du narrateur pour mieux parler d'Ingrid Theyrsen – et, de façon plus générale, du désarroi de l'être confronté à un milieu hostile. *Dora Bruder* ne paraît s'ordonner autour de la jeune fille qu'afin de mieux parler de Modiano. Ce dernier voit, dans les possibilités offertes par le roman, l'occasion inespérée d'effectuer la synthèse, refusée par la réalité, d'un jeu de tensions, rendues maîtrisables par l'écriture : le passé déstabilisant contre le présent mortifère, la vérité contre l'affabulation, ou encore la nécessité du témoignage contre les libertés prises avec le récit.

Les livres de Modiano sont, sans doute, plus intéressants par leur manière de soulever les problèmes et de régler la question de l'Occupation que par les solutions qu'ils proposent. Les hésitations et divergences paraissent plus importantes que les conclusions, forcément réductrices, qui ne représentent jamais qu'un moment du cheminement intérieur de l'écrivain. S'il paraît difficile de toujours pénétrer avec certitude les desseins de celui-ci, il faut en attribuer la cause aux diverses inflexions du questionnement identitaire, indissociable de la réflexion sur les années sombres.

L'auteur des *Boulevards de ceinture* est sans doute le seul écrivain de l'après-guerre à avoir fait preuve d'un tel souci de cohérence dans le choix de ses thèmes. Sa carrière s'ouvre et se ferme par une même question, à savoir la possibilité d'accorder l'existence quotidienne avec le culte nécessaire d'un passé douloureux, légué par les « autres ». L'œuvre évite la répétition et les redites grâce aux fluctuations du thème, indexé sur l'expérience du romancier et ses rapports avec le monde. Sous la diversité des histoires contées, l'Occupation demeure incontestablement présente. Elle semble avoir si bien colonisé l'inconscient, avec son cortège de figures ambiguës ou de drames muets, joués sur fond de terreur diffuse, que les romans tournant délibérément le dos aux années noires semblent moins achevés[1], moins polis que ceux qui prennent celles-ci pour seul cadre. Ils s'articulent certes autour des mêmes thèmes – quête des origines, culpabilité, interrogation sur la duplicité et la trahison ou angoisse irrationnelle de la destruction d'un univers protégé –, mais font la partie belle à l'anecdote, en délaissant la réflexion sur l'écriture comme forme d'élucidation du passé et de justification de l'existence.

La nation française ne semble pas avoir encore chassé tous les démons de son passé. Du procès Papon à la présence de négationnistes sur les listes de l'extrême-droite, lors des élections régionales de mars 1998, les résurgences de l'Occupation sont encore nombreuses. L'écriture romanesque, qui offre une très grande liberté dans le traitement de l'Histoire, en mêlant le parcours individuel des personnages à l'épopée collective, représente, sans doute, la forme la plus apte à rendre compte des débordements du passé. Il paraît intéressant de citer, à titre d'exemple, quelques extraits d'une tribune que Marc Lambron consacrait au choix de Vichy pour son roman, *1941*[2], chronique fictive de cette année par un attaché de du Moulins de Labarthète, à l'Hôtel du Parc. L'écrivain insistait notamment sur l'importance de l'exploration de ce moment, à la fin du XXe siècle, en replaçant, d'une part, son ouvrage dans le cadre de l'histoire littéraire, et en réfléchissant sur les statuts de la fiction et du témoignage historique :

> La « digestion » des fractures historiques par le roman français a suivi pendant des décennies un rythme

---

[1] Nous pensons notamment à *Une jeunesse*, ouvrage atypique, et aux œuvres qui séparent les deux derniers volets de la trilogie : *Chien de printemps, Un cirque passe* et *Du plus loin de l'oubli*.
[2] Marc Lambron, *1941*, Grasset, 1997.

à peu près constant : il faut vingt à quarante ans pour que surgisse une œuvre de fiction qui rende compte d'un épisode charnière. [...] Le grand roman sur 1848, *L'Éducation sentimentale*, est publié en 1869. Et Roger Martin du Gard donne en 1934 la chronique de *L'Été 1914*. [...] autour de 1965 le Nouveau Roman qui régnait, c'est-à-dire une école qui récuse à la fois l'histoire comme événement et l'histoire comme récit. Une forme d'amnésie[1].

On notera l'oubli de l'œuvre de Modiano, qui, à cette époque, relevait le défi des formes d'expression nouvelles pour inventorier les zones d'ombres du passé. Marc Lambron ajoute ensuite :

> Les silences du roman sont des symptômes pour l'historien, et un défi pour le romancier. Ce qui fait que des écrivains peuvent avoir en 1997 le sentiment de défricher certaines scènes [...] que la fiction française, à une ou deux exceptions près (*Le Piège*, d'Emmanuel Bove, *Prénom Clotilde*, de Cécil Saint-Laurent) n'a jamais vraiment traitées. [...]
> Je [...] pense aussi qu'un historien met du romanesque maîtrisé dans son désir de savoir. [...] En somme, l'histoire et le roman sont deux façons de traiter du vertige d'exister[2].

Cette dernière assertion paraît essentielle pour la compréhension de l'œuvre modianienne. Celle-ci tire son importance du renouvellement constant du regard porté sur l'Histoire – et la société dans son ensemble – considérées comme miroir de la conscience. La remise en question de la forme narrative, dans le dernier ouvrage, témoigne de cette évolution : l'écrivain ne désire pas se laisser enfermer dans une structure préétablie soumettant les idées au primat de la forme. Les trente années qui séparent *La Place de l'Étoile* de *Dora Bruder* ont vu, en effet, se succéder les approches littéraires et

---

[1] Marc Lambron, « Le Roman de Vichy », in *L'Histoire*, n° 215, novembre 1997.
[2] *Ibid.*

les modes d'expression. Il reste à savoir si Patrick Modiano, après avoir exploré toutes les déclinaisons de la mémoire et du souvenir, se montrera en mesure de prolonger son travail analytique sans se parodier. Avec le dernier texte, atypique par sa sobriété comme le premier l'était par son outrance et sa démesure, faut-il considérer que le romancier clôt un chapitre de sa création artistique, ou qu'il entend donner à ses interrogations et à ses recherches une nouvelle direction ?

Bibliographie

I) Œuvres de Patrick Modiano
(Le sigle ÉR indique l'édition de référence, lorsque celle-ci n'est pas l'édition grand format. Sauf indication contraire, le lieu d'édition est Paris.)

A) <u>Œuvres romanesques</u> (nous incluons, pour une commodité de classement, les autofictions.)

La Place de l'Étoile, Gallimard, 1968.

La Ronde de nuit, Gallimard, 1969. Collection « Folio », 1976. (ÉR)

Les Boulevards de ceinture, Gallimard, 1972. Collection « Folio », 1978. (ÉR)

Villa triste, Gallimard, 1975. Collection « Folio », 1977. (ÉR)

Livret de famille, Gallimard, 1977. Collection « Folio », 1981. (ÉR)

Rue des boutiques obscures, Gallimard, 1978.

Une jeunesse, Gallimard, 1981.

De si braves garçons, Gallimard, 1982. Collection « Folio », 1986. (ÉR)

Quartier perdu, Gallimard, 1984. Collection « Folio », 1988. (ÉR)

Dimanches d'août, Gallimard, 1986. Collection « Folio », 1990. (ÉR)

Remise de peine, Le Seuil, 1988.

Vestiaire de l'enfance, Gallimard, 1989.

Voyage de noces, Gallimard, 1990. Collection « Folio », 1991. (ÉR)

Fleurs de ruine, Le Seuil, 1991.

Un cirque passe, Gallimard, 1992.

Chien de printemps, Le Seuil, 1993.

Du plus loin de l'oubli, Gallimard, 1995.

Dora Bruder, Gallimard, 1997.

Des inconnues, Gallimard, 1999.

B) <u>Œuvres diverses</u>

Lacombe Lucien (en collaboration avec Louis Malle), scénario de film, Gallimard, 1974.

La Polka (pièce inédite), 1974.

Emmanuel Berl, interrogatoire, suivi de *Il fait beau, allons au cimetière*, Gallimard, collections « Témoins », 1976.

Memory Lane (dessins de Pierre Le-Tan), POL/Hachette, 1981. (récit) Collection « Points-roman », 1983. (ÉR)

Poupée blonde (dessins de Pierre Le-Tan), POL/Hachette, 1983.

Une aventure de Choura (dessins de Dominique Zehrfuss) Gallimard, 1986.

Une fiancée pour Choura (dessins de Dominique Zehrfuss), Gallimard, 1987.

Catherine Certitude (dessins de Jean-Jacques Sempé), Gallimard, 1988.

Paris tendresse (photographies de Brassaï), Hoëbeke, 1990.

Elle s'appelait Françoise, éditions Canal-plus, 1997.

II) Ouvrages consacrés à l'Occupation

A) <u>Analyses et commentaires historiques</u>

a) livres sur l'Occupation :

Jean-Pierre Azéma, *De Munich à la Libération (1938-1944)*, tome XIV de la *Nouvelle Histoire de la France contemporaine*, Le Seuil, 1979.

Jacques Benoist-Méchin, *À l'épreuve du temps* (trois tomes), Perrin, 1980.

Yves Durand, *Vichy, 1940-1944*, Bordas, 1972.

Hervé Le Boterf, *La Vie parisienne sous l'Occupation*, France-Empire, 1974.

Gérard Miller, *Les Pousse-au-jouir du maréchal Pétain*, Seuil, 1975.

Robert Paxton, *La France de Vichy*, Seuil, 1973.

Robert Paxton, *Vichy et les juifs*, Calmann-Lévy, 1981.

Henri Rousso, *Le Syndrome de Vichy (1944-198-)*, Seuil, 1987.

Enzo Traverso, *Les Juifs et l'Allemagne*, La Découverte, 1992.

Wanda Vulliez, *Vichy, la fin d'une époque*, France-Empire, 1997.

b) livres sur la Collaboration :

Jean-Pierre Azéma, *La Collaboration*, PUF, 1975.

Michèle Cotta, *La Collaboration*, Armand Colin, collection Kiosque, 1964.

Jacques Delarue, *Crimes et trafics sous l'Occupation*, Fayard, 1967.

Jacques Delperrier de Bayac, *Histoire de la Milice*, Fayard, 1969.

Jean-Baptiste Duroselle, *L'Abîme*, Imprimerie nationale, 1982.

Claude Lévy, *Les Nouveaux Temps et l'idéologie de la collaboration*, Armand Colin, 1974.

Pascal Ory, *Les Collaborateurs*, Seuil, 1976.

Henri Rousso, *La Collaboration*, HA édit., 1987.

Daniel Veillon, *La Collaboration*, Hachette, 1984.

III) Textes et ouvrages consacrés à Modiano

A) Livres et thèses

Ora Avni, *D'un passé l'autre, aux portes de l'histoire avec Patrick Modiano*, L'Harmattan, 1997.

Olivier Barrot, *Pages pour Modiano*, Éditions du Rocher, 1999.

Xiaone Chen, *Mémoire et quête dans quelques romans de Patrick Modiano*, thèse dirigée par Henri Godard, Université de Paris-VII, 1992.

Françoise Davidovits, *L'Écriture de la nostalgie dans les romans de Patrick Modiano*, thèse dirigée par Jacqueline Levi-Valensi, Université d'Amiens, 1993.

Penelope Hueston et Colin-W. Nettelbeck, *Patrick Modiano : écrire l'entretemps*, Minard, « Archives des lettres modernes », 1985.

Thierry Laurent, *L'Autofiction dans les romans de Patrick Modiano*, thèse dirigée par Pierre Brunel, Université de Paris-IV, février 1995.

Thierry Laurent, *Patrick Modiano : une autofiction*, Presses Universitaires de Lyon, 1997.

Daniel Parrochia, *Ontologie fantôme, essai sur l'œuvre de Patrick Modiano*, Fougères-La Versanne, Encre marine, 1996.

Pierre Srour, *La Métaphysique dans les romans de Patrick Modiano*, thèse dirigée par Marc-Matthieu Munch, Université de Metz, 1994.

Olivier Tardy, *La Quête de l'identité dans les romans de Patrick Modiano*, thèse de doctorat de troisième cycle, dirigée par Michel Malicet, Université de Besançon, mars 1984.

B) Études et articles sur Patrick Modiano :

Jacques Almira, « Toute vie pourrait être sujet de roman », *in Revue des deux mondes*, juin 1991, p. 153-157.

Pierre Assouline, « Modiano, lieux de mémoire », *in Lire*, n° 176, mai 1990, p34-46.

Ora Avni, « Narrative Subject, Historic Subject, *Shoah* and *La Place de l'Étoile* », *in Poetics Today*, XII, 1991.

Jules Bedner, « Modiano ou l'identité introuvable », *in Rapports*, LVIII, 1988, p. 49-67.

Jacques Bersani, « Modiano, agent double », *in La Nouvelle Revue française*, n° 298, 1er novembre 1977, p. 78-84.

Pascal Bonitzer, « Histoire de sparadrap », *in Les Cahiers du cinéma*, n° 250, mai 1974, p. 42-47.

Anneke Brouwer, « L'Emploi des temps verbaux chez Modiano », *in Rapports*, LVIII, 1988, p. 68-73.

Paul-Raymond Côté, « Aux rives du Léthé. Mnémosyne et la quête des origines chez Modiano », *in Symposium*, XLV, p. 315-328.

Norbert Czarny, « La Trace douloureuse. L'Occupation dans *Les Boulevards de ceinture*, *Livret de famille* et *Remise de peine* de Modiano », in *L'École des lettres*, LXXXVII, 14-15 juillet 1991, p. 171-178.

Pierre Daprini, « Le Temps de l'Occupation », in *Australian Journal of French Studies*, XXVI, 1989, p. 194-205.

Gerhard Gerhardi, « Topographie et histoire, Paris et l'Occupation dans l'œuvre de Patrick Modiano », actes du troisième colloque des Universités d'Orléans et de Siegen, Reihe Siegen, Heidelberg, Winter 1995.

Judith Kauffmann, « Modiano, un "juif imaginaire" ? Une relecture de *La Place de l'Étoile* », in *The Hebrew University Studies in Literature and the Arts (Jerusalem)*, XII, 3, 1984, p. 130-145.

Guy Neumann, « Modiano, *La Ronde de nuit* ou le naufrage de l'histoire », in *Australian Journal of French Studies*, XXXVI, 1989, p. 289-298.

Gerald Prince, « Re-Membering Modiano, or Something Happened », in *Substance*, XV, 1, 1986, p. 35-43.

Charlotte Wardi, « Mémoire et écriture dans l'œuvre de Modiano », in *Les Nouveaux Cahiers*, n° 80, printemps 1985, p. 40-48.

Marja Warehime, « Originality and Narrative Nostalgia, shadows in Modiano's *Rue des boutiques obscures* », in *French Forum (Lexington)*, XII, 1987, p. 335-345.

Table des matières

INTRODUCTION 7

PREMIERE PARTIE : 15

L'ECRITURE DE L'HISTOIRE 15

L'OCCUPATION ET SES SEQUELLES (1968-1978) 20
    Le domaine politique.. 20
    Une nouvelle idéologie critique 23
    La mode « rétro ».. 26
    Modiano rattrapé ?... 32
UNE VISION SUBJECTIVE DES ANNEES D'OCCUPATION 35
    Le paysage temporel 35
    Le paysage politique ; voyage en terre de haine.......................... 47
    L'antisémitisme. 54
LES FORMES DE LA COLLABORATION... 59
    La Place de l'Étoile : précis de réaction.................................... 61
    Lacombe Lucien : les exécutants... 63
    La Collaboration mafieuse. 64
    Quelques collaborateurs. 65
    La collaboration artistique. 94
LE « PAYSAGE NATUREL » DE L'OCCUPATION. 107
    Un arpentage du monde. 107
    Une obsession urbaine. 109
    Le cas de Dora Bruder. 115
    Les composants du « paysage naturel ». 117
    Liberté historique et vérité de l'imaginaire : une approche de
    l'autofiction... 121

DEUXIEME PARTIE 127

L'OCCUPATION : 127

UNE REALITE FANTASMEE ; ETUDE DES PROCEDES. 127

Le statut des personnages : de l'archetype au stereotype. 131
- Le protagoniste des romans. 134
- Le tragique de l'Occupation. 137
- Les figures récurrentes. 146

L'Occupation constitue une representation mentale. 152
- Fonctionnement de ce système original : la stylistique des temps. 159
- Une esthétique de l'achronie. 165
- De quelques vacillements ; étude d'un temps : le présent. 170
- L'Occupation dessine un parcours régressif. 178

Une certaine esthetique du passe. 188
- Une écriture de la nostalgie. 190
- L'évocation de la guerre : aux sources du souvenir. 195
- L'édification de la mémoire. 208

TROISIEME PARTIE : 217

L'IDENTITE AU MIROIR DE L'OCCUPATION. 217

Une identite inscrite au cœur de l'Occupation. 227
- Une recherche de la lignée. 227
- Un caractère superficiel. 230
- Glissements permanents de l'identité. 254
- Une ontologie fantôme. 259

Vers une autofiction ? 263
- Une Occupation revue par les lois de l'autofiction. 264
- Un corps en fuite. 278
- « Comment peut-on être juif ? » 284
- Une identité introuvable ? 290
- L'effacement du créateur. 295
- L'interrogation sur le père : un questionnement permanent. 300
- La peur ou le fondement de l'identité. 306

CONCLUSION 313

Collection Critiques Littéraires
dirigée par Maguy Albet et Paule Plouvier

Dernières parutions

TCHEUYAP Alexie, *Esthétique et folie, l'oeuvre romanesque de Pius Ngandu Nkashama*, 1998.
GUERMÉS Sophie, *La poésie moderne*, 1998.
RUSZNIEWSKI-DAHAN Myriam, *Romanciers de la Shoah*, 1998.
DELBARD Olivier, *Les lieux de Kenneth White*, 1998.
DETIS Elizabeth, *Daniel Defoe démasqué*, 1999.
BOUTOUTE Eric, *Sade et les figures du baroque*, 1999.
MAYAUX Catherine (ed.), *Jean Grosjean, poète et prosateur*, 1999.
MIDIOHOUAN Guy Mossito et DOSSOU Mathias D., *La nouvelle d'expression française en Afrique Noire*, 1999.
YEPRI Léon, *Titinga Frédéric Pacere : le tambour de l'Afrique poétique*, 1999.
GAFAÏTI Hafid, *Rachid Boudjedra : une poétique de la subversion*, 1999.
DALZON Christian, *Tom Sharpe, écrivain «populaire», de la farce à l'ironie*, 1999.
LABROUCHE Laurence, *Ariane Mnouchkine, un parcours théâtral*, 1999.
TEODORO Maria de Lourdes, *Modernisme brésilien et négritude antillaise, Mário de Andrade et Aimé Césaire*, 1999.
BASTET Ned, *Valéry à l'extrême*, 1999.
SEMUJANGA Josias, *Dynamique des genres dans le roman africain*, 1999.
LABBE Michelle, *Le Clézio, l'écart romanesque*, 1999.
FOUET Jeanne, *Driss Chraibi en marges*, 1999.
GUILLAUME Isabelle, *Le roman d'aventures depuis* L'Ile au trésor, 1999.
KLEIBER Pierre-Henri, *Glossaire j'y serre mes gloses* de Michel Leiris et la question du langage, 1999.
PARAVY Florence, *L'espace dans le roman africain francophone contemporain*, 1999.
FRIES Philippe, *La théorie fictive de Maurice Blanchot*, 1999.

642782 - Février 2016
Achevé d'imprimer par